Praise for the Novels of Harry Turtledove

Days of Infamy

"[Turtledove] provides brain candy for history buffs.... [*Days of Infamy*] is a gripping book that makes it clear just how lucky the United States was to have things go its way in 1941; it's a read worthy of an all-nighter."
—*Sacramento News & Review*

"Starkly realistic.... This exciting, well-researched alternate history will please history buffs and SF fans alike."
—*Publishers Weekly*

"Demanding, irresistible, and magisterial—to say the very least."
—*Booklist*

"Factions come alive, from the Japanese warriors to the Americans who make Hawaii their home to the natives who find their loyalties torn. Turtledove excels at showing the big picture through the eyes of the individual men and women whose daily lives reflect the urgency and desperation of their times."
—*Library Journal*

"Turtledove captures the feel of the 1940s as he shows the Japanese running roughshod over the unprepared Americans.... While characterization of people and Hawaii is really what drives this novel, Turtledove's descriptions of the military tactics and strategies of the Japanese are never far from the foreground and are enough to please fans of military science fiction."
—*SF Site*

"A gripping and well-told tale.... With this 'what-if?' Harry Turtledove begins what promises to be another of his classic alternate history series.... *Days of Infamy* contains all the hallmarks of Turtledove's work: numerous viewpoint characters, who allow us to see the action from a variety of perspectives; painstaking attention to the details of everyday life in the period; and a story line which—being taken from history—is in many ways far more exciting and engaging than any conventional fiction."
—*SFRevu*

continued ...

"An exciting military thriller . . . another triumph for Mr. Turtledove."
—*Midwest Book Review*

"[Turtledove] clearly has a detailed grasp of history, weaponry, tactics, and the period in general, and brings his story to life through the thoughts, actions, and experiences of these characters. If you like alternate history and particularly Harry Turtledove's style, you will enjoy this book."
—SFcrowsnest

"Harry Turtledove knows how to spin a yarn. . . . When Turtledove is in good form, as he is here, it's like an IMAX® movie of the imagination. . . . This novel holds its ground among his many other series and stand-alone novels. Turtledove writes in a fast-paced multiple perspective, his cast of characters drawing us into the drama and pain of war. . . . Well-drawn, memorable characters."
—*Scifi Dimensions*

"Turtledove has played through versions of [World War II] like a jazzman handed sheet music. You never know what he'll do next, no matter what the score shows. One thing about Turtledove is that though he seems to crank out books like he's a fun factory, the books he cranks out are pretty damn good. . . . [T]hey offer up solid characters and vividly recreated alternate history."
—The Agony Column

In the Presence
of Mine Enemies

"The maven of alternate history layers byzantine complexities into a book with sympathetic characters and a steady buildup of well-managed tension. . . . This novel is more than a little scary, but it has a good deal of hope embedded nicely in the structure."
—*The San Diego Union-Tribune*

"Chilling."
—*East Bay Express* (California)

"Another magisterial alternate history novel from the master of the form. . . . The suspense of the confrontation of good and evil remains intense in Turtledove's hands."
—*Booklist* (starred review)

Ruled Britannia

A *San Francisco Chronicle* Best-of-the-Year Selection
A *Locus* Recommended Read

"Sprinkled with literary jokes, peopled with a lively supporting cast, and filled with engaging plot reversals, *Ruled Britannia* is a smart, enjoyable excercise in 'what if?' "
—San Francisco Chronicle

"[Turtledove's] lines of blank verse are artful combinations of real lines from Shakespeare and the work of some of his contemporaries." *—The Denver Post*

"An amalgam of Elizabethan stagecraft and spycraft: at once elegant and engrossing."
—Home News Tribune (East Brunswick, NJ)

"[A] fascinating what-if. . . . The author revels in complex turns of language and spouts brilliant adaptations of the real Shakespeare's immortal lines. Superbly realized historical figures . . . an intricate and thoroughly engrossing portrait of an era, a theatrical tradition, a heroic band of English brothers, and their sneering overlords." *—Publishers Weekly* (starred review)

"Spectacular. . . . *Ruled Britannia* can stand proudly beside works like Tom Stoppard's *Rosencrantz and Guildenstern are Dead.* . . . It extends this minigenre in new directions, making Shakespeare into a sort of writerly action hero." *—Locus*

"Fascinating. . . . Using Shakespeare as the hero and reluctant catalyst to signal the beginning of the revolution is an inspired plot device, one that guarantees reader interest for more than just Mr. Turtledove's legion of fans." *—Midwest Book Review*

"One of his finest achievements . . . full of scenes that provoke tears, as well as of Turtledove's hallmark good humor. A thoroughly magisterial work of alternate history."
—Booklist (starred review)

"[A] tale of personal heroism and the power of language. Turtledove's command of facts and his understanding of the period allow him to portray his characters with believability, while his prose, liberally salted with Shakespeare's own words, stands as a tribute to both the man and his work." *—Library Journal*

ALSO BY HARRY TURTLEDOVE

"Daimon" in *Worlds That Weren't*
Ruled Britannia
In the Presence of Mine Enemies

DAYS OF
INFAMY

HARRY TURTLEDOVE

A ROC BOOK

ROC
Published by New American Library, a division of
Penguin Group (USA) Inc., 375 Hudson Street,
New York, New York 10014, USA
Penguin Group (Canada), 90 Eglinton Avenue East, Suite 700, Toronto,
Ontario, Canada M4P 2Y3 (a division of Pearson Penguin Canada Inc.)
Penguin Books Ltd., 80 Strand, London WC2R 0RL, England
Penguin Ireland, 25 St. Stephen's Green, Dublin 2,
Ireland (a division of Penguin Books Ltd.)
Penguin Group (Australia), 250 Camberwell Road, Camberwell, Victoria 3124,
Australia (a division of Pearson Australia Group Pty. Ltd.)
Penguin Books India Pvt. Ltd., 11 Community Centre, Panchsheel Park,
New Delhi - 110 017, India
Penguin Group (NZ), cnr Airborne and Rosedale Roads, Albany,
Auckland 1310, New Zealand (a division of Pearson New Zealand Ltd.)
Penguin Books (South Africa) (Pty.) Ltd., 24 Sturdee Avenue,
Rosebank, Johannesburg 2196, South Africa

Penguin Books Ltd., Registered Offices:
80 Strand, London WC2R 0RL, England

Published by Roc, an imprint of New American Library, a division of Penguin
Group (USA) Inc. Previously published in a New American Library edition.

First Roc Printing, November 2005
10 9 8 7 6 5 4 3 2

Copyright © Harry Turtledove, 2004
All rights reserved

ROC REGISTERED TRADEMARK—MARCA REGISTRADA

Printed in the United States of America

I

ON A GRAY, DRIZZLY MORNING IN THE FIRST WEEK OF MARCH 1941, an automobile pulled up in front of the great iron gates of the Imperial Naval Staff College in Tokyo. The young commander who got out was short even by Japanese standards—he couldn't have been more than five feet three—and so slim he barely topped the hundred-pound mark. All the same, the two leading seamen on sentry duty at the gates (both of whom overtopped him by half a head) stiffened to attention at his approach.

"Your papers, sir, if you please." The senior sentry slung his rifle so he could take them in his right hand.

The sentry studied them, nodded, and handed them back. "Thank you, sir. All in order." He turned to his comrade. "Open the gates for Commander Genda."

"*Hai*," the second seaman said, and did.

Genda hurried to the eastern wing of the staff college. He hurried everywhere he went; he fairly burned with energy. He nearly slipped once on the wet pavement, but caught himself. The drizzle was not enough to wash the city soot from the red bricks of the building. Nothing short of sandblasting would have been.

Just inside the door to the east wing sat a petty officer with a logbook. Genda presented his papers again. The petty officer scanned them. *Commander Genda to see Admiral Yamamoto*, he wrote in the log, and, after a glance at the clock on the wall opposite him, the time. "Please sign in, Commander," he said, offering Genda the pen.

"Yes, yes." Genda was always impatient with formality and paperwork. He scrawled his name, then almost trotted down the hall till he came to the stairway. Despite his small size, he took the stairs to the third floor two at a time. He wasn't breathing hard when he came out; he might be little, but he was fit.

A captain on the telephone looked at him curiously as he went past the officer's open door. Genda didn't meet the other man's eyes, or even notice his gaze. All the commander's energy focused on the meeting that lay ahead.

He knocked on the door. "Come in." Admiral Yamamoto's voice was deep and gruff.

Heart pounding, Genda did. He saluted the commander-in-chief of Japan's Combined Fleet. Isoroku Yamamoto returned the courtesy. He was no taller than Genda, but there the physical resemblance between the two men ended. Yamamoto was broad-shouldered and barrel-chested: a wrestler's body, made for grappling with the foe. His gray hair was closely cropped above his broad, hard face. He had lost the first two fingers of his left hand in battle against the Russians at Tsushima in 1905, the year after Genda was born.

After waving Genda to a chair, he asked, "Well, Commander, what's on your mind?" He was no more a time-waster than Genda himself.

Genda licked his lips. Yamamoto could be—often strove to be—intimidating. But the younger man asked the question he had come to ask: "Sir, if war against the United States comes, what do you think of our chances?"

Yamamoto did not hesitate. "I hope this war does not come. If I am told to fight regardless of the consequences, I shall run wild for the first six months or a year, but I have utterly no confidence for the second or third year. I hope we can endeavor to avoid a Japanese-American war."

"You say this in spite of the blow we have planned against Pearl Harbor?" Genda asked. He had been involved in preparing that blow from the beginning.

Admiral Yamamoto nodded heavily. "I do. If we succeed there, the attack buys us time. Maybe it will buy us enough to take the Philippines and the Dutch East Indies and Malaya and form a defensive perimeter so we can hold what we have conquered. Maybe. I do not believe it myself, but maybe."

"If the United States can still use the forward base in Hawaii, matters become more difficult for us," Genda observed. His thick, expressive eyebrows quirked upward as he spoke.

"Much more difficult," Yamamoto agreed.

"Well, then," Genda said, "why do we limit ourselves to an air strike on Pearl Harbor? The Americans will rebuild, and then they will strike back at us."

Yamamoto nodded again. "Every word of this is true. It is one of the arguments I used against the operation. Should hostilities break out between Japan and the United States, it would not be enough that we take Guam and the Philippines, nor even Hawaii and San Francisco. I wonder if our politicians have confidence as to the final outcome and are prepared to make the necessary sacrifices."

That went further than Commander Genda wanted. He said, "May we return to discussing the Hawaii problem?" Yamamoto's smile was almost indulgent. He waved for Genda to go on. The younger man did: "We should follow up on our strike at Pearl Harbor with a landing. If Hawaii is occupied, America will lose her best base. If we make this attack at all, we had better make it decisive."

Yamamoto sat and considered. His face showed nothing. He was an outstanding bridge and poker player. Genda could see why. "Well, Commander, no one will ever accuse you of thinking small," Yamamoto said at last. "Tell me—have you discussed this proposal with Rear Admiral Onishi?"

That was exactly the question Genda wished he would not have asked. "Yes, sir, I have," he answered unhappily.

"And his view is . . . ?"

"His view is that, with our present strength, we cannot take the offensive in both the eastern and southern areas," Genda said, more unhappily still.

"Rear Admiral Onishi is an airman's officer," Yamamoto said. "He is also a very hard-driving, determined man. If he does not believe this can be done, his opinion carries considerable weight. How do you respond to his objections?"

"By saying that half measures will not do against the United States, sir," Genda replied. "If we strike a blow that merely infuriates the enemy, what good is it? Less than none, in my opinion. If we strike, we must drive the sword home all the way to the hilt. Let the Americans worry about defending their West Coast. If they lose Hawaii, they cannot possibly think about striking us."

Again, Admiral Yamamoto showed nothing of what he was thinking. He asked, "How many men do you suppose we would need to subdue Hawaii after the air strike?"

"If all goes well, they should be flat on their backs by then," Genda said. "One division should be plenty—ten or fifteen thousand men."

"No." Now Yamamoto shook his head. His eyes flashed angrily. Genda realized he'd overlooked something. Yamamoto spelled it out for him: "The Americans keep two divisions of infantry on Oahu. Even with air superiority, one of ours would not be enough to root them out. If this enterprise is to be attempted, it must not fail. You are absolutely right about that."

Genda didn't know whether to be ecstatic or apprehensive. The Navy could have pulled together a division's worth of men from its own resources. For a force the size Yamamoto was talking about . . . "Will the Army cooperate with us, sir? Their eyes are on China, and on the south—the Philippines and the Dutch East Indies. And they never like to think of anything new." He spoke with a lifelong Navy man's scorn for the ground-pounders.

"They might like to think about not having to fight the USA so soon," Yamamoto said. "They might. And they might like to think of fighting the Americans from a position of much greater advantage. The advance in the south may be slower if we take this course. But I do believe you are right, Commander. When we hit the Americans, we can hold nothing back. Nothing! The reward for victory in the east could be victory everywhere, and where else have we any hope of finding that?"

Genda could hardly hide his jubilation. He'd been far from sure he could persuade the older man that this was a needful course. Rear Admiral Onishi hadn't been able to see it. But Yamamoto, as his mutilated hand showed, was of the generation that had fought the Russo-Japanese War, the war that had begun with a surprise Japanese attack on the Russian Far Eastern Fleet at Port Arthur. He was alive to the advantages of getting in the first punch and making it count.

Yamamoto was. Were others? Anxiously, Commander Genda asked, "Are you sure you can persuade the Army to play its part in this plan?" Without Army cooperation, it wouldn't work. Yamamoto had rubbed Genda's nose in that. He hated the knowledge. That those Army blockheads might hold Japan back from its best—its only, he was convinced—chance to fight the USA and have some hope of winning was intolerable.

Admiral Isoroku Yamamoto leaned forward a few inches. He was not a big man, and it was not a large motion. Nevertheless, it made him seem to take up the entire room and to look down on Genda from a considerable height when in fact their eyes were level. "You may leave that to me, Commander," Yamamoto said in a voice that might have come from a *kami*'s throat rather than a man's. Genda hastened to salute. When Yamamoto spoke like that, who could doubt him? No one. No one at all.

COAL SMOKE BELCHING FROM ITS STACK, the locomotive pulled into the railroad yard at Esashi, in northernmost Hokkaido. Behind it, the troop train rattled and clattered to a halt. Corporal Takeo Shimizu looked out the window and shook his head. "It's not much like home, is it?"

All the privates in his squad hastened to shake their heads. "Oh, no," they chorused. Shimizu had every right to thump them if they gave him any trouble. He took less advantage of the privilege than some underofficers did. A

round-faced farmer's son, he hadn't been promoted to corporal as soon as he might have because his superiors wondered if he was too easygoing for his own good.

One of the soldiers, a skinny little fellow named Shiro
Wakuzawa, said, "I'd sure rather be back in Hiroshima
right now. It's hundreds of kilometers south of here, and
we wouldn't be shivering in our seats." The rest of the
squad nodded again. A coal-fired stove at the front of the
passenger car did next to nothing to hold the chill outside
at bay.

"No grumbling," Shimizu said. "We will uphold the honor
of the Fifth Division." His squad was only a tiny part of the
division, but he did not want to let the larger unit down in
any way. That was especially true because he didn't want to
lose face before friends, neighbors, and relatives. The whole
division came from the Hiroshima region.

Wakuzawa, who had an aisle seat, leaned forward so he
could look out the window, too. He stared this way and
that, then shook his head in obvious disappointment.

"What were you looking for?" Shimizu asked, curious in
spite of himself.

"Hairy Ainu," Wakuzawa answered. "They're supposed
to live on Hokkaido, aren't they? They have beards up to
here"—he touched his face just below his eyes—"and
down to here." He tapped himself in the middle of the
chest.

Corporal Shimizu rolled his eyes. "And you expect to
find them in the middle of a railroad yard? What do you
use for brains? If they work here, they've got to shave so
they look like everybody else. I'm hairy, too"—he was
proud of his thick beard—"but I shave."

The other soldiers jeered at Wakuzawa. The corporal
had, so they joined in. He looked properly abashed. That
was smart of him. He was just a first-year conscript, with no
rights and no privileges. If he got out of line, they'd give
him lumps. They might give him lumps anyhow, on general
principles.

Lieutenant Osami Yonehara, who commanded the platoon of which Corporal Shimizu's squad was a part, got up

and called, "Everybody out! Get your gear! Form column of fours by the car. Move, move, move!" He was shouting by the time he was done. His officer's sword banged against his hip. He was an educated man as well as an officer, which made the gulf between him and the men he led twice as wide. Shimizu didn't worry about it. Officers gave orders and men obeyed. That was how things worked.

A nasty cold breeze blew down from the north. It felt as if it hadn't touched a thing since it started up in Siberia. Corporal Shimizu's teeth started to chatter. Somebody behind him said, "Why didn't they give us winter uniforms? My balls are crawling up into my belly."

"Silence in the ranks!" Shimizu shouted, to show he was on the job in case one of his superiors heard the grumbler.

"Forward—march!" The command came from Lieutenant Colonel Mitsuo Fujikawa, the regimental commander. March the soldiers did. Shimizu hadn't the faintest idea where he was going. He didn't worry about it. Somebody set above him would know. All he had to do was follow the man in front of him.

Through the streets of Esashi they tramped. Women on their way to shops and workmen gaped at them as they strode past. Some of the workmen had on Western-style overalls and cloth caps. Most of the women wore kimonos, not dresses. Shimizu thought more people back home used Western clothes than was true up here. His slung rifle thumped his shoulder blade at every step. That always annoyed him, and he couldn't do a thing about it.

Around the railroad yard, the buildings were Western style: square, boring structures of brick and concrete. Then the Eleventh Regiment went through an older part of town. Roofs curved and arched. Wood and paper replaced brick. To Shimizu, that made pretty good sense. In an earthquake, brickwork came down on your head. And the purely Japanese buildings looked a lot more interesting than the ones built on Western lines.

When they got to the harbor, Western buildings predominated again. They went with machinery, as they did in the railroad yards. They seemed more solid and sturdy than their Japanese equivalents. And the machinery, or the ideas behind the machinery, came from the West, too. Perhaps it was more at home in familiar structures.

Gulls wheeled and mewed overhead. They descended on fishing boats in vast skrawking clouds, hoping for a handout or a theft. The salt tang of the sea—slightly sullied by sewage—filled Shimizu's nostrils.

He trudged up a pier towards a big merchant ship. Her name—*Nagata Maru*—was painted in hiragana and in Roman letters on her stern. Up the gangplank he went. His boots clanged on the iron plates of the deck. Sailors stared at him as if he were nothing but a monkey. He glared back, but only to show he wasn't intimidated. On land, he knew what he was doing. But this was the sailors' world. Maybe he wasn't a monkey to them. Maybe he was just . . . cargo.

"This way," Lieutenant Yonehara called, and led them down a hatch into the hold. The *Nagata Maru* had been a freight hauler. Now the freight she would haul was men. Double racks of rough, unsanded wood had been run up in the hold. Each one held a straw mat. They had numbers painted on them. Yonehara checked them. "My platoon goes here." He raised his voice to make himself heard over the clatter of more soldiers marching with their hobnailed boots on the steel deck not far enough overhead.

Two of his squads got upper racks, two lowers. Corporal Shimizu and his men were assigned to uppers. He wasn't sure if that was better or worse. They were right under the deck and could bang their heads if they sat up carelessly, but nobody was spilling anything on them from above.

The hold filled and filled and filled. The mats on the racks were very close together. If a man rolled over, he was liable to bump into the fellow next to him. "Packing us in like sardines," Corporal Shimizu said.

Most of his men just nodded. They sprawled on the mats. Three or four of them had started a card game. But a young soldier named Hideo Furuta said, "It could be worse, Corporal."

"How?" Shimizu demanded—he thought it was already pretty bad.

Furuta realized he'd blundered. Anger at his own stupidity filled his broad, acne-scarred face. But he had to answer: "If it were hot, the deck right above us would be like
an oven."

He was right. That would have been worse. Being right
did you little good, though, when you were only a first-year
conscript. Shimizu said, "Why don't you bring us a pot of
tea?" He'd seen a big kettle in the improvised kitchen up
on deck.

"Yes, Corporal!" Thankful Shimizu hadn't hit him, Furuta got down from his mat and hurried up the narrow
aisle towards the ladder that led to the deck. He had to go
belly-to-belly with newly arriving soldiers coming the other
way.

"Hard work!" somebody called after him. That could
mean several things: that the work really was hard, or that
the man calling sympathized with the one stuck with the
job, or simply that the luckless one *was* stuck with it. Tone
of voice and context counted for more than the words
themselves.

After what seemed a very long time, Furuta came back
with a pot of tea. Shimizu thought about bawling him out
for dawdling, but decided not to bother. Given the crowd,
the kid had done the best he could. By the way the men in
the squad praised the tea, they thought the same thing.

Before long, all the soldiers packed into the hold made
it hot and stuffy in there even without the summer sun
beating down on the metal deck above. There were no
portholes—who would have bothered adding them on a
freighter? The only fresh air came down the hatch by
which the men had entered.

Lieutenant Yonehara didn't stay with the platoon. Officers had cabins of their own. Things were crowded even for
them; junior officers like the platoon commander had to
double up. Corporal Shimizu didn't particularly resent their
better fortune. *Shigata ga nai*, he thought—*it can't be helped.*

At last, soldiers stopped coming. Had they crammed the
whole regiment into the *Nagata Maru?* Shimizu wouldn't
have been surprised. The engine began to thump. The ship

began to throb. The deck above Shimizu's head thrummed. Army dentists had given him several fillings. They seemed to vibrate in sympathy with the freighter.

As soon as the *Nagata Maru* pulled away from the pier, the rolling and pitching started. So did the cries for buckets. The sharp stink of vomit filled the hold along with the other odors of too many men packed too close together. Green-faced soldiers raced up the ladder so they could spew over the rail.

Rather to his surprise, Corporal Shimizu's stomach didn't trouble him. He'd never been in seas this rough before. He didn't enjoy the journey, but it wasn't a misery for him, either.

No one had told him where the ship was going. When the authorities wanted him to know something, they would take care of it. Till then, he worried about keeping his squad in good order. The men who could eat went through the rations they'd carried aboard the *Nagata Maru*: rice and canned seaweed and beans, along with pickled plums and radishes and whatever else the soldiers happened to have on them.

Every morning, Lieutenant Yonehara led the men topside for physical training. It wasn't easy on the pitching deck, but orders were orders. The gray, heaving waters of the Sea of Okhotsk and the even grayer skies spoke of how far from home Shimizu was.

When not exercising, the soldiers mostly stayed on their mats. They had no room to move around. Some were too sick to do anything but lie there and moan. Others gambled or sang songs or simply slept like hibernating animals, all in the effort to make time go faster.

The Kuril Islands seemed like an afterthought to Japan: rocky lumps spattered across the Pacific, heading up towards Kamchatka. Etorofu was as windswept and foggy and desolate as any of the others. When the *Nagata Maru* anchored in Hitokappu Bay, Shimizu was unimpressed. He just hoped to get away as fast as he could. He wouldn't even have known where he was if the platoon commander hadn't told him.

He had hoped to be able to get off the freighter and stretch his legs. But no one was allowed off the ship for any reason. No one was allowed to send mail. No one, in fact, was allowed to do much of anything except go up on deck and exercise. Every time Corporal Shimizu did, more ships crowded the bay. They weren't just transports, either. Ships bristling with big guns joined the fleet. So did flat-topped aircraft carriers, one after another.

Something big was building. When the men went back down into the hold, they tried to guess what it would be. Not a one of them turned out to be right.

YOU CAN BE UNHAPPY IN HAWAII as easily as anywhere else. People who cruise over from the mainland often have a hard time believing this, but it's true. The sea voyage from San Francisco or Los Angeles takes five days. They set the clocks back half an hour a day aboard ship, so that each outbound day lasts twenty-four hours and thirty minutes. By the time you get there, you're two and a half hours behind the West Coast, five and a half behind the East.

And then, after Diamond Head and the Aloha Tower come up over the horizon, you commonly stay in a fine hotel. You eat splendid food. You drink . . . oh, a little too much. You don't get drunk, mind. You get . . . happy. You admire the turquoise sky and the sapphire sea and the emerald land. Strange tropical birds call in the trees. You savor the perfect weather. Never too hot, never too cold. If it rains, so what? The sun will come out again in a little while. You want to be a beachcomber and spend the rest of your days there. If you find a slightly brown-skinned but beautiful and willing wahine to spend them there with you, so much the better.

Hawaii is what God made after he'd done Paradise for practice. How could anyone be unhappy in a place like that?

First Lieutenant Fletcher Armitage had no trouble at all.

For one thing, Armitage—called Fletch by his friends— was a green-eyed redhead with a face full of freckles. In between the freckles, his skin was white as milk. He hated the tropical sun. He didn't tan. He burned.

For another, his wife had left him three weeks before. He didn't understand why. He wasn't sure Jane understood why. He didn't think there was somebody else. Jane hadn't said anything about anybody else. She'd said she felt stifled in their little Wahiawa apartment. She'd said he didn't give her enough of his time.

That had frosted his pumpkin—not that frost had anything to do with anything on Oahu. "For Christ's sake, I give you every minute I've got when I'm not with my guns!" he'd howled. He served with the Thirteenth Field Artillery Battalion—the Lucky Thirteenth, they called themselves—in the Twenty-fourth Division. "You knew you were marrying an officer when you said 'I do.'"

She'd only shrugged. She was small and blond and stubborn. "It's not enough," she'd said. Now she had the apartment, and presumably felt much less stifled without him in it. She was talking with a lawyer. How she'd pay him on a schoolteacher's salary was beyond Fletch, but odds were she'd figure out a way. She usually did.

What Armitage had, on the other hand, was a hard cot at Schofield Barracks BOQ and a bar tab that was liable to outdo Jane's legal fees. He had the sympathy of some of the officers and men who knew what had happened to him. Others suddenly didn't seem to want anything to do with him. Almost all of those were married men themselves. They might have feared he had something catching. And so he did: life in the military. If anything could grind a marriage to powder, that'd do it.

He sat on a barstool soaking up whiskey sours with Gordon Douglas, another lieutenant in the battalion. "She knew I was an officer, goddammit," he said—slurred, rather, since he'd already soaked up quite a few. "She knew, all right. Knew I had to take care of . . . this stuff." He gestured vaguely. Just what he had to do wasn't the clearest thing in his mind right then.

Douglas gave back a solemn nod. He looked like the high-school fullback he'd been ten years earlier. He was from Nebraska: corn-fed and husky. "You know, it could be worse," he said slowly—he'd matched Armitage drink for drink.

"How?" Fletch demanded with alcohol-fueled indignation. "How the *hell* could it be worse?"

"Well . . ." The other man looked sorry he'd spoken. But he'd drunk enough to have a hard time keeping his mouth shut, and so he went on, "It could be worse if we spent more time in the field. Then she would've seen even less of you, and all this would've come on sooner."

"Oh, yeah. If." But that only flicked Fletch on another gripe of his, one older than his trouble with his wife (or older than his knowledge of his trouble with his wife, which was not the same thing). "Don't hold your breath, though."

"We do the best we can." Gordon Douglas sounded uncomfortable, partly because he knew he was liable to touch off a rant.

And he did. Fletch exploded. "Do we? *Do* we? Sure doesn't look that way to me. This is a hell of a parade-ground army, no bout adout it." He paused, listened to what he'd just said, and tried again. "No . . . doubt . . . about it." There. That was better. He could roll on: "*Hell* of a parade-ground army. But what if we really have to go out there and fight? What will we do then, when we're not on parade?"

"We'd do all right." Douglas still sounded uncomfortable. But then he rallied, saying, "Besides, who the hell would we fight? Nobody in his right mind would mess with Hawaii, and you know it."

Down the hatch went Armitage's latest whiskey sour. He gestured to the Filipino bartender for another one. Even before it arrived, he went on, "All this shit with the Japs doesn't sound good. They didn't like it for beans when we turned the oil off on 'em."

"Now I know you're smashed," his friend said. "Those little fuckers try anything, we'll knock 'em into the middle of next week. I dare you to tell me any different."

"Oh, hell, yes, we'd lick 'em." No matter how drunk Fletch was, he knew how strong Hawaii's defenses were.

Two divisions based at Schofield Barracks, the Coast Artillery Command with its headquarters at Fort DeRussy right next to Waikiki Beach, the flyboys at Wheeler right by the barracks complex here, and, just for icing on the cake, the Pacific Fleet . . . "They'd have to be crazy to screw with us."

"Bet your ass," Douglas said. "So how come you've got ants in your pants?"

Armitage shrugged. "I just wish . . ." His voice trailed away. He wished for a lot of things that mattered more to him right now than just how prepared the men at Schofield Barracks were to turn back an attack unlikely ever to come. And those weren't ants in his pants. He and Jane had been married for five years. He was used to getting it regularly. These past three weeks had been a hard time in more ways than one. He sipped at the drink. "Life's a bastard sometimes, you know?"

"Plenty of people in it are bastards, that's for goddamn sure," Gordon Douglas agreed. "You keep the hell away from 'em if you can, you salute 'em and go, 'Yes, sir,' if you can't. That's the way things work, buddy." He spoke with great earnestness.

"Yeah. I guess." Fletch's head bobbed up and down. He didn't feel like nodding. He felt like crying. He'd done that only once, the night he moved out of the apartment and into BOQ. He'd been a lot drunker then than he was now. Of course, he could still take care of that. The whiskey sour vanished. He signaled for a refill.

"You're gonna feel like hell tomorrow morning," Douglas said, also putting his drink out of its misery. "If they have live-fire practice, you'll wish your head would fall off." That bit of good advice didn't keep him from reloading, too.

Armitage shrugged. "That's tomorrow morning. This is now. If I'm drunk, I don't have to worry about . . . anything."

"Look on the bright side," his friend suggested. "If we were back home, there might be snow on the ground already."

"If you were back home, there might be snow on the ground," Fletch said. "That's *your* worry. I'm from San Diego. I don't know any more about it than the Hawaiians do."

"You grew up in a Navy town," Douglas said. "You're here where they've got more goddamn sailors than anywhere else in the world. So what the hell are you doing in the Army?"

"Sometimes I wonder," Armitage said. If he had one more whiskey sour, he was going to start wondering about his own name, too. The only thing getting drunk didn't make him wonder about was Jane. She was gone, and he wouldn't get her back. That was why he was drinking in the first place. It didn't seem fair. He turned his blurry focus back to the question. "What the hell am I doing in the Army? Best I can right now. How about you?"

Gordon Douglas didn't answer. He'd put his head down on the bar and started to snore. Fletch shook him awake, which wasn't easy because he kept wanting to yawn, too. They lurched back to BOQ together. Patrolling sentries just kept patrolling; it wasn't as if they'd never seen a drunken officer before, or even two.

The next morning, aspirins and most of a gallon of black coffee put only the faintest of dents in Fletch's hangover. He managed to choke down some dry toast with the coffee. In his stomach, it felt as if it were all corners. Douglas looked as decrepit as he felt, a very faint consolation indeed.

And they did go through live-fire exercises. Having a 105mm gun go off by his head did nothing to speed Fletch's recovery. He gulped more aspirins and wished he were dead.

JIRO TAKAHASHI AND HIS TWO SONS carried tubs full of *nehus* onto the *Oshima Maru* as the sampan lay tied up in Kewalo Basin, a little west of Honolulu. Takahashi, a short, muscular, sun-browned man of fifty-five, had named the fishing boat for the Japanese county he'd left around the turn of the century. He watched the minnows dash back and forth in the galvanized iron tubs. They knew they weren't coming along for a holiday cruise.

He wondered if his sons knew the same. "Pick up your feet! Get moving!" he called to them in Japanese, the only language he spoke.

Hiroshi and Kenzo both smiled at him. He didn't see that they moved any faster. They should have. They were less than half his age, and both of them were three or four inches taller than he was. They should have been stronger than he was, too. If they were, he hadn't seen it. They didn't have the fire in their bellies, the passion for work, that he did. He didn't know why. It wasn't as if he hadn't tried to give it to them.

Hiroshi said something in English as he set his tub down on the deck. His younger brother answered in the same language. They'd both been educated in American schools on Oahu. They used English as readily as Japanese, even though Jiro had sent them to Japanese schools after the regular schools ended. They went by Hank and Ken as often as by the names he'd given them.

They both laughed—loud, boisterous, American laughs. Jiro shot them a suspicious glance. Were they laughing at him? They sometimes used English to keep him from knowing what they were saying.

All over Kewalo Basin, big diesel engines were growling to life. Blue-painted sampans glided out of the basin and into the wide Pacific. The blue paint was camouflage. The fishermen hoped it fooled the tuna they caught. They knew good and well it fooled other fishermen who might try to poach in fine fishing spots.

Back when Jiro first came to Hawaii, sampans had been sail-powered. Diesels let them range much farther a-sea. Takahashi muttered to himself as he started the *Oshima Maru*'s engine. He liked to be one of the first boats out of the basin. Not today, not when he'd had to drag his boys out of bed. Did they think the tuna were going to sleep late, too?

Up at the bow, the two of them were tossing a hollow glass globe as big as their heads back and forth. The net float had drifted here all the way from Japan. A lot of sampans carried one or two of them, sometimes more. They showed up around Kauai more often than anywhere else: some trick of the currents, no doubt.

Jiro hauled in the mooring line and got the *Oshima Maru* going. His sons went right on tossing the float back and forth. He finally lost patience with them. "Will you two knock off that foolishness?" he shouted.

"Sorry, Father," Hiroshi said. He didn't sound sorry. He didn't look sorry, either. He had a silly grin on his face.

Grimly, Jiro steered the *Oshima Maru* south and west. "Careful, Father," Kenzo said. "You don't want to end up in the defensive sea area."

The last three words were in English, but Jiro understood them. Kenzo meant the three-mile-square region south of the Pearl Harbor outlet that the Navy had declared off-limits to sampans. The Navy patrolled aggressively to make sure the fishing boats stayed out of it, too. If you got caught in the defensive sea area, you were sure to get a warning and an escort out; you'd probably also draw a fine.

"You think I'm going to give the Navy my money?" Jiro asked his younger son. "Am I that dumb?"

"No, Father," Kenzo answered. "But accidents can happen."

"Accidents. Oh, yes. They can happen," Jiro Takahashi said. "They can, but they'd better not." Straying into the defensive sea area wouldn't be an accident, though. It would be a piece of stupidity Jiro had no intention of allowing. His boat went where it was supposed to.

A seaplane buzzed by overhead. A Navy man with a radio was probably reporting the *Oshima Maru*'s position. *Well, let him*, Jiro thought. *I'm not in their restricted area, and they can't say I am.*

On went the fishing boat. Pearl Harbor and Honolulu sank below the horizon. Jiro and his sons ate rice and pork his wife, Reiko, had packed for them. They drank tea. Hiroshi and Kenzo also drank Coca-Cola. Jiro had tried the American drink, but didn't think much of it. Too sweet, too fizzy.

It was the middle of the afternoon before they got to a spot Jiro judged likely. He couldn't have said why he thought it would be good. It felt right, that was all. Some combination of wind and waves and water color told him the tuna were likely to be here. When he was a boy, he'd gone out with his father to fish the Inland Sea of Japan. His father had seemed able to *smell* a good catch. When Jiro asked him how he did it, he'd just laughed. "If you know fish, you know where they go," he'd said. "You'll figure it out."

And Jiro had. He glanced over to his strapping sons. Would they? He didn't want to bet on it. Too many things distracted them. He could get them to fish with him, and even to do a good enough job while they were here. But he could have trained a couple of Portuguese cowboys from a cattle ranch on the Big Island to do that. It wouldn't have made them fishermen, and it didn't make Hiroshi and Kenzo fishermen, either. To them, this was only a job, and not such a good one. To Jiro, it was a way of life.

He cut the motor. The *Oshima Maru* drifted silently on the light chop. Not far away, a booby plunged into the sea. It came out with a fish in its beak. That was a good sign. The booby wasn't big enough to catch a tuna, of course, but it caught the sort of fish on which tuna fed. If they were here, the tuna probably would be, too.

Nodding to his sons, he said, "Throw in the bait."

Hiroshi tipped one of the tubs of minnows over the side. The little silvery fish, still very much alive, made a cloud in the water. Hiroshi and Kenzo and Jiro dropped their long lines into the Pacific, lines full of gleaming barbless hooks that a hungry tuna might mistake for a minnow. Greed killed. Jiro understood that. The tuna didn't, which let him make a living. He wondered if his sons did. Compared to him, they'd had things easy. How much good had that done them? Jiro only shrugged.

Hiroshi and Kenzo went back and forth, mostly in English, now and then in Japanese. Jiro caught names: Roosevelt, Hull, Kurusu. He hoped the Japanese special envoy would find a way to persuade America to start selling oil to

Japan again. Cutting it off seemed monstrously unfair to him. He didn't say that to his sons. They saw everything from the U.S. point of view. Arguing over politics was usually more trouble than it was worth.

What Jiro did say was, "Now!" He and his sons hauled the lines back aboard the *Oshima Maru*. A lot of them had small Hawaiian striped tuna, locally called *aku*, writhing on the hooks. They'd been after minnows and found something harder, something crueler. The three men worked like machines, gutting them and putting them on ice.

Jiro grabbed an especially fine striped tuna. His knife flashed. What could be fresher, what could be more delicious, than sashimi cut from a still-wriggling fish? A slow smile of pleasure spread over his face as he chewed. He offered some of the delicate flesh, almost as red as beef, to his boys. They ate with him, though they didn't seem to enjoy it quite so much as he did. He sighed. They gobbled down hamburgers and french fries whenever they got the chance. That wasn't the food he'd grown up on, and it tasted strange to him. To them, it was as normal as what they got at home.

Once the last of the catch was on ice, he said, "Back to it." He and Hiroshi and Kenzo dumped the guts overboard and spilled another tub of *nehus* into the Pacific. The lines with their freight of hooks followed. The fishermen waited while the *aku* struck. Then they hauled in the lines and began gutting fish again.

A shark snapped past just as Kenzo pulled the last of the tuna into the *Oshima Maru*. He laughed. "Waste time, shark!" he said in English. That was another fragment of the language Jiro followed, mostly because both his boys said it all the time. *Waste time* meant anything futile or useless.

They fished till they ran out of bait. Not all the sharks wasted time; they brought in several tuna heads, the wolves of the sea having bitten off the rest of the fish. That always happened, most often after they'd been working for a while. The minnows drew the tuna, and the tuna—and the blood in the water from their guts—drew the sharks.

But it was a pretty good day. When Hiroshi said, "Let's go back," Jiro nodded. They'd done everything they could do. They would get a good price from the men at the Aala Market. These tuna were too good to go to the canning plants. Once the dealers bought them, they'd be sold one by one, mostly to Japanese restaurants and Japanese housewives. Chinese and Filipinos would buy some, and maybe the odd *haole* would, too, though Jiro grimaced when he thought about what whites did to such lovely fish. He'd heard of tuna salad. He'd never had the nerve to try it.

The sun had just set when the *Oshima Maru* tied up in Kewalo Basin once more. Dealers—some Japanese, some Chinese (and mixed outfits, like Oshiro and Wo)—came aboard to examine the catch. They said what they could to disparage it, to bring down the price, but the *aku* were too good to let them get away with much. Jiro went home with almost twenty dollars in his pocket. He wished he could do that well every day.

WHEN THE USS *ENTERPRISE* SAILED for Wake Island on the morning of November 28, the carrier had done so under Vice Admiral William Halsey's Battle Order Number One. Right from the start of the cruise, torpedoes had had warheads mounted. Planes taking off from the carrier's flight deck carried loaded guns. They had orders to shoot down any aircraft not known to belong to the USA. All of Task Force Eight, which included three heavy cruisers and nine destroyers along with the *Enterprise*, had ammunition ready at the guns. Planes patrolled out to two hundred miles around the task force. Halsey insisted the Japanese were liable to attack without bothering to declare war.

Now the task force was bound for Pearl Harbor again. Nothing untoward had happened. They'd delivered Marine Corps Fighter Squadron 211 to Wake without any trouble. No one had seen any airplanes that didn't look American. No one had spotted any subs, either, and subs worried Halsey even more than enemy aircraft did.

Lieutenant James Peterson thought all the extra excitement was just a bunch of hooey. He wasn't shy about saying so, either. The fighter pilot, a rangy six feet two, was rarely shy about saying anything. "Anybody who thinks the Japs have the nerve to try us on for size has to be nuts," he declared, swigging coffee with some of the other pilots. "We'd kick their ass from here to Sunday. They aren't a bunch of dummies. They've got to know that as well as we do."

"The Bull thinks they're up to something," said another pilot, a j.g. named Hank Drucker. "He wouldn't have put out that Battle Order if he didn't." Several men nodded at that. If Halsey thought something, they were convinced it had to be true.

But Peterson remained unquelled and unconvinced. "I think he put it out just to keep us on our toes," he said. "What the hell could the Japs do to us?"

"Halsey's worried about submarines," Drucker said. "One torpedo amidships can put a pretty fair crimp in your plans."

"Yeah, but why would they do anything like that?" Peterson demanded. "It makes no sense. They couldn't sink enough of our ships to hurt the Pacific Fleet very much—and then they'd be eyeball-to-eyeball with us, and we'd be all pissed off."

"They're already pissed off at us." Lieutenant Carter Higdon had a Mississippi drawl thick enough to slice. Despite it, he was the brains of the squadron. When he was off duty, he was working his way through a beat-up copy of *Ulysses*. He went on, "We've cut off their oil. We've cut off their scrap metal. Somebody tried doing that to us, how would we like it?"

"I'd kick the son of a bitch right in the slats," Peterson said.

"I think you just shot yourself down, Jim," Drucker said, a split second after Peterson realized the same thing.

He got out of it as best he could: "But I'm an American, goddammit. Those slant-eyed bastards haven't got the balls for anything like that."

"Here's hopin' you're right," Higdon said. "But I reckon

we'll be steamin' west for real before too long, get the war going in the Philippines or somewhere like that. If they don't get their oil from us, where will they get it? Only other place is the Dutch East Indies—and if they go there, they'll go loaded for bear."

Several pilots nodded. The Dutch East Indies had hung like ripe fruit waiting to be picked ever since the Germans overran Holland the year before. And Vichy France, also under the Nazis' thumbs, had given Japan the right to base troops in French Indochina. Of course, if Vichy had said no, the Japs would have gone in anyhow. This way, France maintained a ghostly sort of sovereignty over the area. Peterson wondered how happy that made the froggies.

"You think we ought to fight if the Japs do go into the East Indies?" Drucker asked Higdon. "Me, I'll be damned if we ought to pull the Dutchmen's chestnuts out of the fire."

"If they do get that oil, it's us next," Higdon said, turning *next* into a two-syllable word. "We're the only ones who can worry them. Holland and France are down for the count, and England's got bigger worries closer to home. If Hitler takes Moscow and knocks the Russians out this winter, he'll turn on England with everything he's got next spring."

The argument went on and on. Sometimes it was arguing in the wardroom, sometimes a poker game, sometimes argument *and* poker. Finally, Peterson got tired of it and went up onto the flight deck. His shoes thumped on the six-inch wooden planks. When the *Enterprise* was a-building, there'd been talk about armoring the flight deck as the British were doing, but it hadn't come to anything.

Color-coded cotton jerseys and cloth helmets told off the deck crew by function. Sailors in blue handled parked planes, those in yellow directed them while they moved, while those in red were the repair and crash crews. A couple of fire watchmen in suits of fuzzy white asbestos moved among them, looking like snowmen out for a stroll. Peterson wouldn't have wanted that job for beans, especially not in warm weather.

Of course, when the fire watchmen went to work, they had more heat to worry about than what they got in the tropics. They watched the world through thick panes of smoked glass. Diving suits might have been heavier and more restrictive than what they wore. Peterson couldn't think of anything else that came close. No, he wouldn't have swapped jobs with them for anything.

One of them waved a gauntleted hand. Automatically, Peterson waved back. The fire watchman's head was turned in his general direction, so he assumed the wave was for him. He might have been wrong. Trying to judge what a man meant when you couldn't see his face wasn't easy.

He laughed out loud. "What's funny, sir?" asked a repair crewman in a red jersey.

"I was just thinking I'd like to wear one of those goddamn fire suits the next poker game I get into," Peterson answered. "Long as I keep the faceplate closed, who's gonna know I'm raising on a busted flush?"

The sailor contemplated that, then grinned. "Don't tell those firewatch bastards. They'd up and do it."

"Who'd play with 'em if they did?" Peterson asked.

"Sir, we got us somewhere close to three thousand men on board," the sailor replied. "You don't figure some of 'em are suckers?"

"Well, yeah, but you're not supposed to say so out loud. Otherwise, you *will* keep 'em out of the games," Peterson said. They grinned at each other.

Peterson looked out to sea. A fresh breeze blew his sandy hair back from his face. The air was the freshest in the world. He didn't consciously notice the salt tang of the sea, but it braced him even so. Off to port, a cruiser kept station with the *Enterprise*. A couple of destroyers prowled ahead, alert for periscopes—and, with their listening gear, for subs lurking below the surface.

A couple of gooney birds glided by on wings that seemed almost as long as a Wildcat's. The big birds bred on Midway and some of the other islands in the northwestern part of the Hawaiian chain. In the air, they were nonpareils. On land . . . They came in as if they'd blown both tires and had a wheel go out from under them. They were almost as ungainly taking off, too. They needed a headwind and a long running start. Otherwise, they couldn't get airborne at all.

More destroyers followed the carrier at the heart of the task force. Peterson turned and peered over the *Enterprise*'s stern. That pointed him more or less in the direction of Japan. What *were* Tojo's boys up to? Could they really be contemplating war with the USA? Peterson still had trouble believing it. Wasn't all their tough talk just a bluff? With the America Firsters and the other isolationists running around loose and making a big noise in the papers and on the radio, weren't the Japs trying to scare FDR into giving them what they wanted?

"Dammit, that's still the way it looks to me," Peterson muttered. If the President just stood firm, Japan would pull in its horns. The Japs had a million soldiers bogged down in China, for Christ's sake. Why would they take on another country that was bigger than they were? It made no sense.

"Prepare to land a plane!" blared from the loudspeakers, and then, "Landing a plane!"

The squat F4F Wildcat came in from astern. The landing officer stood facing it. He held out the wigwag flags so they and his arms made a straight line out from his shoulders. He dipped to the right; the Wildcat straightened up. Jim Peterson laughed. If that wasn't Ike Greenwald coming in, he'd eat his socks. Ike always carried one wing low. The landing officer straightened and moved the flags in small circles. The fighter sped up. The landing officer dropped the flags to his sides. The plane dove for the deck.

Tires smoked as they struck. The tailhook caught an arrester wire. The pilot killed the roaring engine. The stinks of sizzling rubber and exhaust ruined the clean air for a moment. The man in the cockpit rolled back the canopy and climbed out. Sure as hell, it was Greenwald. Nobody else on the *Enterprise* was built quite so much like a soda straw. People said he could sleep in the barrel of a five-inch gun. That wasn't fair, though he might have managed in an eight-incher.

"Nice landing," one of the sailors on the flight deck called to him.

He grinned sheepishly. He never knew what to do with praise. Peterson would have milked it for all it was worth. Greenwald just said, "I didn't crash the crate, and I didn't smash me. I'll take it."

Another Wildcat roared off to keep the combat air patrol at full strength. The plane dropped towards the Pacific as it sped off the flight deck, then steadied and began to climb. Peterson watched it with affection. The Wildcat was a pretty good machine. It measured up fine against land-based American fighters. That had to mean the Japs didn't have anything that even came close.

OSCAR VAN DER KIRK WAS A BUM. He knew it. He was proud of it, as a matter of fact. He was a big blond man in his late twenties, his hair bleached even paler by constant exposure to sun and sea, his hide tanned almost as brown as a Hawaiian's.

He hadn't intended to turn into a bum. He'd graduated from Stanford in 1935: an English major with a history minor. His folks thought he should have studied accounting instead. But he was a second son, a kid brother, and Roger showed plenty of aptitude and eagerness for the family construction business when—if—Dad ever decided to retire. So, while disappointed, Oscar's folks weren't furious. They let him do what he wanted.

It was hard to be furious at Oscar anyhow. He had not a mean bone in his body. An aw-shucks smile made girls' hearts melt. He'd studied coeds at least as much as Chaucer and Herodotus, and he'd got good grades in them.

As a graduation present, his folks gave him a trip to Hawaii. They booked him into the Royal Hawaiian, right on Waikiki Beach. The grounds were splendidly landscaped, with coconut palms and banyan trees insulating the great pink pile from the encroachments of the outside world. The room ran twenty dollars a day—this when millions would have got down on their knees and thanked God to make twenty dollars a week. Oscar had never had to worry about money—and he didn't worry about it now.

Next door to the Royal Hawaiian stood the Outrigger Club, which since 1908 had been dedicated to the art and science of surf-riding. The proximity of club to hotel was the reason Oscar went from new-minted baccalaureate to bum in the course of two short weeks. He watched in open-mouthed awe the first time he saw men glide the big surf-boards over the waves and up onto the white sand of the beach.

"By God, I'm going to try that!" he said. Nobody at the Royal Hawaiian took any particular notice of the remark. Quite a few visitors said they wanted to learn to ride the surf. A good many of them actually did it. A handful did it enough to start to know what they were doing.

The next morning, Oscar was out in front of the Outrigger Club half an hour before sunup. It didn't open till eight. The man who let him in smiled and said, "Hello, *malihini*. You look eager."

Malihini meant stranger or tenderfoot. Without the smile, it might have been an insult. Oscar wouldn't have cared if it were. He nodded to the man, who was then the same shade of brown he would later become himself. "Teach me!" he said.

He learned to ride the surfboard on his belly, and then kneeling, and then, at last, standing. Skimming over the waves was like nothing he'd known in all his life. It was as if God had given him wings. Was this how angels felt? He didn't know about angels. He did know this was what he was meant to do.

He was supposed to go home in two weeks. He cashed in his return ticket instead, and moved to digs much less impressive—and much less expensive—than the Royal Hawaiian. He stretched his money as far as it would go, to stay in Hawaii as long as he could. His only luxury (though to him it was a necessity) was more surf-riding lessons.

When the money he got from the ticket ran out, he worked on the docks for a while, and surfed almost every waking minute when he wasn't working. Before long, he didn't need to take lessons any more. Before much longer, he was giving them. By the time winter came, he was as good as men who'd been riding the waves as long as he'd been alive.

That was what he thought, anyway, till he followed the Outrigger Club members' winter migration to the north shore of Oahu. There he found waves like none he'd seen, like none he'd imagined, near Honolulu. They rolled down across the North Pacific all the way from Alaska. And when they came ashore at Waimea and some of the other spots the club members knew, some of them were as tall as a three-story building.

Riding waves like that wasn't just sport. If it went wrong, it was like falling off a cliff—except then the cliff fell on you. More than once, he came to the surface gasping and gouged and scraped from a tumble against the sand. He lost two front teeth when somebody else's surfboard hit him in the face. That was, if anything, a membership pin. Half the really accomplished surfers at the Outrigger Club sported either bridgework or a space where their incisors had been.

He never did go back to northern California. His family wrote anguished letters for a while. He assured them he was fine. After a while, they gave up and stopped writing. He dropped them little notes every so often—whenever he happened to think of it. He *was* a good-natured fellow. As time went by, though, he thought about anything outside of Oahu less and less often.

He acquired a nickname: Smooth Oscar. He acquired a scar on his leg from a jagged chunk of coral. He acquired a series of lady friends from among the tourists who came from Seattle or St. Louis or Savannah to learn to ride the surf. The lessons were intimate enough to start with, and often got more so after the sun went down. The ladies, almost all of them, went home happy. Oscar smiled a lot.

When times were good, he got enough money from the lessons to make ends meet. When they weren't so good, he went back to the docks or washed dishes in one of Honolulu's nine million greasy spoons or worked in the cane and pineapple fields that filled the middle of the island. When he wasn't out on the ocean, he didn't much care what he did.

One day when he was, by his standards, flush, he paid a hundred bucks for a 1927 Chevy hardtop with no rear window. What the former owner perceived as a deficiency was to Oscar an asset. It let him stow his surfboard much more conveniently. The board, of three-inch-thick koa wood, was eleven feet long and not the easiest object to transport. After seeing how handy the missing window proved, three or four of his fellow surfers knocked the back glass out of their jalopies.

Oscar had been brought up bourgeois. Every so often, he wondered what the hell he was doing with his life. But all the doubts flew away when he rode along at the crest of a wave—or when he rode one of the girls he'd taught to kneel on a board in the wahine surf near the Moana Hotel in Waikiki. He was having a good time: that was what he was doing. Who needed anything more?

He snagged a lot of lessons towards the end of 1941. He'd been short on cash, and winter brought the tourists out from the cold parts of the country. But when his latest girlfriend threw a vase at his head after he didn't ask her to marry him the night before she sailed back to Los Angeles, he decided the time had come to get away from it all for a little while.

He loaded his board into the Chevy. With him rode Charlie Kaapu, a large, smiling, half-Hawaiian fellow who also lived for the surf and a good time. Charlie's surfboard was six or eight inches longer than Oscar's. They tied a red rag to the back of it to keep cars behind them from running into them, then took off for the north coast and whatever they found there.

"Peace and quiet," Oscar said, more plaintively than usual. "I told that Shirley it was only for fun, but she didn't want to listen." He took a hand off the wheel to touch his right ear, the only part of his anatomy the vase had grazed. Four inches to the left and he would have been very unhappy. As things were, he wouldn't be able to go barefoot in his apartment till he swept up all the broken glass.

Charlie Kaapu laughed at him from the backseat. "Women hear what they want to hear. Don't you know that by now?"

"I ought to," Oscar said. "I mean, she was fine for a week or two, but forever?" He shook his head. "She'd drive me nuts. Hell, I'd drive her nuts."

"They put out for you, they think it's gotta be for life," Charlie said, and then, philosophically, "She's gone now. You don't gotta worry about it no more."

"Yeah." Oscar spoke with a mixture of relief and regret. He was glad Shirley'd got on the liner and out of his hair— no doubt of that. But he still wished things had gone better. He didn't like ugly scenes. They weren't his style. A kiss on the cheek, a pat on the fanny, a good-bye from the pier as the ship headed back to the mainland . . . That was how he liked things to go, and how they usually went.

He got out of Honolulu, went past the back side of Pearl Harbor, and drove up the Kamehameha Highway towards the north coast. The drive wasn't so pleasant as he would have wanted. He got stuck behind a snorting convoy of olive-drab Army trucks chugging up to Schofield Barracks. Not only did they slow him down, but the exhaust made his head ache. He hadn't had *that* much to drink the night before . . . had he?

Pineapple fields stretched out along the right side of the road, pineapple and sugarcane to the left. Most of the time, he would have smelled the damp freshness of growing things. Diesel stink made an inadequate substitute.

They rattled past Wheeler Field, off to the left of the highway. Charlie pointed to the planes drawn up in neat, tight rows on the runways. "Pretty snazzy."

"Yeah," Oscar said again. "Nobody's gonna get at 'em or do anything to 'em." He drove on for a little while, then asked, "You think anything's gonna come of this war scare, Charlie?"

"Beats me," Charlie Kaapu answered. "Everybody's pretty stupid if us and the Japs do start fighting, though."

Oscar nodded. He said, "Yeah," one more time. The trucks pulled off to the left, the way to Schofield Barracks. He stepped on the gas. The Chevy went a little faster: not a lot, since the only way it could have hit fifty was to go off a cliff. But he was glad not to have to breathe fumes any more. Smiling, he lit a cigarette and passed Charlie the pack.

The Dole pineapple plantation north of Wahiawa was one of the biggest in the world. Most of the workers in the fields were Japanese and Filipinos. Having put in some time there himself, Oscar had seen enough to feel sorry for them.

He stopped for gas in Waialua, just short of the ocean: eighteen and a half cents a gallon at the Standard Oil station. That made him grumble—Hawaii was more expensive than the mainland. Up at Haleiwa, on the Pacific, he had to stop his car just short of a narrow bridge buttressed by double arches of steel. Another convoy of trucks was heading to Schofield Barracks, these diesel snorters loaded with men who'd been enjoying leave on the north shore.

Even before the last truck came through, Charlie Kaapu was doing some snorting of his own. He pointed north, past the last of the olive-drab monsters. "You see that, Oscar? You see, goddammit? Ain't got no fuckin' surf!"

"Could be better," Oscar agreed. "Could be worse, too. I figure—what, five-six feet?"

"Something like that," Charlie said, still disgusted. "Hell, I can piss higher'n that. I wanted some *big* waves."

"Maybe they'll come," Oscar said hopefully. "Maybe there's a storm up north blowing like hell. Maybe they'll be twenty or thirty feet by tomorrow. And besides, this still isn't too bad."

"Ha!" Charlie Kaapu said. "We could do this out by Diamond Head. You gonna tell me I'm wrong?"

"No." Oscar couldn't, and he knew it. "But we're here, so we might as well make the best of it." He'd been making the best of it ever since he got to Hawaii. He saw no reason to change now. "Tell you what—I'll go on to Waimea Bay. It'll be better there than anywhere else along this coast."

"Okay, go ahead," Charlie said. "We've come this far.

What's another few miles? Anyway, looks like we'll just find more soldiers if we stay around here."

He wasn't wrong about that, either. The Army used Waialua Bay as a place to give its men rest and recreation. It looked to have taken most of them back to Schofield Barracks in the truck convoy that had blocked the bridge, but not all the olive-drab tents had disappeared from the beach here. The trucks would have to come back for the rest of the men.

When they got to Waimea, though, the surfers had things to themselves. Oscar parked the Chevy across the road from the beach. He and Charlie pulled their surfboards out of the car, stuck them under their arms, and carried them down towards the sea. Oscar's toes dug into the sand. It was softer than any he'd known on a California beach. He knew he'd feel that more on the return trip, when he was going uphill. Now . . .

Now he didn't want to think about the return trip. Easier to get out into the ocean when the waves weren't so fierce. The surfboard went into the water. He lay down atop it and paddled with his arms. Ten feet away, Charlie Kaapu was doing the same thing.

After Oscar had paddled out far enough, he turned the board around. The swells pushed him back towards the shore. He scrambled upright on the bobbing, tilting, darting surfboard and rode the crest of a wave all the way up onto the beach.

He looked around for Charlie. There he was, separated from his surfboard, which washed ashore without him. "Surf's not *too* easy, is it?" Oscar called.

His friend gave him the finger. "This shit can happen down by Diamond Head, too," Charlie said. He wasn't wrong about that, either; he'd lost *his* front teeth within a couple of miles of Waikiki.

They surfed all day. Oscar wiped out several times. He'd known he would, and didn't worry about it. When the sun sank down towards Kaena Point, they put the boards back into the Chevy and walked into Waimea. A chop-suey house there gave them a cheap, filling supper.

"You don't want to drive back in the dark, do you?" Charlie Kaapu hinted.

Oscar smiled. "No. I was thinking we'd sleep in the car, put the boards on the roof, and go at it again first thing in the morning."

Charlie's face lit up. "Now you're talking!"

Sleeping in the Chevy was a cramped business, but Oscar had had practice. Charlie hadn't, or not so much, but he managed. His snores escaped through the glassless rear window.

Those same snores helped wake Oscar around sunup. Yawning, he sat up in the front seat and stretched. He did some more stretching after he got out of the car, to work the kinks from his neck and back. He walked over and pissed at the base of a coconut palm. Only the waning gibbous moon looked down at him from low in the west.

His belly growled. He wished he'd thought to bring along something for breakfast. Nothing in Waimea would be open so early. And this was Sunday morning, too, so it was anybody's guess if anything would be open at all.

He couldn't do anything about that. All he could do was put his board in the water. He looked out to the Pacific and muttered under his breath. The waves were no better than they had been the day before. If anything, they were a little flatter. Oscar shrugged. What could you do?

When he got his board off the roof of the Chevy, the noise woke Charlie Kaapu. The big half-Hawaiian extracted himself from the car. As Oscar had, he stretched and yawned. "What time is it, anyway?" he asked.

"I don't know." Oscar didn't wear a watch. But a glance at the sun gave him a fair idea. "About half past seven, I guess."

Charlie looked out to sea. He made the same sort of mutters as Oscar had. Then he went off to take a leak by the same palm tree. When he came back, he got down his surfboard, too. "We're here. We might as well give it a go," he said resignedly.

"Yeah." Oscar nodded. "I was thinking the same thing." He crossed the road and headed down the beach towards the water. Charlie Kaapu followed.

Oscar had a couple of good rides in. The second time, Charlie went off his board. He had a scowl on his face when he recaptured it. He stood there at the edge of the sea, dripping and fuming. Then he frowned, looking north. "What's that noise?"

After a moment, Oscar heard it too: a distant drone that put him in mind of mosquitoes. He also looked north. He pointed. "There they are. That's a hell of a lot of airplanes. The Army or the Navy must be up to something."

The airplanes flew in several groups. Some went south through the central valley. Others took a more southwesterly course. They were plenty high enough to make it over the Waianae Range. Oscar briefly wondered why they were all coming off the ocean. Then he shrugged again. What the military did wasn't his worry. He and Charlie went back to their surf-riding.

LIEUTENANT SABURO SHINDO PILOTED HIS ZERO back toward the *Akagi*. Exultation filled the commander of the second wave's fighters. The first two attacks had heavily damaged the ships at Pearl Harbor and punished the airfields on Oahu. *Now*, Shindo thought, *now we finish the job*.

There was the carrier, with some of the fleet's screen of destroyers and cruisers and battleships. And there were the transports, steaming south towards Oahu as fast as they could go. Shindo's lips skinned back from his teeth in a fierce grin. He was usually on the phlegmatic side. Not today. Today he felt like a tiger. And by tomorrow morning, the Japanese would be landing on the island.

Meanwhile, he had to land on the *Akagi*. Another Zero came in just ahead of his. The deck crew manhandled the plane to one side. The landing officer signaled for Shindo to continue his approach. He did, concentrating on the man's signals to the exclusion of everything else. The carrier's deck was pitching and rolling in front of him. The man on it could gauge his path better than he could himself. Learning that lesson was the hardest thing any Navy flier did.

Down went the flags. Shindo dove for the *Akagi*'s deck.

The arrester hook caught a wire. His Zero jerked to a stop. He shoved back the canopy, scrambled out of the plane, and ran for the carrier's small portside island. "Admiral Nagumo!" he called. "Admiral Nagumo!"

Admiral Chuichi Nagumo came out onto the deck to meet him. He was a stocky man in his mid-fifties, with a round face, two deep vertical lines between his eyes, and thinning hair cropped close to his skull. He was a big-gun admiral, not a flying man, which sometimes worried Shindo. He'd got command of the Pearl Harbor expedition by seniority: the usual Japanese way. So far, though, he'd handled things as smoothly as anyone could have.

"All is well?" he asked now. Tension stretched his voice taut.

"All is very well!" Shindo flashed a grin at Minoru Genda and Mitsuo Fuchida, who'd come out onto the flight deck behind Nagumo. Fuchida, the air commander, was a couple of years older than Genda, taller, with long, horsey features. Shindo pulled himself back to the admiral's question: "Yes, sir, all is very well. We need to launch the third wave right away, to smash the dock facilities and the fuel tanks and to hit Schofield Barracks for the Army's benefit."

"Where are the American carriers?" Nagumo demanded.

That was the one fly in the ointment. They hadn't caught any of the carriers in port. Shindo gave the only answer he could: "Sir, I don't know."

Those lines between Admiral Nagumo's eyes got deeper yet. "You are thinking about what happens to Hawaii," he said heavily. "I am thinking about what happens to my fleet. What if the Americans strike us while we linger here?"

From behind him, Commander Genda said, "Sir, we have six carriers. At most, the Americans have three, and they probably aren't concentrated. We have the best fliers in the world. They have . . . less than the best. If they find us, *they* will be the ones to regret it."

"So you say." Nagumo still sounded anything but happy. Shindo had yet to hear him sound happy since the fleet sailed from Japan. Even the astounding damage the first two waves of attackers had caused did nothing to cheer him. He went on, "I tell you, gentlemen, if it were not for the landing forces accompanying us, I would turn around and sail for the home islands now."

Commander Fuchida couldn't hide his horror. "Sir, we have a job to finish!" he exclaimed.

"I know," Nagumo answered. "And I will stay, and I will carry it through. Those are my orders, and I cannot abandon the soldiers. But what I told you is no less true. We are in danger here."

"So are the Americans," Shindo said. Genda and Fuchida both nodded. At last, reluctantly, so did Admiral Nagumo.

II

THE MESSAGE CAME IN TO THE *ENTERPRISE* FROM ONE OF
the scouts just after eight in the morning: "White 16—Pearl
Harbor under attack! Do not acknowledge."

Aboard the carrier, rage boiled. "Those little slanty-
eyed cocksuckers want a war, they've got one!" Lieutenant
Jim Peterson shouted to whoever would listen.

"You were the one who said they wouldn't fight." Three
people reminded Peterson of that at the same time.

He was too furious to get embarrassed at being wrong.
"I don't give a shit what I said," he snarled. "Let's knock
the yellow bastards into the middle of next week."

But that was easier said than done. Everyone knew the
Japanese were somewhere off the Hawaiian Islands—but
where? Had they come down out of the north or up from
the south? The *Enterprise* couldn't even ask the harried
men at Pearl Harbor what they knew. As soon as that hor-
rifying message came in, Admiral Halsey slapped radio silence on the whole task force. No Japs were going to spot
the carrier and her satellites by their signals.

In the wardroom, the pilots drank coffee and cursed the
Japanese—and also cursed the Pearl Harbor defenders,
who'd shot down some of the scouts trying to land in the
middle of the attack.

The ships steamed furiously towards Pearl Harbor.
They'd been about two hundred miles northwest of Oahu

when they got the dreadful news—about seven hours at top speed. And they were making top speed. Bull Halsey was not a man to hang back when he saw a fight right in front of his nose—far from it. He wanted to get in there and start swinging. The only trouble was, he had no more idea than anybody else where to aim his punches.

As the minutes passed and turned into hours, fury and frustration built aboard the *Enterprise*. The news in the wardroom was fragmentary—people on Oahu were clamping down on radio traffic, too—but what trickled in didn't sound good. "Jesus!" somebody said after the intercom piped in yet another gloomy report. "Sounds like Battleship Row's taken a hell of a licking."

"*That* won't end the world," Peterson said. "The Navy's needed to get rid of those wallowing tubs for years." He spoke like what he was: a carrier fighter pilot. Billy Mitchell had proved battleships obsolete twenty years earlier. Nobody'd paid any attention then. It sounded as if the Japs were driving home the lesson. Would anybody pay attention now?

"You're a coldhearted bastard, Peterson," a lieutenant named Edgar Kelley said. "It's not just ships, you know. It's God knows how many sailors, too."

"Yeah? So?" Peterson scowled at the other pilot. "If they didn't get it now, they sure as hell would when they took their battlewagons west to fight the Japs. Carrier air would take 'em out before the carriers came over the horizon." He didn't think of himself as coldhearted. But if you weren't a realist about the way the world worked, you'd take endless grief in life, sure as hell you would.

Just after noon, a cry not far from despair came over the intercom: "Third wave of attackers striking Pearl!"

That was followed almost immediately by Admiral Halsey's unmistakable rasp: "Boys, we've got to give the land-based air a hand. The Japs have knocked out a lot of it on the ground, and I'll be double-damned and fried in the Devil's big iron spider before I let those monkeys have it all their own way when I can give 'em a lick. Go get 'em! I only wish I were up there with you."

Cheering, the pilots ran for their Wildcats. Peterson's was third in line. He fired up the engine even before he'd closed the canopy and fastened his safety belts. The fierce roar of the 1,200-horsepower Wright radial engine filled him. His fingernails, his bones, his guts all shook with it. It made him feel not just alive but huge and ferocious— *he* might have been making that great noise, not his plane.

A red flag hung from the bridge: the signal that the *Enterprise* was about to launch her airplanes. No men in blue jerseys were left on the deck but the two who stood by to remove the chocks from the squadron leader's wheels. Sailors in yellow smocks formed a line across the deck.

What might have been the voice of God thundered from the island: "Prepare to launch planes!"

The sailors in blue whipped away the chocks. The lead Wildcat rolled forward, a man in yellow walking backwards just ahead of it, leading it on to a point midway up the flight deck. A little ahead of the island stood another man in a yellow jersey. This one held a checkered flag in his right hand.

That biblically amplified voice roared again: "Launch planes!"

As the man with the flag turned his free hand in a grinding motion, the squadron leader gunned his engine. When the note suited the sailor in yellow, he dropped the flag. The plane sped down the deck and zoomed off into the air. The next fighter taxied up to the takeoff line. At the flagman's orders, the pilot built up the boost on his engine. The flag fell. The Wildcat roared away.

Then it was Peterson's turn. The sailors in blue jerseys pulled away the chocks. Up to the line he went, following the man in yellow. The flagman made his grinding motion. Peterson gave his engine the gun. Down went the flag. Peterson whooped with delight. Acceleration shoved him back in his seat as the fighter raced down the *Enterprise*'s flight deck.

As always when he went off the end of the deck, there was that sickening lurch, that moment when he wondered whether he'd go into the sky or into the drink. But the Wildcat climbed after the two planes that had taken off ahead. Peterson whooped again. This was where he was meant to be, what he was meant to do.

More fighters rose from the carrier. They formed in pairs: leader and wingman. Peterson's wingman was a j.g. named Marvin Morrison. He had a squeaky tenor voice that broke when he got excited, which happened frequently. It sounded in Peterson's earphones now: "We're going to clean the Japs' clocks for them."

"Oh, hell, yes," Peterson agreed. "If they want a war, Marv, we'll give 'em all the war they want—you bet your ass we will."

Similar outraged chatter crackled through the squadron. Along with the outrage was a sense of astonishment: how *could* the Japanese, with their buck-toothed, bespectacled pilots and their lousy scrap-metal planes, dare to take on the United States of America? The fighter pilots also monitored radio traffic from Pearl Harbor. When one frantic officer relayed rumors that the Japs had German pilots doing some of their flying for them, Peterson nodded to himself. The little yellow men couldn't have done it all on their own. Say what you would about the Nazis, but they'd shown the world they knew what the hell they were doing when it came to war.

He saw the thick black smoke rising into the blue tropical sky when he was still a devil of a long way out from Pearl. More and more of it came up every minute, too. "Jesus," he said softly. With or without help from Hitler's Aryan supermen, the Japs had done something really terrible here.

Radio from Pearl Harbor abruptly cut off. He didn't think it was silence imposed by command. More likely, a bomb had wrecked the transmitter—the signal went away in the middle of a word.

As Peterson drew closer to Oahu, he saw more smoke rising from the Marine Corps airfield at Ewa, west of Pearl Harbor. In fact, people in Honolulu used *Ewa* as a synonym for *west*, the same as they used *Waikiki* for *east*. Till he got close, though, the small smoke from Ewa was lost in the greater conflagration of Pearl Harbor.

And the closer he got, the worse those fires looked. The tank farms had to be burning, sending untold millions of gallons of fuel oil up in smoke. Peterson swore softly, more in awe than in anger. This was a disaster, nothing else but. Somebody'd been asleep at the switch, or it never could have happened. Heads would roll among the big brass. They'd have to. But that did nobody one damn bit of good now.

"Bandits!" In Peterson's earphones, that was more a cry of exultation than a mere word. "Bandits dead ahead!"

He peered through the bulletproof windscreen. Sure as hell, there they were: shiny silver planes with meatballs on their wings and sides. They were tiny as toys now, but swelled even as he watched. "Come on, Marv!" he called to his wingman. "Time to go hunting!"

"I'm right with you," Morrison answered.

Peterson more than half expected the Japs to run away. Now they'd have to fight, after all, not just kick somebody while he was down. Did they really have the balls for that? But they'd seen the planes from the *Enterprise*, too, and here they came.

His thumb tensed on the firing button on top of the stick. Just when he thought he had the first of the enemy fighters in his sights, though, the Jap did a flick roll and zoomed upwards. *Christ, but he's maneuverable*, Peterson thought, and then, with a twinge of alarm, *He climbs like a son of a bitch, too*.

He gave his Wildcat full throttle. If the Jap wanted to dogfight, he'd play along. Marvin Morrison stuck to him like a burr, the way a good wingman was supposed to. Several of the Wildcats were shooting now, flames spurting from the four .50-caliber machine guns each one carried. A Japanese fighter fell from the sky trailing smoke and flame. Peterson whooped.

But the enemy planes were firing, too, and the shells from their wing-mounted cannon bit chunks out of the fighters from the *Enterprise* when they hit. And they seemed to be able to hit whenever they pleased. Peterson rapidly discovered that dogfighting the Japs was a mistake. It was like trying to pick up water with a fork. Their fighters could turn inside his and outclimb him as if the Wildcat were nailed to the mat.

This isn't right, he told himself. *What the hell are they doing with hotter planes than we've got?*

"I'm hit!" Morrison wailed in his earphones. "I'm going down!" The wingman's Wildcat spun towards the ground and the sea far, far below. Flames licked back from the engine cowling towards the cockpit.

"Get out!" Peterson screamed. "Get out while you can!" But he didn't think Marvin Morrison could.

And then he had to stop worrying about Marv and try to save his own skin. The Jap he'd been hunting had been hunting him, too. Now the bastard was on his tail. Peterson jinked like a maniac, but he couldn't shake the enemy or turn the tables on him. Tracers flashed past. Peterson tensed, not that that would do him any good if a shell slammed through his armored seat and into his back.

Machine-gun bullets stitched across his wing. Two cannon shells hit his engine, one right after the other. It quit. None of his cursing and clawing brought it back to life. All of a sudden, he was flying the world's most expensive glider.

He'd told his luckless wingman to get out. Now he had to follow his own advice—if he could. He pushed back the canopy. The slipstream tore at him as he unfastened his harness. Then he was out, and past the tail that could have cut him in half, and falling free . . . right through the middle of this mad aerial combat. A couple of tracers seemed close enough to touch as he plunged earthward.

He probably pulled the ripcord sooner than he should have. The jolt of the parachute opening made the world go red for a moment. He tried to steer himself towards land and away from the Pacific. He had a Mae West, but even so. . . . Better the jungle than the sharks.

Oh, Jesus, here came a Jap fighter, straight for him. Was that the pilot who'd shot him down? One burst from the bastard's machine guns and he was a dead man. The fighter roared past. The man in the cockpit waved to him as it went by.

Peterson waved back with a one-finger salute. Fortunately, the enemy flier either didn't see it or didn't know what it meant. He flew back into the fight instead of returning to wipe out the insult in blood.

Like bad-tempered dandelion fluff, Peterson floated down. He spilled air from the chute and swung his weight this way and that, fighting not to go into the drink. And he didn't. He came down on the fairway of a golf course about a quarter of a mile from the sea.

Two gray-haired men advanced on him with upraised five-irons. "Surrender!" they shouted.

In spite of everything, he almost burst out laughing. Here he was, taller than either one of them, fairer than either one of them—and they thought he was a goddamn Jap because he came out of the sky. "Get me to a car and get me to an airfield," he growled. "If they can find a plane for me, I've got some more fighting to do."

The golfers gaped at him as if he'd started spouting Japanese. If they'd lived here a while, they might even have understood some Japanese. Did they understand English? "I think he's an American, Sid," one of them said, as if announcing miracles.

"You're right, Bernie," the other declared after cogitations of his own.

Peterson felt like murdering them both. Instead, they drove him back towards Ewa. To the east, the flames and smoke of the U.S. Navy's funeral pyre climbed higher into the air every moment. Soot floated down like black rain.

IN HIS ZERO, LIEUTENANT SABURO SHINDO watched Pearl Harbor go up in smoke below him. *This* was the blow Commander Fuchida had wanted to strike: the blow against the harbor's great tank farms and repair facilities. Even if the invasion of Oahu failed by some accident, the Americans would have a devil of a time getting much use out of their forward base in the Pacific. The channel was plugged, too, with ships sunk trying to steam out and fight. The Japanese task force wouldn't have to worry about sorties, not for a while.

Shindo flew at four thousand meters. The thick, black, greasy smoke had already climbed past him. How high would it go? How far would the pall spread? He couldn't begin to guess. He also couldn't see the ground as well as he would have liked, for the smoke obscured it. The very success of the attack was ruining reconnaissance.

"We were attacked by carrier-based aircraft flying in from the west," Shindo said into the radio. He knew the carriers wouldn't answer, but Admiral Nagumo, Commander Genda, and Commander Fuchida urgently needed to hear. "Repeat: attacked by carrier-based aircraft from the west. Approximate bearing 290 degrees from Pearl Harbor. Range unknown, but not likely to be far. Out."

His lips curled up at the corners in the disciplined beginnings of a smile. He'd knocked down two Wildcats himself. The pilot of one had managed to get out and get his chute open; he thought he'd killed the other American flier in the cockpit. The enemy was brave—no doubt about that. But Shindo had quickly seen he and his men were better trained. And the Zero could fly rings around the slow, stubby Wildcat.

Shindo laughed softly. He knew how the Americans looked down their noses at Japan and what she made. Well, the arrogant white men had got themselves a little surprise today.

Back aboard the task force, they'd be launching a flight of Nakajima B5N2s. They'd held the torpedo bombers out of the third wave just in case American carriers showed up. Now at least one was on the board. Shindo would have bet there was only one, or the enemy would have thrown more fighters at his force.

The plan called for his planes to plaster Schofield Barracks after they'd finished with Pearl Harbor. But he knew he could fly along the bearing from which the Wildcats had come and have a good chance of finding the carrier that had launched them. The B5N2s would be coming from much farther away. They wouldn't know where along that bearing the carrier might lie, so they'd have to waste time searching.

Shindo made up his mind. He pulled half a dozen Zeros and ten Aichi D3A1 dive bombers out of the Schofield Barracks attack and ordered them off to the west with him. If that carrier was there, he wanted to be in at the kill. Taking it out might be the most important thing the Japanese Navy did.

There was Ewa down below. Planes still burned on the runways, where they'd been lined up almost wingtip-to-wingtip: a perfect target. The Americans had a couple of antiaircraft guns up and working. They fired at Shindo's detachment, but the shell bursts didn't come close.

On he flew, out over the Pacific. It was so much bluer and more beautiful than it had been around Japan. The air above Oahu had smelled sweet and spicy before battle began. This was a wonderful place. It would make a fine addition to the Japanese Empire. But to make sure it did, where was that carrier?

If I'm on a wild-goose chase. . . . Alone in the cockpit, Shindo shrugged. If he was, he was. He had to take the chance.

There was Kauai, off to the northwest of Oahu. The Garden Island, its nickname was. He'd run into that in an intelligence briefing. It was supposed to be even lovelier than Oahu. Shindo wondered if that were possible.

Then all thoughts of Kauai, all thoughts of beauty, vanished from his head. There south of the island were ships, their white wakes very visible as they steamed towards Oahu at full speed. Shindo's heart thuttered with excitement. Now—was the U.S. carrier with them? Yes, that had to be it, there at the heart of the flotilla. The escorting ships—were those battleships, or only cruisers?

He couldn't tell. He didn't care, or not much. The carrier counted for more than all the others put together. He radioed its position to his own fleet and to the torpedo bombers that already had to be on the way.

Then he spoke to the pilots he led: "The carrier is your

first priority. Attack it at all costs. Only after it is destroyed will you worry about any other ships. *Banzai* for the Emperor!"

Answering *Banzai!*s dinned in his earphones. The American ships swelled as he drew closer to them. Flame and smoke burst from the guns of the forward vessels. They'd spotted him, then. Black puffs of smoke dotted the sky ahead. They hadn't quite found the range. But they would. They would.

"Enemy fighters ahead!" a Zero pilot yelled.

Shindo swore, but only mildly. Of course the American carrier would have a combat air patrol overhead. Zeros orbited the Japanese task force, too—just in case. "Our job is to keep those fighters off our dive bombers," he radioed to his comrades. "We are expendable. They are not. Let's go." He didn't shout *Banzai!* again. He was not a showy man.

The Zero's engine roared as he brought it up to full combat power. He and his fellow fighter pilots left the D3N1s behind as if they were nailed to the sky. There were the Wildcats, boring in on them. He'd already seen the American Navy fliers had courage and to spare.

What they didn't have was enough in the way of airplanes under them. The Zeros slashed into the enemy planes. One Wildcat after another tumbled towards the Pacific. A Zero fell, too, and then another. The Japanese fighters were lighter and faster and more maneuverable than the Americans, but the Wildcats could take more punishment and keep flying.

There—Shindo turned quicker and harder than any Wildcat could hope to do. His thumb came down on the firing button. The twin 20mm cannon in his wings roared. A tracer round scored a line of what Japanese pilots called *ice candy* across the sky. Shells blew holes in the Wildcat just behind the cockpit. No plane could survive punishment like that. Spinning wildly, flames pouring from it, the American fighter went down.

Where were the dive bombers? In the fight to keep the Wildcats off them, Shindo had lost track. Then the glint of sun off a cockpit let him spy them. They'd gone into their attack run, stooping on the frantically zigzagging carrier like so many falcons.

In these cerulean seas, the American Navy's camouflage scheme—dark gray below and light gray above—left something to be desired. It was better suited to gloomier climes farther north. Even from his height, Shindo could make out the planes on the flight deck. Whether the carrier was going to fly them to Oahu or launch a strike against his task force, he didn't know. Too late now, either way.

Antiaircraft fire snarled up at the diving Aichis. One of them was hit, caught fire, and spiraled into the Pacific. Its bomb went off when it struck, sending up a white geyser of water. But the rest of the dive bombers pressed on fearlessly. They released their bombs one after another and pulled up and away.

"*Banzai!*" Shindo shouted when the first bombs exploded. But they were near misses, one astern, the other to port. The carrier kept dodging, staggering across the sea like a drunk. It did not save her, though. The next three bombs *were* hits: one near the stern, one on the island, and one not far from the bow. The bursts of flame and great clouds of black smoke showed him the difference between what he'd thought a hit looked like and the real thing.

The hit near the stern, among the airplanes loaded with fuel and torpedoes and bombs, was the one that devastated the carrier. Secondary explosions followed almost at once as the munitions, bathed in fire, went off on their own. Engines damaged, the stricken ship slowed to a crawl. Brave men crewed her, though. The antiaircraft guns that hadn't been knocked out kept firing at the Japanese planes.

Seeing their comrades' success, the last three dive bombers pulled up without dropping their bombs. "What are you doing?" Shindo called to them.

"Sir, the carrier is dead in the water," one of those pilots replied. "We request permission to attack a battleship instead."

"I think they're cruisers," Shindo said. "But even if they are battleships, the carrier is the primary target." He looked down at it. The Aichi pilot was right; it could not move at all. Still, the Americans were supposed to be very clever, very skillful, at damage control. Shindo made up his mind. "Two of you will strike the carrier again. The third may use his bomb against a cruiser. Do you understand me? All three of you—speak up!"

"Aye aye, sir!" they chorused.

"Obey, then." Shindo radioed the rest of the D3A1s: "Go back to the ships. If you pass the torpedo bombers coming this way, give them a course."

The three bomb-laden Aichis climbed back up into the sky, then dove once more. As Shindo had commanded, two of them attacked the carrier. One missed even though the target lay dead in the water. The other bomb, though, struck square amidships. Shindo thought afterwards that that one might have been enough to sink her all by itself. She began to list to starboard. The list quickly grew. Whatever men remained aboard her could do nothing to stop it.

Shindo was so intent on watching her that the fire and smoke suddenly spurting from a cruiser's—or was it a battleship's?—superstructure took him by surprise. "*Banzai!*" an excited young pilot shouted in his earphones. "That is a very solid hit!"

"Yes, it is," Shindo agreed. He ordered the remaining D3A1s back to the carriers, and all the Zeros except his own. If he spotted the torpedo bombers, he could guide them down to the American ships. He throttled back. His plane had more endurance than the dive bombers, especially when he wasn't going all out in combat. He could afford to loiter here for a while. And he wanted to watch that carrier sink.

She went to the bottom about twenty minutes later. A few boats and rafts bobbed in the water. He supposed individual men were floating and swimming, but he was too high to spot them. Destroyers and cruisers, including the damaged one, gathered to pick up survivors.

Then the ships scattered. They couldn't possibly have finished picking up all the men from the carrier, but they abandoned them and started throwing up flak. Saburo Shindo spotted the torpedo bombers a couple of minutes later. How had the Americans known about them so soon? Had a cruiser launched a scout? If so, wouldn't he have seen the slow, clumsy plane catapulted off its ship and shot it down? But if not, how had they done it? Did they have detection gear the Empire of Japan lacked?

That was a question for later. Now Shindo dove on a cruiser and strafed the deck, doing everything he could to distract it from the oncoming Nakajimas. Tracers sizzled all around him. He counted himself lucky that he wasn't hit. If he had been, he'd intended to try to fly his plane into one of the U.S. ships.

Lieutenant Fusata Iida had tried that sort of thing at Kaneohe. He'd said before the attack began that he would do his best to strike an enemy target if he was shot down. He *had* been hit, and he'd aimed his Zero at a hangar housing flying boats. He hadn't been able to hit it, but he'd made the effort. His spirit deserved praise.

One of the Nakajima B5N2s caught fire and tumbled into the Pacific. The planes had to fly low and straight to launch their torpedoes. It made them dreadfully vulnerable. Had the Americans here still had any fighters flying, things would only have been worse. Their ships maneuvered desperately. Two destroyers almost collided. "Too bad!" Shindo exclaimed, seeing they would miss. If the foe had hurt himself, that would have been sweet.

Another torpedo bomber exploded in midair—a big shell must have hit it. But torpedoes splashed into the sea one after another. Here the B5N2s had open water of unlimited depth. This wasn't a problem like the one Pearl Harbor itself had presented. The narrow, shallow lochs at the American base had made the Japanese modify their torpedoes so they wouldn't bury themselves in the bottom after they fell from their planes.

No such worries here. Just white wakes in the water, straight as arrows. Shindo cursed when a dodging destroyer managed to evade one of those arrows. But then he shouted, "*Banzai!*" again—a torpedo hit the damaged cruiser amidships. The cruiser shuddered to a stop. A de-

stroyer was hit, too, and her back broken. She sank faster
than the carrier had.

And there was another cruiser (or battleship? Shindo
could still hope) hit, her bow torn off by the force of the
blow. Shindo wished for more bombers to finish off the
whole flotilla. He shrugged, then let out another cheer as a
second destroyer was struck. Despite the cheer, he knew
the carrier-based planes were lucky to have accomplished
this much. The American carrier was dead. That mattered
most. The Japanese Navy also had a swarm of submarines
in Hawaiian waters. Maybe they could finish off some of
the U.S. ships that had escaped the torpedo bombers.

That wasn't Shindo's worry, or not directly. He'd done
everything he could here. The surviving Nakajimas were
flying back towards the northeast. He followed them, as
he'd trained to do. They had better navigation gear than he
did. He smiled as he buzzed along over the Pacific. It
wasn't as if he had to worry about American pursuit. No,
everything had gone just like a drill.

THE FIRST ATTACKS ON OAHU passed Schofield Barracks
by. Listening to the radio, looking at the smoke rising from
nearby Wheeler Field, Fletcher Armitage was almost in-
sulted. "What's the matter?" he exclaimed. "Don't they
think we're worth hitting, the lousy yellow bastards?"

Little by little, the brass started waking up from the hay-
maker they'd taken. Orders came for units to move to their
defensive positions. The Twenty-eighth Infantry Regiment
headed for Waikiki. The Ninety-Eighth Coast Artillery
Regiment (Antiaircraft) rolled out for Kaneohe, on the
windward side of Oahu. And, along with the Nineteenth
Infantry Regiment, the Thirteenth Field Artillery Battalion
hurried up to the north shore, to defend the beach between
Haleiwa and Waimea.

They hurried, that is, once they got everything ready to
roll. That took a while. Along with everybody else, Armitage discovered war was different from drills. The sense
of urgency was much higher. Unfortunately, it made a lot

of people run around like chickens that had just had a meeting with the hatchet and chopping block.

"Come on, goddammit!" Fletch screamed at a sergeant fifteen years older than he was. "You know how to hitch the gun to the truck. How many times have you done it?"

"About a million, sir," the sergeant answered quietly. "But never when it counted, not till now." He looked down at his trembling hands as if they'd betrayed him.

That wasn't the only foul-up, small and not so small, in the battalion—far from it. Armitage thanked God things weren't worse. At last, all the 105mm guns and their limbers were attached. All the men who would fire them had piled into the trucks. All the infantrymen in the accompanying regiment had their rifles and ammunition and helmets. They started north from Schofield Barracks a little before two in the afternoon.

They had barely begun to move when the antiaircraft guns still at the barracks began pounding away, throwing shells up into the sky. Through the roar and rumble of the trucks' diesel engines, Armitage hadn't been able to hear any airplanes overhead. "Are they shooting for the fun of it?" he asked whoever would listen to him.

He got his answer less than a minute later, when bombs started bursting not far away. The truck stopped, so suddenly that the soldiers in back were pitched into one another. "Holy shit!" somebody shouted.

Fletch was shouting too, in a fury at the driver: "What the hell are you doing? Keep going!"

"I can't, sir," the man answered. "Truck two ahead of this one just got blown to hell and gone. Road's blocked."

"Well, get off the road and go around him," Armitage raged.

"I'll try, sir," the driver said dubiously.

Armitage wished he could see better. With the olive-drab canvas cover over the back of the truck, he might as well have been inside a Spam can for all the visibility he had. Then a fragment of bomb casing ripped through the canvas about six inches above his head. He decided he didn't want a view all *that* badly.

The driver let out a frightened howl: "Fighters! Jap fighters!"

They were coming in low, plenty low enough for Fletch to hear *their* motors over the noise the trucks were making. He heard their machine guns and cannon going off, too. And, half a heartbeat later, he heard the driver scream.

He had other things to worry about, though. Machine-gun bullets finished the job of shredding the canvas. They did a pretty good job of shredding men, too, and metal as well. Four or five soldiers in the rear compartment started screaming and shouting and cursing, all at the same time. Something hot and wet splashed Fletch's ear and the side of his face. The iron stink of blood filled the compartment.

More screams followed when the truck ran into the one in front of it. Next to getting strafed by a Zero, though, a collision was a small thing. The diesel engine didn't go up in flames the way a gasoline-powered motor would have. Even so, Fletch said, "We've got to get out of here."

Nobody argued with him. In fact, soldiers scrambled over him to escape. Some of them were wounded, others just panicked. By the time he got out, blood splashed the front of his uniform, even if he wasn't hurt himself.

Japanese planes still buzzed overhead. Here came a fighter, low, flames winking on and off as its machine guns shot up the U.S. column. "Get down!" people were shouting. "Hit the dirt!"

Fletch was damned if he would, even after a bullet slammed into a man less than ten feet away with a noise like a baseball bat hitting a watermelon. The luckless soldier clutched at himself and crumpled. Fletch yanked the .45 from his belt and banged away at the Jap. He had about as much chance of hitting the speeding fighter as he did of taking wing himself, but he gave it his best shot.

Infantrymen started firing at the enemy, too. That actually gave him a little hope. Put enough lead in the air and it was liable to do some good. Meanwhile, though, the handful of enemy planes were cutting the column to ribbons. Bombers pounded it from on high, while the fighters swooped low to strafe again and again. At every pass, men died and vehicles caught fire.

Somebody not far away moaned, "Where the hell are *our* airplanes?"

"You stupid asshole!" Fletch pointed south, towards the funeral pyre of Wheeler Field. "Where the fuck do you think they are? This has got to be the worst sucker punch in the history of the world."

A bomb screamed down, louder and louder. With artillery fire, it meant the shells were headed right for you when the sound behaved like that. Armitage didn't know if bombs worked the same way, but he didn't want to find out by experiment, either. Now he did throw himself flat, a split second before the bomb burst.

Blast picked him up and slammed him down again like a professional wrestler. It tried to tear his lungs out through his mouth and nose. Dazed, he tasted blood. Concussion could kill without leaving visible injury. As he staggered upright again, he realized that had almost happened to him.

Closer to the crater the bomb had dug, men hadn't been so lucky. Some of what he saw might have come straight from a butcher's shop. Butcher's meat, though, didn't scrabble frantically, trying to put itself back together. Butcher's meat didn't scream for its mother, either.

Fletch bent over and was noisily sick. Then he yelled, "Corpsmen! We need some corpsmen over here!" That shout was rising everywhere.

He bent again, this time by an injured man. With clumsy fingers, he put on a wound bandage to slow the soldier's bleeding. Then, almost stabbing himself in the process, he gave the man a morphine injection. The wounded soldier sighed as the drug began to take hold.

Next to him, a sergeant was using a bayonet to cut another wounded man's throat. Considering what the bomb had left of the young man, Armitage only nodded. The sergeant was doing him a favor.

After plunging the bayonet into the ground three or four times to clean it, the sergeant looked over to him.

"How the hell are we supposed to get to our deployment area now, sir?" he asked.

The column was an abbatoir. Trucks burned. Others lay on their side or upside down. Guns had been flipped about like jackstraws. "Sergeant, I'll be damned if I can tell you," Fletch answered. "Truth is, I've been too busy trying to stay alive the last few minutes to care about anything else."

"Yeah," the noncom said. "But we better start caring PDQ, don't you think?"

Fletch looked around again. He saw ruin and wreckage and slaughter. He looked up to the sky. He didn't see any more Japanese planes, for which he heartily thanked God. But that didn't mean the bastards with the meatballs wouldn't come back again. He also didn't see any American planes. That didn't surprise him. The Japs must have swept them away like kids in second grade erasing a blackboard. How the hell was his force supposed to do anything if the Japs could hit it from above whenever they pleased?

He had no idea, none in the whole wide world. But he managed a nod he hoped wasn't too downhearted. "Yeah, Sergeant. You're right. We've got to try."

JIRO TAKAHASHI TOOK THE *OSHIMA MARU* OUT on Sunday just like any other day. The idea of the Sabbath meant nothing to him. The Sabbath was for *haoles*, who'd invented the silly notion. As far as he was concerned, work was work, and one day as good for it as another.

Maybe Hiroshi and Kenzo had different ideas. If his sons did, they'd never had the nerve to say anything about them. If he'd sent them out in the sampan while he stayed home and slept, they might have. As things were, his example pulled them along. If he was willing—even eager—to get out of bed before sunrise and head for Kewalo Basin, how could they tell him they didn't want to? They couldn't. They hadn't yet, anyhow.

Some sampans were coming in even as the *Oshima Maru* put to sea. A few men went fishing by night, trailing lights in the water to lure *nehus* and the tuna that fed on them. They were first to market with their catch, and so got good prices. But their expenses were higher, too—Jiro didn't have to worry about a generator or the fuel to run it or light bulbs. The work was harder at night, too, though that fazed him much less than the extra cost did.

He set a tub of minnows down in the bottom of the sampan. A fairy tern swooped down to try to steal some of the little fish. He waved his hat. The white bird with the big black eyes flew off towards Waikiki.

"Waste time, bird!" Hiroshi said. Kenzo laughed. Jiro only shrugged. He got the *Oshima Maru*'s engine going. The sampan shook and thudded with the diesel's vibration. Out to sea they went. The sky had just started turning pale yellow, out there beyond Diamond Head. Pink would follow, and then the sun.

Today, he got out early enough to suit him. He'd cleared the defensive sea area well before sunrise. Today, other old-school fishermen would be complaining about their lazy, good-for-nothing sons. Not even Jiro could find anything wrong with his boys this morning. They'd done everything he wanted, and done it in good time, too.

He didn't tell them so. He didn't want them getting swelled heads. Besides, why should he praise them for merely doing what they were supposed to do? If he did, then they'd want praise for every little thing. They'd expect it, but they'd be disappointed. He wasn't the sort to throw praise around. He never had been, and he never would be.

They chattered back and forth in incomprehensible English as the *Oshima Maru* skimmed over the water. When they needed to talk with him, they switched to Japanese. That was almost always pure business. They didn't waste a lot of time on chitchat with him. This past week, with no progress in the talks in Washington, the impulse to talk had dried up even more than usual. For all his efforts to make them into good Japanese, they saw things from the USA's point of view.

Jiro looked ahead, trying to spot a good fishing ground. Hiroshi did the same, even if he wasn't so good at it. Kenzo stared over the sampan's stern, back in the direction from which they'd come. Jiro almost told his younger son, "Waste time!" but figured he'd be wasting his breath.

Then Kenzo pointed north towards Oahu and spoke one word: "Look!"

The urgency in his son's voice made Jiro turn around. "Oh, Jesus Christ!" he exclaimed, an oath he used even though he was a Buddhist and Shintoist, not a Christian. Those black clouds on the horizon couldn't be good news.

"That's not Honolulu. It's too far west," Hiroshi said. "That's Pearl Harbor. I wonder if some of the ammunition there blew up or something."

Maybe he would make a proper fisherman one of these days after all. He was dead right about the direction from which the smoke was rising. Kenzo said, "I wish we had a radio on board. Then we'd know what was going on."

As far as Jiro was concerned, a radio for the boat was more expensive than it was worth. He said, "Whatever's going on up there, it's got nothing to do with us. We have a day's work ahead of us, and we're going to do it."

Neither Hiroshi nor Kenzo argued with that. If they'd tried, he would have knocked their heads together, and so what if he would have had to stand on tiptoe to do it? Some things simply needed doing, and he would have done what needed doing here without the least hesitation.

As things were, the *Oshima Maru*'s diesel kept pounding away. Most of the smoke to the north vanished below the horizon. Jiro forgot about it. He'd find out what it was when he got home. In the meantime, there were fish to catch. If his sons wanted to go on about Pearl Harbor while they worked, he didn't mind—as long as they did work.

He steered the sampan to what he thought would be a good spot. Boobies plunged into the sea nearby. That said there were small fish around. Where there were small fish, there could be tuna to feed on them. He killed the motor. The sampan glided to a stop, alone on the Pacific— alone but for that nasty smoke smudge in the north, anyhow. Whatever had happened to Pearl Harbor, it wasn't anything small.

Again, Jiro made himself shove that aside. He picked up a tub of bait minnows and poured them into the ocean. Away they streaked: little silver darts racing in all directions.

"Come on," he told Hiroshi and Kenzo. "Let's get the lines in the water and see how we do today."

The fishing lines followed the bait. To Jiro's eyes, those big, barbless hooks didn't look much like minnows. Tuna, fortunately, were less discriminating.

As soon as he and the boys started hauling in the lines, he knew it would be a good day. Fat *aku* and bigger *ahi* hung from the hooks like ripe fruit from a branch. Take them off, gut them, store them, throw more minnows in the water to lure more tuna to their doom. . . .

Noon came and passed, and the fishermen hardly even noticed. Most days, Jiro and his sons would break for lunch no matter how things were going. Not today. Today the younger men seemed as much machines as their father. Jiro began to think the weight of fish they were taking might swamp the *Oshima Maru*. He shrugged broad shoulders. There were worse ways to go.

Kenzo broke the spell about one o'clock, again by pointing north towards Oahu. He said not a word this time, nor did he need to. Those great black greasy clouds spoke for themselves. Even from here, miles away, they boiled high into the sky, swelling and swelling.

Hiroshi whistled softly. "That is something really, really big," he said. "I wonder if one of the battleships blew up, or if they have a fire in their storage tanks."

"*I* wonder how many people are hurt," Kenzo said. "Something that big, they're not going to get off for free."

Jiro Takahashi didn't say anything. He just eyed the smoke. When the *Oshima Maru* couldn't hold another *aku*, he started the motor and steered the sampan back towards Kewalo Basin. He was not a man to go guessing wildly when he didn't know. But he wondered whether any accident, no matter how spectacular, could have caused that kind of conflagration. He also wondered what had, what could have, if an accident hadn't.

Hiroshi pointed east across the water. "There's another sampan coming in. Maybe they'll know what's going on. Will you steer towards them, Father?"

Most of the time, Jiro would have gruffly shaken his

head and kept on towards Honolulu. The ever-swelling black clouds to the north, though, were too big and too threatening to ignore. Without a word, he swung the *Oshima Maru* to starboard.

The other skipper steered his disreputable, blue-painted fishing boat to port. He waved a dirty white cap in the direction of the *Oshima Maru* and shouted something across the water. Jiro couldn't make out the words. He cupped a hand behind his ear. The other skipper shouted again. Jiro snorted in disgust. No wonder he couldn't understand— the other man was speaking English.

"He says, what's going on at Pearl Harbor?" Kenzo reported.

Hiroshi didn't hide his disappointment. "I was hoping he'd be able to tell us," he said in Japanese, then switched to English to yell back at the other sampan. The men on board pantomimed annoyance. They'd wanted to find out what was going on from the Takahashis.

Kenzo called in English towards the other sampan, too. Then he return to Japanese: "We'll run into more boats when we get closer to the basin."

"*Hai. Honto,*" Jiro said. And it was true. Somehow, though, his younger son contrived to speak Japanese with English intonations. It wasn't Kenzo's accent; the teachers at the Japanese school had made sure he spoke better than Jiro, who was a peasant from a long line of peasants. But anyone with an ear to hear had to notice the influence of the other language on he way he put his sentences together. They weren't exactly wrong, but they were . . . different. Jiro didn't know what to do about it. Hiroshi had the same problem, but not so badly.

Both sampans skimmed north over the waves. Sure enough, other *Maru*s were also making their way back to Kewalo Basin. (To the Japanese, anything that floated was a *Maru*. *Haoles* got a laugh out of their calling sampans ships rather than boats.) On one of them, the crew were all but jumping out of their dungarees.

Hiroshi pointed to the excited men. "They'll know."

"Yes." Jiro swung the rudder. The *Oshima Maru* wasn't

the only sampan making for that one, either. Now Jiro raised his voice. "What is it?" he yelled, and waved northwest, in the direction of Pearl Harbor.

The four fishermen on the sampan had a radio. News tumbled out of them, some of it in English, some in Japanese. Jiro didn't get all of it. But he understood enough: the Empire of Japan had attacked the U.S. Navy at Pearl Harbor, and had struck a devastating blow.

His first reaction was pride. "This is how Admiral Togo hit the Russians in Manchuria when I was young," he said.

Hiroshi and Kenzo didn't say anything for a little while. Then, gently, his older son answered, "But, Father, you weren't living in Manchuria when they attacked it."

"A surprise attack is a dirty way to start a war," Kenzo added, not gently at all. "That's how Hitler does things."

Jiro blinked. In the *Nippon jiji* and *Jitsugyo no Hawaii* and other local Japanese-language papers—the ones he paid attention to—Hitler got pretty good press. The writers worried more about Communists. Wasn't it the same in English?

He pointed out what was obvious to him: "This isn't Hitler. This is *Japan*."

His sons looked at each other. Neither of them seemed to want to say anything. At last, Hiroshi did: "Father, we're Americans." Kenzo nodded.

I'm not! The words leaped into Jiro's mouth. They were true. Both his sons had to know it. Even so, he didn't say them. If he had, something would have broken forever between the two boys and him. Sensing that, he kept quiet. Reiko would have understood, but she was of his generation, not his sons'.

Hiroshi went on speaking carefully: "This attack is going to be bad for all the Japanese in Hawaii—all the Japanese on the mainland, too. The fat cats will think we wanted it. They'll think we were all for it. And they'll make us pay." His brother nodded again, nothing but gloom on his face.

"When have things been good for the Japanese in Hawaii?" Jiro asked. "When have the big shots not made us pay? And things would have been even worse if the Japanese government hadn't complained and made the planters live up to their contracts. All that was before you were born, so you don't remember. But it happened."

"Don't you see, Father? That doesn't matter now," Kenzo said. "We're at war with Japan."

We're at war with Japan. The words stabbed Jiro like a dagger. They put him and his sons on opposite sides of a chasm. What he hadn't said, Kenzo had. *He* wasn't at war with Japan. Japan was his country. It always had been, even if he hadn't lived there since he was young. The *haoles* who ran Hawaii had made it very plain that they didn't believe he was an American, or that he could turn into one.

His sons might think themselves Americans. The *haoles* who ran the islands didn't think they were. There weren't enough jobs for Japanese who had the education to fill them. They couldn't move up in society. They couldn't join the Army, either. No Japanese were allowed in the Twenty-fourth or Twenty-fifth Divisions, though every other group in Hawaii had members there. Kenzo and Hiroshi had to know that. But they didn't want to think about it.

And Jiro didn't want to think about what the attack on Pearl Harbor might mean, or about what might happen in its aftermath. Because he didn't, he steered the *Oshima Maru* back towards Kewalo Basin without another word. The time for a real quarrel might come later. He didn't want it now, out on the open sea.

The other sampans hurried north along with his. The one with the radio was a bigger boat, with a bigger engine. Minute by minute, it pulled away. That proved its undoing. A buzz in the sky swelled into a roar. A dark green fighter with unmistakable U.S. stars on wings and fuselage swooped down on the lead sampan. Machine guns roared. The fighter streaked away.

"Oh, Jesus Christ!" Jiro exclaimed once more. His sons stared in horror. The other sampan lay dead in the water.

Jiro brought the *Oshima Maru* up alongside it. Two of the fishermen aboard were gruesomely dead, one almost cut in half by bullets, the other with his head blown open. One of the others was clutching a wounded leg. "They thought we were invading!" he moaned. The fourth fisherman, by some miracle, hadn't been hit, but stood there in shock, a dreadful amazement frozen on his face.

"Come on," Jiro told his boys, trying to ignore the stink of the blood that was everywhere on the shattered sampan. "We've got to do what we can for them."

"What if that plane comes back?" Kenzo quavered.

Jiro shrugged fatalistically. "What if it does? It shows you what the *haoles* think of how American you are, *neh?*"

Neither Kenzo nor Hiroshi had anything to say to that. Gulping, they scrambled onto the other sampan.

"COME ON! COME ON!" Lieutenant Yonehara shouted. "Move! Move! Move! You can't waste a minute! You can't even waste a second!"

A great stream of Japanese soldiers emerged from the hold of the *Nagata Maru*. Once upon a time, during his brief schooling, Corporal Takeo Shimizu had heard something about the circulation of the blood. There were little things inside the blood that swirled through the body over and over again.

Corpuscles! That was the name. He wouldn't have bet he could put his finger on it, not after all these years. He felt like a corpuscle himself, one out of so very many. Corpuscles, though, weren't weighted down with helmets and bayoneted rifles and packs that would sink them like stones if they couldn't make the journey from the transport to the landing barges coming alongside.

It was black night, too, which didn't make things any easier. The *Nagata Maru* had charged forward all through the day and after darkness came down. The ship and the other transports unloading their cargoes of soldiers and equipment were supposed to be near the north coast of Oahu. Shimizu hoped their captains and navigators knew what they were doing. If they didn't . . .

Someone stepped on his foot. That gave him something more urgent than captains and navigators to worry about. "Watch it," he growled.

"So sorry," a soldier said insincerely.

"So sorry, *Corporal*," Shimizu snapped. The soldier, whoever he was, let out a startled gasp. It was still too dark to recognize faces, and Shimizu hadn't been able to tell whose voice that was, either.

The *Nagata Maru* rolled and pitched in the Pacific swells, rising and falling six or eight feet at a time. Behind Shimizu, somebody noisily lost the supper he'd had the evening before. The sharp stink made the corporal want to puke, too. Again, though, he had other things to worry about. The swells wouldn't make boarding the barges any easier.

His platoon commander didn't seem worried. "This isn't bad, men," Lieutenant Yonehara called. "We could board in seas twice this high!"

"Oh, yeah? I'd like to see you try it," said a soldier protected from insubordination by darkness. Another soldier stepped in the new puddle of vomit and cursed monotonously.

Yonehara's platoon did keep advancing towards the rail, so Corporal Shimizu supposed other men from the regiment were going down the side of the ship and onto the barges. It was either that or they were all going over the side and drowning. They could have done that back in Japanese waters, if it was what the High Command had in mind. They wouldn't have needed to come all this way.

"Wait!" a sailor called. The tossing didn't seem to bother him a bit. "Another barge is coming alongside. That's the one you'll go into."

Corporal Shimizu wondered how he could tell. It was as dark as the inside of a pig. Something hard and cold caught him just above the belly button—the rail. Automatically, his hands reached out to take hold of it. His right hand closed on iron, his left on rope: part of the netting down which he'd scramble when the word came.

He stood there, hoping the pressure behind him wouldn't send him over the side before he was supposed to go. Without warning, the sailor slapped him on the back. "Down you go," the fellow said. "Hurry! Don't hold things up."

"*Hai*," Shimizu said. He swung over the rail, hanging on for dear life while his boot found the net. If he'd been a monkey, able to grasp with feet as well as hands, everything would have been simple. As things were, he clambered down slowly and carefully.

"Hard work!" said a soldier scrambling down beside him. Corporal Shimizu nodded. This time, that was true literally as well as metaphorically.

The Daihatsu landing craft bobbed in the Pacific beside the *Nagata Maru*. It was about fifty feet long, with a beam of ten or twelve feet. Its hull was made of steel, supported by heavy wooden braces. It had twin keels riveted on to the hull. Except for the two machine guns at the bow and the steel shield protecting the wheel, it could have been a fishing boat going after sardines on the Inner Sea.

Getting down into the barge from the transport was tricky. Shimizu clung to the net. He didn't want to get squashed between the two vessels. If he did, they'd scrape him off the steel.

"Come on!" a man on the barge called encouragingly. "Lean out. I'll grab your boots and keep you safe."

Leaning out, taking his feet out of the net, was the last thing Shimizu had in mind. Glumly, he realized he had no choice. With the burden he was bearing, how long could he hang on with arms and hands alone? How soon would he go into the water? "Hurry up!" he called to the fellow in the barge.

"I've got you," the man answered, and so he did. "Let go. You'll come in."

Reluctantly, Shimizu obeyed. He was falling . . . into the barge. He laughed in relief as he straightened up. "*Arigato*," he said.

"*Do itashimashite*." The other man waved away his thanks. "Don't pay back—pay forward. Help your friends coming down."

That was good advice, and Corporal Shimizu took it. No one got crushed between the *Nagata Maru* and the landing barge. There were a couple of close calls, passed off with laughs and bows and exclamations of, "Hard work!"

The whole company squeezed onto the barge. Shimizu wouldn't have believed it if he hadn't seen it with his own eyes. Lieutenant Yonehara seemed pleased. "All according to plan," he said. "We should start for Oahu any minute now."

"I thought we were going to Hawaii," a soldier said.

"Oahu is one of the islands of Hawaii," the platoon leader explained. "It's the one with the good harbor, and the one where the Americans have all their soldiers. Once we take it away from them, all the Hawaiian Islands are ours."

It all sounded very easy when Lieutenant Yonehara put it like that. Shimizu let out a soft sigh of relief. He wanted it to be easy. People said the planes from the carriers had done a good job of hitting the harbor and the rest of the island's defenses. Shimizu had been in the Army long enough not to trust what people said. This time, though, he hoped rumor told the truth.

The diesel engine at the stern of the landing barge took on a deeper note. The barge pulled away from the *Nagata Maru*. Another took its place. The motion was fierce—up hill and down dale, much worse than it had been in the freighter. Shimizu's stomach lurched. *I won't be sick*, he told himself sternly. A few soldiers did puke up whatever was in their bellies.

Twilight began turning the eastern sky pale as the barge—one of a whole flotilla of invasion craft—lumbered towards the shore. Most of the other landing craft carried soldiers, as Shimizu's did. Some had howitzers or light tanks aboard. Shimizu hoped they were well chained down. If they shifted, they could capsize their barges and take them to the bottom.

Other men worried about other things. "If American planes come overhead right now, we're sitting ducks," a sergeant said. Nobody could contradict him, for he wasn't wrong. What pilot could want a better target than wallowing invasion barges?

"Will the Americans be waiting for us on the beach?" Shiro Wakuzawa asked.

That was another good question. Shimizu didn't know how to answer it. It was a day now since the carrier task force had started pounding Oahu. Would the Americans think it was just a hit-and-run raid, or would they expect an invasion to follow the attack from the air? Shimizu would have, but he didn't know how Americans thought.

Lieutenant Yonehara found his own way to deal with the question: "Whether they are on the beach or not doesn't matter, Private. If they are, we'll beat them there. If they aren't, we'll move inland and beat them wherever we find them. Plain enough?"

"Yes, sir. Thank you, sir." Wakuzawa would goof off whenever he got the chance, but he wasn't foolhardy enough to show an officer disrespect. A man who did that soon regretted the day he was born.

The sky grew ever lighter. Soldiers pointed ahead and exclaimed, "Land!"

"Well, what did you expect when we got into the barges?" Shimizu demanded. "That they'd dump us in the middle of the sea?" The men laughed. Some of them probably hadn't thought much about getting into the barges one way or the other. A lot of soldiers were like that: they took things as they happened, and didn't worry about them till they happened.

"It's so warm, and the air smells so good," Private Wakuzawa said. "The weather sure is better than it was when we left the Kurils."

"*Hai!*" Several soldiers agreed with him. Maybe Siberia had worse weather than the Kurils did, but maybe not, too. After all, most of the weather those northern islands got blew straight down from Siberia.

The machine guns at the landing barge's bow began banging away. Shimizu followed the lines of tracers rising up into the brightening sky and saw his worst nightmare—everybody's worst nightmare—realized. Three American fighter planes were swooping down on the fleet of barges. Their guns started winking. Bullets kicked up spurts of water. Screams from other barges said not all the bullets were splashing into the Pacific.

But then the American planes suddenly broke off the attack. They darted away. Zeros swooped down on them like falcons after doves. Takeo Shimizu let out a wordless cry of joy and relief. An American fighter caught fire and cartwheeled into the sea. Another went down a moment later. Shimizu didn't see what happened to the third, but it didn't come back. Nothing else really mattered.

"If I ever meet those Zero pilots, I'll buy them all the *sake* they can drink," Private Wakuzawa exclaimed. "I thought we were in trouble."

"The Navy will not let us down," Lieutenant Yonehara said. He might have said much more than that; Wakuzawa had shown not just a lack of confidence but a lack of martial spirit. But the platoon leader dropped it there. Maybe he'd had a moment of alarm, too. Shimizu knew *he* had, even if he'd kept quiet about it.

He peered south. The sun came up over the horizon, spilling ruddy light across the golden beaches dead ahead, the palm trees just behind them, and the jungle-clad mountains a little farther inland. The sight was one of the most beautiful Shimizu had ever seen. It all seemed so peaceful. It wouldn't stay that way for long.

Waves broke on the beach. They looked like pretty good-sized waves to Shimizu. Could the barge get through them without flipping over? He hoped so. He'd find out any minute now.

A few machine guns on the shore started shooting at the invasion barges. The barges shot back. Something bigger and heavier threw shells at the Japanese—those were big splashes rising from the sea. Zeros dove at the beach. Dive bombers appeared overhead. They swooped down, too. The shelling suddenly stopped.

Some of the machine guns kept firing. Two bullets ricocheted off the shield that protected the sailor at the wheel. A soldier howled when another one, instead of ricocheting, struck home. Shimizu had fought in China. He'd seen plenty of gunfire worse than this. It was just something a soldier went through on the imperial way. To the new men, it must have seemed very heavy and frightening.

Shiro Wakuzawa said, "The Americans won't have any ammunition left for when we come ashore if they keep shooting like this."

"Oh, I think they'll save a bullet or two," Shimizu said. "Maybe even three." Some of the first-year soldiers, taking him seriously, gave back solemn nods. Most of them, though, joined the men who'd been in the Army longer and laughed.

Somebody pointed to the water, right where the waves began breaking. "Are those people? What are they doing? They must be out of their minds!"

Two nearly naked men rode upright on long boards towards the beach. Bullets must have whipped past them in both directions. They seemed oblivious. They skimmed along on the crest of a wave, side by side. Shimizu stared at them, entranced. He'd never dreamt of such a skill.

"They must be Americans. Shall I knock them down?" asked a machine gunner at the bow of the barge.

"No!" Corporal Shimizu was one of the dozen men shouting the same thing at the same time. He added, "They might almost be *kami*, the way they glide along."

"Christians talk about their Lord Jesus walking on water," Lieutenant Yonehara said. "I never thought I would see it with my own eyes."

The two men reached the beach still upright on their boards. Then they did the first merely human thing Shimizu had seen from them: they scooped the boards up under their arms and ran. That was also an eminently sensible thing to do. Machine-gun bullets kicked up sand around their feet. Not all the men on the landing barges must have felt as sporting as the soldiers on this one. But Shimizu didn't see them fall. Maybe they really were spirits. How could an ordinary man be sure?

His own barge came ashore, much less gracefully than the surf-riders had. It didn't quite bury its bow in the sand, but it came close. He staggered. He didn't know how he stayed on his feet. Somehow, he managed. "Off!" the sailors were screaming. "Get off! We have to go back for more men! Hurry!"

He scrambled out of the barge and jumped down. His boots scrunched in the sand. Some Americans were still shooting from the plants—almost the jungle—on the far side of the road. Machine-gun and rifle muzzles flashed malevolently. A bullet cracked past Shimizu's head, so close that he felt, or thought he felt, the wind of its passage.

He couldn't run away. There was no *away* to run to, not at the edge of a hostile beach. He ran forward instead. If he and his comrades didn't kill those Americans, the Americans would kill them instead. "Come on!" he shouted, and the men in his squad came.

Oscar van der Kirk and Charlie Kaapu spent their Sunday morning surf-riding at Waimea Beach and grumbling that the waves weren't bigger. Every so often, one of them would look up at the planes flying back and forth overhead. At one point, Charlie remarked, "Army and Navy must have a hair up their ass. That's the biggest goddamn drill I ever saw. Has to cost a fortune."

"Yeah," Oscar said, and thought no more about it. Six-foot waves weren't so much, not when he'd been hoping for surf three or four times that size, but you could still find all sorts of unpleasant ways to hurt yourself if you didn't pay attention to what you were doing.

Finally, his stomach started growling so loud, he couldn't stand it any more. He and Charlie went into Waimea for something to eat. It wasn't a big town. There weren't a lot of choices, especially on a Sunday. As they usually did when they were up there, Oscar and Charlie headed for Okamoto's siamin stand. For a quarter, you could get a bowl of noodles and broth and sliced pork and vegetables that would hold you for a hell of a long time.

Old man Okamoto looked faintly apprehensive when they walked in. Oscar wondered why. They hadn't cadged a meal off him in a year and a half, and they'd paid him back for that one the next time they were here. They ordered their noodles and sat down to wait while the gray-haired little Japanese man ladled them out of the big pot he kept bubbling in back of the counter. He set the bowls on the table along with the short-handled, big-bowled china soup spoons every Japanese and Chinese place in Hawaii seemed to use.

"Thanks, Pop," Oscar said, and dug in. He and Charlie both ate like wolverines. He was halfway down the bowl before he noticed old man Okamoto had the radio tuned to KGMB, not to the nasal-sounding Japanese music he usually listened to. KGMB should have been playing music, too, if of a more normal sort. It wasn't. Instead, an announcer was gabbling into the mike. He sounded as if he'd have kittens right there on the air.

That was how Oscar—and Charlie, too—heard about Pearl Harbor. "Jesus," Charlie said. Then he spooned up some more siamin. Oscar nodded. He went on eating, too. After a couple of minutes, he glanced over to old man Okamoto. No wonder the old guy was nervous! If the Japs had done that down there, he probably counted himself lucky that his neighbors hadn't come by with pitchforks and tar and feathers.

Oscar laughed. Like most old-country Japanese, Okamoto had come to Hawaii to work in the fields. He'd been running this place for as long as anybody could remember, though. You had to be crazy to think of him as a danger to the United States. His neighbors must have felt the same way—no sign of tar and feathers.

"Your KGMB time is eleven forty-eight," the man on the radio said, his voice getting shriller every minute. "We have been ordered off the air by the United States Army, so that our signal does not guide Japanese airplanes or parachutists. We will return only to transmit official bulletins and orders. Please stay calm during this period of emergency."

This time, Charlie laughed first. Oscar followed suit. The radio signal cut away to sudden, dead silence. How would the horrible news, followed by the station's disappearance, make anybody stay calm?

Something else crossed his mind. Japanese parachutists? What would happen if the Japs invaded Oahu? He hoped the Army would trounce them. What else was it here for?

But suppose it didn't. It sounded as if the Japs had landed on things with both feet. Suppose . . .

Oscar eyed old man Okamoto again, more thoughtfully this time. If the Japanese Empire's soldiers came to Oahu, how *would* the local Japanese respond? He'd heard Army and Navy brass had sleepless nights about questions like that.

But it was their worry, not his. He and Charlie got to the bottom of their bowls at the same time. "What now?" Charlie asked.

"I don't want to go back to Honolulu right away. Everybody's gotta be going nuts down there," Oscar answered. "Besides, if the Japs are shooting up Wheeler and Schofield and Kaneohe, God knows if we can even get there from here. We might as well hang around and surf and hope the waves get better. What do you think?"

Charlie nodded. "Suits me. I was gonna say the same thing, but some *haoles*, they figure they all the time gotta *do* stuff, you know what I mean?"

"If I saw anything I could do, I'd do it," Oscar said. "You want to join the Army right now?" Charlie shook his head. Oscar shrugged. "Okay. Neither do I. In that case, we might as well do what we're doing." He left a dime on the table for old man Okamoto as he and Charlie headed out to his car.

By the time they got back to the beach, Oscar could see smoke rising in the south up over the mountains. He whistled softly. That was a hell of a lot of smoke. He and Charlie were both shaking their heads when they paddled out into the Pacific. No wonder the fellow on the radio sounded as if he'd just watched his puppy run over by a cement mixer. The Japs must have blown up everything that would blow.

They rode the waves all afternoon, then went back into Waimea for supper. Okamoto's seemed to be the only place open, and nobody but them was in it. Along with siamin, Oscar bought a loaf of bread and a couple of Cokes for breakfast the next morning. Getting the old man to understand *a loaf of bread* wasn't easy, but he managed.

He and Charlie slept in the car again that night. Some time after midnight, truck noises and swearing men woke them up. "The Army," Oscar said, and went back to sleep.

Army or no Army, it never occurred to him not to go into the water at dawn the next morning. It didn't occur to the soldiers to try to stop them till they were already in the ocean and could pretend not to hear. When fighter planes zoomed by overhead right afterwards, Oscar wished he'd listened.

He didn't know whether he spotted the incoming barges before the Army men on the beach did or not. He did discover getting stuck in a crossfire was no fun at all. By what would do for a miracle till a bigger one came along, he and Charlie made it back to shore alive. They piled into his Chevy and got the hell out of there.

III

JIM PETERSON HADN'T THOUGHT THE JAPANESE WOULD HIT Hawaii. He would have been glad to have his fellow fliers from the *Enterprise* tell him what a damn fool he'd been, but he didn't think many of them were left alive. Nobody was saying much about what had happened to the carrier, either.

And nobody was letting him get back into combat. The only Wildcats on Oahu were the couple that had survived the flight in from the *Enterprise*. They already had pilots. "Put me in anything, then!" Peterson raged after the golfers whose round he'd interrupted brought him to the Marine Corps Air Station at Ewa, west of Pearl Harbor. "I don't care what I'm in, as long as I get another swing at those little yellow bastards!"

They wouldn't listen to him. The first thing they did was send him to the dispensary tent, where a harried-looking medic confirmed that yes, he was still breathing, and no, he didn't have any bullet holes in him. That done, they took him out to the airstrip. It was nothing but wreckage, some still burning.

"You see?" a Marine Corps captain said. "You aren't the only one who wants another shot at the Japs—but you're gonna have to wait in line, just like everybody else."

"Jesus!" Peterson said. And it could have been worse. The *Enterprise* had taken some of the Marine pilots and plants from Ewa to Wake Island just before the Japs came in. Otherwise, they might have got stuck on the ground, too. "What the hell are we going to do?"

"Beats me," the captain answered.

"They kicked us in the nuts, and we weren't even looking!"

"Sure seems that way." The Marine seemed to take a certain morose satisfaction in agreeing with him. "And it's not just this base, mind you." He waved to the east. It looked like hell over there—literally. The pall of thick, oily black smoke filled that half of the sky. "Sons of bitches didn't just hit the fleet. They got the tank farms, too. God only knows how many million gallons of fuel going up in smoke."

"Up in smoke is right," Peterson said. Little by little, the sheer scale of the disaster began penetrating even his stubborn soul. "For God's sake, if you can't do anything else, give me a rifle and a helmet and let me shoot at 'em."

For the first time, the Marine officer looked at him with something approaching approval, not barely concealed annoyance. "That, now, that may be arranged—if it turns out there's anybody to shoot at."

Peterson stared at him. "If they've done this much, you think they *won't* follow it up with an invasion? They'd have to be crazy not to." He was a born zealot; his views swung from one extreme to the other with the greatest of ease.

Supper was an oddly carefree meal, featuring some of the best lamb chops Peterson had ever eaten. Supper also featured hot-and-cold running booze. Admiral Halsey sometimes winked at the rules against shipboard alcohol, but Peterson had been mostly dry for a while now. The whiskey and rum and gin and Irish coffee added something to the rumors coming in from around the island. Some of the Marines believed everything, no matter how gloomy. Some refused to believe anything.

"Only stands to reason," one of them insisted. "If the Japs plastered us and Pearl Harbor, they couldn't have had much left over to do anything else."

"Bullshit," said the captain who'd shown Peterson

around. "If they did that much down here, they aren't going to forget about Schofield and Wheeler and Kaneohe. They'll hit everything."

Reports seemed to bear him out. With the radio off the air, though, Peterson found it hard to be sure of anything. He supposed the big wheels here knew what was really going on. He hoped they did, anyhow. They should have— phones were still working, even if the radio had been yanked. But whatever they knew, they weren't talking. That by itself seemed to say the news wasn't good.

Peterson got a cot in a tent that night, and counted himself lucky. When reveille sounded, he thought for a moment he was back aboard the *Enterprise*. Then memory returned. He was swearing as he bounced to his feet. A Marine climbing out of another cot a few feet away nodded sympathetically. "Yeah, Navy, it's a bitch, isn't it?" he said.

"A bitch and a half," Peterson answered. "What the hell do we do now?"

"Might as well have breakfast," the Marine said practically. "Soon as the brass wants anything from us, I figure they'll let us know."

Breakfast was bacon and eggs and hash browns, not much different from what Peterson would have eaten on the *Enterprise*—she hadn't been at sea long enough to switch from fresh to powdered eggs. But the walk to the mess hall reminded him where he was and what had happened. The west was light, but in the east the sun couldn't penetrate the smoke rising from Pearl Harbor. They hadn't even slowed down the fires there during the night. How much fuel was burning?

He'd just got a second cup of coffee when air-raid sirens began to howl. He sprang up and followed the Marines as they ran for shelter. Most of them made for a nearly finished swimming pool not far away. "First time I ever jumped into one of these when it was dry," he said.

He got a laugh. Minutes later, though, bombs started whistling down. Being on the receiving end and unable to hit back was anything but funny. A few antiaircraft guns banged away, but the enemy airplanes were high in the sky. Peterson didn't think any of them got hit. No U.S. planes rose to challenge them. No U.S. planes at Ewa could.

"This isn't how it was yesterday morning," said one of the Marines in the pool. "Then they came in with fighters, right over the rooftops. We shot back with Springfields, .45s, anything we could get our hands on. Didn't do a hell of a lot of good, not as far as I could see."

The bombers didn't linger very long. After ten or fifteen minutes, they droned away. The Marines and Peterson emerged from their makeshift shelter. A bomb had knocked over the old Navy airship mooring mast the Marines used for a control tower. Another had hit the enlisted men's barracks, which the Zeros had shot up the day before. One end had fallen down, and what was still standing was on fire. And that second cup of coffee never got finished, because the mess hall had taken a direct hit.

Bombs had hit the asphalt X of the runways, too. If Ewa had had any flyable planes, they wouldn't have been able to get off the ground till the craters were repaired. "Son of a bitch!" Peterson said, looking around at the devastation. "*Son* of a bitch!"

"That's about the size of it," agreed the captain who'd taken charge of him the day before. He hadn't been in the pool, and Peterson hadn't seen him at breakfast, either. By his drawn features, he hadn't had any sack time the night before. He went on, "You were talking about drawing a helmet and a rifle and making like a soldier. Were you serious about that?"

"Hell, yes," Peterson answered without hesitation. But then he thought to ask, "How come?"

"About what you'd expect," the Marine officer answered. "The Japs are on the island."

LIEUTENANT SABURO SHINDO DIDN'T MUCH CARE for flying combat air patrol above the Japanese task force. As far as he was concerned, that was a job for the float planes from the battleships and cruisers that had accompanied the aircraft carriers to Hawaii. But Admiral Nagumo had ordered differently, and so Shindo buzzed along with his engine throttled back to be as miserly with fuel as he could.

He would rather have been strafing the American soldiers on Oahu and finishing the job of knocking out the U.S. aircraft on the island. But he was not the sort of man to protest orders. When Commander Genda told him to take charge of the patrol, he'd just nodded and saluted and said, "Aye aye, sir."

In a way, he could see the need. They'd sunk one carrier. But they thought three or even four had been based at Pearl Harbor. If planes from any of those showed up at the wrong moment . . . well, life could get more interesting than Shindo really wanted. He preferred things to go according to plan.

His eyes darted now right, now left, now center. He kept flicking them here and there. If anything was in the sky to see, he wanted to make sure he didn't miss it. Stare straight ahead all the time, and even important things wouldn't register.

He'd been flying for a couple of hours, and almost dismissed the float plane off to the west as one of his countrymen. But the lines weren't quite right. Neither was the color—Japan seldom painted her aircraft that oceanic blue.

"That's an American plane!" The words crackled in his earphones. One of the other pilots had spotted it too, then. "It's seen us. I'll shoot it down!"

"No!" Shindo said sharply. "No one is to shoot at that airplane until I do. The rest of you, continue on your normal patrol."

Had another man given orders like that, the fliers under him would have thought him out for glory, out to run up his own score. With Lieutenant Shindo, that was unimaginable. He gunned his Zero towards the American plane.

The enemy pilot took awhile to spot him. No doubt the Americans were paying more attention to the ships spread out ahead of them. That was their duty, after all. Not until just before Shindo fired a machine-gun burst at him did they realize they had company. Only after the burst did the pilot turn towards the west and try to escape. The radioman, who also had charge of the rear-facing machine gun, shot back at the Zero.

Shindo pulled back out of range, as if afraid. Then he made a couple of feckless lunges at the float plane. He fired each time, but his bursts went wide. "What are you doing, Lieutenant?" one of the other fliers demanded. "For heaven's sake, finish him. Do you want him to get away?"

"No," Shindo said, and said no more for a little while. Then he radioed the carriers: "Enemy aircraft's bearing is 280. I say again, 280. Along that bearing, we will find American ships, and we may also find planes on the way to attack us."

He got no acknowledgment. He'd expected none. Even if the enemy had spotted them, the carriers needed to maintain radio silence, especially if a U.S. carrier had launched against them.

Now that he had the bearing, he could end the little farce he'd been playing out. He felt proud he'd been the one to get it here as well as from the Wildcats near Pearl Harbor the day before. He climbed and then dove. The enemy gunner couldn't fire at him without shooting off his own tail. Shindo put several cannon shells into the float plane's belly. This held no sport. It was simply killing: a part of war. The American plane tilted in the air. Smoke poured from it. The pilot fought for control—fought and lost. Down towards the water he fell. He and his gunner had both been brave and skillful. Flying a scout plane against the best carrier-based fighter in the world, that hadn't helped them a bit.

The next question was twofold. What could the task force throw at the U.S. ships off to the west? And what were the Americans throwing at them?

COMMANDER MITSUO FUCHIDA COUNTED HIMSELF LUCKY. If his Nakajima B5N1 hadn't come back to the *Akagi* to refuel at just the right time, he wouldn't have been able to join in the search for the newly suspected American ships. The Japanese air commander shook his head. Somewhere off to the west, there *were* American ships; they weren't just suspected. That float plane hadn't come from nowhere. How many ships and of what sort remained to be seen, but they were there.

As soon as the deck officer gave him the signal, he gunned the bomber towards the *Akagi*'s bow. There was, as usual, that sickening dip when the bomber went off the flight deck, that moment of wondering whether it would splash into the sea instead of rising. But rise it did. Fuchida took it up to join the rest of the scratch attack force Admiral Nagumo and Commander Genda were throwing together.

B5N1s loaded with bombs, B5N2s with torpedoes slung beneath their fuselages, Aichi dive bombers, and Zeros to shepherd them along all mustered together. Fuchida was glad the Zeros had longer range than most fighters; they'd probably be able to protect the attack aircraft all the way to the target. If the American plane had found the Japanese fleet, surely the Japanese would be able to return the favor.

Fuchida waited impatiently for planes to fly off the six Japanese carriers and join the attacking force. He was never one to like loitering—he wanted to go out there and hit the enemy. And the Americans would not be idle. If one or more of their carriers was with that force, they would have launched as soon as they got word their scout had located the fleet that was punishing Oahu.

After half an hour, he radioed, "I am commencing the search," and flew off to the west with the planes already in the air. A timely attack with fewer aircraft was better than a great swarm that came too late. Somewhere north and west of Kauai, the enemy waited.

Forty-five minutes went by. Then one of the pilots with him exclaimed, "Airplanes! Airplanes almost dead ahead!"

Almost dead ahead they were: a little north of the course on which the Japanese were flying. As they got nearer, Fuchida saw they were about the same sort of force as the one he led: torpedo planes and dive bombers with fighters flying cover. Those fat, stubby fighters weren't

Wildcats. They had to be Brewster Buffaloes, the U.S. Navy's other carrier-based fighter planes.

Wildcats had proved themselves no match for Zeros. What about Buffaloes? *We'll find out*, Fuchida thought. "Odd-numbered Zeros, attack the U.S. planes," he ordered. "Even-numbered Zeros, stay with our force." As nine or ten Zeros peeled off, the sun shone brightly on the Rising Suns on their wings and fuselages. Some of the stumpy Buffaloes turned to meet them. Fuchida sent a message back to the task force: "From size of enemy force, estimate it comes from one carrier. Repeat, from *one* carrier."

American fighters began tumbling in flames. The Buffaloes couldn't climb and dive with the Zeros. They couldn't turn as tightly, either. Fuchida smiled. He knew white men thought Japan built junk. But whose planes survived and whose spun helplessly towards the Pacific? Junk, was it?

Then the Zeros were in among the American attack aircraft. The U.S. torpedo bombers were simply sitting ducks: too slow to run away and too poorly armed to fight back. His own B5N2s far outdid them. Zeros hacked down several in swift succession. The dive bombers were better at both evading and defending themselves. Fuchida couldn't fault the American pilots' courage. He'd seen that from the beginning. But courage went only so far. Without skill and an adequate airplane under you, courage was only likely to get you killed.

A handful of the Brewster Buffaloes tried to come after the Japanese bombers and torpedo planes. Again, the covering Zeros had no trouble driving them off or shooting them down, though they did damage one Aichi dive bomber enough to make it turn back.

Commander Fuchida swung his planes a few degrees north of their previous course. He also ordered them to spread out more widely, to give themselves the best chance of finding the American ships. They droned on. Somewhere out here, in this vast ocean . . .

* * *

FROM THE *AKAGI*'S BRIDGE, Commander Minoru Genda swept the western sky with field glasses. Fuchida's planes had crossed paths with the American attack force about forty-five minutes after flying west. That had been about forty-five minutes before, which meant the Americans should find the Japanese task force . . . now, more or less.

Beside Genda, Admiral Nagumo looked thoroughly grim—but then, Nagumo usually looked that way. "This could prove very expensive," he said.

Genda shrugged. "Yes, sir," he said; he couldn't openly disagree with his superior. But he went on, "We are as ready for the attack as we can be. We have fighters overhead. All the antiaircraft guns are manned. The ships are tightly buttoned up. We can give a good account of ourselves. We have been very lucky so far. When we war-gamed this attack, we thought we might well lose a couple of carriers. As long as Operation Hawaii succeeds, it will be worth it."

The twin lines between Nagumo's eyes got deeper. "Easy for you to speak so lightly of losses, Commander. This is not your task force." Genda looked down at his shoes for a moment, accepting the rebuke.

A yeoman rushed onto the bridge. "Destroyer *Tanikaze* and combat air patrol report enemy aircraft in sight!" he exclaimed.

Tanikaze, right now, was the westernmost of the destroyers screening the task force. She would have sent the signal by blinker unless her captain disobeyed orders. The planes had to use radio. Could the Americans pick them up?

Too late to worry about it now—no sooner had the yeoman spoken than black puffs of antiaircraft fire started filling the western sky. "Now the Anglo-Saxons will see what we can do," Genda said.

"*Hai.*" Chuichi Nagumo nodded heavily. "And we will also see what they can do."

"So far, they haven't done much. We can stop them," Genda said confidently.

The first glimpse he got of American planes was of the

smoke and fire trailing from one as it splashed into the Pacific. All at once, the *Akagi* started maneuvering like a destroyer, to make herself as difficult a target as she could. The deck beneath Genda's feet thrummed as the big ship's engines went up to full power.

Akagi's antiaircraft guns started firing. Genda couldn't see what they were shooting at, but their crews had a much broader view of the action than he did. He hoped they shot well.

All five other carriers were dodging, too, as were the supporting ships in the task force. As far as Genda was concerned, the Americans were welcome to go after destroyers or cruisers or even the two battleships that had sailed from Hitokappu Bay. In the new calculus of naval warfare, carriers were all that mattered.

Bombs splashed down around one of those carriers—Genda thought it was the *Kaga*, but he wasn't sure. Then, amidst the tall columns of white water the near misses threw up, he saw a swelling cloud of black smoke. The ship was hit, how badly he had no way to guess. A dive bomber streaked off towards the west, a Zero hot on its tail. That was an uneven contest. The dive bomber did a flat roll and splashed into the sea. But its crew had hurt their foes before falling. Commander Genda nodded a salute to brave men.

Somebody on the bridge screamed, "Torpedo plane!" and pointed to starboard. Automatically, Genda's head whipped that way. The U.S. aircraft was plainly on its attack run, zooming straight towards the *Akagi*. Antiaircraft fire converged on it. A Zero dove towards it. Its pilot ignored all distractions. He needed to be perfectly aligned to drop his torpedo, and perfectly aligned he was.

Genda watched the fish fall from the plane, watched it dive into the Pacific. The Japanese had had to expend a lot of sweat and engineering on their torpedoes to make sure they didn't go too deep and bury themselves in the mud under the lochs of Pearl Harbor. Here on the open ocean, that mattered not a bit. The American torpedo could dive as it pleased. It would come up soon enough to strike.

Not fifteen seconds after the torpedo plane launched its missile, the Zero shot it down. That was, of course, fifteen seconds too late. The *Akagi* turned sharply to starboard, to try to present the smallest possible surface to the torpedo. Some men on the bridge prayed. Others cursed. Some did both at once.

Neither would do any good now. Everything depended on that American pilot's aim. Genda gritted his teeth. He feared the enemy flier had known exactly what he was doing, and had done it well. He'd thrown his life away like a ten-sen coin to make sure he had the proper line. Which meant . . .

Thump! The impact echoed through the carrier. But it was only a thump, not the boom Genda had tried to brace himself against.

"A dud!" Half a dozen men said it at once. Smiles of glad relief filled the bridge. Minoru Genda laughed at himself. Maybe prayer had more to do with how things went than he'd thought.

"Some *kami* watched over us there," Admiral Nagumo said, which amounted to the same thing.

Another yeoman rushed onto the bridge. Bowing to Nagumo, he said, "Sir, *Kaga* signals bomb damage from two hits towards the stern. It would have been much worse, her captain says, if the hangar deck hadn't been empty of planes."

Nagumo and Genda and everyone else who heard that nodded. Planes waiting to take off were fires waiting to happen. And, like the rest of the carriers, the *Kaga* had already used up a lot of the munitions she'd brought to Hawaii. That helped make her less inflammable, too. Nagumo asked, "Does she still have power? What speed can she make?"

Genda added, "Can she land planes?" Nagumo, a big-gun admiral down to his toes, would not think of a question like that.

But Nagumo was the task-force commander, and the yeoman answered him first: "Sir, the engine room has taken some damage, but she can make fifteen knots. The engineers are doing all they can with repairs." Having said that, the rating turned and bowed to Genda. "There is damage on the flight deck, sir. Right now, the ship cannot land planes. Again, the crew does hope to make repairs and keep her battleworthy."

"Tell them to do all they can. Until we seize airstrips on Oahu, we have to have our flight decks clear," Genda said. Saluting, the yeoman hurried back to the blinker.

The action seemed over. A few escort vessels were still firing, but Genda couldn't see that they had any targets. The American planes that had attacked the task force had either gone down or fled.

Admiral Nagumo spoke in wondering tones: "All this fighting, and we have yet to set eyes on an enemy ship."

"True, sir." Genda nodded. He could hardly blame Nagumo for his surprise; there had never been a naval battle fought beyond gunnery range before, not in all the history of the world. After a moment, he went on, "The Americans haven't seen our ships, either. That doesn't mean we can't hurt them."

"*Hai.* That's true, too." Nagumo still sounded surprised.

COMMANDER MITSUO FUCHIDA STARED OUT ACROSS the Pacific. More than anything else, he wanted to be the man who spotted the Americans' flotilla. So he thought, anyway, till another flier shouted out that he saw ships. Then Fuchida discovered that he'd been wrong. Discovering the enemy was all very well. Destroying him was more important.

"Look for the carrier—or maybe carriers," he radioed to the pilots in the bombers and dive bombers and torpedo planes. "Worry about other ships only after you've wrecked the carrier force. Bombers, line up behind your leaders."

In training for the attack on Pearl Harbor, the Japanese had discovered that most of their high-altitude bombardiers were not very accurate. They had not had the time to train them all up to the same standard. Instead, they'd assigned the best crews as leaders, and had the others follow them precisely and bomb just where they had. That had dramatically improved their percentage of hits. Now they would try it again.

"There!" A pilot's voice cracked with excitement. "That ship is launching planes!"

For a moment, Fuchida didn't see them. Then the glint of sun off metal or glass drew his eye towards the enemy planes, tiny in the distance. Yes, the ship that was launching them had a flight deck, but she also had smooth, almost rakish lines that showed the hull had originally been intended for a battleship or battle cruiser. The *Akagi* and the *Kaga* were the same sort of conversion. The Americans, if Fuchida remembered rightly, had started the *Lexington* and the *Saratoga* as battlewagons before changing their minds.

Which one was that, down below? He shrugged. It hardly mattered. Now that the Japanese had spotted her, they had to hit her.

He and his comrades had been spotted, too. The ships around the carrier started throwing up antiaircraft fire. Most of them began taking evasive action. The carrier stayed headed into the wind so she could go on sending up planes. That made her easier to pick out from the others.

"Each group—attack the target," Fuchida ordered. "Fighters, accompany the torpedo planes." They were the ones that had to fly low and straight. They most needed fighter protection. Fuchida went on, "Lead bombers—line up on the enemy carrier."

He was a lead bomber himself. He used the voice tube to ask his bombardier how he should set the bomber's course. "Five degrees to the left, sir," the man said at once, and then, half a minute later, "Another five degrees."

Fuchida obeyed with machinelike precision. For the time being, he was not his own man, only an extension of the bombardier's will. Tracers climbed from the ships below, reaching for his plane. Flak burst in black clouds. Some of the explosions came close enough to shake the bomber, making it rise and dip in the air. He was flying straight and level, which gave the gunners a splendid target. He kept on even so. The mission was all that mattered.

Then the B5N1 leaped again. "Bombs gone!" the bombardier cried exultantly.

The bombardiers flying behind Fuchida would do their best to launch their bomb loads from the same spot as he had. Now the bomber was his again. He could speed up, slow down, jink, dive, or climb to evade the ferocious anti-aircraft fire coming up from the Pacific.

And he could pay attention to the rest of the attack on the carrier. Down tumbled the bombs, till they disappeared against the background of the ocean. Zeros and Buffaloes were dueling at lower altitude. Several planes aimed straight for the carriers. Those would be the B5N2s with their torpedoes. One of them caught fire and crashed, then another—shot down, no doubt, by American fighters. The rest bored in on the enemy ship.

Bombs began bursting around the carrier. Was that a hit? Commander Fuchida couldn't be sure. The big ship dodged desperately. She didn't seem to be slowing down. If any of the bombs had struck home, they hadn't done much damage. Fuchida's curses made his disappointment echo in the cockpit.

Where were the Aichi D3A1s? The dive bombers shouldn't miss, especially when the enemy fighters were pulled down towards the sea battling Zeros and attacking torpedo planes. That gave the Aichis a free run at the target.

Just about all the bombs from the high-altitude bombers had fallen now. Fuchida had thought some of them hit. The splashes couldn't have come closer to the carrier. But she emerged from those columns of water still twisting and dodging at top speed. Hitting a moving target from four kilometers up wasn't easy. *We should have done it, though.* Fuchida bit his lip in mortification.

Without warning, the carrier staggered, as a man might after an unexpected blow to the face. A plume of water rose from her port side. "Hit!" Fuchida screamed, unable to hold in his delight. "That's a torpedo hit!"

The American carrier slowed to a crawl. The Aichis chose that moment to dive on her. The pilots in those planes were the best Japan had. They'd been training for months. When they struck, they didn't miss. Bombs burst all around the carrier—and on her flight deck, too.

"*Banzai!*" The fiercely joyous cry burst from Mitsuo Fuchida. "*Banzai! Banzai!*" A moment later, he remembered his duty, and radioed back to the Japanese task force: "Enemy carrier heavily damaged. Black smoke rising. I can see flame through it. She is listing to port, more and more as I watch. She lies almost dead in the water now. . . ." He switched to the frequency the fliers used: "Anyone who still has bombs, use them against the American battleships or cruisers."

Only a few bombs fell. He'd expected nothing different. The carrier was the main target, and the Japanese had devoted most of their effort to wrecking her. *Schwerpunkt*, the Germans called the point of concentration. The fliers had done what they had to do. Fuchida circled over the carrier like a vulture over a dying ox. The list stabilized; some alert engineer must have begun counterflooding. But that only meant she sank on an even keel instead of rolling over. No more than half an hour went by from the first torpedo hit to the moment she slid beneath the waves.

One of the battleships or cruisers down there was on fire. The Japanese might not have had much to throw at the carrier's escorts, but they'd done damage. Fuchida radioed the news to his carriers. He eyed the fuel gauge. It was getting low. No—it had got low. Where his was low, some of the others' would be lower. Time to head back to the task force. Yes, they'd done what needed doing.

LIEUTENANT FLETCHER ARMITAGE SUPPOSED he was lucky to be alive. That was about as much luck as he could find in the situation. He shook his head wearily. One hand scrabbled through his pockets, looking for a pack of cigarettes. He found it. He still had his gun, too. Compared to what a lot of his fellow artillerymen had gone through, he was a lucky fellow.

He pulled out the Chesterfields. He couldn't come up with a Zippo or matches, but that didn't matter. He sprawled in front of a little fire somewhere not far south of Haleiwa. He got the cigarette going from that and sucked harsh smoke into his lungs.

"Can I scrounge one of those off you, Lieutenant?" asked a sergeant who sounded every bit as exhausted as Fletch felt.

"Why the hell not?" Fletch held out the pack.

"Thanks." The sergeant lit his cigarette, too. In the red, flickering firelight, he looked as if he hadn't slept for a week. That was impossible, as he proceeded to prove: "Was it just yesterday morning when the Japs started jumping on us?"

"Yeah." Out of somewhere deep inside him, Fletch dredged up a raspy chuckle. "Time flies when you're having fun, doesn't it?"

"Boy, no kidding." The sergeant took another drag and blew out a cloud of smoke. "I never figured we'd get up to Waimea Bay, and then I never figured we'd get off the goddamn beach, either."

"That's about the size of it," Armitage agreed. "Nobody ever said anything about what a high old time you have when the other bastard's got air support and you don't."

The Japs had strafed the detachment twice more on the way up to Waimea Bay. By the time they were done, hardly any trucks would still move. That reduced the Army to going on foot or commandeering cars from motorists coming up Kamehameha Highway, motorists who had no idea there was a war on till they drove straight into it. Some of them hadn't been very happy about giving up their automobiles. Rifles and bayonets, though, turned out to be mighty good persuaders. Pack as many soldiers into a car as it would hold—and then a couple more—and tie a cannon to the rear bumper and you could go. The car's motor and transmission and suspension might not be worth much afterwards, but who gave a damn?

Of course, bomb craters and the wrecks of shot-up cars in the road north hadn't made things any easier. And they were coming up past the Dole plantation, where the pineapples grew right to the side of the road. Getting by on the

shoulder wasn't easy, because most places there wasn't any
shoulder to speak of.

Some of the workers in the fields were Filipinos. Fletch
hadn't worried about them. They were on his side. But
what about the Japs who stared impassively at the Army
men from under their broad-brimmed straw hats? What
were they thinking? He couldn't tell. All he knew was, he
didn't want to turn his back on them. Maybe that was foolishness. Maybe they were as American as hot dogs and
apple pie. And maybe he didn't feel like taking chances,
just in case they weren't.

Nobody'd counted on having to do part of the way from
Schofield Barracks to Waimea Bay in the dark. Now that
Armitage looked back on it, nobody'd counted on quite a
few things. Almost all the drills he'd been through had
made the unconscious assumption that everything would
go pretty much according to plan. When things turned out
not to go that way, a lot of people had no idea what to do
next.

Fletch smoked his Chesterfield down to a tiny little
butt, then crushed it out. He laughed, not that there was
anything much to laugh about. Things were going according to plan, all right. The only trouble was, the plan had
been drawn up in Tokyo, not Honolulu or Washington.

Somewhere up ahead, a machine gun fired off a burst. It
wasn't an American machine gun; it sounded different. Of
its own accord, Fletch's hand started for the .45 on his right
hip. "It ain't so bad, sir, when you hear shit going off ahead
of you," the sergeant said. "When it's on your flank, that's
when you've got to look out for your ass."

Armitage considered that. After a moment, he nodded.
"Makes sense." He laughed again, this time with something
approaching genuine amusement. "Remember those two
goddamn beach bums, stuck in the water between us and
the Japs?"

"I'm not likely to forget 'em," the sergeant answered.
"Poor sons of bitches didn't know whether to shit or go
blind."

Caught between the Devil and the deep blue sea was

what Fletch had been thinking, but it boiled down to the same thing. And the surf-riders had been *on* the deep blue sea. With the Americans and the Japs both shooting at them and past them at each other, he didn't know how they'd missed getting chopped into hamburger, but they had. They'd even managed to disappear in their jalopy. There were plenty of times over the past day when Fletch wished he could have done the same.

He supposed the main reason the beach bums were still breathing was that Japanese planes had come overhead just then. Getting bombed and strafed had distracted the Americans from the surf-riders—and, rather more to the point, from the barges full of Japs wallowing towards shore just then.

Had all the Americans been in position as planned, and had the Japs not been plastering them from the skies, they would have massacred the invaders before the barges ever got to the beaches. As things were . . .

As things were, they'd done their best. They'd hurt the Japs. Fletch had planted a shell right on a barge carrying a field gun and watched it turn turtle. But a Japanese bomb had upended the gun right next to his and blown its whole crew to red rags, while a strafing fighter coming in at tree-top height had put more artillerymen out of action.

And then the Japanese soldiers had got onto the beach. That wasn't supposed to happen. In all the drills, the invaders were repelled. Whoever'd worked out those drills had been an optimist. The Japs got on the beach, and then they were running up off the beach, shooting rifles and light machine guns and whatever else they had with them.

They'd even had a tank or two clatter down off a big barge. Their tanks didn't look very impressive—they weren't a patch on the M3s the Forty-first Tank Company at Schofield Barracks had. But they were where they needed to be, and the M3s weren't. Machine-gun bullets bounced off them. Their cannons were popguns, but they could take care of machine-gun nests and shell unprotected field guns. And Fletch had discovered it was damned hard to hit a moving target with a 105mm gun.

He lit another Chesterfield. God only knew where he'd get more after the pack was empty, but he'd worry about that later. Now he needed the smoke. "We did everything we could," he said. "I really think we did." He sounded dazed and disbelieving even to himself.

"Yeah." The sergeant nodded. "I guess maybe we did. It wasn't enough, though. Those fuckers are on the island now. How the hell we gonna kick 'em off?"

"Beats me." Armitage yawned. "All I know is, I'm falling asleep sitting up."

"Go ahead, Lieutenant. I'll shake you in a couple of hours so I can get some shuteye, too," the noncom said. "Or maybe I'll shake you sooner, in case we gotta fall back again."

He didn't say anything about shaking Fletch if the Americans started advancing. Plainly, he didn't think they would. Fletch knew he should have reproved him. But he didn't think the Americans would start advancing in the middle of the night, either. They hadn't quite come to pieces when the Japs got ashore, but some of them had sure retreated at a pace faster than a walk.

Yawning again, Fletch finished the cigarette and stretched out by the fire. Back on the mainland, it would be cold. A lot of places, it would be snowing. He didn't even worry about a blanket here. He closed his eyes and let sleep club him over the head.

He didn't know how much he'd had when a hard hand on his shoulder prodded him back to consciousness. He did know it wasn't nearly enough. "What the hell?" he asked muzzily. He felt slow and stupid, almost drunk.

"Sorry, sir." The sergeant didn't sound very sorry. "There's shit going on off to our left. If the Japs turn our flank and get on the road behind us—"

"We're screwed," Fletch finished for him. The sergeant nodded. The fire had died down to crimson embers: barely enough to let Fletch make out the other man's face. If the Japs got on the road behind them, they might escape through the fields. Their precious gun, though, would be lost. Right now, Fletch wouldn't have parted with that gun for all the gold in Fort Knox. He didn't know how many others were left. He didn't know for sure if any others around here were left. "Okay," he said. "We'll pull back."

What they had to pull back with was a 1935 De Soto, taken at gunpoint from a Japanese family out for a drive. Compared to the snorting truck that had hauled the gun partway north, it was ridiculously underpowered. But compared to a horse or a dozen poor bloody infantrymen, it was a miracle of rare device.

The miracle's engine coughed into life when Fletch turned the key. He wondered if the noise would bring a volley of gunfire his way, but it didn't. Shells as long as a man's arm clattered and clanked on the floorboards. The car couldn't pull the gun and the limber both. Artillerymen put their feet on the ammo. As Fletch put the De Soto in gear, he tried not to think about what would happen if a Jap fieldpiece hit the car. *Boom! Right to the moon!* was what occurred to him.

He reached for the light switch, then jerked his hand away as if the switch were red-hot. Now *that* would have been Phi Beta Kappa! "The Japs are trying to kill you, Fletcher my boy," he muttered. "You don't have to try and kill yourself, too."

He couldn't go faster than about ten miles an hour, not if he wanted to stay on the road. Of course, even ten miles an hour would have taken him all the way down to the south coast in a little more than two hours. He didn't get that far, or anywhere close. After ten minutes or so, he came to a roadblock manned by some nervous infantrymen. They seemed glad to see he had the gun—and even gladder that he wasn't a Jap.

Fletch was pretty goddamn glad they weren't Japs, too, only he did his best not to let on. He and his men piled out of the De Soto and added the gun to the roadblock's strength. By sunup, if not sooner, he figured he'd be in action again.

"MARTIAL LAW!" SHOUTED POSTERS ALL OVER HONOLULU. Jiro Takahashi didn't read English. His sons made sure he understood. "It means the Army's in charge," Kenzo said at breakfast Monday morning. "It means you have to do whatever soldiers tell you to do."

"It means we're going to land in trouble for being Japanese," Hiroshi added.

"When have we not been in trouble for being Japanese?" Jiro asked. If his son was bitter, so was he.

"They attacked the United States. They hit us when we weren't even looking." Kenzo sounded furiously angry at Japan.

Jiro felt furiously angry at his younger son. Kenzo had everything backwards. As far as Jiro was concerned, Japan was *we* and the Americans were *they*. Jiro looked to his wife for support. He didn't have to look far for Reiko. The tiny kitchen of their cramped apartment barely held the four of them. Reiko just said, "Eat your noodles, all of you. Drink your tea. Whether it's war or whether it's peace, work doesn't stop. You've got to go to the sampan."

She was right. Her refusal to come right out and take Jiro's side left him punctured anyway. She'd been born in Oshima County, just as he had; her home village was only about fifteen miles from his. Surely she felt as Japanese as he did. What difference did it make that they'd lived in Hawaii for decades and probably never would go back to the old country? None—not as far as he could see. But Reiko didn't want to quarrel with the boys, no matter how foolishly they behaved.

Hashi flying, Jiro finished the soba noodles. He'd been surprised to discover there were Americans who ate buckwheat groats, but he didn't know of any who made them into noodles. He drank some of the hot water in which the noodles were boiled; it was supposed to be very healthy. And he gulped his tea. Then he jumped to his feet. He barked at his sons: "Come on! We haven't got all day!"

To his dismay, they got done no more than a few seconds after he did. When they rose, they loomed over him. How could he feel he was in charge when he had to look up at them to tell them anything? But all Hiroshi said was, "We're ready, Father."

Down to the street they went. When they got there, Jiro coughed as if he'd smoked a pack of Camels all at once. Horrible, choking black smoke swirled through the air. For all he could see, it might as well have been nighttime. The smoke made his eyes burn and sting, too. It left greasy soot everywhere it touched.

His sons made almost identical disgusted noises. They pulled bandannas out of their pockets—Hiroshi's red, Kenzo's blue—and tied them over their mouths. That struck Jiro as a good idea. All he had was a dirty white handkerchief. He used it. Everything would be dirty in short order. Maybe the hankie kept some of the nasty smoke out of his lungs. He could hope so, anyhow.

The streets were crowded. It was Monday morning, after all. But people moved as if in slow motion. In the black, stinking murk, you had to. Otherwise, you'd get run into on the sidewalk or run over in the street. Cars had their lights on, but the beams didn't pierce more than a few feet of haze.

"Go to hell, you goddamn Japs!" somebody yelled in English. Jiro understood the sentiment well enough. He squared his shoulders and kept walking. Above the bandannas, his sons' eyes blazed. He wasn't even sure the curses had been aimed at them. They were far from the only Japanese on the streets.

A lot of intersections had policemen posted to keep traffic moving. Honolulu's cops sprang from every group in the islands: *haoles*, Hawaiians, Chinese, Japanese, Filipinos, Koreans (which Jiro found revolting, but Koreans weren't subject to Japanese authority here). Normally, the police got obeyed because they were the police. Now people who weren't Japanese swore at the Japanese cops—and sometimes, if they were ignorant, at the Chinese and Koreans, too. When the cursers guessed wrong, the policemen angrily shouted back. Stoic as samurai, the officers who were Japanese ignored whatever came their way.

Some of the intersections that didn't have cops had soldiers. They wore helmets and carried bayoneted rifles, and looked nervous enough to shoot or skewer anybody who rubbed them the wrong way. They were cursing Japanese as loudly as any civilians. Jiro pretended not to hear; arguing with armed men struck him as suicidal madness. His sons muttered to themselves, but not loud enough to draw notice.

The Aala Market was half deserted. That shook Jiro. He hadn't thought anything could keep the dealers away. Only the smell of fish lingered at full strength.

He and Hiroshi and Kenzo went on to Kewalo Basin. But more soldiers waited, along with a few fishermen who'd arrived ahead of the Takahashis. Some of them, the younger ones, were talking with the soldiers in English. Jiro's sons joined the discussion. After a little while, Hiroshi's voice rose in anger. One of the soldiers aimed a rifle at his chest. Jiro sprang forward to push his son out of harm's way. But Hiroshi took a step back on his own, and the soldier lowered the Springfield. He and Hiroshi went on speaking English, not quite so furiously.

"What's going on?" Jiro asked. The soldier scowled at him, probably for speaking Japanese. He ignored the man. It was the only language he could speak, and he needed to know.

"We can't go out." Hiroshi's voice was hard and flat.

"What? Why not?" Jiro exclaimed. "How are we supposed to make a living if we can't go out? Are the Americans crazy?" As he always did, he used the word to label other people. It didn't apply to him or, as far as he was concerned, to his family.

"We can't go out because the Army doesn't trust us," Hiroshi answered. "It doesn't trust any Japanese. Didn't you see that yesterday, when the airplane shot up that other sampan? It could have been us just as easily. The soldiers are afraid we'll go out and tell the Japanese Navy what's going on here, or maybe that we'll go out and bring back Japanese soldiers."

"That's . . ." Jiro's voice trailed away. He couldn't say it was mad or impossible, for it was neither. He hadn't thought about actually helping Japan against the United States, but the idea didn't disgust him. Maybe some other

fishermen *had* thought about it. How could he know? If
they had, they would have kept their mouths shut. That was
only common sense.

And some sampans, bigger than the *Oshima Maru*, could
range out five hundred miles, maybe even more. They could
surely find the Imperial Navy. They could bring back soldiers, too, if their skippers were so inclined. If a boat could
carry tons of fish, it could also carry tons of men, and each
ton was ten or twelve fully equipped soldiers.

"That's an insult, that's what it is," Kenzo said. "I'm
loyal, you're loyal, we're all loyal." He raised his voice:
"*We're all loyal!*" Then he spoke in English, probably repeating the same thing.

The fishermen nodded. Some of them said, "*Hai!*" Others said, "Yes!" More protests in English followed.

For all the good those protests did, the Japanese men
might have been talking to a bunch of stones. The American soldiers glared at them and shook their heads. One, an
older man with stripes on his sleeve, made pushing noises
with both hands. *Go away*, he was saying. Even Jiro had no
trouble understanding that.

Fishermen who spoke English kept arguing. Jiro started
to turn away. He saw they could argue till they turned blue
in the face without persuading the men in uniform. Then
another soldier ran up shouting something in English. Jiro
could make out *Japs*, but nothing more. All the soldiers exclaimed, some of them hotly. So did the fishermen.

"What does he say?" Jiro asked. Most of the time, not
knowing English didn't bother him. Every once in a while,
he felt the lack.

Grimly, Kenzo answered, "He says Japanese soldiers
have landed on the northern beaches. We've been invaded."

"Oh." Jiro took the news in stride. "It's part of war, *neh?*
If America could, she would invade Japan, wouldn't she?"
But, as he knew very well, America couldn't. If that didn't
show which country was mightier . . .

His sons didn't seem to see it like that. They both turned
away from him. Hiroshi said, "I'm not going to translate

that for the soldiers, Father. And you're lucky I'm not, too, or we'd all end up in trouble."

Kenzo added, "This is our country. We were born here. We like it here. We don't want anything to do with Japan now that she's at war with us."

Another fisherman, a weathered fellow of Jiro's generation named Tetsuo Yuge, shouted angrily at the two younger Takahashis: "How dare you talk to your father like that? If my boys were that rude, I'd be ashamed of myself—and of them."

Jiro wondered what the other fisherman's sons would say if they were here. One of them worked at a gas station; the other was a bank clerk. They thought of themselves as Americans, too; Tetsuo had complained about it. Jiro said, "War makes everybody crazy for a while. Sooner or later, things will straighten out."

Several of the tall American soldiers put their heads together. When they separated, the man with stripes on his sleeves shouted in English. Some of the younger men, the ones who understood what he was telling them, started to walk off. Kenzo translated: "He says we have to leave. He says this place is off-limits for civilians. That's Army talk—it means we're not allowed here."

"Can he do that?" Jiro asked doubtfully. He didn't like the idea of leaving the *Oshima Maru* tied up where soldiers who hated Japanese could do whatever they wanted to her.

But both his sons nodded. Hiroshi said, "It's martial law. If the soldiers say we have to do it, we have to do it. The only ones who can change things now are other soldiers."

"This would never have happened if Japan hadn't jumped on us," Kenzo said.

"What are we going to do without a day's catch? What are we going to do without a day's pay?" Jiro asked. "And how long will the soldiers"—he almost said *the American soldiers*, but judged that would cause more trouble than it was worth—"keep us from going to sea? What will we do for money if it's a long time?"

Those were good questions, important questions. Jiro knew that. Neither of his sons had any answers. He didn't see what else they could do but go back home. Reiko would have a lot of questions for them then. Jiro didn't have any answers, either.

JANE ARMITAGE WAS GLAD they'd called off school for the day in Wahiawa. Half the kids in her third-grade class were Japs. They were bright and eager. They were respectful, and they mostly worked harder than *haoles*. But she didn't think she could stand the sight of so many slanty-eyed faces right now.

She'd had a devil of a time getting used to what people in Hawaii looked like when she came over with Fletch. Columbus, Ohio, wasn't like this at all. In Columbus, the Negroes mostly stayed in Bronzeville on the east side of town. Elsewhere, even Italians were out of the ordinary. Her own blond, blue-eyed good looks were as normal as sunshine. Not here. Hawaii was different. Coarse black hair and swarthy skin were the expected; she was the one who stood out.

When she caught herself wondering how Fletch was doing, she grimaced. Without the war, she wouldn't have given a damn. Without the war, she would have just waved bye-bye if he jumped off a cliff. But she didn't want the Japs blowing him up. Even for her, that went too far.

She wondered if he was sober. If he wasn't, he'd be sorry. If he was . . . he'd be in the war, and he might be sorry anyway. "Shit," Jane said crisply. Inside the apartment she no longer shared with him, who'd hear her swear?

Bright sunlight streamed in through the window. It would be another warm day—not hot, for it probably wouldn't get to eighty, but warm. Tonight, it would drop into the sixties, which was as cold as it ever got. Columbus might have snow on the ground. Jane hadn't needed any time at all to get used to the weather.

The window was open. Why not, when the air was the sweetest in the world? But along with the smells of flowers that bloomed all year around, the stink of smoke came in today. The Japs had jumped on Wheeler Field and then on Schofield Barracks with both feet. By what the breeze said, some of those fires were still burning.

And what the Japs had done to Pearl Harbor! The smoke in the south blotted out a big part of the sky. It reached up towards the sun, and looked so very thick and menacing, it might bring down night at noon if it climbed high enough to blot out the source of light and warmth.

After lighting a cigarette, Jane turned on the radio, a fancy set Fletch had bought with money that could have been better spent elsewhere. So Jane had thought at the time, anyhow. Now she did some more swearing when the ordinary bands brought in nothing but silence and static. The Hawaiian stations were still off the air, then. She switched to the short-wave tuner. She'd never dreamt how desperately she could crave news from the outside world.

As she turned the dial, she got more static in snarling bursts, and then a man speaking a language she didn't understand—Italian, she thought, or possibly Spanish. Whoever he was, he sounded full of himself, and also full of hot air. Jane spun the dial some more.

She got a squawky, singsong Oriental language next, and then a program of dance music that could have come from almost anywhere on the planet. Music wasn't what she was after now, though. The next station she found featured somebody—Hitler?—bellowing in German. She understood some German; she'd studied it at Ohio State. But this fellow used a dialect she had trouble following, and he was going a mile a minute. All she could do was pick up a word here and there. She gave the dial another twist.

English at last! A strong, New York–accented voice said, "—Twelve-thirty this afternoon, President Roosevelt asked Congress to declare war against the Empire of Japan. He called December seventh, the date of the Japs' unprovoked attack against Pearl Harbor in the Territory of Hawaii, 'a date which will live in infamy.'"

Jane looked at a clock on the mantel. It was half past eight here. Washington was five and a half hours ahead of

Hawaii time, so the President had spoken about an hour and a half before.

"Swift Congressional approval of the request is expected," the announcer went on. "There are rumors that the Japs are trying to land soldiers in the Hawaiian Islands, but these are so far unconfirmed. If they prove correct, it is expected that the soldiers of the Hawaiian Department will drive the invaders into the sea."

"They'd better!" Jane exclaimed. She thought about her not-former-enough husband and his friends, all of whom drank too much. She thought about the stories they told of their ignorant, inept enlisted men. She thought about how they always complained the government didn't spend enough money on paper clips, let alone on important things. And she thought about how they were going to be the ones who threw the Japs back into the sea.

She started worrying in earnest then.

"Outrage continues pouring in around the country at the dastardly Japanese deed," the newscaster said. Jane had never heard anyone actually use the word *dastardly* before. It sounded like *bastardly*, which sure as hell fit the situation.

The newsman went on yammering about Japanese attacks in the Philippines and other places she couldn't have found without a big Rand McNally to give her a hand. Then he talked about what the Germans were doing in Russia. It sounded as if the Russians were trying to counterattack, but it had sounded like that before, and Hitler's troops were in the suburbs of Moscow.

Jane turned off the radio and did the breakfast dishes. There weren't many; she'd had cornflakes and a glass of apple juice. Even so, she paused with the Bon Ami–soaked dishrag. The cereal and the juice both came from the mainland. If the Japs really were trying to invade Oahu, how would ships from the States get here? How much food did Hawaii have on its own? How much could it grow if it had to?

She laughed. "How much pineapple and sugarcane can we eat?" That wasn't a joke. Hawaii grew more pineapple than any other place in the world, and lots and lots of sugarcane. But because the Territory grew so much cane and pineapple, it didn't grow a whole lot of anything else.

Off to the west, antiaircraft guns started booming. Jane's mouth twisted into a sour grimace. That she could tell they were antiaircraft guns proved she'd spent too much time with Fletch Armitage. Field guns had a different report—deeper and more prolonged—and didn't fire so quickly.

What could Fletch tell about anything that mattered to her? Not a thing, not as far as she could tell. All that mattered to him were guns and booze and the bedroom—and he hadn't been nearly so good there as he thought he had.

Muttering to herself, she finished the dishes. The thought that had come to her while she was washing the cereal bowl wouldn't go away. Maybe a trip to the grocery would be smart, to stock up on things just in case. She wished Wahiawa had a Piggly Wiggly, the way Honolulu did. You could do all your shopping in one trip at the supermarket. With a corner grocery, you were never sure ahead of time what they'd have and what they wouldn't.

And Japs ran most of them. She'd learned not to give that a second thought. Now she was going to have to unlearn it again. Things had changed. Exactly how they'd changed . . . well, she'd just have to wait and see.

A quarter to nine was too early to go to the store. There was another reason to wish for a Piggly Wiggly. Stores like that opened earlier and stayed open later than little family businesses.

She spent an hour or so cleaning the apartment. That was all it needed. Keeping it clean was a lot easier with Fletch gone. The Army was supposed to have made him neat, but it had fallen down on the job. Or maybe it was just that, while he lived with her, he expected her to do all the work, and he didn't care how much it was. Whatever it was, she was glad to be out from under it.

When she did come out trundling a little metal folding grocery cart behind her, she found the streets of Wahiawa full of soldiers. Since the town was right next door to two divisions of Army men, that wasn't the biggest surprise in the world. But they usually came here to get drunk or get laid or pawn something for the cash they needed to get drunk or get laid.

These weren't men on leave out for a good time. They wore the steel derbies that made them look like British soldiers from the Great War and carried rifles with fixed bayonets. And they had the air of men who knew damn well they were doing something important and something that might be dangerous.

Jane was glad she'd chosen to walk. The soldiers were setting up roadblocks and barricades in the streets, which snarled traffic to a fare-thee-well. Horns blared. "What the hell are you doing?" a fat, middle-aged man shouted from behind the wheel of his Ford.

A sergeant who usually dealt with a swarm of privates had no trouble putting one mouthy civilian in his place. "What are we doing?" he echoed. "We're making sure you don't get your stupid ass shot off, that's what. And this is the thanks we get? The horse you rode in on, too, buddy." He spat in magnificent contempt.

The fat man deflated like a leaky balloon. Jane had all she could do not to giggle. Years as an Army wife had acquainted her with the talents of sergeants. This one turned back to his men. They hadn't missed a beat. As soon as they had their barricade finished, they hauled a cannon up behind it. It wasn't one of the bigger guns Fletch dealt with, but an antitank weapon. Seeing its snout pointing north gave Jane pause.

When she got to the grocery store, she discovered she wasn't the only one who'd had the same idea. The line stretched out the door. Some of the women in it were *haoles*, others Japanese or Chinese or Filipino, though there were just a couple of the latter. Most of the Filipinos on Oahu were men brought in to work in the fields. They sometimes brawled because they didn't have enough women to go around—or got into knife fights over the ones there were, or over fighting cocks, or over nothing in particular. Jane didn't have much use for Filipinos.

Two Japanese women right in front of her chattered in their own language. She'd heard Japanese almost every day since coming to Hawaii. She took it as much for granted as the perfect weather or the funny birds or the palm trees. She had taken it for granted, anyhow. Now she eyed the women suspiciously. What were they saying? What were they thinking? If the Japs got this far—almost inconceivable, but for the soldiers in the streets—what would they do?

The white housewife who came out of the store was loaded down with so many groceries, she could hardly walk. She gave the Japanese women a hard stare. "Goddamn lousy Japs," she said, and trudged on.

They plainly understood English. They stared after her, their flat, narrow-eyed faces unreadable, at least to Jane. For close to a minute, neither of them said anything in any language. Then they started speaking again—in Japanese. Jane didn't know whether to want to applaud them or kick them in the teeth.

By the time she got into the grocery store, it looked as if a swarm of locusts had been there ahead of her. *And so they have*, she thought, *and I'm another one*. She bought canned vegetables and Spam and yams and potatoes and crackers—everything she could think of that would keep for a while. Well, almost everything: try as she would, she couldn't make herself get a sack of rice. Other *haoles* weren't so fussy. Jane shrugged. She liked potatoes better anyhow. She bought toilet paper and Kleenex and soap, too.

She brought her cart up to Mr. Hasegawa. He totaled everything up, not on a cash register but with a pencil on the back of an old envelope. "Twenty dallah, fo'ty-t'ree cent," he said at the end of his calculations.

On impulse, she asked him, "What do you think of all this?"

His face closed down, the same way those of the Japanese women outside the store had. "Very bad," he said at last. "We have war, where get more groceries?"

That undoubtedly wasn't a tenth of what was on his

mind, but it wasn't far removed from what Jane and the other panic shoppers were thinking, either. She set a twenty and a one on the counter. The storekeeper gave her a half-dollar, a nickel, and two pennies. She bumped her little cart out of the grocery store and headed home.

One of the soldiers manning the antitank gun sent a wolf whistle after her. She ignored him, which only made him laugh. Getting mad at them—letting them see you were mad at them—just encouraged them. Fletch had been right about that.

What else had Fletch been right about? Jane angrily shook her head. No matter how much her in-the-process-of-becoming-ex-husband had known about soldiers and artillery pieces, he hadn't known a goddamn thing about being a husband. If he'd been married to anything, it was the Army, not her.

She looked back at the soldiers. She looked south at the appalling black smoke rising from Pearl Harbor—and west at the smaller smoke clouds from Wheeler Field and Schofield Barracks. All she'd done to Fletch was throw him out of the apartment when she couldn't stand living with him another minute. Being married to the Army was liable to get him killed.

FLETCHER ARMITAGE STUCK A FRESH FIVE-ROUND CLIP in his Springfield and worked the bolt to chamber the first cartridge. He wanted something that would hit from farther away than he could throw a rock. He still had the officer's .45 on his hip, but he hadn't used it for a day or two. The soldier who'd been issued the rifle wouldn't miss it; a Japanese shell had cut him in half.

The roadblock south of Haleiwa to which he'd added his gun hadn't held the Japanese for long. They hadn't come straight at it. He could have slaughtered a million of them if they had. Instead, they'd gone around, through the cane and pineapple fields. The bastards were like water or mercury; they flowed through the tiniest gaps in the American line—and came out shooting on the other side.

He still had the 105mm gun. He still had the De Soto

that hauled it, too. The windshield had been shot out of it. A bullet hole went through both rear doors. The round hadn't gone through any of the men in the backseat. Fletch didn't know why it hadn't. Maybe God was on his side after all. But if He was, why had He turned so many Japs loose on Oahu?

A bullet from off to the left cracked past his head and ricocheted off the barrel of the field gun. He ducked, automatically and much too late. He had no idea whether the bullet was American or Japanese. If many more came from that direction, though, he'd have to pull up stakes and fall back again . . . if he could. If he couldn't, he'd fall back without it, and take along the breech block so the Japs couldn't turn the piece around and start shooting it at his side.

More shooting did come from off to the left, but most of it came from two American machine guns. They fired noticeably faster than their Japanese counterparts. Maybe the Japs, instead of flowing through a hole, had walked into a buzz saw this time. Fletch's lips skinned back from his teeth in a savage grin. Jesus, he hoped so!

And so it seemed, for the shooting moved farther north. "My God," one of the artillerymen said wearily. "I didn't think them slanty-eyed fuckers knew how to back up."

"I don't think they're doing it on purpose. I think we're doing it to them. There's a difference," Fletch said. The artilleryman paused in the act of lighting up a cigarette long enough to nod.

A wild-eyed foot soldier burst out of the cane to the left of the Kamehameha Highway. Half a dozen men around the gun swung their rifles towards him. He didn't seem to notice how close a brush with death he'd just had. All he did seem to notice was the single silver bar on each of Fletcher Armitage's shoulders. "Thank God!" he said. "An officer!"

"What the hell?" Fletch said. Most of the time, enlisted men wanted nothing to do with officers. They hoped their superiors would leave them alone. When a PFC actually came looking for a first lieutenant, something was rotten in the state of Denmark.

"Sir, come with me, please." The PFC sounded close to tears. "There's something you need to see."

"What is it?" Fletch asked.

The soldier shook his head. "You got to see it, sir. Christ almighty!" He gulped as if fighting his stomach.

Fletch had already seen much more than he ever wanted to. War was nothing like the sanitized version the Army had got ready for in the drills on the mainland and around Schofield Barracks. People didn't just get killed. They got blown to pieces. They got chopped to shreds. They got holes punched through them—not neat, tidy holes but ones that poured—often gushed—blood. Fletch had smelled shit and burnt meat, sometimes from the same wounded man. He'd heard shrieks that would haunt him as long as he lived—which didn't look like it would be long.

By the PFC's grime and the stubble on his chin, he'd been fighting from the very beginning of this mess. How could he not have seen and smelled and heard the same kinds of things as Fletch had? How could he not be getting hardened to what war did? What he'd seen just now, though, had shaken him to the core.

Which meant that either he was shell-shocked or that it was going to shake Fletch to the core, too. For his own sake, Fletch rooted for shell shock. But he went into the cane field with the soldier. Stalks rustled. Bugs chirped. One of them lit on him. He brushed it away, trying to walk as softly as he could.

"Eddie?" the PFC called, cradling his Springfield. "You there, Eddie?"

"Wish to hell I wasn't," another soldier answered from not far ahead. "You find an officer, Bill?"

"A lieutenant," the PFC—Bill—said, damning with faint praise.

"Bring him on." Eddie didn't seem inclined to be fussy. "I'm with poor goddamn Wilbur. Ain't no Japs around—now."

Following Bill, Fletch pushed the last little way through the cane. Eddie was a stocky, swarthy private who looked straight out of Hell's Kitchen or some other equally charming slum. He stood guard over a corpse. The dead man's hands were tied behind his back, which Fletch saw first. Bill said, "Jap bastards caught poor Wilbur alive. Go on around, sir. Take a look at what they done to him."

I don't want to do this. I really *don't want to do this* went through Fletch's mind eight or ten thousand times as he took the four or five steps that let him see what the Japanese had done to the American soldier they'd captured. And he was right. He was righter even than he'd imagined. "Fuck," he said softly, the most reverent, prayerful obscenity he'd ever heard.

They'd bayoneted Wilbur again and again, in the chest and in the belly—but not in the left side of the chest, because that might have pierced his heart and killed him faster than they wanted to. And after he was dead (Fletch hoped like hell it was after he was dead) they'd yanked down his trousers, cut off his penis, and stuffed it into his mouth. And they must have been proud of their handiwork, too, because they'd stuck a piece of cardboard by his head. On it, one of them had written, in English, HE TAKE LONG TIME DIE.

"Fuck," Fletch said again. "What do you need me for?"

"What do we do with him, sir?" Eddie sounded like a lost kid, not at all like a tough guy.

"Bury him," Fletch answered at once, his mouth running ahead of his brain. His wits caught up a moment later: "Bury him, and for Christ's sake don't tell anybody just what happened to him. But spread the word: you really don't want the Japs to take you alive."

Eddie and Bill both nodded. "Yes, sir," they said together, seeming relieved somebody was telling them what to do. Then Bill asked, "What about the Geneva Convention, sir?"

"I don't know. What about it?" Fletch pointed to the mutilated, degraded remnant of what had been a man. "How much do you think the Japs care about it? Why don't you ask Wilbur here?"

They both flinched. "What do we do if we catch one of them?" That was Eddie.

Fletch looked down at the dead American soldier again. He knew what he was supposed to say. What came out of his mouth was, "Whatever you do, don't come asking an officer beforehand, you hear me?"

"Yes, *sir!*" Where nothing else had, that got Bill and Eddie's enthusiastic approval.

IV

WHILE AT ANNAPOLIS, LIEUTENANT JIM PETERSON HAD taken a lot of military history. Back around the time of Christ, he remembered, the Roman Empire had tried to conquer the Germans. (That looked like a damn good idea nowadays; too bad it hadn't worked.) Augustus sent three legions into the middle of Germany under a bungling general, and they didn't come back. The Emperor howled, "Quintilius Varus, give me back my legions!"

Peterson felt like howling, "General Short, give me back my airplanes!"

Yes, the Japs had sunk the *Enterprise* and the *Lexington*, but they'd both gone down swinging. They'd shot down enemy planes. A couple of surviving pilots claimed the *Lexington*'s aircraft had nailed an enemy carrier, maybe even two.

But the Army? Before the Japs struck, the Army had lined up its fighters and bombers wingtip-to-wingtip. Scuttlebutt said the illustrious General Short had been scared of saboteurs. Peterson didn't give a damn about scuttlebutt. What Short had done was set up the bowling pins. And when the Japs did show up, they knocked just about every one of them down.

Not that the Navy came off smelling like a rose. There was plenty of blame to go around, as far as Peterson could tell. Looking back on it, Admiral Kimmel's decision to have most of the Pacific Fleet in port every weekend seemed something less than brilliant. If Hirohito's boys had somebody keeping an eye on Pearl Harbor—and anybody with two brain cells to rub together would have—they'd spot the pattern lickety-split. And, again, the USA paid because the Japanese were on the ball when its own top officers weren't.

Peterson also wondered why the hell neither the Army nor the Navy had spotted the enemy carriers before they launched their planes. *Someone* should have been looking off to the north. That was the logical direction for the Japs to pick if they were crazy enough to attack the United States at all. Peterson hadn't thought they would be.

Crazy? The slant-eyed bastards were raking in the chips. "Shows how goddamn smart I am," he muttered inside the Pearl Harbor BOQ, where he'd gone from Ewa. It was, at the moment, a tent city. Japanese bombs had blown the original structure to hell and gone.

Why this is hell, nor am I out of it. Peterson had taken English Lit, too. Lines like that stuck in the mind as firmly as Augustus' anguished cry. This one was a pretty good description of what things were like at Pearl Harbor right now. Everybody wore gauze of some sort over his nose and mouth. Despite the Americans' best efforts to douse the flames, the fuel-tank farm still burned a week after it was bombed. Noxious smoke filled the air. It got on everything and everybody, and made men look as if they were in blackface for a minstrel show.

Distant thunder came from off to the north. The only trouble was, that wasn't thunder. It was an artillery duel, the Japs versus the U.S. Army. Again, scuttlebutt was the only way to get a handle on what was happening if you weren't at the front. On the rare occasions the radio said anything, it belched out optimistic twaddle that made Peterson want to puke. He knew bullshit when he heard it.

Gossip and rumor said the Americans were falling back. The way the distant thunder didn't seem quite so distant argued that gossip and rumor knew what they were talking about. They also said you didn't want to try to surrender to the Japs. Peterson didn't know about that. He'd talked to people who'd talked to people who'd talked to people who said they'd seen this, that, and the other thing. Maybe they had, maybe they hadn't. There were party games where you passed a sentence around the room from mouth to mouth. It always came back to the person who'd started it garbled beyond recognition. The rumor just didn't make any sense to Peterson. If the Japanese abused American prisoners of war, wouldn't the USA declare open season on captured Japs? Who'd want to start anything like that?

His doubts weren't what propelled him out of BOQ. Nobody had yet figured out how to get him into action. He'd been patient as long as he could stand. Now he intended to start pounding on desks and shouting at people till he got what he wanted. That was the strategy of a four-year-old throwing a tantrum, but it often worked. The squeaky wheel got the grease. Peterson wouldn't just squeak. He'd scream.

He winced when he emerged from the tent. Hawaii had always struck him as paradise on earth, or as close as anybody was likely to come. The thought was profoundly unoriginal, which made it no less true. Here, hell had visited itself on paradise. The noxious smoke swirled everywhere, now thicker, now thinner, depending on the vagaries of the breeze. Maybe the gauze mask Peterson wore helped some, but he still had a permanent nasty taste in the back of his throat, while his eyes felt as if somebody'd thrown ground glass into them.

Heavy black fuel oil fouled the turquoise waters of the harbor. The floating fires were finally out. That helped a little, but only a little. The Navy's proud battlewagons lay shattered and broken, their terrible grace and beauty turned to trash: *Oklahoma* capsized; *West Virginia* and *California* sunk; *Arizona* not just sunk but with her back broken, too, her bridge and foremast all twisted and askew and blackened by the conflagration that had raced over her. And *Nevada*, or what was left of her. Yet another armor-piercing bomb had struck her in the third wave of the attack, after she beached herself near Hospital Point, and started fires that still smoldered. She might be salvageable, but it would be a long, slow job.

Bombs had savaged the lush greenery on Ford Island, too, toppling palm trees and showing the earth all naked and torn. *This is what war looks like. This is what war feels like. This is what war smells like*, Peterson thought. It wasn't the way he'd imagined it at Annapolis. It wasn't even the way he'd imagined it when that goddamn Jap shot him down. That had been a duel in the air, a fair fight— except that his Wildcat was a lumbering pig when measured against the machine the Jap flew. This . . . Nothing even remotely fair about this. Japan had kicked the USA right in the nuts, and this was the aftermath.

Peterson wanted with all his heart to visit the same devastation on Tokyo. He couldn't. His country couldn't. He was painfully aware of that. But Japanese soldiers were within reach on Oahu, and getting closer all the time. He could pay them back for some of what they'd done to Hawaii.

That they might do the same to him never crossed his mind. He'd spent his whole military career training as a pilot. Ground combat was a closed book to him, though one he wanted to open.

If they tell me no, goddammit, I can steal a Springfield and a bike and head for the fighting myself, he thought. *Hell, I don't even need a bike. I can hoof it. This isn't what anybody'd call a big island*. Being ready to contemplate ignoring orders spoke strongly about how frazzled he was.

Bombs had hit the dispatching office, too. *Is there anything around here bombs haven't hit?* But the clerks—the pen-pushers and rubber-stamp stampers and typewriter jockeys without whom the military couldn't function but who often thought themselves the be-all and end-all instead of the men who did the fighting and dying—the clerks persisted, even if they had to go to tents, too. Some of them had died here. Some of them might even have fought here.

"I'm sorry, Lieutenant. No chance for a plane. We haven't got any planes to give you right now," a yeoman said through his own muffling of gauze.

Peterson knew nobody had any planes. He'd heard nothing but how nobody had any planes since those gray-haired geezers from the golf course got him to Ewa. "Let me have a rifle, then," he said. "Let me have a rifle and a helmet and permission to go north. There's a war on up there."

Unlike the Marine captain over at Ewa, the yeoman shook his head. "We don't want to do that, sir. If we get planes, we don't want to find out that all the people trained to fly them have turned into casualties in the meantime."

"Are you out of your goddamn mind?" Peterson exploded. "Where the hell are you going to get more planes from? Pull 'em out of your asshole? Everybody and his mother-in-law says the Japs have blown all the planes in Hawaii to hell and gone. What did I join the Navy for if you won't even let me fight?"

The yeoman turned red. "Sir, I have my orders," he said stolidly. "And if you don't mind my saying so, sending you to the front with a rifle is about like putting a doughboy into a fighter cockpit and expecting him to shoot down Japs."

"My balls!" To Peterson, ground combat looked simple. You aimed at a Jap, you shot the son of a bitch, and then you aimed at the next one. What was so complicated about that? Flying a plane, now, was a whole different business. *That* took skill and training.

With a shrug, the yeoman said, "However you want it, sir. If you like, I'll bump you on to Lieutenant Commander McAndrews. I don't have the authority to change orders like that. He does."

"Bring him on!" Peterson said eagerly.

Lieutenant Commander McAndrews still had an office in a real building to call his own. As it did everywhere, rank had its privileges. McAndrews, a jowly man in his late forties, looked at Peterson as if he were a cockroach in the salad. "So you want to go off and be a hero, do you?" he said in a voice like ice.

"No, sir. I want to serve my country, sir." Peterson could yell and cuss at the yeoman—he outranked him. The shoe was on the other foot here. He had to move carefully. "They won't let me get back into an airplane. If they would, I'd gladly fly. But the enemy is *here*. I want to fight him."

"You may not be doing yourself any favors, you know," McAndrews said. "Things aren't going so well. The Army may have promised more than it can deliver." He sniffed, as if to say one couldn't expect anything else from the Army. By all the signs, the rivalry between Navy blue and Army khaki counted for more with him than the war against Japan.

Maybe that made sense in peacetime. Peterson had had plenty of rude things to say about the Army, too. What Navy man didn't? But you could take it too far. "Good God, sir!" he said. "In that case, they need all the help they can get."

McAndrews eyed him curiously. "Are you really so eager to get yourself killed, Lieutenant?"

"No, sir," Peterson answered. "What I'm eager for is killing those little yellow bastards who jumped on our backs when we weren't looking."

"Your spirit does you credit," McAndrews said, but not in a way that made it sound like a compliment. "It is policy not to risk those men who have skills that may be valuable in the future. . . ."

"How? Where? We haven't got any airplanes to speak of, and we have got more pilots than we know what to do with," Peterson said. "Sir."

"If I have more money than I know what to do with, Lieutenant, I don't throw some of it in the fire," McAndrews said coldly. "Do you?"

"I don't know, sir. I never had more money than I knew what to do with." As a matter of fact, Peterson had done the equivalent of throwing his money in the fire plenty of times. When he was in port, he spent it on booze and broads and bright lights. What else was it good for?

"I was speaking metaphorically." Lieutenant Commander McAndrews' tone declared that Peterson wouldn't recognize a metaphor if it bit him in the leg. He might have accused the younger man of eating with the wrong fork. "But if you are mad enough to want to go . . ."

"If somebody doesn't go stop the Japs up there, sir, don't you think they'll come down here?" Peterson asked. "What happens if—no, *when*—they do?"

By the horrified expression that washed across McAndrews' face, he hadn't even imagined that. A lot of possibilities about the Japanese hadn't occurred to Americans till too late. Peterson knew all about that; he was one of the Americans those possibilities hadn't occurred to. Maybe McAndrews hadn't let himself think about this one. He looked as if he hated Peterson for making him think about it.

Five minutes later, Peterson had in his possession an order releasing him for ground combat "in the best interest of the Navy and the United States of America." McAndrews' eyes said he hoped Peterson stopped a bullet with his teeth. Peterson didn't care. Regardless of what McAndrews thought, he had what he wanted.

WHEN THE AMERICANS PULLED OUT OF HALEIWA, they'd done their best to wreck the airstrip near the little town on the north shore of Oahu. They'd dynamited the runways to try to make sure planes couldn't land or take off on them. A lot of pick-and-shovel men would have needed a long time to get the airstrip ready for operations again, and the Japanese Army didn't have that kind of manpower to spare.

As Lieutenant Saburo Shindo took off from that airstrip, a smile wreathed his usually impassive features. The Americans hadn't been as smart as they thought they had. When they pulled out of Haleiwa, they'd left behind a couple of bulldozers and a steamroller. With those, Japanese military engineers had been able to repair the airstrip in a couple of days, not several weeks.

The smile faded a little as he gained altitude. There sat one of the dozers, painted a friendly civilian yellow, by the side of a runway. Such a casual display of U.S. wealth bothered Shindo a little, or more than a little. That wealth of earth-moving equipment wouldn't have been casually available in a Japanese small town. His countrymen had been able to take advantage of it, yes. But they couldn't come close to producing it themselves. Attacking a nation that could was worrying.

With a shrug, Shindo dismissed such worries from his mind. They were things to keep an admiral or a cabinet minister up in the wee small hours, not a lieutenant. As a matter of fact, nothing much kept Shindo awake at night. He looked forward, not back.

Forward lay the American positions. U.S. forces were trying to form a line between Oahu's two mountain ranges, the Waianae in the west and the Koolau in the east. They seemed to assume the land outside the mountain ranges didn't matter much. So far, they hadn't managed to stop the Japanese advance, but they had slowed it down.

Black puffs of antiaircraft fire appeared behind Shindo's Zero. The Americans were much more alert than they had been when the fighting started. They still didn't lead the Japanese fighters enough. They couldn't believe how fast Zeros were.

Shindo dove on a U.S. artillery position in front of Wahiawa. Sooner or later, the Yankees were bound to figure out that the Japanese had a land-based airstrip and weren't just flying off carriers any more. When they did, 105mm guns here had no trouble reaching Haleiwa. Knocking them out was important.

He dove on the guns. The Americans realized they had an important position here, too, though they might not have realized why. Tracers from machine-gun fire spat past the stooping Zero. Shindo couldn't do anything about them, so he ignored them. If they knocked him out of the sky, that was fate, karma. If they didn't, he would carry out his mission.

His thumb came down on the firing button. He was better at shooting up ground targets than he had been when the fighting here began. He didn't overshoot any more. As with everything else, practice made perfect. The men around the American guns scattered. Some of them fell. One or two snatched up rifles and banged away at him. That was brave. It was also futile.

Or so Shindo thought till a sharp clank told him somebody's bullet had struck home. He pulled up, eyeing his instrument panel. No fuel leak showed. His eyes flicked to left and right. His wing tanks weren't on fire, either. All the controls answered. The round must have hit somewhere harmless. In the privacy of the cockpit, he allowed himself a sigh of relief.

The Americans wasted weight on self-sealing fuel tanks and armored pilot's seats. That cost them speed and maneuverability. Japan's fliers had been inclined to laugh at them on account of it. Lieutenant Shindo still was . . . but less so than when the fighting started. Yes, the extra weight hurt performance. But Shindo had seen U.S. planes take hits that would have sent a Zero down in flames and keep on flying as if nothing had happened. There were advantages on both sides.

Half his attention was on the ground as he looked for more strongpoints to shoot up. The other half was in the air. Every so often, the Yankees sent up some of their few surviving fighters. They weren't much if you knew they were coming, but they could give you a nasty surprise if they got on your tail before you knew it. The pilot who didn't learn to check six in a hurry usually didn't last long enough to learn at his leisure.

Shindo didn't spot any trouble this time. As usual, the Japanese had the skies over Oahu to themselves. All he had to worry about was ground fire. That didn't bother him much. He had its measure.

A column of olive-drab trucks was heading north up the highway that ran through the center of the island. The column wasn't moving anywhere near so fast as it might have. Southbound refugees, some on foot, others in automobiles, clogged the road. Shindo laughed. He'd seen that before. Americans had no discipline. They refused to keep refugees off the road by whatever means necessary, as Japanese soldiers surely would have. And they paid the price for their softness, too.

Radial engine roaring, the Zero dove on the road. Shindo cut loose with the fighter's machine guns and cannons. It was like stamping on an anthill. People down there scattered in what seemed like slow motion—far too slowly to evade bullets and shells.

Fire and smoke erupted from truck and automobile engines. The plume was tiny compared to the one rising from Pearl Harbor, but every little bit served its purpose. Those soldiers wouldn't get where they were going when they wanted to get there. That ought to help the Japanese move forward.

On the way back to Haleiwa, Shindo spotted an American machine-gun nest spitting tracers at Japanese foot soldiers. A tank would have taken care of it, but none seemed close by. The pilot felt as if he were looking for a policeman when he really wanted one. He had to do the job himself. And he did, swooping down on the gunners from behind. They might have died before they even knew they were under attack.

Behind the Japanese lines, commandeered cars carried soldiers here and there. Again, Shindo's side took advantage of the enemy's wealth. He wished his own country had a larger share of wealth for itself. Getting that larger share, of course, was what this war was all about.

Shindo was used to coming in on the rolling, pitching deck of a carrier. Landing at a strip on dry land felt ridiculously easy, as if he were back in flight school. The only thing the signalman had to do was guide him into one of the earth-banked revetments engineers had made with the bulldozers. They kept his plane safe from anything but a direct hit. As soon as the Zero was in the U-shaped shelter, camouflage nets covered it. The Yankees wouldn't spot it from the air.

"How did it go?" a groundcrew man asked after Shindo climbed out of the fighter.

"Routine," he answered. "Just routine."

MACHINE-GUN BULLETS STRUCK FLESH with wet slaps. The noise reminded Fletcher Armitage of the last few fights he and Jane had had before she threw him out of the apartment. When she slapped him, though, his head had only felt as if it would fly off his shoulders. When a real machine-gun bullet hit . . .

The Zero roared away to the south, bound for more mischief. It was low enough to the ground to kick up dust. Fletch fired a last futile shot at it. The fellow piloting it was an artist, which didn't keep Fletch from hoping he'd burn in hell, and soon, too.

He had more immediate things to worry about, though. Two of his precious, irreplaceable gunners were down, one clutching his leg and moaning, the other ominously still. A quick glance told Fletch nobody could help the second man this side of Judgment Day. He'd caught a slug in the back of the head, and spilled his brains out in the dirt. The only good thing you could say about such an end was that it was quick. He'd never known what hit him.

The artilleryman with the leg wound, by contrast, screamed about God and his mother and shit, all of which amounted to the same thing: he was in pain and didn't like it. "Hold still, Vic," Fletch said, kneeling beside him. "I'll get a bandage on you." A week earlier, he might have lost his lunch trying. Not any more. He'd had practice. What was that line from *Hamlet*? *Custom hath made it in him a property of easiness*, that was it. Old Will had known what he was talking about there, sure as hell.

"Hurts. Hurts like shit," Vic said.

"Yeah, I know." Fletch used his bayonet to cut away the khaki cloth of the other man's uniform—one of the few things a bayonet was actually good for. He could see the artery pulsing inside the wound. It looked intact. If it weren't, Vic probably would have bled to death.

Fletch dusted the gash with sulfa powder. He couldn't sew it shut, but fumbled in one of the pouches on his belt and produced three safety pins. They'd help hold it closed, anyhow. He got a bandage over the wound, then stuck Vic's syringe of morphine into his thigh and pressed down on the plunger.

A couple of minutes later, Vic said, "Ahh. That's better,

sir." He sounded eerily calm. The drug had interposed a barrier between his torment and him.

"We'll take him now, sir," someone behind Fletch said.

He looked up. There were two corpsmen, Red Crosses prominent on their helmets and on armbands. "I wish you guys got here sooner," he said.

The man who'd spoken gave back a shrug. "It's not like there's nothing going on for us, sir." He looked weary unto death.

His buddy nodded, adding, "Goddamn Japs shoot at us regardless of these." He tapped the Red Cross emblems. "Bastards don't give a shit about the Geneva Convention."

"Tell me about it!" Fletch exclaimed. The memory of the American soldier the Japanese had captured rose in him again. His stomach churned. "You don't want to let yourselves get caught," he told the corpsmen.

They nodded in unison. "Yeah, we already know about that," one of them said. They got Vic onto a stretcher and carried him away. "Come on, buddy—the docs'll fix you up."

That left Fletch to figure out how to fight his gun without two more trained men. He had untrained infantrymen jerking shells now. His gun wouldn't shoot as fast as it had before, but he could still get out two or three rounds a minute. If he had to lay the gun by his lonesome . . . then he did, that was all.

He muttered to himself. Even from here, the piece could reach all the way to the north shore and into the Pacific. And how was it being used? As a direct-fire gun, banging away at whatever targets he could see. He had no idea where the rest of the 105s in the battery were. The two guns close by belonged to another outfit. They'd been shot up worse than his crew. And that was par for the course. If anything, it was better than par for the course. He'd taken everything the Japs could throw at him, and he was still in the fight. A hell of a lot of people weren't.

In the cane fields off to the northeast, a Japanese machine gun started hammering away. The Japs were aggressive with their automatic weapons. They pushed them right up to the front and went after U.S. infantry with them. He didn't care to think what they would have done with Browning Automatic Rifles. So far, they hadn't shown any signs of owning weapons like those. He thanked God for small favors.

Aiming the gun at a target by himself was only a little faster than dying of old age. And he hadn't finished the job before shouts of, "Tank! Tank!" from right in front of him made him give it up.

From everything he'd heard, the U.S. M3 wasn't anything special compared to what the Germans and the Russians were throwing at each other these days. M3s could usually make the Jap machines say uncle, though. That truth would have pleased Fletch more if any of those U.S. tanks were in the neighborhood. They weren't. If anything was going to stop this snorting Jap beast from running roughshod over the infantrymen, it was his gun.

"Armor-piercing!" he shouted to the foot soldiers he'd dragooned into his service.

"Which ones are those, sir?" one of them asked.

"Shit," Fletch said. But he said it under his breath; it wasn't the infantrymen's fault that they didn't know one kind of round from another. "The ones with the black tips. Shake a leg, guys, or that son of a bitch is going to—"

That son of a bitch did start shooting first. Fletch and his makeshift crew threw themselves flat. Fragments of sharp, hot steel snarled overhead. Standing up while you were getting shelled was asking to get torn to pieces. Sometimes you had to, but you never wanted to.

An American machine gun opened up on the tank. For all the good their bullets did, the soldiers at the gun might as well have thrown marshmallows at the Japanese machine. A tank that wasn't armored against machine-gun fire had no *raison d'être*.

"French, yet," Fletch muttered. But the machine gun did do one thing: it distracted the Japs in the tank from the distant artillery piece to the annoyance right at hand. Fletch didn't know if that was what the machine gunners had had in mind. He doubted it, as a matter of fact. But it let him get to his feet and yell till his crew did the same. "Come on, you bastards! They've given us a chance. They're human, by God! They can make mistakes, just like us."

The Japs hadn't made very many, damn them. By sheer dumb luck, the tank wasn't very far from the line on which the 105 pointed. Fletch swung the barrel to bear on it. Range was about seven hundred yards. He turned the altitude screw. The muzzle lowered, ever so slightly. "Fire!" he shouted.

The gun roared. Flame shot from the muzzle. The shell kicked up dirt in front of the tank and a little to the left. "Short!" one of the infantrymen shouted—they were starting to learn the ropes.

Now—had the Japs seen the shot? Fletch didn't think so. They went on banging away at the machine gun. "Armor-piercing again!" he said. "Quick, goddammit!" As the shell went into the breech, he corrected his aim—or hoped he did. The tank wasn't going very fast, but this gun wasn't made for hitting any kind of moving target. He'd already seen that. "Fire!"

Boom! The 105 went off again. The foot soldiers who served it flinched. They usually remembered to cover their ears, but they didn't know opening their mouths helped at least as much when it came to beating an artillery piece's noise.

But then they started making noise of their own, screaming, "Hit! Hit! Jesus God, that's a hit!" and, "You nailed that fucker, Lieutenant! Nailed his ass good!"

Fletch didn't think any tank in the world, U.S., British, German, or Russian, could stand up to a 105mm AP round. This Japanese hunk of tin didn't have a prayer. He couldn't have aimed it better if he'd had the most highly trained crew in the world and tried for a week. It struck home right at the join between hull and turret, and blew the turret clean off the tank and a good six feet in the air. Ammo in the turret started cooking off, while the hull erupted in a fireball. The crew never had a chance, not that Fletch wasted much grief on them.

"You see how that Jap tank tipped his hat to our gun?" one of the infantrymen yelled.

Fletch laughed his head off. It was a pretty good line, and all the better because it came from somebody so raw. But that wasn't the only reason. He felt giddy, almost drunk, with relief. The odds had favored the tank, not him. All he had to protect him from fragments was a flimsy shield. He'd had to be dead accurate to kill before he got killed—and he'd done it.

And, as far as he could tell, doing it did neither him nor the American position one damn bit of good. A couple of hours later, he got the order to fall back to the outskirts of Wahiawa. The Army would try to make another stand there.

OSCAR VAN DER KIRK'S LIFE SWAYED back and forth between something approaching normality and something approaching insanity. Some of the tourists the war had stuck on Oahu still wanted surf-riding lessons. He gave them what they wanted. Why not? He needed to pay his rent just like anybody else. His landlord, a skinflint Jap named Mas Fukumoto, would have flung his scanty belongings out in the street the day after he failed to pay.

He'd had the crummy little apartment on Lewers Street for a couple of years now, after getting the heave-ho from another place much like it. All that time, of course, he'd known Mas Fukumoto was a Jap. He'd known Fukumoto was a skinflint, too. As a matter of fact, he'd never known a landlord who wasn't a skinflint. The one who'd tossed him out when he got behind was Irish as Paddy's pig.

But to think of Mas Fukumoto as a skinflint Jap now was to think of him as an enemy—as *the* enemy—in a way it hadn't been before December 7. Oscar didn't know Fukumoto wasn't loyal to the United States. He had no reason to believe his landlord wasn't, in fact. That didn't keep him—and a lot of Fukumoto's other *haole* tenants—from giving the man a fishy stare whenever they saw him.

And even when Oscar paddled out into the Pacific—warm despite its being the week before Christmas—with a wahine from Denver or Des Moines, he couldn't help seeing and smelling the black, stinking smoke that still rose from the Navy's shattered fuel tanks at Pearl Harbor.

The wahines mostly didn't care. They'd come to Hawaii to forget whatever ailed them on the mainland. They intended to go right on forgetting, too. And when they couldn't forget, they said things like, "Well, but that's all going on way up there. Everything's pretty much okay down here in Waikiki and Honolulu, right?"

That was a strawberry blonde named Susie. She'd come to Hawaii from Reno to forget about a recently ex-husband, and she was doing quite a job of it, too. She was ready for any kind of lessons Oscar wanted to give her. He had a sure instinct about such things.

He wondered if saying something would mess up his chances. Lying there on the surfboard with her, he shrugged a tiny shrug. She wasn't the only fish in the sea. He said, "Wahiawa's only half an hour away. The north coast is only an hour away—a buddy of mine and I were surf-riding up there when the Japs landed. They were shooting at us."

Susie looked back over her slightly sunburned shoulder at him. Her eyes were blue as a Siamese cat's. "What was that like?" she asked.

When the bullets started flying back and forth, I pissed myself. Nobody but me'll ever know, because I was dripping wet anyway, but I damn well did. "Not a whole lot of fun," he answered out loud, which was not only true but sounded tough and not the least bit undignified. He wondered if the same thing had happened to Charlie Kaapu. No way to ask, not ever.

What he said seemed to satisfy Susie. She made a little noise, almost a purr, down deep in her throat. "I'm glad they missed," she told him.

"Me, too," Oscar said, and she laughed. If he lowered his chin a couple of inches, it would come down on her cotton-covered backside. He decided not to. Unlike some of the women to whom he gave lessons, Susie didn't need much in the way of signals. He paddled out a little while longer (so did she, not very helpfully), then swung the surfboard back towards the beach. "This time, we're going to get you up on your knees on the board, okay?"

"What happens if I fall off?" she asked.

"You swim," he answered, and she laughed. He started paddling shoreward. "Come on. You can do it. I'll steady you." And he did, kneeling behind her with his hands on her slim waist. That was a signal of sorts, but it was also line of duty, and she could ignore it if she wanted to. She laughed again. She wasn't ignoring anything—except the Japs. Oscar wished he could do the same.

Actually, her sense of balance was pretty good—plenty good enough to keep her kneeling on the board with only a little support. The surf wasn't very big—Oscar had chosen this place with care. But she got enough of the roller-coaster thrill to let out a whoop as they neared the beach.

"Wow!" she said when the surfboard scraped to a stop on the soft sand. There were stars in her eyes. She turned back and gave him a quick kiss. "Thank you."

"Thank *you*," he said, keeping any hint that he'd expected it out of his voice. If they knew you knew, they got coy. "Want to try it again?"

"Sure," she said, "unless you'd rather just go on back to my room instead."

Even Oscar hadn't thought she'd be that brazen. Sometimes the ride lit a fire, though; he'd seen that before. He said, "Well, you've paid for two hours of lessons. Afterwards . . . I don't have anything else going on, so. . . ."

"I like the way you think—among other things," she said. "Okay, we'll do that."

And they did. By the end of the lesson, she was kneeling unsupported. She did fall off on one run, but struck out strongly for the shore. When the lessons were done, she gave Oscar her room number. He took the board back to the Outrigger Club, then went over to the hotel.

If he'd gone in with her, the house detective would have had to notice. This way, the fellow just tipped him a wink and looked in the other direction. All along Waikiki Beach, the house dicks and the surf-riding instructors had their informal understandings. A few dollars every now and then, a few drinks every now and then, and nobody got excited about anything. *No huhu*, Charlie Kaapu would have said.

Oscar knocked on the door. "It's open," Susie called. He turned the knob. She lay on the bed, naked and waiting.

"Jesus!" he said. "What if I'd been the plumber or something?"

Those blue eyes went wide in some of the phoniest innocence he'd ever seen. "That depends," she said throatily. "Is the plumber here good-looking?" Oscar's jaw dropped. Susie's laugh was pure mischief. "Since it's you, how's *your* plunger?"

"Let's see," he managed, and slipped off his trunks. By the way she eyed him, he passed muster. He got down on the bed beside her. She slid towards him. He rapidly discovered she had no inhibitions hidden anywhere about her person. Once she got back to the mainland, she'd probably rediscover them. He'd known more than a few other women who left them behind in San Pedro or San Francisco or Seattle. This one seemed an extreme case—not that extremes couldn't be extremely enjoyable.

He was poised to find out just how enjoyable she could be when sirens started wailing and bells started clanging. "What the hell is that?" Susie exclaimed, and then, "Whatever it is, for God's sake don't stop now."

But Oscar said, "That's the air-raid siren. We'd better get in the trenches." Having been under fire once, he didn't care to repeat the experience. He'd helped dig some of the trenches that marred the greenery around the hotel buildings.

Susie stared at him. "Don't be silly. They wouldn't bomb Waikiki. We're *civilians*." She spoke the last word as if it were a magic talisman.

"Maybe they wouldn't, not on purpose," Oscar said, though he wasn't convinced. "But Fort DeRussy's just Ewa from the Waikiki hotels." She sent him a blank look. "Just west," he explained impatiently, adding, "If they bomb that and they miss . . ."

Susie reached out and gave him a regretful squeeze. "Okay, I'm sold," she said, all the kitten gone from her voice. "The trenches." She ran for the bathroom, and emerged in her bathing suit by the time Oscar had his on again.

They weren't the only scantily dressed people hurrying down the hallways. The sharp, flat *boom!* of a bomb bursting not far away made several people—not all of them women—scream and made everybody hurry faster. More bombs went off as Oscar and Susie raced across the lawn and scrambled down into a trench.

Antiaircraft guns at the fort added to the din. Sure enough, DeRussy was what the Japs were after. Most of their bombs fell on it—most, but not all. When a bomb burst on the hotel, it made a noise like the end of the world. Sharp fragments of hot metal hissed and screamed by overhead. The ground shook, as if at an earthquake. Blast stunned Oscar's ears. As if from very far away, he heard Susie say, "Well, you were right." She kissed him— more, he judged, from gratitude than passion.

And then an armor-piercing bomb, or maybe more than one, penetrated the reinforced concrete protecting the coast-defense guns in the fortress and their magazines. The explosions that followed made the ones from the bombs themselves seem like love pats. Chunks of cement and steel rained down out of the sky. Shrieks said some of them came down in trenches. Oscar wondered how many men Fort DeRussy held—had held, for they were surely dead now.

The raid lasted about half an hour. The antiaircraft guns kept firing for five or ten minutes after bombs stopped falling. Shrapnel pattered down out of the air along with debris from the fort. Oscar wished for a helmet. That stuff could smash your skull like a melon.

Despite the secondary explosions, people started climbing out of the trenches. "Christ, but I want a drink!" somebody said, which summed things up as well as Edward R. Murrow or William L. Shirer could have done.

Susie let out a wordless squawk of dismay. She pointed at what had been her room and was now nothing but smoking rubble. Oscar gulped. If they'd ignored the sirens and gone on with what they were doing, they might have died happy, but they sure would have died.

Then Susie found words: "What am I going to do? All my stuff was in there. God damn the dirty Japs!"

Oscar heard himself say, "You can move in with me for a while if you want to." He blinked. He'd taken in stray kittens before, and once a puppy, but never a girl. It wasn't even that he was all that crazy about Susie. If it hadn't been for the war, they'd have screwed each other silly for a few days and then gone their separate ways. But he didn't see how he could leave her stranded here with nothing but the bathing suit on her back.

By the way she eyed him, she was making some calculations of her own. "Okay," she said after a few seconds. "But it's not like you own me or anything. Whenever I want to walk out, I'm gone."

"Sure," Oscar said at once. "I don't have any trouble with that. If you start driving me nuts, I'll hold the door open for you. In the meantime, though . . ." He stuck out his hand. "Uh, what's your last name?"

"Higgins," she said as she shook it. Her hand almost got lost in his, but she had a pretty good grip. "What's yours?" He told her. "Van der Kirk?" she echoed, and started to laugh. "You're so brown, I would've figured you for a dago."

He shrugged. "I'm out in the sun all the time. That's one of the reasons I like Hawaii. You want to see the place? It's only a few blocks *mauka* from here." Susie Higgins looked blank again. "North. Towards the mountains," Oscar told her. Hawaiian notions of directions had baffled him, too, when he first got to Oahu. Now he took them for granted. But he was on his way to becoming a *kamaaina*— an old-timer—here; he wasn't a just-arrived *malihini* any more, the way Susie was. "Come on," he said, and she went with him.

The apartment building plainly didn't impress her. Well, it didn't much impress Oscar, either. She did seem surprised when he opened his door without a key. Once she walked in, she said, "Oh, I get it. You don't bother to lock it because you don't have anything worth stealing."

"Only things I own that are worth anything are my car and my surfboard, and my car isn't worth much," Oscar answered with another shrug. "You don't *need* much to live here."

Susie didn't say anything about that. Even so, he got the idea she wasn't going to stay there forever, or even very long—she was a girl who liked *things*. He could tell. What she did say was, "You want to lock the door now?"

"How come?" he said, and then, "Oh."

She laughed at him. He deserved it. He laughed, too. She said, "We were doing something or other when that air raid started." As if to remind him what, she peeled off her bathing suit.

The bed was narrow for two, but not too narrow. Things were going along very nicely when a great roar made the walls shake and the window rattle—it was a miracle the window didn't break. Susie squealed. Oscar needed a bit to recover. John Henry the Steel-Driving Man would have needed a moment to recover after that. He'd just started again when another identical roar made Susie squeal again.

This time, though, it didn't unman him, for he'd realized what it was: "More things blowing up at Fort DeRussy, that's all."

"That's *all?*" Susie exclaimed. "Jesus!"

Oscar didn't answer, not with words. After a while, he managed to distract her, which he took as a compliment to himself—distracting somebody from the thunder of those explosions was no mean feat. Susie's gasp said he hadn't just distracted her—he'd got her hot. A moment later, Oscar exploded too. He stroked his cheek. "Not so bad," he said, and tried to believe it. What the hell had he got into, getting into Susie? Well, he'd find out.

AN AMERICAN SOLDIER SHOWED HIMSELF. Corporal Takeo Shimizu's rifle jumped to his shoulder. He steadied on the target, took a deep breath, and pulled the trigger. *Just like a drill,* he thought as the Arisaka rifle kicked. The American crumpled. Shimizu ducked down deep into his foxhole in the pineapple field outside of Wahiawa.

He didn't feel particularly proud of himself for shooting the enemy. The Americans were brave. He'd seen that since coming ashore. They were braver than he'd expected, in fact, even if some of them did try to surrender instead of fighting to the death. That made for amusing sport.

But shooting them hardly seemed fair. Hadn't anyone taught them anything about taking cover? He was one of the veterans in his regiment who'd fought in China. You never saw the Chinese bandits till one of them put a bullet between your eyes. They didn't have a lot of rifles, and even less in the way of heavy weapons, but they made the most of what they had, and of the ground on which they fought.

The Yankees, by contrast, were very well armed—better than Shimizu's own men, probably. If their air power hadn't been knocked out, they would have been tough to shift. But they didn't seem to know what to do with what they had—and they paid the price for it, again and again.

Machine-gun bullets snarled over Shimizu's head. He laughed. The Americans must have thought he'd stay upright waiting to get shot. They were like someone who covered his belly when you hit him there, then covered his face when you hit him *there*. They didn't know what was coming next, and they didn't think their foes did, either. And they paid the price for being so naive.

Behind Shimizu, a mortar started going *pop-pop-pop*. The bombs came down around the machine-gun position the Yankees had incautiously revealed. Shimizu hoped they knocked out the gunners. Even if they did, though, they were unlikely to put the gun out of action. A machine gun wasn't so complicated that ordinary soldiers couldn't handle it.

Lieutenant Yonehara crawled up to Shimizu's foxhole. Yonehara had pineapple leaves fixed to his helmet to make him harder to spot. His belly never came up higher off the ground than a snake's. He pointed south. "Do you see that white frame house, Corporal?"

Shimizu warily raised his head for half a heartbeat. Then he ducked back down again. "Yes, sir. I see it. The one about a hundred meters behind the enemy line?"

"*Hai*," Yonehara said. "That is the one. It's on high ground. Our company has been ordered to seize it. You will prepare your men to take part in the attack."

"Yes, sir," Shimizu said: the only thing he could say when he got an order like that. No, not quite, for he did add a few words that expressed his opinion of the order: "Hard work, sir."

"Yes, hard work," Yonehara agreed, his voice not without sympathy. "Colonel Fujikawa feels it is necessary, however. I will lead the attack. We will use the sword and bayonet if that is what it takes to clear the Americans from their positions."

A bayonet made a handy tool for gutting a chicken. If you stabbed it in the ground, the socket held a candle. Shimizu had yet to fight with his. But if the lieutenant led, he would follow. "Yes, sir," he said. And if the Americans didn't run, he would give them the bayonet—unless he shot them from close range instead.

"At my order," Yonehara said, and crawled away. Shimizu passed the news to his men.

Mortar fire picked up. From farther back of the line, field guns started pounding the American position. When Lieutenant Yonehara shouted, "Forward!" Shimizu jumped out of his foxhole and ran towards the American line.

"My squad, with me!" he yelled. They too came out of their holes. Pride filled him. Truly he sprang from a warrior race. How could the Americans hope to stop his comrades and him?

He got the answer to that sooner than he wanted. The Americans hoped to stop them with sheer firepower. The machine gun that had been shooting at him opened up again. So did others that had been silent till then. Onrushing Japanese soldiers fell as if scythed. A bullet tugged at Shimizu's sleeve, as if to tell him he had to go back or go down.

He kept going forward nonetheless. The platoon commander had given the order, and he had to obey. Lieutenant Yonehara had drawn his *katana*. The sword blade shone in the sun. It could lop off an arm, or a head—if Yonehara ever got close enough to use it. No sooner had that thought crossed Shimizu's mind than a bullet caught the lieutenant in the face and blew out the back of his head. He crumpled as if all his bones had turned to water.

Seeing him fall was like waking from a fevered delirium. Corporal Shimizu looked to his right and to his left. A lot of the company was down. Like him, the men still on their feet wavered. If they kept on advancing, they wouldn't waver. They would die. Shimizu could see that perfectly well. Machine-gun bullets didn't care whether you were a warrior. They'd kill you any which way.

But the soldiers had been *ordered* to advance. Shimizu wondered how to change that. The officer who'd given him the order was dead, but the thing itself remained very much alive. Bullets couldn't slaughter an order, only the soldiers who tried to obey it. No one had ever trained Shimizu or any other Japanese soldier in retreating. If he ordered the survivors to fall back, they might not obey him.

All that ran through his head in less than a heartbeat. And then, fast as lightning, he found the answer. "Men, we're going to recover our positions!" he shouted. That didn't say a word about retreat. It got the message across even so. And it gave the soldiers an honorable way to get back to the foxholes and trenches from which they'd emerged.

They took advantage of it, too. Shimizu might not have called it a retreat, but a retreat was what it was. They dragged the wounded back with them and left the dead where they had fallen. American fire stung them all the way back to their starting point.

A private jumped into Shimizu's foxhole with him. Akira Murakami was a first-year soldier, still wet behind the ears—or he had been till combat started. Nobody who'd landed on Oahu was wet behind the ears any more, not like that. But Murakami's eyes were wide and staring as he asked, "What will they do to us for . . . for coming back?" He wouldn't say *retreat*, either.

"We tried our best," Shimizu said. "Maybe a tank could take that house. Infantry can't, not by itself." Murakami only shrugged. He didn't dare contradict a corporal, but he didn't believe him, either. Shimizu went on, "Besides, what can they do to us that the Yankees' machine guns wouldn't have?" *That* got home. The young soldier shivered and nodded.

No one ever said a word about the retreat. An hour and a half later, Aichi dive bombers screamed down out of the sky. They pulverized the position the luckless company hadn't been able to overrun. The order to advance went out again. With the defenses shattered, the Japanese had no trouble pushing forward toward Wahiawa.

Why didn't they send in the bombers before the Americans chewed us up? Shimizu wondered. But he had no one he could ask that question. It stayed unspoken. The fight went on.

HAVING GOT WHAT HE'D ASKED FOR, Lieutenant Jim Peterson quickly discovered it wasn't all it was cracked up to be. Since he was still a young man, he fondly imagined this discovery to be unique to himself. Everyone around him was too busy trying to stay alive to tell him any different.

The Navy might have been willing to slap a tin hat on his head, toss him a rifle, and send him off to the front. Once he got there, the Army showed itself less than delighted to have him. A sergeant looked at him and said, "Sir, you're going to have to shed those captain's badges before you get a bunch of people killed."

"Captain's . . . ? Oh." A Navy captain—which had been Peterson's first thought—was the equivalent of a bird colonel in the Army. But the two silver bars of a Navy lieutenant matched an Army captain's rank emblem. Peterson said, "I didn't come here to command a company."

"Damn good thing," the sergeant said. Put him in Navy blue and he'd have made a good CPO. He paused to light a King Sano, then went on, "Up here, your rank don't mean shit—pardon my French—on account of you don't know anything. If you were a Marine . . . But you're not. Tell you the truth, what's likely gonna happen is that you'll get shot for nothing."

"If I can take out a couple of Japs first, it won't be for nothing," Peterson said savagely. "I'm no infantry officer, but I can shoot. I know how to take orders, too."

For the first time, the sergeant looked at him as if he were something more than a fly in the soup. Peterson realized he'd said the right thing, even if it was at least half by accident. After blowing a meditative smoke ring, the sergeant said, "Okay, sir. That's fair enough. As of now, you're Private, uh"—he looked down to check the paperwork in front of him—"Private Peterson. That suit you?"

"You bet!" Peterson said. The sergeant looked at him. He realized something more was expected. "Uh, yes, Sergeant!" This man was suddenly his superior.

"Okay." The noncom nodded. "Now, then, like I told you, get rid of those silly-ass silver bars."

That was an order. He'd claimed he knew how to take them. "Yes, Sergeant," he said again, and removed them. He felt younger with them in his pocket, as if nothing that had happened since Annapolis counted any more. In some pretty basic ways, it didn't. He also felt weaker, which made sense. Everybody could tell him what to do now. It was like his first year at the Naval Academy, only worse. Then he'd been bound for officer's status. Now he'd chucked it out the window.

"Tell you what I'm going to do," the sergeant said meditatively. "I'm going to send you to the garrison guarding Kolekole Pass, off to the west of Schofield Barracks. That'll help me peel some trained soldiers out of there and put 'em in a part of the line where there's more going on."

Peterson realized he'd just been handed the Army equivalent of the coast defense of South Dakota. He started to say that he'd come up here to fight, not to make it easier for somebody else to. The words didn't pass his lips. Privates didn't get to make protests like that. The sergeant undoubtedly knew more about how things were going than he did. He managed a nod. "All right, Sergeant."

"There you go," the noncom said. "That's almost always the right answer. Truck full of beans and stuff heading over there pretty soon. You hustle, you can scrounge a lift. And you better hope you don't see too many Japs there. You do, we're in deep shit. Go on, scram. I got more things to worry about besides you."

Off Peterson went. He did catch the truck, and rode in the cab with the driver. The kid behind the wheel was named Billy Joe McKennie, and hailed from somewhere deep in the South. He said, "If'n them Japs"—it came out *Jayups*, the first time Peterson had ever heard it as a two-syllable word—"try comin' over the Waianae"—a name that had to be heard to be believed—"Mountains, they'll have to come through us'ns, an' I don't reckon they kin."

"How do you know they won't try somewhere else?" Peterson asked.

McKennie might not speak much real English, but he understood it. He looked at Peterson as if he were crazy. "On account of a goat'd have trouble gittin' over them mountains, let alone a lousy Jap."

The truck rumbled through Schofield Barracks. The east-west road that cut the immense base in half remained intact. The barracks, and all the other buildings around the facility, had taken a hell of a beating. Burned-out cars and trucks had been hastily dragged off the road. They sprawled alongside it, a terrible tangle of twisted metal. Peterson didn't like to think about the men who'd been inside them when they were hit.

West of the base, the land began climbing towards the mountains. The closer Peterson got to them, the more he started to think Billy Joe McKennie had a point. They weren't especially tall, but they rose swift and steep. And they were covered with the thickest, most impenetrable-looking jungle he'd ever seen. He couldn't have named half the plants—hell, he couldn't have named any of them—but he wouldn't have wanted to try pushing through that maze of trees and ferns and thorny bushes.

Halfway through Kolekole Pass, the road stopped. The mountains loomed up on either side. The American detachment faced west. It boasted some field guns, several nicely sited machine guns, and a couple of command cars—soldiers called them peeps—with pintle-mounted machine guns of their own for mobile firepower.

Peterson helped McKennie and the soldiers already at the strongpoint unload the truck. Nobody seemed to find anything out of the ordinary about him. He pulled his weight. When McKennie drove off, a whole squad of men rode in the back of the truck.

"We give away a dozen and we get one back," grumbled the major in charge of the garrison. By the disgusted look on his face, this wasn't the first time that had happened. "Pretty soon we'll have all the guns in the world and not a soul to shoot 'em."

He stood in no serious danger of having all the guns in the world. Whether he'd run out of men was a different question. The question related to it was whether he ought to have any men there at all. The more Peterson looked at those mountains, the more he suspected the garrison was what the Army did instead of snapping its fingers to keep the elephants away.

"Sir, I don't think Tarzan of the Apes could come at us through country like this," he said.

The major blinked. Then he grinned. "You never can tell with Tarzan," he said. "He got around a lot—that lost Roman city and. . . ." He went on and on. Peterson realized he'd run into an Edgar Rice Burroughs fanatic. The major shifted to John Carter on Mars, then to Carson Napier on Venus. Peterson had to listen to him, and listen, and listen. The officer started talking about Burroughs himself, who, it turned out, spent a lot of his time on Oahu.

If Peterson was any judge, Burroughs came to a place like this to escape his fans. There probably was no escape, though. *No escape for me, that's for sure*, Peterson thought unhappily. The major didn't seem to want to run dry.

At last, he did. That let Peterson escape, and it let him look east across the center of Oahu. He could trace the front all the way over to the Koolau Range on the other side of the island. It wasn't that far. If the Americans could hold the Japs north of Schofield Barracks and Wahiawa, he thought they had a decent chance.

Kolekole Pass would have made a hell of an observation post. Peterson started to say something about that, then hesitated. A Navy lieutenant could make such suggestions. What about a buck private in the Army? Wasn't he supposed to keep his mouth shut and do as he was told? That was what he would have wanted from an ordinary seaman in the Navy. He buttoned his lip.

A little later, he heard the major talking into a field telephone. The officer was pinpointing the location of a Japanese artillery position. Peterson laughed at himself. Old Granny Army didn't need him to teach her how to suck eggs.

Off in the distance, artillery boomed. Machine guns rattled. Rifles crackled like fireworks. Here in the pass, everything was quiet. Soldiers played pinochle or acey-deucey. Birds chirped. Peterson could no more name them than the trees in which they perched.

It was quiet duty. Considering what was going on only a few miles away, it was miraculously quiet. Most of the men seemed delighted to be out of anything more dangerous. Peterson muttered and fumed. He wanted to have a go at the Japs, not sit here twiddling his thumbs in a place where they were anything but likely to show up.

After fuming till the sun swung down towards the horizon, he decided to beard the major after all. The man heard him out. Then he said, "No. I'm sorry, Private. I commend your initiative. It does you credit. But the answer is still no. We are serving a necessary function here. I would sooner be in combat myself. But I am doing what was ordered of me, and you will do what is ordered of you. Is that clear?"

"Yes, sir," Peterson said. That the man was obviously right only made his refusal more galling.

They had beans for supper, beans and roast pork. The beans couldn't have come off of Peterson's truck; they'd been soaked before they were boiled. They weren't anything fancy, but they were okay. As for the pork, everybody smiled and ate in a hurry. Peterson suspected the pigs had been liberated from some little local farm. No one said anything, though, and he didn't think he'd make himself popular by asking a whole lot of questions.

He rolled himself in his blanket and fell asleep on the ground. Some of the soldiers had mosquito netting. He didn't. He wondered how high a price he'd pay for that. He tossed and turned, trying to get comfortable. Snores rose around him. The Army men had no trouble sleeping on bare ground. If he'd got used to sacking out in a bunk every night, that was his hard luck.

And then, some time around midnight, shouts woke everybody who'd managed to fall asleep. "Out! Out! Out!" the major yelled. "We've got to get out of here before we get cut off and surrounded!"

"What the fuck?" somebody said, which perfectly summed up what Peterson was thinking.

"The Japs," the major said, which was no shock: Mussolini's men, for instance, were a hell of a long way away. But what followed *was* a shocker: "Goddamn slanteyes landed on the west coast, and they're over the mountains behind us. That's why we're pulling out."

"Did they get through Pohakea Pass south of here?" a soldier asked.

"No. They're over the goddamn *mountains*, I tell you. Don't ask me how—they must be part monkey. But most of what we've got is up at the front. God only knows how we'll stop 'em, or even slow 'em down. Gotta try, though. Come on, get moving!"

Peterson scrambled out of his bedroll. Maybe he'd see action after all. It didn't occur to him to wonder if that was what he really wanted.

SOME CIVIL WAR GENERAL—Fletch Armitage was damned if he could remember who—had said raw troops were as sensitive about their flanks as a virgin. Some things hadn't changed a bit in the past eighty years.

Fletch looked west, towards the Waianae Range. He was damned if he could see how anybody human could have got over those steep, jungle-covered mountains. For all he knew, the Japs *weren't* human. But they were over the mountains, and square in the U.S. Army's rear with . . . how many soldiers? Fletch had no idea, and he didn't think any other Americans did, either.

Too many—that was certain. They weren't just on the Army's flank. They were in its rear. And if the Americans couldn't pull back in a hurry and form some kind of new line farther south, they were probably history, and ancient history at that.

Pulling back meant giving up Wahiawa, leaving it to its fate. Plenty of people in the town didn't intend to be left. Refugees packed the roads. Fletch had seen that before, when the people from Haleiwa and Waimea ran away from the oncoming Japs. This was worse. More people lived in Wahiawa. Japanese fighters had a field day shooting up the Kamehameha Highway. They didn't seem to care whether they blasted soldiers or civilians. Why should they? They spawned chaos with every cannon shell, with every burst of machine-gun fire.

As the beat-up De Soto with his gun in tow slowly—so slowly—rattled south through Wahiawa, Fletch looked now this way, now that. One of the infantry privates newly hauled into artilleryman's duty said, "Sure is a pretty place. Sure is a shame, letting the Japs have it."

"I wasn't looking at the town," Fletch said tightly. He was looking for his more or less ex-wife. If he spotted Jane, he intended to shoehorn her into the car. Okay, she didn't love him any more. But after what he'd seen, he wouldn't have left a dying, half-witted dog to the mercy of the Japs. Maybe Jane would thank him for getting her out of there. Maybe she'd try to spit in his eye. He didn't give a damn either way. If he saw her, she was going.

But he didn't see her. All he saw was Wahiawa. He didn't think it was all that lovely. It was the sort of town that grows up alongside any Army base, full of cheap, hastily run-up buildings that held businesses designed to separate soldiers from cash: bars; hamburger stands; chop-suey joints; tailors' shops that sold cheap, loud clothes; tattoo parlors; dives that called themselves burlesque houses but were really brothels. To make matters worse, the Japs had bombed and shelled the place. No, it wasn't lovely in his eyes.

But it wasn't so ugly as a base-side town back on the mainland would have been, either. Palm trees swayed in the breeze. Hibiscus didn't care that it was December.

Blooms of gold and red and white brightened the day. Fletch didn't know the names of a lot of the other flowers busily blooming in the middle of winter. Mynah birds and zebra doves and red-headed, gray-backed cardinals from South America added to the tropic scenery.

Fletch wished he could hop out of the car and run over to the apartment where he'd lived till not so long before. He knew he couldn't. Rescuing Jane if he saw her on the street would have been one thing. Abandoning his gun to go after her would have been something else again: dereliction of duty.

A couple of hundred yards ahead, dirt fountained into the air. Another shell came down, and another, and another. Most of the column there was civilian. People scattered, screaming. "*Son* of a bitch," Fletch said softly.

"Sir?" the dragooned infantryman said.

"Those aren't the bursts the Japs get from their usual field pieces." Armitage spoke with authority. He'd earned the right; he'd seen what the enemy's guns could do. U.S. troops had mountain howitzers that broke down into loads light enough for one or two soldiers to manhandle them forward no matter what the terrain. Evidently, the Japs did, too. He thought about manhandling even mountain guns over the Waianae Range. Who could have dreamt the Japs could manage such a thing?

Who could have dreamt the Japs would strike at Hawaii in the first place? Oh, the people in charge of the Army and Navy here had played with the idea before. But it was only play, and everybody here had treated it that way. The trouble was, Japan hadn't. She'd been dead serious about it.

And now we're paying the piper, Fletch thought. He gave the car some gas. When he shifted up into second, gears clashed. The De Soto wasn't made for towing an artillery piece. It would break down altogether pretty soon. In the meantime, he'd get what use from it he could. If a shell from one of the mountain howitzers came down on him . . . then it did, that was all. He had to get the gun free if he possibly could.

He did it. A spent shell fragment clanged off his fender,

but he got through, skirting potholes all the way. Down towards Pearl Harbor and Honolulu he drove, wondering where the next stop would be.

JANE ARMITAGE STAYED IN HER APARTMENT when the Japanese Army entered Wahiawa. She didn't know what the Japs would do to civilians. She especially didn't know what they would do to white female civilians. She didn't want to find out the hard way, either.

She couldn't help looking out the window. Was that skinny little man skulking along the street really a soldier? He looked as if he ought to be in the eighth grade. He wore short pants. His legs seemed skinny as matchsticks. By his size, the big Americans she was used to should have been able to tie him in knots and throw him away. But a helmet that looked too large perched on his head. He carried a rifle, and had the air of a man who knew what to do with it.

He looked up towards the window. Jane drew back, not wanting him to see her. He must not have, for he kept going. Two more Japs followed him a moment later. One was even skinnier, the other stocky and strong-looking but still very short. The stocky soldier had an American canteen bumping on his hip.

Occasional shots rang out. The Americans had pulled out hours before. Maybe the Japs weren't sure about that. Maybe they were shooting people for the fun of it, or to put the fear of God into the ones they didn't shoot. Jane laughed shakily. *They sure know how to get what they want, don't they?*

She wondered if she should have headed south before the Japs came in. What she'd seen and heard from the refugees out of Waimea and Haleiwa had made her decide to sit tight. The Japanese had shelled them and shot at them and strafed them from the air. All they had was what they could carry. American soldiers had commandeered a lot of their cars. And the Army men might have shot the refugees who tried to refuse to give them up.

What had really made Jane decide to stay in Wahiawa

was the fear that fleeing wouldn't do any good. The Japs seemed only too likely to take all of Oahu. If they did, where would she be better off? In her own apartment, or somewhere on the road with only the clothes on her back? The choice had looked obvious.

Now that she'd gone and made it, she wished she hadn't. Part of the island remained free, but not her part. If she was wrong, if the Army could somehow stop the Japs . . .

She wondered how Fletch was doing. She hoped he was still alive and fighting, at least as much because an artilleryman could really hurt the Japs as because, up till fairly recently, she'd loved him. She hadn't seen him in the American retreat through town. Who could say what that proved, though, or if it proved anything?

Time crawled by. The gunfire gradually sputtered into silence. And then a man shouting something broke the silence. As he got closer, Jane managed to make out what he was saying: "Everyone come to the corner of Makani and California at four o'clock. The Japanese commander will give the rules for the occupation. Makani and California! Four o'clock! Rules for the occupation! You have to be there!" Whoever he was, he spoke good English, with only a slight Japanese accent.

Was he an invader who'd learned the language in college on the mainland? Or was he a local Jap doing what the occupiers told him? Would the local Japs do what the occupiers told them? Were they cheering to see the Stars and Stripes come down and the Rising Sun go up? *Some of them are, I bet*, Jane thought furiously.

She wondered if she ought to go listen to the Jap commander, or if the order was a trick or a trap. Reluctantly, she decided she had to take the chance. If the Japs gave more orders at this gathering, she didn't want to get shot for not knowing what the rules were. Makani and California was only a few blocks east of Kamehameha Highway, and only a few from her building. She locked the door behind her when she left, not that that would do much good against a rifle butt.

Other people were also coming out of hiding. Jane

waved and nodded to the ones she recognized. They all tried to pretend the Japanese soldiers prowling the streets weren't there. The Japs just eyed the *haoles*. They talked with the Japanese who'd lived in Wahiawa. Some of those Japanese answered, too. Tone of voice was plenty to tell Jane the shoe was on the other foot, all right.

One of the local Japanese, a man who ran a nursery, stood on a table with a Jap officer at Makani and California. The local man translated for the invader: "Major Hirabayashi says that from now on you must bow to all soldiers of the Empire of Japan. You must make way for them on the street. Soldiers may stay with people here. If they do, you will be responsible for their room and board."

The locals muttered at that. They did no more than mutter, though, not with soldiers all around. Major Hirabayashi went on, "All guns must be turned in. Anyone found with a gun after three days' time will be executed. Also, all food in Wahiawa will be shared. When ordered, you will deliver your supplies to a central distribution point. Anyone caught hoarding after that will also be executed."

More mutters. A dull horror washed over Jane. So much for what she'd bought. If only she lived in a house with a yard. She could have buried some by dead of night. Not with only an apartment around her, and lots of nosy neighbors. *Maybe I should have run away after all.*

V

THE *OSHIMA MARU*'S PLANKING THROBBED UNDER JIRO Takahashi's feet. Diesel growling at the sampan's stern, it scooted out into the Pacific. Takahashi was happy. "Now we get to go work again," he said. Staying at home without working had been harder on him than all the backbreaking labor he went through here on the ocean.

His sons seemed less delighted. "Merry Christmas," Hiroshi said, in sarcastic English. Jiro had always bought the boys presents at Christmastime. Why not? Everybody else did. But for the presents, though, the day meant nothing to him. What difference did a *haole* holiday make?

In Japanese hardly less sardonic, Kenzo added, "You know why they've let us go out again, don't you, Father?"

"I don't care why," Jiro said. "Isn't it good to breathe clean air?" The tank farms at Pearl Harbor had mostly burned themselves out by now, but acrid, eye-stinging haze still filled the air in Honolulu. No sooner had Jiro praised the air away from the city than he lit a cigarette. "Have to be careful with these," he remarked. "They're starting to run low."

"They're starting to run low on everything," Kenzo said. "That's why they've let the sampans out. They really *need* the fish we bring back."

"As long as there's diesel fuel, we'll do all right," Jiro said. "Lots of things can happen to a fisherman, but he probably won't starve."

"How long will there be diesel fuel?" Hiroshi asked. "It comes from the mainland just like everything else. It came from the mainland, I mean. Nothing's going in or out, not any more."

"If Japan wins, she can send us diesel fuel," Jiro said.

To his annoyance, Hiroshi and Kenzo both laughed at him. "Don't you remember, Father?" his older son said. "One of the big reasons Japan got into a fight with the United States was that we wouldn't sell them oil any more. They won't have any to spare for Hawaii." Kenzo nodded in agreement with his brother.

Jiro glared at his sons. He *had* forgotten about the oil embargo. Not only were they rude for laughing, they were right, which made it three times as bad. And, to Hiroshi and Kenzo, the United States was *we* and Japan was *they*. Jiro had already bumped into that, but he liked it no better now.

Hiroshi rubbed his nose in the point: "Everything except pineapple and sugar comes from the mainland, just about. If we need blue jeans or shoes or canned milk or canned corn or flour for bread or—or—anything, they have to ship it in."

"Remember when they had the dock strike on the West Coast five years ago?" Kenzo added. "We were down to two weeks' worth of food by the time it ended—and that was when things were coming in from the East Coast, and from Australia and Japan, too. Where will we get supplies now? We'll start going hungry a lot faster."

"All right. All right." Jiro wanted to cuff both of them. He couldn't. They were grown men, and both bigger than he was. And they were so very, very different from him. He wondered what he'd done wrong. If he'd been a better father, wouldn't he have had sons who were more Japanese?

He busied himself on the sampan, not that there was much to do. The engine chugged away. It was noisy, but it was reliable. He almost wished it would have broken down. That would have given him the excuse to haul out the tool kit and tinker with it. Then he could have ignored his milkshake-guzzling, hamburger-munching boys. As things were, he just stared back towards the receding bulk of Oahu.

Hiroshi said something in English. Kenzo laughed. Neither of them bothered to translate for Jiro. *They must be talking about me*, he thought resentfully. They thought they knew everything and their old man didn't know anything. Well, by the look of things, they'd backed the wrong horse in the war. Every day the rumble of artillery came closer to Honolulu. The Japanese advanced. The Americans retreated. They couldn't retreat much farther, or they'd go into the Pacific.

He felt the way the *Oshima Maru* bumped over the waves. He watched terns and boobies and frigate birds. He remembered gulls raucous over the Inner Sea when he was young. They could guide a fisherman to schools of smelt or mackerel. But gulls, except for rare vagrants, didn't come to Hawaii. A man had to use what other birds gave him.

There were boobies, plunging into the sea. Japanese dive bombers must have looked like that when they swooped down on the American ships at Pearl Harbor. They hadn't gone into the sea, though; they'd pulled up and flown away to strike again and again. "*Banzai!*" Jiro said softly. "*Banzai!*" He didn't think his sons heard him. That was just as well.

He steered towards the boobies. One of them came to the surface with a foot-long fish writhing in its beak. Jiro nodded. He waved to Hiroshi and Kenzo. They'd already started dumping *nehus* into the water and getting the lines ready. They did know what needed doing.

Thrilled to be free, unaware of the fate awaiting so many of them, the minnows swam off in all directions, silver flecks under the blue of the sea. And bigger flashes of silver rose to meet them. Some of those fish would get themselves a meal. Some would bite down on silver hooks, not silver scales. Instead of getting meals, they would become meals themselves.

Across miles of ocean, booms came from the north. "Are those the coast-defense guns again?" Kenzo asked.

That would have been Jiro's guess, too. But Hiroshi

shook his head. "I don't think so," he said. "I think those are some of the ships in Pearl Harbor, shooting at the Japanese as they come farther south."

"You notice they couldn't get *out* of Pearl Harbor," Jiro said. Both his sons sent him stony looks. He ignored them. He knew it was true, and so did they, however little they liked it. The very day the war started, Japanese bombers in the third wave had sunk two light cruisers in the channel leading from the harbor to the Pacific. That had corked the bottle and made sure the rest of the ships stayed put. Since then, Japanese planes had pounded them again and again.

Some of the ships still had working guns. Every so often, they opened fire. They were heavier artillery than any based on land except the coast-defense batteries. Jiro suspected Japanese planes would return before long. After that, very likely, fewer Navy guns would fire on his country's soldiers.

My country's soldiers, Jiro thought again, and nodded to himself. Yes, Japan was his country. It always would be. And if Hiroshi and Kenzo didn't like that or couldn't understand it, too bad.

The fish didn't seem to care about the distant artillery. When the Takahashis pulled in the lines, they had plenty of *aku* and *ahi* on them, as well as a few *mahimahi* that had come to join the feast. The frenzy of gutting them and getting them into storage came next.

Then it was more minnows over the side, and fish guts, too, and the lines went back into the Pacific with them. The guts, Jiro knew, would draw sharks, but sharks were also good to eat, even if a lot of *haoles* were too dumb to believe it. He didn't think he would have any trouble selling them, not today.

He and his sons brought in fish till the sun sank low in the west. Then Jiro started up the diesel again and took the *Oshima Maru* back to Kewalo Basin. "Now we see how we do," he said as they tied up there.

"We see how scared people are, you mean," Hiroshi said. Jiro only shrugged his aching shoulders. In the end, it all boiled down to the same thing.

Along with the Japanese and Chinese buyers in the marketplace, there were also tall American soldiers with bayonets on their rifles. Fear stabbed at Jiro when he saw them. Were they there to enforce price controls or, worse, to confiscate the fish the Takahashis had worked so hard to catch? If they were, Jiro was damned if he intended to go out again the next morning. He'd built his life on the cornerstone of hard work, but hard work with the expectation of fair pay for it. If he didn't get his reward, what point to putting to sea?

But the soldiers only kept order. They needed to keep order, too, because the buyers sprang at Jiro, Hiroshi, and Kenzo like starving wolves. They frantically bid against one another. By the time they were through, Jiro had three times as much money in his pocket as he'd imagined in his fondest dreams.

He had so much money, he was tempted not to take home some especially fine *ahi* for Reiko. But the thought of what his wife would say if he didn't was plenty to conquer even greed. "We'll be rich!" he said to his sons. "Rich, I tell you!" He could think about the money he *had* made, if not the bit of extra cash that would have been in his pocket if he'd sold the rest of the tuna.

Then Hiroshi spoiled even that, saying, "No, we won't. The buyers will just jack up the price they charge. Everybody's jacking up the prices he charges. Look at that." He pointed to the window of a *haole* grocery store they were walking past. He and Kenzo both read English fluently, which Jiro didn't. "Flour is half again what it was when the war started. Rice the same. Onions are double. And look at oranges—a dollar thirty-five a dozen! That's two and a half times what they were before, easy."

Some of Jiro's glee evaporated. Then it returned, or a portion of it did. "Yes, the prices are up, but what I got paid is up even more."

"How much did you shell out for diesel fuel?" Kenzo asked.

Jiro scowled. "Old man Okano is a highway robber," he said. But this time his glee didn't come back. He knew he couldn't have got a better price from anybody else, Japanese, Chinese, or *haole*. Diesel fuel was heading straight through the roof. The Army needed a lot of it, and, as his sons had said, no more was coming in from the mainland. And gasoline was going up even faster than diesel fuel. Which meant . . .

"All right, we won't get rich," Jiro said. He was less upset than he might have been. He wouldn't have known what to do as a rich man anyhow.

Kenzo asked, "What happens when there is no more fuel? Can we take the engine off the sampan and rig a mast? Hiroshi and I don't know anything about handling a sail."

"I've done it, back when I was young," Jiro said. "I think I can still manage. I'd want somebody who really knows what he's doing to see to the rigging, I expect." He stuck a hand in his pocket. Something like that wouldn't come cheap. His imagined wealth seemed to be dripping away even faster than he'd got it.

THE DAY AFTER CHRISTMAS, Joe Crosetti reported to the San Francisco Naval Aviation Selection Board. A big blond Swede named Lundquist chaired the board. He looked at Joe's papers and smiled. "Are you any relation to Frankie Crosetti, young man?" he asked.

Joe smiled, too, in a resigned way. If he had a dime for every time somebody'd asked him if he was related to the Yankees' shortstop, he might have been making more dough than Frankie was. "No, sir, not that I know of," he answered. "Oh, there may be some kind of connection between his family and mine back in the old country, but it's nothing anybody can prove."

"Okay. Doesn't matter one way or the other," Lundquist said. "I wondered, that's all. How old are you, son?"

"I'm nineteen, Mr. Lundquist." Crosetti knew he looked younger. He was five-seven and on the skinny side, with a narrow, swarthy face and a thick shock of curly black hair. He did have a five-o'clock shadow that came out at three, but it was five after nine in the morning now; he'd got to the board as soon as it opened, and he'd shaved just a couple of hours before.

"You graduated from high school . . . ?"

"A year and a half ago, sir. My diploma's in with my papers."

"All right. And what are you doing now?"

"I'm a mechanic at Scalzi's garage, sir," Joe answered. "My old man's a fisherman. Sometimes on weekends I go out with him. I used to do it every summer and Christmas vacation till I got this job."

"So you know your way around the water, do you?"

"A little bit, maybe. I'm an okay sailor, but I'm not a *sailor*, you know what I mean?"

Lundquist and the rest of the men on the board looked at one another. Joe tried to figure out what that meant, but he couldn't. The chairman said, "When you were in high school, did you play any sports?"

"Yes, sir," Joe answered. "I played second base on the baseball team, and I was a backup guard on the basketball team."

"No football?"

Joe shook his head. "I like playing touch in the park, but I'm not a great big guy." That was an understatement. "I didn't have a prayer of making the team. How come you want to know?"

"Teamwork," Lundquist told him. "Basketball is good, football's even better. Baseball shows coordination, but less of the other."

One of the other men spoke up: "Second and short need it more than other positions. They have to work together if they're going to turn double plays." His wiry build suggested he might have been a middle infielder in his day. Whether or not, he was dead right, and Joe nodded. He and Danny Fitzpatrick, his shortstop, had taken endless ground balls and practiced 6-4-3 and 4-6-3 double plays till each knew in his sleep what the other was going to do.

Lundquist scribbled a note. He asked, "Have you got any flying experience?"

"No, sir," Joe admitted, wondering how much trouble

the admission would get him in. Again, he couldn't tell what Lundquist was thinking. The man had one of the deadest pans Joe had ever seen; he wouldn't have wanted to play poker against him.

"But you do drive a car as well as work on them?" Lundquist persisted.

"Oh, yes, sir," Joe said. "I've had my license since I was sixteen."

"Any accidents?"

"No, sir."

"Tickets?"

"Just one." Joe thought about lying, but they could check. The ticket might not wash him out. If they nailed him in a lie, he figured that was all she wrote.

The selection-board chairman shuffled through his folder. "I see you have your letters of recommendation in place." He looked over each of them in turn. "Your boss and your two high-school coaches. They know you pretty well?"

"If they don't, nobody does." Joe wondered if he should have tried to get letters from important people—judges or politicians, maybe. The only trouble was, he didn't know anybody like that. *I'm an ordinary Joe*, he thought, and grinned a little.

"One more question," Lundquist said. "Why do you want to do this?"

"Why? Sir, the day after the Japs jumped on Pearl Harbor, my old man tried to join the Army. He wanted to hit back, and so do I. They wouldn't take him—he's forty-five, and he's got a bad back and a bad shoulder. But I was so proud of him, I can't even tell you. And what he did got me thinking. If we are going to hit back at the Japs, who'll get in the first licks? Pilots flying off carriers, looks like to me. So that's what I want to do."

The man who looked as if he'd played second or short remarked, "Kid's got a head on his shoulders." That made Joe feel about ten feet tall. He tried not to be dumber than he could help, but he was no big brain. If they wanted guys with high foreheads and thick glasses to fly their fighters, he was out of luck.

"Why don't you step outside?" Lundquist told him. "We need to talk about you behind your back for a little while." Joe did a double take when he heard that. Lundquist was a cool customer, but maybe he was okay underneath.

Joe could hear them muttering about him in there. If he put his ear to the door, he might make out what they were saying. He didn't do it. It was something else where getting caught would land him in hot water. Not doing it turned out to be smart. Ten seconds later, two guys in sailor suits turned the corner and came past him. They paid him no more attention than if he were part of the linoleum. But if he'd been leaning up against the door, that would have been a different story.

He wanted a cigarette, but didn't pull the pack of Luckys out of his pocket. He didn't want to have a butt in his mouth when they called him back in, and it'd be just his luck to get halfway down the smoke when the door opened.

Again, that turned out to be the right move, because a couple of minutes later the door *did* open. "Come on in, son," Lundquist said. "Have a seat." As usual, his face gave no clue to what he was thinking. He might have been about to give Joe what he wanted, or to arrest him and send him to Alcatraz.

Silence stretched. Joe craved that cigarette more than ever. It would have calmed his nerves, slowed his pounding heart. Finally he couldn't stand it any more, and said, "Well?"

"Well, we're going to make you an appointment with the psychological officers," Lundquist said. "If they don't say you've got an unfortunate tendency to raise hedgehogs in your hat, we'll see if the Navy can make a flyboy out of you."

"Thank you, sir!" The words seemed cold and useless to Joe. What he really wanted to do was turn handsprings.

"No promises, mind you, but you don't look too bad," Lundquist said.

The man who looked like a middle infielder added, "You had all your paperwork in order the first time you came in. That's a good sign right there—you'd be amazed how many people have to try three times before they bring us everything we need. No promises, no, but my guess is you've got what it takes."

"See the petty officer at the door," Lundquist said. "Make yourself a psych appointment for right after the first of the year. Good luck to you."

Joe thanked him again and left the conference room. His feet hardly seemed to touch the ground. He might have been flying even without a fighter under him. The petty officer, who had an impressive array of long-service hashmarks on his sleeve, set up the appointment for testing. That Joe had passed the selection board didn't impress him. By all appearances, nothing impressed him.

Out in the street, Joe half expected people to stare at him and point and say, *There's the kid who's going to shoot Tojo's medals off his chest.* They didn't, of course. To them, what he'd accomplished didn't show. The gray-haired man at the street corner who wore a helmet and an armband with CD—Civil Defense—on it was visibly part of the war. Joe wasn't.

On the same corner, a kid in short pants was peddling the *Examiner.* "More Jap landings in the Philippines!" he bawled, over and over. "Read all about it!" Joe gave him a nickel and took a paper.

He read the *Examiner* as he walked back to the garage where he worked. Lots of people had their noses in newspapers, far more than had read as they walked before the war started. Every so often, they'd bump into each other, mutter excuse-mes, and keep on reading as they walked.

Not much of the news was good. The Navy was laying mines outside harbors on the East Coast to try to keep German subs away. Congressmen were fuming that blackout regulations weren't strict enough and were being ignored. The Nazis and Reds were both claiming victories in Russia.

Rooting for the Russians felt funny. Joe's old man had admired Mussolini before he got too chummy with Hitler, and couldn't stand Stalin. But the USA and the Soviet Union were on the same side now, like it or not.

"How'd it go, Joe?" his boss asked when he walked in.

"Pretty good, Mr. Scalzi, I think," Joe answered. Dominic Scalzi's family and the Crosettis both came from the same village south of Naples. That wasn't the only reason Joe had a job there, but it sure didn't hurt. He went on, "Thanks again for your letter. I had all my ducks in a row, and they really liked that."

"Good, kid. That's good." Scalzi lit a Camel. Joe couldn't see how he smoked them; they were strong enough to grow hair on your chest. The garage owner was a short, round man with a graying mustache. He blew a smoke ring, then sighed out the rest of the drag in a blue-gray cloud. "I shoulda told 'em you were a lousy good-for-nothing. Then they wouldn't take you, and you could go on workin' for me a little longer."

"Probably not much," Joe said. "If I don't end up a Navy flier, the draft'll get me pretty soon."

"I said a little longer." Dominic Scalzi was a precise man, a good thing for a mechanic to be. He jerked a thumb at the little washroom off to one side of the work area. "Go on and change into your coveralls. Long as you're here, I'm gonna get some work outa you. See if you can clean the gunk outa Mr. Jablonski's carburetor, will you? He's been pissing and moaning about it for weeks."

"I'll try," Joe said. "You want to know what I think, I think the carb on a '38 Plymouth is a piece of crap."

"I don't give a damn what you think. I just want you to clean out the son of a bitch." Scalzi's uniform was an almost navy blue, but all it had on it was *Dom* machine-embroidered over the left breast pocket. Joe's was just like it except for the name.

He grabbed a hasty cigarette of his own while he changed out of his jacket and slacks and into the scratchy denim coveralls. Before he came out, he flushed the butt down the toilet. He figured on soaking the carburetor in gasoline before he got to work on it. Gasoline and cigarettes didn't mix.

Once he'd soaked everything with the gasoline, he went after the valves and springs and made sure no deposits could interfere with their functioning. Then he reassembled the carb. His hands knew what to do, almost without conscious thought on his part. He had the carburetor back on the engine before he really noticed what he was up to.

The key was in the ignition. He started up the Plymouth, listened, and nodded to himself. The car sounded a hell of a lot better than it had when old man Jablonski brought it in. He waved to his boss. Scalzi came over, wiping his greasy hands on a rag. He listened, too, and gave Joe a thumbs-up. Joe grinned. It was turning into a pretty damn good day.

CORPORAL TAKEO SHIMIZU LIKED THE WAY things were going nowadays much better than he had a week earlier. The attack over the western mountains had made the Americans fall back for their very lives. They still hadn't pieced together a line to match the one they'd held in front of Schofield Barracks and Wahiawa. With a little luck, they wouldn't be able to.

They hadn't quit, though. A Yankee machine gun up ahead spat death across a pineapple field. Shimizu crouched in a foxhole. Sooner or later, a grenade or mortar bomb would take care of the machine-gun crew. Then he'd advance again. Or, if one of his officers gave the order, he'd advance sooner than that. And if the machine gun blew out his brains or chopped his legs out from under him . . . in that case, like it or not, one of the chowderheads in his squad would get a star on each of his red-and-gold collar tabs.

Meanwhile . . . Meanwhile, Shimizu lit a cigarette from a pack he'd taken off a dead American. The tobacco was amazingly smooth and mild. *Any way you look at it, the Americans live better than we do*, he thought. He made twenty yen—about four dollars and sixty cents—a month. He wondered what an American corporal got paid. More than that, or he missed his guess.

Cautiously, he stuck his head up for a look around. He saw where the machine gun was: in a sandbagged position behind a creek. Whoever'd sited it had known what he was doing. If there were no mortars handy, he didn't see how anyone could knock it out. The gunners would shoot a man with grenades before he got close enough to fling them.

He ducked down in a hurry. He wasn't going to order anybody forward to throw his life away. Lieutenant Yonehara had done that, and what had it got him? Nothing but a grieving family back home.

Of course, Colonel Fujikawa or some other officer could order the men to advance, and they would have to go. What would happen to them afterwards? That was in the hands of karma. So Shimizu told himself, anyway.

"This way! Forward! It's clear over here!" The shout came in Japanese, from ahead and to the right. It wasn't just Japanese, either. It was Hiroshima dialect—from Shimizu's own part of the country—and old-fashioned Hiroshima dialect at that. It sounded like somebody who'd never been off a farm in the back of beyond till the Army grabbed him. Shimizu would have thought only old grannies talked like that nowadays.

But if there was a way forward . . . He sprang out of his hole, shouting, "Come on, men! Let's drive the Yankees back again!"

He wasn't the only one who'd emerged. Quite a few soldiers had heard that shout. They all jumped up and started running ahead and to the right. And the American machine gun and nearby riflemen remorselessly chopped them down. Shimizu had learned better than to stay on his feet very long under fire like that. He threw himself flat and, still on his belly, started scraping himself a new hole in the ground.

Amid the screams of the wounded, somebody yelled, *"Zakennayo!"*—a pungent, all-purpose obscenity—and then went on, "Must be one of those Hawaii Japanese!"

Shimizu dug harder. He muttered, *"Zakennayo!"* too. They'd told him before he set out that there were more people of Japanese blood in Hawaii than any other group. From what he'd seen, that was likely true. Most of them had roots around Hiroshima, too. That was why the Fifth Division, which drew its manpower from that region, was on Oahu now. And they'd told him the Hawaii Japanese would be delighted to see these islands come under the Rising Sun.

That . . . wasn't so obvious. Some of the older men and women seemed glad enough to see the Japanese. A lot of the younger ones, the ones born here, seemed anything but. This fellow had just got several soldiers shot. *If we get our hands on him . . .* Shimizu thought longingly.

He cursed again as he threw dirt in front of himself. The Americans and the damned Hawaii Japanese had suckered him. He squeezed the entrenching tool till his knuckles whitened. Of course the bastard sounded as if he came from the dark side of the moon. Most of the Japanese here had old-fashioned accents. They or their ancestors had been peasants to begin with, and the language here hadn't changed with time as it had in Japan.

He'd just got the foxhole half as good as the one he'd left behind when mortar bombs did start whistling down around the American machine gun. Those bursts sounded sweet to him—but not sweet enough to make him stick his head up out of that foxhole. If he did, the Yankees were liable to blow it off for him.

"You got 'em. It's safe. Come on!" The alluring Japanese voice came from ahead of him. This time, he sat tight. What *could* they do to that fellow if they caught him? He'd be even more fun to play with than an ordinary captive.

Soldiers were yelling, "Down! Stay down! It's a trick!" But Shimizu heard feet running through the field. He also heard the machine gun stutter to life. Curses and screams followed. So did the thuds of bodies crashing to the ground. Shimizu added his own curses to the din. Now he was swearing at his own men at least as hard as at the Americans. If that voice had fooled them once—well, they weren't expecting it. But if it fooled them twice . . .

"Stay down, *baka yaro!*" he yelled. Dumb assholes they were, almost dumb enough to deserve getting shot.

More mortar bombs fell around the machine-gun nest. "You can't hit a damn thing!" that lying Japanese voice jeered. Maybe, on the principle that everything it said was full of crap, the mortars really had put the American machine gun out of action. Maybe—but Corporal Shimizu didn't stick his head up to find out.

He didn't hear any signs that the men around him were trying to advance, either. He breathed a sigh of relief. Some of them could learn after all. The ones who couldn't had paid the price for their stupidity.

After a while, the machine gun started up again, this time sending a stream of bullets over to the left. When another machine gun there answered the fire, Shimizu did look out from his hole. A tank rumbled through the pineapple field, straight towards the American machine gun. Its bow gunner shot back at the Yankees. Enemy bullets clanged off its armor, now and then striking sparks but doing no harm.

The snorting mechanical monster stopped. The cannon in the turret bellowed. The shell burst just in front of the sandbags shielding the American gun. The enemy soldiers were brave. They kept right on shooting at the tank. It did them no good. The cannon spoke again. Sandbags flew. The machine gun kept firing even after that, but not for long. The tank's bow and turret-mounted machine guns had a clear shot at the Americans now.

Corporal Shimizu sprang from his new foxhole. "Come on!" he shouted. "Move fast! Maybe we can catch that Hawaii Japanese and give him what he deserves!" If anything would get the men out of their holes and advancing, that ought to do the trick.

And it did. They splashed through the creek and past the shattered machine-gun nest. Not many riflemen had backed up the machine gunners. The Japanese soldiers gained several hundred meters before enemy fire forced them to hit the dirt and dig in again. Shimizu was proud of the dash they showed. But the man who'd tricked them got away. He didn't know how lucky he was—or maybe he did.

LIKE MOST NINETEEN-YEAR-OLDS in Honolulu, Kenzo Takahashi had Japanese friends and *haole* friends and Chinese friends and Filipino friends and friends who were a

little bit of everything. Everybody was packed together
with everybody else in school. A good many kids had parents who wished their friends came only from their own
group. But that wasn't how things worked in Hawaii—
which was why so many kids were a little bit of everything.

With his friends who weren't Japanese (and even, a lot
of the time, with the ones who were), Kenzo was just Ken.
That suited him fine; Ken was a good American name, and
he was at least as American as he was Japanese. When he ate
with his parents, he used *hashi* to shovel in rice and raw
fish. When he wasn't with his parents, he was likely to order
fried chicken or spaghetti and meatballs. He liked them
better. So did Hiroshi.

Since the attack on Pearl Harbor, though . . . All of a
sudden, his *haole* friends didn't want to know him any
more. It wasn't just that he was spending most of his time
out on the *Oshima Maru*, either. He was—he'd never worked
so hard in his life—but that wasn't the point.

Going home from Kewalo Basin, he'd sometimes see
people with whom he'd sat for four years in math and English and history and science classes. He'd see them . . .
and, if they were white, they'd pretend they didn't see him.
Sometimes they would even turn their backs so he couldn't
possibly miss the point. That cut like a knife.

And he knew those *haoles* and their folks were lining up
to buy the fish he and his father and brother brought in.
They didn't mind doing that at all. Oh, no, especially not
when the fish the sampans brought in was the only fresh
food coming into Honolulu these days.

What really hurt was when Elsie Sundberg acted as if
she'd never set eyes on him in her life. Thanks to the won-
ders of alphabetical seating, he'd had the desk right behind
hers in just about all the classes they took together. The alphabet could have played plenty of worse tricks on him:
Elsie was blond, blue-eyed, and curvy, a cheerleader for the
football team. She got better grades in English and history;
he was stronger in science and math. They'd spent a lot of
time coaching each other. They'd gone to a few movies together, held hands. He'd kissed her once. He'd thought

about asking her to the prom, but by the time he got up the nerve to do it the star halfback beat him to the punch. She'd sounded genuinely sorry when she told him no.

And now . . . now he was nothing but a lousy Jap to her. It made him want to cry, or else to go out and kick something or somebody.

"It's not right, goddammit," he raged to Hiroshi later that evening. "I'm as much an American as she is." The one advantage of having parents who'd never learned English was that he and his brother could use it without fear of eavesdropping.

His brother made a small production of lighting a cigarette. Only after a long, meditative drag did he answer, "It's tough, all right. Some of that same shit's happened to me, too."

"Tough? Is that all you can say? What's the good of trying to be an American if the stinking *haoles* won't let you?" He pointed to the pack of Chesterfields. "Let me have one of those."

Hiroshi did, and leaned close to give him a light. After they were both smoking, Hiroshi said, "Well, what other choice have you got? Do you want to stand up and cheer for Hirohito the way Dad does?"

"Jesus Christ, no!" Kenzo exclaimed. "That's just embarrassing."

"It's worse than embarrassing these days." Hiroshi dropped his voice even though his and Kenzo's folks couldn't understand. "It's damn near treason."

"Yeah. I know," Kenzo said heavily. "But you can't tell him anything. He won't listen." He sucked in smoke, then blew it out in a ragged cloud. What with the blackout and the radio being off the air almost all the time, the night was almost eerily quiet. That made it easy for him to hear the thunder in the middle distance—except it wasn't thunder. The boom of the guns got louder and louder, closer and closer, as the days went by. "What do we do if . . . our side doesn't win?"

"I don't know." His brother smoked his cigarette till the butt got too small to hold between his lips. Some people

were even using toothpicks or alligator clips to hold tiny
butts and squeeze an extra drag or two out of them. Tobacco wouldn't last forever. Nothing in Honolulu would
last forever. If Hawaii fell, nothing would last very long.
Hiroshi stubbed out the remains of the Chesterfield and
stared down at the ashtray. "What *can* we do? Try and keep
our noses clean. Try and keep Dad from busting his but-
tons 'cause he's so proud."

"It's a good thing the sampan's going out again," Kenzo
said. "If Dad's on the ocean, he can't be on the streets.
Somebody'd knock his block off for him."

"Or maybe not, depending on where he is," Hiroshi
said. "As long as he stays Ewa side of Nuuanu Avenue, he
won't do too bad."

Kenzo only grunted. That was a half truth. Older Japanese like his father often pulled for their native country.
Most of the younger ones were as American as Hiroshi and
himself. And none of the Chinese and Koreans and Filipinos who helped crowd Honolulu's Asian district had any
use for Japan. That had sometimes led to fights even before
Pearl Harbor. Now . . .

Off in the distance, the thunder that wasn't thunder
rumbled again. Kenzo grunted again. "What do we do if . . .
if the Japanese Army marches into Honolulu?" There.
He'd said it.

"What *can* we do?" his brother said. Kenzo shrugged.
He had no answer. He'd hoped Hiroshi would.

SABURO SHINDO LOOKED DOWN ON HONOLULU from his
Zero. Even from his height, he could see olive-drab trucks
rolling through the city. The time had come—as far as he
was concerned, the time was long since past—to give the
Americans a lesson. He wondered why his superiors had
held off for so long. He'd heard a lot of Japanese lived in
Honolulu. Maybe the powers that be hadn't wanted to hurt
them, or hoped they could somehow get the Americans to
give up. It hadn't happened. As far as Lieutenant Shindo
was concerned, the best way to make somebody give up
was to kick him in the teeth till he did.

Honolulu was about to get kicked in the teeth.

The place was defended. Puffs of black smoke from antiaircraft guns were already pocking the sky around the fighters Shindo led, and around the bombers flying above them. Antiaircraft guns were a nuisance. But they were only a nuisance. The Americans had next to no combat aircraft left. That was what really mattered.

Waggling his wings to the rest of the Zeros, Shindo dropped his fighter's nose and dove on the city below. The other planes followed. Those olive-drab trucks—and the cars, and the buildings past which they drove—swelled from ant size to toy size to the real thing. Now the antiaircraft fire was above his planes. He laughed. The Yankees couldn't depress their guns fast enough to stay with him.

As if trying to make up for that, small-arms fire reached for the Zeros. All the machine guns and rifles and pistols on the ground seemed to go off at once. Muzzle flashes and tracers sparked below Shindo. As usual, he ignored them. Odds were, all that stuff would miss him. Nobody could lead a speeding plane enough; people with small arms shot behind aircraft they aimed at. And if, by bad luck, this once they didn't . . . Ground fire had already winged Shindo's plane once. It could have been worse. But he couldn't do anything about it one way or the other.

Come to that, he'd had to learn to shoot at ground targets. He was pretty good at it now. He didn't know whether that truck convoy heading west through the center of town was carrying men or supplies or ammunition. He didn't care. He shot it up any which way.

Flames exploded from some of the trucks. *Gasoline*, he thought. The less the Americans had, the less good they could get out of their cars and trucks and tanks. He pulled up and went around for another pass. A bullet banged through the Zero's fuselage, about a meter behind where he sat. Sure as sure, put enough rounds in the air and some would hit. The plane kept flying. This one hadn't hit anything important.

The truck convoy burned merrily. Soldiers scrambled out of some of the vehicles. Some of them fired into the sky. Others ran for cover. He shot up not only the convoy but as many cars on the street as he could. Now he wasn't just aiming to impede military traffic, though he wanted to do that. His orders were to make Honolulu howl. The louder the city howled, the likelier the American commanders were to raise the white flag.

As Lieutenant Shindo pulled up, acceleration and a contemptuous grin thrust his lips back from his teeth. Japanese officers wouldn't give a damn about how loud civilians howled. They'd fight to the last man, whatever the odds. But the Americans were soft, decadent, effeminate. They let extraneous factors like civilians affect even important things like war. Well, they would pay for it.

Shindo automatically checked six. A pilot who didn't do that all the time would regret it. Even though he didn't think the Americans could put any more fighters in the air, habit was unbreakable.

One of his Zeros went down. It sent a fireball and a column of black smoke up into the sky. The building it had hit was starting to burn, too. Even in death, the pilot did damage. Shindo nodded, saluting his courage. The dead man's spirit would go to the Yasukuni-jinja—the Shrine for Establishing Peace in the Empire—at Kudan Hill in Tokyo.

The Nakajimas and Aichis that flew with the fighters were bombing the city now. What civilian terror could do, it would do. Shindo hoped it would make the Americans give up. He was an economical warrior. He didn't believe in expending more on objectives than he had to.

Shindo spoke to his fellow fighter pilots on the all-planes circuit: "Mission accomplished. Now we return to the carriers." They mostly weren't landing on carrier decks any more; still, security persisted.

Oahu was so small, it made the war seem a miniature painting. Even Haleiwa airstrip, on the north coast of the island, was less than ten minutes' flying time from Honolulu. The front wasn't that far north of the local capital and Pearl Harbor. The gap between the Waianae Range and the Koolau Range widened from north to south, which meant the Americans had to hold a longer line and stretch themselves thinner as they fell back. Japanese soldiers might have been the best in the world at taking advantage of weak spots in the enemy's defenses. Other armies had more in the way of heavy equipment, yes. If Japanese pilots hadn't had complete control of the air and smashed up a lot of American heavy equipment before it got into action, this would have been a much tougher fight. But nobody could match the Japanese at infiltrating.

Shells burst on and near the roads north of the front. Sensibly, the Americans were trying to deny the Japanese the use of them. The Yankees had fought reasonably well and with considerable courage since the first crippling blows they'd suffered. But those were plenty to bury them in a deep, deep hole.

Here came Haleiwa. It had the advantage of being out of range of most American artillery. The Japanese still couldn't use Wheeler Field. Even U.S. mortars could reach the runways south of Schofield Barracks. But the more planes and fuel and equipment the Navy ferried off the carriers and onto dry land, the sooner some of the precious big ships could be released for other duty.

Down came the Zero for a smooth landing. Not for the first time, Shindo thought how easy landing at an ordinary airstrip was compared to a carrier landing. He got out of the fighter and jumped down. Groundcrew men in khaki coveralls dragged his Zero into a revetment. One after another, the fighters that had followed him to Honolulu came in. He counted them, nodding as the last plane's landing gear kicked up dust. He'd lost one, but no more.

He went to the command tent. Commanders Genda and Fuchida sat in front of a card table probably purloined from a Haleiwa house. The map they were examining also had to be local, for it was printed in English. It was larger and more detailed than any Japanese-language map of Oahu that Shindo had seen. He pointed. "Where did you get it?"

Minoru Genda looked up, a smile half mischievous, half bemused on his face. "From a service station," he answered. "They give them away."

"*Bako yaro*," Shindo said, thinking anyone had to be a stupid jerk to give away something that strategically valuable.

"How did it go?" Genda asked.

"Routine, for the most part," Shindo answered. A stolid man, he'd described the opening day's raids on Pearl Harbor much the same way. He went on, "We lost one fighter; I saw it go down. I don't know if the antiaircraft got any of the bombers. And how do things look on your fancy new map?"

"They're sending more and more sailors up from Pearl Harbor to fight in their line as infantry—trying to get some use out of them," Mitsuo Fuchida said. "You can give a man a rifle, but that doesn't turn him into a soldier."

"*Hai. Honto.*" Shindo bent closer to the map. English meant nothing to him, but he knew the topography of Oahu—and his superiors had already started marking up the map in Japanese. "What's our next move? Another raid on Honolulu, or does some part of the front need special softening up . . . ?"

OSCAR VAN DER KIRK'S PARENTS had raised him to be polite no matter what. He paid no attention to a lot of what they'd taught him, especially the stuff they'd tried to drive home with a sledgehammer. But being—and staying—polite was part of what they were, and they'd made it part of what he was. Most of the time, it didn't matter. If anything, it was an asset more often than not.

It handicapped him with Susie Higgins.

He rapidly figured out why she'd got divorced. He'd had trouble living with her for even a few days, and he was a hell of a lot more easygoing than most guys. What did puzzle him was how she'd got married in the first place. Oh, she was cute, and she was fun in the sack, but lots of girls were cute and fun in the sack. Who knew that better than a Waikiki beach bum?

She was also all smiles and happiness—as long as you did exactly what she wanted. When you didn't, you soon discovered she was hard and rough as a steel file underneath.

Hadn't the guy she'd briefly been hitched to figured that out before she marched him down the aisle and got him to say *I do?*

Evidently not, poor bastard.

She quickly lost interest in surf-riding, even though she could have been good at it. "Why do you want to go out there every single day?" she demanded. "Don't you get bored?"

He stared at her as if she'd suggested getting bored with sex. "Good Lord, no," he said. "Besides, some of the people stuck in the hotels still want lessons. How else am I going to make any money?"

Susie sent him a suspicious stare. "You just want to meet some gal who'll give you a throw," she whined.

"I've got a gal," he said. "Don't I?"

"You damn well won't if you don't pay more attention to me," Susie said.

"You come with me," Oscar suggested—reasonably, he thought.

"You come shopping with me," Susie said.

That wasn't reasonable, not to him. "The Japs have blown up half the stores, and how are you going to get anything you buy back to the mainland?" Oahu would fall. He could see it, even if Susie couldn't.

She started to cry, which left him flummoxed—he'd never had to worry about that with stray kittens. "God damn you," she choked out. "You don't care about anything, do you? You didn't even care that yesterday was New Year's."

"Was it?" Oscar knew when Christmas had been. To celebrate, he'd bought some tuna from a Jap fisherman so he and Susie could have a Christmas dinner that didn't come out of a can. He wasn't much of a cook, but he could manage tuna steaks. Till Susie came to Hawaii, she'd never set eyes on fresh tuna. Remembering when the tuna dinner had been, Oscar had to count on his fingers to work out that yesterday really had been January first. A little sheepishly, he said, "Well, happy 1942."

"Yeah, sure," Susie said bitterly. "I wish to God I'd never

come here. The Japs are gonna . . ." She didn't say what the Japs were going to do. Instead, she dissolved into fresh tears. Maybe she *could* see the writing on the wall. She wasn't dumb, just spoiled as three-day-old potato salad.

Oscar realized he was supposed to do something, even if he wasn't quite sure what. He tried stroking her hair, which was what they did in the movies when a girl started crying. Susie turned and snapped. She didn't actually bite, but only because he jerked his hand away in a hell of a hurry.

"What do you care? Why do you give a damn?" she demanded. "As long as you can ride your stinking surfboard, so what if the Japs are in charge of things?"

He gave her a dirty look, but no more than a dirty look. He was too easygoing to relish screaming rows, let alone to smack her in the jaw. He wondered if something like that would knock some sense into her stubborn little head, but all he did was wonder.

Tears came harder than ever. "What are we going to do?" she wailed.

What do you mean we, *Kemo Sabe?* thought Oscar, who'd followed *The Lone Ranger* on the radio till he ended up in Hawaii—the local stations didn't carry it. But that wasn't fair. Nobody'd held a gun on him when he invited Susie here after the bomb blew her room to hell and gone. Oh, he'd had ulterior motives, but still. . . .

"I'll take care of you the best I can," he said.

Scorn blazed from her blue, blue eyes. "You can't even take care of yourself, Oscar."

"Oh, yeah? What do you call this?" His wave encompassed the apartment.

"What do I call it?" Susie spoke with deadly precision. "Not much, that's what I call it. This isn't *life*. This is just . . . drifting. Existing."

She was right, of course. Oscar knew that. It was part of what had attracted him to Hawaii in the first place. "Happens I like it," he said mildly. And even the most easygoing temper can fray. His voice rose: "If you don't, sweetheart, you can just darn well hit the highway." He pointed to the door.

He more than half hoped Susie would storm out through it. She didn't. She went pale under her sunburn. "Where would I go? What would I do?"

Go down to Hotel Street. Stand on a corner. Show a lot of leg. I don't care if the Japs are bombing downtown Honolulu right this minute—somebody'll pick you up in jig time. But Oscar swallowed that instead of saying it. Susie might have round heels—she hadn't wasted any time falling into bed with him—but she wasn't a pro.

What Oscar did say was, "Well, if you want to keep on staying here, try acting like it, okay?"

"Okay," she said in an unwontedly small voice. Off in the distance—not so very far in the distance—artillery rumbled. Susie involuntarily turned towards the sound. Then, with what looked like a distinct effort of will, she looked back to Oscar. "What do we do if . . . the Japs win?"

No, she wasn't so dumb. She could see what was in front of her nose, anyhow. "I don't know, babe," Oscar answered. "The best we can, I guess."

"They're going to, aren't they?"

"Sure looks like it to me." He didn't fancy it any more than she did. He didn't see much point in lying to her, though.

"I wish I'd never come here!" She'd said that before.

"Yeah, well . . ." Oscar shrugged. "A little too late to worry about it now, don't you think?" He thought it was a lot too late himself. He didn't tell her so. It would only have upset her more, and what could either one of them do about it? Not a damn thing, not that he could see.

JIM PETERSON HAD BEEN EAGER to get into the fighting. He'd been so eager, he'd volunteered to go from Navy officer to doughboy in one fell swoop. Now he'd seen some of the war up close, and he had only one conclusion—he'd been out of his goddamn mind.

He crouched somewhere in the cane fields north of Pearl City. A Jap machine gun was hammering away much too close. Bullets snarled past him. He'd acquired an entrenching tool from a skinny blond corporal who wouldn't need it any more. He dug like a man possessed. In an air fight, you had the advantage if you got the edge in altitude. Here on the ground, the deeper your hole, the better off you were.

By the time I'm done, this one will be deep enough to bury me in, he thought. Then he swore under his breath. That wasn't how he'd wanted to put it. No matter what he'd wanted, though, it was liable to be true.

Half the men holding this part of the line were sailors. They had plenty of spunk. As he'd been, they were eager for a crack at the enemy. But they didn't know the first thing about taking cover or supporting one another or ... anything about being an infantryman. Peterson didn't know much: only what he'd learned falling back from Kolekole Pass. But what he'd learned since the Japs sent their men into the Army's rear made him a seasoned veteran next to most of these guys.

He'd trained and trained and trained to fly a Wildcat. He knew how hard, how complex, that was. He'd never dreamt there was anything particularly hard about being an infantryman. He knew better now. Quite a few of these gobs would turn into pretty fair foot soldiers if they lived long enough. A hell of a lot of them would get killed before they learned what they needed to know.

A wet, slapping noise meant a bullet had struck home somewhere close by. The howl the wounded man let out meant it hadn't killed him right away. "Hang in there, Andy!" an American yelled. "I'll bring you in!" He came crashing forward through the growing sugarcane. All he thought about was saving his buddy. Saving himself never crossed his mind—either that or, more likely, he had not the foggiest idea how to do it.

"Get down!" Peterson shouted. "Get down, you stupid fool!" Maybe he said something stronger than *fool*; he didn't remember afterwards. Whatever he said, it didn't do a damn bit of good. The Japanese machine gunner was no doubt a louse, a stinker, a rotten, dirty son of a bitch. But he was no fool. If the American was generous enough to give him a perfect target, he'd take it. He squeezed off a quick, tidy burst—three or four rounds. The American who'd intended to rescue Andy crashed down before he got real close to him.

He wasn't dead, either. He started moaning for his mother. And *another* brave, stupid fellow hurried up to try to rescue both wounded men. He had no more idea how to go about it than the first would-be hero had, and he got shot, too.

"Oh, for Christ's sake!" Peterson muttered under his breath. They were liable to get bled white, greenhorns going forward and getting nailed till they ran out of greenhorns or the Japs ran out of ammo. The Japs hadn't shown any signs of running short.

If you want something done right, do it yourself, went through Peterson's mind. He did some more muttering, this time of the sulfurous sort. All three of those wounded men were screaming and moaning. He couldn't just leave them out there. They'd attract more suckers for that Jap to murder. Either that, or he'd start shooting them up for the fun of it. Peterson had seen a few samples of what the Japs called fun, and heard about more. He wouldn't have wished them on a mad dog.

Before he could ask himself what the hell he was doing, he scrambled out of his foxhole and crawled towards the wounded men. His belly scraped along the ground like a lizard's. He'd learned a thing or two, if not three. He wished he didn't have his rifle slung on his back. But one of the things he'd learned was that he couldn't afford to be taken alive. If the Japs wanted him, they'd have to pay for him—and he intended to save the last bullet for himself.

He almost bumped noses with a mongoose. Which of them was more surprised and appalled would have been hard to say. The mongoose scurried away. It reminded him of a weasel: all slithery grace. Heart thumping, he crawled on.

The thrashing in the cane up ahead wasn't coming from any mongoose. "Hey, up there!" Peterson hissed. "Who's hit worst?"

One of the men just kept calling for his mother. Another one, though, said, "Take Steve. He got a slug in the chest." That took balls: lying there shot and saying somebody else was worse off than you.

Steve turned out to be the one who wanted his mother. Andy had a wounded leg, the third guy a shattered right arm. "You can crawl," Peterson told him. "Follow me back."

"I don't want to leave Andy," the sailor said through clenched teeth—he wore a U.S. Navy armband on the left sleeve of a khaki shirt. He couldn't do much with one good arm, but Peterson didn't waste time arguing with him. He figured Steve would buy his plot if he wasted time.

Going back was ten times as bad as coming forward had been. He had to drag the wounded man behind him. After a while, Steve stopped moaning. Peterson wished he would start again. He didn't want to think he might be dragging a corpse. And, just to make matters worse, the Japanese machine gunner started spraying bullets around again. They made little *clip-clip-clip* noises as they cut through the cane. Peterson knew what kind of noises one of them would make if it cut through him. He knew what kind of noises he would make then, too.

A jumpy American almost shot him when he got back into the lines. He managed to persuade the kid that he wasn't Hirohito's brother-in-law. Steve was still breathing; Peterson managed some weary pride at that. Stretcherbearers took the injured man away.

"You did good, soldier," a sergeant said to Peterson, and then, his voice rising in surprise, "Hey! Where the hell you going?"

"Two more wounded out there," Peterson answered. "If I bring one, the other can make it back on his own. He's standing guard on his buddy."

"You bring him back and I'll make you a corporal on the spot," the sergeant promised.

For a Navy lieutenant to be thrilled at the prospect of getting two stripes on his sleeve was one of the more surreal things that had happened since the Japs hit Pearl Harbor. But Peterson was. He crawled back into the cane, hoping he would find Andy and the man whose name he didn't know.

They were still making noise, so it wasn't too hard. But he must have got overenthusiastic moving towards them, because the Jap machine gunner sent a long burst slicing after him. He flattened out like a toad after a truck ran over it.

Working a Springfield one-handed was a bastard, especially if that one hand was your left. But Andy's buddy had found a way. He'd propped the muzzle end of the rifle on a rock and aimed it in the direction of the Japanese. "Look at young Tom Edison," Peterson said. The man with the wounded arm managed a grin.

Instead of dragging Andy, Peterson got him up on his back. Andy was healthy enough to let out a yelp when he did. The Jap with the machine gun started shooting again.

A bullet hit. Peterson heard it. He didn't feel it, though. Andy didn't jerk. Awkwardly, Peterson looked behind him. The man with the wounded arm had been coming after him and Andy. Now the fellow sprawled bonelessly, his brains splashed over the dirt.

"Aw, shit," Peterson said softly. He brought Andy in. That sergeant saw him do it, and gave him the two stripes and a threaded needle. Two out of three wasn't bad. So he told himself, again and again. But remembering the guy who'd stopped a machine-gun round with his ear sucked all the pride out of the promotion. *That could have been me*, dinned in Peterson's head. *Sweet Jesus, that could have been me.*

COMMANDER MITSUO FUCHIDA LOOKED DOWN on Honolulu from his Nakajima B5N1. "Now, remember," Fuchida told his bombardier, "we don't want to hit too far inland this time, and we don't want to hit too far west. That's the Japanese part of town."

"Yes, sir." The bombardier sounded more resigned than anything else. Fuchida tried to remember how many times he'd told the man the same thing. More than he should have? Probably.

The Americans kept throwing up antiaircraft fire. They showed more spirit than Fuchida had expected. He'd thought they would surrender once they realized Japan had got the upper hand. But they were still putting up the best fight they could. It wouldn't be enough. Fuchida could see that. He suspected the enemy could, too. That didn't keep the Americans from making the fight.

A shell burst near the Nakajima. The plane staggered in the air. Fuchida didn't hear any shrapnel bang the fuselage or wing. "There's the Aloha Tower," he told the bombardier. "Do you see it?"

"Yes, sir," the man replied. "Shall we go after the docks again?"

"Yes. Plenty of warehouses there. The sooner the Americans get hungry, the sooner they do what we want."

Down went the stick of bombs. The B5N1 bounced in the air, not so rudely as it had from the near miss by the shell. Fuchida watched the bombs tumble towards their target. The bursts sent up clouds of smoke and dust. "Ha!" the bombardier said. "I think one of those hit the tower itself."

"Nicely done." Fuchida wanted to keep his crewman happy. He didn't care about the Aloha Tower one way or the other. It mounted no guns; as far as he knew, it stored no food. Still . . . "If you did hit it, that will be a blow to the Americans' pride."

"*Hai*," the bombardier said. "Pride is about all they have left, *neh?*"

"They still have soldiers and guns," Fuchida pointed out.

The bombardier laughed. "Fat lot of good those have done them."

In a strictly military sense, he was right. But the Japanese were monitoring radio stories from the mainland about the "Heroes of Hawaii." The Americans here might be doomed to failure. They still made good propaganda, and helped distract the people of the USA from the advances General Homma's army was making in the Philippines and the rapid push down the Malayan peninsula towards Singapore against the British.

Things are going our way, Fuchida thought. *We have to*

keep moving fast. If we let up, if we let our enemies catch their balance, we could be in trouble. But so far, everything is fine.

Other bombers were pounding the docks and the area just inland from them. Unopposed bombers could do dreadful things to cities. The Germans had shown as much over Rotterdam and Belgrade. Now Japan, having swept away American air power in Hawaii and the Philippines, was teaching the same lesson to Honolulu and Manila.

Fuchida wondered if the rumors he'd heard could be true. Had the Americans in the Philippines really let their planes get caught on the ground? The Japanese hadn't hit them from Formosa till a day after fighting opened here in Hawaii. People said General MacArthur was supposed to be a good commander. If he'd been caught with his pants down like that, though . . . A Japanese officer would have slit his belly to atone for the disgrace. The Americans seemed to lack the idea of seeking an honorable death.

They lacked all sorts of notions of honor. And yet no one could fault the courage with which they'd fought here in Hawaii. The contrast left Fuchida puzzled. How could courage come into being without honor?

The other thing that puzzled him was how so much courage sprang from so much wealth. The homes, the swarms of motorcars, the vast numbers of telephones and radios . . . All of it made a Japanese stare in astonished disbelief. The meat and vegetables in the shops had been a surprise, too, but they were starting to run low. Put everything together and it was amazing the Yankees weren't too soft to fight. Somehow, though, they weren't.

Fuchida swung the B5N1 back to the north for the short hop back to Haleiwa. All hops here were short, which saved fuel. Not all of what the bomber was burning had come off the *Akagi*. Quite a bit was taken from captured filling stations. The Americans, with all the petroleum in the world at their fingertips, hadn't thought to destroy much of what was in that stock to keep the Japanese from using it.

More antiaircraft shells burst around the bomber as Fuchida flew over the front. The Americans were falling back into the high ground that covered Honolulu from the north. They might be hard to root out of there. Fuchida shrugged in the privacy of the cockpit. The Army had done a good job so far—better than he'd expected. It should be up to this, too.

"Wish we had some more bombs on board, sir, so we could drop some on these fellows' heads," the bombardier said.

"We have people paying attention to them, I promise," Fuchida said dryly.

"I know that, sir," the bombardier answered. "But I want to do it myself."

"Every man in his place," Fuchida said. But the bombardier showed fine martial spirit. Of course the Japanese had it. They were a warrior race, schooled in the ways of *bushido*. It was the Americans who should have been without it. But they made warriors, too. Fuchida shrugged again. However strange that was, it was the truth.

He landed at that first captured airstrip by Haleiwa. Elsewhere in the north, combat engineers were making new runways with captured earth-moving equipment. Ordinary American builders had more bulldozers and other heavy machinery than Japanese military engineers—another example of American prodigality, or maybe just of American wealth.

"How did it go, sir?" a groundcrew man asked as Fuchida climbed out of the bomber.

"According to plan," he answered, and laughed—he sounded like Lieutenant Shindo. But it was true. "Just according to plan."

"Lousy Jap!" Kenzo Takahashi heard that shout every time he stuck his nose outside. "Lousy stinking Jap!"

It had been bad before. It was worse now that the Japanese were bombing Honolulu. That brought the war home to people for whom, even after Pearl Harbor, it hadn't seemed quite real. Hard to deny reality when you were out on the street because your house, and maybe your wife or your son, too, had been blown to smithereens.

The only good thing about being out on the street in Honolulu in January was that you wouldn't freeze, the way you might somewhere on the mainland. If you had a sweater, that was plenty. Even if you didn't, you'd get by. But if you were on the street and you saw a young man with golden-brown skin, high cheekbones, slanted eyes, and coarse black hair, you weren't going to wish him the top of the morning and ask him how he was.

"I'm not a Jap. I'm an American!" Kenzo had tried protesting the first few times people showered abuse on him. It had got him exactly nowhere, accomplished exactly nothing. It just made people yell at him even more. It had also almost got him into a couple of fistfights.

One of those would have happened if a cop hadn't broken it up. The policeman, a *haole*, hadn't wanted his thanks. "I ain't got much use for you, neither, kid," he said, "but there's too much real shit going on to waste time with pissant stuff. Get the hell out of here." Kenzo got.

He told Hiroshi about it. He didn't tell his father. He knew what his old man would have said: that it proved he ought to be saluting the Rising Sun and not the Stars and Stripes. He couldn't stomach that.

"I *am* an American, dammit," he raged, "even if the *haoles* can't see it."

"Yeah, I know. Me, too," Hiroshi said. "But you know what? It's not just the *haoles* yelling at us these days. It's everybody—Chinese, Koreans, Filipinos." His grin was haggard.

Kenzo only grunted. Part of that fell under *what can you expect?* Japan was at war with China, ruled Korea, and now had invaded the Philippines. But it still stung. Just as *haoles* in Hawaii looked down their noses at everybody else (with the partial exception of the Hawaiians themselves, and they weren't competition), the Japanese here thought themselves better than Koreans and Filipinos, and probably Chinese, too.

"You know how bad it is?" Hiroshi said. Kenzo shook

his head. His brother said, "Even the Puerto Ricans are yelling, 'Goddamn Jap!' these days."

"Oh, Jesus Christ!" Kenzo said, unconsciously echoing his father. There weren't many Puerto Ricans in Hawaii. The ones who were there were seen as thieves and crooks and grifters by everybody else. The story was that the governor of Puerto Rico lo these many years ago, asked for a shipload of laborers, had provided it by emptying the local jails and whorehouses. Kenzo didn't know if the story was true, but everybody told it.

Getting out on the Pacific in the *Oshima Maru* was something of a relief. Kenzo had never imagined he would think something like that. But his father, however loopy the old man's ideas were, didn't hate him. The other advantage of going to sea was not being there when the bombs went off. That didn't help so much, though, because Kenzo still worried about his mother.

As they pulled out his of Kewalo Basin, Hiroshi said, "Father, why not bring Mother on the sampan? That way, we'd all be safe together."

"I said this," Father answered. "She told me she didn't want to come. What am I supposed to do, drag her?"

Hiroshi didn't say anything to that. Kenzo wouldn't have known what to say to it, either. They just stood there listening to the engine. The sampan had enough fuel to get to Kauai or Maui, but so what? What difference did that make? Even if they got Mother aboard, they'd be nothing but refugees. And, for all Kenzo knew, the Japanese Army was already on the other islands. Even if it wasn't, it probably would be soon. The U.S. Army hadn't garrisoned them. They couldn't put up any kind of a fight.

Oahu, now, Oahu had put up a hell of a battle. *And a whole lot of good it's done anybody, too*, Kenzo thought bitterly. The fighting here couldn't go on much longer, either. The diesel throbbed under his feet. For how long would his father be able to keep it fueled? How much longer would the food last? What would people do when it started running out?

Starve, was what occurred to Kenzo. That might be a

reason to get off Oahu: the other islands had fewer people, and might have bigger reserves. Or they might not—with fewer people, maybe they'd got less in the way of supplies to begin with. That was probably how things went, all right. They seemed to be going the worst way they could.

VI

THE GARDENER WHO SPOKE FOR MAJOR HIRABAYASHI IN Wahiawa was named Tsuyoshi Nakayama. Some people called him Yosh. Till this mess started, Jane Armitage hadn't called him anything. She'd never had anything to do with him. What she and a few other *haoles* were calling him these days was Quisling. They were careful about where, when, and to whom they said it, though. Let the wrong ears hear and . . . Jane didn't know what would happen then. She didn't want to find out, either.

To give Nakayama his due, he didn't seem to relish being the occupiers' mouthpiece. He didn't shrink from the job, though. What the Japs told him to do and say, he did and said. They'd confiscated guns and food just after they took the town. Radios lasted only a couple of days longer. If Jane had had a little one, she might have tried to hide it. She didn't have a prayer with the big, bulky shortwave set. When a Japanese soldier carried it away, she felt as if he were stealing the world from her.

She soon discovered she was lucky she hadn't tried anything cute. Mr. Murphy, the principal at the elementary school, had had two radios. He'd given the Japanese one and secretly hung on to the other. Not secretly enough—somebody ratted on him.

Through Yosh Nakayama, Major Hirabayashi called the people of Wahiawa into the streets. Mr. Murphy, hands tied behind his back, stood in front of Hirabayashi. The officer spoke in Japanese. Nakayama translated: "This man disobeyed an order of the Imperial Japanese Army. The punishment for disobeying an order is death. He will receive the punishment. Watch, and think about him so this does not happen to you."

Two soldiers forced Mr. Murphy down to his knees. The principal looked astonished, as if he couldn't believe this was happening to him. He didn't seem afraid, which also argued that he didn't believe it. Surely the Japs would call it off once they'd taught him his lesson.

Major Hirabayashi drew his sword. Jane had seen it there on his hip before. She hadn't thought about it; it seemed about as useful in modern war as a buggy whip. Now, all at once, she noticed that the major had lovingly kept it sharp. The blade was slightly curved. The edge glittered in the sun.

Hirabayashi raised the sword above his head. With a sudden, wordless shout, he swung it in a gleaming arc of death. It bit into—bit through—Mr. Murphy's neck. The principal's head leaped from his shoulders. Blood fountained, amazingly red. Some of it splashed the soldiers who'd held the American. Mr. Murphy's body convulsed. The spasms went on for a couple of minutes. His head lay in the street. It blinked once before the features slackened into death's blankness.

Somehow, that blink sickened Jane worse than all the gore and the flopping. Had he *known* what had happened to him, even if just for a few seconds?

Some people in the crowd—women and men both—screamed. Several threw up. Some made the sign of the cross. A hulking six-footer who ran a hardware store keeled over in a faint. His wife, who barely came up to his chin, kept him from smashing his face on the asphalt.

Hirabayashi wiped his bloody blade on Mr. Murphy's trousers, then slid it back into the scabbard. He shouted something angry-sounding in Japanese. "You will obey," Yosh Nakayama translated. "If you do not obey, you will be sorry. Do you understand?" No one said anything.

Hirabayashi shouted again, even louder. Nakayama said, "He wants to know if you understand."

A ragged chorus of yeses rose from the crowd. Some of the people who'd crossed themselves did it again. Major Hirabayashi grunted again and turned his back. Nakayama gestured to the locals: it was over.

Singly and in small groups, they straggled back to their homes. Jane was alone—and had never felt more alone in her life. She'd seen Mr. Murphy every day since getting her teaching job here. He wasn't the most exciting human being ever born—what principal was?—but he was solid, competent, plenty likable if you didn't happen to be a fourth-grader in trouble.

Now he was dead. For a radio, he was dead.

Hardly anyone talked about the—murder? execution?— as the crowd drained away. Part of that, no doubt, was shock. And part of it probably had to do with fear over who might be listening. Somebody you'd lived across the street from for the last twenty years might sell you down the river to the Japs. How could you know, till too late? Why would you take the chance?

People in Russia and Nazi Germany and the countries Hitler had overrun had to make calculations like that. Americans? Even a month earlier, Jane never would have believed it. But if you didn't make those calculations, or if you got them wrong . . . you might be the next Mr. Murphy.

And it wasn't just the local Japanese you had to look out for. Jane had seen more than one *haole* sucking up to the occupiers. Some people had to be on the ins with whoever was in charge. If it was the usual authorities, fine. If it was a bunch of bastards with guns—and with swords; oh, yes, with swords—well, that was fine, too. There was one more thing Jane wouldn't have believed till she saw it with her own eyes.

She locked the door behind her when she got to the apartment. She hadn't been in the habit of doing that till the Japs came. It wouldn't help her a hell of a lot now, either. The rational part of her mind knew that. She locked the door anyway, because she wasn't feeling any too rational these days.

She wished she could fix herself a good stiff drink. But Fletch had taken most of the booze when he left (she'd been glad to see it go, too—then), and the rest had been confiscated along with the food. She was stuck with her own thoughts, no matter how much she hated them. The thunk of the sword as it slammed into Mr. Murphy's neck . . . That last blink after he was—after he had to be—dead . . .

"Oh, Jesus," she moaned: as close to a prayer as had passed her lips in years.

The worst of it was, she'd have to go out again for supper. The communal meals had started off bad, and were getting worse as stocks of this and that began to run out. She was damned if she knew what they would do in a few months.

"Damned is right," Jane muttered. And damnation might not wait for months. It might be only weeks away. She wondered how much food other people had given up, and how much the Japs had taken from groceries. How long would it last? How long *could* it last? "We'll find out."

She also wondered whether the occupiers gave a damn. Wouldn't they be just as happy if everybody on Oahu except maybe their few special friends starved to death? Then they wouldn't have to worry about keeping an eye on them any more.

With that cheery thought echoing in her head, she went to supper. It was rice and noodles and local vegetables and a small chunk of cheese that was starting to be past it. Before the Japs came, the food would have appalled her. Now all she cared about was that it filled her belly. Quantity had routed quality.

People had chatted over meals. No one said much this evening. Mr. Murphy's death hung over Wahiawa the way that cloud of black smoke had hung over Pearl Harbor for so long. Jane went straight home when she finished eating. She'd been on dishwashing detail the week before. All the women in town took turns at it. Not for the first time, Jane wondered why nobody had included the men. Who was going to suggest it to Major Hirabayashi, though? That . . . chopped the head off that idea. *Stop it!* she told herself fiercely. But she couldn't.

Two days later, somebody knocked at the door. Fear shot through her. These days, a knock on the door was likely to mean trouble, not a neighbor wanting to borrow a stick of butter. The knock came again: loud, insistent. Jane trembled as she went to open the door. She'd started taking in another lesson Americans should never have had to learn.

Tsuyoshi Nakayama stood there, with two younger local Japanese behind him. "You are Mrs. Jane Armitage?" he said. Jane nodded. He made a checkmark on a list. "Where is your husband, Mrs. Armitage?"

"I don't know. We were getting a divorce when—when the war started," Jane answered. That was true. No one could say it wasn't. She didn't want to tell him she'd been married to a soldier. Who could guess what he or Hirabayashi might do if she did? He could find out if he poked around. But even if he did, she hadn't lied.

The gardener just shrugged now. "You live here alone, then?" he asked. Jane's head went up and down again. Yosh Nakayama nodded, too. He wrote something else on the list. What was it? Jane couldn't tell. Not knowing alarmed her. Nakayama looked up. "We may run short of food," he said.

This time, Jane nodded eagerly. If he wanted to talk about food, he didn't want to talk about Fletch. Everybody had to worry about eating. Not everybody had to worry about a husband in the Army.

"I am going to give you turnip seeds and pieces of potatoes with eyes," Nakayama said. "You will plant them. You will grow them. You will take care of them. We hope we can start growing things to eat soon enough to keep from getting too hungry."

"Plant them where? How?" Jane asked. She didn't know the first thing about farming. *But it looks like I'm going to find out.*

"You have been assigned a plot," Yosh Nakayama told her. "I have tools for you." The young men behind him carried a spade, a hoe, a rake, and a trowel. They thrust them at Jane now. Nakayama went on, "Plenty of people here know what to do. Ask them. They will be in the fields, too. And the seeds come with instructions. Follow them. Follow them with care."

"Turnips?" Jane couldn't remember the last time she'd eaten a turnip. Back in Ohio, they fed hogs more often than people.

Nakayama shrugged. "They grow fast. You can eat the root and the greens. We have to do whatever we can. We will all be hungry soon. Other people will raise beans and corn and squash and whatever else we have. We need to work hard. Otherwise, we will be worse than hungry."

What about the Jap soldiers? Will they help us farm? But Jane didn't have the nerve to ask the question. She accepted the seeds and the quartered potatoes. All she did ask was, "Where will my, uh, plot be?"

"I will show you. Come on." He led her downstairs and out to the street. A whole stretch of lawn had been divided into sections with stakes and twine. Yosh Nakayama pointed to one of those sections. "This is yours. You will clear it and plant it."

"Clear it?" Jane echoed. The gardener just nodded impatiently. Jane looked down at her hands. They were nice and soft. The only callus she had was a small one on the middle finger of her right hand: a writer's callus. That was going to change if she had to dig out all that grass and plant vegetables. She sighed, not too loud. "What about bugs and things?"

"It is a problem," Nakayama admitted. Hawaii was chockfull of all kinds of bugs. You couldn't ship local fruit to the mainland for fear of turning them loose there. He went on, "We do have to try, though. If we don't try, we try starving instead. Which would you rather do?"

Jane had no answer to that, none at all.

FLETCHER ARMITAGE STARED IN DISMAY at the De Soto that had hauled his 105 down from the north coast of Oahu to not far from the outskirts of Honolulu. The De Soto sat on the grass, sad and lopsided. Fletch was glad the burst of Japanese machine-gun fire had missed him and his crew. And so it had, but there were fresh holes in the car, and three of its tires were flat.

One of the infantrymen he'd collared into serving the gun came up beside him and said, "Sir, if it was a horse, I'd shoot it."

"Yeah." Fletch had fixed flats before, but he saw no way in hell to do it this time. Two of those inner tubes didn't just have holes in them. They'd been chewed to pieces. Then he brightened. "Tell you what, Clancy. There's houses around here. If you and your buddies bring me back wheels with fresh tires on 'em, I won't care where they came from."

He'd started breaking rules when he commandeered the De Soto in the first place. He was ready to keep right on doing it if that meant he could go on hitting back at the Japs. Maybe somebody would make him go stand in a corner later on. He'd worry about that then, if there was a then.

"I'll see what we can do, Lieutenant," Clancy said with a grin. "Hey, Dave! Arnie! Come on!" He appreciated larceny. By now, he and his pals made pretty fair artillerymen, too. *Baptism by total immersion*, Fletch thought.

The soldiers grabbed their rifles and hurried off. If some civilian didn't fancy watching the wheels from his car walk with Jesus, a Springfield was a terrific persuader. Fletch hoped the men found a Jap to rob, not a *haole*. That wasn't fair, but he didn't give a damn. Every time he saw an Oriental face, he suspected its owner was on the enemy's side.

Airplanes droned by, high overhead. He gave the Japanese bombers the finger. That was all he could give them. Even as he did it, he knew a certain amount of relief: they weren't going to drop anything on *him*. If not for the Japs' air power, he thought the Army would have held them. *Yeah, and if ifs and buts were candied nuts, we'd all have a hell of a Christmas.*

As things were, the Americans were losing hope. He could feel it. They'd thought they could stop the Japs in front of Schofield Barracks and Wahiawa. Then those enemy soldiers appeared in their rear—and they hadn't been the same since. He had to admire the Japs who'd got over the Waianae Range. That didn't mean he didn't want to kill them all, but he knew they'd pulled off something astonishing. After its hasty retreat from a line that was just coming together, the U.S. Army simply hadn't been the same.

If it got shoved off the hills here, the next stops were Pearl Harbor and Honolulu. Fletch wondered if he'd have to aim his 105 up Hotel Street at the advancing Japanese. Soldiers and sailors would fight like madmen to hang on to the red-light district . . . wouldn't they?

He heard more airplane engines. These weren't droning—they were screaming. Fletch dove for a hole in the ground. He hadn't been on the receiving end of a dive-bomber attack for a while. He could have done without the honor now, too. The Japs cared for his opinion as much as they usually did.

One of the planes shot by overhead almost low enough for him to reach up and snag the fixed landing gear. The bomb went off much too close. It slammed his face down into the dirt. He spat mud, and tasted blood when he did it. That didn't surprise him. He was probably also bleeding from the nose and ears. He counted himself lucky: he was still breathing.

And, with luck, he still had his gun crew. Clancy and Dave and Arnie were off scrounging tires. Fletch climbed out of the hole. His dive left him even filthier than he had been a minute before. *They said it couldn't be done*, he thought vaguely. He felt vague, all right, as if he'd just taken a Joe Louis right to the jaw. Blast could do that to you.

Then, looking around, he couldn't decide whether to laugh or cry. The bomb had flipped the commandeered De Soto over on its back like a turtle, except turtles didn't catch fire when that happened to them. With or without new tires or wheels, it wasn't going anywhere ever again. That was almost funny.

But the bomb had also knocked his gun over on its side.

The 105 weighed almost two and a half tons on its carriage. That hadn't been enough to keep it upright. One wheel still spun lazily. Fletch wanted to kick the piece. He couldn't fire it. He couldn't move it.

"I can't do shit," he said, and heard himself as if from very far away.

Then he remembered the De Soto had been carrying ammunition. He yelped, sprang back into the hole in the ground, and flattened himself out again. Sure as hell, the shells started cooking off one after another as the flames got to them. That probably made for a spectacular fireworks display, but you wouldn't have wanted to watch from too close. Fletch, hugging the ground as shell fragments screeched past overhead, was much too close.

When the booming stopped, he cautiously looked up from the hole. He might have been a groundhog, curious about his shadow. What he was curious about was the De Soto, and whether any pieces of it bigger than a bobby pin were left. As far as he could tell, the answer was no.

Ten minutes later, the men from the gun crew came back, each of them rolling along a wheel with tire and inner tube on it. They stared at the overturned gun and at what was left of the car that had drawn it. "Fuck, Lieutenant," Clancy said, "why didn't you tell us to bring back a whole automobile?"

"Please accept my apologies, gentlemen," Fletch said with what he thought was commendable dignity. "If you can get one, please do. Some rope would be nice, too. Maybe we can get the gun back on its wheels." He thought he would need to do that pretty damn quick if he was going to do it at all. It wasn't just that he wanted to keep shooting at the Japs, though he did. But it looked as if the Army was going to retreat again, and he wanted to hang on to the gun if he possibly could. He'd brought it this far, after all.

What went through his head was, *Yeah, and a hell of a lot of good it's done me.* What had he accomplished with the 105? Oh, he'd blown up a tank. And he'd probably killed or maimed a bunch of Japanese soldiers he'd never seen. But so what? If he'd done anything really worth bragging about, would the U.S. Army have been down here on the outskirts of Honolulu? If everybody'd done something really worth bragging about . . .

If that had happened, some scout plane would have spotted the Japanese carriers and the invasion force before they plastered Oahu. The carriers would have been attacked and driven off or sunk. If the landing force had managed to hit the beach, it would have been slaughtered right there. As soon as the Japs wrecked the fleet and, worse, wrecked the local U.S. air power, that was the ballgame right there.

Clancy and Dave and Arnie didn't worry about such things—or if they did, they didn't show it. "We'll find you a ride, Lieutenant," Dave said. "Ain't nothin' to get all hot and bothered about." He nudged his pals. "Come on, guys. Let's get it done." Off they went, with as much swagger as if they were still fighting at Waimea.

Fletch wearily shook his head. He wished he could keep his pecker up like that. Japanese artillery started pounding the positions in front of him. The Jap guns were poorly sited; he could see their muzzle flashes. If he'd had anything to shoot back with, he would have made them sorry. But all he could do right now was watch. Few of their shells came back far enough to get close to him. None came close enough to make him dive for cover. He would have for some of them when the war got started. Misses that would have terrified him then he took for granted now.

What he didn't take for granted were men straggling away from the line the Japs were shelling. They looked as if they'd had themselves a bellyful of war and didn't want any more. "Get back to your positions!" he shouted at them. "What the hell do you think you're doing?"

Some of them just kept walking. They weren't running, but they weren't going to fight any more, either. One man said, "It don't make no fuckin' difference now. Shit, we're licked." Two or three others nodded.

"Get back to your positions," Fletch snapped. "That's an order, goddammit."

They ignored him. He didn't know what to do. If he picked up his rifle and tried giving that order again . . . Quite a few of them had rifles, too. They might not want to use them against the Japs any more, but he didn't think they'd be shy about turning them on him.

What was an army when soldiers stopped obeying officers? It wasn't an army any more, that was for damn sure. It was just a mob. That had happened to the Russians and the Germans at the end of the last war. Now Fletch saw it here.

The soldiers trudged past him. More followed in their wake. The Americans had done everything they could here. Now some of them—a lot of them—were deciding they couldn't do any more, and might as well save their own skins.

Was anybody still *at* the front? Would the Japs be along in another ten minutes? Fletch didn't want to meet them by himself. Unlike a lot of his countrymen, though, he didn't want to run away from them, either. He stood irresolute, peering north and west.

A shiny maroon Ford convertible drove up against the tide of retreating men. Clancy waved to Fletch. "Ain't this some snazzy hot rod?" he yelled from behind the wheel.

"It'll do," Fletch said, grateful his merry men hadn't got the hell out of there in that snazzy hot rod. "You have rope?"

Dave and Arnie hopped out of the Ford. Dave displayed a coil. He and Fletch fixed it to the gun, while Arnie tied the other end to the car's front bumper. Fletch waved to Clancy, who put it in reverse. The rope came taut. The tires spun, kicking up dust. Fletch figured either nothing would happen or the dead weight would pull the Ford's bumper off. But when the 105 stirred a little, hope also stirred in him.

He rushed to the gun and started pushing with all his might. "Come on, goddammit!" he yelled to Arnie and Dave. They joined him, grunting and straining. "We can do it!" *Maybe we can do it.* "Put your backs into it!"

"Give us a hand, you lazy bastards," Arnie growled at

three retreating soldiers. For a wonder, they did. For an even bigger wonder, the gun thumped over into its wheels.

Sweat ran down Fletch's face. He'd pulled something in the small of his back. He didn't give a damn. "That's the way," he panted. "Let's get her hitched up and. . . ." He stopped. After that, what else could he do but retreat, too?

THIS IS THE WAY THE WORLD ENDS, Jim Peterson thought. T. S. Eliot hadn't known a thing about it. When the British surrendered to the American colonists at Yorktown, their band had played "The World Turned Upside Down." Peterson's world was turning upside down under his feet. The little yellow men from Tokyo were walloping the tar out of their American foes. That wasn't supposed to happen. It wasn't supposed to be possible. But it was real, real as the stink that rose from him because he hadn't bathed in he couldn't remember how long.

Pearl City lay just north of Pearl Harbor. It housed sailors who'd been stationed there and civilians who'd worked there. It had been a pleasant little town. Now it was on the front line. Palm trees and Norfolk Island pines lay in the streets, uprooted by bombs and shells. What had been nice little homes were now smoldering, bullet-pocked rubble. As far as fighting went, rubble wasn't so bad. It gave better cover than it would have before it got smashed.

"Hey, Peterson," said the sergeant who'd given him his stripes. The man's name was Bill McKinley, and he answered to Prez.

Peterson just grunted. They crouched in a wrecked kitchen, peering out through the glassless window towards the north. A hole in the roof about the size of a cow let in sun and rain—sometimes both at once.

McKinley went on, "You take any money or any other shit off a dead Jap?"

"Nope." Peterson shook his head. "How come?"

"On account of if you did, I was gonna tell you to ditch it," the sergeant answered. "The Japs catch you with any of that stuff, they figured you killed one of their boys. They're even worse on you then than they are any other time."

"Not me." Motion up ahead made Peterson's finger tense on the trigger. Then he relaxed. It was just a mynah bird, hopping across a lawn looking for worms and bugs. The birds had no idea what war was all about. Peterson wished he didn't. He shot McKinley a sidelong glance. "You figure the Japs are going to catch us?"

"Don't get me wrong—I'm still fighting," McKinley said hastily. "But I don't see the cavalry riding over the hill in the last reel. Do you?"

Before Peterson could say anything, a gunshot made him flinch. He hated doing that, but couldn't help it. His only consolation was that almost everybody else did it, too. He said, "Looking at where we're at, I'd say we could use the goddamn cavalry right about now."

"Bet your ass," Sergeant McKinley said. "But if we ain't got it . . ."

That motion behind a hibiscus bush wasn't a mynah. Peterson brought up his rifle, fired, and ducked away from the window, all in one smooth motion. He worked the bolt to chamber a fresh round. The brass cartridge from the last one clinked on the linoleum at his feet.

"You're getting pretty good at this shit, Navy," McKinley said. By now, he knew about Peterson's disreputable origins.

"Up yours, Prez," Peterson said mildly. "You can't say I haven't had practice."

"You're still breathing, so you musta done something right." The sergeant laughed. "If you were in your right uniform, you'd be tellin' me what to do instead of the other way round."

"Damn near makes it worth my while," Peterson said, and McKinley laughed again. An American machine gun a couple of houses over fired a short burst, then a longer one. Very cautiously, Peterson went to the window and peered out. If the Japs were up to something, he wanted to find out what it was. Some men in the dark khaki that they wore were moving a few hundred yards to the north, but he didn't have a clear shot at them. He ducked away again.

"Well?" McKinley asked.

"Nothing much, I don't think," he answered. "I wish to hell this kitchen had two windows so we could look out from more than one place. Way things are, if a Jap sniper draws a bead on that one, he's liable to punch our tickets for us."

"You want to move? It's okay by me," McKinley said.

Before Peterson could answer, he heard freight-train noises in the air. He threw himself flat before the first shells started bursting. Japanese artillery was probably after that machine gun, but that meant it was coming down on his head, too. He was glad McKinley hadn't spoken sooner. If there was anything worse than being upright and out in the open when shellfire started coming in, he didn't know offhand what it might be.

"Just their lousy three-inch popguns," McKinley shouted through the din.

"Yeah, I know," Peterson answered. "But where's *our* artillery?" Most of it had been wrecked, and most U.S. artillerymen were likely dead. Jap fighters and dive bombers had gone after the American guns with everything they had. It made sense. Rifles and machine guns were just nuisances on the battlefield. Artillery killed.

Artillery also pinned down U.S. infantry so Japanese foot soldiers could advance. If you rose up to shoot at the Japs, you asked to get flayed by flying fragments. If you didn't, you had the enemy sliding around your flank.

Peterson and McKinley both rose up. You could take your chances with shellfire. Sometimes you had to. But if the Japs flanked them out of this position, where would they go? Into the Pacific, that was where. They had next to no place left to retreat.

And, sure enough, the Japs were coming. Both Americans fired. The Japanese soldiers went down. Some of them shot back. Others dashed past them, running all crouched over. Then they dove for cover and the ones in the rear advanced.

"Fire and move," McKinley said, slapping in a fresh clip. "It's pretty when you do it well, and those bastards know how."

"Terrific." Peterson snapped off another shot. This was one of the intricacies of ground combat he'd never imagined when he was flying fighter planes. The sailors coming up into the line from Pearl Harbor hadn't, either. Maybe some of them did now. A lot of them had got shot before they could learn.

A shell slammed into the house with a rending crash. The walls shook. Part of the roof that hadn't fallen in did now. A bullet came in through the window and clanged off a pot hanging on the far wall. Peterson waited for the American machine gun to start slaughtering the oncoming Japs. When it stayed silent, he glanced over to Sergeant McKinley. If Prez said this was the place to make a stand, he'd do it. This was part of what he'd signed up for.

But McKinley said, "We'd better fall back a couple of houses. We don't want 'em to go sliding around behind us and cutting us off. That's how you get captured." He made a horrible face.

"Right," Peterson said tightly, and made another one. They did fall back, and fell in with more Americans. It was only a tiny retreat. Now the Japs would have a tougher time breaking through. So Peterson told himself, over and over again. He had a devil of a time making himself believe it.

BY THE TIME THE TRAIN PULLED INTO THE STATION at Durham, North Carolina, Joe Crosetti, who'd never been out of California before, had stared out the window in fascination all the way across the country. Going over the Rockies had been something. Going across the Great Plains had been something, too—miles and miles and miles as flat as if somebody'd ironed them, half the time under a blanket of snow. Seeing all that white was pretty amazing by itself. It had snowed in San Francisco only two or three times in Crosetti's life, and never since he was a kid. But there it was, white and silent and beautiful.

Joe thought so, anyway. Sitting next to him was a guy named Orson Sharp, who'd got on the train in Salt Lake City. "It's just snow, for heaven's sake," he said. He was blond and pink-cheeked and earnest, with the start of a double chin. Aside from that, there was nothing soft about him; he was on the chunky side, that was all, the sort who would have played the line in football.

"Maybe it's just snow to you, but it's *snow* to me," Joe answered. Orson Sharp only shrugged. Joe got the feeling he thought that was funny to the point of being ridiculous, but was too polite to say so. Most fellows his age would have razzed Joe unmercifully if they thought something like that. Crosetti eyed Sharp with something approaching suspicion, wondering what his angle was.

As the train got farther east, it rolled past—sometimes rolled through—forests full of bare-branched trees. That bemused Joe, too. Some of the trees in San Francisco lost their leaves: some, yeah, but not all. These looked like a horde of skeletons with their arms held high.

Streams and ponds had ice on them—not all, but the smaller ones. That was something else Joe hardly ever saw back home. San Francisco never got very hot, and it never got very cold, either. As far as he was concerned, that was the way things were supposed to work.

When he said so, Orson Sharp did laugh. "Maybe where you come from," he said. "In Salt Lake, it can get up over a hundred and down below zero, too. Having the same weather all the time must get boring."

"It's not the same all the time," Joe said. He didn't think so, anyway. Maybe things looked different if you came from somewhere like Utah.

He hadn't needed long to decide Orson Sharp was a strange breed of cat. Trainees bound for Chapel Hill filled the car. Blue language filled the air. Most guys, among themselves, used profanity for emphasis, almost for punctuation. Joe did, and he'd never thought of himself as particularly foul-mouthed. But as far as he could tell, Sharp didn't swear at all.

He didn't drink coffee, either. When they went to the dining car, Joe guzzled the stuff. "Gotta get my heart started some kind of way," he said.

He wondered if Sharp would give him an argument, the

way temperance people did if you had anything good to say about the demon rum. But the would-be flier from Salt Lake just nodded and said, "Whatever you think is right for yourself."

"How come you don't think it's right for you?" Joe asked, quickly adding, "Don't answer if you think I'm sticking my nose in where it doesn't belong." He didn't want to get Sharp mad. Strange breed of cat or not, he seemed a pretty good guy.

And he smiled now. "That's okay. I don't mind. My religion teaches that we shouldn't smoke or drink alcohol or coffee or tea."

"Your religion?" Joe scratched his head. He knew some Jews, and knew they didn't eat pork or, if they were strict enough, shrimp or lobsters or clams, either. But they drank—and they drank coffee, too. And they smoked. Then, probably slower than it should have, a light went on in his head. "You're one of those Mormons, aren't you?"

"That's right." Orson Sharp laughed. "Haven't you ever seen one before?"

"Probably—San Francisco's a big city. But not that I ever knew of." Joe gave Sharp a curious look. Did he have three wives back home? Did his father have three wives, or thirty-three? That was what you heard about Mormons.

He suddenly realized Sharp knew just what he was thinking. "Well?" the other young man said. "No fangs, no horns, no tail."

Joe's ears got hot. He suspected he turned red. To keep from showing it, he raised his coffee cup to his lips. Then he lowered it. Even something as ordinary as drinking coffee all at once felt funny. "Heck with it," he said. "I'm a Catholic. There's people who don't like us, either. But we're all Americans first, right?"

Instead of coffee, Orson Sharp had a glass of apple juice by his plate of bacon and eggs and hash browns. He lifted it as if making a toast. "We're all Americans first. That's just right. And we're not America First, either."

"Damn straight!" Joe exclaimed. "Those damn fools helped the Japs catch us with our pants down in Hawaii.

You listen to them, nothing could ever happen to us, so we didn't have to worry about the war. Shows how much they knew, doesn't it?"

"Most of them have wised up since then," Sharp said, and Joe nodded. Pearl Harbor and the invasion had knocked the bottom out of isolationism. Just about everyone who'd believed in it had come to his senses since. The handful who hadn't were crackpots and chowderheads and pro-fascists: nobody worth paying any attention to.

"Listen," Joe said. "If we get a chance to pick roomies when we get where we're going, you want to stick together?"

"Sure," Sharp said. "Why not?" He stuck out his hand. In the clasp, it almost swallowed up Joe's.

Young Navy officers—ensigns and lieutenants, junior grade—met the train at the Durham station. They divided the newly arrived flying cadets into groups of fifty or so. The ensign in charge of Joe's group was a tall, green-eyed fellow named Don Ward. "I am your mother," he announced in an accent not far removed from where they were. Several people snickered. Ward waited till they were through, then repeated himself: "I *am* your mother. That's what they call my duty. I am supposed to shepherd you all through this here training course, and I aim to do it. I am also supposed to keep you out of mischief, and I aim to do that, too."

He got his charges aboard a bus that barely held them and their luggage. With much grinding of gears, the bus chugged towards Chapel Hill, about twelve miles away. The town proved tiny, the business block hardly more than a block long. Homes seemed pleasant enough, often separated from one another by ivy-covered walls. Except for the cedars, all the trees that would have given shade in the summertime were naked now. Without their leaves on them, Joe couldn't tell one kind from another.

The University of North Carolina dominated Chapel Hill. The bus wheezed to a stop in front of a three-story brick building. A native Californian, Joe didn't like brick buildings; they fell down in earthquakes. He laughed at himself, wondering when North Carolina had last had an earthquake. That would be okay.

"This is Old East," Ensign Ward told his charges. "It's almost a hundred and fifty years old—the oldest state college building in the country."

Maybe he thought people would be impressed to hear that. Joe was impressed, all right, but probably not the way Dillon had in mind. *Wonderful*, he thought. *They're sticking us in a goddamn ruin.*

"Old East will be your home while you're here. You will be four to a room." Ward waited out the groans, then went on, "This is not the worst introduction to Navy life. If you can't get the hang of living in each other's pockets, you probably don't belong here. Ships are crowded places. You need to get used to the idea. If you've already started pairing off, that's okay. We'll try to accommodate you."

Joe caught Orson Sharp's eye. The cadet from Utah nodded. In a voiceless whisper, Joe asked, "Got anybody else in mind?"

Sharp shook his head. "Not yet. How about you?" he answered, just as quietly.

"Nope," Joe said. "Want to trust to luck? Or do you see anybody you especially want to snag?"

"Luck will do," Sharp said. "This looks like a pretty good bunch of guys. How can we go wrong?" He and Joe were about the same age, but Joe felt ten years older. Somehow, the cadet from Utah had missed out on his share of cynicism. *How can we go wrong?* Joe thought. *Just wait and see. You'll find out how we can.* But Orson Sharp expected things to go right, not wrong. Joe didn't know whether to call him a Pollyanna or to envy him his confidence.

They got joined up with Bill Frank, who was from Oakland, and Otis Davis, who'd got on the train in St. Louis. Frank and Davis seemed to be a pair, too. That made Joe feel a little better—at least they weren't guys nobody else wanted anything to do with.

The room . . . wasn't as bad as Joe had expected. That was about as much as he could say for it. It wasn't big enough to swing a cat, but he hadn't looked for anything different there. The iron-framed bunk beds also came as no surprise. It did boast electricity and running water, even if you could tell they were add-ons. The people who'd built the room hadn't thought there would ever be such things.

Whoever built the room hadn't thought there would ever be such things as human beings in it, either. That was how it seemed to Joe, anyhow. The window was tiny and set high in the wall, so it let in only a little light and gave a lousy view. And the place had a peculiar kind of airlessness to it. It felt stuffy with the door open and got downright stifling with the door closed.

Otis Davis said, "I'm glad we'll be out of there before the hot weather comes. This place'd be a bake oven like you wouldn't believe."

"*Gevalt!*" Bill Frank said. "I hadn't thought of that."

"Only goes to show you're from the West Coast," Davis said. "If you came from a place where it gets hot and muggy, you'd know the signs."

"This is a pretty crazy town, not even big enough for a train station," Joe said.

Don Ward stuck his head into the room. "Supper at 1800," he announced. "That's an hour and a half from now. Lights out at 2130. Reveille tomorrow—and every day—at 0530. Tomorrow you'll draw your clothes and do another pile of paperwork. And after that, gentlemen"—his grin went hard and ruthless—"we put you to work."

Joe was still slow at translating military time into what he was used to. He said, "Lights out at half past nine, sir? Is that right?" He hadn't gone to bed that early since he was thirteen years old.

But Ward only nodded. "That is correct, Mr. Crosetti." People didn't have any trouble remembering Joe's last name once they heard it. Accurately interpreting the expression on his face, Ward added, "You'll find enough to do to tire yourself out by then. Trust me, Mr. Crosetti—you will." And, leaving that promise behind, he went down the hall to pass the word to the next dorm room.

* * *

"So sorry, Jiro-san," Tomatsu Okamoto said nervously. "So sorry, but I haven't got any more fuel to sell you. I'm all out."

Flanked by his sons, Jiro Takahashi glowered at the man from whom he'd been buying diesel fuel for years. He'd known this day was coming, but he hadn't expected it so soon. "You had plenty day before yesterday," he growled. "Where did it go? Did you drink it?"

Okamoto laughed nervously. "Not me," he said. "The Army confiscated everything I had left. They said they had to keep their trucks running as long as they could."

"Does anybody else have any?" Jiro asked. "Do you know?"

"I don't know, not for a fact, but I wouldn't bet on it," Okamoto answered. "I'm not a big operator, not even close. If they're down to taking away *my* stock, they've already sucked the others dry."

Jiro nodded. That made more sense than he wished it did. "What am I going to do now?" he asked, not so much of old man Okamoto as of the whole uncaring world around him. "How am I supposed to take the *Oshima Maru* out if I can't get fuel for her?"

"Weren't you talking about knowing somebody who could fit her out with a mast and sail, Father?" Hiroshi said. "It's about time."

"Yes, I was talking about that," Jiro said. "But I don't know how long it will take. I don't know how much it will cost. Jesus Christ!" He clapped a hand to his forehead. "I don't even know if that Doi fellow is still alive."

"If he isn't, it'll take longer," Kenzo said.

Hiroshi laughed. Even old man Okamoto laughed. Jiro glared at his younger son. What kind of a joke was that? An *American* joke, that was what. Jiro didn't think it was funny (though he might have if Okamoto had told it). It was just annoying to him.

"Eizo Doi, the handyman fellow?" Okamoto asked. Jiro nodded. Okamoto said, "He's still around—at least, I saw him three or four days ago. You think he can put a sail on a sampan?"

"I don't know for sure. He's talked about it," Jiro answered. "If he can, I'm still in business, whatever business there is. If he can't . . ." The fisherman spat on the sidewalk. "If he can't, I have to find something else to do."

"Like what?" Okamoto asked with interest. Jiro only shrugged. Except for his stint in the fields, he'd been a fisherman all his life. He didn't know anything else. He didn't want to know anything else.

"What are we going to do if we can't put to sea today?" Hiroshi asked.

Jiro shrugged again. Again, he had no idea. Reiko would be surprised to see him and their sons home so early. Whether she'd be happy to see them . . . That was liable to be another story.

Hiroshi and Kenzo and he had just started back from old man Okamoto's when Japanese bombers appeared overhead. The air-raid sirens didn't begin to wail until after antiaircraft guns opened fire and bombs started whistling down. "Oh, Jesus Christ!" Jiro exclaimed in dismay. His sons both swore in English.

He wasn't so frightened as he might have been. The Japanese planes had been in the habit of dropping most of their bombs farther east, on the *haole* part of town. The ones that had hit around here had seemed like accidents— to everyone except the people they landed on, of course.

But things were different this morning. This morning, bombs rained down all over Honolulu. When one burst a couple of hundred yards ahead, it sounded like the end of the world. If it had burst any closer than that . . .

Kenzo grabbed him by the arm. "We've got to find some cover, Father!"

He was right. Jiro could see that. But where? Farther east, where things were more open, they'd dug air-raid trenches. Not many of those here, not with concrete and asphalt covering so much of the ground. Not many cellars to huddle in, either; hardly any buildings in Honolulu had them.

His younger son pointed to a deep doorway. That would have to do. It would, unless a bomb burst right in front of them—or unless the building came down on top of them. Jiro did his best not to think of such things.

More and more people crowded into the doorway. Women screamed when bombs burst close by. So did several men. Others cursed in a variety of languages. So did several women. Neither the men's screams nor the women's curses affronted Jiro the way they would have under different circumstances. He was almost frightened enough to piss himself. Why should anyone else be different?

Hiroshi pointed up into the sky. "One of them's coming down!" he shouted in Japanese. Then he said what was probably the same thing in English.

Sure enough, a Japanese bomber trailing smoke and fire plummeted out of the sky, swelling enormously as it did. Jiro wondered about the men inside. Were they dead? If they weren't, what were they thinking as they plunged to their deaths? Could they keep the Emperor in their minds? Or did bright panic swallow everything else?

Panic swallowed everything else in the voice of a woman by Jiro as she shrieked, "It's coming down on us!"

Jiro wanted to call her a stupid idiot. He wished he could. But she was right. He started to scream himself when he thought the doomed bomber would smash into the building in whose doorway he huddled. It didn't. It crashed into a laundry half a block away. A fireball erupted—the plane must have had almost a full load of fuel on board. Blazing fragments pinwheeled off and went flying along the street.

"Come on!" Now Jiro grabbed his sons instead of the other way around. "We can't stay here. That fire will burn this whole block."

They had to fight their way out of the doorway. Some people couldn't think of anything but the moment's shelter. But what good was staying in the roasting pan if it was about to go into the oven?

Bombs kept screaming down. The Takahashis weren't safe in the street, either. But they had to get away from the spreading fire—if they could. "This whole part of town is liable to burn!" Kenzo shouted.

"We'd better get Mother out, if we can," Hiroshi said. "I wish she'd been willing to get on the sampan with us."

"So do I," Jiro said. Fear for Reiko rose like a choking cloud within him. Some of it turned to fury. "And I wish the Americans had surrendered a long time ago. They can't win. They can't hope to win. They're the ones who are making Japan do this to Honolulu."

His sons looked at each other. Their shoulders went up and down in identical shrugs. Those could have said, *He may be right.* Jiro didn't think they did. He thought they meant, *He's crazy, but what can you do?* That only made him angrier. Before he could say anything more, though, Hiroshi said, "We can worry about that another time, Father. For now, let's see if we can get back to the apartment and make sure Mother's all right."

Inside Jiro, the rage collapsed. The fear didn't—it kept growing. He nodded brusquely. "Yes. Let's do that."

Kenzo had been right. The burning bomber hadn't started the only fire in the Asian part of Honolulu. Streets and alleys were crowded here. People packed together far more tightly than they did on the *haole* east side. That didn't bother Jiro; to him, it was water to a fish. If anything, Honolulu was less crowded than he remembered cities in Japan being. But once fires got going here, they had no trouble spreading. And the narrow streets and the rubble choking them made it hard for fire engines to come to the rescue.

Bombs kept on falling, too. Jiro ignored them. Some people, like his sons and him, were trying to push deeper into the city to find their loved ones. Others were fleeing towards the Pacific. There, if anywhere, they'd be safe from the spreading flames.

And some people simply lay where they had fallen, struck down by blast or flying fragments of bomb casing or falling debris. In a handful of horrible minutes, Jiro saw more ways the human body could be mangled than he'd ever imagined. He had to step over bodies and pieces of bodies. He had to step over writhing, howling, bleeding people who weren't dead yet, too. Part of him wanted to

help them, but he didn't think he could do much for most.
And if he'd tried, he never would have got back to the
apartment. There were too many wounded, and they would
have taken too much time.

He and his sons were getting close, but the flames and
smoke up ahead were getting thicker. Somebody coming
the other way shouted in Japanese: "Go back! You can't go
any farther. It's all fire up ahead. You'll just kill yourselves."

Jiro and Hiroshi and Kenzo looked at one another.
None of them said anything, or needed to. They plunged
ahead with no more hesitation than that. Jiro knew a moment of somber satisfaction. The boys might not be everything he would have hoped for, but they were no cowards.

Courage, here, helped not at all. The shouting Japanese
man proved right. Fire and smoke blocked the way forward. Jiro coughed and hacked as if he'd smoked a hundred packs of cigarettes all at once. Hiroshi and Kenzo
were coughing, too. But their faces remained grim and determined. They were going to go forward even if it killed
them.

And it was liable to. Jiro realized his sons would retreat
only if he spoke first. He also realized he had to. "We can't
get through this way. Can we go back around and try from
the side?"

"I think we'd better, Father." Soot stained Kenzo's face.
Sweat streaked it. He didn't seem to know he had a burn
on his cheek. "We'd have more of a chance."

They had no chance pushing straight ahead. Jiro could
see that. He led the way. His sons followed. He went west,
not east. The Japanese overhead were still bombing more
heavily towards the east. That was where the *haoles* lived,
where their enemies lived.

Or some of their enemies, anyway. A round-faced man
with Asian features sitting in the street cradled a dead
woman in his arms. Tears ran down his face as he howled
curses to the uncaring sky in singsong Chinese. He didn't
seem to notice when the Takahashis ran by, which might
have been just as well.

The Chinese man would have hated Jiro just then. Jiro didn't hate him. He felt a horrid sympathy for him and with him, in fact. *That could be me, holding Reiko.* He muttered to himself, trying to repel the evil omen.

Panting, he went around a corner—and dug in his heels to stop as fast as he could. Burning cars up ahead made the street an inferno. Heat blasted into his face. He went up another block, only to find another fire.

People were running away, not going towards the flames. Jiro scanned faces, hoping to see Reiko's. He didn't, which only made his fear worse. "Come away, *baka yaro!*" someone yelled at him. "You can't do anything here!"

He looked to his sons. "What do you think?"

"We'll get trapped if we stay much longer," Hiroshi said. "But I'll go on if you want to." Kenzo nodded.

No, they weren't cowards, even if they were . . . Americans. And Jiro's older son had thrown the choice back on his shoulders. He'd hoped one of the boys would make it for him. No such luck. He ground his teeth. "We can't go there," he said. They didn't argue with him. He wished they would have. Because they didn't, he had to spell everything out himself: "If we can't get there, we can't do your mother any good. We have to hope the place isn't burning, and that she got out, and we just haven't seen her."

His sons nodded. Kenzo cursed in English. He was cursing Japan, but Jiro didn't try to stop him. It wouldn't change anything anyhow.

Neither Kenzo nor Hiroshi made the slightest move to withdraw from the advancing flames. Jiro realized they were leaving that to him, too. Part of him wanted to rush forward, into the fire, and embrace oblivion. But Reiko might be all right—and, in any case, the boys needed someone to keep an eye on them and make sure they stayed out of trouble.

"We'd better get away, then," he said. Only when he started back down towards the ocean did Hiroshi and Kenzo move. He reached up to put an arm around each of their shoulders. They weren't everything he'd wanted in sons, but he could have done worse as well as better.

* * *

FLETCHER ARMITAGE SET A HAND ON THE BARREL of his 105. He felt like a cowboy saying good-bye to his favorite horse. He was out of ammunition for the gun. He had no idea where to get more, or how soon it might come up if by some miracle he found out.

After more than a month of fighting as hard as it could, the American Army was visibly starting to come to pieces now. It had done as much as flesh and blood could do—and that hadn't turned out to be enough. Small-arms fire rattled in front of Fletch's position, and off to the left flank, too. The end hadn't come yet, but it was getting closer.

He glanced over to the shiny Ford his infantrymen-turned-gun-bunnies had shanghaied. The car had three flats, the same as the De Soto had had a few days earlier. It wasn't going anywhere. Maybe his merry men could commandeer another one. What point, when the gun had no shells?

If he'd had a horse and needed to deny it to pursuing Indians, he would have shot it. Instead, he took the breech block out of the 105. A stream ran down from the mountains not far from where the gun rested. He carried the heavy steel casting to the bank and threw it in the water. He'd picked a place where the flow was turbulent. As he'd hoped, bubbles and foam hid the breech block from prying eyes. The Japs might get their hands on that 105, but they wouldn't be able to do anything with it.

Wearily, he trudged back to what was now a Quaker cannon. His makeshift crew stood by the gun, waiting to see what happened next. Fletch wished he knew. He said, "Well, boys, I made artillerymen out of you for a while. Now it looks like I've joined the infantry."

Clancy and Arnie and Dave looked at one another. Clancy talked more than either of the other two. "No offense, Lieutenant, but you picked a shitty time to go slumming."

In spite of everything, Fletch laughed. "They say timing's everything." He reached up and touched the Springfield slung on his shoulder. "I haven't quit fighting. I don't intend to, either."

As if to mock him, the rattle of gunfire from the left got louder. It also moved farther south, down towards the sea—*makai*, they said here, without seeming to know that wasn't really an English word. The Japanese were pushing forward, the Americans falling back. That was how it had gone since the beginning. But the Americans couldn't fall back any more, not if they were going to have any real chance of holding on.

They were falling back anyhow. No doubt that said they had no real chance. Fletch scowled. He didn't want to think about that. He said, "We'd better move back towards Honolulu. Things are still holding together there, or they were the last I heard."

"We'd better move back somewhere, that's for damn sure," Clancy said.

The other two enlisted men nodded. Arnie said, "If we don't, the Japs are liable to cut us off."

He stopped right there. He didn't need to say another word. If advancing Japanese soldiers cut them off, they were liable to capture them. Nobody in his right mind cared to chance that.

"Come on," Fletch said harshly. "Let's get going."

Off they went, retreating to the south and east. They weren't the only ones—far from it. Singly and in small groups like theirs, other soldiers tramped along the side of the road or out in the middle of it. Clouds drifted overhead. A spatter of rain fell, though the sun never disappeared. The landscape was one of almost unearthly beauty: jungle-clad hills to the north, palm trees and blossoming hibiscus close at hand, mynahs and bluish-faced zebra doves pecking for whatever they could find, the sapphire sea visible to the south.

Where beauty failed, it failed because of man rather than nature. Ahead, Honolulu lay mired in smoke after the latest Japanese bombing attack. If Fletch turned his head to look west, he could see more ruin in Pearl Harbor. He didn't. He was too stubborn.

But when he looked around, he saw the ugliness in his comrades and himself. They were scrawny and filthy and unshaven. They smelled bad. At least half of them had minor wounds. They all had the hangdog air of beaten men.

That was one more thing Fletch had no idea how to cure. He was sure he had that same hangdog air himself. Oahu *was* going to fall. It would fall sooner, not later, too. And what would the Japs do with all the soldiers they captured then? What would they do *to* them? *Whatever they want to*, Fletch thought, and shuddered.

Somewhere not far away, an officer was shouting frantically, trying to get men to form a defensive line. "Come on, you sorry bastards!" he howled. "We've still got a chance as long as we don't quit!"

Fletch gathered up his erstwhile gun team by eye. "Let's go," he said.

They didn't argue with him. They showed no great enthusiasm, but they went along. Maybe they were also wondering what would happen if and when they had to lay down their arms. That one gnawed at Fletch.

Because it gnawed at him, he shoved it to the back of his mind. He found the loud officer—a captain—behind a bougainvillea hedge. "What do you need, sir?" he asked.

"Fucking everything!" the captain exclaimed. Then he amplified that. Pointing north towards the hills overlooking Honolulu, he said, "We've got to stop the advancing enemy."

"But, sir—" Fletch pointed west, the direction from which he'd come. "The Japs are over there."

"I know *that*, goddammit," the captain said impatiently. "But they're sneaking down through the hills, too, to get on our flank and rear."

Fletch didn't know why he was surprised. If the Japs could get men over the Waianae Range, these lower, less rugged hills would prove no great challenge to them. But he couldn't help asking, "Why didn't we have men up there to stop them?"

"In that jungle? Who would have figured they could get through it?" the captain said, proving some people had trouble learning even from experience. It wasn't the captain's fault alone, of course. His superiors had to have the same attitude. Ostriches eventually pulled their heads out of the sand and ran, didn't they? That only proved they were one-up on the top brass in the Hawaiian Department.

"Uh, sir?" Fletch gestured for the captain to step aside with him for a moment. The other officer did. In a low voice, Fletch said, "Meaning no disrespect, sir, but if they're coming at us from the north and from the west, we are really and truly screwed."

The captain nodded. "Yes, I realize that. And so, Lieutenant? Have you heard an order to surrender?"

"No, sir," Fletch said.

"Neither have I. That being so, we had better keep fighting, don't you think?" As if to underscore the captain's words, mortar bombs started whistling down not nearly far enough away. The captain and Fletch both threw themselves flat on the ground before the first one burst. Jagged fragments of steel hissed and whistled through the air. A soldier cried out, sounding startled and hurt at the same time. The captain started shouting again without raising his head more than a couple of inches: "Stay ready, men! They may try to follow this up with foot soldiers!"

"Christ!" Fletch said. "Are they down this far already?"

Before the captain could answer, Japanese rifle fire did it for him. The Arisaka rifle the Japs used sounded less robust than the Springfield. It was only .256 caliber, and didn't have quite the stopping power of the bigger, heavier American round. The Arisaka had proved plenty good enough, though.

Men began slipping away from the captain's makeshift line. He cursed them with weary hopelessness. Fletch understood that. It was exactly the way he felt himself.

CORPORAL TAKEO SHIMIZU HADN'T KNOWN what to expect from Honolulu. It sprawled ahead of him now, hard by the Pacific. The buildings were large and solid, in the Western style. All the same, it couldn't have held much more than half as many people as Hiroshima, the Japanese city closest to his farm.

Here and there, in little stubborn knots, the Americans

still fought hard. But now that resistance began to feel like the last spasms of some dying thing. The Japanese could bypass the men who did keep battling, because in a lot of places there weren't any. That let them surround the pockets of diehards and dispose of them at their leisure.

When Shimizu sent young Shiro Wakuzawa out to scrounge supplies for the squad as the sun sank in the west, the first-year soldier went off with a sigh. His squadmates murmured, "Hard work!" in sympathy. Shimizu didn't care. Somebody had to do it. He'd done it himself often enough in China, before he got promoted.

Wakuzawa came back with a big burlap sack slung over his shoulder and an enormous smile on his face. "You look like the monkey who found the apple tree," Shimizu said. "What have you got in there?"

"Wait till you see, Corporal-*san*." Wakuzawa let the sack down on the grass by the fire the Japanese had started. The fire was purely force of habit; Hawaiian nights didn't come close to requiring one. As the youngster reached into the sack, he went on, "I came across a grocery store that hadn't been looted empty."

"Ahhh!" the whole squad said as one man. They said it again when Wakuzawa took out three cartons of mild, flavorful American cigarettes. Boxes of crackers followed, and then Wakuzawa's triumph: can after can of meat, its pink glory displayed against a dark blue painted background. Big yellow letters told what it was, but Shimizu couldn't read the Roman alphabet.

"Does anyone know what it says?" he asked.

"It's called 'Spam,' Corporal," Senior Private Yasuo Furusawa answered.

He'd always struck Shimizu as a bookish type. "How do you know?" the corporal asked.

"My father is a druggist in Hiroshima," Furusawa said. "I was learning the trade till I got drafted. Some of the medicines he got came from the West, so I had to learn the characters the *gaijin* use."

The Spam cans opened with keys conveniently soldered to them. The meat inside them looked just like the tempting illustration. The soldiers hacked it into rough slices with their bayonets and ate it on crackers. Some of them toasted the Spam over the fire first; others didn't bother. Shimizu didn't—he was too hungry to care. He wolfed down the meat.

"That's one of the most delicious things I ever ate," Senior Private Furusawa said with a sigh of pleasure.

"*Hai. Honto*," Shimizu agreed; he'd been thinking the same thing. "Even better than sashimi, if you ask me. Why don't we have things like this in Japan?" He took a pack from one of the cartons, opened it, and began to smoke. "This is better tobacco than we get at home, too. We've already found that out."

"It's ours now, by right of conquest," somebody said.

"*Banzai!* for Wakuzawa, who conquered it for us," somebody else added. A soft chorus of "*Banzai!*"s rang out. Shiro Wakuzawa blushed like a schoolgirl. Corporal Shimizu hid a smile. Wakuzawa might be only a lowly first-year soldier, but he was the hero of the moment.

"I don't remember the last time I felt so full," Furusawa said. "I want to go to sleep right where I'm sitting."

Several soldiers incautiously nodded. "You'd better not," Shimizu said. "We'll have sentries out through the night. Never can tell what the Americans might do if they catch us all snoring here. Furusawa, you'll take the first watch."

"Yes, Corporal," the senior private said. That was work, but not too bad. At least he wouldn't have his sleep interrupted, the way the men who came later would.

"And then tomorrow," Shimizu went on, "tomorrow, I think, we push on into Honolulu at last." He wondered how hard the Americans would fight for the city. Clearing them out one house at a time, one block at a time, would be expensive and leave the place in worse ruins than it was already. He shrugged. It would be as it was; he couldn't do anything about it any which way. He rolled himself in his blanket and fell asleep.

He slept through the night—one of the privileges of his rank was that he didn't have to stand sentry. He woke just before sunrise. Hawaii's unfamiliar birds were calling. He got up and stretched, then went behind a tree to ease himself. Spatters of gunfire came from the east, but only spatters. Maybe it wouldn't be too bad. He tried to make himself believe it.

Smoking one of those smooth American cigarettes helped. And then, with the air of a magician pulling a rabbit out of a hat, Shiro Wakuzawa produced three more cans of Spam. They made as fine a breakfast as they had a supper. The other privates in the squad pounded Wakuzawa on the back and told him what a fine fellow he was.

Such displays were beneath a corporal's dignity. But Shimizu was glad to have something good in his stomach, too. He told himself he'd go a little easier—only a little, mind—on Wakuzawa for a while. The kid had earned some respect.

Cautiously, the squad moved forward. Shimizu preferred the fields where they had been fighting to the houses that surrounded him now. Who could say how many big, fierce American soldiers they were hiding?

Things stayed fairly quiet. A machine gun in a brick building made its presence known too soon. If the gunner had held off a little longer, he could have slaughtered the Japanese as they came forward across the grass in front of the building. As things were, they got the chance to take cover.

The gunner seemed to have all the ammunition in the world, and to enjoy hosing it around. Shimizu crouched behind some rubble. He wasn't going to stick his nose out unless ordered. Sooner or later, soldiers to the north or south would outflank that machine gun. Till they did, going straight at it was a recipe for suicide.

About halfway through the morning, the machine gun fell silent. Shimizu sat tight. Maybe the American had run out of ammo after all. Or maybe—and more likely—he was just waiting for his foes to think he had.

But then Senior Private Furusawa called, "Corporal! There's an American soldier coming forward with a white flag!"

That made Shimizu stick his head up. Sure enough, a tall Yankee with a flag of truce strode towards him. A nervous-looking local Japanese man stuck close to the soldier's side. "What do you want?" Shimizu called.

The American spoke in English. Without a word of the language, Shimizu could hear how bitter he sounded. The translator said, "Captain Trexler wishes to seek surrender terms for U.S. forces on Oahu." He spoke old-fashioned Hiroshima dialect. Had he been one of the men fooling Japanese soldiers? If he had, he would pay.

Next to the other, though, that was a small thing. If the Americans were surrendering . . . *If they're surrendering, I won't get shot*, Shimizu thought happily. "I will take the captain back through our lines," he said aloud. The local Japanese spoke in English. With a curt nod, the American came on.

VII

COMMANDER MITSUO FUCHIDA ADJUSTED THE CAP OF HIS white dress uniform as he walked up to Iolani Palace to take part in the surrender ceremony. The cap, with its anchor-and-chrysanthemum badge, felt odd on his head. He was more used to a flying man's leather helmet that covered his ears.

He turned to Commander Minoru Genda, who walked along beside him, also in dress uniform. Honolulu's bright sun flashed from the two silver chrysanthemums on each of Genda's gold shoulder boards. Like Fuchida's, those shoulder boards were striped with an aviator's blue. "Congratulations," Fuchida said. "You are the architect of this day."

Modest as usual, Genda shook his head. "Admiral Yamamoto planned the attack," he said. "And you so ably led the fliers. Both of you deserve far more credit than I do."

Although burly General Tomoyuki Yamashita and his aides stumped along ahead of the Navy officers, Genda said not a word about what the Army had contributed to the conquest of Oahu. Fuchida understood that. He was sure Yamashita had not a single good word for the Navy, either, though without it the soldiers the general led could not have come within five thousand kilometers of Hawaii.

Iolani Palace, luckily, had not suffered much during the Japanese bombardment of Honolulu. Ornamental plaster and cement work covered the brick walls. Cast-iron columns with fancy floral capitals upheld the deep veranda on the second floor. Shorter but otherwise similar columns there—these with a fancy iron balustrade between them—helped support the roof.

Atop the palace, the flags of the United States and the Territory of Hawaii still fluttered. The territorial flag—also the flag of the former Kingdom of Hawaii—amused Fuchida. The Hawaiians had been doing their best to please and appease Britain and the USA at the same time. Red, white, and blue stripes covered most of the field; the Union Jack occupied the canton. Much good such pandering had done the Hawaiians. The United States annexed their islands anyway.

And now Hawaii had a new master. The territorial flag might go on flying. The Stars and Stripes would be coming down. The Rising Sun would wave in their place.

A low, broad stairway led up into the palace. General Yamashita tramped up the stairs as if he intended to capture the place single-handed. Captain Kiichi Hasegawa, skipper of the *Akagi*, led the naval delegation. The *Akagi* and the *Soryu* would stay in Hawaiian waters to defend the new conquest against attack from the American mainland. The damaged *Kaga* was already under repair in Japan. Admiral Nagumo had taken the other three carriers west to aid the Japanese advance through the Dutch East Indies.

At the top of the stairway, an American honor guard came to attention and presented arms as the Japanese dignitaries approached. General Yamashita brushed past the American soldiers as if they did not exist. The Navy officers, Fuchida among them, did the same. How could any men who were surrendering imagine they still kept their honor?

Just inside the entrance stood three weary-looking Americans and a nervous local Japanese man in a business suit. The latter bowed and said, "I am Izumi Shirakawa. I am the interpreter for the Americans. I present to you Admiral Kimmel, General Short, and Governor Poindexter." He turned and spoke in English, explaining what he'd just said.

Admiral Kimmel spoke. Shirakawa turned his words to Japanese: "He says he hopes you will use the Americans in the spirit of bravery with which they fought."

General Yamashita grunted. "Let's get on with it," was all he said. Kimmel's face fell when the interpreter translated that.

Governor Poindexter, who was older than the two military men with him, said, "This way to the Throne Room, gentlemen. That is where the Territorial Legislature meets, and so we thought it fitting that. . . ." He ran down, like a watch in need of winding.

"Where you surrender does not matter," Yamashita said. "That you surrender matters."

Air seemed to leak out of the governor. He turned and walked into the palace. Admiral Kimmel followed. General Short, who wore cavalry breeches tucked into shiny boots, paused for a moment. He had to call back the interpreter, who'd started to go with Poindexter. Short said, "I know that Japan has not signed the Geneva Convention, but I trust you will treat the prisoners of war you are taking in accordance with its usages."

He waited. Fuchida did not think General Yamashita would answer, but one of Yamashita's aides murmured something to him. The Army commander nodded brusquely. "We will do what is necessary to secure these islands," he said. General Short had to be content—or discontented—with that.

Into the palace the Japanese delegation went. Commander Fuchida admired the Grand Hall. "Handsome," he murmured to Genda.

"If you like the old-fashioned European style, yes," answered Genda, whose tastes were modern, even radical.

Fuchida was more conservative. He admired the tall arched doorways with their wooden frames, the portraits of Hawaiian monarchs hung between them, and most of all the splendid staircase ascending to the second floor. The rich brown wood of which it was made seemed to glow under the electric lights. Statues carved from the same wood sprang from the pillars at the bottom of the bannisters.

The Throne Room was all white plaster, red velvet hangings, and red carpet underfoot. The Territorial legislators' desks looked small and silly and out of place in the midst of such magnificence. So did the table that had been brought in for the surrender ceremony.

Flashbulbs popped as the American dignitaries sat down on one side of the table. General Yamashita and Captain Hasegawa took the other. Army and Navy aides on both sides grouped themselves behind their principals.

Yamashita set the instrument of surrender—written in both Japanese and English—on the table. "This surrender is unconditional on your part," he told Short and Kimmel. "All military men in the Hawaiian Islands will yield to the Empire of Japan. They are prisoners. All destruction of military stores and weapons is to cease at once. All civil authority is suspended. All civil functionaries will obey orders from the Japanese military. Any violation of these terms will be punished most severely. Is that clear?"

"May we read the terms?" Admiral Kimmel asked.

"You may read," Yamashita said. "And then you may sign." He hardly bothered hiding his scorn for men who would surrender.

Kimmel—erect, gray-haired, handsome—and Short— pinch-faced, looking stunned at the disaster that had overtaken his side—studied the English half of the document. Fuchida would not have been surprised if the English was imperfect. That did not matter, as long as it was understandable.

When the military men were done, they passed the instrument to Governor Poindexter. His presence here was plainly an afterthought. Their own declaration of martial law had already superseded his authority. Kimmel said, "These terms are very harsh."

"The best way not to get harsh terms is not to lose the fight," General Yamashita said. When Izumi Shirakawa translated that, Kimmel bit his lip and stared down at the table.

"May I say a few words?" Governor Poindexter asked through the interpreter. For a moment, Mitsuo Fuchida thought General Yamashita would refuse. Then the Army commandant gave another curt nod. "Thank you," Poindexter said. "I speak on behalf of the civilians in Hawaii who now come under your control. Food is already in short supply, and will only grow more scarce as time goes by. If we are to avoid starvation, we will need help from the Empire of Japan in feeding our people."

"We will do what we can," Yamashita said. The American official looked relieved. Commander Fuchida had a hard time holding his face straight. Was Poindexter really so naive? Did he think he'd got a promise from Yamashita? Surely anyone could tell that was nothing but a polite phrase intended to keep him quiet. It had worked better than Yamashita probably intended.

"This is the hardest duty of my life," Admiral Kimmel said. "In spite of the handicaps of surprise, isolation, lack of food, and lack of ammunition, we have given the world a shining example of patriotic fortitude and self-sacrifice. We yield now more to save civilian lives than our own. The American people can ask for no finer example of tenacity and steadfast courage than our men have shown."

He looked to Yamashita, perhaps hoping for some sympathetic response. Yamashita said only, "It is over now. You must sign the surrender. The Imperial Japanese Army and Navy will continue to prosecute the war until it formally ends."

Kimmel sighed. "The morning the fighting started, a spent bullet hit me in the chest"—he tapped his left breast pocket with a forefinger—"and fell to the ground at my feet. That round should have killed me."

There was the first thing he'd said that made sense to Fuchida. Of course an officer who'd seen his command caught flat-footed would not wish to go on living afterwards. A Japanese officer in that position would have taken matters into his own hands, but the Americans were soft.

Kimmel looked across the table. General Yamashita stared back stonily. Captain Hasegawa was a livelier man than the Army commandant, but was also junior to him.

He did not give the American admiral whatever he was looking for—atonement, perhaps?—either. Kimmel lowered his head and scratched his name below the English text of the surrender. General Short and Governor Poindexter also signed. The civilian hid his face in his hands. His shoulders shook.

Yamashita and Hasegawa signed for Japan. To Fuchida's surprise, the taciturn Army commandant proved a formidable calligrapher. You never could tell what sort of accomplishments a man hid within himself.

Bombs burst, not too far away. General Short said, "It's over now." He seemed to be fighting tears. "It's over, dammit. Call off your attacks, sir. They aren't needed any more."

"They will stop," Yamashita said. "Those who have surrendered, though, are in no position to make demands. *No* position—do you hear me?"

"I hear you," Short replied. "I'd hoped to hear something worthy of a soldier."

Yamashita growled, down deep in his chest. Something ugly could have happened then. Captain Hasegawa forestalled it by pointing to the two American officers and saying, "Your sidearms."

With a face that might have been carved from stone, Admiral Kimmel took his ceremonial sword from his belt and laid it on the table. Short wore no sword. He pulled a pistol from the holster on his belt and set it beside the sword. More photographs recorded the moment. With ill-disguised greed, Yamashita grabbed the gold-hilted blade. That left the pistol, an ordinary .45, for Captain Hasegawa. He took it with no outward show of anger. Since he'd suggested that the American commanders turn over their weapons, Commander Fuchida thought he should have had first choice.

"Now it is over," Yamashita said, satisfaction in his voice. Shirakawa translated that into English. Yamashita turned to one of his aides: "Order the cease-fire, effective immediately." The interpreter translated that, too. The Army commandant sent him a hard look, but it was done.

Kimmel might have been a dead man talking as he said, "We are your captives, sir. What are your orders for us?"

Maybe he was trying to rouse sympathy in the Japanese. If so, he'd made a mistake. To a Japanese soldier, captives roused nothing but contempt. Yamashita did not bother to hide it as he answered, "Just stay here. You will be taken care of." He gathered up his officers by eye. "Let's go."

Once out in the bright sunshine again, Fuchida looked up at the central flagpole, the tallest of the five atop Iolani Palace. The American flag had come down during the ceremony. The Japanese flag flew there in its place.

Tears stung Fuchida's eyes. Such a gamble—but they'd brought it off. He turned to Minoru Genda. No matter how modest Genda was, he more than any other man had been the man who made this victory possible. Impulsively, Fuchida bowed low. "Congratulations!" he said once more.

Genda returned the bow. "It was for the Empire," he said, but not even his quiet words could hide all the pride in his voice.

RUMORS OF SURRENDER HAD SWEPT THROUGH the Americans still fighting for a couple of days before they turned out to be true. Even then, Fletcher Armitage didn't want to believe them. Neither did the men he'd hauled into serving his now-abandoned 105. "What do you think, sir?" Clancy asked. "Should we steal us some civvies and make like we were never in the Army? I'll be damned if I want to put myself in the hands o' them heathen bastards. I seen what they do to prisoners."

"I'm not going to give you any orders about that," Fletch answered. "If you want to try and disappear, go ahead. I won't say boo. I don't know who you are. But if you try and disappear and the Japs find out who you are, your neck isn't worth a plugged nickel."

Arnie said, "If everybody's surrendering, they'll have to play fair by us, won't they?"

"Get your head out of your ass, man," Dave said. "They're the Japs. They just won. They fucking licked us.

They don't *have* to do shit. They can do whatever they god-damn well want."

Clancy nodded. "That's what I'm afraid of. That's why I'm thinking about bugging out." He glanced over to Fletch. "What are you gonna do, Lieutenant?"

Back when he was still married to Jane, Fletch might have tried to get up to Wahiawa and pretended to be part of a civilian couple with her. *And you might have been an idiot, too*, he thought. *What if one of your neighbors turned you in? You'd get shot, and so would she.*

He shrugged. He didn't have that choice any more. "I'm sticking," he said. "I *am* in the Army, goddammit. But I'm not going to tell anybody else what to do, not for this. Whatever you think gives you the best chance, you go ahead and do it, and good luck to you."

Clancy set his rifle and his tin hat on the ground. "I'm gone," he said. "Good luck back atcha, Lieutenant." He slipped away. Dave followed. Arnie stayed.

They looked at each other. "What the hell happens next?" Arnie asked. "Uh, sir?"

"Beats me," Fletch said. "We had drills and exercises for everything under the sun, but I don't think we ever practiced surrendering." No American had ever imagined that he could taste defeat. After the Japanese landed on Oahu, Fletch's imagination had been expanded.

Somewhere not far away, someone with a loud, official-sounding voice shouted, "Come stack your weapons here! Fighting's done! Come stack your weapons!"

"Jesus," Arnie muttered. He was a little, swarthy guy with a clotted Chicago accent.

"Got to get rid of your piece even if you bug out," Fletch reminded him. "Japs catch you with it, you're history." There were places—the Philippines, for instance—where a man might take to the jungle and go on with the fight. Oahu wasn't a place like that. It had jungles, sure enough, but they didn't have anything to eat in them.

"Jesus," Arnie said again, and then, "They really gonna treat us like prisoners of war now?"

That poked Fletch's worst fears. He remembered too

well what the Japs had done to American soldiers they'd captured. But they couldn't do things like that to all the men who'd surrendered . . . could they? He shook his head. Impossible. "They're supposed to," he answered. "We wouldn't have quit if we thought they wouldn't, would we?"

"I guess not." Arnie still sounded dubious, but he nodded. "Lead the way, Lieutenant."

Rank hath its privileges, Fletch thought. This was one he could have done without. But he had no choice now that he'd decided not to disappear. He trudged along the road towards the man who was shouting about stacking arms. Here in the western suburbs of Honolulu, buildings weren't jammed together the way they were in the city proper. There was more greenery than there were houses and shops. But war had laid its hand here. Shell and bomb craters scarred the ground. Flame had gutted one of the houses Fletch and Arnie walked past. And the sickly-sweet battlefield reek of dead meat was in the air.

Springfields made neat pyramids on the grass, stocks down, barrels pointing up. The soldiers who'd already stacked their weapons were anything but neat. They looked like Fletch and Arnie: dirty, weary, tattered, dejected. They looked fearful, too. "What the hell are the Japs gonna do to us?" was a question Fletch heard again and again. The answer to that one would win the sixty-four dollars, all right. It might win something even better: life.

A few minutes later, somebody pointed west and said, "Here they come." Several soldiers, Arnie among them, crossed themselves.

The Japs advanced cautiously, rifles at the ready. Fletch had seen them before, but they'd only been targets to him. Now, suddenly, they were men. Most of them were shorter and skinnier than their American opposite numbers—most, but not all. They weren't the buck-toothed, bespectacled caricatures he'd more or less subconsciously expected. They looked like the Japanese men who lived in Hawaii.

What a surprise, Fletch thought sarcastically. And yet, in a lot of ways, it *was* a surprise.

"Attention!" shouted the American with the authoritative voice. "Form ranks!"

Some soldiers heeded him. More didn't, but just stood around, waiting to see what happened next. Fletch was one of those. He'd had all the shouting he could stand. A Japanese soldier with a scraggly mustache came up to him. He made himself hold still and nod to the victor.

"*Tabako?*" the Jap asked, holding out his hand. Fletch frowned. "*Tabako?*" the soldier repeated, more insistently this time.

A light dawned. Fletch pulled out a mostly empty pack of cigarettes and handed it to the Jap. The fellow grinned and stuck one in his mouth. Then he looked crestfallen. He mimed striking a match. Fletch fumbled in his pockets. Did he have any matches? He did, and gave them to the soldier. The man lit the cigarette. He seemed happy as a hog in front of a bucket of strawberries.

After a long, almost ecstatic drag, though, he pointed to Fletch's wristwatch. Fletch hesitated. He didn't want to give that up. But he didn't want to get shot or bayoneted, either.

Before he had to make up his mind, a noncom strode over. He said something to the soldier, who answered hesitantly. *Wham!* The noncom hauled off and hit the other Jap a lick that sent his cigarette flying and snapped his head back. *Wham!* This time, it was a backhand across the face. The soldier staggered, but did his best to stay at attention. The noncom screamed what was obviously abuse at him. The Jap soldier stood there, wooden as a cigar-store Indian. A tiny trickle of blood ran from the corner of his mouth. His cheeks looked to be on fire. The noncom belted him one more time, then barked something contemptuous. Face still impassive, the soldier bowed and got the hell out of there.

Jesus H. Christ! Fletch thought. *This is what they do to their own guys. No wonder they're hell on wheels to the poor suckers they catch.*

The noncom looked him over. He made himself stand

there. If he showed any kind of fear, he thought he was a dead man. If this monkey started beating on him, though . . . Well, in that case he would be a dead man, because he intended to jump the Jap. He also intended to take the noncom down to hell with him.

Instead of hitting him, the fellow pointed to his wrist-watch, the same as the ordinary soldier had done. Despite what Fletch had seen the noncom do, he hesitated again. Plundering prisoners was supposed to be against the rules. Maybe it was—if you were a private, and a corporal or sergeant or whatever this bastard was caught you at it. For him, though . . . *To the victors go the spoils.*

A curt word or two of Japanese had to mean, *Make it snappy, Charlie!* The noncom reached out and undid the watchband himself. Fletch didn't knock his hands away, however much he wanted to. The Jap put the watch on his own wrist. When he fastened it, he closed the band a couple of holes farther along than Fletch did. Off he went, peacock-proud.

Other Japanese soldiers were relieving American prisoners of their minor valuables. Seeing his countrymen robbed made Fletch feel a little better. Maybe misery really did love company. And it could have been worse. It wasn't a massacre. That noncom had done worse to the poor greedy private than the Japs were doing to the Americans.

You know you've hit bottom when you're glad 'cause they've only stolen your watch, Fletch thought. He *was* glad, too. Maybe it would be all right, or at least not too bad.

WHEN THE ORDER TO CEASE FIRE and lay down his arms reached Jim Peterson, he was in a house in Pearl City with his back to the sea. He couldn't have stayed there too much longer. Either he'd get killed or he'd be squeezed off into the west—into irrelevance—while the Japs reached the oil-befouled waters of Pearl Harbor.

He was damned if he felt like giving up. He had a good position and plenty of clips for his Springfield. Had he signed up as a ground-pounder only to surrender to the enemy? *What would you have done if you'd stayed aboard the Enterprise?* he jeered at himself. *You'd have been shot out of the sky or gone down with her.*

As a matter of fact, he *had* got shot out of the sky. But he'd had golfers for company, not sharks. The Pacific was a wide and lonely place.

He wondered if he ought to put his lieutenant's bars back on. He might get better treatment if he did. After a moment's thought, he shook his head. He'd signed up to be an infantryman, and he'd go into captivity as one. He knew that was pride talking—perverse pride, probably. He shrugged. He didn't give a damn. Perverse or not, it was his.

"Come out and assemble!" some loudmouth was yelling. "Come out! If the Japs take you later, they'll say you tried to go on fighting after the surrender. You don't want that to happen. Believe me, you don't."

Loudmouth or not, he was much too likely to be right. Regretfully, Peterson slung his rifle and came out of the house. Other similarly draggled men were doing the same thing elsewhere along the block. They'd been in close contact with the Japs. Japanese soldiers were coming out, too, to look them over.

The Japs were about as grubby as the Americans. Their beards weren't so thick, but plenty of them needed shaves, too. Even though neither side showed much in the way of spit and polish, you could sure as hell tell who'd won and who'd lost. The Americans walked with their shoulders slumped and their heads down. They mooched along as if they'd just watched a tank run over their cat. That was about how Peterson felt, too.

By contrast, the Japs might have just conquered the world. They'd sure as hell just conquered one of the nicest corners of it. And boy, were they proud of themselves! They swaggered. They strutted. They grinned. Some of them seemed almost drunk with happiness—or was it relief?

Japanese officers were easy to spot. They were the ones who wore swords. Peterson had seen they really thought they could fight with them, too. At close quarters, he would have preferred a bayonet—it gave more reach. He hadn't

seen any hand-to-hand combat, though. People shot each
other before they got that close. Bayonets were handy
things to have, but they didn't get blood on them very
often.

"Over here!" the loudmouth bawled. "Stack arms!"

One of the Jap officers had a local Oriental with him.
The local gave him a running translation. He nodded in
reply.

Collaborators already, Peterson thought. *Happy day!*
The officer said something in Japanese. The local Japanese
man translated: "Even though you have surrendered and
are dishonored, you must try to remember that you are
men."

That was a dangerous thing to say to soldiers with
weapons still in their hands. For a nickel, Peterson would
have blown that Jap's head off for him. Fear for himself
didn't keep him from doing it. Fear for what would happen
to other Americans all over Oahu did.

His rifle joined others stacked in neat pyramids. Japanese
soldiers watched the Americans giving up their weapons.
Peterson looked down at his hands when the Springfield
was gone for good. He felt naked without the rifle. Whatever the Japs wanted to do to him, they could.

Dishonored? Maybe that officer hadn't been so far
wrong. If losing to these bastards wasn't a humiliation,
what was? As far as he was concerned, the USA should
have been able to lick Japan with one hand tied behind its
back. Maybe it had tied both hands back there, because it
had sure as hell lost.

And what would happen next? How the devil was the
United States supposed to fight a war in the Pacific from
the West Coast? What would happen to Australia and New
Zealand? How could America get soldiers and supplies
down there without going through Hawaii? It wouldn't be
easy—if it was possible at all.

"Hey, you lousy little monkey, keep your goddamn
hands off me!" a soldier with a thick Southern drawl said
angrily. He shoved away a Jap who'd been about to lift
something from him.

Peterson didn't think the Japanese soldiers spoke any English. That didn't matter. The tone and the shove were all they needed. Half a dozen of them jumped the American. All the others close by raised their rifles, warning the rest of the newly surrendered Americans not to butt in.

They stomped the Southerner. It was angry at first, and got angrier when he managed to land a blow or two of his own. That didn't last long, not against six. After he stopped fighting back, it turned cold-blooded and methodical. To Peterson's mind, that was worse. They knew exactly what they intended to do, and they did it. By the time they finished, it wasn't a human being on the ground any more: only dead meat in khaki wrappings. They had blood on their boots and puttees.

To Peterson's surprise, they didn't have smiles on their faces. They hadn't particularly enjoyed what they'd done—which didn't mean they hadn't done it. It was just . . . part of a day's work. That was pretty scary, too.

The Japanese officer watched the whole thing without making a move to interfere and without batting an eye. He spoke in his own language. The local Jap, by contrast, was green and gulping. The officer had to nudge him before he remembered to translate: "Let this be a lesson to you. You are prisoners, nothing more. When a Japanese soldier comes up to you, you are to bow and you are to obey. Do you understand?" Appalled silence answered him. He spoke again, sharply. He didn't have to nudge the local this time: "*Do you understand?*"

"Yes, sir!" It was a ragged chorus, but it plainly said what the Jap wanted to hear. Peterson joined in. He understood, all right. He understood this was nastier trouble than he'd imagined in his worst nightmares.

You should have run away, he jeered at himself. But where could he have run? Oahu had nowhere to hide, except maybe among the civilians in Honolulu. He hadn't been able to stomach the notion . . . and now it was too late.

A Japanese soldier came up to him and waited expectantly. *You are to bow and you are to obey.* Tasting the gall of the defeated, Peterson bowed. *It's only politeness*, he told himself. *It's what they do, too.* It would have been only politeness had the Jap returned the bow. He didn't. He accepted it as nothing less than his due. He deserved it for being on the winning side, and he didn't have to give it back.

He reached into Peterson's pockets. Peterson stood there, stiff as a statue. *You lost. This is what happens when you lose.* The Jap found his Navy rank badges. He kept them. All he cared about was that they were silver. *I really am nothing but a corporal now.* Then the Jap found his billfold. He had fourteen dollars, just about what he'd had when he took off from the *Enterprise*'s flight deck. It wasn't a whole lot of money, and he sure hadn't had any place to spend it since he'd parachuted down onto that golf course.

By the way the Jap clutched the greenbacks in his fist and hopped up and down and jabbered in his own language, he might have broken into Fort Knox. People talked about inscrutable Orientals, but this guy wasn't inscrutable. He was damn near out of his mind with glee.

He was so overjoyed, he even gave the wallet back to Peterson once he'd pocketed the money. "Thanks a lot," Peterson said, sarcastic before he remembered sarcasm might be deadly dangerous. Then he had a rush of brains to the head. He bowed again.

This time, the Jap bowed back. *You're nothing but a lousy prisoner, but I can be polite about robbing you.* That was what it boiled down to. It couldn't mean anything else. *You son of a bitch*, Peterson thought. *You rotten, stinking son of a bitch.*

The other Japs were plundering the rest of the Americans. The prisoners took it quietly. Flies landed on the ruined face of the soldier who'd resented it. The Japanese officer barked a command. The interpreter said, "This way," and pointed. The Americans trudged off into the new world of captivity.

SUSIE HIGGINS LAY ON THE NARROW BED and sobbed. "I wish to God I'd never come here!" she wailed.

Even though Oscar van der Kirk had come to Hawaii years before Susie had, that same thought had occurred to him. He said, "A little too late to worry about it now."

She glared at him. Even with her makeup smeared and tear streaks down her face, she looked good. Not a hell of a lot of women could say that. "What are we going to do? The Japs are taking over the island."

"Yeah, I noticed that," Oscar said. "I don't know what we can do except keep our heads down, try to stay out of trouble, and hope there'll be enough to eat. Have you seen the prices? Food's going up like a Fourth of July sky-rocket."

"*We lost!*" Susie exclaimed. "That wasn't supposed to happen."

"You knew it was going to, same as I did," Oscar answered. "You said so."

This time, Susie glared at him in a different way. She didn't like getting reminded of what she'd already said. "They're *Japs*," she said. "They're not Americans. They're not even white men. They shouldn't be able to do this."

Oscar shrugged. "The guy who owns this building is a Jap. A lot of the people who've made it big for themselves here are Japs—and that's in spite of everything the *haoles* do to hold 'em down. When I first moved here, I thought the same way you do. The longer I've stayed, the more I don't. The Japs can do anything we can do, and I don't give a damn if they're green."

"Are you going to teach them to surf-ride?" she spat.

He grunted. That question had occurred to him, too, and he wished it hadn't. "I guess so. If they want to learn. If they want to pay me," he said slowly. "Their money'd spend just like anybody else's. Lord knows we're going to need it."

"I wouldn't have anything to do with them," Susie said.

"Yeah, well, surf-riding lessons aren't what they'd want from you," Oscar said.

Susie's hand reached out for something to throw. Fortunately, nothing was in reach of where she lay. "And if I gave 'em that, how would it be any different than you giving 'em lessons?"

"It would, that's all." Oscar had to stop and figure out how. He did his best: "Giving lessons is what I do for a living. It'd be like a cabby giving a Jap a ride. The other—if you did that, you'd be doing it 'cause you wanted to, not because it was your job." If he said it was, she'd get up to find something to throw at him. He'd deserve it, too.

Instead of getting up, she changed the subject. She hardly ever came out and admitted she was wrong. This sort of thing was her nearest approach. She asked, "Are you going to watch the victory parade tomorrow?"

"Heck, I don't know. I was thinking about it," he answered. "Why not? It's something to do. I'm not going to cheer or anything."

"Jesus, I hope not," she said. "I bet everybody who's there'll be a Jap, though."

Oscar grunted again. He hadn't thought of that. "I bet you're right. Okay, I'll stay away. Wouldn't that be just what I need, showing up on some lousy Jap propaganda newsreel? If it got back to my folks, they'd never live it down."

"That's more like it," she said. "What'll we do instead?"

"We can go out on the ocean, or else we can stay here. Your call," he said.

She shrugged. "Worry about it in the morning." She got up from the bed and looked at herself in the little mirror over the sink. "Lord! I'm a fright! Why didn't you tell me?"

Then we'd fight over something else, he thought. Aloud, he said, "You always look good to me, babe." That was true enough. He knew exactly what hold Susie had on him. Knowing it didn't make it any less real.

In the morning, he wanted to go out to the Pacific. Susie said, "Go ahead. I just don't feel like it." She looked at him in a way that would have been sidelong except, in a fashion he couldn't quite define, it wasn't. "I don't much feel like anything else today, either," she added, just in case he hadn't got the point.

But he had. He was no dummy, not where people were

concerned. "See you later," he said, and hurried out the door. He trotted down towards Waikiki Beach like a man going towards his beloved. He got his surfboard from the Outrigger Club and was heading across the soft sand of the beach to the sea when somebody behind him let out a yell.

He stopped. There was Charlie Kaapu, also with his surfboard under his arm. "You can't stand the Japs, either, hey?" Charlie said.

"That's . . . part of it," Oscar answered. "Come on—let's go."

They entered the water side by side. Setting his skill against the surf, Oscar didn't have to think about the Japs or anything else. If he had done any thinking, he surely would have taken a tumble. If you were anything but a creature of reflex and reaction on the waves, you were in trouble.

When he and Charlie came up onto the beach after one long, smooth ride, he saw a pair of Japanese officers watching. *Well,* would *I teach a Jap to surf-ride?* he wondered. He didn't want to think about that, either, and plunged into the Pacific again. But the Japanese officers were still there when he got back. So were the rest of his troubles, of course. He knew they wouldn't disappear no matter how he ran. Knowing didn't stop him from running.

After a while, he'd had enough. He walked up the beach to the Outrigger Club. He passed within about ten feet of the two Japs. He wanted to pretend they didn't exist. But they both bowed to him. He'd heard things about how touchy Japs were, so he figured he'd better nod back. That seemed to satisfy them. He'd never been sorry to get a salute for what he did on a surfboard, but he was now.

The apartment was empty when he walked in. A note lay on the bed. He picked it up. *Good luck,* Susie had written. *It isn't fun any more. Nothing is much fun any more.* He stared down at that, then slowly nodded. It wasn't as if she was wrong.

Then he checked the place. She hadn't cleaned him out. Maybe that meant that, in her own way, she had style. Maybe it just meant he didn't own anything she thought worth stealing. He went back and looked at the note again. "Good luck, Susie," he said.

JIRO TAKAHASHI CLIMBED OUT OF THE TENT where he and his sons were living. They were lucky to have even a tent. Their apartment building was a burnt-out wreck. No one had found any trace of his wife. Officially, Reiko was listed as missing. Jiro clung to that. He knew what it meant, knew what it almost had to mean. The less he had to think about that, though, the better.

Escaping the tent felt good. If he stayed in there, he'd just quarrel with Hiroshi and Kenzo again. They blamed Japan for the bombs that had left them without a home and their mother missing or worse. He blamed the Americans for not surrendering once things were hopeless. He also scorned them for surrendering at all. He didn't even notice the inconsistency.

Before the tent city sprang up, this had been a botanical garden. A lot of the trees here had come down for the sake of firewood. At first, the *haole* in charge of the place had fussed about that, but people had to cook food and heat water. What were they supposed to do, go without fire?

"Ha! Takahashi!" There was old man Okamoto. He'd lost his house in the bombing, too. "You going to watch the parade?"

"I don't know," Jiro answered. "It's hard to care about anything any more, you know what I mean?"

"Life is all confused," Okamoto said.

"*Hai. Honto,*" Jiro agreed. Confused he was. When the fighting started, he'd wanted Japan to teach the United States a lesson. *Haoles* had the arrogance to treat Japanese like inferiors. They deserved a comeuppance.

And they'd got it. Oahu belonged to the Empire of Japan. All the Hawaiian islands did. But Jiro had never imagined victory would come at such a high price to *him*. He'd never imagined the war would come home to civilians at all. When you thought of war, you thought of soldiers shooting at soldiers, of airplanes shooting down airplanes, of ships sinking ships. You didn't think of bombs and shells landing on your city, on your home. You didn't think any of your loved ones would go missing, which was only a politer way of saying *get killed.*

You didn't think about that, but you were only a civilian, so what did you know? The officers in the fancy uniforms figured that war involved making your life miserable. They were the ones who gave orders to the soldiers and the airplanes and the ships. What they said went. And if you happened to get in the way . . . well, too bad for you.

"Come on," old man Okamoto said. "I mean, what else have we got to do?"

Takahashi had no answer for that. He could stay here and brood. Or he could stay here and quarrel with his sons, which was a loud, external kind of brooding over *whose* officers in fancy uniforms were to blame for the way things were in Honolulu.

"All right," Jiro said, his mouth making up its mind before his brain did. "Let's go."

To get to King Street, down which the parade would run, they had to walk down Nuuanu Avenue through the bombed-out part of town. Scavengers picked through the ruins for whatever they could salvage. Jiro walked on, his face hard and set as a stone. He would not think of Reiko lying there lost in the wreckage. He would not think that her body added to the stench of death still lingering here.

He would not—but he did.

King Street wasn't too badly damaged. Here and there, buildings had broken windows, or perhaps plywood where windows had been. Takahashi didn't see any craters in the street itself. Rising Sun flags fluttered from lamp poles. Okamoto pointed to one of them and said, "The Japanese consulate had people putting those up yesterday."

"Really?" Jiro said. "I know the consul a little. I've sold Kita-*san* tuna fairly often—whenever I had some that was particularly good. And Morimura, the chancellor at the consulate, knows a good piece of fish, too."

"I wouldn't be surprised," Okamoto said. "Morimura drives all over the place. Did you ever notice? I wonder how much spying he did for Japan."

"I don't know anything about that," Jiro said. "I was out on the ocean. I only paid attention to him when I had fish I thought he might like."

"Well, he did. He bought gas from me plenty of times," Okamoto said. "And Oahu's not a big island. You can do a lot of driving here without using much gas. So if you're filling up twice a week, or even three times, you're doing a *lot* of driving."

Before Takahashi could answer, a Japanese boy who couldn't have been more than six handed him a small Japanese flag on a stick. "Here, mister," the boy said in English. He gave Okamoto a flag, too, and then went on up the sidewalk passing them out.

Following the kid with his eyes, Jiro took in the other people who'd come to watch the Imperial Japanese Army's victory parade. Almost all of them, unsurprisingly, were Japanese themselves. Most of them were of his generation, the generation that had been born in Japan. A few men and women in their twenties and thirties accompanied them, but only a few.

"Here they come!" People pointed west. Jiro craned his neck to see better. He'd watched U.S. military parades often enough, so he had some idea what to expect. This one didn't seem too different, not at first. Standard-bearers carrying Japanese flags led the procession. Half a dozen tanks followed them.

The tanks were both more and less impressive than Jiro had expected. They weren't very big. But they'd plainly seen combat. They were splashed with mud and other stains. Their yellow-green paint was chipped and scarred by American bullets. Still, the bullets hadn't penetrated their armor. The tanks were here. They'd won.

Here and there, someone would clap or shout out, *"Banzai!"* Most of the crowd stayed quiet, though. That made Jiro notice the absence of a marching band. He'd never paid much attention to the ones in American parades. Now, to his surprise, he found himself missing them.

Japanese officers stood in open cars and waved to the crowd. Unlike the tanks, the cars hadn't come from Japan.

They were convertibles with Hawaii license plates. That didn't bother Takahashi too much. If you won, you captured what you needed. Japan had won.

Behind the tanks and the officers came regiment after regiment of Japanese soldiers. More "*Banzai!*"s and applause rang out for them. They marched proudly, eyes straight ahead, faces expressionless, bayoneted rifles on their shoulders.

"They look brave. They look tough," Jiro said to old man Okamoto. The other Japanese nodded.

And then sudden silence slammed down on the crowd. After the neat ranks of imperial soldiers, and plainly included as a contrast, shambled a swarm of American prisoners. The U.S. Army men went up the street in no particular order. They were skinny. They were dirty. They were unshaven. Their uniforms were torn and filthy. Most of them trudged along with their heads down, as if they didn't want to meet the eyes of the people staring at them.

For as long as anyone but the oldest residents could remember, Americans had ruled the roost and called the shots in Hawaii. The sight of those prisoners—and the smell of them, for they hadn't bathed any time lately, which became only too clear as they went by—said one era had passed here and another was beginning. The handful of Japanese guards who herded the Americans along seemed a different and superior species.

Still more Japanese soldiers followed the prisoners. "Not bad," Okamoto said. "Funny watching all those *haoles* go by like so many sheep."

"I was thinking the same thing," Jiro answered. "They didn't let Japanese join their divisions here. Now they're paying the price."

"That's the truth." But Okamoto lowered his voice and added, "We're all paying the price now. It's going to be a hungry time."

Takahashi nodded. "I've got to get that Doi fellow to put a mast on my sampan. That's not going to wait any more. If I can catch fish, I won't starve." Soup kitchens fed

the refugees in the botanical garden. There wasn't enough
to go around, and what there was wasn't very good.

"Bound to be a good idea for you. Nobody knows
where fuel's going to come from now," Okamoto said. He
nudged Jiro. "Nobody will know what you eat that you
don't bring in, either. You're lucky."

"Some luck," Jiro said. No home, his wife missing and
probably dead . . .

No matter what he thought, old man Okamoto nodded
this time. "Yes, lucky. Your children are alive, and fishermen
don't starve any more than cooks do."

"I won't be a fisherman any more if Doi can't rig the
sampan." As always, saying that frightened Jiro. He'd been
a fisherman as long as he could remember. His father had
started taking him out on the Inland Sea when he was a
very little boy. If he couldn't be a fisherman, what could he
be? Anything at all?

Okamoto shrugged. "He'll manage. He'd better manage. If we don't get boats out there, nobody eats."

Jiro grunted. That was too likely to be true. As stocks of
everything got shorter, prices went on soaring. But if
Okamoto or anybody else thought the sampan fleet could
feed Oahu by itself . . . Jiro knew what a dream that was.
There weren't enough sampans. There probably weren't
enough fish, either. And the sampans wouldn't be able to
go out nearly so far with sails as they could with their
diesels. Or if they did go out as far, they wouldn't be able
to do it so often.

"Japan can't want us to starve," Jiro said.

Another shrug from Okamoto. "Why should she care?
As long as she's got soldiers and airplanes here, what difference do we make? We're just a nuisance."

Shaking his head, Jiro said, "That can't be so. You and I,
we're Japanese, too." Old man Okamoto only shrugged
again.

AT OHIO STATE, JANE ARMITAGE had read *Candide*. The
advice the naive hero had got could be boiled down to one

phrase: *tend your garden*. While Jane was in college, she'd never understood what important advice it could be. She did now. Now she had a garden of her own.

Her little plot of turnips and potatoes had sprouted. With luck, they would grow fast. She eyed the turnip greens. The only people she'd ever heard of who ate such things were niggers. She shrugged. If you got hungry enough, you'd eat almost anything.

A mynah bird fluttered down and landed in her plot. It pecked at something: a bug. "Good for you," Jane said. "Eat lots of bugs. Get fat." Were mynahs good to eat? She wouldn't have been surprised if, somewhere on the island, some people were already finding out.

And then there were zebra doves. The blue-faced birds were so tame, you could grab them with your bare hands. They made pigeons seem smart by comparison. They weren't very big, but they were meat. And they were all over the place. They ate anything that wasn't nailed down. She'd shooed them out of the plot more times than she could count. If she didn't shoo them . . . If she grabbed them or netted them . . .

Could I wring their necks? Could I pluck them and gut them? She wasn't a farm girl. She'd never dealt with chickens or hogs or anything like that. She suspected that gutting a zebra dove might make her lose her lunch. But if she had no lunch to lose, if she was empty in there . . . And after she'd done it a few times, wouldn't she get used to it?

Something brown and low to the ground skittered towards the mynah bird, which fluttered away. The mongoose reared up in almost palpable frustration. Jane didn't worry about him. He didn't care about turnips or potatoes or any of the other crops different people were growing. He might assassinate some zebra doves, but that was as far as he went towards being a pest.

Jane wished he would have gone as far as assassinating rats. That was why people had brought mongooses here in the first place. But the mongooses preferred eating birds that were out and about during the day, as they were. Rats came out at night. Traps didn't do much to discourage them. Jane had known about rats back in Columbus. Nothing did much to discourage them.

A Japanese soldier tramped by. Jane bent and dug out a weed with her trowel. She didn't want the Jap paying any special attention to her, either because he thought she was lazy or because he liked her looks. Bad things could happen both ways.

He kept going. She breathed a silent sigh of relief. Some of the local Japanese women had got friendly, or more than friendly, with the new occupiers. And, to Jane's shame, so had a few of the local white women. *If you can't join 'em, lick 'em*, she thought scornfully. The heat that rose to her cheeks after that had nothing to do with the warm sun in the sky. That was the sort of thing Fletch would have said.

As she got rid of another weed, she wondered how Fletch was doing. However much she wanted not to, she couldn't help herself. They'd been together most of her adult life, and apart for not very long. She was used to worrying about what was going on with him. She didn't want him dead, just out of her life. She'd got that. For all she knew, he *was* dead, whether she wanted him that way or not.

A shadow made her look up. There stood Yosh Nakayama, watching her. Major Hirabayashi's local go-between nodded. "You do well," he said in his slow, careful English. "Plot looks good."

"Thanks," Jane said. She didn't want to collaborate with the Japs and their quislings, but she didn't want to get them angry at her, either. *Very* bad things happened if the Japs got mad at you.

"Hope everything grows fast," Nakayama said. "Hope food we have lasts till it does."

"Aren't the Japanese"—Jane was careful not to say *Japs* to a Jap—"bringing in supplies?"

"For their own men, yes. For anybody else . . ." Nakayama shrugged. "They don't have a lot of ships to spare." By the way he said it, that was liable to be an understatement.

"What do we do if . . . if things run out?"

The Hawaiian Japanese man shrugged again. "Eat sugarcane. Eat pineapple. Eat whatever birds and fruit we can. Then we start to starve." He didn't wait for any more questions. With a curt nod, he walked away to inspect the work of some other involuntary gardener.

Jane eyed the zebra doves even more thoughtfully than she had before.

She worked till almost sundown. Her hands had blistered at first. Now they were starting to callus. Her nails were short, and had dirt under them. Her face was sunburned, her hair a sweaty mess. She didn't worry as much about that as she'd thought she would. All her neighbors were in the same boat. And if that boat happened to be the *Titanic* . . . She shoved the thought aside.

She still had running water in her apartment. She didn't have hot water, though, and she couldn't even make any on the stove. Like the water heater, the stove ran on natural gas. There was no more natural gas for them to run on. A cold shower in January would have been an invitation to double pneumonia—to say nothing of frostbite—in Columbus. Here in Wahiawa, it was refreshing, as long as she didn't linger under the water too long.

No more shampoo, either. Jane did still have a couple of bars of Ivory left after the one she was using. What she would do once the last suds gurgled down the drain, she didn't know. Her mouth twisted as she brushed her hair in front of the mirror. Figuring out what she'd do then wasn't very hard. One of her pupils could have done it with no trouble at all. She'd be filthy and she'd stink, that was what.

Other such worries were cropping up, too. She was almost out of Kotex pads. Like everything else, those came, or had come, from the mainland. What would she use without them? Rags, she supposed. What else was there? Her mouth twisted again, harder this time.

She put on a sundress to go to the communal supper. It was fairly clean: she didn't do farm work in it. Most people dressed a little nicer than usual for supper. Some didn't bother.

A couple of Japanese soldiers with rifles on their shoulders strode up the street towards her. She got out of their way and bowed, holding the pose till they'd gone past. They mostly didn't bother people who followed the rules they'd set. Mostly. But you never could tell. That was part of what made them so scary.

Supper was rice and noodles with a little tomato sauce and some canned mushrooms for flavor. Dessert was canned pineapple. That had been the only dessert for some time. Jane was sick of it, but ate it anyhow. Her body cried out for all the food it could get. Supper wasn't really enough. When she finished, she didn't feel she was starving any more, but she didn't feel full, either.

Everybody else seemed as tired as she was. Nobody said much. Nobody said anything at all about the Japs. Early on, a woman had cursed them at a communal meal. A couple of days later, she abruptly stopped showing up. No one had seen her since. Somebody had listened to her. Somebody had betrayed her. Nobody knew who, or even whether the informer was Japanese, Chinese, or *haole*. Nobody was inclined to take a chance. *The first lesson of tyranny: shut up and keep your head down*, Jane thought.

Something with eyes that glowed in the dark startled her as she was walking home. After a moment, she realized it was only a cat. She relaxed and walked on. And then, all unbidden, a phrase she'd heard in an Italian restaurant in Columbus popped into her mind: *roof rabbit*. The fellow who'd said it had laughed. So had the girl with him. Maybe an occasional cat had gone into the pot back in the old country. People in America didn't do things like that . . . did they?

What Jane thought was, *A lot more meat on a cat than on one of those little zebra doves*. Spit flooded into her mouth. It had been a while since she'd tasted meat. Then tears stung her eyes. Was this what hunger, and fear of hunger, did to people? She nodded to herself, there in the night. So it seemed.

CORPORAL TAKEO SHIMIZU STOOD IN A LONG LINE at a Japanese field post office in Honolulu. The package he carried was addressed to his parents. The line moved with the glacial pace of post-office lines everywhere. He didn't care. He'd expected nothing different. Sooner or later, he'd get to the front of it. He didn't have anything else going on in the meantime.

At last, he came up to a clerk. The man looked even more bored than Shimizu felt. "Contents of the package?" he asked. By his tone, he couldn't have cared less.

"Souvenirs of war: an American flag and a bayonet I took from the rifle of a dead Yankee," Shimizu answered. "I want my honorable parents to see that I have not been idle here."

The postal clerk grunted. Had he seen any combat while the Japanese were overrunning Oahu? Shimizu wouldn't have bet on it. Some people always managed to land soft jobs behind the lines. The clerk threw the package on a scale. "Postage is seventy-five sen," he announced.

Shimizu gave him a one-yen coin and got his change. The clerk put stamps on the package. They were, Shimizu saw, American stamps. But they had a blue overprint that said *Hawaii* in Japanese characters. One was also overprinted *50*, the other *25*.

"Our islands now," Shimizu said, not without a certain pride. He'd earned the right to be proud, as far as he was concerned. The Hawaiian Islands were Japanese now because of him and men like him.

"*Hai.*" The clerk sounded indifferent. He didn't quite yawn in Shimizu's face, but he came close. What were you to do with such people? *Yes, my friend, have you ever seen machine-gun fire?* Shimizu wondered. *How would you like it if you did? Would you still be bored? I doubt it.*

He stepped away from the clerk. Another Japanese soldier walked up with a bigger, heavier package than the one he'd just mailed. What was in that one? *Clothes, maybe*, Shimizu thought. Shirts and trousers would make very good spoils of war to send home.

When Shimizu went outside, a white woman was walking up the street towards him. She hastily dipped her head—it wasn't much of a bow, but it would do—and got out of his way. He walked past her as if she didn't exist.

He'd never seen a white woman before he landed on Oahu. He could count the times he'd seen white men on the fingers of one hand.

A local Japanese man about his own age who wore American-style clothes did a better job of bowing. With him, Shimizu felt he could unbend a little: "This is the prettiest country in the world. You're lucky to live here all the time."

"Please talk slow," the local said. "Talk only little Japanese. So sorry." He wasn't kidding. He didn't just have a peasant accent, either. He had the sort of accent an English-speaker would. He might look Japanese on the outside, but he was American where it counted.

Corporal Shimizu felt betrayed. "Why didn't your parents teach you the way they should have?" he asked angrily.

The young man flinched as if Shimizu had threatened him with a bayonet. "So sorry," he said again. He sounded tolerably Japanese when he brought out the stock phrase. But then he went on, fumbling for words and butchering his grammar: "Grandfather, grandmother come here. Father, mother born here. They speak Japanese with grandfather, grandmother, speak English with me. Speak Japanese when no want I to know what they meaning. I learn some, not much. English number one here."

"Disgraceful," Shimizu said. What was even more disgraceful was that the young local didn't even understand the word. Shimizu tried again: "Bad."

Yes, the local got that. He bowed again, repeating, "*Gomen nasai.*" Shimizu didn't care if he was sorry or not. He jerked his thumb down the street. The young man hurried away.

When Shimizu got back to his company's encampment, he was still in a foul mood. "What's the matter, Corporal-*san?*" Shiro Wakuzawa asked. "You look like you could bite nails in two."

"I'll tell you, that's how I feel," Shimizu said. The story of the young man who could hardly speak Japanese poured out of him. "And he was happy that way!" he raged. "Happy!

English number one here, he said—'English *ichi-ban*.' " He mocked the way the local spoke. "And he couldn't even understand when I told him what a disgrace he was."

"So sorry, Corporal," Wakuzawa said. That did nothing to make Shimizu feel better. It just reminded him of the Hawaiian Japanese stuttering apologies. Private Wakuzawa went on, "Everything is pretty crazy here, though. Some of the policemen in Honolulu are Koreans. Koreans, if you can believe it! And everybody, even the Japanese, even the whites, has to do what they say."

"Koreans? That is crazy," Shimizu agreed. Korea had been part of the Japanese Empire longer than he'd been alive. Any Japanese knew Koreans were hewers of wood and drawers of water, and that was about all. They got drafted into the Army, but as laborers and prison guards. They weren't good for anything else. Shimizu wouldn't have wanted to go into battle alongside Koreans with rifles in their hands. He said, "Americans have to be a little screwy to let something like that go on. I bet we take care of it now that we're in charge."

"I hope so, Corporal," Wakuzawa said. "If anybody thinks I'm going to do what some Korean tells me to do, he'd better think twice."

"Oh, no." Shimizu shook his head. "Maybe they call themselves Americans, not Koreans. I don't care if they do. Maybe they call themselves policemen. I don't care about that, either. We are soldiers of the Imperial Japanese Army. We obey no one except our superiors in the Army. If some Korean cop—or even a real American cop—tries to tell you what to do, kick him in the teeth."

Wakuzawa was a skinny little fellow with a ready smile. He couldn't look very fierce no matter how hard he tried. But he did his best now. "*Hai*, Corporal-*san!*" he said, and mimed a kick at someone taller than he was.

Shimizu laughed out loud. "I don't think you'd get him in the *teeth* with that, but it would probably do the job." He slapped the private on the back. In Japan, that would have been an unheard-of familiarity between noncom and first-year soldier. Here in easygoing Hawaii, it seemed natural enough.

KENZO AND HIROSHI TAKAHASHI USED SHOVELS and rakes and hoes to clear rubble from the streets of Honolulu. Till the *Oshima Maru* put to sea with sails taking the place of her engine, that was the most use they could be. The job also paid well: three full meals a day, plus a dollar.

The work was steady, if you liked that sort of thing. Kenzo didn't. "Is this why we graduated from high school?" he asked bitterly, filling the shovel full of broken bits of brick and dumping them into a waiting wheelbarrow.

His older brother shrugged and added a shovelful of his own. "It's what we've got," Hiroshi answered. "If we don't pitch in, the town just stays a mess."

"Yeah, I suppose so," Kenzo said. He and Hiroshi didn't just speak English—they made a point of speaking English. He wondered if it was a point the rest of the men in the labor gang understood, or even cared about. Like any outfit in Honolulu, the rubble-clearing party had men of every blood and every mix of bloods in it. Some of them used English, some the pidgin that did duty for English among those who didn't speak it very well, and some the languages of their homelands. The straw boss was a Hawaiian Japanese who was fluently profane in both his own language and an English that was almost but not quite pidgin.

"No waste time!" the straw boss shouted. "You waste your time, you waste my time. You waste my time, you be sorry!"

This was harder work than fishing. Kenzo hadn't thought anything could be. It never got as frantic as pulling tuna off the line and gutting them one after another, but it never let up, either. One shovelful after another, the whole day long . . . "The guys who built the Pyramids worked like this," he said.

Hiroshi shook his head. "They didn't have wheelbarrows."

Kenzo grunted. He sounded very much like his father

when he did it, though he would have brained anybody who said so with his shovel. He said, "Well, you're right. It could be worse. I wouldn't've believed it."

"Keep an eye peeled for cans," Hiroshi added. "Guys who built the Pyramids didn't have those, either."

This time, Kenzo refused to back down. "They didn't know how lucky they were," he said.

The rule was that any cans found intact had to go into the communal food store. Nobody paid attention to the rule unless Japanese soldiers were close by to enforce it. Otherwise, an older rule prevailed: finders keepers. Of course, half the time you didn't know what you'd found till you got it open. Labels didn't last, not when big chunks of the city had turned into wasteland. Corned-beef hash? Canned peaches? Tomato soup? Nobody was fussy, not these days.

Every so often, Japanese soldiers would march past. When they did, the laborers had to stop what they were doing and bow. Kenzo ground his teeth at showing the invaders a respect he didn't feel. Like most Japanese his age in Hawaii, he'd always felt more ties with America than with the old country. Japan had been something for his father to talk about nostalgically. But the war had made sure no *haole*, no Chinese, no Korean—nobody—would ever treat him as anything but a damn Jap.

After lowering his spade one more time to bow to some soldiers, he noticed something interesting. "You see what I see?" he asked Hiroshi in a voice not much above a whisper.

"What's that?" his brother said, just as quietly.

"They don't come around by ones or twos any more," Kenzo said. "They're always in bunches—like bananas."

"Heh," Hiroshi said—about as much laughter as the crack deserved. "I can tell you how come, if you really want to know."

"Sure," Kenzo said. "Spit it out."

Hiroshi paused till the straw boss went by. He didn't stop shoveling. Neither did Kenzo. The straw boss went on to yell at somebody else. The two Takahashis looked busy enough to suit him. Once he'd moved out of earshot, Hiroshi said, "They don't go around by ones or twos any more because they got knocked over the head when they did—always where nobody could see anything or find out what happened."

"Yeah?" Kenzo asked eagerly.

"Yeah," his brother said. "No way to take hostages or anything when they haven't got any idea who done it." He threw another shovelful of wreckage into the wheelbarrow, then stopped when he took a look at Kenzo's face. "Don't you go getting any dumb ideas, now!" He wagged a finger at Kenzo.

"If I'm going to knock anybody over the head, I'll start with Dad," Kenzo said. Hiroshi snorted as if he'd been joking. To show he wasn't, he went on, "Even after what they did to Mother, he still went to their stinking parade."

"Hell, you know Dad," Hiroshi said. "He stands up and whinnies when he hears 'Kimigayo.'"

That made Kenzo snort. It damn near made him giggle. He could picture his father—picture him all too well—as an aging cart horse responding to the Japanese national anthem. "Damn you," he said, still snorting. "Now I'm going to want to give him a lump of sugar whenever I see him."

"Well, go ahead," Hiroshi said. "We're short on all kinds of stuff, but we've got sugar. Sugar and pineapple. How long can we eat 'em?"

"Here's hoping we don't have to find out, that's all." When Kenzo thought about food, he didn't feel like joking any more. He went back to work. If he was busy, he wouldn't have to think so much. And laborers were getting fed well . . . so far, anyhow.

Japanese soldiers weren't the only people on the streets. There were also scroungers, men and women picking through the ruins for whatever they could grab. Both laborers and soldiers chased them when they saw them. But the scroungers were like mongooses; they were good at not being seen.

And there were ordinary people trying to lead ordinary lives in times that were anything but ordinary. They often had a faintly lost air, as if they not only couldn't believe how much things had changed but also refused to acknowledge it. Most of the people like that seemed to be *haoles*. They'd been on top so long, they'd come to take it for granted. They didn't know how to cope now that Hawaii was under new management. They seemed to think this was all a bad dream. They'd wake up pretty soon, and everything would be fine. Except it wouldn't.

Kenzo froze with his shovel in midair. Up the street towards him came Elsie Sundberg and a couple of other girls. The last time she'd seen him, she'd pretended she hadn't. The memory of that still burned. Would she do it again? He didn't think he could stand it if she did, even though she wasn't exactly his girlfriend and never had been.

He knew just when she recognized him. She half missed a step, then turned to one of her friends and said something Kenzo was too far away to catch. The other girls just shrugged, which told him nothing.

Elsie squared her shoulders. She kept walking. When she came to where Kenzo was working, she nodded and said, "Hello, Ken. How are you?"

He felt like cheering. Instead, he nodded back. "I'm okay. How are you? Is your family all right?"

"I'm . . . here," she answered. That could have meant anything. "My family's safe, yes. How about you? I see your brother's here."

"Yes." Kenzo nodded jerkily. "And my father's fine. My mother . . ." He didn't go on. His face twisted. *I won't cry in front of her. I won't*, he told himself, and somehow he didn't.

"Oh, Ken! I'm so sorry!" All of a sudden, Elsie sounded like the girl he'd known for so long, not the near-stranger who thought he was nothing but a Jap.

One of the girls she was with, a brunette named Joyce something who'd graduated a couple of years ahead of her and Kenzo, said, "I didn't know the Japs did anything to their own."

He gripped the handle on the shovel very tightly. *She*

probably hasn't got any brains to knock out, he told himself. He made himself hold still. It wasn't easy. Neither was holding his voice steady as he answered, "I'm not a Jap. I'm an American, just as much as you are—or I would be if you'd let me."

By the way Joyce looked at him, he might as well have spoken to her in Japanese. Elsie's other friend rolled her eyes, as if to say she'd heard it before and didn't believe a word of it. Kenzo waited to see what Elsie would do. She eyed him as if she were seeing him for the first time. In a way, maybe she was. She said, "Take care of yourself. I've got to go."

And she did. Joyce wagged a finger at her. She just shrugged. The straw boss yelled, "You work, Takahashi, you lazy *baka yaro!*" Kenzo did. Maybe the world wasn't such a wretched place after all.

VIII

Lieutenant Saburo Shindo strode along the runway at Wheeler Field. His boots clumped on concrete. The wreckage of American warplanes caught on the ground had been bulldozed off to the grass alongside the runways. Japanese technicians attacked the wrecks with pliers and wrenches and screwdrivers and wire-cutters, salvaging what they could. A lot of Japanese flight instruments were based on their American equivalents. In a pinch, the American ones might do. And spare parts, wherever they came from, were always welcome.

Turning to Commander Fuchida, Shindo said, "The Americans had so much here!"

"*Hai.*" Fuchida nodded. "We knew that before we started this."

"We knew it, yes, but did we *know* it?" Shindo said. "Did we feel it in our bellies? I don't think so. If we had *known* how much they had, would we have had the nerve to try what we tried?"

This time, Fuchida shrugged. "What you have is one thing. What you do with it is something else. And we had the advantage of surprise." He waved to the shattered hulks of airplanes. "Once we caught them on the ground, they never had the chance to recover."

"Yes, sir," Shindo said. "That was the point of the exercise, all right."

Fuchida turned away, towards the northeast. "Now we make them come to us. If they want to fight a war in the Pacific from their own West Coast, they're welcome to try." He paused, then resumed: "Commander Genda was right. If we'd struck the fleet and gone away, they would have used *this* for their advance base, not San Francisco, and who knows what they might have interfered with? But Hawaii shields everything we're doing farther west."

"Oh, yes. We make good progress in the Philippines and the Dutch East Indies, they say." Shindo paused, for the first time really hearing something. "Commander Genda, sir?"

"That's right," Fuchida answered, a small smile on his face.

"But I thought the plan for the attack on Pearl Harbor came from Admiral Yamamoto," Shindo said.

"And if you ask Genda-*san* about it, you'll go right on thinking the same thing," Fuchida told him. "I sometimes think Genda is much too modest for his own good. But I happen to know he was the one who persuaded Yamamoto to follow up the air strike with an invasion. He'll say Yamamoto was the one who persuaded the Army, and that was what counted. But he gave Yamamoto the idea."

"I had no idea," Shindo murmured. "Genda has said not a word of this."

"He wouldn't. It's not his style," Fuchida said.

From what Shindo knew of Genda, that was true. To Genda, the operation counted for more than anything else, including who proposed it. Shindo suddenly snapped his fingers: an unusual display for him. "Something I've been meaning to ask you, sir—have the technicians made any more sense of the wreckage we found at that Opana place?"

"Not so much as I'd like," Fuchida answered. "Whatever it was, the Americans didn't want us to know anything about it. They did a good, thorough job of destroying it after we landed."

"I can make a guess," Shindo said. Fuchida gestured for him to go on. He did: "When we attacked the first American carrier—the one that turned out to be the *Enterprise*—she had fighters up and waiting for us before we got there. We didn't see any American patrol planes as we flew towards her. I don't think there were any. I think the Americans have instruments that let them spot planes at some very long distance."

Fuchida frowned thoughtfully. "And you think the Opana installation is one of these?"

"Opana is a logical place for one," Shindo replied. "It's as far north as you can go on Oahu, near enough. Any attack was likeliest to come from the north. And the Yankees would do a good job of destroying something that important."

"If they had that kind of device there, why didn't it find our first attack wave?" Fuchida asked. "It didn't, you know. Our surprise was complete."

Lieutenant Shindo shrugged this time. "Maybe something went wrong with it. Maybe the Americans just didn't pay any attention to it. They were like those big birds that stick their heads in the sand."

"Ostriches," Fuchida supplied. "They don't really do that, you know."

"So what?" Shindo shrugged once more. "The Americans did, and that's what counts."

"Yes." Fuchida turned towards the northeast once more. "They did a bad job of scouting, and it cost them. We'd better not imitate them, or it will cost us, too. We'll need long-range patrols to make sure they don't try to cause trouble."

"Can we afford the fuel to do a proper job of it?" Shindo asked.

"The cost of using up the fuel is one thing. The cost of *not* using it up is liable to be something else again," Fuchida said. "Or do you think I'm wrong? If you do, don't be shy."

Lieutenant Shindo was seldom shy. He was, if anything, unusually forthright for a Japanese. Because he didn't ruffle easily, he didn't think anyone else should, either. But he shook his head now. "No, sir, you're not wrong. It's just one of the things we've got to think about."

"Oh, yes." Fuchida mimed letting his shoulders sag, as if the weight of the world lay heavy upon them. But then he gestured, not just at the technicians stripping U.S. airplanes but at all of Wheeler Field. "So many things to think about. And this would be much harder if not for everything we've captured from the Americans."

"I've thought the same thing ever since I saw the bulldozers and other earth-moving equipment we used to fix the airstrip up at Haleiwa," Shindo said.

"And that was just civilian stuff: what the local builders used," Fuchida said. "The military gear is even better, though a lot of it got ruined in the fighting and the Americans sabotaged what they could of the rest."

"By what I've seen, they might have done a better job with that," Shindo said.

Now Commander Fuchida shrugged again. "They're rich," he said, and said no more. Lieutenant Shindo inclined his head in silent agreement. He understood exactly what his superior meant. Because the Yankees had so much, they didn't seem to realize how valuable even their scraps and leavings were to the Japanese. Along with the earth-moving machinery, they'd left plenty of automobiles behind as they fell back from the northern part of Oahu, and they hadn't torched all the filling stations, either. The Japanese had made good use of both the cars and the precious gasoline.

The same held true elsewhere. Hawaii had an astonishing telephone network: there was a phone for every ten people in the islands. In Japan, the figure was more like one for every sixty people; outside of Tokyo, it wasn't far from one for every hundred people. You could talk to anyone here, or any place on the islands, almost instantly. The Americans took that so much for granted, they hadn't bothered to destroy the phone lines or the switching system. That would make it much easier for Japan to defend its conquests. Japanese soldiers slept in U.S. barracks that hadn't been blown up to deny them to the invaders. They lived softer than they would have at home. The list went on and on.

Fuchida kept looking towards the American mainland. "Sooner or later, they will try to come back," he predicted.

"Let them try," Shindo said. "We'll give them a set of lumps for their troubles, and then they can try again." He and Fuchida smiled at each other. The sun shone down brightly. It was a perfect morning. But then, what morning wasn't perfect in Hawaii?

ONCE UPON A TIME, in the dim and vanished days before the war came to Oahu, Kapiolani Park had been a place where tourists and locals could get away from the frenzy of Waikiki for a little while. Lying by the road out to Diamond Head, the expanse of grass and trees had featured, among other things, a fancy band shell where the Royal Hawaiian Band played on Sunday afternoons.

Now, barbed wire and machine-gun towers ringed Kapiolani Park. Japanese soldiers patrolled the perimeter. In the park itself, tents sprouted like a swarm of toadstools. This was what being a prisoner of war meant.

A mynah hopped along the grass between the tents, head cocked to one side as it studied the ground for worms and grubs. Fletcher Armitage studied the mynah the same way the bird studied the ground, and with the same hunger. He had a rock in his hand.

He also watched his fellow captives. If he knocked the bird over, could one of them grab it before he did?

That was an important question. Everybody on Oahu was going to get hungry by and by. Fletch had seen as much before the surrender. For POWs, though, by and by was already here. The Japanese fed them a little rice or noodles every day. Sometimes green leaves of one sort or another were mixed in with the mess. More rarely, so were bits of fish. Even when they were, the day's ration wouldn't have kept a four-year-old healthy, let along a grown man.

"Come a little closer, you stupid bird," Fletch murmured. Mynahs took people pretty much for granted. Why not? People had always let them alone. People had . . . till they started getting hungry.

Fletch's belly growled at the thought of mynah meat.

He'd never been fat. He was getting skinnier by the day. He'd traded his belt for a length of rope and half a dozen cigarettes. He'd smoked all the cigarettes the day he got them. The rope would go on holding up his pants after he got too skinny for the belt to do him any good.

Closer came the mynah, and closer still, till it got within about six feet of him. Then it paused, tilting its head to one side and watching him with a beady black eye. It was fairly tame, yes, but not suicidally so like a zebra dove.

"Come on," Fletch crooned. "Come on, baby." The mynah bird kept on casing him. It came no closer. He crooned curses when he decided it wasn't going to. He'd just have to take his best shot.

He let fly with the rock. The motion of his arm startled the bird. It was already on the wing and squawking when the rock thudded down somewhere close to where it had been. Would he have hit it if it hadn't taken off? Maybe. Maybe not, too.

Coming out with some curses that weren't crooned at all, Fletch turned away in disgust. "Too bad, buddy," said a soldier in a tent across the narrow track. "Woulda been good, I bet."

"Yeah," Fletch said. "It would've been." The rest of the day looked black and gloomy. If he'd made the kill, he could have had a few bites of real meat, even if mynahs weren't anything to make you forget fried chicken. Now he'd have to get by on rations alone. The only trouble with that was, a man couldn't possibly do it.

He went over and picked up the rock before somebody else got hold of it. It was a good size for clouting birds. Some time before too long, he'd get another chance. *Don't blow it*, he told himself sternly.

How smart were birds? How long would they take to figure out that they'd suddenly become fair game? How long before they started staying away from Kapiolani Park? If they did, that would be very bad.

The Japs didn't bother bringing drinking water into the park. They just left the drinking fountains in place. *Generous of them*, Fletch thought sourly. If a man had to stand in line for an hour just to wet his whistle . . . well, so what? That was no skin off the Japs' noses.

Anyone who wanted to wash had to do it at the drinking fountains, too. That meant anything resembling real washing was impossible. Fletch noticed the stink less than he'd thought he would. When everybody smelled, nobody smelled. And everybody sure smelled here.

Rank had no privileges in line. As far as Fletch could see, rank had no privileges anywhere in the camp any more. If enlisted men obeyed officers, it was because they respected them or liked them, not because they thought they had to. And if they didn't, what could the officers do about it? Not much. The Japs wouldn't back them up. The Japs didn't care what happened here.

Slowly, slowly, the line snaked forward. Fletch sighed. He was thirsty. He was tired. And he was hungry. Anyone who was hungry enough to want to eat a mynah bird was hungry, all right. Unless he caught a mynah or a dove, he'd stay hungry till he got supper. He shook his head. He'd stay hungry after he got supper, too, because it wouldn't be nearly enough.

His turn at the water fountain finally came. He drank and drank and drank. If he drank enough, he could trick his belly into thinking he was full, at least for a little while. He splashed water on his face and hands, too.

"Come on, buddy. Shake a leg," the soldier behind him growled. Reluctantly, Fletch moved away from the fountain. The breeze off the ocean a few hundred yards away dried the water on his face. As usual, the weather was perfect: not too hot, not too cold, moist but not too humid. Diamond Head towered in the middle distance. The inside of the dead volcano was supposed to be honeycombed with tunnels, fortified beyond belief. When the rest of Oahu was hostage to the Japs, though, that hadn't turned out to matter a whole hell of a lot.

A bunch of things everybody had thought would be important hadn't turned out to matter a whole hell of a lot. The innate superiority of the white man to the Oriental was one that occurred to Fletch. Here in this POW camp, he didn't feel very goddamn superior.

The Japs went out of their way to rub it in that he wasn't, too. A squad of guards strode through the camp, bayonets glittering on their rifles. Americans scrambled to get out of the soldiers' way. Along with everybody else, Fletch bowed when the guards passed him. Everyone had learned that lesson in a hurry. The Japanese set on and savagely beat anybody who forgot. A couple of Americans were supposed to have died from their mistreatment. Fletch didn't know if that was true, but he wouldn't have been surprised. The Japs didn't give a rat's ass whether Americans lived or died.

Fletch sat down in front of his tent. There wasn't much else to do. In fact, there wasn't anything else to do. Hunger left him slow and lethargic. A fly landed on his arm. Slowly and lethargically, he brushed it away. There seemed to be more flies in the POW camp every day. That only made sense; the latrines got fouler every day. Fletch didn't know how many thousands of prisoners were jammed in here. Enough so that their wastes overwhelmed the lime chloride the Japs deigned to sprinkle into the latrine trenches.

How long before they ran out of lime chloride altogether? How long before they ran out of chlorine for treating the drinking water? Probably not long—like damn near everything else, the chemicals came, or had come, from the mainland. What would happen when they did run out? *Dysentery* was the word that came to mind.

After half an hour or so, Fletch heaved himself to his feet. The one drawback to filling yourself full of water was that you didn't stay full. It worked its way through. He trudged off towards the slit trenches. He might as well have been moving in slow motion. He didn't have the energy to hurry.

He stood at the edge of a trench, unfastened his fly, and eased himself. Out beyond the barbed wire, Japanese soldiers kept an eye on him and on the other Americans using the slit trenches. Fletch caught a guard's eye as he put himself back in his pants. *Yeah, you son of a bitch, I've got a bigger one than you do*, he thought. He turned away.

Such games were dangerous. If he got too obvious, the

Japs were liable to understand exactly what he meant. Then there'd be hell to pay. He ambled off. The guard didn't start yelling or open fire, so he'd got away with it.

"Fletch! Is that you? I thought sure you were dead!"

"Gordy! I'll be goddamned. I thought you were, too." Fletch pumped Gordon Douglas' hand. Then both men seemed to decide at the same instant that that wasn't good enough. They clung to each other as if each were drowning and the other a life preserver. Douglas was dirty, and thinner than Fletch ever remembered seeing him. Seeing him at all was great, though. "How the hell did you end up in one piece?"

The other artillery lieutenant shrugged. "Half the time I ask myself the same thing. They started shooting us up when we were just going out of Schofield Barracks."

"Yeah, us, too," Fletch broke in. "You would have been in the truck convoy right in front of mine, or maybe right behind it."

"Behind it, I think." Douglas rubbed at a nasty, half-healed scar on his arm. "But Jesus God, Fletch, you can't do shit when the other guy's got planes in the air and you don't. You're dead as what comes out of a Spam can."

"I found that out, too," Armitage said. "We didn't get to our position till the Japs were already hitting the beaches, and that was too late."

"Shit, you did better than we did," Douglas said. "We never made it to Haleiwa at all. It can't be more than fifteen fucking miles, but we never fucking got there. Air attacks, traffic on the road coming south, wrecks to try and go around—except sometimes you couldn't go around them. You had to clear 'em—by hand—and that took forever."

"Tell me about it!" Fletch exclaimed. "Our truck got shot up. We commandeered a civilian car. You should've heard the Nips in it howl when we threw 'em the hell out. Try towing a 105 with one of those babies if you want a fun time."

"You kept your piece? You don't know how lucky you are," Douglas said. "We had a bomb burst right under ours

early that second morning. Took out most of my crew. I was
farther away—that's when I got this." He rubbed the scar
again. "They slapped a bandage on it, but after that I was
an infantryman, and a piss-poor infantryman, too, let me be
the first to tell you."

"I had all ground-pounders on the gun except for me by
the time we folded up," Fletch said. "They learned the ropes
pretty good."

"When it's root, hog, or die you learn or you go under."
Douglas shrugged. "I learned, too, or learned enough. I
must've—I'm still here."

Fletch didn't say anything to that. From what he'd seen,
who lived and who died when bombs and bullets started flying was often—not always, but often—a matter of luck. Instead, he waved at what had been the charming Kapiolani
Park and was now the anything but charming POW camp.
"Yeah, we're here, all right, and ain't it a garden spot?"

Gordon Douglas only shrugged again. "The goddamn
monkeys didn't murder us all after we surrendered. Far as
I'm concerned, that's a step up from what they could've
done. Step up from what I figured they'd do, too. Some of
the shit I saw—" He spat, but didn't go into detail.

All Fletch did was nod and say, "Yeah." He scratched at
himself. He was itching more and more as time went by.
Fleas? Lice? Bedbugs? All of the above? Probably all of the
above. Then he waved at the camp again. "They didn't
need to murder us all at once. Looks like they're gonna do
it by inches instead." He poked Douglas in the belly. The
other man had always had trouble keeping the pounds off.
He didn't any more. "You're skinnier than you used to be.
So am I."

"Don't remind me," Douglas said. "They give us this
horrible slop, and they don't give us enough of it, and it's
the most delicious stuff in the world when you get it, on account of then you feel a little less empty for a little while."

"I know. I know. Oh, God, do I know." Fletch looked
towards the kitchen tents. He knew how long it was till supper, too—knew to the minute even without a watch. Too
long. Too goddamn long.

* * *

WHEN OSCAR VAN DER KIRK and Charlie Kaapu got their surfboards from the Outrigger Club, Charlie asked, "You giving lessons today?"

"This afternoon, yeah. Not now," Oscar answered. "How about you?"

His *hapa*-Hawaiian buddy only shrugged. "Not now."

Oscar always thought of himself as a happy-go-lucky guy. Next to most of the population of Hawaii, much less the mainland, he was. Next to Charlie Kaapu, he might have been a Rockefeller or a du Pont. "Charlie, what the hell *do* you do for money?" he asked.

Charlie shrugged. "Never have much. Never worry much. Too much worry, too much *huhu*, waste time." He slapped his rock-hard belly. "I don't starve yet."

"Yeah." Oscar's voice rang a little hollow. Before the Japs took over, that would have been a joke. It wasn't so funny now. People were short of everything from pasta and tomatoes to toilet paper. That wouldn't get better, only worse. Every once in a while, even though she'd walked out on him, he wondered how Susie Higgins was doing and where her next meal was coming from. He didn't waste a whole lot of grief on her, though. She was the kind who'd always land on her feet—or, if she had to, on her back.

His toes dug into the sand as he and Charlie walked down to the Pacific. Waikiki Beach was crowded this morning—not with tourists, the way it usually was, but with fishermen. Swarms of people with a rod and reel, and quite a few people with just a rod and a length of line and a hook, were out trying their luck.

A man in a straw hat, a loud floral shirt, and Bermuda shorts hauled a silvery fish out of the water. It wasn't very big, but all his neighbors stared jealously. He stashed the fish in a creel he kept between his feet. Nobody was going to take his prize away from him.

"Excuse us. 'Scuse us," Oscar said over and over, pushing past the fishermen to get into the sea. Charlie was more direct. He used his surfboard's nose to clear a path for himself. A couple of fishermen gave him nasty looks. He looked

right back at them. They muttered to themselves, but that
was all they did. Charlie hardly ever got into fights. That
was mostly because nobody was crazy enough to want to
take him on.

A hook splashed into the water right by Oscar's shoulder as he paddled out to sea. That wouldn't have been any
fun if it had bitten into him. He scowled back towards the
beach, but he couldn't even tell which would-be Izaak Wal-
ton had launched it.

He breathed a sigh of relief when he and Charlie got
out of range of such missiles. "Well, they won't catch us instead of their minnows," he said.

"Yeah," Charlie said, and then, "That one guy got a real
fish. Don't see that all the time, not off Waikiki Beach."

"These days, you take whatever you get," Oscar said.
Along with their surfboards, he and Charlie had hand nets
and canvas sacks to hold whatever they caught. They could
get a lot farther out to sea than the optimists who fished
from the water's edge. Or maybe they weren't optimists.
Maybe they were just hungry men doing what they could.
Anything was better than nothing.

Were he giving a lesson, Oscar would have turned back
towards shore long since. But he wasn't. Oahu receded behind him. The breeze came off the land. He wrinkled his
nose. At just about the same time, Charlie said, "What's
that stink?"

"It's got to be the prisoners' camp in Kapiolani Park,"
Oscar answered. "I can't think of anything else it could
be."

Charlie Kaapu grunted. "That's a nasty business."

"Everything that's happened since the Japs landed is a
nasty business," Oscar said. Charlie grunted again. He
didn't say anything more, so Oscar took it for a grunt of
agreement.

Off in the distance, a couple of fishing sampans headed
out to sea. The light breeze filled their sails. More and more
sampans were abandoning engines for the wind. Without
fuel, what good were engines? Without fuel, what good was
anything? Oscar's Chevy sat on the street. It wasn't going

anywhere. Even if he could get gas for it, the battery was sure to be dead by now.

He was jealous of the sampans for the same reason the surf fishermen were bound to be jealous of him. As he could get fish the men on the beach couldn't, so the sampans could find fish he'd never see. "Hey, Charlie!" he called.

Charlie Kaapu looked up from his paddling. "What you want?"

"You think we could rig a little mast and sail on a surfboard? That would let us get a lot farther out to sea than we can like this."

Charlie thought it over, then shook his head. "Waste time," he said. Oscar shrugged. His friend might well be right.

Something nibbled his finger. He looked into the water. A minnow darted away. Oscar laughed. His hands and feet were the bait he fished with. Even as he laughed, though, he also scanned the sea. Fish he wanted to catch weren't the only sort out there. The Pacific also held fish that wanted to catch him. Sharks big enough to be dangerous were rare. Some people on the mainland imagined surfriders devoured every day. That was a bunch of hooey. But a man who ignored the risk was a fool, too. It was like not watching the road when you got behind the wheel.

"What do you think?" he asked Charlie after a while. "We out far enough?"

Charlie looked back towards the shore. "I guess maybe. We don't get anything, we can paddle some more."

"Okay." Oscar stopped paddling and let his arm trail in the water. He fluttered his fingers. Now he wanted fish to come up to him. *Here, isn't this an interesting piece of seaweed?* That was what he wanted to put across to the fish. *I should be writing radio spots*, he thought.

A fish came up to see what he was selling. He had the net in his other hand. He didn't advertise the net. He made a swipe with it—and the fish got away. "Oh, shit," he said without too much heat. Such mishaps happened all the time.

Charlie made a swipe of his own. He hauled something

silvery out of the sea. As he stuffed it into his sack, he sent Oscar a sly smile. Oscar took his hand out of the water and flipped Charlie off. They both laughed. No mystical native talent had let Charlie catch a fish where Oscar failed. Before long, Oscar would be smiling and Charlie cussing. They both knew it. There wasn't any point in getting excited. If you weren't patient, you'd never make it as a fisherman.

After a while, Oscar caught a little ray. Before he came to Hawaii, he would have thrown the bat-winged fish back. A few visits to Chinese and Japanese restaurants, though, had convinced him ray and even shark could be pretty tasty if you did them right. And he couldn't be too choosy these days anyhow.

A swarm of minnows flashed by, like shooting stars under the surface of the sea. Oscar and Charlie looked up, the same hopeful expression on both their faces. Minnows wouldn't swim that way unless something was after them. And whatever was after them might really be worth catching.

Oscar swiped with his net. He let out a whoop—his catch almost tore the handle out of his grasp. He hauled a mackerel up onto his surfboard. A few seconds later, Charlie caught one, too. They both stuffed the fish into their sacks and thrust the nets into the sea again. If there were more, they wanted them. And there were. Oscar got another one in nothing flat. *I eat today*, he thought.

Lots of people in Honolulu had such worries these days. Unlike most of those people, Oscar had had them before. He'd spent a lot of time living from hand to mouth. There was a difference, though. When he'd worried about going hungry before, it was because he'd been short of money. Now he was short of food, and so was everybody else.

He went on fishing even after he caught the second mackerel. What he didn't eat today could go into the little icebox in his room for tomorrow. Or he could trade it for other food, or sell it to get the money he needed to pay the rent. He wondered if his landlord would take fish for the rent in place of cash. Before the war started, the idea would have been ridiculous. Not any more.

"Well, shall we head back?" he asked at last, after a long dry stretch.

"Why not?" Charlie Kaapu said. "Plenty for today." He worried about tomorrow even less than Oscar did.

They turned their surfboards towards the shore and began to paddle again. That was work: familiar work, but work. Oscar thought some more about putting a sail on the surfboard. It wouldn't be pretty, but he was damned if he could see why it wouldn't work. You did what you had to do. If you were making your living as a surf-rider, that was one thing. If you were using your surfboard mostly as a fishing boat, that was something else again.

Waikiki Beach neared. The fishermen still cast their lines upon the water. Oscar glanced over to Charlie. "Shall we give 'em a show?" he said.

"What else we got to do?" Charlie answered.

They rode the breakers back to the beach. Oscar was used to standing up on a surfboard supporting a skittish tourist. Doing the same thing with a net in one hand and his sack of fish in the other was no *huhu*. Beside him, Charlie Kaapu might have been the incarnation of Kuula, the Hawaiian god of fishermen. You got the feeling nothing could make him come off his surfboard. That feeling might be wrong; Charlie could take a tumble like anybody else. But Oscar didn't think he would, not this time.

And he didn't. Neither did Oscar. They glided smoothly up onto the sand. The fishermen gave them a smattering of applause. Somebody reached into his pocket and tossed Oscar a quarter. Oscar caught it out of the air with his net. That won him some more cheers. He would have got more still if he could have balanced the coin on the end of his nose.

He shrugged as he walked back to his apartment. He was a performer when he got on a surfboard. If he got paid for being a performer, what was wrong with that?

A JAPANESE OFFICER SHOUTED in his own language. Along with the rest of the prisoners in the Pearl City camp, Jim Peterson waited for the English translation. He didn't have to wait long. As usual, a Hawaiian-born Jap about his own age stood next to the officer. The local wore a sharp shark-skin suit. He seemed happy as a clam to serve his new bosses.

"You will be moved," he said. "You will go to the north and central part of the island. Some of you will work in the fields. You will be well fed and well treated."

Peterson turned his head ever so slightly towards Prez McKinley, who stood beside him. "Yeah, and the check is in the mail," he said out of the side of his mouth.

McKinley snickered. He didn't do it very loud, though. Guards watched the POWs. If you got out of line, they beat you. They stomped you, too, and hit you with sticks. They'd already killed at least one American. Nobody wanted to give them any excuse to go to work.

And there were probably prisoners who couldn't be trusted. Peterson didn't like thinking so, but it was the way to bet. Some people were out for themselves, first, last, and always. *If you can't beat 'em, join 'em. If you can't lick 'em, lick their boots.*

The Jap with the sword on his hip shouted some more. The quisling in the sharkskin suit translated: "This move will begin in one hour. All able-bodied prisoners must go. It is an order from the Japanese Imperial Army." The way he said it, God might have handed it to Moses on a tablet of stone.

"What about the wounded? What about the sick?" somebody called.

Questions—the mere idea that there could be questions—seemed to surprise both the translator and the officer. The officer growled something. If it didn't mean, *What the devil was that?* Peterson would have eaten his hat. The local Jap spoke nervously in Japanese. The officer said something else. The translator returned to English: "They will come when they are fit. Until then, they stay here."

"They could put most of 'em on trucks and bring 'em along," McKinley said as the gathering broke up.

"They could, yeah, but why would they?" Peterson answered. "They can't have a whole lot of fuel here. You think they're going to waste it on Americans? You think they're going to waste it on American *prisoners*, for crying out loud?"

"For crying out loud is right," McKinley said. "Don't know what the hell I was thinking. I musta been outa my tree."

"For Japs, they're being damn nice to give us an hour to get ready," Peterson said. "It's not like I've got a lot to pack. Outside of the clothes on my back, what I've got is a canteen and a deck of cards."

"Take 'em," Prez McKinley said. "You can kill a lot of time with cards. And fill up the canteen before you start. God knows whether those monkeys'll give us anything, no matter what they say."

That made more sense than Peterson wished it did. Rations had been anything but abundant here. And the Japanese didn't bother to hide their contempt for the men who'd surrendered. Any American who gave them even the slightest excuse got beaten up. As far as the Japs were concerned, they were on top, the prisoners were on the bottom, and anybody who didn't remember that was how things were supposed to work was asking for it.

He had to stand in line to fill the canteen. He had to stand in line for everything in the prison camp. *Might as well be in the service or something*, he thought wryly. The one faucet the POWs were allowed to use was at the back of what had been a park building. Two Japs in a sandbagged machine-gun nest kept an eye on the queue.

McKinley had a canteen, too. He rubbed his chin, which was sporting a pretty fair crop of grizzled whiskers. "Christ, what I wouldn't do for some shaving soap and a razor," he said.

Peterson nodded. "Oh, yeah. We're all going to look like we play for the House of David before too long."

They set out when the Japanese officer blew a whistle. It felt like about an hour to Peterson. He didn't know for sure, having been relieved of his watch. The Jap had one on his wrist. Peterson wondered if he'd worn it when he got here, or if he'd stolen it since. He sure didn't want to know badly enough to ask, though.

The Japanese soldiers nervously eyed the prisoners as they came out of the barbed-wire enclosure the Japs had thrown up around the park. The soldiers gestured with their rifles: this way. Every one of the rifles had a bayonet fixed to it. The long blades gleamed in the sun. They weren't worth much in combat, but for sticking a prisoner who couldn't fight back they'd do just fine.

Along with the other men, Peterson started to walk. The journey north was like running a newsreel backwards: the farther he went, the more distant in time the remains of the fighting were. Things seemed to go in waves that hadn't been apparent while he crouched on the landscape with a rifle in his hand. A stretch of ground would look as if a giant had been stamping on it with hobnailed boots. That would be a place where the Americans had tried to make a stand. Then he would go forward through a few hundred yards of relatively unchewed terrain. After that would come another battered stretch of ground that would in fact have been the previous U.S. line.

Once they got out of Pearl City and onto Kamehameha Highway, there were places where the retreating Americans had blown up the road to keep Jap-run vehicles from moving forward along it. Not all the holes had been repaired. Some of them were ten feet deep and thirty feet across. The prisoners, naturally, tried to go into the fields on either side to get around them.

The guards shook their heads and gestured with their rifles. *"Kinjiru!"* they shouted.

Kinjiru! meant something like, *You can't do that!* It was one of the bits of Japanese Peterson had started picking up, however little he wanted any. "What do they want us to do, Prez?" he asked Sergeant McKinley. "Go through the goddamn hole? That's nuts."

Nuts or not, it was what the Japs had in mind. "You make," said one of them who knew a few words of English. "You go in."

Plainly, none of the prisoners wanted to do that. They piled up at the edge of the crater. The guards did some more yelling. Some of the gestures they used were pretty

explicit. *If you don't go in, you're going to get it.* Not a POW
went forward, though.

"They can't shoot all of us," somebody said. Jim Peterson wished he were sure of that. For the moment, though,
it seemed to be true.

One of the guards went pelting off towards the rear.
"The most junior man," McKinley remarked.

"Yeah, I noticed," Peterson said. By now, he'd got the
hang of reading Jap Army rank badges. The more gold and
the less red in the background, the higher the grade. Within
each grade, the more stars, the higher the rank.

For most of an hour, the standoff continued. Then that
poor miserable private, his tunic now all sweaty, returned
with the Japanese officer who'd started the parade and his
interpreter. He looked things over, then spoke in his own
language. The interpreter said, "He says you have to the
count of five to obey the order you have been given. After
that, the guards will begin to shoot. They will not stop
shooting until you obey."

"*Ichi*," the officer said. The interpreter held up one finger. "*Ni*." Two fingers. "*San*." Three . . . The guards raised
their rifles to their shoulders and stared down the barrels.

Peterson didn't find out how to say *four* or *five* in Japanese. With almost identical frightened moans, half a dozen
prisoners in the front ranks plunged down into the crater.
They floundered over to the other side and started scrambling up towards the asphalt once more. Other men followed them. As soon as a couple made it up onto the
highway again, they reached into the hole in the ground to
help their buddies climb out.

Along with everybody else, Peterson went through the
hole. He was filthy and weary by the time he made it to the
other side. Going around would have saved time. It would
have been ever so much easier. But it wasn't what the Japs
wanted.

"You know what they're doing?" he said as the march
north resumed.

"Lording it over us, you mean?" Prez McKinley said,
trying without much luck to get the dirt off his tunic.

"Yeah, that, too," Peterson answered. "But they're *breaking* us, taming us, like you'd break a mustang or something."

McKinley muttered to himself. It sounded like, "Try and break me, will they?" And maybe he had a point. But maybe not, too. If the Japs could get the Americans to do what they wanted without making a fuss for fear something worse would happen if they didn't, wouldn't that be enough to keep them happy? What more could they want, egg in their beer?

Plenty of people were out in the fields, cutting down sugarcane and pulling up pineapple plants. The Big Five, the companies that had run Hawaii ever since the annexation, were probably having heart attacks. What the Big Five thought was the least of Jim Peterson's worries. What he saw here actually made some sense. If Hawaii couldn't import what it needed from the mainland, it would have to grow its own food. People were taking the first steps in that direction, anyhow.

Yes, but can they grow enough soon enough? he wondered. All he could do was give a mental shrug. He didn't know. At least they were trying.

On went the POWs. A few people in the fields waved to them. That took guts, with Japanese soldiers watching the prisoners and others watching the laborers. Peterson wanted to wave back. He didn't, though; it might have drawn the Japs' notice to people who weren't afraid to show they didn't like the occupiers.

They were nearing the turnoff for Wheeler Field when a soldier who'd been visibly dragging for a while went over to the side of the road and sat down on his haunches. "Can't—go on—for a while," he panted. "Get my breath—catch up later." His face was gray with fatigue. Peterson wondered if he'd been hiding a wound.

Two guards rushed over to him. "*Kinjiru!*" they shouted. One of them made a motion with his rifle: *get up*.

"So sorry, soldier-*san*," the American soldier said, shaking his head. "Can't do it. Too damn tired. Let me rest—a little. Then I'll come."

"*Kinjiru!*" the guards yelled once more. The one who'd

gestured did it again. When the American didn't get up, they both kicked him. He howled and rolled over onto his side. They waited a moment, then kicked him again. He groaned. With an effort, he made it to his hands and knees. They waited a minute or so. When he didn't get to his feet, they kicked him some more. Plainly, they were ready to kick him to death if he didn't straighten up and fly right.

He must have figured that out at about the same time Peterson did. With another groan, he heaved himself up onto his pins. He stood swaying like a cypress in a hurricane, but he didn't fall down. One of the guards shoved him back into the pack. Two POWs caught him and held him upright; otherwise, he would have fallen on his face. The other guard used his rifle to urge the whole gang of prisoners forward again.

The exhausted soldier had a devil of a time going forward. The guards watched him like wolves eyeing a sickly elk that couldn't keep up with the herd. If he fell again, he was theirs.

He saw it, too. "You better get away from me, boys," he croaked. "If they decide to shoot me, they might hit one of you by mistake."

Rage kindled in Peterson. "Fuck 'em all," he said. "We'll get you there, goddammit." He draped the flagging man's arm around his shoulder. "We'll take turns."

"I've got him next," Prez McKinley said. Other men clamored to volunteer. The Japs didn't make a fuss. As long as everybody kept up, they didn't care how. Peterson strode ahead, taking his weight and a good part of the other man's till Prez cut in on him, almost as if at a dance.

This'll work as long as most of us are sound enough to help the ones who aren't, he thought. *Good thing Oahu's a small island. They can't take us too far. This might turn into a death march if they could.*

As the sun sank down towards the Waianae Range, a couple of trucks forced their way through the column of prisoners. They were U.S. Army vehicles, the white star on the driver's-side door hastily painted over with a Japanese meatball. "Goddamn guards didn't want to shoot *them* for going around the holes in the road," Peterson whispered to Prez McKinley.

"Oh, hell, no," McKinley whispered back. "They got Japs driving 'em. You suppose they've brought rations for us?"

"That'd be nice," Peterson said. In spite of the Japanese officer's promise, the prisoners had got no food as they tramped up Kamehameha Highway. Peterson's stomach was growling like an angry bear.

But instead of rations, the trucks disgorged machine-gun teams, who deployed onto high ground from which they could rake the throng of prisoners. A Buick came up a few minutes later. In it were the Japanese officer and his local stooge. The officer spoke in his own tongue. The translator turned it into English: "If anyone tries to escape, we will open fire on all of you. You are responsible for one another. See to it."

"Where's our food?" The question came from half a dozen places in the crowd.

The local obviously didn't want to translate it into Japanese. But the officer nudged him, just as obviously asking what was going on. The local Jap spoke. So did the officer. The fellow in the sharkskin suit said, "You disgraced yourselves with disobedience at the first hole in the road. Going hungry is the price you pay. You should be thankful it is no worse."

Jim Peterson was anything but thankful. With all those machine guns staring down at him, though, he couldn't do a thing about the way he really felt.

JIRO TAKAHASHI AND HIS SONS looked over the *Oshima Maru*. As she bobbed in the light chop in Kewalo Basin, she hardly seemed like the same sampan. A tall mast and a gaff rig changed her into something much more graceful than she had been with a diesel stuck on her stern. That she was also much slower than she had been and dependent on the breezes seemed almost an afterthought.

"She's ready," Eizo Doi said. The handyman cracked his knuckles, producing a noise alarmingly like a machine-gun burst. "You sure you know what you're doing with her, Takahashi-*san*? If you don't, you should only take her out a little ways the first few times, till you get the hang of it."

"I'll manage," Jiro said. "I helped my father man a boat on the Inland Sea. How to place the sail and which line to pull, they'll come back to me soon enough. What I really need to do is show the boys how everything works."

Kenzo said something to Hiroshi in English. Jiro caught the words *Moby Dick*. Was that some sort of strange obscenity he'd never heard before? He knew what a dick was, but the moby part went right over his head.

"Please yourself," Doi said. "Just don't get in trouble before you finish bringing me my fish." The way things were these days, most people were happier to get paid in food than in cash. As supplies got tighter, mere money bought less and less. Nimble as a mongoose, Doi hopped up onto the wharf. "Good luck," he told Jiro, and bowed. The fisherman returned it.

Half a beat slower than they should have, so did his sons. *No, they aren't properly Japanese at all*, Jiro thought with yet another mental sigh. Eizo Doi was polite enough to pretend he hadn't noticed they were slow. He ambled off towards another sampan. Jiro wondered if he was doing anything these days besides putting masts and sails on boats that couldn't use their engines any more.

Jiro stepped down into the *Oshima Maru*. Hiroshi and Kenzo followed a little more slowly. They couldn't act as if they knew it all here, because they damn well didn't. "Okay, Father. What do we do?" Hiroshi asked. The first word was English, but Jiro got it.

"Here—you go to the rudder for now. You know what to do with that, *neh*?" Jiro said, and his elder son nodded. Jiro turned to Kenzo. "All right, you come with me."

"I'm here," Kenzo said.

"Good. First we find which way the wind is blowing," Jiro said. For the moment, that was easy: it came off the hills in back of Honolulu, and would waft the *Oshima Maru* out to sea. Once the sampan sailed out onto the Pacific, though, things would get more complicated. "Next thing to remember is, mind the booms. They can swing and knock you right into the water."

"*Hai*," Kenzo said. Jiro looked back towards the stern. Yes, Hiroshi was listening. Good. He would need to know, too.

Jiro went on, "We set the foresail to one side of the mast and the jib on the other." He did that, then tied the booms to the belaying pins Doi had mounted on the rail. "Now we cast off, and we're ready to go." He brought in the rope that bound the *Oshima Maru* to the wharf.

Light as a feather, the sampan glided out of Kewalo Basin. Hiroshi steered well enough—he *did* know how to do that. Even so, a look of surprise and delight spread over his face. "She feels so different!" he exclaimed.

And she did. Before, with the motor pushing her forward, she'd been a creature of straight lines. If the small waves were moving at an angle to her path, she'd just chopped through them. Not any more. Kenzo noted another essential difference: "She's so quiet, too!"

Jiro had got used to the relentless pounding and throbbing of the diesel. Without it, the *Oshima Maru* might have been a ghost of her former self. All he heard were the waves and the distant squawks of seabirds and the breeze thrumming in the lines and bellying out the sails. The sampan also felt different underfoot. He'd always got the engine's vibration through the soles of his feet. They'd told him as much about how it was running as his ears did. Now all he felt was the boat's pure motion. He smiled. He couldn't help himself. "I'm younger than you are," he told his sons. "I'm with my father on the Inland Sea."

Kenzo and Hiroshi looked at each other. They probably thought he was crazy. They often did. He didn't care. He could see the rising sun on those crowded waters, the headlands that looked so different from the jungled slopes of Oahu, sometimes a flight of long-necked cranes overhead. . . . He hadn't thought about cranes in years, or realized how much he missed them.

He ran straight before the wind for a while, and talked his sons through adjusting the sails to compensate as it shifted slightly. He showed them how, if you wanted to swing to port, you had to swing the mainsail to starboard. It seemed backward, but they soon saw it was what needed doing.

"There's a lot more to think about now," Hiroshi said.

"Oh, yes," Jiro agreed. "Of course, you *are* thinking about it now, and that makes it seem harder. After you've done it for a while, you won't need to wonder what to do. You'll just do it." He wasn't doing things automatically himself—no, not even close. Part of him might have been that fourteen-year-old out on the Inland Sea with his father. The rest was a middle-aged man trying to remember what went where, and why. His father's boat had been rigged differently. He knew the principles here, but none of the details were the same. He didn't want his sons seeing that.

Kenzo asked, "If the wind is still off the mountains when we come back to the basin, how do we get there?"

"We tack," Jiro answered. "It means we slide in at an angle. You can't sail straight against the wind, but you can go against it. I'll show you."

"All right." Kenzo's voice was uncommonly subdued. Jiro almost laughed in his son's face. Yes, the old man still knew a few things the young one hadn't imagined. That always came as a painful surprise to the younger generation.

A tern soared down and perched at the very tip of the mast. It stared at the Takahashis out of big black eyes that seemed all the bigger because the rest of it was so perfectly white. "That never would have happened when we had the diesel," Hiroshi said.

"Of course not. There wouldn't have been any place for it to land then," Jiro said. Hiroshi stirred as if that wasn't exactly what he'd meant, but he didn't try to explain himself. As far as Jiro was concerned, that was fine.

Jiro had his sons practice setting the sails with the wind astern and at either quarter. They got the hang of it pretty fast. They knew the *Oshima Maru* and how she had handled; that helped them now. What Jiro didn't let on was that he was learning almost as much as they were. No, he hadn't handled sails in a lot of years himself.

But he did remember enough to send the sampan on two long, gliding reaches into the wind. "You see how we beat back towards the shore?" he said. Hiroshi and Kenzo both nodded. They seemed impressed. Jiro was impressed that he'd remembered enough to manage to do that, too. He had more sense than to show it, though.

However serene the sampan was under sail, she wasn't swift. Jiro had come to take the noisy, smelly diesel for granted. It got him where he needed to go, and got him there pretty quick. Now she took a lot longer to reach likely fishing grounds. "We'll probably have to spend the night in the boat," Hiroshi said.

"Well, so what?" Kenzo answered. "It's not like we've got anything much to come home to." Jiro and Hiroshi both grimaced, not because he was wrong but because he was right.

They spilled minnows into the Pacific. They had fewer than usual. The boats that had caught the *nehus* were diesel-powered, too. All three Takahashis had netted these themselves, using chopped-up bits of rice from their own rations as bait. Then the fishing lines with their big, silvery hooks went into the sea. Jiro hoped for a good catch, to make up for the rice they'd lost.

"One more problem with the new sail," Kenzo said. "People can see us for a long way."

He was also right about that. Like most sampans, the *Oshima Maru* was painted a blue somewhere between sea and sky, not least because the color made it hard for competitors to find her. But what good did the camouflage do when the mast and sail stuck up there like a Christmas tree? It *did* work both ways. If three or four other boats could spy the sampan, Jiro could see them, too.

What he wanted to see was what he'd caught. He felt like shouting when the first few hooks yielded *aku* and *ahi* both. He and his sons worked like men inhabited by demons. They gutted fish and chucked them into storage one after another. Jiro noted that Hiroshi and Kenzo set aside a prime *ahi*, as he did. When they'd finished the lines, they all gorged on strip after strip of flavorful tuna. It was always delicious, and all the more so after days of the horrible slop the soup kitchens served.

Hiroshi and Kenzo ate with every bit as much gusto as Jiro. They might prefer hamburgers to sashimi, but anybody in his right mind would prefer sashimi to the bowls of rice and noodles and beans, all overcooked together, they'd been getting. That kind of food might keep you alive, but it made you wonder why you went on living. This . . . This was worth eating.

"Ahhh!" Jiro smiled and smacked his belly. "I've missed that."

Kenzo nodded. Hiroshi was still chewing. "Me, too," he said with his mouth full.

"We'll use the guts and things for bait this time," Jiro said. "That'll draw more sharks, but nobody these days will turn up his nose at shark meat. We don't sell just the fins now."

"Food is food," Hiroshi agreed. "Even the *haoles* aren't so fussy now. Maybe they'll call it something like 'sea steak' "—he said the words in English, then translated them into Japanese—"so they don't have to think about what they're really eating, but they'll eat it."

When they drew in the lines this time, they did catch some sharks, but they also got one of the nicest *ahi* Jiro had ever seen, even better than the one he'd feasted on before. He started to cut more sashimi from it, but paused with his knife poised above its still-glittering side. "Go ahead, Father," Kenzo said. "You took it off the hook, so it's yours. It'll be good." He smacked his lips. He was eating more raw fish.

Jiro shook his head. "I'll choose another. This one I think I'll save for Kita-*san*."

His sons looked at each other, the way they often did when he said something they didn't like. He waited for them to start shouting at him for having anything to do with the Japanese consul. To his surprise, they kept quiet. He supposed it was because he'd sometimes brought fish to the consulate before the war started. They couldn't say he was doing it to curry favor with Kita now.

Kenzo did sigh, but all he said was, "Have it your way. You will anyhow."

"*Arigato goziemasu.*" Jiro made the thank-you as sarcastic as he could. Then he cut strips of tender, deep pink flesh from another *ahi*. Maybe that fish wasn't quite so perfect as the one he'd set aside for the consul, but it was plenty good enough for him.

He and his sons threw the offal from the second run into the sea as bait for a third. They didn't do so well this time; they already taken most of what that stretch of the Pacific had to offer. After they'd stowed what fish they had caught, Jiro turned the *Oshima Maru*'s bow towards the shore—actually, towards the northeast rather than due north. He'd have to tack all the way home unless the wind shifted.

"*Will* we need to spend the night on the ocean?" Hiroshi asked.

"Maybe. I don't know yet. It all depends on the wind," Jiro answered. Actually, that wasn't quite true. It also depended on how tired he was. If he decided he had to roll himself in a blanket before the sampan got back to Kewalo Basin, well, then, they wouldn't come in till morning.

But the wind stayed steady, and the *Oshima Maru* handled better than Jiro remembered his father's boat doing back when he was a boy. Sampans weren't pretty—which was, if anything, an understatement—but they were seaworthy. He steered the boat into Kewalo Basin a little past nine o'clock. Mars, Saturn, and Jupiter shone in the night sky, Mars farthest west, Jupiter almost straight overhead. The moon, nearly full, glowed in the east and had done its share to help him home.

Japanese soldiers waited by the wharfs, where armed Americans had stood before. They weighed the Takahashis' fish and gave them their price based on that weight, not on quality. To Jiro's relief, they didn't quarrel when he and his sons took some fish off the *Oshima Maru*. "Personal use?" a sergeant asked.

"For us, *hai*, and to pay the man who added the mast and sails to the sampan, and a fine tuna for Kita-*san*, the Japanese consul," Jiro answered.

"*Ah, so desu.*" The sergeant bowed. "I am sure he will be glad to have it. Kind of you to think of him." He waved Jiro and Hiroshi and Kenzo on into Honolulu. Jiro thought about pointing out to his sons how useful that *ahi* had proved, but he didn't. They wouldn't pay any attention.

Eizo Doi was glad to get thirty pounds of fish when the Takahashis knocked on his door, but had his own worries: "Where am I going to freeze all of it? It's more than my freezer will hold."

That wasn't Jiro's problem. After he and his sons left Doi's house, Hiroshi and Kenzo went back to their tent in the botanical garden. They wanted nothing to do with Kita or the Japanese consulate. Jiro kept walking north up Nuuanu Avenue to the corner of Kuakini Street. The Japanese consular compound there had become one of the nerve centers of the imperial occupation of Hawaii; Iolani Palace was the other.

Like the rest of Honolulu, the consular compound remained blacked out. Jiro didn't understand why. No American plane could hope to bomb the city and return to the mainland. He wasn't even sure a U.S. plane could carry bombs all the way from the mainland to Hawaii. But the Japanese military could be just as unreasonable as its American counterpart.

"Halt!" a sentry called from out of the darkness. "State your name and business." When Jiro did, the sentry said, "Ah. Go on in. You'll be very welcome, especially after the torpedoing."

"Torpedoing?" Jiro said. "What's this? I've been out on the ocean all day without a radio."

"A damned American submarine sank the *Bordeaux Maru* this afternoon," the soldier told him. "She was bringing supplies to the island, but. . . . Karma, *neh?* The Americans want everyone here to starve. That's why I said Kita-*san* would be so glad to get your tuna."

He opened the door for Jiro, who took the *ahi* inside. Nagao Kita, the consul, was a short, stocky, round-faced man. He was in animated conversation with three or four Army and Navy officers, but broke off when he saw Jiro.

"Takahashi-*san!*" he said, and the fisherman was proud this important personage had remembered his name. A broad smile spread across the consul's face. "What have you got there, my friend? Doesn't that look beautiful?"

"It's for you, sir," Jiro said, "and maybe for these gentlemen, if you feel like sharing."

"Yes, if I do," Kita said, and laughed. The officers were ogling the splendid *ahi*, too. A Navy captain licked his lips, then tried to pretend he hadn't. Kita stepped up and took the fish from Jiro. The consul gave him a more than polite bow. "Very kind of you to think of me, Takahashi-*san*, very kind. I won't forget it, believe me. When I have the chance, you can bet I'll think of you."

Delighted, Jiro returned the bow. "I'm sure that's not necessary, sir."

"I think it is." Having received the tuna with his own hands, Kita called for one of his aides to take charge of it. He turned back to Jiro. "I'm afraid you'll have to excuse me now. We have to figure out what to do about the miserable business this afternoon."

He didn't say what the business was. Jiro didn't show he knew. That might have landed the sentry in hot water. He just nodded and said, "Of course, sir," and turned to go.

"I won't forget you," Kita promised. "You're a reliable man." As Jiro pushed through the blackout curtains that kept light from escaping when the door opened, he felt ready to burst with pride. The consul thought he was reliable! The Emperor might have just pinned the Order of the Rising Sun on his chest.

JOE CROSETTI'S INSTRUCTOR IN ESSENTIALS of naval service was a graying lieutenant named Larry Moore. He had a face as long as a basset hound's, and normally about as doleful, too. When he came into the classroom wreathed in smiles one morning, Joe figured something was up.

And he was right. Lieutenant Moore said, "Gentlemen, yesterday the *Grunion* sent a Jap freighter to the bottom off the north coast of Kauai. We *are* starting to hit back at those slanty-eyed so-and-sos."

A savage cheer—almost a growl—rose from the throats of the flying cadets. Joe joined in. Several young men clapped their hands. Orson Sharp raised his. When Moore pointed to him, he said, "Sir, are the Japs making any effort to bring in supplies for the civilians in Hawaii, or is everything they're shipping in for their garrison?"

"That's . . . not entirely obvious," Moore said after a brief pause. "But that ship could have been carrying munitions or aircraft as readily as rice for soldiers or civilians."

"Yes, sir." As usual, Sharp was punctiliously polite. "Were there secondary explosions after the torpedo hit?"

"I don't know one way or the other, so I can't tell you," the instructor answered. "If you'd be so kind, though, you might tell me why you're wasting grief on a bunch of damn Japs."

Most cadets, if challenged that way, would have lost their temper or backed down. Orson Sharp did neither. "Sir, I'll wave bye-bye to all the Japs we send to the bottom. But there are an awful lot of hungry people in the Hawaiian Islands. If they're going to get hungrier, I am sorry about that."

Lieutenant Moore studied him. Sharp hadn't been disrespectful or insubordinate in any way. He had an opinion, and he'd come out with it. If it wasn't one the instructor happened to share . . . Well, was this still a free country or not? No, Joe realized, that wasn't the right question. The country was still free. How freely anyone in the Navy could speak up was a whole different ballgame.

At last, Moore said, "Well, we'll let it go this time, then." He sounded like a governor pardoning a prisoner who probably didn't deserve it. After another moment or two, Moore went on, "Where were we? Oh, yes. We were going to talk about yesterday's quiz. About half of you didn't know that a chief bosun can't be tried by summary courtmartial. Well, gentlemen, he can't. A chief bosun is a warrant officer, which means the rules for ratings don't apply to him."

Bill Frank, who was sitting to Joe's left while Sharp sat to his right, whispered, "Did you get that one?"

Joe nodded infinitesimally. "Yeah," he whispered back. "How about you?"

"I think I blew it." His roomie put a world of pathos into five almost inaudible words.

Lieutenant Moore went over the quiz item by item, concentrating on the ones a lot of cadets had missed. Along with courts and boards, essentials of naval service covered ranks and their duties, naval customs and usages, and all the endless formalities that let officers and ratings work together smoothly. Joe had seen a commander tromp all over a j.g. for something dumb the junior officer did one morning, then play bridge with him that night as if nothing had happened.

He didn't fully understand how that worked. If anybody had been so bitingly rude to him, he would have wanted to brain the son of a bitch with a tire iron, not play cards with him. But the career Navy men seemed able to build a wall between what happened on duty and what happened off. Of course, they'd had years of practice. That kind of discipline didn't come naturally. Without it, though, a lot of guys would have grabbed tire irons.

The instructor might have been reading his thoughts. "A ship is a very crowded place," Moore said. "The sooner you start thinking like Navy men, the better you'll fit in when you go to sea. We have round holes, gentlemen. People who insist on being square pegs don't have an easy time of it." He was looking at Orson Sharp as he said that.

When they got out of essentials of naval service, they had to hustle to make it to introductory navigation. Joe liked that least of the three academic courses in the program; it showed him he hadn't paid enough attention in geometry and trig. But plenty of other cadets were struggling harder than he was.

"I hope you didn't get Moore mad at you," he said to Sharp as they hurried from one building to another.

"So do I, but I won't lose any sleep over it," the cadet from Utah replied. "I had a legitimate question."

"I guess so," Joe said.

Sharp's eyes said Joe had just flunked a test. "Don't you

care what happens to the civilians in Hawaii? They've got a tough row to hoe."

"Well, yeah," Joe admitted. "But isn't kicking the Japs out the best thing we can do for them? Odds are, whatever that freighter was carrying was going to the Jap Army or Navy, not to civilians."

"Maybe. I suppose we have to hope so." Sharp sounded no more convinced than Joe had a minute earlier. "They can't let everybody starve, though."

"Who says they can't?" Joe retorted. "Look what the Nazis are doing in Russia." Sharp winced but didn't carry the argument any further, from which Joe concluded he'd won the point.

Any pride in his prowess disappeared in introduction to navigation. He butchered a problem—and he did it on the blackboard so everyone could see. "I'm afraid that answer is just exactly 180 degrees off, Mr. Crosetti," the instructor said. "In other words, you couldn't be wronger if you tried. Take your seat." Ears blazing, Joe did. The instructor looked around. "Who sees where Mr. Crosetti went astray here?" Several people raised a hand. The instructor pointed. "Mr. Sharp."

Orson Sharp solved the problem with what looked like offhand ease. He wasn't having any trouble in the class. When he sat down, he didn't act as if he'd just shown Joe up. Maybe he didn't even feel that way. Joe knew he would have were their positions reversed. That made him resent his roomie even if Sharp didn't resent him.

After the lecture, the instructor gave out more problems, these for pencil and paper. Joe thought he did pretty well on them. *You probably did, but so what?* he jeered at himself. *Everybody already watched you show what a jerk you could be.*

He breathed the heady—and chilly—air of freedom again when he got out of class. As far as he could tell, he'd never make it back to his carrier if he took off from one. But when he said that out loud, Orson Sharp shook his head. "I saw what you did. You took the tangent instead of the sine—just a little goof. You won't do it with your neck on the line."

"I hope not," Joe said. Sharp perplexed him almost as much as his mangled navigation. Maybe the other cadet really wasn't mad at him after all. Did that mark almost inhuman restraint or a genuinely good person?

The cadets' other academic class was identification and recognition: how to tell bombers from fighters, cruisers from battleships, and Allied planes and ships from the ones that belonged to the Axis. They'd already had to learn the silhouettes of some new German and Japanese planes that hadn't been known when they started the course.

Joe eyed blown-up photos and drawings with something less than his usual attention. He kept thinking about the question he'd asked himself between classes. *How do you identify and recognize a genuinely good person?* It wasn't as if that were something he had to worry about every day. He knew too well that *he* didn't fill the bill. Orson Sharp might.

Despite absentmindedness, he got out of the class without embarrassing himself again. Along with the other cadets, he trooped over to the cafeteria—now styled the galley in deference to the influx of Navy fliers—for lunch. The choice was between chicken à la king (which the cadets universally called *chicken à la thing*) and creamed chipped beef on toast (which had an older and earthier nickname). Joe chose the chicken. Sharp filled his plate with the beef.

At every table, some wit tapped out *dot-dot-dot, dash-dash-dash, dot-dot-dot*, the Morse for SOS. People snorted. Orson Sharp looked puzzled. "What's going on?" he asked.

Pointing to Sharp's plate, Joe said, "You know what they call that stuff."

"No. What?" The kid from Utah seemed more confused than ever.

As the pseudo-distress calls went on and on, Joe fought not to roll his eyes. Sharp really had led a sheltered life. Patiently, Joe spelled it out for him: "Shit on a shingle. S-O-S."

"Oh." A light went on in Sharp's eyes. "No, I didn't

know that. Well, at least it makes sense now." He dug in. "I don't care what they call it. I think it's good." As usual, he didn't let being different from the other cadets faze him. He had his own standards, they suited him, and he stuck to them.

After lunch came athletics. Orson Sharp knocked people into next week on the football field. Joe played offensive end and defensive back. Bigger guys tried to run over him. He tried not to let them. Along with everybody else, they both got knocked around by the dirty-fighting instructors. Swimming felt strange to Joe. He already had a pretty good crawl, but they wanted him to use a modified breaststroke because it kept his head out of the water better. He did his best to learn it. He'd gained five pounds since coming to Chapel Hill, all of it muscle.

And when the lights went out at half past nine, he fell asleep as if he'd been clubbed.

IX

ACCELERATION PRESSED LIEUTENANT SABURO SHINDO back into his seat as he roared off the *Akagi*'s flight deck. He'd had the mechanics install steel plates in the back and bottom of the seat. A lot of Japanese pilots disdained the extra weight: it made their Zeros slower and less maneuverable. The Americans had carried much more armor than he did. It had saved a lot of pilots, or at least let them bail out. It hadn't saved Hawaii, but he still thought it was a good idea.

Surrounded by a screen of destroyers, *Akagi* patrolled northeast of Oahu. The Japanese had also commandeered some big fishing sampans, mounted radios on them, and posted them in a picket arc close to a thousand kilometers out from the Hawaiian Islands. No carrier-based bomber could fly that far and return to the ship that had launched it. The United States wasn't going to catch Japan napping, the way Japan had caught the USA.

Just in case the boats in that picket arc had missed something, Shindo watched the sky like a hawk. Some people slacked off when they didn't expect to run into trouble. Shindo wasn't one of those. Routine meant routinely capable, routinely excellent, to him.

He also glanced down at the ocean every now and again. Losing the *Bordeaux Maru* was a wake-up call for the Japanese Navy. That had happened more than three weeks ago now. The submarine that got the freighter was bound to be long gone. That didn't mean others hadn't come to take its place, though. Shindo couldn't sink one if he spotted it on the surface: the Zero didn't carry bombs. But he could shoot it up. If his machine guns and cannons filled it full of holes, it couldn't submerge. Then it would be easy meat for bombers or destroyers.

Here, though, nothing marred the Pacific but the ships of the Japanese flotilla and their wakes. The rest of the ocean seemed glassy smooth. There was hardly any chop; the wind was the next thing to a dead calm. No big swells were rolling down out of the north, either, as they had been when the task force moved on Hawaii. Had those been much worse, the barges would have had trouble landing, and the invasion might have turned into a fiasco. Admiral Yamamoto had bet against the *kami* of wind and wave, and he'd won.

Shindo called the other fighter pilots flying combat air patrol: "Anything?"

A chorus of "No"s resounded in his earphones. Some pilots were even tempted to take the radio out of a plane to save weight. Shindo had issued stern orders against that. As far as he was concerned, staying in touch counted for more than the tiny bit of extra speed and liveliness you might gain from saving the kilos the radio weighed. Some people had grumbled about it, but he'd stood firm.

A sudden spurt of steam down below, foam and spray everywhere as a great bulk heaved itself out of the water. Excitement coursed through Shindo. Was that a broaching submarine? A few seconds later, the Japanese flier started to laugh. That was no submarine—it was a breaching whale. The war between Japan and the USA meant nothing to it. To it, the ocean mattered only for krill. Men had other ideas, though. One of those ideas had put Shindo in a fighter plane and taken him far from home.

He listened to excited radio calls from the other pilots who'd seen the whale. "I was going to dive on it and shoot it up," somebody said.

"Shame to waste all that meat without a factory ship close by," someone else replied.

That made people laugh. Shindo smiled a thin smile inside his cockpit. Better when the men were happy and laughing. They paid closer attention to what was going on around them. Right here, right now, that probably didn't matter. No Yankees were likely to be within hundreds of kilometers. But you never could tell.

Throttled back, a Zero could stay in the air for more than two hours. Shindo and his comrades buzzed along in great spirals around the *Akagi* and the destroyers that covered her. The whale was the most interesting thing any of them saw. Shindo didn't yawn as he flew—he was far too professional to let down on the job—but it was a long way from the most exciting patrol he'd ever led.

He took the flight back to the carrier after its replacements had risen into the air. Nobody felt like yawning landing on a rolling, pitching flight deck. Shindo made himself into a machine, automatically obeying the signals of the landing officer at *Akagi*'s stern. The man on the ship could judge his course better than he could. He knew that, however little he cared to admit it even to himself.

When the landing officer's wigwag flags went down, Shindo dove for the deck. He bounced when he hit, so that the Zero's hook missed the first arrester wire. But it snagged the second one. The fighter jerked to a stop.

Shindo pushed back the canopy and scrambled out. The deck crew took charge of the Zero, shoving it to one side, away from the path of the incoming planes behind it. Shindo sprinted for the island. The motion of the deck under his feet seemed as natural as the motion of air in his lungs.

Commander Genda greeted him just inside. "Anything unusual?" he asked.

"No, sir." Shindo shook his head. "About the most interesting thing we saw was a whale. We wondered if it was a Yankee sub, but it was only a whale."

"All right," Genda said. "The splash the big ones make when they come to the surface can confuse you at first. But the Americans don't build subs with fins and flukes." He chuckled.

Shindo managed another thin smile. Fins and flukes . . . Where did Genda come up with such nonsense? The smile didn't last long; Shindo's smiles seldom did. He said, "Forgive me for saying so, sir, but I'm afraid this patrol is costing us more fuel than it's worth. How likely are we to encounter the enemy?"·

Genda only shrugged. "I don't know, Lieutenant. As a matter of fact, you don't know, either. That's why we're here: to help find out how likely we are to run into the Americans sticking their long noses where they don't belong. We learn something if we meet them . . . and we learn something if we don't."

"Yes, sir," Shindo said, an answer a subordinate could never go wrong in giving to his superior. His own opinion he kept to himself. If Genda wanted it, he would ask for it.

He didn't. He just said, "Prepare your report. We'll put it together with all the others and see what kind of picture it makes."

"Yes, sir," Saburo Shindo said again, and gave Genda a salute as mechanically perfect as his landing a few minutes before. As he had then, he followed someone else's will rather than his own. He shrugged, if only to himself. A lot of military life involved following someone else's will.

THE SUN SANK TOWARDS THE PACIFIC. Jim Peterson took a nail out of his mouth and used it to fasten a plank to a two-by-four. He wished he were using his hammer to smash in a Jap's skull instead. The guards, though, were on the other side of the barbed wire as the POW camp rose near Opana— about as far north as anyone could go on Oahu. From there, it was nothing but ocean all the way up to Alaska. Peterson could look up and see waves rolling onto the beach.

He drove another nail to make sure the plank stayed securely fastened. He might have to stay in the barracks he was building. He wanted to make sure the building kept off the rain. He didn't have to worry about making sure the place was warm, the way he would have on the mainland. A good thing, too, because the Japs couldn't have cared less if their prisoners froze.

He fastened another plank, and another, and another. He worked till a Jap outside the wire blew a horn. The bastard must have thought he was Satchmo Armstrong; he put some Dixieland into the call that let the POWs knock off for the day. And wasn't that a kick in the nuts—a Jap who liked jazz? Peterson had run into some crazy things in his time, but that might have taken the cake.

The prisoners lined up to return their tools. The guards kept track of every hammer and saw and chisel and axe and screwdriver and pliers they issued each morning. If the count didn't add up when the tools came back, there was hell to pay. They'd beaten the crap out of a guy who tried to stick a chisel in his pocket and walk off with it. You had to be nuts to think you'd get away with something like that, but young Einstein had taken a shot at it. He'd paid for his stupidity, too; he was still laid up in the infirmary.

Peterson turned in the hammer without any fuss. No matter what he wanted to do with it, he couldn't, not with armed Japs ready to kill him if he got cute with the sergeant in charge of checking off the tools on a chart full of incomprehensible squiggles.

Prez McKinley stood a couple of men behind Peterson in line. He gave the Jap sergeant his saw. Then he and Peterson got bowls and spoons from their tent and headed for the chow line. The march up to Opana had taught them sticking with a buddy was a good idea. The Japanese had hardly bothered to feed the POWs on the trek across the island. What the guards did give out, the strong had tried to snatch from the weak. Two men together were stronger than any lone wolf could be. Nobody had robbed the two of them. They'd got to Opana in fair shape. Some of the weaker, hungrier men had lain down by the Kamehameha Highway and, too weary to go on, let the Japs do them in.

Here at the camp, having a buddy proved even more important than it had on the road. A buddy could hold your place in line if nature called or if you were busy trying to make some scheme pay off. A buddy might help you escape, too. Prisoners were duty-bound to try to get away. Nobody seemed hot to try it, though. Even under the

Geneva Convention, the power holding prisoners could punish would-be escapees who failed. Since the Japs hadn't signed the convention, no one was eager to find out what they'd do.

"I wonder what sort of gourmet treat we'll have tonight," Peterson said. "The pheasant under glass, do you think, or the filet mignon?"

"Shut the fuck up," said somebody behind him in line.

"Hey, I can dream, can't I?" Peterson tried to stay pleasant.

"Not while I gotta listen to you, goddammit." The other prisoner didn't bother.

It could have turned into a brawl. The main reason it didn't was that Peterson was too worn and hungry to take it any further. He told McKinley, "Some people can't take a joke," but he didn't say it loud enough for the angry POW in back of them to hear.

"Filet mignon . . . Hell, I didn't know whether to laugh or to want to deck you myself," McKinley answered. "Your belly's empty, you take food serious."

Peterson decided he must have stepped over a line if that was the most backing his friend would give him. Joking about steak and pheasant here felt like joking about somebody's mother on the outside. You were asking for trouble if you did. But if you couldn't joke, wouldn't you start going nuts?

Such thoughts vanished from his mind when the chow line started snaking forward. His belly growled like a wolf. He had to clamp his lips together to keep drool from running down his chin. The spit flooding into his mouth reminded him that he took food as seriously as Prez McKinley, as seriously as the son of a bitch who'd resented what he'd said, as seriously as all the other sorry bastards cooped up here with him. The most beautiful prisoner-of-war camp in the world—but who gave a damn?

He looked down at his bowl. It was cheap, heavy earthenware, glazed white. It had probably come from a Chinese restaurant. He'd eaten chop suey out of bowls just like it plenty of times. Thinking about chop suey made him want to drool, too. *I really* was *out of line with that crack*, he decided.

Cooks slapped stuff into POWs' bowls. Peterson wondered how they'd landed the job. Had they been cooks before the surrender, or had the Japs just pointed and said, "You, you, and you"? Either way, he was jealous of them. If anybody here came close to getting enough to eat, it had to be the cooks.

Plop! A ladleful of supper went into a bowl. *Plop!* Another ladleful, one man closer to Peterson. *Plop!* Another. *Plop!* Another. And then *plop!*—and it was his turn.

He stared avidly at the bowl as he carried it away from the chow line. Just behind him, McKinley was doing the same thing. Rice, some broth, some green things. He didn't think the green came from proper vegetables. Some of it looked like grass, some like ferns, some like torn-up leaves boiled in with the rice. He didn't care, not one bit. He drank every drop of the broth and made sure he ate every grain of rice and every bit of greenery—whatever the hell it was—the cook doled out to him.

He was still hungry when he finished—hungry, yes, but not *hungry*. Even partial relief might have been a benediction from on high. "Jesus!" he said. "That hit the spot."

"Hit part of the spot, anyway," McKinley answered. His bowl was as perfectly empty and polished as Peterson's. "Give me about three of those, and some spare ribs to go with 'em. . . ." Before the surrender, he wouldn't have talked so reverently about anything but women. People had taken food for granted then, fools that they were.

The two men carried their bowls over to what looked like a horse trough. For all Peterson knew, it had been a horse trough once upon a time. He sloshed his bowl in the water, and his spoon, too. You did want to keep things as clean as you could. Otherwise, you were asking for dysentery. With so many men packed so close together, you might come down with it anyhow, but you were smart to try not to.

After supper came the evening lineup and count. Nobody got to sack out till the Japs were happy with it. Some of the guards couldn't count to twenty-one without undoing their fly, which didn't make things any easier. It started to rain while the Americans stood in their rows. Nobody tried to get away from the rain. That might have fouled up the count and left them out there longer yet. At least it wasn't a cold, nasty rain, like so many on the mainland. Not even the Japs could ruin the weather. Peterson stood there with rain dripping from his nose and ears and chin and the ends of his fingers. He felt sorry for the guys who wore glasses. They probably went blind after a few minutes.

Finally, the Japs decided no one had escaped. The sergeant in charge of the count gestured. The men in the first couple of rows could see him. When they peeled off, the rest of the Americans did, too.

Peterson and McKinley had been smart enough to pitch their tent on the highest ground they could find. The rain wouldn't get the ground inside too muddy. Besides, it would probably stop before too long. A little on, a little off, a little on . . . There was the tent. "Home, sweet home," Peterson said, not altogether ironically.

"Right," Prez McKinley answered. They dried off as best they could and rolled themselves in their blankets. Sleep slugged Peterson over the head.

LEARNING TO HANDLE THE SAILS that had sprouted on the *Oshima Maru* kept Kenzo Takahashi busy. He and Hiroshi were both surprised to find their father a good teacher. Most of the time, their old man lacked the patience to teach well. Not here: he took everything one step at a time, and didn't ask them for more than they knew how to do. "It's his neck, too," Kenzo said in English as they came in after a fair fishing run.

"That's part of it," Hiroshi said, also in English. "The other part is, he's learning it at the same time as he's showing us. He doesn't have it down pat himself. If he did, he'd think we ought to know it just like that." He snapped his fingers.

Kenzo didn't need long to think it over. "Well, you're right," he said.

"What are you two going on about?" their father asked in Japanese. "You talking about me again?"

He knew they did that. He wasn't a fool, however much Kenzo wanted to think of him as one. He didn't have much education, but that wasn't the same thing. "No, not about you—we were talking about the sampan and sailing," Kenzo said, the second part of which held some truth.

Jiro Takahashi let out one of the grunts he used to show he didn't believe a word of it. "You could do that in Japanese."

"We feel more at home in English," Hiroshi said, and that held nothing but the truth.

It got another grunt from the senior Takahashi. "Foolishness," he said. "Foolishness any old time, but especially now. Japanese is the language everybody needs to know."

He succeeded in getting his sons to stop speaking English for a while. Kenzo didn't want to say anything in any language. Was Japanese going to drive English into second place in Hawaii? It would if Japan won the war and kept the islands. From all the news, that looked to be the way to bet right now. Wake Island and Midway were gone. The Philippines were going. Singapore had just fallen, finishing the British collapse in Malaya. And the Japanese were rampaging through the Dutch East Indies. The Dutch, the Australians, and the Americans seemed able to do little to stop them.

"Wouldn't that be just our luck?" Hiroshi said—in English—to break that long silence. "We spend our whole lives trying to turn into Americans, and just when we start to get good at it it turns out not to be worth anything."

"Funny," Kenzo said. "Funny like a crutch."

"You think I was kidding?" his brother asked.

"No." Kenzo left it at that. Would he have to spend the rest of his life trying to make himself Japanese? The New York Yankees meant more to him than the Emperor did. On the mainland, spring training would be starting soon. The closest that came to Hawaii was the Cubs' springtime home on Catalina Island near Los Angeles.

He and Hiroshi brought the *Oshima Maru* into Kewalo

Basin. Their father watched everything they did, but said not a word. That had to mean they'd done it right. If they'd messed up, they would have heard about it.

As usual these days, Japanese soldiers took charge of the catch. Onto the scales it went, and the Takahashis got paid by weight. Also as usual, nobody fussed when they took some fish for themselves and for Eizo Doi. "Personal use?" a noncom asked Kenzo.

"*Hai*. Personal use," he answered. The formula kept the soldiers happy. Kenzo saw speaking fluent Japanese *was* especially useful just now. He would sooner have slammed the sampan into a pier than admitted that to his father.

It was late in the afternoon, but not too late. They'd brought in as much fish as the *Oshima Maru* would hold. People hurried here and there, trying to get on with their lives as best they could. More than a few of them sent jealous glances towards Kenzo and his brother and father. If they hadn't been three stalwart men walking together, they might have had trouble.

A girl coming out of a side street waved and called, "Ken!"

"Hi, Elsie," he answered, not sorry to see her without her stuck-up friends. "How are you doing?"

The *haole* girl shrugged. "Okay, I guess. I'm looking for a job. Nobody has enough these days, but there isn't much out there." She shrugged again. "Everything's gone to pot since . . . since the surrender."

What had she almost said? *Since the Japs took over?* Something like that, Kenzo supposed. Well, she hadn't said it. He asked, "Are you getting enough to eat?"

"Nobody's getting enough to eat these days except people like you who catch your own," Elsie said. "It's not too bad. We're not starving or anything." *Not yet* hung in the air. "But we're hungry some of the time." By the way she said it, she'd never gone hungry before.

Neither had Kenzo. Elsie was right about that. A fisherman's family might not have much money, but the Takahashis had always had food on the table. Impulsively, Kenzo held out a nice *aku*. The striped tuna was as long as his forearm. "Here. Take this back to your folks."

She didn't say, *Oh, you shouldn't*, or anything like that. She reached out and took the fish by the tail. What she did say was, "Thank you very much, Ken. This means a lot to me."

"Be careful with it. Don't let anybody get it," he told her. She nodded, then hurried away with the prize.

"What did you go and do that for?" his father said. "Now we have to tell Doi we're short this time."

"So we give him some extra next time," Kenzo answered. "He knows we're good for it. He'd better, everything we've brought him so far."

"You're sweet on this girl, *neh?*" his father said.

How am I supposed to answer that? Kenzo wondered. If he said he wasn't, his old man would know he was lying. If he said he was, his father might pitch a fit. He might have pitched a fit any old time. With Japanese soldiers on the streets of Honolulu, with civilians of all colors scrambling out of their way and bowing as they went by . . . "Maybe some," Kenzo said cautiously.

"Foolishness. Nothing but foolishness." But his father left it there.

Hiroshi was the one who spoke up, and he did it in English: "Dad may be right. Is this a smart time to show you like a *haole* girl?"

"Jesus Christ! Not you, too!" Kenzo said.

His brother flushed. "I didn't say it wasn't a smart time to like her. I know you like Elsie, for crying out loud. I said it wasn't a smart time to *show* you like her—and you know why as well as I do."

As if to make his point for him, four or five more Japanese Army men turned the corner and came up the street towards the Takahashis. Kenzo had taken men in U.S. uniforms for granted. Getting used to the new occupiers was harder. Bowing didn't grate on him the way it had to on *haoles*, though. He'd grown up with it, and took it for granted.

"I'm not going to do anything stupid," Kenzo said.

"Good. Make sure you don't," Hiroshi told him.

Since it was still daytime, they went to Eizo Doi's shop

instead of his home. The place was tiny; if you weren't looking for it, you wouldn't find it. A sign over the door said HANDYMAN in English in small letters. The hiragana characters for the same thing were twice as tall.

Doi was tinkering with a bicycle's chain and sprocket when Kenzo and his brother and father came in. "You have an icebox here?" Jiro Takahashi asked.

"*Hai*," Doi answered. "Come on in back. So you make me lug the fish home, do you?"

"We didn't want to knock on your door when you weren't home—might scare your wife," Kenzo's father said. The handyman nodded. Kenzo grimaced. Nobody would have said that before the Japanese took Hawaii. Times had changed, and not for the better. Kenzo kept that to himself. He didn't know who all of Eizo Doi's friends were. Being wrong about such things could cost much more now than it had when the Stars and Stripes flew over Iolani Palace.

The handyman's back room was even more crowded than the part of the shop where he worked: a dark jumble of handmade shelves full of a ridiculous variety of spare parts and odd tools and stuff that looked like junk to Kenzo but presumably was or might prove useful to Doi. Kenzo knew a couple of other handymen. They accumulated odds and ends the same way. If you weren't part pack rat, you were in the wrong line of work.

Hiroshi pointed to the icebox—no, it was a refrigerator, for a plug snaked out of it. "Did you make that yourself, Doi-*san?*" he asked. Kenzo couldn't tell whether his tone was meant to be admiring or appalled.

"*Hai*," the handyman said again, looking pleased. "It's not that hard. I got the motor from a drill press, the compressor from . . . I don't remember where I got the compressor. But I put everything together, and it works."

"That's what counts," Kenzo's father said.

When Doi opened the refrigerator door, Kenzo saw a couple of bottles of beer and other things he had more trouble identifying. By the way some of those looked, he didn't want to know what they'd been once upon a time. They'd been in there much too long. Doi happily piled fish on the shelves, which might have started their careers as oven racks. If he wasn't going to worry about it, Kenzo wouldn't, either.

After the Takahashis left the place, Kenzo said, "See? He didn't care about that *aku*. I bet he didn't even notice."

His father shook his head. "He noticed. Or if he didn't, his wife will when he takes the fish home. But you were right—they know we're good for it sooner or later."

Sooner or later. The phrase made Kenzo look to the northeast, towards the American mainland. Sooner or later, the USA would try to take Hawaii back. He was sure of that. When, though? And how? And what were the odds the Americans would succeed? Kenzo had no answers for any of those questions. He was sure of one thing, though: it wouldn't be easy.

IN BACK OF IOLANI PALACE stood a barracks hall. Once upon a time, when Hawaii was an independent kingdom, it had housed the Royal Guards. Commander Minoru Genda had seen a photograph of the Guards in the palace: big men in fancy uniforms with hats that made them look like British bobbies standing at attention beside and behind a battery of polished brass field pieces.

Now the Iolani Barracks held only one man: a prisoner. Walking slowly across the brilliant green lawn towards the building—with the crosses set into its square, crenellated towers, it looked more like a medieval European fortress than a barracks—Genda turned to Mitsuo Fuchida and said, "This is a bad business."

"*Hai.*" The man who'd commanded the air strikes against Oahu nodded. "I don't know what else we can do, though. Do you?"

"No, I'm afraid not." Genda sighed. "But I wish I could think of something. And I wish we hadn't been chosen as witnesses." He sent a defiant stare up towards the taller Fuchida. "Go ahead, call me soft."

"Not you, Genda-*san*. Never you." Fuchida walked along for a couple of paces before continuing, "I might say that of some other men. I might also say you would do well

not to say such things to officers who aren't lucky enough
to know you the way I do."

Genda bowed. "*Domo arigato*. This is good advice."

They went in through the rounded entranceway. The
courtyard inside the barracks was a long, narrow rectangle
paved with flagstones. Several Navy officers already stood
inside it. Some of them looked grim, others proud and righ-
teous. Also waiting in the courtyard was a squad of special
Navy landing troops, in square rig with infantry rifles and
helmets (though those bore the Navy chrysanthemum, not
the Army star) and white canvas gaiters that reached their
knees. They were all impassive as so many statues.

Two more witnesses came in after Genda and Fuchida.
Genda was relieved not to have been the last. Captain
Hasegawa of the *Akagi*, the senior officer present, spoke in
a loud, official-sounding voice: "Let the prisoner be brought
forth!"

Out of one of the rooms at the far end of the courtyard
came four hard-faced guards leading a young Japanese
man. *Such a pity*, Genda thought. A couple of the nearby
officers let out soft sighs, but only a couple.

Captain Hasegawa faced the young man. "Kazuo Sakamaki, you know what you have done. You know how you
have disgraced your country and the Emperor."

Sakamaki bowed. "*Hai*, Captain-*san*," was all he said. He
was—he had been, before his summary court-martial—an
ensign in the Japanese Navy. He'd commanded one of the
five two-man midget submarines Japan had launched against
Pearl Harbor as part of the opening attack. Four were lost
with all hands. Sakamaki's crewmate had also perished.
But Sakamaki himself had floundered up onto an Oahu
beach—*and been captured by the Americans*.

Hasegawa nodded to the guards and the special Navy
landing troops in turn. "Let the sentence be carried out."

"Captain-*san*"—Sakamaki spoke once more—"again I
request the privilege of atoning for my dishonor by taking
my own life."

The skipper of the *Akagi* shook his head. "You have

been judged unworthy of that privilege. Guards, tie him to the post."

With another bow, Sakamaki said, "Sir, it is not necessary. I will show you I do know how to die for my country. *Banzai!* For the Emperor!" He came to stiff attention, his back touching the post driven between two flagstones.

For that, Hasegawa gave him a nod if not a bow. The senior officer turned to the special landing troops. "Ready!" he said. The guards hurried out of the line of fire. "Aim!" Hasegawa said. Up came the rifles, all pointing at Sakamaki's chest. "Fire!"

As the rifles roared, Genda thought Sakamaki shouted, "*Banzai!*" one last time. His mouth opened wide and he yelled something, but the word was lost in the fusillade. Sakamaki staggered, twisted, and fell. Red had already spread over the front of his prison coveralls. It soaked the back, where the exit wounds were. The young man jerked and twitched for a minute or two, then lay still.

Captain Hasegawa nodded to the firing squad. "You did your duty, men, and did it well. You are dismissed." They saluted and marched away. The skipper of the *Akagi* held up a piece of paper for the officers who'd witnessed Sakamaki's execution. "I will need your signatures, gentlemen."

Along with the others, Genda wrote his name under the brief report that described Kazuo Sakamaki's failure to die in battle, his humiliating capture (it said he'd asked the Americans to kill him, but they'd refused), the court-martial following the Japanese victory, the inevitable sentence, and its completion. There on the page, everything seemed perfectly clear-cut, perfectly official. Genda didn't look at Sakamaki's body. He couldn't help noticing the air smelled of blood.

"Thank you, Commander," Hasegawa said when Genda returned the pen to him. "One more loose end cleared up."

"*Hai.*" As far as Genda was concerned, that was acknowledgment, not agreement.

After the officers signed the report, they left the barracks one by one. Genda waited on the grass till Mitsuo

Fuchida came out. A small bird with a gray back, a white belly, and a crested head of a red even brighter in the sun than Kazuo Sakamaki's blood hopped along three or four meters away from him, pausing every once in a while to peck at an insect. When he took a step towards it, it fluttered away. He was probably more frightening than the thunderous volley of rifle fire had been a few minutes earlier.

Here came Fuchida. The red-headed bird flew away. Genda and Fuchida walked slowly back towards Iolani Palace. After a while, Fuchida said, "I didn't know he tried to get the Americans to finish him."

"Neither did I," Genda said heavily.

"Too bad they didn't—it would have saved him the disgrace," Fuchida said. "But you can't count on the enemy to take care of what you should have done yourself."

"I suppose not," Genda said. It wasn't that his friend was wrong. It was only that . . . He didn't know quite what it was, only that it left him unhappy rather than satisfied. "Too bad all the way around."

"Can't argue with you there," Fuchida said. "Think of his poor family. All the other men on the midget submarines died as heroes, attacking the Americans. Their son, their brother, was the only captive. How can you live something like that down?"

"If the officials are kind, they'll bury the report and just tell the family he died in Hawaii," Genda said. "I hope they do."

"That would be good," Fuchida agreed. "Still, though, even reports that should be buried have ways of getting out."

He wasn't wrong, though Genda wished he were. "Witnessing one of those will last me forever, even if he did die bravely," Genda said. "I hope I don't get drawn for the same duty twice. Plenty of other work I'd rather be doing."

"Can't argue about that, either," Fuchida said. "A man with a clean desk is a man who doesn't get enough thrown at him." Genda nodded. They both headed back towards their desks, which were anything but clean.

* * *

IN JAPANESE, THE NAME OF HOTEL STREET came out as three syllables: *Hoteru.* Corporal Takeo Shimizu wasn't fussy about how he said it. He just wanted the chance to get there as often as he could. Before the war came to Oahu, the street had been geared to making American soldiers and sailors happy. It had taken some damage during the fighting, but hadn't needed long to start doing the same job for the new masters of Hawaii.

Before letting the men from Shimizu's squad go on leave, Lieutenant Horino, the platoon commander who'd replaced Lieutenant Yonehara, lectured them: "I do not want any man here disgracing himself or his country. Do you understand me?"

"Yes, sir!" the men chorused.

"You will be punished if you do. Do you understand *that?*"

"Yes, sir!" they said again.

"All right, then. See that you remember it," Horino said.

"Salute!" Shimizu called. Like him, the other men made their salutes as crisp and perfect as they could. Some officers would forbid a soldier to go on leave if they didn't like the way he saluted. Shimizu didn't think Lieutenant Horino was that strict, but why take chances?

Horino returned those precise salutes with one that wasn't much more than a wave. A sergeant would have slapped a common soldier till his ears fell off for a salute like that. But officers lived by different rules. "Dismissed," Horino said. Then he unbent enough to add, "Enjoy yourselves."

"Yes, sir," the men said, Shimizu loud among them. He wasn't sure that had been an order—how could someone command you to have a good time?—but he wasn't sure it hadn't been, either. Again, why take chances? Lieutenant Horino strode away, sword swinging on his hip. Shimizu eyed the men he'd led since before they got on the transport back in Japan. "You have your passes? The military police are bound to ask you to show them." He had his, in his tunic pocket.

"Yes, Corporal. We have them," the soldiers said. Shimizu waited. One by one, they dug them out and displayed them.

When he'd seen all of them, he nodded. "All right. Let's go. You all know what the lieutenant meant about not disgracing yourselves?" He waited. When no one said anything, he spelled it out for them: "Don't get the clap."

"Corporal-*san*?" Senior Private Furusawa waited to be recognized. Only after Shimizu nodded to him did he go on, "Corporal-*san*, the Americans are supposed to have medicines that can really cure it."

Since his father was a druggist, maybe he knew what he was talking about. Or maybe he didn't. Shimizu only shrugged. "If you don't get a dose in the first place, you won't have to worry about that, will you?"

Unlike some of the men in the squad, Furusawa was smart enough to know a dangerous question when he heard one. "Oh, no, Corporal," he said hastily.

"Good. And remember to salute all your superiors, too." Shimizu looked the men over one more time. He didn't see anything wrong with anybody's uniform. "Come on. Let's go."

They followed him like ducklings hurrying on after a mother duck. That made him proud; even if he was only a corporal, he had a fine string of common soldiers in tow. The civilians the men passed on the street didn't care that he was only a corporal. They scrambled out of the squad's way. The Japanese among them knew how to bow properly. The Chinese and whites didn't, but orders were not to make a fuss about it as long as they tried to do it right.

Here came a reeling sergeant who'd had a good time somewhere. "Salute!" Shimizu said, and the whole squad did in unison. He hoped everyone did it well. That might not matter, of course. If the sergeant felt like topping off his leave by slapping common soldiers around (and maybe even a corporal, too), he could always find an excuse to do it. But he only returned the salutes and kept on going. He was singing a song about a geisha named Hanako. Shimizu remembered singing that song when he'd got drunken leave in China.

As soon as he and his squad got to Hotel Street, military policemen rushed up to them like mean farmyard dogs. "Let's see your passes!" they shouted, their voices loud and angry.

Shimizu produced his. One by one, his men did the same. The military policemen scowled as they inspected each pass. But there was nothing wrong with any of them. All the information was there, and in the proper form. The military policemen had no choice but to give them back and nod; grudgingly, they did. "Salute!" Shimizu said again. Again, the men obeyed.

"You keep your noses clean, you hear me?" one of the military policemen growled. "If you end up in trouble, you'll wish your mothers never weaned you. Do you understand me?"

"*Hai*, Sergeant-*san!*" chorused Shimizu and the men he led. They must have been loud enough to satisfy the sergeant, for he and his pal went off to harass some other soldiers. Shimizu pitied anyone they found without proper papers.

But that wasn't his worry. A lot of places that had served food were closed. There wasn't a lot of food to serve. Bars were open, though. Some of them sported freshly painted signs in hiragana and also, Senior Private Furusawa said, in Roman letters boasting that they served sake. Shimizu was sure it wasn't sake imported from Japan. They grew rice here. Some of it had probably been taken out of the food store and turned into something more entertaining. He wondered whose palm had been greased to make that happen, and with how much cash. *More than I'll see any time soon*, he thought mournfully.

Almost all the bright, blinking neon signs were in English. One looked as good as another to Shimizu. "I'm going in here," he said, pointing to one bigger and fancier than most. "Who's coming with me?"

Only a couple of men from the squad hung back. "I

want to start off with a woman," one of them said. The other nodded.

"You'll last longer if you do some drinking first," Shimizu said. They shook their heads. Shimizu shrugged. "Suit yourselves, then. But if you aren't back at the barracks when you're supposed to be, you'll wish those military policemen were beating on you. Have you got that?" He tried to sound fierce, and hoped he succeeded. He really was too easygoing to make a good noncom.

The bar was dark and cool inside, and already full of Japanese soldiers and sailors. The bartender was an Asian man. He spoke Japanese, but oddly; after a little while, Shimizu decided he had to be a Korean. "No, no whiskey, *gomen nasai*," he said when the corporal asked. "Have sake, have sort of gin."

"What do you mean, sort of?" Shimizu inquired.

"Made from fruit. Made from fruit here, understand. Is very good. *Ichi-ban*," the bartender said.

A drink was one yen or twenty-five cents U.S. money—outrageously expensive, like everything else in Oahu. "Give me some of this gin," Shimizu said. "I want something stronger than sake." He dropped a U.S. quarter on the bar. The silver rang sweetly. The bartender set a shot in front of him.

He knocked it back. He had all he could do not to cough and lose face before his men. The stuff tasted like sweet paint thinner and kicked like a wild horse. It might have been a mortar bomb exploding in his stomach. He liked the warmth that flowed out from his middle afterwards, though.

His men followed his lead. The bartender poured them shots, too. Like Shimizu, they gulped them down. They weren't so good at hiding what the stuff did to them. Some of them coughed. Senior Private Furusawa said, "My insides are on fire!" Private Wakuzawa seemed on the edge of choking to death. Somebody pounded his back till he could breathe easily again.

By then, Shimizu had recovered his equilibrium—and the use of his voice. He hardly wheezed at all as he laid down a new quarter and said, "Let me have another one."

"The corporal's a real man!" one of his soldiers said admiringly.

Shimizu drank the second shot as fast as the first. The stuff didn't taste good enough to savor. It didn't hurt so much going down as the first shot had. Maybe he'd got used to it. Or maybe the first assault had stunned his gullet. He managed a smile that looked as if he meant it. "Not so bad," he said.

"If he can do it, so can we," Furusawa declared. He put a yen on the bar. "Give me a refill, too." The rest of the soldiers who'd come in with Shimizu followed suit. They also did better the second time around. Most of them did, anyway: even in the gloom inside the bar, it was easy to see how red Shiro Wakuzawa turned.

"Are you all right?" Shimizu asked him.

He nodded. "*Hai*, Corporal-*san*."

Another question occurred to Shimizu: "How much drinking have you done before this?"

"Some, Corporal-*san*," Wakuzawa answered. *Not much*, Shimizu thought. He didn't push any more, though. Sooner or later, the youngster had to get hardened. Why not now?

They all had another couple of drinks. Shimizu could feel the strong spirits mounting to his head. He didn't want to get falling-down drunk or go-to-sleep drunk, not yet. Plenty of other things to do first. He gathered up his men. "Are you ready to stand in line now?" They nodded. He pointed to the door. "Then let's go."

Under the Americans, prostitution had been officially illegal, which didn't mean there hadn't been plenty of brothels on Hotel Street. It only meant they had to be called hotels. The Japanese were less hypocritical. They knew a young man needed to lie down with a woman every so often. They thought nothing of importing comfort women to serve soldiers in places where there weren't many local girls (and they didn't wonder, or even care, what the comfort women—usually Koreans—thought). Here in Honolulu, they didn't have to worry about that.

"Senator Hotel." Senior Private Furusawa spelled out the name of the place. The line of men waiting to get in stretched around the block. Some of them—most of them, in fact—had been drinking, too. Nobody got too unruly, though. Ferocious-looking military policemen kept an eye on things. You wouldn't want them landing on you, not before you got what you were waiting for.

A soldier started singing. Everyone who knew the tune joined in. Shimizu hadn't drunk enough to make them sound good. Some of the soldiers from his squad added to the racket. "You sound like cats with their tails stepped on," he told them. They laughed, but they didn't stop.

More men got in line behind Shimizu and his soldiers. The line moved forward one slow step at a time. He wished he'd had another drink or two. By the time he went in, he'd be half sobered up.

More military policemen waited inside, to make sure there was no trouble. A sign said 16 YEN, 4 DOLLARS, 5 MINUTES. Four dollars! He sighed. Almost a month's pay for him. Two months' pay for the most junior privates. No one walked out.

He gave his money to a gray-haired white woman who could have looked no more bored if she were dead. She wrote a number—203—on a scrap of paper and shoved it at him. "Is this the room I go to?" he asked. She shrugged—she must not have spoken Japanese. One of the military policemen nodded. Shimizu sighed again as he went up the stairs. He'd hoped to pick a woman for himself. No such luck.

When he found the cubicle with 203 above it, he knocked on the door. "*Hai?*" a woman called from within. The word was Japanese. He didn't think the voice was. He opened the door and found he was right. She was a brassy blonde, somewhere a little past thirty, who lay naked on a narrow bed. "*Isogi!*" she told him—hurry up.

Five minutes, he reminded himself. Not even time to get undressed. Part of him wondered why he'd bothered to do this. But the rest of him knew. He dropped his pants, poised himself between her legs (the hair there was yellow, too, which he hadn't thought about till that moment), and impaled her.

She didn't help much. For all the expression on her face, he might have been delivering a package, not plundering her secret places. Because he'd gone without, he quickly spent himself anyway. As soon as he did, she pushed him off. She pointed to a bar of soap and an enameled metal basin of water. He washed himself, dried with a small, soggy towel, and did up his pants again. She jerked a thumb at the door. "*Sayonara*."

"*Sayonara*," he echoed, and left. A military policeman in the hallway pointed him towards another set of stairs at the far end. Down the hall he went, trying to ignore the noises from the numbered cubicles on either side. A minute earlier, he'd been making noises like that. He felt a strange mixture of afterglow and disgust.

These stairs led out to an alley behind the Senator Hotel. It smelled of piss and vomit. A military policeman standing near the exit said, "Move along, soldier."

"Please, Sergeant-*san*, I came here with friends, and I'd like to wait for them," Shimizu said. He was a corporal himself, not a miserable common soldier, and he spoke politely. The military policeman grudged him a nod.

Over the next five or ten minutes, the soldiers from Shimizu's squad came out. Some of them came happy, others revolted, others both at once like Shimizu himself. "I don't think I'll do that again any time soon," Shiro Wakuzawa said.

"Of course you won't—you won't be able to afford it," somebody else told him, adding, "The only thing worse than a lousy lay is no lay at all." The whole squad laughed at that. It explained why they'd stood in line better than anything else could have done.

"Move along," the military policeman said again, this time in a voice that brooked no argument.

"Salute!" Shimizu told his men, and they did. Some of them were clumsy, but the military policeman didn't complain. When they got to the end of the alley, they turned left to go back up to Hotel Street. "You all still have money?" Shimizu asked. Their heads bobbed up and down. "Good," he said. "In that case, let's drink some more." Nobody said no.

*   *   *

WHEN OSCAR VAN DER KIRK PAUSED at the water's edge on Waikiki Beach to assemble his contraption, the men fishing in the surf paused to stare at him. One of them said, "That's the goddamnedest thing I ever set eyes on."

"I never saw anything like it," another agreed.

"Glad you like it," Oscar said. Because he was a happy-go-lucky fellow, he made them smile instead of getting them angry. It did look as if his surfboard's mother had been unfaithful with a small sailboat.

He'd had to find a Jap to do the work. That made him queasy in a way it wouldn't have before the war started. He'd paid that Doi character twenty-five bucks—which happened to be all the cash he had—plus a promise of fish when he went out to sea. Doi didn't speak a hell of a lot of English, but he had no trouble at all with numbers.

What if I stiff him? Oscar wondered, not for the first time, as he fit the small mast and sail to the surfboard. Only a Jap, after all . . . But a Jap wasn't *only* a Jap, not these days. If the handyman had any kind of connections with the occupiers . . . Well, that might not be a whole lot of fun.

And besides, Doi had giggled like a third-grade girl when he finally figured out what the deuce Oscar was driving at. "*Ichi-ban!*" he'd said. Oscar knew what that meant, as any *kamaaina* would. How could you stiff a guy who got so fired up about your brainstorm? Oh, you could, but how would you look at yourself in the mirror afterwards?

Into the Pacific went the—whatever the dickens it was. Oscar didn't know what to call it any more. It wasn't exactly a surfboard, not now. But it wasn't quite a boat, either. *Neither fish nor fowl*, Oscar thought. It would be pretty foul, though, if he couldn't get any fish. Wincing to himself, he went into the Pacific.

Till he got out past the breakers, he lay on his belly and paddled as he would have with a wahine on the surfboard instead of a mast (he didn't—he wouldn't—think about Susie Higgins). But once he made it out to calm water . . . Everything changed then.

He stood up on the surfboard. He could do that riding a

wave as tall as a three-story building. It would have been child's play for him here even without the mast, but the tall pole did make it easier. And then he unfurled the sail.

"Wow!" he said.

The breeze came off the mainland, as it usually did in the morning. The sail filled with wind. Oscar had had an argument with Eizo Doi about how big to make it. He'd wanted it bigger. The handyman had kept shaking his head and flapping his hands. "No good. No good," he'd said, and he'd pantomimed a capsizing. He'd been right, too. Oscar tipped the hat he wasn't wearing to the Jap.

Even the small spread of canvas Doi had put on the mast was plenty to make the surfboard scoot along like a live thing. And the breeze was none too strong. A real wind would have made the board buck like a bronco. Oscar wouldn't have wanted to try to control it. This, though, this was as right as Baby Bear's porridge.

An hour with the surfboard—*sailboard?* Oscar wondered—took him farther out to sea than he could have gone paddling half the day. The northern horizon started to swallow Diamond Head and the hills behind Honolulu. Fishing sampans rarely bothered putting out lines or nets where they could still see the shore, but nobody without one could come even this far. With luck, that meant Oscar had found a pretty good spot. He furled the sail and glided to a stop.

The Japs who went out in sampans used minnows for bait. Oscar didn't know where to get his hands on those. Next best choice would have been meat scraps. But meat scraps were worth their weight in gold these days. People were eating dog food and cat food. They'd be eating dogs and cats pretty damn quick, too. For all Oscar knew, they already were.

He couldn't even cast bread upon the waters. Bread was as extinct as the *mamo* birds that had given Hawaiian kings yellow feathers for their cloaks. Oscar had to make do with grains of rice. With luck, they would lure small fish, and the small fish would lure bigger ones—although nobody turned up his nose at even small fish these days.

"Come on, fish," Oscar said, scattering the grains. "Pretend it's a wedding. Eat it up. You know you want to."

He had the net he'd used when he went out with Charlie Kaapu. And he had a length of line with a motley assortment of hooks on it that Eizo Doi had thrown in with the mast and sail. What he didn't have was any bait for the hooks. *I should have swatted flies or dug up worms or something*, he thought. *Next time. I'm making it up as I go along.*

Glints of silver and blue in the water said the rice was luring fish of some sort, anyhow. He started swiping with the wide-mouthed net. Sure as hell, he caught flying fish and other fish he had more trouble naming and some squid that stared reproachfully at him. He wasn't wild for squid himself—it was like chewing on a tire—but he knew plenty of people weren't so fussy.

When he drew in the line, he felt like shouting. It had four or five mackerel on it, and a couple of dogfish, too. He wouldn't have eaten shark before he came to Hawaii, either, but he knew better now. Besides, flesh was flesh these days. He wasn't about to throw anything back.

He hadn't seen any bigger sharks sliding through the sea. These days, their streamlined deadliness put him in mind of Jap fighter planes, a comparison that never would have crossed his mind before December 7. Any surf-rider had to be alert for them. A surf-rider with a crate full of fish had to be a lot more than alert. Now he had to get the fish back to Oahu.

That might also turn into an adventure. The breeze was still blowing from the north. If he kept on running before it, the next stop was Tahiti, a hell of a long way away. He felt like Mickey Mouse as the sorcerer's apprentice in *Fantasia*. Had he started something he didn't know how to finish?

"Making it up as I go along," he said again, this time out loud. The sampans went out and came back. He ought to be able to do the same . . . but how? He tried to dredge up memories of high-school trig and physics. Triangles of forces, that's what they were called. What to do with them, though?

Memory didn't help much. Maybe experiment would. If he set the sail so he ran before the wind, he was screwed. That meant he had to set it at some different angle. His first effort got him moving parallel to the shore. That didn't hurt, but it didn't help, either. If he swung the sail a little more . . .

Bit by bit, he figured out how to tack. He didn't have the seafaring lingo to describe what he was doing, even to himself. That made things harder. But his confidence grew as each successive reach brought him closer to land.

Beginner's luck carried him back almost exactly to the point from which he'd set out. There were the waves rolling up onto Waikiki Beach. He started to take down the sail and mast and ride in on his belly.

He started to—but he didn't. He'd thought of surfsailing to let him get farther out to sea than he could with an ordinary surfboard. A slow grin spread over his face. That was why he'd thought of it, yeah, but did anything in the rules say he couldn't have some fun with it, too?

"You don't want to lose the fish," he reminded himself, and lashed the crate to the mast with a length of his fishing line. He stood by the mast, too, holding on to it with one hand, adjusting the sail so it kept on pushing him shoreward.

People on the beach were pointing to him. They had to wonder what the hell kind of contraption that was out there on the Pacific and what he was doing with it. *I'll show 'em*, he thought, and rode in on the crest of a breaker, skimming along as graceful as a fairy tern. He didn't even think about what would happen if things went wrong, and they didn't. He came up onto the soft white sand feeling like Jesus—hadn't he just walked on water?

The surf fishermen actually gave him a hand. "That's the goddamnedest thing I ever saw," one of them said, nothing but admiration in his voice.

Oscar grinned again. "It is, isn't it?"

COMMANDER MITSUO FUCHIDA MUTTERED TO HIMSELF as he walked up to Iolani Palace. Commander Minoru Genda

sent him a quizzical look. Fuchida's mutters—and his mis-
givings—coalesced into words: "I don't like getting dragged
into politics. I'm an airman, not a diplomat in striped
trousers."

"I don't like it, either," Genda said. "But would you
rather leave the political choices to the Army?"

That question had only one possible answer. "No,"
Fuchida said. The Army had the political sense of a water
buffalo. The unending strife in China proved that. Half of
Japan's resources, manpower and manufacturing that could
have been used against the United States, were tied down
in the quagmire on the Asian mainland, a quagmire of the
Army's making. Maybe Japanese rule here wouldn't mean
antagonizing everybody in sight. Maybe. Fuchida dared
hope.

Japanese soldiers had replaced the American honor
guard at the palace. They presented arms as Fuchida and
Genda came up the stairs. Once inside, the two Navy officers climbed the magnificent inner staircase—Fuchida had
learned it was of koa wood—and into King Kalakaua's Library, which adjoined the King's Bedroom. The Army officers waited for them there. Fuchida had trouble telling
Lieutenant Colonel Minami from Lieutenant Colonel Murakami. One of them had a mustache; the other didn't. He
thought Minami was the one with it, but he wasn't sure.
Maybe Minami and Murakami had trouble telling him and
Genda apart, too. He hoped so.

The Library was another fine specimen of late-Victorian
splendor. The chairs featured elaborately turned wood,
leather upholstery, and brass tacks polished till they
gleamed like gold. There were book stands of walnut and
of koa wood, all full of leather-bound volumes. Along with
those of officials from the Kingdom of Hawaii, the walls
boasted photographs of Prime Ministers Gladstone and
Disraeli and the British House of Commons.

"Busy," was Genda's one-word verdict.

"I like it," Fuchida said. "It knows what it wants to be."

Murakami and Minami just sat at the heavy green-
topped desk in the center of the room. For all they had to

say about the decor, they might have been part of it themselves. *Army boors*, Fuchida thought as he sat down, too.

Two minutes later, precisely at ten o'clock, a large, impressive-looking woman of about sixty with heavy features and light brown skin strode into the room. In a long floral-print dress and a big flowered hat, she made a parade of one—in fact, of slightly more than one, because Izumi Shirakawa, the local Japanese who'd interpreted for the Americans at the surrender ceremony, skittered in behind her. He might have been a skiff following a man-of-war with all sails set.

Fuchida and Genda rose. Half a second slower than they should have, so did Minami and Murakami. All four Japanese officers bowed in unison. The impressive-looking woman regally inclined her head to them. Fuchida spoke to the interpreter: "Please tell Her Highness we are pleased to greet her here."

Shirakawa murmured in English. Princess Abigail Kawananakoa replied loudly and clearly in the same language. Shirakawa hesitated before turning it into Japanese. The woman spoke again, even more sharply than before. Shirakawa licked his lips and said, "She, ah, thanks you for the generosity of welcoming her to the palace her family built."

"She has her nerve," Lieutenant Colonel Murakami said indignantly.

"Yes, she does," Fuchida said, but he was smiling. He found himself liking the Hawaiian (actually, half-Hawaiian, as her father had been an American businessman) princess. She was the widow of Prince David Kawananakoa, who was Queen Kapiolani's nephew. Fuchida looked back to the interpreter. "Tell her we appreciate her very kind greeting."

Through Shirakawa, the princess said, "I suppose you asked me—no, you told me—to come here because you want something from me."

That made both Minami and Murakami splutter. This time, Fuchida had all he could do not to laugh out loud. He *did* like her. She had a great sense of her own importance,

and wasn't about to let anyone get the better of her. The
Army officers didn't know what to make of that. They
thought she should have been groveling at their feet, and
didn't see that her sturdy independence might make her all
the more useful to Japan.

Minoru Genda did. He said, "Tell me, Your Highness, do
you remember the days when the Americans put an end to
the Kingdom of Hawaii and annexed these islands?"

"I do," Princess Abigail Kawananakoa replied at once.
"I was only a girl, but I remember those days very well."

"How do you feel about them?" Genda asked.

For the first time, the princess hesitated. "Things are not
always simple," she said at last. "Look at me if you do not
believe that. I have both bloods in me. That is what Hawaii
is like these days. And what I thought then and what I
think now looking back are two different things."

Lieutenant Colonel Minami opened his mouth. Fuchida
was sure what he would say and how he would say it. He was
also sure Minami could not do worse if he tried for a week.
Forestalling the Army officer, he said, "And yet you still
have your disagreements with the American government."

"With *this* American government, certainly." Princess
Abigail Kawananakoa let out a disdainful sniff. "How anyone could agree with that man in the White House has always been beyond me, though many people seem to."

"You were Republican National Committeewoman for
Hawaii," Fuchida said after checking his notes. The title
translated only awkwardly into Japanese. He had no idea
what a committeewoman might do, especially when Hawaii
was only an external territory of the USA, not a province—
no, a state: that's why they call it the United States, he reminded himself.

"I was," she agreed. "And I have stayed a Republican
even though my party is no longer in the majority. I do not
abandon causes once I undertake them."

There was the opening Fuchida had hoped for. "And
have you abandoned the cause of the Hawaiians, Your
Highness?"

Again, Princess Abigail Kawananakoa hesitated. At

last, she shook her head. "No, I have not abandoned it. How could I? I am one of them, after all."

Now Fuchida could ask the question Lieutenant Colonel Minami would have tried too soon: "Since things have changed here, do you not think you could do most for them as Queen of a restored Kingdom of Hawaii?"

She looked at him. She looked through him—he got the feeling she could see the wall behind him through the back of his head. She said, "If I were to be Queen of Hawaii, I would rule; I would not just reign. I am no one's figurehead, sir: not the Americans', and not yours, either. Could I be anything more than a figurehead?"

The only possible answer to that was no. Japan wanted pliable puppets like the Emperor of Manchukuo. The Japanese told him what to do, and he told his people. That caused less friction than if a Japanese governor gave orders in his own name. A Queen of Hawaii would serve the the same function. Even the whites would be happier about orders from her than from General Yamashita.

A Queen of Hawaii, yes, but plainly not *this* Queen of Hawaii. Still, Fuchida did his best: "You would serve the interests of your people, Your Highness, and the interests of all the people of Hawaii, if you accepted."

When Abigail Kawananakoa shook her head, her jowls wobbled. Oddly, that made her seem more impressive, not less. She said, "If I accepted, I would serve the interests of the Empire of Japan. I do not doubt that you make the offer in a spirit of goodwill, but I must decline. Good morning, gentlemen." She rose from her chair and sailed out of the King's Library, Izumi Shirakawa again drifting along in her wake.

"She is a widow, *neh?*" Lieutenant Colonel Murakami said.

"*Hai.* For many years," Fuchida answered.

"I can see why," the Army man said with a shudder. "I would rather die than live with a woman like that, too." Fuchida and Genda both laughed; Fuchida wouldn't have guessed Murakami had a joke in him.

Lieutenant Colonel Minami said, "What do we do now?

We've got orders to start up the Kingdom of Hawaii again. How can we do that if we have no royal backside to plop down on the throne?"

"We'll manage." Genda sounded confident. "This woman isn't the only person with connections to the old royal family, just the one with the best connections. Sooner or later, one of the others will say yes, and we'll have the backside we need."

"This princess would have been a nuisance even if she did say yes," Fuchida said. "We're better off without her." None of the other Japanese officers told him he was wrong.

WHEN JANE ARMITAGE DUG HER FIRST TURNIP out of the ground, she was as proud as she had been when she first got her driver's license. She might have been prouder now, in fact. The driver's license had given her the freedom of the open road. That first turnip, and the other white-and-purple roots that came out of the ground with it, gave the promise of freedom to keep on living.

If she'd seen her turnips in a grocery-store bin before the war, she wouldn't have spent a nickel on the lot of them. They weren't much for looks. Bugs had nibbled them, and they were generally ratty. Jane didn't care, not these days. Beggars couldn't be choosers.

Tsuyoshi Nakayama studied the pile with grave approval. "You have done well," he said, and wrote a note on a piece of paper in a clipboard he carried.

"Thank you." Jane had never imagined a Jap gardener's opinion could matter to her. But Nakayama knew how to grow things, even if he was the occupiers' go-between in Wahiawa. Jane knew in her belly—quite literally knew in her belly—how important that was.

"Because you have done so well, take a dozen turnips back to your apartment," Nakayama said. "Take greens, too. The rest will go to the community kitchen."

"Thank you!" Jane exclaimed. Food of her own! He could have given her no greater reward. Or could he? Doubt set in. "How am I supposed to cook them? I don't even have hot water, let alone a working stove."

"You can make a fire. You can boil water." The local Jap was imperturbable. "Or you can leave them there, and they will all go to the kitchen."

"Oh, I'll take them," Jane said quickly. "Will you watch the pile till I get back?" Yosh Nakayama nodded. Like her, he knew others would make turnips disappear if someone didn't keep an eye on them.

Jane picked what looked like the biggest and best turnips. Then she discovered that carrying a dozen of them was no easier than carrying a dozen softballs. She thought about making two trips, but doubted whether Nakayama would put up with such inefficiency. Instead, she tucked her blouse into her dungarees and dumped the turnips down her front. She looked ridiculously lumpy, but so what?

When she got to the apartment, she hid the turnips in as many different places as she could find. Even if someone broke in, he might not steal them all. And she locked the door behind her when she went out again. She hadn't bothered lately, but now she had valuables in there again.

Valuables! Before the invasion, she would have turned up her nose at turnips; she'd thought of turnip greens as nigger food, if she'd thought of them at all. No more. Before the invasion, she'd been worried about the beginnings of a double chin. Where so many fears had grown, that one had shriveled and blown away. Nowadays, her jawline was as sharp as anyone could want. Her cheekbones stood out in sharp relief under her skin. She didn't know anyone in Wahiawa who wasn't skinnier than before the war began. From what doctors said, that would add years to people's lives. Some of the days Jane put in felt like years.

To give Yosh Nakayama his due, he was skinnier than he had been before the war started, too. He wasn't living off the fat of the land for helping the Japs. In his weathered face, the prominent cheekbones put Jane in mind of the Old Man of the Mountain in New Hampshire. Nothing else in Hawaii reminded her of New England.

"Thank you for keeping an eye on things," she told him.

He nodded gravely. "You're welcome. I do it for everybody, you understand, not just for you."

"Of course." She was glad he wasn't interested in her in particular. That could have got awkward. If she said no and he didn't like it, would he make sure she didn't eat? Would he get her in trouble with the occupiers? The nasty possibilities were endless.

Three men with wheelbarrows came up and started loading her turnips into them. When the wheelbarrows were full, they wheeled them off in the direction of the community kitchen. A few turnips were left. Jane wondered what would become of them. She needn't have. One of the men, a Filipino, came back and loaded in those last few. Sweat ran down his face as he said, "Hard work!" Away he went, panting a little.

Nakayama looked after him, an odd expression on his face—so odd that Jane asked, "What is it?"

"We say, 'Hard work!' in Japanese, too. I wonder if Carlos knows that. With us, it can mean the work really is hard, or it can mean you complain about what you have to do, or it can mean you are sorry about what someone else has to do."

Jane hadn't expected a Japanese lesson. She also hadn't had the faintest idea what the Filipino's name was. To her, he was only a face in the crowd, and not a handsome face, either. But Nakayama knew. He knew who she was, too. He probably knew who everybody in and around Wahiawa was. That had to make him all the more valuable for Major Horikawa and the rest of the Japs.

"Your potatoes, I think, do well, too," he said. Touching the broad brim of his straw hat, he went off to talk with another cultivator.

How do I cook those turnips? Jane wondered over and over. Only two answers came to her. She could build a fire in the open—and risk having more company than she wanted. Or she could build one in the oven of her gas stove. It might make a fair imitation of the coal-burner her family had had when she was a little girl.

She tried that. It worked, though the kitchen got smoky

and she wouldn't have wanted to do it every day. Boiled turnips, even with salt, were uninspiring. But they were better than nothing, and a welcome addition to the slop from the community kitchen. When you got right down to it, what counted for more than a belly that didn't rumble? Not much. No, not much.

X

JIRO TAKAHASHI WANTED TO SPEND AS MUCH TIME OUT ON the ocean as he could. When he was on the Pacific, he wasn't in that miserable tent in the botanical garden. When he was out there, he didn't quarrel so much with his sons, either. They talked about things that had to do with the *Oshima Maru*, not so much about politics and what it meant to be a Japanese or an American. That was all to the good, because he didn't see eye to eye with Hiroshi and Kenzo.

And he found he liked sailing the sampan. He'd put to sea with her with the diesel for so long, he'd come to take it for granted. You pointed her bow in the direction you wanted to go, started the engine, and away you went. It took about as much skill as drawing a straight line with a pencil. (Knowing where you wanted to go was a different story. *That* took skill.)

When you sailed, though, every move you made depended on something outside the sampan. If the breeze shifted and you wanted to keep going in the same direction, you had to shift the sails to account for the change. If the wind died, you couldn't go anywhere. If you were running against it, you had to go like a drunken crab, zigzagging now one way, now the other, traveling ever so much farther—and slower—than you would in a straight line.

His sons had got the hang of handling the sails as fast as he could have wanted. He remained better at it than they did, though. He knew it, and so did they. After one long tack closer to the wind than the beamy sampan had any business getting, Kenzo said, "That was very pretty, Father."

"It was, wasn't it?" Jiro found himself smiling. He called back to Hiroshi at the rudder: "We're going to come about. Are you ready?"

His older son nodded. "*Hai*, Father."

"All right then—now!" Jiro swung the sails from one side of the mast to the other. He and his sons ducked as the boom slid by, then quickly straightened again. Hiroshi shifted the rudder to help guide the *Oshima Maru* onto her new course. The sails filled with wind. They were off on the other tack. Jiro's smile got broader.

"You couldn't have done that better if you tried for a week," Kenzo said admiringly. Jiro bowed slightly at the praise. It warmed and embarrassed him at the same time. He knew he'd done well, too. But a proper Japanese would have said something more on the order of, *Not bad*. Kenzo's extravagant compliment was much more American.

One bad thing about even the most perfect tack: it brought the sampan closer to Kewalo Basin. However crabwise she traveled, the *Oshima Maru* neared land each passing minute. Jiro didn't want to come ashore. But there wasn't much point to fishing if you didn't bring the catch home.

He cut another strip of dark pink meat from the fat belly of an *ahi*. He and his sons ate better on the Pacific than they did on land—one more reason to want to stay at sea. The tuna's flesh was almost as rich as beef.

Kenzo also cut himself some *ahi*. As he chewed, he said, "We'll have Doi paid off before too long."

"Well, yes." Jiro nodded. "The way things are now, though, it doesn't matter that much. So we get a little more money. So what? What can we buy with money these days?"

"Not much." But Kenzo couldn't help adding, "That's because we're cut off from the mainland—the mainland of the United States. That's where we got everything we needed, and that's why we're in the mess we're in."

"Before long, the Greater East Asia Co-Prosperity Sphere will make up for the things we can't get from the USA," Jiro said stubbornly.

His younger son rolled his eyes. "Don't hold your breath."

Even on the Pacific, politics reared its ugly head. "We'll see," was all Jiro said; he didn't feel like fighting. For a wonder, Kenzo took it no further, either. But the silence as they glided into the basin had the charged quality of the air just before a thunderstorm.

When they tied up at one of the quays, work kept them too busy to quarrel. The Japanese soldiers in charge of taking the fish weighed the catch and paid the Takahashis. As usual, the sergeant in charge of the detail asked, "Personal use?" when the fisherman took fish off the *Oshima Maru*.

"*Hai*," Jiro said. "And I have some for the honorable Japanese consul, too."

The sergeant bowed to him. "Yes, you've done that before—I remember. It shows a true Japanese spirit and feeling." Delighted, Jiro bowed back. Whatever his sons were thinking, none of it showed on their faces. The sergeant waved them all away from the sampan harbor.

Their first stop, as usual these days, was Eizo Doi's shop. As they were going in, a tall, suntanned *haole* came out. He saw the fish they were carrying and started to laugh. He said something in English. Kenzo nodded and answered in the same language. They went back and forth for a little while. Then the white man walked off with a smile and a wave. "What was that all about?" Jiro asked.

"He said he's paying Doi off for putting a sail on his surfboard, of all the crazy things," Kenzo answered.

"That *is* peculiar," Jiro agreed. "But he could go out a lot farther with the sail than without it. If he doesn't have a boat, I suppose it would be the next best thing."

Kenzo nodded. "That's what he said."

Jiro talked about it with the handyman after they gave him his fish. "Yeah, I thought the *haole* was a *baka yaro*," Eizo Doi said. "Who besides a prime jerk would come up with something that weird? But he says it works pretty well, and he gave me some good mackerel. These days, you don't complain about any food you get."

"*Hai. Honto*," Jiro said, and then, "You're getting so much fish from so many people, you could do some dealing on your own."

"It's against occupation regulations," Doi said. For a moment, Jiro thought that meant he wasn't doing it. Then the fisherman realized Doi hadn't said any such thing. If he was dealing on the side, keeping quiet about it was a good idea.

After they left the handyman's, Jiro and his sons went their separate ways. They headed back to the tent while he went on up Nuuanu Avenue to the consulate. Hiroshi and Kenzo wanted nothing to do with that. Jiro hadn't tried to persuade them to join him, even if that might have looked good to the occupying authorities. He knew he would have got nowhere.

By now, the sentries outside the compound recognized him. They nudged one another as he came up the street. "Hey, it's the fisherman," one of them said. "What have you got today, Fisherman-*sama*?" He and his pals laughed. Jiro smiled, too. Lord Fisherman sounded ridiculous. With Oahu so hungry these days, though, the fancy title was less absurd than it might have been.

"See for yourselves." Jiro held up a good-sized fish with a long, high dorsal fin and a body blue and green above and golden below. The soldiers exclaimed—its like hardly ever got up into Japanese waters. "They call this a *mahimahi* here," Jiro said. "It's very good eating, as good as any tuna."

"If it tastes as good as it looks, it'll be wonderful," said the sentry who'd called him Lord Fisherman. "But you can't tell by looks. The *fugu*'s the ugliest fish in the world, near enough, but it's the best eating—if you live through it, anyway."

Jiro nodded. "That's the truth." The *fugu* was a puffer fish that blew itself up into a huge, spiny ball to keep other fish from eating it. Its flesh was uniquely delicious—and deadly dangerous, for the puffer also produced a paralyzing poison. Skilled chefs knew how to cut away the dangerous entrails and leave only the safer meat behind. Dozens of Japanese fishermen killed themselves every year trying to prove they knew how to do the same thing.

"Well, I'm sure the consul will be glad to see you. Go on in," the sentry said.

"Thanks," Jiro said, and he did.

Secretaries and clerks exclaimed at the *mahimahi*. Jiro wondered how much fish Nagao Kita shared with them. That was something he couldn't ask. It was the consul's business, not his. He didn't get to see Kita, either. "So sorry, Takahashi-*san*," a clerk told him. "He's in consultation with Army officers right now."

"He's come out before," Jiro said.

"Not this time, I'm afraid. They're . . . very serious, these Army men," the clerk said. Jiro got the feeling he didn't care for the Japanese officers at all. The fellow continued, "Morimura-*san* will take charge of the fish, though."

"Ah." Jiro brightened. "That will do."

He liked the chancellor at the consulate. Tadashi Morimura was young to hold such a responsible post—he couldn't have been more than thirty. He had a long face, handsome in a slightly horsey way, and had lost the first joint of his left index finger in some accident. "Thank you very much, Takahashi-*san*," he said. "That is a very thoughtful gift for the honorable consul. I know he will be glad to have it." He didn't say anything about whether Kita would share, either.

"I am glad to be able to help. I know times are hard," Jiro said.

"They will get better." Morimura rose from behind his desk. He was of slightly above medium height, which made him several inches taller than Jiro, and wore a sharp Western-style suit. "I am going to put the—*mahimahi*, did you say?—in the icebox for now, to keep it fresh for Kita-*san*. Please don't go—I'd like to talk for a little while."

"Of course," Jiro said. "It is a privilege to talk to such an important man."

"You give me too much credit," Morimura said with becoming modesty. "Please wait. I'll be right back." He was almost as good as his word. *Maybe he has to make room in the icebox*, Jiro thought as he sat in front of the desk. *It's a big fish*. When Morimura came back, he offered Jiro a cigarette from a gold case.

"Thank you, Morimura-*san*." Jiro bowed in his seat. He hadn't tasted tobacco in a couple of weeks. He savored the first drag. "That's very good."

"Glad you like it. It's the least I can do." The younger man lit a cigarette, too. After blowing out a long plume of smoke, he asked, "Where did you catch such an interesting fish?"

"It was southwest of here, sir," Jiro answered. "We sailed for about half a day—we had a nice strong breeze to take us along."

"How many other sampans did you see while you were on the fishing grounds?"

"All told? Let me think." Jiro puffed on the cigarette, smoking as slowly as he could to stretch out the pleasure. It did help him concentrate. "There were . . . five or six. Those were just the ones I could see, you understand. Bound to be plenty more out there."

"Yes, I understand," the consular official said. "Were they all sailing boats? Did you see any that had motors?"

"No, sir. Not one with a motor." Jiro didn't need to think about that. "Where would a boat with a motor get fuel?"

"Well, you never can tell," Morimura replied—and what was that supposed to mean? "But I thank you very much for telling me what you saw . . . and for the *mahimahi*, too, of course. Kita-*san* will also be very grateful for the fish. I'll be sure to tell him you were the one who brought it."

He let Jiro finish the cigarette, then eased him out the door. Jiro scratched his head. Unless he was crazy, Morimura cared more about the sampans that he'd seen than about the lovely fish. Jiro wondered just what exactly the chancellor at the consulate did to earn his pay.

KAPIOLANI PARK WAS A BIG PLACE. Before the Japs turned it into a POW camp, it had had plenty of trees—mostly pines. A lot of them had already come down to give the Americans firewood. Now, as a pair of prisoners banged away with axes, another pine swayed as if in a strong breeze.

Fletch Armitage stood in a good-sized crowd watching the amateur lumberjacks. It gave him something a little out of the ordinary. Two squads of Japanese soldiers also watched the tree-fellers—and the other prisoners. They were there to make sure the axes didn't disappear into the camp after the job was done. None of the Americans got close to them. When other trees came down, everyone had seen that they had short fuses.

"No more shade," a prisoner near Fletch said sadly. Fletch nodded, but his heart wasn't in it. He liked shade as much as the next guy, but you didn't have to have it in Hawaii, the way you would in a place where the sun could knock you dead. He was as pale as anybody in the camp, but even he could see that firewood counted for more. He wondered what the POWs would do when no more trees were left inside the barbed-wire perimeter.

A crackle like distant machine-gun fire snapped his attention back to the pine. "Timberrrr!" yelled one of the woodcutters—a cry he'd surely learned at the movies and not in the great north woods. Down came the tree, and slammed into the grass. Fletch wished it would have fallen on the Japs, but no such luck. They were too canny to let themselves get smashed.

The sergeant in charge of the guards collected the axes. Only after he had them both did he shout something in Japanese to his men. They chose volunteers—that was what it amounted to—and handed out saws. The POWs they'd picked went to work turning the fallen pine, which had to be sixty or seventy feet tall, into chunks of wood convenient for cooking food and boiling water. The guards watched these prisoners no less intently than they had the axemen. As far as they were concerned, saws were weapons, too.

Watching a fallen tree turned into firewood was less interesting than watching it fall in the first place. Along with most of the crowd, Fletch drifted away. If he hung around, there was always the chance that the Japs would find work for him, too. The Geneva Convention said officer prisoners genuinely had to volunteer to work, but the Japs hadn't signed it and respected it only when they wanted to. They didn't feed him well enough to make him feel like doing anything more than he had to.

"How's it going, Lieutenant?" That was Arnie, the ersatz artilleryman who'd surrendered along with Fletch.

"What could be better? It's the beachfront by Waikiki, right?" Fletch said. "I'm just waiting for the waitress to bring me another gin and tonic."

Arnie grinned. He was skinnier than Fletch remembered. Of course, Fletch was probably skinnier than he remembered, too. He just didn't get to see himself very often. Arnie said, "You got a good way of looking at things."

"My ass," Fletch told him. "If I had a good way of looking at things, I would have gone over the hill with Clancy and Dave."

"Wonder what the hell happened to 'em?" Arnie said.

"Whatever it is, could it be worse than staying in the Royal Hawaiian here?" Fletch asked. He got another smile out of Arnie. Considering how things were in the camp, that was no mean feat.

But nobody was laughing a couple of days later. The guards started shouting for a lineup in the middle of the morning. That was out of the ordinary. By now, Fletch had learned to view anything out of the ordinary with suspicion. The Japs didn't break routine to hand out lollipops.

He hoped there'd been an escape. Most of him hoped so, anyhow. People who left the perimeter on work details talked about "shooting squads": groups of ten where, if one man ran, all the others got it in the neck. That was a brutally effective way to convince prisoners not to try to make a break—and to stop the ones who did want to try. There were no shooting squads inside the camp, though. If somebody'd dug a tunnel and sneaked off, more power to him.

Fletch's hopes sank when the guards didn't count and recount the men lined up in neat rows. They would have if they thought they were missing people, wouldn't they? The commandant scrambled up onto a table in front of the POWs. As soon as he got up there, all the prisoners bowed. There would have been hell to pay if they hadn't. Much less athletically, a local Japanese in a double-breasted suit that didn't go with his tubby build clambered onto the table with the officer.

The Jap commandant shouted in his own language. He had one of those voices that could fill up as much space as it had to. A whole regiment could have heard his orders on the battlefield. The interpreter tried twice as hard and was half as loud: "We have captured four American soldiers. They did not surrender at the proper time. This makes them nothing but bandits. We treat bandits the way they deserve. Let this be a lesson to all of you."

Guards marched in the four Americans. *Poor bastards*, Fletch thought. They'd been stripped to the waist. Their faces and torsos showed cuts and bruises. The Japs must have worked them over after they were caught. One of them staggered like a punch-drunk palooka. How many times had they hit him in the head? If he didn't know everything that was going on around him, maybe he was luckier than his buddies.

None of them was Dave or Clancy. Fletch was glad of that. And then, in short order, he wasn't glad of anything any more. To him, *hung by the thumbs* had always been a joke, something people said but nobody would ever do.

The Japs weren't kidding. They tied ropes to a horizontal length of wood that had to be twelve feet off the ground, and to the Americans' thumbs. They were viciously precise about it, too, making sure their captives had to stand on tiptoe to keep their thumbs from taking all their weight. Once they'd tied them, they gagged them. And then they walked away.

Another shout from the camp commandant. "Dismissed!" the interpreter said.

Japanese soldiers stood guard around the four Americans. They made sure none of the ordinary POWs drew near. The men they'd captured just hung there, without food, without water, without hope. Fletch didn't need long to realize the Japs intended to let them die there. Every so often, one of them would sag down off his toes as weariness overcame him, only to be jerked up again by the agony in his hands. The rags tied over their mouths didn't muffle all the noises they made.

It took six days before they hung limp and unmoving. The guards cut them down with bayonets. They crumpled to the ground. Even after that, though, one of them tried to roll himself up into a ball. The Japs stared at him, gabbling in their own language. One of them ran off to get an officer.

When the officer came back with him, he took a look at the feebly wiggling American, then snapped out a command in his own language. "*Hai!*" the guards chorused. Three of them raised their rifles and aimed them at the man they'd made into an example. The Arisakas barked together, too. After that, the American didn't move any more.

With gestures, the guards ordered some of the POWs to drag the dead bodies to the burying ground. There already was one, for men who came down sick and couldn't find the strength to get better on what the Japs fed them—and for men the Japs killed one way or another.

Fletch was the third man a guard pointed at. He didn't try protesting that the Japanese couldn't make him work. If he had, he figured two more POWs would have dragged him to the burying ground. The corpse whose ankle he had hold of didn't weigh much; all the water was gone from it.

"You damn sorry son of a bitch," he said.

"Oh, yeah?" The corporal who had the other leg shook his head. "He's liable to be the lucky one. It's over for him. How long will it last for us?" Fletch had no answer. The dead man's head bumped along the ground. *Will that be me one day?* Fletch wondered. He had no answer for that, either.

"Where are you going?" Hiroshi Takahashi asked.

"Away from here. Any place at all away from here," Kenzo answered. They were both speaking English to keep their father from knowing what they were saying. "I can't stand hanging around this miserable tent." He didn't come right out and cuss; his dad knew what swear words were, all right.

"You better be back before we go out again, that's all I've got to tell you," Hiroshi warned.

"Yeah, yeah." Kenzo ducked out of the tent before his brother could nag him any more. The way his father kept taking fish to the Japanese consulate, and the way he kept coming back looking as if he'd just had tea with Hirohito . . . Some of the reverence for the Emperor Kenzo had learned as a little boy still lingered, but knowing that Hirohito reigned over a country at war with the USA carried more weight. No matter what his old man thought, Kenzo remained determined to stay an American.

He had to bow, though, when a Japanese patrol marched up the street towards him. He'd learned how to do that properly as a little boy, too. The noncom who headed up the patrol recognized him as a countryman and bowed back, which he wouldn't have done for a *haole*. That made Kenzo angry, not proud, but he didn't show what he was thinking.

He bowed again several times as he walked through Honolulu. His route would have looked random to someone who didn't know the city well—and who didn't know what had happened in it and to it since the Rising Sun went up over Iolani Palace. Since almost all food was supposed to go into community kitchens, the markets that had sprung up here and there were highly unofficial. Sometimes the Japs closed down one or another. More often, the people who ran them figured greased palms were part of the cost of doing business.

Fish here (sure as hell, he'd seen Eizo Doi selling some of what he got), taro there, rice somewhere else, yet another place for fresh vegetables . . . Yeah, you had to know your way around. You had to know your way around when you were buying, too, or you'd lose your shirt. The way things were these days, people with food they could sell had the whip hand.

But Kenzo wasn't looking to buy. Going out on the *Oshima Maru* kept him fed. It also gave him food to bargain with. If he wanted a coconut, he could trade a flying fish for it. He didn't need to lay out a stack of greenbacks fat as his fist. You could still buy almost anything if you had enough money, but *enough* swelled every day. People bargained frantically. Kenzo heard curses in half a dozen languages.

Whenever he saw a blond girl about his own age, he tensed. Was it . . . ? Whenever he got close enough to tell, he added some curses of his own to the electric air because, again and again, it wasn't. He began to wonder if he was wasting his time. That only made him shrug. How could he be wasting it if he was doing what he wanted to do?

And then, when he was almost sure he wouldn't run into Elsie Sundberg, he did. She was carrying a cloth sack that looked heavy, but that didn't show what it held. *Smart*, Kenzo thought—a lot smarter than carrying food out in the open. The hungrier people got, the likelier they were to steal.

He waved. For a moment, Elsie didn't think that was aimed at her. For another moment, she looked alarmed that she'd caught an Oriental's eye. Then she recognized him. He almost laughed at the look of relief that passed over her face before she smiled and waved back. He picked his way towards her past hard-faced sellers and excitable buyers.

"Hi," he said. "How are you? How are things?"

"Hi, yourself," Elsie answered. "Not . . . too bad. I want to thank you again for that fish you gave me. That really helped my whole family a lot."

"No *huhu*." Kenzo did laugh then. Why not? A Jap tossing a Hawaiian word to a *haole* girl . . . If that wasn't funny, what was? "Hope people aren't giving you a rough time." *Hope the Japanese aren't treating you the way whites treated local Japs before the war*. He wondered why he hoped that. Wasn't turnabout fair play? But Elsie had never treated him like a Jap—not till things got strange after the shooting started, anyhow, and then only for a little while.

She shrugged now. "Sign of the times," she said, which neatly echoed what he was thinking.

"You have any trouble getting that tuna home?" he asked.

Elsie shrugged again. "A little. But I was lucky. There were cops around both times, so things didn't get too messy. If those so-and-sos had got any pushier, I would've kicked 'em right where it hurts most. I was ready to." She did her best to look tough.

Back in high school, Kenzo wouldn't have imagined her best could be that good. But everybody'd had some painful lessons since then. "That's the way to do it," he said. "Uh—you want company taking your stuff home today?"

She hesitated, much the same way she had when he waved to her across the makeshift market. Then, as she had that time, she smiled again, smiled and nodded. "Sure, Ken. Thanks."

"Okay." Now he paused. "Your folks gonna start pitching a fit when you come up to the front door with a Jap?"

She blushed. He watched in fascination as the color spread up from her neckline all the way to the roots of her hair. But, yet again, she didn't need more than a moment to gather herself. "Not when it's somebody I went to school with," she said firmly. She eyed him. "Is that good enough for you?"

"Yeah." This time, Kenzo answered right away. She would have got mad at him if he hadn't, and she would have had a right to. "You ready to go or you need more stuff?"

"I'm ready." As if to prove it, Elsie hefted the bag. "Come on."

Kenzo had hustled till he was almost breathless, hoping to run into her. Now that he'd succeeded, he had trouble finding things to say. Honolulu wasn't a great big city; every step brought him that much closer to good-bye, which was the one thing he didn't want to tell her.

Elsie did her best to help, asking, "How are your brother and your father?"

"Hank's okay." Kenzo used the name by which Hiroshi was known to *haoles*. "My dad . . ." He didn't know how to go on with that. At last, he said, "Dad was born in the old country, and he's . . . he's happier with the way things are now than we are."

"Oh." She walked on for a little while. "That must make things . . . exciting to talk about." Like him, she was looking for safe ways to say inherently unsafe things.

"Exciting. Yeah." He laughed, not that it was funny. "Things get so exciting that most of the time we don't talk about anything but fishing. You don't want to whack somebody over the head with a brick on account of fishing."

"I guess not." Elsie took another few steps. He realized she had to feel as wary around him as he did around her. "You're lucky that you're able to go out there, especially with so many people hungry."

"Some luck," he said bitterly. "If I were really lucky, I'd be in college now. Then I could be working on a degree instead of a line full of hooks. Of course, afterwards I'd probably go out fishing with my old man anyway, because who's gonna hire a Jap with a degree?"

"Was it really that bad?" Elsie was white. She hadn't had to worry about it. She hadn't even had to know the problem was there.

"It wasn't good—that's for darn sure," Kenzo answered. "Lots more Japanese with good educations than places for them to work. You put somebody with a university degree in a shoe store or a grocery or out on a sampan and he starts wondering why the heck he bothered. You let him watch somebody with green eyes and freckles get the office job he's better qualified for and he won't be real happy about it."

Quietly, Elsie said, "It's a wonder you aren't happier about how things are now."

"I'm an American," Kenzo said with a shrug. "That's what everybody told me, even before I started going to school. People told me that, and I believed it. Heck, I still believe it. I believe it more than the Big Five do, I bet." The people who ran the Big Five—the firms of Alexander and Baldwin, American Factors, C. Brewer and Company, Castle and Cooke, and the Theo. H. Davies Company—pretty much ran Hawaii, or they had till the war, anyhow. They ran the banks, they ran the plantations, they did the hiring, and they did the firing. And the higher in their ranks you looked, the whiter they got.

Another proof of who'd been running things here for the past fifty years was the neighborhood they were walking through as they neared Elsie's house. These large homes—mostly of white clapboard with shingle roofs—on even larger lots were nothing like the crowded shacks and tenements west of Nuuanu Avenue, the part of town where Kenzo had grown up. They didn't shout about money; they weren't so rude or vulgar. But they admitted it was there, even the ones that had been wrecked or damaged in the fighting. And the people who lived in them were white.

Somebody had neatly mowed the Sundbergs' front lawn. Kenzo wondered whether Elsie's father pushed the lawn mower every Sunday morning or they had a gardener. Before the war, he would have bet on a gardener. Now? He admitted to himself that he wasn't sure.

The front door opened before he and Elsie got to it. Mrs. Sundberg looked a lot like Elsie. Like her daughter, she also looked alarmed for a moment—what was this Jap doing here? Then, even without Elsie telling her, she realized which Jap he was likely to be, and her face cleared. "Mr. Takahashi, isn't it?" she said politely.

"That's right, Mrs. Sundberg." Kenzo was polite, too.

"Thank you for the fish you gave us. It was very generous of you," she said. He nodded; he'd expected something like that. But she went on in a way he hadn't expected: "It's good to see you here. Now we can give you something, too."

"Huh?" he said, which was not the most brilliant thing that could have come out of his mouth, but she'd caught him by surprise.

She smiled a slightly superior smile—a very *haole* smile. Elsie, who hadn't got that trick down pat yet, giggled instead and then said, "Come on in, Ken."

Mrs. Sundberg's smile slipped a little, but only a little, and she put it back fast. "Yes, do," she said. "We have lemonade, if you'd like some. Elsie, you get it for him, and I'll go out back and do the honors."

Inside, the house was pure New England: overstuffed furniture with nubbly upholstery, lots of turned wood stained a color close to dark cherry, and more pictures on the wall and knickknacks on tables and shelves than you could shake a stick at. "Thanks," Kenzo said when Elsie did bring him some lemonade. That *didn't* surprise him. Lots of people had lemon trees, you couldn't do much with lemons but squeeze them, and Hawaii did still have plenty of sugar—if not much else. She carried a glass for herself, too. He sipped. It was good.

Mrs. Sundberg came back inside with half a dozen alligator pears, the rough skin on some dark green, on others almost black. "Here you are," she said proudly.

"Thank you very much!" Kenzo meant it. Alligator pears—some people called them avocados—were a lot harder to come by than lemons. He couldn't remember the last time he'd had any.

"You're welcome," she said. "The darker ones are ripe now; the others will be in a few days. Feel them. When they start to get soft, they'll be ready to eat."

"Okay. That's great. Thanks again." Kenzo was glad she'd given him a number he could share evenly with his brother and his father. Had she done it on purpose? Probably; she wouldn't miss a trick like that. He'd told Elsie what his living arrangements were, and that his mother hadn't made it. If Elsie'd mentioned it even once, Mrs. Sundberg wasn't the sort who'd forget.

He thought she would hover over him and her daughter, but she didn't. She went off into the back of the house somewhere. Somehow, that left him more on his best behavior than if she had hovered. He and Elsie talked about people from high school while they drank their lemonade.

When he finished his, he said, "I better go."

Elsie didn't say no. She did say, "Thanks for walking me home. That was nice of you," which was almost as good.

"It's okay. It was good to see you." That was about a tenth of what Kenzo meant. Gathering his courage, he tried again: "Could we maybe, uh, see each other some more one of these times?"

He'd already seen she wasn't as good as her mother at masking what she thought. He didn't need to be a private eye or somebody like that to read what she was thinking. She'd known him a long time, but he was Japanese. He was Japanese, but she'd known him a long time—not quite the same as the other. Being Japanese meant something different now from what it had before December 7. Whatever it meant, he wasn't a collaborator, or no more than you had to be to survive when the place where you lived was occupied. And so . . .

"Yes, we can do that," she said.

"Swell!" He grinned like a fool. "So long." He didn't think his feet touched the ground at all as he went down the walk and out to the street.

THE TRAIN CHUGGED TO A STOP. "Pensacola!" the conductor shouted. "All out for Pensacola!"

Joe Crosetti leaped up from his seat. He grabbed his duffel bag from the overhead rack and slung it over his shoulder. All his worldly goods in a canvas sack—he felt proud, not impoverished. And he was so excited, he could hardly stand still. "Pensacola Naval Air Station!" he said. "Wings! Wings at last!"

Orson Sharp shouldered his duffel, too. "Keep your shirt on, Joe," he said mildly. "They're not going to let us fly this afternoon."

"Yeah, but soon," Joe said. "We *can* fly here. We're *gonna* fly here. It's not like Chapel Hill, where we couldn't."

"Okay," his roommate said. Joe had the feeling he was hiding a laugh, and wondered if he ought to get mad himself. But then, as the swarm of cadets surged towards the door, he forgot all about it.

The last time he'd got off a train, it was in the middle of a North Carolina winter. He liked spring in Florida a hell of a lot better. He got a glimpse of the Gulf of Mexico. Just that glimpse told him he didn't know as much about the ocean as he thought he did. The Pacific off San Francisco could be green. It could be gray. It could even be greenish blue or grayish blue. He'd never seen it, never imagined it, a blue between turquoise and sapphire, a blue that was really *blue*. The color made you want to go swimming in it. People went swimming off of San Francisco, too, but they came out of the water with their teeth chattering when they did.

Beside him, Orson Sharp said, "I've never seen the ocean before."

That made Joe blink. To him, this was a variation on a theme. To the kid from Utah, it was a whole new song. "You wanted to be a Navy flier before you even knew what all that wet stuff was like?" Joe said.

Sharp didn't get angry or embarrassed. "I figured I'd find out what I needed to know." He was hard to faze.

"Buses! Buses to the Air Station this way!" somebody shouted. Cadets started heading *this way*. In the middle of the crowd and short, Joe didn't even see which way the shouter pointed. He just went along, one more sheep in the flock. If everybody else was wrong, he'd be wrong, too, but he'd have a lot of company. They couldn't land on him too hard unless he goofed all by his lonesome.

The buses were where they were supposed to be. A placard in front of the first one said, TO PENSACOLA NAVAL AIR STATION. This time, the flock had done it right. Cadets lined up to get aboard. The Navy was even bigger on lining up than grade school had been.

Joe got a little look at Pensacola as the bus rolled south and west towards the Naval Air Station. A lot of the streets had Spanish names. He remembered from an American history course that Florida had belonged to Spain once upon a time, the same as California had. He shook his head in wonder. He'd never expected that to matter to him—when would he get to Florida? But here he was, by God.

Oaks and palms and magnolias all grew here. The air was mild and moist, although this extreme northwestern part of Florida wasn't a place winter forgot altogether, the way, say, Miami was. Frame and brick buildings, some with big wrought-iron balconies on the upper stories, lined the streets.

"Reminds me a little of New Orleans," said somebody behind Joe. The comparison would have meant more to him if he'd ever been to New Orleans.

Whites and Negroes walked along the sidewalks and went in and out of shops and homes. They seemed not far from equal in numbers. As it had been in North Carolina, that was plenty to tell Joe he was a long way from home. Colored people in San Francisco were few and far between.

Because of the name, he'd figured the Naval Air Station would lie right next to the town. But it didn't; it was half a dozen miles away. On the way there, Joe's bus passed a massive fort of brickwork and granite. "This here is Fort Barrancas," the driver said, playing tour guide. "The Confederates held it for a while during the War Between the States, but the Federals ran 'em out."

Joe had heard people talk about the *War Between the States* in North Carolina, too. In San Francisco, it had always been just the Civil War. Cadets from the South seemed a lot more . . . serious about it than those from other parts of the country. Of course, their side had lost, which doubtless made a difference.

"Over there across the channel on Santa Rosa Island is Fort Pickens," the driver went on. "It could've touched off the war if Fort Sumter didn't. The Confederates never did take it, even though the fellow who attacked it was the same man who'd built it before the war. They kept Geronimo the Apache there for a while after they caught him, too."

Leaning out past Orson Sharp, Joe got a glimpse of Fort Pickens. It had five sides, with a bastion at each corner. Even now, it looked like a tough nut to crack. He imagined gunfire sweeping the sand of Santa Rosa Island and shivered a little. No, trying to take a place like that wouldn't have been any fun at all.

And then he forgot all about the Civil War or the War Between the States or whatever you were supposed to call it. Along with the gulls and pelicans fluttering over Fort Pickens, he spotted an airplane painted bright yellow:

a trainer. The buzz that filled the bus said he wasn't the only one who'd seen it, either. Excitement blazed through him. Before long, *he'd* go up in one of those slow, ungainly machines—except it seemed as swift and sleek as a Wildcat to him.

Pensacola Naval Air Station itself was a study in contrasts. The old buildings were *old*: brickwork that looked as if it dated from somewhere close to the Civil War. And the new ones were *new*: some of the plywood that had gone into hangars and administrative buildings hadn't been painted yet, and hadn't started weathering yet, either. And out beyond the buildings sprouted a forest of tents.

The driver might have been reading Joe's mind. "You gentlemen will be staying in those for a while, I'm afraid," he said. "We're putting up real housing as fast as we can, but there's a lot going on, and we've had to get big in just a bit of a hurry, you know."

That got laughs all through the bus. A couple of years earlier, nobody'd wanted to hear about national defense, much less talk about it. Now nobody wanted to pay attention to anything else. But making up for lost time was no easier, no more possible, than it ever was.

Brakes groaning, the bus stopped. The cadets shouldered their duffels again. As they descended, a lieutenant commander came out of the closest old brick building and greeted them with, "Welcome to Pensacola Naval Air Station, gentlemen. You will have no mothers here. We assume you're old enough to take care of yourselves till you show us otherwise—at which point we're liable to throw you out on your ear. Now if you'll line up for processing. . . ."

Processing here was for the cadets about what it was for a cow going through the Swift meat-packing plant in Chicago. Joe didn't end up with USDA CHOICE stamped on his backside, but that was almost all he escaped. The paperwork he filled out made what he'd done at Chapel Hill seem like the kindergarten course. "We ought to drop this stuff on the Japs," he grumbled to Orson Sharp. "It'd smash 'em flatter than a ten-ton bomb."

"It can't be helped." Sharp took everything, even

bureaucratic nonsense, in stride. Joe didn't know whether to admire him or to want to clobber him.

They shared a two-man tent a good deal more spacious than their four-man dorm room. Joe looked at a mimeographed handout a bored petty officer had given him. He rolled his eyes up to the heavens and let out a theatrical groan.

"For heaven's sake, what is it?" Sharp asked. Any other cadet in the group would have said something more pungent than *for heaven's sake*.

"Listen to this." Joe read from the handout: "'Flight training and academic preparation will continue in the ratio of three parts to two. Academic subjects to be covered will include the following: navigation, ordnance and gunnery, indoctrination, recognition, communications, and airplane engines.' We're stuck with more classes, for cryin' out loud." He would have been more pungent himself with anybody but his roommate. He refused to admit that Orson Sharp was a good influence on him.

"Well? We need to know all those things." Sharp was so reasonable, he could drive anybody nuts.

"I thought we were done with notebooks and desks and tests. Lord knows I hoped we were." Joe refused to cheer up, even though he already knew a lot about engines.

"I'm not thrilled, either, but we can't quit now. We just have to go through with it." Sharp wasn't wrong. Joe didn't clobber him. He couldn't have said why, not to save his life.

COMMANDER MINORU GENDA WAS WORKING in a Honolulu office that had once housed a U.S. Navy officer. The space was larger and better appointed than anyone below flag rank would have had in Japan, but nothing out of the ordinary here. His work was nothing out of the ordinary, either. That left him slightly discontented. He wouldn't have minded leaving Oahu and going on to fight in the Philippines or the Dutch East Indies. Things were too quiet here. He wanted new problems to sink his teeth into.

He hadn't had that thought more than ten minutes before an excited radioman ran into his office and exclaimed,

"Sir, one of our picket boats has sighted two American carriers heading towards these islands!"

"Well, well," Genda said. That was a surprise. He hadn't expected the Yankees to try to raid Hawaii. "Give me more details."

"Sir, there are no more details," the radioman answered. "The picket boat's signal cut off in the middle of the message."

"*Ah, so desu.* I understand." Genda nodded. No, he wouldn't be able to get more details from the picket boat's crew. No one this side of the Yasukuni Shrine for the spirits of the war dead would. Now he had to think about what to do to make sure the Americans paid for their folly. "*Akagi* and *Soryu* have been notified?"

"Oh, yes, sir," the radioman said. "Captain Hasegawa says he wants to let the American ships come closer before he launches his attack against them. The Americans will have to come closer if they're going to strike at Oahu."

"*Hai. Honto,*" Genda said. That was why the picket boats were out there, some more than a thousand kilometers north and east of the island. No carrier-based bombers could fly that far and return to the ships that had launched them. Genda looked at his watch. It was almost three. He wouldn't have been surprised if the Americans intended to run in towards Oahu all through the night, as the Japanese strike force had done back in December. Thinking out loud, he went on, "We caught them by surprise, though. They won't play the same trick on us. We'll be ready and waiting tomorrow morning."

"Yes, sir," the radioman said. "Do you need me to pass anything on to either of our carriers?"

"Just one thing—good hunting."

THE AIRSTRIP BY HALEIWA had to be one of the most beautiful in the world. Out beyond the grass and the palm trees and the beach was the vast turquoise expanse of the Pacific. Neither the beauty nor the perfect climate did anything to salve Lieutenant Saburo Shindo's temper. When he looked north to the Pacific, he saw only an opportunity he would not have. The Americans stuck their head in the tiger's mouth when he happened to be ashore. Others aboard the *Akagi* and the *Soryu* would hunt them at sea. As for him . . .

Feeling like a caged tiger himself, he paced back and forth at the edge of the runway. The pilots drawn up at attention there followed him with their eyes. He glared at them, then deliberately stopped so they had to look west, into the sinking sun, to see him.

"I hope we will be unlucky," he said. "I hope the men on our carriers will find the Americans and sink them before they can make their night run towards Oahu. But if the carrier pilots fail, we will see American planes overhead early tomorrow morning. Do you understand?"

"*Hai!*" the fliers chorused.

"You had better," Shindo snarled. "Because you will be up and waiting for them when they arrive. You will be waiting for them, and you will make them sorry they dared come anywhere near this island. Do you understand *that?*"

"*Hai!*" they chorused again.

Shindo scowled. "All right, then. I will be up there with you, and I will be watching. Anyone who lets an American escape—even one American, do you hear?—will answer to me. I am more dangerous to you than any stinking Yankee pilot ever born. Do you understand *that?*"

"*Hai!*" the pilots said once more.

"Good. You'd better." Shindo turned his back. "Dismissed." He heard the men muttering, but he didn't look at them again. Let them mutter. As long as they were worrying about him, they wouldn't worry about the enemy. That was what he had in mind.

JANE ARMITAGE BROKE A NAIL weeding her potato patch. She hardly bothered to swear. That wasn't because she didn't want to seem unladylike. She couldn't have cared less. These days, though, a broken nail was nothing to get excited about. She looked down at her hands. Before the war started, the only mark they'd had was a small callus on the side of her right middle finger: a writer's callus. Now hard yellow calluses banded her palms. Her fingers were battered and scarred. Her nails ... didn't bear thinking about. They'd been a disaster even before she broke the latest one. She bit it off short and reasonably straight—why wait to go back to the apartment and dig out a manicure scissors? Then she got back to work.

Pretty soon she'd be able to knock off for the day. The sun was sliding down towards the Waianae Range. A shower would be—not quite heavenly, not without hot water, but welcome even so. Then she could go have supper. She was amazed how important food had become in her life now that she didn't have enough of it. Just thinking of supper was enough to make her stomach rumble. It would go on rumbling after she ate, too.

Never enough ... Everyone in Wahiawa got thinner by the day. That had to be true of everyone on Oahu, everyone in the Territory of Hawaii, but Jane hadn't gone outside of Wahiawa since the fighting started. She felt as if she'd fallen back through time like someone in an H. G. Wells story. What was she but a peasant from the Middle Ages, tied to her little plot of land?

She paused again in her weeding. This time, it wasn't a broken fingernail but a distant droning in the sky. She frowned. The Japs didn't fly all that much, certainly not so much as the Army Air Corps had before Hawaii changed hands. Maybe they didn't have as much fuel as they would have liked. Or maybe they just didn't think they had anything to worry about. Whatever the reason, they didn't.

And the swelling drone didn't sound as if it came from Japanese planes. Jane had heard enough of them to know what they sounded like. She looked up. Coming out of the northeast, over the Koolau Range, was a V of big, two-engine, twin-tailfinned airplanes. She stared at them, hardly daring to hope that. ...

They flew right over Wahiawa, low enough to let her make out the stars on their wings. They were! They were American planes!

Jane wanted to yell and scream and dance, all at the same time. She heard cheers here and there. She heard them, but she didn't do anything except go on staring up at the sky. Too many people were out and about. Someone might see her and report her to the Japs if she celebrated too hard. You never could tell, and you didn't want to take a chance.

How had they got here? They looked too big to be carrier planes. Had they flown all the way from the Pacific Coast? If they had, they surely couldn't carry enough gas to get back. What were they going to do?

What they were going to do now was attack Wheeler Field, not far southwest of Wahiawa. A few antiaircraft guns started shooting at them, but only a few. The Japs must have been as taken aback as the Americans were when the war started. Would some Japanese politician stand up in whatever they used for a parliament and make a speech about April 18, the way FDR had about December 7? *By God, I hope so!* Jane thought savagely.

Crump! Crump! Crump! Yes, that was the noise of bursting bombs. Jane had become altogether too well acquainted with it to harbor any doubts. *Give it to 'em! Give it to the lousy sons of bitches!* She didn't say a thing. She thought her head would burst with the effort of holding those loud, loud thoughts inside.

Not everybody bothered. She heard an unmistakable Rebel yell. And somebody shouted, "Take that, you fucking slant-eyed bastards!" She didn't recognize the voice. She hoped nobody else did, either.

A column of greasy black smoke rose into the sky, and then two more in quick succession. They weren't anything like the massive pall that had marked Pearl Harbor's funeral pyre, but they were there. The bombers had hit something worth hitting.

The dinner bell rang, summoning people all over Wahiawa to the community kitchen. Jane's amazement grew by leaps and bounds. For a few wonderful minutes, she hadn't even realized she was hungry.

COMMANDER MINORU GENDA snatched up the jangling telephone in his office. "*Moshi-moshi!*" he said impatiently.

An excited voice gabbled in his ear. Genda's impatience gave way to astonishment. "But that's impossible!" he exclaimed. More gabbling assured him that it wasn't. "How the—?" He broke off. He heard bombs going off in the distance, not at Wheeler Field—that was too far away for the sound to carry—but off to the west. *Hickam!* he thought in dismay. "So sorry, but I've got to go," he told the officer on the other end of the line, and hung up before the man could squawk any more.

He rushed downstairs and out onto the sidewalk in front of his office building. The sun was dropping down toward the Pacific. Genda caught glints of light off airplane wings. He knew the silhouette of every plane Japan made. Those weren't Japanese aircraft.

They were, they could only be, American. He watched them drone east past the southern edge of Honolulu. He knew every carrier-based U.S. warplane by sight, too. He had to. The planes he saw weren't any of those, either.

Other people also realized they belonged to the USA. The whoops and cheers that rang out all over Honolulu told him as much. If he'd had any doubts that Hawaii wasn't fully reconciled to Japanese occupation, those whoops would have cured them.

Those weren't carrier-based aircraft. They were . . . "*Zakennayo!*" Genda exclaimed. He seldom swore, but here he made an exception. Those were U.S. Army B-25s.

A million questions boiled in his head. *How did they get here?* came first and foremost. They didn't have the range to fly from California. The answer to that one formed almost as fast as the question did. The Americans must have flown them off one of the carriers the picket boat had spotted. Genda bowed slightly towards the U.S. bombers in token of respect. That had taken imagination and nerve.

But the next question was, *How do they aim to recover their planes and their air crews?* He couldn't imagine that the United States would send men off on a suicide mission. He also couldn't see how the USA planned to get them back. He scratched his head. It was a puzzlement.

Yet another good question was, *What are we doing*

about this? The Japanese didn't seem to be doing very much. A few antiaircraft guns started firing. A few puffs of black smoke stained the sky around the B-25s. Genda saw no signs that any of them was hit.

He also saw no fighters going after them. Had the Yankees blasted all the runways on Oahu? Genda couldn't believe it. There weren't nearly enough American bombers to do anything of the sort. More likely, they'd just caught the Japanese with their pants down. Nobody had expected the raiders till tomorrow morning. The Americans had pulled a fast one—the B-25s, with their greater range, could launch far sooner than the usual carrier-based planes would have.

The *Akagi* and the *Soryu* would be rushing north to meet the American carriers . . . which probably wouldn't be anywhere near so far south as the Japanese thought they were. And Japanese fighters based here on Oahu didn't seem to be reacting very well at all.

The Yankees may have done us a favor, Genda thought. This was—this could only be—a raid, a pinprick, an annoyance, a stunt. It wouldn't and couldn't settle anything. He imagined U.S. newspapers with headlines like WE STRIKE BACK AT HAWAII! People on the American mainland would cheer—and would have the right to.

But what would happen if and when the Americans seriously attacked Oahu? Genda didn't know whether they could. But now he was sure as sure could be that they wanted to. They weren't going to accept what had happened in the central Pacific as a *fait accompli*.

We weren't ready here, Genda thought. *We weren't ready, and they've embarrassed us. They've made us lose face.* That wouldn't happen again, though. Genda intended to be one of the men who made sure it wouldn't happen again. If the Yankees returned, they wouldn't find Oahu too flustered to fight back. The island would be ready to repel them.

Meanwhile, still without much harassment from the ground or from the air, the B-25s buzzed off in the direction of Diamond Head. No matter what Genda might plan for the future, today belonged to them. Genda went back up to the office as fast as he'd hurried down to the street. Yes, today belonged to the Americans. He got on the telephone to do his best to ensure that tomorrow wouldn't.

CHOW TIME. HORRIBLE GLOP. Not enough of it—nowhere near enough of it. Fletch Armitage didn't care. He looked forward to every meal he got in the Kapiolani Park POW camp with greater anticipation than he ever had when he was going to some pretty fancy restaurants back on the mainland.

He didn't need to be Albert Einstein to figure out why. These days, he had an insider's understanding of relativity. When you were already well fed, even the finest supper could be only so nice. And when you were hungry, any food at all, even food you would have turned your nose up at when times were better, couldn't be anything less than wonderful.

In those days, more good food had been just a surfeit. Fletch had wondered when he would start to get a potbelly. Here and now, every grain of rice kept him breathing for another—how long? A minute? Five minutes? Who could say? But he would rather have had a T-bone with all the trimmings than Jane wearing nothing but a smile.

He wondered how she was. Had she stayed in Wahiawa or fled in front of the oncoming Japanese? Fletch had no way to know, of course. He had no way to know which would have been better, either. The Japs had gleefully strafed refugees, and in the end there'd been no way to stay in front of them. Had there been, he wouldn't have been standing in line in a POW camp.

A fly landed on his arm. He slapped at it. It buzzed away. Then his ear caught another buzz, this one up in the sky. He wasn't the only one who heard it, either. Somebody pointed west, towards downtown Honolulu. Somebody else said, "What the hell are those?"

Since the planes were coming out of the sun, what they were wasn't obvious for a little while. But then somebody else said, "Fuck me if they ain't B-25s!"

As soon as the soldier said it, Fletch knew he was right. Those sleek lines and twin tail booms couldn't have belonged to any other aircraft. Fletch wished Hawaii would have had a few squadrons of them instead of the lumbering Douglas B-18s that weren't fast enough to run or well enough armored to fight. Then he wondered what difference it would have made. The Japs would have shot up the B-25s on the ground, too.

And then—and only then—Fletch wondered what the hell B-25s were doing flying over Japanese-occupied Oahu. He wasn't the only one slow on the uptake—far from it. The cheering in the camp had hardly started before he was yelling his head off. Everybody was yelling a few seconds later, yelling and shaking hands and pounding buddies on the back.

Not more than ten seconds later, the machine guns on the guard towers around the camp cut loose. The prisoners inside hit the dirt with the unanimity of conditioned reflex. Only after Fletch lay flat did he poke his head up for a split second to see what the hell was going on. The Japs in the towers weren't shooting at their captives. They were blazing away at the bombers.

"Dumb assholes," said a sergeant lying next to Fletch. "Those planes are too high up for small arms to hit."

"Let 'em waste ammo," Fletch said. "At least it's not coming in on us." The sergeant nodded.

The B-25s flew on by. East of Diamond Head, they swung up towards the north. That was when Fletch started trying to figure out not only what they were doing but how they'd got here. They couldn't have taken·off from San Francisco. They wouldn't have made it to Oahu in the first place, let alone had a prayer of getting back. Could the big, hulking brutes have flown off a carrier? He wasn't sure; he was no Navy man. But he would have bet the farm the stork hadn't brought them.

Quite a few of the POWs *were* Navy men. Some of them swore up and down that no Army bombers could have got airborne off a carrier's short flight deck. They couldn't come close to explaining how else the bombers had arrived over Oahu, though. As that sank in, their protests faded.

The cheering didn't last long. A captain—Army variety, not Navy—said, "You wait and see—the Japs'll make us pay for yelling for our own goddamn side."

"Of course they will. They've lost face," another officer said.

Fletch found that horribly likely. What could be more embarrassing than enemy bombers showing up over an island you thought you owned? *Surprise, guys*, Fletch thought. The Japs cared more about prestige than Americans did, too.

Slowly, the chow line started snaking forward again. Here and there, men had dropped mess kits when they dove for cover as the guard-tower machine guns opened up. They squabbled over which one was whose and over who'd been a clumsy idiot and stepped on one: all serious business because it centered on food.

No juicy T-bone for Fletch or anybody else at the Kapiolani camp—just rice and leaves that might have been vegetables or might have been weeds, and not enough of either. He hated it and he wanted more, both at the same time. But however unsatisfactory a supper it made, he felt better afterwards than before. For a little while, his body was only yelling at him that it was hungry. It wasn't screaming, the way it usually did.

Here and there, prisoners whistled or hummed "The Star-Spangled Banner" and "America the Beautiful" and "God Bless America" and other patriotic songs. Nobody sang the words out loud. That would have been asking for trouble. Some of the guards knew English, and some of the local Japanese had thrown in with the occupiers. Even the tunes were dangerous. Fletch admired the POWs who showed what they were feeling without wanting to irritate the occupiers. He didn't doubt that everybody felt the same way. Why stick your neck out to show it?

And one flight of bombers couldn't be anything more than a nuisance to the Japs. They might remind Hawaii—and Tokyo—that the USA was still in the fight, but they weren't about to bundle the Empire of Japan back across the Pacific. *Too bad*, Fletch thought, eyeing the barbed wire surrounding him. *Too goddamn bad.*

LIEUTENANT SABURO SHINDO wasn't usually a man to show what he felt. Right now, though, he was furious, and making only the barest effort to hide it. The officers set over him had talked about an American attack at first light tomorrow morning. He'd been ready to meet that. He'd had his fellow fighter pilots at Haleiwa ready to meet it, too.

They hadn't been ready for the single U.S. bomber that swooped low over the airstrip here now as afternoon passed into evening, dropped a stick of bombs, and roared off to the south. Had there been three bombers instead of one, they could have wrecked the whole field. Bombs from the one were bad enough. No Zeros could take off till those holes got filled in.

"*Isogi!*" Shindo shouted at the bulldozer operator. The Army noncom tipped his hat to show that he *was* hurrying. Blue, stinking diesel smoke belched from the bulldozer's exhaust pipe. The lowered blade shoved dirt into one of the last holes in the ground. The big, snorting machine tamped the dirt down flat with the blade and with its caterpillar treads.

Pick-and-shovel men would have taken a couple of days to repair the damage. Shindo knew that. Here, the sun still stood in the sky, though it sank towards the western horizon with each passing minute. And each passing minute meant one minute fewer in which he could hope to gain revenge.

As if moving in slow motion, the bulldozer cleared the runway. "Let's go!" Shindo shouted to his men. They ran for their fighters. As soon as Shindo slammed his canopy shut, a ground crewman spun his prop. The Zero's engine roared to life. Obeying another ground crewman's signals, Shindo taxied out of the revetment that had saved the plane from damage and out to the runway.

He gave the Zero the gun. It bounced a couple of times as it ran over the hasty repairs the bulldozer had made, but he had no trouble getting into the air. He grudged the time he had to wait for his comrades to join him. As soon as they'd all taken off, they streaked away to the northeast after the now-vanished American bombers.

Where? Shindo didn't know, not exactly. He was going on dead reckoning and gut instinct and the sketchy reports he'd got from other parts of Oahu. Any of those might have been wrong. All of them might have been wrong, and he knew it only too well. If they were . . . If they were, he'd see nothing but sky and ocean till he ran low on fuel or ran out of light.

He admired the Yankees' nerve. They'd got everybody on Oahu jumping like fleas on a hot plate. *Including me*, he thought sourly. He still hadn't figured out how they intended to get picked up. He couldn't believe they'd be able to land on a carrier, even if they'd left from one. Would they ditch in the ocean and trust to luck? That seemed to stretch trust further than it ought to go.

"There, Lieutenant!" An excited voice in his earphones made him stop puzzling over it. "Isn't that them, about ten o'clock low?"

"*Hai.*" Shindo, by contrast, sounded perfectly calm. He estimated the American bombers' course and radioed it back to Oahu. It might help the Japanese carriers and their planes find the ships that had launched the B-25s. That done, he said, "Now we make them pay."

It wouldn't be easy. They had scant daylight left. And the bombers had seen them, too. The B-25s dove for the deck. They had a very fair turn of speed. They weren't as fast or as maneuverable as the Zeros (nothing was as maneuverable as a Zero except the Japanese Army's Hayabusa fighter, which was much more lightly armed), but they didn't dawdle.

They also showed they had teeth. The machine gunners in their dorsal turrets blazed away at Shindo and his comrades. And those were heavy machine guns. A Zero must have got in the way of a few rounds, for it tumbled into the Pacific trailing smoke and flame. One reason Zeros were so fast and maneuverable was that they were lightly built. When they got hit, they paid the price.

Shindo chose a B-25. He gave it a burst from his own machine guns. Those were just rifle-caliber weapons. He made hits. He was sure of that. But the bomber kept flying as if nothing had happened to it. Sturdy construction and armor plate might make a plane slow and sluggish, but they too had their advantages.

Another Zero cometed into the sea. Shindo swore. Who was supposed to be shooting down whom? He brought another bomber into his sights. This time, he opened up with his twin 20mm cannon. A couple of hits from them would knock anything out of the sky. Getting the hits was the problem. They fired none too fast and carried only a limited store of ammunition.

Get in close, he thought. That was the fighter pilot's number-one rule. Get in close enough and you couldn't miss. Shooting at long range was the most common and worst mistake novices and bad pilots made. Once the enemy filled your windscreen, you didn't scare him when you opened up. You killed him.

The Americans knew that as well as Shindo did. Tracers streaked past his Zero. But they had to aim guns in turrets, which wasn't easy. He pointed his fighter's nose at the B-25 and started shooting. Chunks flew from the bomber. For a long, dreadful moment, he thought it would keep going all the same. But it heeled over and smashed down into the ocean. Even then, though, it left only an oil slick, not a floating patch of fire like a Zero. Another place the Yankees added weight was in self-sealing fuel tanks that really worked.

Three more B-25s—and another Zero—went into the Pacific before Shindo broke off the attack. If he and his comrades were going to get back to Oahu with any light in the sky, they had to turn south now. The bombers kept on heading northeast, as if they intended to fly to California. They couldn't get there, though. Shindo wondered again what they *did* intend to do.

As he made for Oahu, he also wondered if he'd pursued too long. And then he saw that the ground crew at Haleiwa had lit up the airstrip with parked cars and trucks and a searchlight that had stood in front of a movie theater. His landing was a long way from elegant, but he made it.

A ground crewman with a flashlight guided him to a revetment. He killed the motor, leaped out of his Zero, and ran for the radio in the headquarters tent. He wanted to find out whether carrier-based aircraft could catch the enemy's ships.

Other pilots came to listen with him. A couple of hours later, they got a nasty jolt. Instead of the Japanese finding the American carriers, a U.S. sub found the *Soryu*. The Yankees must have hoped the Japanese would charge after them, hoped and had submarines lying in wait. Now Shindo listened anxiously, fearing the carrier would sink. Not till after midnight was it plain the ship would survive. Two torpedoes had struck her, but only one exploded. Had they both . . . But they hadn't, and the *Soryu* limped back towards safer waters.

With her came the *Akagi*. There would be no pursuit of the U.S. raiders after all. However they intended to recover their planes and crews, they could go ahead and do it.

XI

DOOLITTLE RAIDS HAWAII! the newspaper headlines
screamed. TAKES JAPS BY SURPRISE! Only when you got to
the fourth paragraph of the story did you discover that six
of his sixteen B-25s had been shot down. The rest of what
was in the paper was a paean to the heroism of the crews
that had been rescued after they ditched in the Pacific—
and, in slightly smaller measure, to the heroism of the destroyer crews that had done the rescuing.

Joe Crosetti understood that. Like every cadet at the
Pensacola Naval Air Station, he wished he'd been along
with Jimmy Doolittle and his intrepid flyboys. He was sick-
jealous of the fliers, as a matter of fact. How horribly unfair that they'd got to go and he hadn't! Just because they'd
been flying for years while he was only now beginning to
get up in the air . . .

That they'd lost more than one plane in three and about
one man in two (for several crewmen had been shot even
on B-25s that kept flying to the ditching point) fazed him
not at all. It hadn't fazed them either. They were all volunteers. The papers made that very plain. He couldn't imagine anybody in the country who *wouldn't* have stepped up
to the plate there.

He burbled about the attack standing on the runway
next to the Boeing Stearman he'd soon be taking up. Like
all Navy trainers, the tough little biplane was painted bright

yellow so nobody could mistake it for anything but what it
was. People not training in Stearmans called them Yellow
Perils, not altogether in jest. They were dangerous to their
pilots and dangerous to those around them.

"If you will bring yourself back from the Hawaiian Islands to the business at hand, Mr. Crosetti . . ." said the instructor, a lieutenant from Pittsburgh named Ralph
Goodwin.

"Uh, yes, sir. Sorry, sir." Joe wasn't the least bit sorry.
"Can you imagine the look on the Japs' faces when we
buzzed 'em?"

Goodwin had cool blue eyes and a manner that spoke
of money. "Can you imagine the look on *your* face when I
give you a downcheck for wasting your time—and mine?"

"No, sir," Joe said quickly.

"All right, then. Why don't you hop on in? We'll run
through the checks."

"Aye aye, sir." Joe scrambled up into the Stearman's
rear seat. It went up and down like a barber chair, to adjust
to trainees of different heights. The man who'd taken the
plane out last must have been big, because Joe had to raise
it three or four inches. He clipped the parachute pack to
the flying harness.

Lieutenant Goodwin, meanwhile, had taken his place in
the front seat. "You squared away there?" he asked.

"Uh, just about, sir." Crosetti reached up and adjusted
the mirror attached to the upper wing. He might have been
fooling with the rearview mirror on a car somebody else
had been driving. When he got it fixed the way he wanted
it, he said, "All ready now."

"Okay. Let's run through the checklist, then," Goodwin
said.

"Right." Joe hoped he hid his lack of enthusiasm.

By the way the instructor snorted, he didn't hide it well
enough. "You do this every time you plop your fanny
down in an airplane, mister—every single time. The one
time you forget, the one thing you forget, will always be
the one you wish you hadn't. A Stearman's a very forgiv-
ing plane—you can do a lot of things that'd send you

home in a box if you tried 'em in a hotter machine. But no airplane ever made will forgive out-and-out stupidity. And even if you don't feel like running through the checks, I do—'cause it's my neck, too."

Ears burning, Joe mumbled, "Yes, sir."

"Okay." Goodwin sounded amused, not angry. "Seems about two cadets out of three are like that. They get the hang of it, though. Let's go through the list."

Through it they went, everything from the attachment of Joe's safety belt to pedals and stick to throttle and magneto with the motor running. Everything checked out the way it was supposed to. "All green, sir," Joe said above the roar of the seven-cylinder radial.

"Looks that way to me, too," Goodwin agreed. "Take her over to Runway Three-West and let the tower know you'll be going into the air."

"Three-West. Aye aye, sir." Slowly and carefully, Joe taxied to the end of the required runway. A plane was meant to fly, not to waddle along on the ground; taxiing was nothing like driving a car, the way he'd thought it would be. He exchanged formalities with the control tower. He also looked down the runway to make sure nobody else was landing on it or taxiing across it. That *was* like automobile traffic: charging out from a stop sign without looking was liable to get you creamed. "Seems all clear, sir," he said to Goodwin. He wasn't far enough along to take off without the instructor's permission.

"So it does. Get us airborne, Mr. Crosetti."

Joe advanced the throttle. The engine's roar got louder and deeper. The Stearman shot down the runway. Actually, the little biplane was one of the most sedate airplanes ever manufactured, but it didn't seem that way to him. Even though he was still on the ground, he kept one eye glued to the airspeed indicator. When it showed he was going fast enough, he pulled back on the stick. The Yellow Peril lurched into the air.

"Smoothly, Mr. Crosetti, smoothly," Goodwin said. "You're not bulldogging a steer."

"Yes, sir." Joe thought he'd made a great takeoff. He was flying, wasn't he?

"It's, like learning to drive a car," Goodwin told him. "After you get enough hours, you won't need to tell your hands and feet what to do. They'll know by themselves, and they'll do everything together. It'll seem like second nature—if you don't kill yourself before then, of course."

That comparison made sense to Joe. It also told him he wasn't as far along as he'd thought. He remembered how ragged he'd been the first few times he got behind the wheel. A few less than perfect turns here—and the instructor's sardonic comments accompanying each one—went a long way towards cutting him down to size.

But he *was* flying! Even if he wasn't such hot stuff yet, he was up in the air and learning what he needed to learn so he could go out and shoot down Japs one of these days. There was the Naval Air Station, and the woods and swamps behind it, and the blue bay in front, and the even bluer Gulf of Mexico out beyond the bay. Birds got a view like this all the time. The Stearman could outperform any bird ever hatched. (Even had it carried machine guns, it would have been helpless against anything this side of a Sopwith Camel, but Joe didn't dwell on that.)

Much sooner than he wanted to, he was coming in for a landing. "Gently," Goodwin urged. "Smoothly. You're juggling eggs. Cadets make ninety percent of their mistakes in the last twenty feet. If you only knew where the hell the ground is, you'd be Charles Lindbergh."

"I don't want to be Charles Lindbergh," Joe snapped. Lindbergh had done everything he could to keep the USA out of the war till the Japs jumped Hawaii. He'd been the Nazis' teacher's pet. And he'd been mighty quiet since December 7.

"Okay, you'd be Jimmy Doolittle," Lieutenant Goodwin said equably.

"That's more like it."

Jimmy Doolittle Joe wasn't, or not yet, anyhow. The Stearman bounced hard when he put it down. His teeth clicked together. The instructor said something Joe hoped didn't go out to the control tower. He brought the recalcitrant beast to a stop and killed the engine.

"Well, sir?" he asked unhappily into the sudden silence that seemed so loud.

But Goodwin had recovered his sangfroid in a hurry. "Well, Mr. Crosetti, you're learning, that's all," he said. "I've seen men at your stage of training do better, but I've seen plenty do worse. You've got plenty of work ahead of you, but you can get where you want to go."

Joe knew where he wanted to go: where Jimmy Doolittle had gone before him. Doolittle had raided. Joe wanted to take Hawaii back all by his lonesome. He wouldn't. He couldn't. He knew that. But it was what he wanted.

COLONEL MITSUO FUJIKAWA had been promoted for bravery after the conquest of Hawaii. But, even though Corporal Takeo Shimizu's regimental commander now wore three stars on his collar tabs instead of two, he looked anything but happy. Like the rest of the men in the regiment, Shimizu stood at stiff attention on the grass of a park doing duty for a parade ground. His face held no expression. He stared straight ahead. He might have been carved from wood.

It wasn't going to help him. He could feel that in his bones. Nothing would help the soldiers, not after what had happened a few days before.

Colonel Fujikawa prowled back and forth. Once upon a time, Shimizu had seen a picture of a *daimyo* hunting a tiger with a spear in Korea three and a half centuries earlier. The great noble wore fancy armor and a tall headgear with a floppy tip. Shimizu remembered that, but what he *really* remembered was the ferocity that blazed from the tiger. He'd never seen anything like it since—not till now.

Even when Fujikawa stopped pacing, he still looked ready to roar and to spring. Instead of roaring, though, he spoke softly, and somehow made that more wounding than the loudest shouts could have been.

"You are in disgrace," he hissed. "Disgrace! Do you hear me? *Do you hear me?*"

"*Hai!* We hear you, Colonel!" The men spoke as if they were part of a perfectly trained chorus. In an abstract way, Shimizu was proud of them—but only in an abstract way, because no matter how perfect they were, that wouldn't do them any good, either.

"Disgrace!" Colonel Fujikawa said once more. "You are disgraced, I am disgraced, the whole Japanese Army in Hawaii is disgraced, and the Japanese Navy in and around Hawaii is disgraced, too. And do you know why?"

Everyone knew why, of course. Shimizu knew why all too well. This time, though, no one said a word. It was as if, if no one admitted what had happened, somehow it wouldn't have happened after all.

But Colonel Fujikawa was intent on plumbing the depths of their iniquity. "The Americans—the *Americans!*—made us lose face. They bombed Oahu. They torpedoed one of our carriers. And most of their bombers escaped. It is an embarrassment. It is a humiliation. It is a disgrace, truly a disgrace."

As one man, the soldiers of the regiment hung their heads in shame. Shimizu lowered his at the same time as everybody else. Even as he did, though, he wondered why this was his fault. What could an infantry noncom do about bombers overhead except jump for cover and hope he didn't get killed? Nothing he could see.

The regimental commander went on, "The captain of the picket boat that spotted the American carriers was fished out of the water after the enemy sank it. He has committed suicide to atone for his failure to see that they had long-range bombers aboard. The commander of the antiaircraft defenses on this island has also committed suicide, to atone for *his* failure to shoot down even a single enemy airplane."

Now real fear ran through the regiment. Honorable *seppuku* was always a way out after failure. Saying good-bye to everything was not only honorable, it was also easier than living on as an object of scorn to everyone around you. But how far would that particular form of atonement reach?

Colonel Fujikawa said, "Common soldiers, form two ranks facing each other. Move, you worthless wretches!"

They moved. Now they knew what was coming. It would be bad, but it could have been worse. After a while, Fujikawa would decide it was over.

"Sergeants and corporals, face one another," Fujikawa added.

Shimizu didn't let the dismay he felt show on his face. He'd been through this mill before, too. Who hadn't? Officers hadn't, that was who. Unlike enlisted men, officers were presumed to be gentlemen. Here, now, they stayed at their stiff brace.

When Shimizu turned to face Corporal Kiyoshi Aiso, who led another squad in his platoon, Aiso's face was as expressionless as his. The other noncom was a long-service soldier; he had to be close to forty. But his weathered skin and the broad shoulders that bulged under his tunic said he'd grown strong with the years, not soft.

Now, at last, Fujikawa shouted: "Each man, slap the face of the man in front of you! Take turns!"

Corporal Aiso was senior, which meant he got to go first. Shimizu braced himself. Aiso let him have it, right across the cheek. In spite of being braced, Shimizu staggered. His head rang. He shook it, trying to clear his wits. Aiso hadn't held back, not even a little bit.

Then the other corporal stood at attention and waited. Shimizu slapped him hard. Aiso's head flew to one side. He shook his head, too. Shimizu came to attention in turn. "The same cheek or the other one?" Aiso asked politely.

"Whichever you please. It doesn't matter one way or the other," Shimizu answered.

Aiso hit him lefthanded, which meant his head snapped to the right this time. The older soldier was just as strong with his off hand as with his good one. Shimizu asked whether he had a preference. Aiso just shrugged. Shimizu, a thoroughly right-handed man, struck his left cheek again.

Usually, the noncoms would have kept the common soldiers at it, making sure they didn't slow down and making sure they didn't pull their blows. The noncoms were also caught in the web of humiliation today. The regimental officers stalked through the ranks. "Harder!" they shouted. "Keep at it! Who told you you could slack off? What kind of soldier do you think you are?"

Unless Shimizu concentrated, he saw two of Corporal Aiso. He hoped he was just as blurry to the older man. His whole face felt on fire. He tasted blood in his mouth, and he wasn't sure whether that was blood or snot dribbling from his nose. Probably both. Aiso wasn't trying to box his ears, any more than he was trying to box those of the other corporal. That didn't mean they didn't get walloped now and again. Even Shimizu's palm started to sting from giving too many blows.

He couldn't have told how long it went on. Privates started falling over. Cursing officers kicked them. Nobody was trying to get away with faking, not this time. Only when a polished boot in the belly or the spine failed to prod them to their feet were they suffered to stay on the ground.

At last, contemptuously, Colonel Fujikawa yelled, "Enough!"

Corporal Aiso had his arm drawn back for another blow. Shimizu hardly cared whether it landed or not. After so many, what difference did one more make? But Aiso stayed his hand. Shimizu swayed. Stubbornly, he kept on his feet. He didn't care to crumple where his squad could see him do it. Since most of them were still upright, he would have lost face by falling.

He felt as if he'd lost his face anyway. At the same time, he wished he *could* lose it. Then he wouldn't have to feel it any more.

"Go clean yourselves up," Colonel Fujikawa commanded. "You are disgusting. The way you look is a disgrace to the Japanese Army, too."

And whose fault is that? Shimizu wondered blearily. But he would never have said such a thing, not even if the Yankees were disemboweling him with a dull, rusty bayonet. Discipline ran deep. After bowing to Corporal Aiso—who returned the courtesy—Shimizu gave his attention, or as much of it as he had to give, back to his squad.

All of them were on their feet now. He didn't know who had fallen and then got up again. He didn't intend to ask, either. That would make whoever might have gone down lose face. The whole regiment had lost face. The whole Hawaii garrison had lost face. What point to singling out one or two common soldiers after that?

Heads up, backs straight, they marched off to the barracks. Once there, they lined up at the sinks to wash their bloody faces, rinse out their bloody mouths, and soak their tunics in cold water to get the bloodstains out of them.

"I thought my head was going to fall off." Shiro Wakuzawa spoke with more pride than anything else.

"We all did," Shimizu said. The men he led nodded, one by one. His rank usually exempted him from such spasms of brutality. Not this time, though. He was as bruised and battered as any of them. No one could say he hadn't been through it. No one could say he hadn't come through it, either. For now, he was one of them.

Senior Private Furusawa said, "If the Americans come again, we'll be ready for them."

"Of course we will. Who'd want to go through this more than once?" Even after the abuse Wakuzawa had taken, he could still joke.

"How could the Americans come again?" somebody else said. Shimizu was splashing his face with cold water—which hurt and felt good at the same time—and couldn't tell who it was. The soldier went on, "They can't try another raid like that. Furusawa's right. We'd smash them flat."

Shimizu pulled away from the faucet blowing like a whale. He shook his head, which made drops of water fly everywhere—and which also reminded him how sore he was. "If the Americans come again, they won't just raid," he said. "They'll run in a pack like wild dogs, and they'll try to take Hawaii away from us."

Some of the soldiers in his squad nodded again. Others, men who hurt too much for that, softly said, "*Hai*."

WRITING THE REPORT on how the Americans had caught the Japanese garrison on Oahu flat-footed fell to commander Mitsuo Fuchida. He felt more as if the duty had fallen *on* him. Before sitting down in front of a blank sheet of paper, he went to pick Minoru Genda's brain. Genda was one of the few men on the island with whom he could speak frankly.

"It's not very complicated," Genda said. "They did something we didn't expect, that's all. You can't get ready for what you don't anticipate."

"Easy enough to say," Fuchida answered. "What do I do for the other forty-nine and three-quarters pages of the report, though?"

As it usually did, Genda's smile made him look very young. "You can tell General Yamashita and Captain Hasegawa that we won't get fooled again."

Fuchida bowed in his seat, there in Genda's office. "*Domo arigato*," he said, spicing the thanks with all the sarcasm he could. "We'd better not. If we do, we'll all have to open our bellies." He wasn't joking, or not very much. The garrison had put itself through a painful orgy of self-reproach. If it was humiliated again . . . much more blood would flow than had this time.

"They *are* going to come sniffing around these islands. They haven't given up, the way we hoped they would," Genda said. "Carrier raids, submarines, maybe even flying boats, too."

"We need better ways to detect them," Fuchida said.

"The picket boats did their job, *neh?*" Genda said. "The skipper of that one was too hard on himself, I think. Why blame him for not looking out for B-25s when nobody else did, either?"

"Picket boats can only do so much," Fuchida insisted. "Things can sneak past them, or their skippers can make mistakes. Yes, I know we all made the mistake, but we should have *known* what the Yankees were up to before they got here."

"How?" Genda asked reasonably.

"I don't know," Fuchida said. "Or maybe I do. Have the engineers ever figured out what that installation up at Opana was supposed to do before the Americans wrecked it?"

"Whatever it was supposed to do, it didn't do it," Genda

pointed out. "We caught them napping. They had no idea we were there till the bombs started falling. You were the one who signaled *Tora! Tora! Tora!* to show we'd taken them by surprise."

"No, it was Mizuki, my radioman," Fuchida said.

"And here I thought you were a Navy man, not a damn lawyer," Genda said.

"I *am* a Navy man," Fuchida said. "As a Navy man, I want to know about that installation."

"I don't have a whole lot to tell you. I don't think the engineers have a whole lot to tell you, either," Genda said.

Commander Fuchida started to get angry. "They damn well ought to by now, Genda-*san*. They've had months to unravel it. Have they found documents talking about what it does?"

Genda only shrugged. "I don't think so."

"They should have!" Fuchida exclaimed. "If they haven't, the Americans must have destroyed them. And why would the Americans destroy them? Because they must show the Opana installation was important. What other possible reason could they have?"

"You'd better be careful," Genda said. "Next thing you know, you'll hear little men who aren't there talking behind your back."

"So you think I'm crazy, do you?" Fuchida growled. "I'll tell you what I want to hear. I want to hear the Americans who worked at that thing, whatever it was. They'll know, and we can squeeze it out of them. Some of them—a lot of them, probably—will just be enlisted men. They won't much care what they blab."

"Go ahead, then. Find them. Interrogate them. You're not going to be happy till you do," Genda said. "Get it out of your system. You'll feel better then." He might have been recommending a laxative.

"I will," Fuchida said. "And you'll see—something important *will* come from this."

With another shrug, Genda said, "It could be. I'm not convinced, but it could be. I hope you're right."

"I intend to find out," Mitsuo Fuchida said.

* * *

JIM PETERSON WAS IN A FUNK. So were a lot of the POWs up at Opana. They'd got less of a look at the American bombers that had raided Oahu than just about anybody else on the island. Peterson knew why. Opana was nowhere. It wasn't even worth flying over.

Nothing he could do about it. Nothing anybody could do about it. All the prisoners could do was sit behind barbed wire, look out at the green countryside all around them and the blue Pacific to the north, and slowly starve to death.

He almost wished the Japs would stop feeding them altogether. Then it would be over. The way things were, he felt himself losing ground a quarter of an inch at a time. Everything he did, everything he thought about, centered on the miserable breakfast and lousy supper he'd got.

"You know," he said to Prez McKinley one afternoon a few days after the raid, "I don't hardly think about women at all any more."

The sergeant let out a grunt. Peterson thought it was surprise. "Me, neither," McKinley said. "I like pussy as well as the next guy—bet your ass I do. But I don't think I could get it up with a crane right now."

"Same here," Peterson said. "Pussy's the best thing in the world when your belly's full. When it's not . . . you forget about women." He fooled with his belt. Day by day, his waistline shrank. He closed the belt several holes tighter than he had when he got here. Pretty soon, even the last hole would be too loose, and he'd have to trade the belt for whatever he could get and use rope to hold up his pants. *And after a while, I'll have enough rope to hang myself with, too*, he thought. Surprisingly few men here had killed themselves. Maybe they wouldn't give the Japs the satisfaction.

McKinley looked northeast, the direction from which the B-25s had come, the direction in which the mainland lay. "I wonder if they're really gonna try and take Hawaii away from the Japs again."

"Don't wonder if. Wonder when," Peterson said. "They

haven't forgotten about us. That's one thing those bombers showed."

"Wonder if they can do it, too," McKinley said.

It was Peterson's turn to grunt. The Japs shouldn't have surprised the defenders here. They had, but they shouldn't have. He couldn't imagine an American armada catching the new occupiers asleep at the switch. How much damage could the Japs do before a landing party hit the beach? Even if Americans did land, the Japanese would fight like rabid weasels to hold on to what they'd taken.

At lineup the next morning, the Japanese didn't release the POWs to breakfast once they had the count straight, the way they usually did. Standing there at attention in his row, Peterson eyed the guards with suspicion. What the devil were they up to now?

A nervous-looking Oriental in Western clothes—plainly a Jap from Hawaii—came into the camp along with more guards and the commandant. The Japanese officer spoke in his own language. The local turned it into English: "The following prisoners will make themselves known immediately. . . ." The commandant handed him a piece of paper. He read off half a dozen names.

Looking confused, a lieutenant and several privates stepped out of ranks. Peterson wondered what the hell they'd done, and whether the Japs were about to make a horrible example of them. He'd already seen enough examples to last him the rest of his life, and several lifetimes yet to come.

But, to his surprise and relief, nothing dreadful happened. Guards came up to the men and hustled them away, but that was all. They didn't beat them or kick them or anything of the sort. They weren't gentle, but Peterson had a hard time imagining gentle Japs. They were businesslike, which in itself was out of the ordinary.

After the handful of prisoners were taken away, things went back to normal. The rest of the swarm of POWs queued up for breakfast. They had something new to buzz about. Somebody not far from Peterson said, "Those guys hadn't even hardly left home before."

"What's that supposed to mean?" somebody else asked.

"They were stationed at some kind of installation right around here, and this is where they ended up, too," the first man said. "Small world, ain't it?"

"Well, I'll be a son of a bitch," Peterson said as a light went on inside his head.

"What's up?" Sergeant McKinley asked. What he'd heard didn't mean thing one to him.

In a low voice, Peterson said, "Ever hear of radar, Prez?"

"I dunno. Maybe." McKinley screwed up his face in concentration. "Some kind of fancy range-finding gear, right?"

"Yeah." That was as much as McKinley, a born ground-pounder, needed to know. As somebody who'd got paid from flying off a carrier deck, Jim Peterson knew a good deal more. Among the things he knew was . . . "They had a radar station up here at Opana."

"Yeah?" McKinley thought about that for a little while. "You think the Japs are gonna squeeze those guys about it?"

"Wouldn't be surprised," said Peterson, who would have bet the mortgage on it. "They don't know much about that stuff." As far as he'd heard, the Japanese hadn't known anything about radar. It looked as if they'd figured out there was stuff they didn't know.

"Well, shit," McKinley said. "I thought those suckers were lucky on account of the guards didn't work 'em over right then and there. Shows what I know. They're gonna get the third degree from professionals, aren't they?"

"Can't tell you for sure," Peterson said grimly, "but that's how it looks to me, too." He looked around. "You probably don't want to talk about it a whole hell of a lot. You don't want to say that name, either. Otherwise, the Japs may decide to find out how much *you* know about it."

"Well, shit," McKinley said again, in a different tone of voice. He looked around, as if expecting a guard to be listening over his shoulder. Peterson would have worried even more about other POWs. Knowing who could be trusted wasn't always easy. McKinley nodded, at least half to himself. "Gotcha."

"Attaboy, Prez."

The chow line crawled forward. As usual, there wasn't enough to eat and it was lousy. Also as usual, everybody emptied—indeed, polished—his mess kit. The only thing worse than not enough food was no food at all. Camp rations came altogether too close to that, but they weren't quite there.

Fighters on patrol buzzed overhead. The Japs were bound to be taking that much more seriously since the American raid. Peterson glanced up at the warplanes, then all at once eyed them seriously. "Goddamn!" he exclaimed.

"Now what?" Prez McKinley asked.

Peterson pointed to the fighters. "Those aren't Zeros." He spoke with complete authority. He'd earned the right, by God, not just through study but because a Zero had knocked his Wildcat out of the sky. "They've got to be planes from the Japanese Army instead."

"Yeah? And so?" Prez didn't see the point. He was shrewd, no doubt about that, but he really did have a non-com's narrow view of the world. He was also an infantryman. What happened in the air and on the water didn't mean so much to him.

Peterson spelled things out: "No way in hell those could've flown here all by themselves. Stinking slanty-eyed bastards had to ship 'em in. This place is like a great big old aircraft carrier right out in the middle of the Pacific, and the Japs are sure as hell making the most of it."

"They'll ship in planes. They'll ship in gas and ammo for 'em. They'll ship in enough chow for their own guys." McKinley pointed to one of the guards. Sure enough, the man hadn't missed any meals. "What does everybody else get? Hind tit, that's what."

"Yeah." Peterson wondered how much more weight he could drop and still keep going. He didn't know, but he had little doubt he'd find out.

BY NOW, OSCAR VAN DER KIRK got more envious comments than astonished ones when he assembled his sailboard on Waikiki Beach. He wasn't the only one who'd made the conversion any more; several others, Charlie Kaapu among them, had imitated him. He didn't mind. There seemed to be enough fish to go around. Some of the others were using the boards more for sport than for fishing. He'd seen people do some pretty spectacular things. The more he watched them, the more he felt like doing spectacular things himself. He'd already tried one the first day he came in, but they were outdoing him now.

Beside Oscar, Charlie planted his newly converted sailboard's mast in its socket. "You were one sly *haole* to come up with this scheme," Charlie said admiringly. "I didn't think it would work when you started talking about it, but I was wrong."

Oscar shrugged. "What's being a *haole* got to do with it? Hawaiians were the ones who started this whole surf-riding business in the first place."

"That was a long time ago," Charlie said, which seemed to make sense to him even if it didn't make a whole lot to Oscar. He added, "We were okay as long as we were just in the game against us, you know what I mean? But then *haoles* came along, and you knew how to do all this stuff we couldn't, and so we pretty much stopped trying to figure out new stuff on our own."

Was that why Hawaiians and *hapa*-Hawaiians were the way they were? Oscar had no idea. A lot of them just seemed to drift without trying to make much of their lives, though.

Since Oscar had spent most of the time since coming to Hawaii drifting through life, he couldn't very well blame them. He made sure his mast was firmly seated, then said, "Let's go on out."

Fishermen stepped aside to let them go into the surf. Oscar wondered if there was any beach on Oahu that didn't have its complement of fishermen these days. Unless he missed his guess, there wasn't. Fishing wasn't just a sport any more. It was a vital part of feeding the island, just like the gardens that had sprung up everywhere. If you didn't have access to fish or to garden vegetables, what did you get? Rice, and not very much of it.

Into the water he slid. As usual, the Pacific was not too hot, not too cold. "Just right," he murmured. Not for the first time, he thought of Goldilocks and the three bears.

He and Charlie paddled out to sea, guiding their surf-boards over the waves till they could stand up and unfurl their sails instead. "This is really something, you smart son of a bitch," Charlie called. "You could make sailboards for everybody in the world, make yourself a million dollars."

He might even have been right—had Oscar had the idea at another time. As things were . . . "There's this little thing called the war."

"Oh, yeah. I remember that." By the way Charlie said it, he hadn't remembered till Oscar reminded him. Oscar laughed, wishing that could be true. He would never be able to forget those horrible moments off Waimea, stuck in the crossfire between the Japanese invasion force and the American defenders on the shore. He'd never forget piss-ing himself in terror, either.

Not even Charlie Kaapu knew about that. A sudden thought occurred to Oscar. He glanced over at his friend. Could Charlie have done the same thing? Maybe wonder-ing about it was just misery loving company—but if Char-lie hadn't been scared to death out there, too, he wasn't human.

I'll never know for sure, Oscar thought. *I can't ask him. And if he did, he can't ask me, either. Just one of those things.*

Charlie took to sailboarding as if it were his idea and not Oscar's. That was no great surprise; any surf-rider could adapt to the addition of the sail pretty fast. But Char-lie also seemed to enjoy skimming along over the waves under wind power as if he'd thought of it. Of course, Char-lie enjoyed everything he did. If he didn't enjoy it, he didn't do it.

"You ever see that blond wahine any more after she move out?" he asked.

"Susie? Nope, not lately." Oscar shook his head and shrugged. "She was fun in bed, but she was kind of rugged any other way."

"Yeah, well, dames are like that sometimes." Charlie took everything in stride. "Enjoy 'em while you can, then kiss 'em good-bye." He'd kissed a lot of women good-bye. So had Oscar, but Charlie never let it bother him. "No *huhu*," he said now. It might have been his motto.

Oscar looked back over his shoulder. Oahu receded behind him—much faster than it would have before he'd had his surfboard altered. "We ought to split up," he said. "It's not that I don't love you" —Charlie boomed laughter and blew him a kiss— "but we both ought to bring in as many fish as we can."

"Oh, yeah." Charlie didn't argue about that. Hunger was something even he took seriously. "See you later, alligator." He slanted off towards the west, as slick as Vaseline on the sailboard.

Am I that good? Oscar wondered. He shrugged again. He probably wasn't quite that stylish, but he got the job done even so. He swung a little towards the east, to put as much room between himself and Charlie Kaapu as he could.

He had a pretty good day fishing—not a great day, but a pretty good one. He got plenty of fish for himself, some for Eizo Doi, and some to sell. The Japs hadn't got around to regulating sailboarders the way they did with the men who fished from sampans. He could take what he didn't give to the handyman and sell it in one of the unofficial markets. A little cash was always nice. Food that wasn't fish or rigidly rationed rice was even nicer.

Doi bowed to him when he brought fish to the handyman's cramped little shop. "You good fella, you keep make pay," the Japanese man said in what was intended for English.

"Sure I do," Oscar said. "I always pay my bills." That was pretty much true, too. Sometimes he took a little longer than he might have—he'd had plenty of spells of living hand-to-mouth even before the war—but he never forgot. When he had money (or, here, fish), he got out of hock.

"Good, good," Doi told him. "Some fella, even some Japanese fella—not all Japanese fella, but some Japanese fella—get sails, forget make pay." His face twisted as if he were smelling his fish a week from now.

After leaving Doi's, Oscar headed for one of the open-air outfits that had been replacing grocery stores and supermarkets since the war started. Most of them were in the Oriental part of town west of Nuuanu Avenue. *Haoles* came here to buy and sometimes, like Oscar, to sell, but few markets sprang up in their neighborhoods. It was as if they were saying such things were good enough for Japs and Chinamen, but not for them. Or maybe the Asians just took to huckstering more naturally than whites did.

Fish always went fast. Oscar got some cash and some fruit. Dietitians would probably tell him he wasn't eating a balanced diet, but he didn't care. He would have murdered for a big greasy hamburger and french fries, but nobody except a few millionaires could get beef any more.

Greenbacks in his pocket, fruit in a cloth bag, he started back towards Waikiki. No buses ran; they had no fuel. Some enterprising Orientals propelled pedicabs and pulled rickshaws, but Oscar couldn't stomach riding in something like that. Using a man like a draft horse—even paying a man to use himself as a draft horse—stuck in his craw. It didn't stop a lot of prosperous *haoles*. It didn't stop a lot of Japanese officers, either. Of course, from what Oscar had seen, the SPCA would have landed on them like an avalanche if they'd treated draft animals the way they treated their own troops. And that said nothing about what happened to the American POWs.

"Oscar! Hey, Oscar!" Across the street, Susie Higgins waved to him. She was wearing an electric-blue silk sundress she sure hadn't had when she was living in his apartment.

"Speak of the devil," he said, and then, louder, "Hi, Susie." He didn't know what to do or say after that. Most of the time, he didn't need to worry about running into ex-girlfriends after a fling had had its day. They got on an ocean liner or a Pan Am Clipper flying boat, and that was that. Susie would have done the same thing but for the small detail of the Japanese invasion. He trotted over to the other side of the street. Dodging a horse-drawn wagon full of greens was a hell of a lot easier than jaywalking when a truck would just as soon knock you flat as let you cross. "How are you?" he asked, adding, "You look good."

She'd always looked good. She looked better now. She'd acquired a proper Hawaiian suntan, which the bright blue silk only played up. She cocked her head to one side and gave him a saucy smile. "So do you—good enough to eat, in fact."

"Promises, promises," he said. Susie laughed out loud. Oscar knew he had to play it light. If he didn't, he might want to haul off and belt her, and people would talk. "How are you doing these days?" he asked, and then, "*What* are you doing these days?"

"I'm taking dictation—and the accent isn't on the first syllable, either, you nasty man." She wrinkled her nose and winked at him. "Happens I'm an A-number-one secretary. Even if all my references are back on the mainland, I showed Mr. Underhill what I could do."

"I'll bet you did," Oscar said, again lightly. She made as if to hit him. He made as if to duck. They both laughed this time. Oscar wouldn't have been surprised if she was a first-class secretary. She'd be good at anything she set her mind to. She sure as hell screwed as if they were going to outlaw it day after tomorrow.

"What are you up to?" she asked.

"Some surfboarding lessons. Some sailboarding lessons. You know about sailboards?" He waited till she nodded, then struck a pose and went on with what he hoped was pardonable pride: "I invented 'em. And I do some fishing, and I trade the fish for other stuff."

"*You* thought of sailboards?" Susie said. Now Oscar nodded. She grinned at him. "That's swell. I've seen some guys using them. Maybe I've even seen you out there on the water—who knows?"

"Like you'd care." Oscar did his best to sound as if he was still teasing. It wasn't so easy now.

"I might," Susie said. "How do you know unless you try to find out?"

"And get slapped down for my trouble? Fat chance."

"Hey, we had fun." Susie might have been challenging him to deny it, and he couldn't. She continued, "Maybe we could have some more."

"We'd just start fighting again." Now Oscar dared her to tell him he was wrong.

"Maybe we wouldn't," she said—if that meant she thought he was wrong, it didn't mean she thought he was very wrong.

He'd thought he would gloat, but he didn't. All he said was, "What's wrong with the fellow you're taking dictation from?"

Even as he said it, he wondered if it would make her mad. It didn't. She answered matter-of-factly: "Underhill? He's got a Chinese wife he's crazy about and three little kids. It happens." Her shrug held all sorts of knowledge.

They had had fun—in bed. Anything else? As he'd said to Charlie, anything else had been trouble. So did the one make up for the other? Maybe it did. She hadn't stolen from him, anyway, and she'd had plenty of chances. He thought it over. "Heck, come along if you want to," he said, knowing he'd probably regret it but not right away.

"You still have that apartment in Waikiki?" Susie asked. When he nodded, she said, "Why don't you come to my place instead? It's a lot closer."

"Okay." Oscar was nothing if not agreeable.

He was so agreeable, Susie made another face at him. "Listen, buster," she said, "do you know how many guys would give their left one for an invite like that? Do you?" She sounded half joking, half belligerent.

"Probably a bunch," Oscar answered. "If they start beating down the door, can I go out the window?"

"You're a terrible man." Susie Higgins scowled. "Come on, before I change my mind like you deserve."

Her apartment was roomier than his, and likely more expensive, too. He wondered in what coin she was paying for it, but then shook his head. Whatever she was, she wasn't a pro. And she was getting by, where plenty of people who'd been here a lot longer were having all sorts of trouble.

As soon as she closed the door behind her, she pulled the sundress off over her head. "We had fun, didn't we?" she repeated.

Oscar caught her to him. "Sure," he said . . . agreeably.

CAPTAIN KIICHI HASEGAWA GLOWERED at Commander Minoru Genda. "The Army is being very difficult," complained the senior naval officer in Hawaii.

"Yes, sir," Genda said—usually a safe answer when a superior was fuming.

"Here in my own quarters on *Akagi*, I can tell you what I really think of those people," Hasegawa said. "You won't run off at the mouth."

"No, sir," Genda said. That was also safe when it turned out to be agreement.

Hasegawa reached into a desk drawer and pulled out a bottle of whiskey. He rummaged a little more and came up with two glasses. He poured a knock for himself and another for Genda, sliding the second across the desk. "*Kampai!*" he said.

Genda echoed the toast. The whiskey glided smoothly down his throat and started a small fire in his belly. "What can you do, sir?" he asked.

"I can't do a damned thing," Hasegawa answered. "General Yamashita outranks me. He's stubborn as an ox, and not much smarter."

"Sir"—now Genda spoke with considerable urgency— "the Army and the Navy have to get along here. We need both services to defend the island, and each needs to know what it must do and what the other will do."

"Yes, yes." Hasegawa said it, but he didn't mean it.

Sensing as much, Genda spoke more urgently still: "The Americans divided responsibility here, too. They didn't do a very good job of it. That's one reason these islands are ours now. Do you want to imitate them?"

With that, he did get Captain Hasegawa's attention. Hasegawa took a meditative sip from his drink and then said, "At least the Americans had the sense to make a Navy man the senior officer in the islands."

So that's what's eating you, Genda thought. Aloud, he said, "Nobody here can do anything about that, sir. The only people who can change the command setup are in Tokyo."

"Don't I know it!" Hasegawa said bitterly. "They don't want to listen to me. They especially don't want to listen to me after the Yankee bombers raided us. All they want to do is bring in more soldiers and more Army airplanes. As if we didn't have to drag the Army to Hawaii kicking and screaming!" He gulped down the whiskey and poured himself another healthy dose.

Trying to put the best face he could on it, Genda said, "Now the Army understands how important it was to seize these islands."

"Maybe," Hasegawa said. "Then again, maybe not, too. The Army just has to say, 'Take this and that from Japan to Honolulu.' The Army just has to say it. The Navy has to do it. And once the men and the airplanes get here, does the Army worry about the food and fuel we have to haul in to keep everything the way it's supposed to be? Not likely! The Army seemed to think we can bring in everything easy as you please."

"I've been keeping track of the food situation, sir," Genda said. "It's not quite as bad as it was right after the surrender."

"Yes, I know that," Hasegawa agreed. "Things can hardly help growing here. That will take care of itself once we clear the land that was planted with sugarcane and pineapple and turn it over to rice and other real crops, crops people can eat. But you can't plant gasoline bushes, dammit."

Genda had been keeping track of that, too. Genda kept track of everything he could; it was part of his nature. When he said, "We have . . . enough," he put things in the best light he could.

"We have enough to go from one routine day to the next, yes," Hasegawa said. "Do we have enough if we really have to fight? I don't have much good to say about the Yankees. We licked them just the way we should have. But they will never lose because they run short of *things*. Can we say the same?"

Genda wished Japan could. He knew she couldn't. That was what this war was about: getting the Japanese Empire the oil and the rubber and the tin—the *things*—it needed to stay a great power. He said, "Once we win, we will be able to say that. It will be true then."

"Then, yes. Now?" Hasegawa rolled his eyes. "The Prime Minister can afford to worry about then. I have to worry about now. I know I am only an ignorant sea captain, but the way it looks to me is, if now isn't the way we want it, then won't be, either."

It looked the same way to Genda. He said so, adding, "If we didn't have to keep bringing in more soldiers and more Army airplanes, we could bring in more supplies for what's already here instead. That would serve us better in the long run."

"We should be able to do both, *neh?*" Hasegawa said.

"Yes, we should." Genda let it go at that. He knew—as Hasegawa undoubtedly did, too—the Japanese didn't have enough shipping capacity to let them bring in reinforcements and fully supply them, too. "If we could make sure American submarines didn't trouble us . . ."

Hasegawa looked as unhappy as Genda felt. The first time a U.S. sub sank a Japanese freighter, it had been news, a chance to complain about America's inhumanity. It had happened several times since then, and Japan hadn't said a word. Acknowledging each sinking would have been the same as admitting the shoe was starting to pinch. American bombers from the mainland couldn't bother Hawaii. American submarines setting out from the West Coast had no trouble at all.

"The Army has complained that we don't stop all submarines before they make trouble for us," Hasegawa said.

"Let the Army try it! Good luck to them!" Genda burst out. "We do what we can. We use convoys. We zigzag. We escort with destroyers. We use all the tricks we learned in the Mediterranean and the Indian Ocean in the last war."

"Yes, I know," Hasegawa said unhappily. "They aren't always enough."

"That's because we're finding out what kind of tricks the Americans learned then—and since," Genda added.

Captain Hasegawa sent him a sour stare. "Commander, this operation is more your brainchild than anyone else's— and that includes Admiral Yamamoto. We did everything we had to do to take these islands. Frankly, we did more than I thought we could do. Why can't you be contented now?"

"Two reasons, sir," Genda answered. "The first is, I hoped losing Hawaii would knock all the spirit out of the Americans and knock them clean out of the war before it really got started. We can see that hasn't happened. They're still fighting. They haven't figured out what they want to do and how they want to do it yet, and we have to hope they will take a long time before they do. That leads me to the second worry. Taking these islands was one sort of problem. Holding them is a very different one."

"Oh, yes," Hasegawa said in a voice like iron. "*Oh*, yes. Holding Hawaii is the reason we have to put up with these Army bumpkins."

Genda managed a thin smile. "They would say, *Taking Hawaii is the reason we have to put up with these Navy snobs.*"

"I don't give a shit what the Army says." Hasegawa sounded more like a bumpkin than a snob. "I want to be replaced. I've already told Tokyo as much. They need to send a Navy man out here who has the rank to deal with Yamashita. Until they do that, I have no faith that these islands can be held, because the Army will make a hash of it."

Genda couldn't say what he was thinking, not to a superior officer. He would have spoken his mind with Mitsuo Fuchida, and was pretty sure Fuchida would have done the same with him. But not with Captain Hasegawa, especially since Genda thought the senior Navy man in Hawaii had made a frightful mistake. Genda was sure Hasegawa would be relieved of his post here. He'd just done his best to make himself impossible. But Genda didn't think the Navy would send out an admiral to counterbalance the Army commandant. That would have to go through the Cabinet, and Hideki Tojo, the Prime Minister, was a general himself.

When Genda didn't say anything, Hasegawa had to know what was in his mind. The *Akagi*'s skipper didn't push him on it. He just said, "That will be all, Commander."

"Yes, sir." Genda rose, saluted, and left the captain's cabin. Like any ship's compartment, the cabin had a heavy steel waterproof door. Genda closed it as gently as he could. It thudded into place even so. The sound of metal meeting metal seemed much more final than he would have wanted.

WHENEVER MAJOR HIRABAYASHI SUMMONED the people of Wahiawa at an unusual time, Jane Armitage started worrying. After watching Mr. Murphy get it in the neck—literally—she feared the Jap in charge of this part of the island would offer up another object lesson. One of those had been a thousand too many.

Yosh Nakayama stood up on a table to translate for Hirabayashi. The gardener's face was impassive as he turned the major's excited Japanese into far more stolid-seeming English. "The Japanese Empire announces that the island of Corregidor has surrendered to imperial forces under General Homma. The Empire also announces the fall of Port Moresby in New Guinea." He had to go back and forth with Hirabayashi several times before he got that one straight.

Jane knew where New Guinea was, but couldn't have said where on the island Port Moresby lay to save herself from Hirabayashi's sword. She knew New Guinea wasn't far from Australia. If the Japs were taking towns there, were they looking to go after the Land Down Under next?

Could anybody stop them? Up until the day she threw Fletch out, he'd insisted that the USA could kick Japan around the block. She'd thought he knew what he was talking about. On the evidence so far, he'd been as misguided a soldier as he had been a husband.

"*Banzai!* for the Japanese Empire!" Nakayama said.

"*Banzai!*" the people of Wahiawa said. Jane hated herself

for joining the cheer. You couldn't get out of it, though. Bad things happened to people who tried. It wasn't even safe to mouth the word without saying it out loud. Somebody would be watching you. Somebody would be listening to you. You couldn't show your thoughts anywhere, not if they weren't the sort of thoughts the Japs wanted you to have.

She looked around the crowd. More than a few people in Wahiawa had cheered when the American bombers flew over the town on their way to plaster the Japanese planes at Wheeler Field. There were missing faces these days. What had happened to the men and women who'd disappeared? The people who knew weren't talking. Not knowing only made their fate more frightening to everyone else.

And who had betrayed them? Obviously, you were a fool to trust any of the local Japanese. That didn't mean none of them was trustworthy. Some of the younger ones really were patriotic Americans. But others pretended, and were good at pretending. Finding out who belonged to which group could cost you your neck. Much less dangerous to think of all of them as menaces.

Much as Jane wished it did, that didn't mean all whites were reliable. Some of them didn't even bother to hide their collaboration. They, at least, were honestly disgusting. The snakes hiding in the grass were the ones that killed when they bit, though.

As for Chinese and Filipinos, they barely entered into Jane's calculations. She'd had little to do with them before the war started, and she still had little to do with them. To her, they were more nearly part of the landscape than people in their own right.

Major Hirabayashi spoke in Japanese once more. "You can go now," Yosh Nakayama said laconically. The local commandant had probably said something like, *You are dismissed*. That was how people who ran things talked. The only thing Nakayama had ever run was his nursery. He didn't talk fancy.

Jane despised him less than she had when he first became Hirabayashi's right-hand man. He did what he could for Wahiawa. He passed on the Jap's orders without glorying in them and without seeming to imagine they came from him. She would have thought more of him if he'd chosen to have nothing to do with the major, but he could have been worse.

She wanted to go back to her apartment, put her feet up, and do nothing for a while. What she wanted to do and what she had to do were two different things. It was back to the potato plot to weed and to pick bugs off the plants and to smash them once she had picked them off.

Every time she looked at her hands, she wanted to cry. Those calluses, those short, ragged, black-rimmed nails . . . Things would have been even worse if everybody else's hands weren't about the same. As Jane worked, she watched tendons jut and muscles surge under her skin. She'd lost weight; she didn't think she had an ounce of fat anywhere on her body. But she was stronger than she'd ever been in her life.

Of course, she was also working harder than she ever had in her life. Teaching third grade was nothing next to keeping a garden plot going. Somewhere not far down her family tree were farmers. That was true of almost everyone. Now she understood why they'd gone to town and found other lines of work. What she didn't understand was why anybody who didn't have to grow crops did. You had to be starving or nuts to break your back like this every day . . . didn't you?

On her way to the plot, two Japanese soldiers came up the sidewalk towards her. She stepped aside and bowed as they tramped past. They walked by as if she didn't exist. That was better than when they leered. When they leered, she had all she could do not to run away. There hadn't been a lot of rapes in Wahiawa, but there had been some. One of the women had had the courage to protest to Major Hirabayashi afterwards. It hadn't done her any good. Nobody was going to punish the Japs for anything they did to locals.

Once Jane was weeding with her head down, she felt a little safer. Not only was she less visible, but other locals

were around her. They would squawk if Japanese soldiers
tried to drag her away. How much those squawks would
help . . . She tried not to think about that.

In fact, she tried not to think about anything. If she
didn't think, she could get through a minute at a time, an
hour at a time, a day at a time. Whatever happened, it
would simply be . . . gone. And with most of what happened these days, it was better that way.

AS USUAL, JIRO TAKAHASHI WAS BY HIMSELF when he took
fish up to the Japanese consulate. He wished Hiroshi or
Kenzo would come with him, but he didn't try to talk them
into it. He'd given up on trying to talk them into anything
that had anything to do with politics or with the war. Their
ideas were as fixed as his. (That wasn't precisely how he
looked at it, of course. To him, they were a pair of stubborn
young fools.)

He bowed to the guards outside the building. They returned the courtesy. "It's the fisherman!" one of them said.
"What have you got today, Fisherman? Anything especially good?" He licked his lips.

Laughing, Jiro shook his head. "Just some *ahi*. It was a
pretty slow run, out there on the ocean."

"*Ahi* is good," the guard said. "Not that we ever get more
than a mouthful—and not even that very often. Eh, boys?"
The other Japanese soldiers mournfully nodded agreement.

"Ah, too bad." Jiro sounded sympathetic, but he wasn't
much surprised. No doubt Consul Kita and Chancellor
Morimura kept what they wanted from the presents he
brought. Only when they were satisfied would any go to
the people who made them safer and more comfortable.
That wasn't very nice, but it was the way the world worked.
It always had been, and it probably always would be.

"Well, it's not your fault," the guard said, and bowed
again. "Go on in." He stepped aside. One of the other soldiers opened the door for Takahashi.

Inside the consulate, a secretary smiled to see him.
"Good day, Takahashi-*san*," the man said. "Would you like
to say hello to the consul?"

"Yes, please, if he's not too busy," Jiro answered. "If he is, I can leave the fish with the chancellor." He wouldn't entrust them to an underling like this fellow. With food in Hawaii so tight these days, that was asking to have some of his gift disappear before the people for whom it was intended ever saw it.

"Well, he's talking with a reporter from the *Nippon jiji*," the secretary answered. "Let me ask him what he wants to do. Please excuse me for a moment." He got up and went into a back room. When he returned, he was smiling. "Kita-*san* says please join him. Come with me."

"Ah, Takahashi-*san*," the Japanese consul said when the fisherman walked into his office. He turned to the reporter, who wore a Western-style sport jacket with a gaudy print. "Mori-*san*, you ought to be talking to this fellow, not to me. He'd have some interesting stories to tell you. I can guarantee that."

"Would he?" The reporter turned in his chair and looked Takahashi over. "Hello, there, I'm Ichiro Mori. I write for the *Nippon jiji*."

"Oh, yes. Very pleased to meet you, Mori-*san*." Jiro dipped his head. "I've seen your name in the paper many times."

"You flatter me." Mori had an easygoing voice and a ready grin. He was the sort of man you couldn't help liking at first sight. "So you're a Takahashi, eh? What's your first name?"

"Jiro," Takahashi answered, and the other man—who was a few years younger than he—wrote it down.

"How long have you been in Hawaii, Takahashi-*san*?" Mori asked.

"More than thirty years now."

"*Ah, so desu!* That's a long time. Where were you born? Somewhere not far from Hiroshima, by the way you talk."

"*Hai.*" Jiro nodded. "Yamaguchi prefecture. I call my sampan the *Oshima Maru*, after the county I come from. I learned to be a fisherman there; my father took a boat out onto the Inland Sea."

"Have you been fishing ever since you got here, then?"

"Oh, no. I worked in the sugar fields. That's what they brought us over to do. I had to save my money for a long time before I could buy a boat and get away." Jiro laughed reminiscently. "They weren't very happy about it—they didn't want cane pickers leaving. But I'd met my contract, so they couldn't keep me."

"You settled down here? You have family?"

"I'm a widower," Jiro said, and no more about that. After a brief pause, he added, "I have two sons."

"Do they speak Japanese, I hope?" the reporter asked. "Some of the people born here can't say a word in what should be their own language."

"Not my boys." Pride rang in Takahashi's voice. "I made sure they learned it."

"Good. That's very good." Mori scribbled notes. "And you're happy the way things have turned out here? Are your sons happy, too?"

Jiro glanced over to Nagao Kita. The consul was from Japan. Would he want to hear that Hiroshi and Kenzo thought of themselves as Americans? Not likely! Jiro didn't want to hear it himself. He spoke of his own views first: "Would I bring fish here if I weren't happy?" That let him think about what he would say next: "My sons work too hard to worry much about politics."

"Hard work is always good," Mori agreed. "What did you think when the Rising Sun came to Hawaii?"

"I was proud," Jiro answered. His boys hadn't been proud. He didn't think the gulf between them would ever close. He added, "I waved a flag in the victory parade. The soldiers made a brave show."

"So you were there for the parade? What did you think of all the Yankee prisoners? Weren't you happy to see that their day in the sun was over?"

What did *I think?* Jiro wondered. Mostly, he'd been amazed. He'd never imagined filthy, ragged, beaten American POWs shambling through Honolulu. "The Japanese soldiers who were guarding them certainly were a lot sharper," he said. "I told you, I was proud of all they had done. They were heroes for the Emperor."

"'Heroes for the Emperor,'" Ichiro Mori echoed, beaming. He turned to Consul Kita. "That's a good phrase, isn't it?"

"*Hai*, very good," Kita agreed. "Takahashi-*san* has a way with words."

"Oh, no, not really." The fisherman's modesty was altogether unfeigned.

"Can you stay for a little while, please?" Mori asked him. "I'd like to call a photographer over here and get your picture."

"A photographer? My picture? For the newspaper?" Jiro said, and the reporter nodded. In a daze, Takahashi nodded back. He'd never imagined such a thing. He'd never thought of himself as important enough to land in a newspaper. He read the *Nippon jiji*. Reading about himself in it . . . He felt himself swelling up with pride. *This* would show his boys!

The photographer got there in about twenty minutes. He was a wisecracking fellow named Yukiro Yamaguchi. He took photos of Jiro by himself, with the fish he'd brought, with Consul Kita, and with the consul and the fish. By the time he got done popping flashbulbs, green and purple spots danced in front of Jiro's eyes.

Blinking to try to clear his sight, he bowed to Yamaguchi. "Thank you very much."

"No *huhu*, buddy," the photographer answered, casually dropping a Hawaiian word into his Japanese. "No *huhu* at all."

KENZO TAKAHASHI HAD NEVER PAID a whole lot of attention to Honolulu's Japanese papers. Like most people his age, he preferred the *Star-Bulletin* and the *Advertiser* to *Nippon jiji* and *Hawaii hochi*. All papers had shrunk since the war, the English-language ones much more than their Japanese counterparts. Not surprisingly, the occupiers gave what wood pulp there was to papers that would back their line a hundred percent.

But when Kenzo saw his father staring out at him from the front page of the *Nippon jiji*, he spent a dime to get a copy—the paper had gone up since the fighting started, too. Sure as hell, there was Dad, holding an *ahi* and clasping the Japanese consul's hand. Kenzo didn't tell the newsboy he was related to the man in the paper. The kid, a few years younger than he was, might have hated him. Or he might have congratulated him, and that would have been worse.

What the devil had Dad said? Kenzo had no trouble reading the Japanese as he walked along. He hadn't much wanted to learn it—he would rather have had fun after American school let out—but he'd conscientiously gone and done it, as Hiroshi had before him. And he'd lived in a neighborhood where there were so many Japanese signs and posters and ads that he couldn't very well forget it once he had learned.

Now he wished he had. There was his father praising the Emperor, praising the courage of the Japanese soldiers who'd conquered Hawaii, saying he'd been proud of the victory parade, and telling the world the American soldiers they'd paraded with them were a bunch of decrepit wrecks. He also had good things to say about the way Japan was running Hawaii and about the Greater East Asia Co-Prosperity Sphere.

"Oh, Dad," Kenzo said, wishing he'd never seen the picture, never bought the paper. "*Oh*, Dad."

Maybe it wasn't treason. Maybe. But if it wasn't, it sure came close. Kenzo wondered how many words the reporter had put in his old man's mouth. Would his father recognize the Greater East Asia Co-Prosperity Sphere if it trotted over and bit him in the leg? Maybe he would, at that. He'd talked about it once.

The Greater East Asia Co-Prosperity Sphere damn well had bitten all of Hawaii in the leg, and wouldn't let go. And here was Dad, a smiling propaganda tool for the occupiers. He couldn't have known what he was doing. He must have said the first things that popped into his head when the reporter—Mori, that was the lousy snake's name—asked him questions. But how it had happened didn't much matter now. That it had happened did.

Kenzo started to crumple up the *Nippon jiji* and throw it in the trash. He started to, but he didn't. Instead, he carefully folded the paper and put it in the back pocket of his dungarees. One of the things that no longer came into Honolulu harbor was toilet tissue. He could put that miserable story to good use. Not the picture—he'd tear that out first. But the story? Hell, yes. And the soft pulp paper would be an improvement on the scratchy, coated stuff they put in the outhouses by the botanical garden.

"Oh, Jesus Christ!" Kenzo muttered, deliberately ignoring how much he sounded like his father when he said it. To think he'd been reduced to worrying about how he could comfortably wipe his ass! Before December 7, he would have taken the answer for granted. Before December 7, he'd taken all kinds of answers for granted. What did that prove? It proved he'd been pretty goddamn dumb, that was what.

Here came a squad of Japanese soldiers. Kenzo got out of their way and bowed. By now, he did that automatically. But he couldn't help noticing that one of them was reading a copy of the *Nippon jiji*. How could he, when the soldier held it open to read an inside page so Dad's picture was right there looking out at him?

What did the soldiers think when they read a piece like the one Ichiro Mori had written? Did it make them think all the people who lived on Hawaii were glad they'd come? Or did they just go, *Oh, more crap*? Had they seen so much of this garbage that they recognized it for what it was? Kenzo didn't know.

He hoped all the people who saw the story wiped their asses with it. Then they would forget about it. If the USA got Hawaii back, people who said stuff like this would be remembered. Dumb as Dad was, Kenzo didn't want that.

XII

Fletch Armitage looked longingly past the barbed wire surrounding Kapiolani Park. Waikiki was almost close enough to reach out and touch. Honolulu wasn't much farther. *If I could get past the wire . . .*

Escape was a POW's duty. He'd had that drilled into him. But even the Geneva Convention let garrisons that recaptured escaped prisoners punish them. And the Japs cared as much about the Geneva Convention's rules as a bunch of drunks in a barroom brawl cared about the Marquis of Queensberry's. They'd already made that very, very clear.

And so . . . Fletch looked. A mynah flew over the barbed wire. The scrounging was bound to be better on the other side. Fletch had never dreamt he could be so jealous of a stupid, noisy bird.

After a little while, he turned away. Contemplating freedom just hurt too much. He laughed, not that there was much to laugh about. In one sense of the word, there was no such thing as freedom anywhere in the Territory of Hawaii, and there hadn't been since the surrender. In another sense . . . Fletch would gladly have traded places with anybody outside the camp. He didn't think anybody out beyond the wire would gladly have traded with him.

He mooched back towards his tent. A slow Brownian motion was always on display in the camp. Some prisoners who had nothing else to do would drift towards the wire to get a glimpse of what things were like out beyond it. Others, having seen as much as they could stand, sadly drifted into the interior once more. You never could tell where any one man would be, but the traffic pattern hardly ever changed.

Here and there, POWs bent over a card game or a makeshift checkerboard or a race between two or three crawling bugs—anything to make the time go by. Most of the captives, though, just sat around letting it go by as it would. A lot of them were too hungry to have the energy for anything unessential. They came fully alive twice a day, at breakfast and supper, and banked their fires the rest of the time.

I'm not far from that myself. Fletch contemplated his own hand. He ignored the filth; nobody here could get as clean as he wanted. What he noticed were the bones and tendons thrusting up against the skin. The flesh that had softened his outlines melted off him day by day, leaving only the basics behind.

He saw the same thing on other men's faces, which displayed more and more of the hard uplands of nose and cheekbones and chin as time went by. No doubt the same was true of his own mug, but he didn't get to see that very often. Not seeing himself was a small mercy: in a place singularly lacking larger ones, something to cherish.

Ducking into the tent was another small mercy. If he stayed outside for very long, he burned. Oahu never got too hot, but sunlight here was fiercer than it was anywhere on the mainland because it was more nearly vertical. Back before the fighting started, he'd gone through a lot of zinc-oxide ointment. It hadn't helped much, but nothing else had helped at all. Since then, he hadn't had much choice. Some guys tanned almost native-Hawaiian brown. Fletch just scorched, over and over again.

He didn't have to wait till after sundown to emerge, though thoughts of Bela Lugosi crossed his mind every now and then. The sun was sinking towards Waikiki as he came out to line up for supper. That was funny if you looked at it the right way; people in Honolulu often used *Waikiki* as a synonym for *east*, the same as they used *Ewa* for *west*. But now he'd moved far enough Waikiki of Honolulu that Waikiki was Ewa of him.

POWs gossiped in the chow line, almost as they would have back at Schofield Barracks. What energy they had came out now. They were hungry, but they knew they'd soon be . . . less hungry for a little while, anyway.

Somebody behind Fletch said, "Do the Japs really feed you better if you go out on a work detail?" Fletch pricked up his ears. He'd heard the Japs did that, too. They'd damn near have to. They couldn't expect to get much work out of people who ate only the horrible slop they dished out here.

Another prisoner answered, "Yeah, they do, but only if you meet their work norms. And they set those fuckers so high, you do more shit to meet 'em than they give you extra food."

"Sounds like the Japs," the first man said.

Fletch found himself nodding. It sure as hell did. The Russians had a name for workers who went over their norms. Some of the left-wingers at Schofield Barracks had used it now and again. What the hell was it? Fletch scowled, trying to remember. Sta-something . . . He snapped his fingers. Stakhanovites, that was it!

Feeling smart was almost as good as feeling full. After supper, Fletch shook his head. Feeling full would have been better. But feeling smart *was* almost as good as feeling not quite so empty, which was the most camp rations could achieve.

After the morning count, a local Japanese came into camp and, speaking good English, did indeed call for volunteers for work details. He got them, more than he could use. Lots of men figured things were so bad here, they had to be better somewhere else.

Fletch wasn't convinced. Here he ate next to nothing, but he also did next to nothing. If he ate a little more but did a lot more, wouldn't he just waste away all the faster? That was how it looked to him.

The Japs had boasted about their victories in the Philippines and New Guinea. Taking Hawaii had let them run wild farther west, and had kept the United States from doing one damn thing about it. Fletch could see that very clearly. But the USA hadn't given up. The B-25s that had visited Honolulu were proof of that. Sooner or later, he was convinced, the Americans would try to retake Hawaii. He wanted to be around when they did.

If that meant sitting around on his can doing very little and eating very little, then it did, that was all. He'd been in more than enough poker games to know that bucking the odds was the fastest way to lose. From where he sat, going out on a work detail looked to be bucking the odds. How many of those who went would come back? Ma Armitage hadn't raised her boy to be a fool. Fletch hoped she hadn't, anyway.

CORPORAL AISO WAGGED A FINGER in Takeo Shimizu's face. "Be careful when you go out on patrol," the veteran warned. "Something's in the air. Don't trust any of the locals. Don't even trust the local Japanese. Some of them are like bananas."

"Bananas?" Shimizu scratched his head.

Kiyoshi Aiso nodded. "*Hai.* Bananas. Yellow on the outside, white on the inside. They may look like us, but they think like Americans."

"*Ah, so desu!* Now I understand. Bananas!" Shimizu wondered who'd come up with that. It was pretty funny.

Aiso might have been reading his mind. "You may laugh now, but you won't if you run into trouble. And don't go wandering off by yourself or let your men do anything dumb like that. Somebody knocked a soldier over the head and stole his rifle the other day."

"My men and I will be careful," Shimizu promised. "Why did the Americans want a Japanese rifle? Even after all the sweeps we've done, I think this little island has more small arms on it than all of Japan put together."

"I wouldn't be surprised," Aiso said. "Whoever slugged the soldier was probably after him first and took the rifle as an afterthought."

Shimizu nodded. That made sense. He warned his squad the same way the older corporal had warned him. The men all looked attentive. He looked like that whenever a superior addressed him, too. He knew it didn't necessarily mean anything. Half the time he'd been thinking about something else, no matter what his face said. Half the squad was likely to be thinking about something else now.

"Let's go," Shimizu barked, and off they went.

They made a fine martial spectacle, backs straight, helmets all just so, bayonets gleaming in the sun. Locals scrambled to get out of their way and bowed as they tramped past. People of Japanese blood did it right. The others? They obeyed the requirement, but they still didn't really understand what they were doing.

Back and forth went Shimizu's gaze. Trouble might come from anywhere, Aiso had said. If somebody'd been brave— or foolhardy—enough to take on a fully armed Japanese soldier, the other noncom was right, too. Shimizu wondered whether the attacker had killed the soldier. Shimizu hoped so, as much for the man's sake as for any other reason. Anyone who suffered a disgrace like that was better off dead.

A policeman escorted a fisherman with a string of silvery fish along the street. Otherwise, *he* would have been a real candidate for getting clobbered. The policeman was white, the fisherman Japanese. Because of his job, the policeman retained the pistol he'd worn before Honolulu changed hands. But, like anyone else here, he bowed when the Japanese soldiers marched by.

Senior Private Furusawa said, "I still don't like seeing Americans walking around with guns."

"Policemen don't worry me too much," Shimizu said. "They're watchdogs, not wolves. They'll do what the people in charge of them tell them to do—and we're the people in charge of them now."

"*Hai*," Furusawa said. That wasn't agreement; it was only acknowledgment that he heard the corporal. Shimizu knew as much. He shrugged, ever so slightly. Furusawa didn't have to agree with him. The senior private did have to stay polite, and he had.

Cars sat next to the curb, quite a few of them on flat tires. Hardly any rolled down the street these days; fuel was too short for that. Even seeing them immobilized, though, reminded Shimizu of how different Hawaii was from Japan. Honolulu wasn't anywhere near as big as Hiroshima, but it boasted far more automobiles. They were perhaps the most prominent mark of American wealth.

The corporal shrugged again. *Who cares how rich the Yankees were? We beat them anyway. They were easier to beat* because *they were rich. It made them soft.* Men set above Shimizu had said that a great many times. They'd said it so often, they undoubtedly believed it. He wasn't so sure. The Americans he'd fought hadn't shown any signs of softness. They'd lost, but nobody could say they hadn't fought hard.

Everything seemed quiet this morning. That was the idea behind patrolling. Marching through Honolulu, making the Japanese presence felt, was the best way to stop trouble before it started. Remind the locals that the Army was keeping an eye on them and they wouldn't get gay. Leave them alone, and who could say what might happen?

A pretty woman with yellow hair bowed as the soldiers went by. The light cotton dress she wore covered much less of her than would have been proper back in Japan. Several of Shimizu's men gave her a thorough inspection. He looked her over himself. If they decided to drag her into a building and enjoy her one after another, who could stop them? Nobody. The fright on her face as she bowed said she knew it, too.

"Keep going, you lugs," Shimizu said. "Maybe another time." A couple of the soldiers sighed, but they obeyed. Honolulu hadn't been treated as roughly as Chinese towns were when they fell . . . and Shimizu, a good-natured man, preferred his women willing.

It was midafternoon when they headed back towards the barracks. Nothing much had happened on patrol, which didn't break Shimizu's heart. He approved of routine while he was prowling the streets. Anything that wasn't routine was too likely to be messy and dangerous.

Getting back in the company of lots of Japanese soldiers felt good. It meant he didn't have to look over his shoulder and wonder whether all hell would break loose when he rounded the next corner.

So he thought, anyway, till a freight-train noise in the air made him throw himself flat. His body recognized that sound before his mind did—and before the incoming shell burst less than a hundred meters away. Most of his men hit the dirt, too. Few who'd met artillery forgot it in a hurry.

Another shell crashed down by the barracks, and another, and another. Only after the third or fourth burst did Shimizu wonder where they were coming from. Out of the south, by the sound, but what lay south of Honolulu? The Pacific, nothing else.

"Submarine!" someone shouted, his voice half heard through the crashing impacts and the screams of wounded men.

Submarine! Shimizu swore. *I should have thought of that myself.* A sub could sneak close to shore, surface, use its deck gun against whatever it felt like shooting up, and then disappear under the sea again.

That had hardly crossed Shimizu's mind before the shelling stopped. He cautiously raised his head, ready to flatten out again in a hurry if more rounds roared in. But the bombardment did seem to be over. He looked around. The men in his own squad were scrambling to their feet. None of them seemed more than scratched.

Not all the Japanese by the barracks were so lucky. Injured soldiers went on shrieking their pain up to the uncaring tropical sky. And others weren't men at all any more, but disjointed chunks of meat. Someone's foot lay only a couple of meters from Shimizu. The body from which the foot had come was nowhere to be seen. Men who hadn't been hurt started bandaging their comrades and tying off bleeding wounds with tourniquets to try to keep people alive till doctors could see to them.

The barracks had taken a beating, too. Windows were shattered. Walls had holes in them. The building didn't seem to be burning. Shimizu wondered why. Dumb luck was the only thing that occurred to him.

He looked out towards the ocean. He saw no submarine, but it wouldn't have surfaced for a second longer than it had to. It was bound to be underwater now, crawling away after striking its blow.

A few minutes later, airplanes started buzzing over the ocean south of Honolulu. One of them dropped a stick of bombs—or would they be depth charges? Even distant explosions set Shimizu's nerves on edge. He wondered whether that pilot had really seen something or was blowing things up just to be blowing them up. Either way, he'd never know.

Shiro Wakuzawa came up to him. Sounding surprisingly cheerful, the youngster said, "One good thing, Corporal-*san*."

"What?" Shimizu asked. "What could be good about a mess like this?"

"Simple, Corporal: it's not our fault," Wakuzawa answered. "Whatever they do, they can't blame this on us poor soldiers. The Navy? *Hai*. Us? *Iye*." He shook his head. "If they can't blame it on us, they can't make us wallop each other on account of it."

"You hope they can't, anyway. If they want to bad enough, they can do whatever they please," Shimizu said. Private Wakuzawa looked alarmed—and had reason to. Shimizu went on, "But I think you're right. This one's the Navy's fault. I'm glad I'm in khaki right now."

WHEN GENERAL YAMASHITA SUMMONED Captain Tomeo Kaku to Iolani Palace to confer with him, Captain Hasegawa's replacement asked—ordered, really—Minoru Genda to accompany him. Genda understood that. He sympathized with it. His superior was brand-new here, and naturally wanted someone along who sympathized with his side of things, to say nothing of someone famous for having facts at his fingertips.

All the same, Commander Genda could have done without the honor.

Had the Navy sunk the American submarine, things wouldn't have been so bad. The enemy would have paid for his daring. But there was no sign that the Yankees had paid even a sen. That one flier had bombed what he thought was a sub. Afterwards, though, there'd been no oil slick and no floating debris. Odds were he'd attacked a figment of his excited imagination.

Up the stairs to the palace entrance trudged Captain Kaku. He was a stumpy man with bulldog features, less friendly and casual than Hasegawa. One pace to the rear, one pace to the left, Commander Genda followed him. The guards—Army men—at the top of the stairs gave grudging, halfhearted salutes. They weren't quite insolent enough to be called on it, but their attitude still stung. They might as well have shouted that Navy men deserved no better.

Kaku affected not to notice. Because he chose to do that, Genda had to match his self-control. It wasn't easy. Despite his slight stature, Genda was a fiercely proud man.

"What can we do?" Kaku murmured as they walked into the entry hall. "We deserve to be mocked. First those bombers, and now this!" He let out a long, sad sigh. He'd taken over for Captain Hasegawa only the day before the submarine raid, but plainly saw it as his fault.

They went up the koa-wood staircase to King Kauakala's Library. The last time Genda was in the room, he and Mitsuo and Fuchida and a couple of Army officers had asked Princess Abigail Kawananakoa if she wanted to become Queen of Hawaii. As far as Genda knew, plans for reviving the monarchy hadn't gone any further after she said no. Someone needed to keep working on that. Other potential sovereigns were out there.

But the monarchy could wait. Now Major General Tomoyuki Yamashita sat behind King Kauakala's ponderous desk. Yamashita was a ponderous man himself, and only looked more massive looming over that formidable piece of furniture. He had set one chair in front of the desk, intending to leave Captain Kaku out there alone and vulnerable to take whatever he felt like dishing out.

The general shot Genda a baleful glance. Genda wondered whether Yamashita would order him out or make him stand. By Yamashita's scowl, he was thinking about one or the other. But he must have decided either would have been too raw. Grudgingly, he pointed to another of the leather-backed chairs against the wall. Genda set it beside the one meant for Captain Kaku. The two Navy officers sat down together.

"Well?" Yamashita growled. "What do you bunglers have to say for yourselves?"

"If it weren't for our 'bungling,' sir, you wouldn't be sitting where you are right now," Genda said.

Now Yamashita looked at him as if he were a bug in the rice bowl. "If that submarine had decided to aim for this building, I could have been killed sitting where I am right now."

"I am very sorry about that, General," Captain Kaku said. "Submarines are hard to detect and hard to hunt. That makes them good for nuisance raids like the one the other day. I am glad the boat did not turn its gun this way."

Genda wouldn't have missed General Yamashita. He didn't think Kaku would have, either. The forms had to be observed, though. Too much truth was destructive of discipline.

"How do you propose to make sure this sort of outrage doesn't happen again?" Yamashita demanded. "Aside from the damage it does, look at the propaganda it hands the Americans."

"So sorry, General," Kaku repeated. The Americans had handed Yamashita a stick, and he was using it to beat the Navy.

"We are increasing patrols, sir," Genda put in. "The new Kawanishi H8K flying boats will help. They have much longer range and greater endurance than the H6Ks they're replacing. We're flying them out of the Pearl City base that the Yankees set up for their Pan American Clipper planes."

"There are no guarantees, sir," Kaku added, "but they do have a better chance than anything else we've got."

"They're heavily armed, too," Genda said. "If they spot a sub, they also have a good chance of sinking it." He paused for some quick mental calculations, then nodded to himself. "They might even be able to reach the U.S. mainland from here. That would pay the Yankees back for what they did to us. If we could drop bombs on San Francisco, say . . ."

He'd captured Yamashita's imagination. He'd hoped he could. "*Could* they get there and back?" the general asked.

"It would be right on the edge of their range if they took off from here," Genda answered. "They could do it more easily if we had a submarine out in the Pacific to refuel them."

"Could you arrange that with Tokyo?" Yamashita asked, suddenly eager.

Genda and Kaku looked at each other. Neither one smiled. "Possibly," Kaku said. "It might take some persuading, but possibly. If you would add your voice, Yamashita-*san*, that would be bound to help." Genda still didn't smile, though how he didn't he couldn't have said. After what the Americans had done here, Tokyo would leap at the chance to strike back. He was sure of that. Regaining lost face would appeal to the Navy and Army both.

Major General Yamashita nodded. "You may be sure that I will."

Once Captain Kaku and Genda were out on the lawn outside the palace, the new skipper of the *Akagi* did smile, in relief. "That went better than I hoped it would," he said. "Thank you very much, Commander."

"My pleasure, sir," Genda answered with a polite bow.

JIM PETERSON DIDN'T NEED LONG after volunteering for an outside work detail to realize he'd made a mistake. He'd thought nothing could be worse than the POW camp by Opana. That only proved he'd been sadly lacking in imagination.

He and his fellow suckers were set to work repairing a stretch of the Kamehameha Highway. The Japs had graders and bulldozers. If they hadn't brought their own, they had the ones they'd captured here. They didn't want to use them. Maybe they were short on fuel. Maybe they just wanted to find a new way to give their prisoners hell. The whys didn't really matter. The what did.

The POWs had picks and shovels and hods and mattocks and other hand tools. They broke rock. They carried rock. They flattened chunks of rock till they had a roadway. At first, they'd all been eager to show the Japs what they could do. That hadn't lasted long. Soon sense prevailed, and they started doing as little as they could get away with.

That didn't mean they didn't work. Oh, no—far from it. The Jap guards were harder on them than the whip-cracking overseers in *Gone with the Wind* were on the slaves. Peterson had no trouble figuring out why, either. If a slave died, his owner was out a considerable investment. If a POW died here . . . well, so what? Plenty more where he came from.

There was more food at the start and end of each day. Nobody could have done hard physical labor on what the Japs fed POWs in camp. Trouble was, there wasn't *enough* more food to make up for the labor the men on the work detail did. Every day, Peterson's ribs seemed to stand out more distinctly.

And he had to keep an eye on everybody else in his shooting squad. The Jap who'd come up with that scheme had to be a devil who got up and sharpened his horns every morning the way ordinary men shaved. If anybody took off for the tall timber, the whole squad bought the farm. You couldn't believe the Japs were kidding, either. They'd shoot nine guys because one had run. Hell, they'd laugh while they were doing it, too.

Peterson particularly worried about a fellow named Walter London. London had been skinny the first time Peterson set eyes on him back in the camp. Unlike most POWs, he hadn't got any skinnier. He was an operator, a guy who could come up with things like cigarettes or aspirins . . . for a price, always for a price. He looked out for number one— and there was no number two in his book. That made him dangerous. He wouldn't care what happened to the rest of the shooting squad, not if he'd disappeared over the horizon before anybody knew he was gone.

Everybody watched him. Everybody watched everybody else, but everybody *especially* watched him. He noticed, of course. Only a fool wouldn't have. Walt London might have been—probably was—a slimy son of a bitch, but he was nobody's fool. One morning, he asked, "How come I can't even take a dump by myself without somebody handing me some leaves to wipe my ass?"

The other members of the shooting squad looked at one another. For a few seconds, nobody seemed to want to take the bull by the horns. Then Peterson did: "That way, we know we'll have the pleasure of your company after you pull up your pants, Walter."

London donned a look of injured innocence. He might have practiced in front of a mirror. "I don't know what you're talking about," he said.

Now Peterson's voice went cold and flat. "You lie like a wet rag. Anybody with two brain cells to rub together would know what I'm talking about. You may be a bastard, but you're not a jerk. If you start pretending you are, is it any wonder nobody trusts you?"

"I'm not gonna bail out on you guys," London protested.

"See? You did know what I was talking about after all. How about that?" Peterson's sarcasm flayed. Walter London turned red. Peterson didn't care. He drove his point home: "But you're right. You're *not* gonna bail out, because we're not gonna let you. If you get away, you kill all nine of us. But if you try and get away and we catch you, you don't need to worry about the Japs. We'll goddamn well kill you ourselves. Isn't that right, boys?"

He got nods from the rest of the shooting squad. He wore only the corporal's stripes he'd earned not long before the American defense on Oahu collapsed. But he still talked like an officer. He knew how to lead. The others responded to that, even if they didn't quite know what they were responding to.

Hate blazed from Walter London's eyes. Peterson looked back at him with nothing at all in his own. London wilted—under the hate lay fear. "Honest to God, I'm not going anywhere," he said.

Push him too hard now, Peterson judged, and he might bolt for the sake of getting everybody else shot. With a broad, insincere smile of his own, Peterson said, "Okay. Sure thing."

Later, one of the other men in the shooting squad, a PFC named Gordy Braddon, sidled up to him and said, "That asshole still wants to cut out on us."

"Yeah, I know," Peterson said. "We'll watch him. If he does try and disappear, we'll nab him, too. I'm not about to let a punk like that put me in my grave."

Braddon had tawny hair, a long-jawed face, and an accent that said he came from Kentucky or Tennessee. His chuckle sounded distinctly cadaverous. "You bet you won't, on account of the Japs won't bother throwin' you in one if they shoot you 'cause London goes south."

"All the more reason not to let him, then," Peterson said. Braddon chuckled again and slipped away.

Nights were bad. The rest of the shooting squad had to keep watch on Walter London. That meant giving up part of their own sleep when they were desperately weary. London proved how shrewd he was. If he'd kept complaining and kicking up a fuss, the other men would have been sure they were doing the right thing. He didn't. He didn't say boo, in fact. He just slept like a baby himself. He might have been saying, *If you want to waste your time, fine. Go ahead. I don't intend to waste mine.* That was a damned effective way to take revenge.

Fighting to keep his own eyes open, watching the other POWs snoring away in the middle of the night, Peterson hated him right back. If London were square, he wouldn't have needed to waste his time like this. *Yeah, and if ifs and buts were candied nuts, we'd all have a hell of a Christmas.*

He felt the exhaustion less in the nighttime than he did the next day. One morning when he was particularly frazzled, Braddon handed him three or four small, greenish fruits—they couldn't have been much above the size of his thumbnail—and said, "Here. Chew on these."

Peterson did. They were bitter enough to make his face

pucker up. "What the hell are they?" he asked, wondering if the other man was playing a nasty practical joke on him.

"Coffee beans," Braddon answered. "Stuff grows wild here."

"Oh, yeah?" Peterson let the juice run down his throat. Sure as hell, his heart started beating faster and his eyes opened up. Admiringly, he asked, "How the devil did you recognize 'em?"

"My ma kept tryin' to grow 'em in Memphis," Braddon said. "Didn't work. Winters are mild, but they aren't *that* mild. Every time we got a hard frost, it'd kill 'em off. But she kept after it, Ma did. Hell, for all I know, she's still tryin'."

"Damn," Peterson said reverently. He couldn't remember the last time he'd had coffee. Not too long after December 7—he was sure of that. Since he'd gone so long without, the stuff kicked him hard now, almost like Benzedrine. He felt like a new man, and the new man felt ready to go out there and bust his ass. It wouldn't last—he was sure of that—but he'd make the most of it while it was there.

FLYING ABOARD ONE OF THE THREE KAWANISHI H8Ks that droned east and north through the darkness awed Commander Mitsuo Fuchida. Part of his excitement was over the mission. The Americans had dared to strike at Hawaii from the air. Now Japan would pay the same kind of visit to the U.S. mainland.

Some good *kami* must have taken hold of Minoru Genda's tongue when he proposed the raid to General Yamashita. It was the perfect way to pay the Yankees back for their insolence. As soon as Fuchida heard about it, he knew he had to come along. And here he was, heading straight for North America.

The rest of the awe was devoted to the plane in whose copilot's seat he flew. The H8K was, quite simply, the best flying boat in the world, and nothing else came close. The airplane was about three-quarters the size of one of the China Clippers that had traveled from the U.S. West Coast to Hong Kong and Macao, but it was half again as fast as they were. It cruised at better than 320 kilometers an hour, and could get up over 460 at top speed.

It packed a wallop, too. Along with the bombs waiting in the bomb bay, it carried five 20mm cannon and five more machine guns. Any U.S. fighter that jumped an H8K was liable to get a very nasty surprise. Not only that, the flying boat, unlike a lot of Japanese planes, was well protected, with self-sealing fuel tanks in the hull and a good fire-extinguishing system. As far as Fuchida could see, the designers had thought of everything.

He said as much to the pilot, who sat to his left. Lieutenant Kinsuke Muto grinned a crooked grin. "Oh, they did, Fuchida-*san*," Muto said. "The only trouble was, it took them a while, or the plane would have been in service a long time ago."

"I heard something about this last year, but not too much," Fuchida said. "I was busy training for the Hawaii operation. Tell me more, please."

"Busy? I'll bet you were, sir—just a little." Muto laughed out loud, then went on, "Well, you know we wanted something better than the H6K: faster, with longer range, and a plane that wouldn't catch fire the first time a bullet came anywhere near it." He laughed again, not that it was funny; attacks against the Dutch East Indies and New Guinea had shown that the H6K turned into a torch when the enemy started shooting at it.

Fuchida leaned forward in his seat to lay a gentle hand on the instrument panel in front of him. "We have what we wanted, too."

"*Hai.* We do—*now*." Lieutenant Muto stressed the last word. "But it wasn't easy. The first flight tests showed the beast was unstable at takeoff and a disaster on the water generally. They had to do a total redesign on the lower hull, and it set them back for months."

"Ah, is that what the trouble was?" Fuchida said. "I knew there was a delay, but I don't think I ever heard why. It was worth waiting for, though—the plane handles beautifully on the water now. I saw that when we took off from Pearl City."

Muto snorted. "Hardly a tough test, sir. The water inside Pearl Harbor is going to be calm, no matter what. But wait till you see this baby out on the open ocean. It's just as good there."

"You know best," Fuchida said. He had a hasty familiarization with the H8K. He'd been bound and determined to come on this mission, but he hadn't wanted to be dead weight while he was along.

The radioman brought tea to Fuchida and Muto. He hesitated for a moment, wondering which man to serve first: Fuchida had the higher rank, but Muto sat in the pilot's chair. The two of them pointed to each other. They both laughed.

"Give it to Muto-*san*," Fuchida said. "He's the captain of this ship. I'm just excess baggage."

Muto took a cup of tea. A moment later, Fuchida had one, too. He looked out the window. There was nothing much to see: only black ocean below and dark blue sky above. He couldn't spot the other two flying boats. He was in the leader, while they trailed his plane to either side.

After sipping, Fuchida asked, "How long till we reach the mainland?"

"Another couple of hours," Lieutenant Muto answered. "Long before then, though, we'll use the Yankees' radio stations to home in on our target."

"Oh, yes. Of course." Fuchida nodded. "I did the same thing with the Honolulu stations when we hit Pearl Harbor. They even told me the weather was good."

"That must have been handy. You speak English, then?" Muto said.

"I speak some, yes," Fuchida told him. "And it was very handy. I'd been wondering how to find out what sort of cloud cover they had down there. It would have made a difference in how high we flew. I'd been wondering—and the Americans went and told me."

"I hope they do it again. San Francisco can be a foggy town, I hear," Muto said. "I don't want to have to drop my bombs any old place. I want to hit something worthwhile in the harbor there."

"Don't worry. The Americans will be chattering away,"

Fuchida promised. "They don't have anything that can reach Hawaii from the mainland and get back, so of course they won't think we have anything that can reach the mainland from Hawaii."

Lieutenant Muto grinned at him. "Surprise!"

"*Hai*." Mitsuo Fuchida grinned back.

On they went. The throbbing of the four Mitsubishi fourteen-cylinder radial engines seemed to penetrate Fuchida's bones. He flew the plane for a couple of minutes when Muto got up to answer a call of nature. He knew he'd be doing more on the way back. Even in a speedy H8K, San Francisco was ten hours from Honolulu. He held course and altitude. That he could do, and do well enough. He wouldn't have wanted to be at the controls if American fighters attacked the flying boat, or if he had to put it down at sea.

Muto returned and took over again. Fuchida leaned back in his chair. He could doze if he wanted to. He did for a while, to stay fresh for the return flight. Then the radioman hurried up with something written on a scrap of paper. The number had to be the new course for San Francisco. Muto glanced down at it, nodded, murmured, "*Arigato*," and swung the plane's nose a little to the north.

"Our navigation was pretty good," Fuchida said, seeing how small a correction he made.

"Not bad," Muto agreed. He pointed out through the forward window. "Demons take me if that's not the California coast."

Sleepiness fell from Fuchida like a discarded cloak. He leaned out and peered into darkness. Sure enough, those lights ahead marked the edge of land—the edge of a continent dreaming it was immune from war. He laughed softly. "This is what the Americans call blackout."

"They'll get better at it once we've been here and gone, I expect." Muto laughed, too. "Of course, that will be a little too late."

Fuchida had heard that German submarines were having a field day sinking freighters silhouetted against the bright lights of the U.S. East Coast. He hadn't known whether to believe it. He did now.

A few minutes later, the flying boats approached San Francisco from the south. An English phrase occurred to Fuchida: *lit up like a Christmas tree.* The city probably wasn't so bright as it would have been in peacetime, but it was plenty bright enough. Fuchida said, "The harbor is on the eastern side of the city, on the bay, not here by the ocean."

"Yes, I know," Muto answered, and then spoke over the intercom to the bombardier: "Are you ready? We are going into the bombing run."

"Ready, yes, sir." The reply sounded in Fuchida's earphones as well as Muto's.

Nobody on the ground paid any attention to the three flying boats. No searchlights tried to spear them. No anti-aircraft fire came up at them. If anyone had any idea at all that they were there, he had to assume they belonged to the USA. A street that ran diagonally through the heart of San Francisco guided them straight to the harbor.

Not even the piers with warships tied up alongside them were properly blacked out. Fuchida grinned. *We've caught them napping again,* he thought. But then the grin slipped. Two could play at this game—the Yankee B-25s and the U.S. submarine had surprised the Japanese in Hawaii.

"Bombs free!" the bombardier exclaimed. The H8K grew livelier as it got lighter, but to a much smaller degree than Fuchida's B5N1 had over Pearl Harbor. The flying boat was a far heavier plane. Fuchida hoped the other two Japanese aircraft were also bombing. He couldn't tell. He had a good forward view, but not to the side or behind.

Lieutenant Muto swung the flying boat in a sharp turn back towards Hawaii. "I think, Fuchida-*san,* we've just worn out our welcome," he said.

"*Hai. Honto,*" Fuchida agreed gravely.

"Hits! We have hits!" That wasn't the bombardier—it was the rear gunner, who manned the 20mm cannon in the tail turret. Of all the crew, he had the best view of what was going on behind the H8K. A moment later, he added, "The other two planes still have bombs left. They're unloading them on the city."

"Good. Very good," Muto said. "The Americans think they're immune from war. They need to learn they're not."

After the flying boats dropped their bombs, a few antiaircraft guns did start shooting. None of the bursts came anywhere near the Japanese planes. Lieutenant Muto whooped exultantly. So did the radioman. As the California coast vanished behind the H8Ks, he said, "The Yankees will never catch us now!"

Mitsuo Fuchida was less sure of that than his comrades. They didn't know about the interrogations of the U.S. soldiers from the strange installation near Opana. The USA had a way to track planes through the air electronically. Fuchida gathered his own country was also working on such devices, but Japan didn't have them up and running yet. If one was operating anywhere near San Francisco, it might guide fighters after the flying boats.

He shrugged. If that happened, it happened. Even if it did, fighters wouldn't have an easy time finding the H8Ks in the darkness. And the Japanese planes, though slower and less maneuverable than U.S. fighters, were armed well enough to give a good account of themselves.

The danger of pursuit shrank with each passing minute. Fighters had only limited range. If they wanted to get home again, they couldn't go too far out to sea. The flying boats, on the other hand . . .

Muto leaned back in his seat. "Copilot, would you like to hold this course for a few hours and let me grab a little sleep?"

"Of course. My pleasure." Fuchida admired the smooth way Muto gave orders to a superior officer.

"Good. *Domo arigato*," Muto said. "Wake me at once if there's any trouble, of course, or when the radioman picks up the signal from the *I-25*."

"I'll do that," Fuchida promised, most sincerely. Yes, indeed, trying to land the flying boat on the Pacific was the last thing he wanted to do. Muto closed his eyes. He started snoring inside a few minutes. Fuchida admired him again, this time for his coolness.

Fuchida kept an eye on the compass and the airspeed

indicator and the altimeter. He held the course Muto had given him. Every minute put San Francisco five and a half kilometers farther behind the flying boat, Honolulu five and a half kilometers closer. Too bad so many kilometers lay between them.

He was proud that their navigation to the U.S. mainland had worked out so well. The flight wouldn't have been easy by daylight, let alone with most of it at night. Fuchida laughed. Three Japanese flying boats would have got a rather warmer reception if they'd appeared over San Francisco with the sun still in the sky.

In any case, the round-trip between Honolulu and San Francisco was about twenty hours. Without a layover—again, unlikely!—much of it had to be by night.

After about three and a half hours, Lieutenant Muto yawned and stretched and opened his eyes. He looked over at Fuchida and asked, "How is everything?"

"Fine," Fuchida answered. "We were going on to the Panama Canal from San Francisco, weren't we?"

"The Panama Canal?" Muto's eyes flashed to the compass. Only after he made sure of the course did he laugh. "You know how to wake a fellow up in a hurry, don't you, Commander?"

"I try," Fuchida said. Lieutenant Muto clucked in mock reproach and shook his head. Though Fuchida had been joking, he couldn't help looking back towards the southeast. The Panama Canal lay in that direction. If Japan could put it out of action, that would be a tremendous blow to the USA. If the Americans had to ship everything around South America . . .

Regretfully, he shook his head. The Panama Canal was more than twice as far from Honolulu as San Francisco was: out of range even for an H8K. The Canal would be well defended, too, and the Americans would move heaven and earth to repair whatever damage it suffered. Attacking it was nice to think about. So was making love to a beautiful movie actress. In real life, neither was likely to be practical.

Little by little, the sky began to grow light. They were

flying away from the sunrise, which slowed it, but it came anyway. Even when dawn did arrive, though, there was nothing to see but sky above and an endless expanse of ocean below. Fuchida checked the fuel gauge. They'd filled every tank to overflowing before takeoff. Even so, they didn't have enough left to get back to Honolulu.

Half an hour later, the radioman's voice sounded in Muto's earphones, and in Fuchida's: "I have the signal from the *I-25!*"

"*Ichi-ban!*" Muto exclaimed. The relief in his voice said he must have been watching the needle drop towards empty, too. "What is the bearing?"

"Sir, we're going to need to swing south about five degrees," the radioman replied. "We'll all keep our eyes peeled after that. By the strength of the signal, I don't think we're very far away."

"Pass the word to the other planes on the low-power circuit," Muto said. "No one's likely to pick it up here, and no one's likely to be able to do anything about it even if he does."

"*Hai*," the radioman said.

A crewman on one of the other flying boats first spotted the surfaced submarine. His radioman passed the word to Fuchida's H8K and Muto the third one. Then Fuchida and Muto both pointed out the window at the same time. Muto brought the flying boat down to the water. Spray kicked up from the hull as it landed. Suddenly, its motion took on a new character. For a plane, it had an excellent hull. For a boat . . . Fuchida gulped. *I am a good sailor*, he told himself sternly.

Muto taxied up alongside the *I-25*. Sailors on the sub's deck waved to the flying boat. "How did it go?" somebody shouted. Muto and Fuchida waved and grinned. The sailors clapped their hands. They yelled, "*Banzai!*"

Then they got down to business. The *I-25* carried fuel for the last leg of the flying boats' return to Honolulu. Two sailors in a boat ran a hose from the submarine to the H8K. Fuchida listened to fuel flowing into the tanks. When the plane had enough to get back to Honolulu, the sailors disconnected the hose.

Muto taxied out of the way. The other two flying boats refueled in turn. When all three had got what they needed, the submarine sailed away. Fuchida breathed a silent sigh of relief when the H8Ks got airborne once more after long takeoff runs that put him in mind of geese sprinting along the surface of a lake before they could get airborne. The flying boats had been hideously vulnerable as they bobbed on the surface of the Pacific. Now they were in their proper element again, and could take care of themselves.

They came back to the Pan American Clipper base about four in the afternoon. Japanese officers waited for them as if they really were tourists coming to Hawaii from the West Coast of the USA. Applause and shouts of, "*Banzai!*" greeted them as they got out of the planes.

"Radio in the United States is going mad!" a signals officer yelled. "The Yankees are saying this was as big an embarrassment as Pearl Harbor!"

Fuchida and Muto bowed to each other. Then they both yawned. Together, they started to laugh.

COMPASSIONATE LEAVE WAS THE LAST THING Joe Crosetti wanted. But here he was, tearing across the country on the fastest trains he could get. Most of the bombs the Japs had dropped on San Francisco came down on the harbor or near it. As they were leaving, though, they'd emptied their racks—and one of those afterthoughts had landed on the house where Uncle Tony and Aunt Maria and their four kids lived. One of the kids was still alive, though he'd lost a leg. He'd been blown into a tree across the street, which doubtless saved his life. The rest of the family? Gone.

In the harbor, the Japs had damaged a cruiser, a destroyer, and two freighters, and they'd sent another freighter to the bottom. Nobody'd laid a glove on them, not so far as anyone could tell. They'd come out of the night, done their dirty work, and then disappeared again.

To Joe, the ships mattered much less than his family. Had his aunt and uncle's house not been hit, he might have given the enemy grudging credit for a nice piece of work. Not now. Now the war was personal. He did want to string up the San Francisco civil-defense authorities, who must have been asleep at the switch when the Japs came in. Had they had their radar on? Had they watched it if they had? Not likely, not by what had happened.

No one paid any special attention to him as he rolled west across the country. Men in uniform were a dime a dozen. More were soldiers than sailors, and more sailors were ratings than officers, but Joe wasn't unusual enough to draw notice. That suited him fine. He preferred being alone with his thoughts.

His own family lived only a few blocks from what had been Uncle Tony's house. The bomb could have blown up his mom and dad as easily as his aunt and uncle. He couldn't see anything but dumb luck that had kept it from doing just that—and there was a thought he would rather not have had.

His train got into the Southern Pacific station at First and Broadway in Oakland at two in the morning on the day of the funeral. His father waited on the platform for him. Dad was in his usual fisherman's dungarees; he wouldn't change to a suit till later.

They embraced. Dad hadn't shrunk, exactly, but he seemed frailer than he had before Joe started flight training. Joe didn't stop and think how much more muscle he'd added since then; he wasn't built like a middle infielder any more.

His father kissed him on the cheek, saying, "Good to see you, boy. I wish it wasn't for something like this."

"Jesus, so do I!" Joe said. "Those dirty, stinking bastards. I—"

"You go pay 'em back, that's all," his father said. "Those other pilots, they can yell, 'Remember Pearl Harbor!' when they give the Japs what-for. You, you yell, 'Remember Tony and Maria and Lou and Tina and Gina!'—and Paul, too, dammit!"

"I will," Joe said. "I've got a picture of 'em in my wallet. Whenever I go up, it goes up with me." He wished he were flying planes hotter than the sedate trainers at Pensacola. You had to crawl before you could walk and walk before you could run, but he wanted to run like Jesse Owens—run right at the Japs and run right over them.

"Okay, Joey." His father set a hand on his shoulder. "Come on, then. I'll take you back to the house. That all your stuff?"

"Yeah." Joe slung the duffel bag over his shoulder. "They teach us to travel light." He yawned. "I'd like to sleep for about a week when I get home."

"Funeral's at ten," Dad warned.

"I know. I'll want to take a bath, too." After so long on the train, Joe felt grubby all over. "Be nice to get in the tub for a change. I haven't had anything but showers since I went back East."

At that hour, the parking lot was almost empty. Next to no traffic was on the roads. They went back to San Francisco on the Bay Bridge. Joe remembered the hoopla with which it had opened in 1936. It was a hell of a lot more convenient than the ferry that had linked San Francisco and the East Bay. It would have been, anyhow, if they could have gone faster than the crawl the new, strict blackout regulations imposed.

Something else occurred to Joe. "You all right for gas, Dad?" He hadn't paid much attention to gas rationing since becoming a cadet. He didn't have a car, so it wasn't his worry.

His father shrugged. "It'll be okay. And this—this is more important than crap like that." Joe bit his lip and nodded.

He was damned if he could figure out how his old man navigated in the pitch blackness. Masking tape covered all but the narrowest strip of headlights. What was left didn't let you see far enough to spit. Dad managed, though. He didn't clip any of the other cars groping their way through the night, and he got back to the house with no wrong turns anywhere.

After months of bunks and cots, Joe's bed seemed ridiculously soft. Lying down on it made him feel like a kid, as if he'd shed years. He wondered if the ticking of the alarm clock on the nightstand would bother him. It did—

for ninety seconds, maybe even two minutes. After that, he heard nothing.

When the alarm clock went off, he had to figure out what it was and how to turn it off. Reveille had been rousting him since he joined the Navy. He realized he didn't have to change out of his pajamas before he went to breakfast. Now *there* was luxury.

His mother burst into tears when she saw him. His brother Carl was sixteen, and stared at him in awe. His sister Angie was twelve. She just seemed glad to have him back. He shoveled down breakfast with the single-minded determination he would have shown back in Pensacola. Carl gaped. Dad grinned. His mother brought him seconds. In Pensacola, he would have overloaded his plate the first time around.

With all the talk at the breakfast table, he didn't have time for a bath after all. He zipped through the shower and put on his dress uniform. When he came downstairs again, his mother started crying for a second time. Carl's eyes damn near bugged out of his head. His brother and father wore almost identical black suits. Joe ignored the faint smell of mothballs.

They all piled into the car to go to church. When they got there, they found reporters waiting outside. Joe hadn't expected that. *Goddamn vultures*, he thought. Along with the rest of his family, he pushed past them without a word.

Relatives and friends and neighbors packed the church. Joe solemnly shook hands again and again. Dominic Scalzi set a hand on his shoulder. "Garage ain't the same without you, kid," the mechanic said. "Guy who's filling your slot ain't half as good. But what you're doing, it's important. You make all of us proud." His suit gave off that chemical tang, too.

"Thanks, Mr. Scalzi." Joe's mind was only half on what his ex-boss was saying. "Excuse me, please." He went over and sat down with his folks. There were the coffins, looking dreadfully final—and all the more so because they were closed. He knew what that meant: the mortician hadn't been able to clean up the bodies enough to let anybody look at them.

Even in the wool dress uniform, he shivered. He'd seen more than one Yellow Peril crash, and he'd seen what happened afterwards. The first time, he'd thrown up right on his shoes. To imagine something like that happening to his aunt and uncle and his cousins . . . His hands slammed shut into fists. He felt as if he'd let them down.

That was ridiculous. The logical part of his mind knew as much. A funeral, though, wasn't made for the logical part of the mind.

The Mass helped steady him. The genuflections and the sonorous Latin were made, not to drive grief away, but to put it in channels made for its flow. The dry tastelessness of the Communion wafer on his tongue brought the ritual to a close. When the priest intoned, "*Ite, Missa est,*" at the end, he did feel better.

But then came the funeral procession and the burial itself. He was a pallbearer, of course. He was young and strong and healthy, and he'd been twenty-five hundred miles away from where he could do anybody any good. Watching and hearing dirt thud down on the coffins made him bury his face in his hands.

"It's okay," his father whispered in a ravaged voice. "This once, it's okay."

Joe shook his head. It wasn't okay. It wasn't going to be okay. If it were okay, he would still have been back at Pensacola, and his relatives would have been going on about their business. Instead, he was here, five of them lay in holes in the ground, and the sixth wouldn't get out of the hospital for at least another two weeks. Tears dripped out between his fingers and fell on the green graveyard grass.

After the burial, everybody went back to his folks' house. People packed it to overflowing. The war was supposed to have made things hard to come by. The food his mother set out and the booze his father set out made a mockery of that. He wondered how big a hole they'd dug for themselves with such a big spread and with the cost of five funerals. As soon as he did, he shrugged the thought away. At a time like this, you didn't stint.

Everybody kept pressing drinks on him. If he'd drunk all of them, they would have had to carry him aboard the eastbound train on a stretcher. He poured down enough to put a thick glass canopy—like that of a fighter plane—between himself and the slings and arrows of outrageous fortune. Then he walked around with a half-filled glass in his hand, which kept most people from offering him a new full one.

They kept telling him—sometimes in alarmingly explicit detail—what to do to the Japs when he got the chance. He would nod and try to move on. He wanted to do all those things to them. But nobody here seemed to have the slightest idea that the Japs were liable to shoot back.

With everything from Hawaii to Burma lost, with Japanese troops and planes at Port Moresby looking across the Coral Sea towards Australia, Joe didn't see how people could be so blind, but they were. *Civilians*, he thought. He hadn't had much to do with civilians the past five months. He had been one of them. No more. He wasn't a naval officer yet—he wasn't what he was going to be—but he sure wasn't what he had been, either.

Late that night, his father drove him back across the Bay to Oakland. Dad had put away a lot of booze, too, but not even the craziest drunk—which he wasn't—could do anything too drastic at the speeds blackout permitted. "Take care of yourself, Joey," Dad said on the platform. "Take care of yourself, *but pay those bastards back*."

"I will," Joe said. *I hope I will.*

He had no trouble sleeping sitting up, not that night he didn't. When he woke, the sun was hitting him in the face. His head felt as if someone were dancing on it with a jackhammer. He dry-swallowed three aspirins. Slowly, the ache receded. Coffee helped, too.

After so much time cooped up in a seat, Joe felt like an arthritic orangutan when the train pulled into the Pensacola station again. He had trouble straightening up to grab his duffel bag from the rack above the seat. All his joints creaked and popped.

When he got out, he found Orson Sharp waiting for him on the platform. "Hey, you didn't have to do that," Joe said, touched. "I was gonna flag a cab."

Sharp looked at him as if he'd suddenly started speaking Japanese. "We're on the same team." He might have been talking to a moron. "I borrowed Mike Williams' De Soto. Big deal. If you don't help the guys on your team, why should they help you?"

Joe didn't see anything he could say to that, so he just nodded. By the time they'd left the station and gone out into the potent Pensacola sun, he found a couple of words: "Thanks, buddy." He'd left family behind in San Francisco. Now he realized he'd come back to family, too.

PLATOON SERGEANT LESTER DILLON had been a Marine for twenty-five years. He'd seen a hell of a lot in that span. He'd gone over the top half a dozen times in France in 1918 in the desperate fight that hurled the Kaiser's men back from their final drive on Paris and towards their own border once more. The last time, a German machine gun took a bite out of his left leg. He'd celebrated the Armistice flat on his back in a military hospital.

Since then, he'd been in Haiti and in Nicaragua and at the American legation in Peking. He'd served aboard two destroyers and two cruisers. If he hadn't joined the Corps, he didn't know what he would have done with his life. Ended up in trouble, probably. He was a big sandy-haired guy with cold blue eyes in a long, sun-weathered face, and he'd never been inclined to take guff from anybody. If he'd stayed a civilian, he might have knocked somebody's block off and done a stretch—or maybe more than one stretch— in the pokey.

Now he sat in San Diego twiddling his thumbs and waiting for the rest of the country to get off the dime. He was ready to hit the beach on Oahu tomorrow. The Navy wasn't ready to get him there yet, though, or to make sure that the

Japs didn't strafe him or drop bombs on his head or otherwise make life difficult for him.

But things were starting to move. Camp Elliott held so many Marines, it was bursting at the seams. The Navy had bought an enormous rancho up the coast from San Diego. What would be Camp Pendleton would have enough room to train troops even on the scale this war would require. But Pendleton wasn't ready yet. The contractors swore up and down that it would be come September, which did nobody any good right this minute.

He sat in the enlisted men's club nursing a Burgie and smoking a Camel. Across the table from him sat Dutch Wenzel. The other platoon sergeant had almost as much fruit salad on his chest as Dillon did. He was three or four years younger than Les, a little too young to have seen France, but he'd done plenty of bouncing around since. He took a pull at his bourbon and soda. A White Owl sent a thin plume of fragrant smoke up from the ashtray in front of him.

"It's a bastard," Dillon said. "We could tear the Japs a new asshole if we could just get at 'em."

Benny Goodman lifted out of the radio. Wenzel paused to savor the clarinet solo and to blow a smoke ring. "Army didn't," he observed.

"Yeah, well, that's the Army for you." Like any Marine worth his salt, Les Dillon looked down his nose at the larger service.

"Little yellow bastards aren't bad." Wenzel liked playing devil's advocate.

"Fuck 'em. You were in China, too, right?" Dillon didn't need to wait for the other man to nod. The Yangtze service ribbon was blue in the center, with red, yellow, and blue stripes on either side. "Okay, you saw the Japs in action, didn't you? They're brave, yeah, okay, but no way in hell they can stand up to us. Besides, their tanks are a bunch of junk."

"Six months ago, people said the same thing about their planes," Wenzel remarked.

"That's different," Dillon said. "With their tanks, it's really true."

"They're liable to have better ones by the time we can get over there," Wenzel said.

Dillon grimaced. That was a cheery thought. He sipped at his beer. After a moment, he brightened. "Well, so will we. The Army just had Stuarts in Hawaii, and they didn't have very many of 'em. A Lee'll make a Stuart say uncle any day, and a Sherman . . . !" With reasonable armor and a 75mm gun in a proper turret, a Sherman was a very impressive piece of machinery.

Dutch Wenzel nodded. "Okay. I'll give you that one," he said. "But the Japs won't be sound asleep when we hit the beach, the way the Army was when they landed."

Now he admitted the Army hadn't done everything it might have to defend Oahu. The Navy hadn't, either. If Dillon could have got his hands on General Short and Admiral Kimmel, he would have given them worse what-for than the Japs were, and scuttlebutt said the Japs were hard as hell on prisoners. For that matter, the Marines at Ewa and Kaneohe hadn't done enough to stop the enemy, either. *You get caught with your pants down, that's what happens to you*, Dillon thought unhappily.

"I just wish we could get at them," he said, and finished the Burgermeister. Sucking foam off his upper lip, he went on, "Sooner or later, we will. And when we do, I want to be the first guy off the boat."

"First guy to get his ass shot off, you mean," Wenzel said. Dillon lazily flipped the other noncom the bird. He knew Wenzel was as eager to get within rifle range of the Japs as he was.

Two days later, his company commander summoned him to his office. Captain Braxton Bradford was as Southern as his name; he had a Georgia drawl thick enough to slice. "How would you like to make gunnery sergeant, Dillon?" he asked, stretching Les' surname out into three syllables.

"What do I have to do, sir?" Dillon asked eagerly. He couldn't think of anything he wanted more than a second stripe on the rocker under the sergeant's three.

"Hoped that might get your attention." Captain Bradford pointed north. "We're gonna need us a hell of a lot of new Marines. All of those boots are gonna need somebody to show 'em how to *be* Marines. That there's one of the things a gunny is for."

"Oh." Les thought for a moment, but only for a moment. "Thank you very much, sir, but I'll pass."

Bradford's eyebrows came down and together. His nostrils pinched. His lips narrowed. He would have scared a boot out of ten years' growth. Dillon already had all his growth. After machine-gun fire, nothing a captain did or said could be more than mildly annoying. Bradford kept on trying his level best to intimidate: "Suppose you tell me why, Sergeant."

"Yes, sir," Dillon said stolidly. "They're going to throw the old breed at the Japs in Hawaii. If I'm up there at that Camp Pendleton place, I won't get to go. If I stay where I'm at, I will." He threw away the promotion without the least regret. He wanted some things more than that second stripe on the rocker after all.

It was Captain Bradford's turn to say, "Oh." He did his best to hold on to his glower, but his best wasn't good enough. "Goddammit, I can't even get angry at an answer like that."

"Sorry, sir," said Dillon, who wasn't sorry one bit.

Bradford's sour smile showed a gold front tooth. "Now tell me one I haven't heard. You think of anybody who'd take a promotion to go on up to this new place, or maybe to Parris Island or Quantico?"

"Nobody I know, sir," Dillon answered. "You can always ask, though."

"Officers all over Camp Elliott are asking—other places, too, for all I know," Bradford said. "Lots of good people turning 'em down. You aren't the only one. In a way, that's good. We want our first team on the field against the Japs. But we want first-raters showing the boots the ropes, too. If mediocre people show 'em what being a Marine's all about, they're liable to make mediocre Marines."

"Yes, sir." Dillon said no more. With officers, the less you said, the better off you were. He didn't disagree with

Captain Bradford. He knew what was important to him, though—knew very plainly, if he'd turned down a promotion to keep it. And he had.

Bradford studied him. "Nothing I can do to make you change your mind, Sergeant?"

"No, sir." Les almost added another, *Sorry, sir*. But that would have been laying it on too thick.

The company commander made a disgruntled noise down deep in his throat. "All right. Go on. Get the hell out of here."

Dillon thought about asking Bradford if *he* felt like going to Camp Pendleton. He didn't do that, either, though. He just saluted with machinelike precision, did an about-face, and left the captain's office.

As usual, the sun was shining. As usual, it wasn't all that warm even so. It would get up into the low seventies today, and that was it. San Diego had a milder climate than Los Angeles did, even if it was more than a hundred miles down the coast from the bigger city. Mission Bay and the ocean currents and the prevailing winds all had something to do with it. Les didn't know the wherefores, or worry about them. He just knew it stayed mild almost the whole year around.

He was stripping a BAR that afternoon when Dutch Wenzel came up to him. "So," Wenzel said, "you a gunny?"

"Fuck, no," Les answered. "You?"

"Nah." Wenzel shook his head. "Somebody else is gonna have to whip them boots into shape."

"That's what I told Bradford, too." Les set down the oily rag he was using and wiped his hands on a cleaner one. "We're the ones who're gonna have to take those islands away from the Nips. This is what I signed up for, and I'll be damned if I'm gonna miss it."

"I'm with you." Wenzel turned and looked southwest. "Matter of fact, I figure I will be with you. You hit the beach, I'll either be in the same landing craft or the next one over."

"Gluttons for punishment, that's us," Dillon said. The other platoon sergeant laughed, for all the world as if he'd been joking. Dillon went on, "Hell, you haven't even got shot up. You really want a Purple Heart that bad?"

"Look who's talking," Wenzel retorted. "You got it once, and you're dumb enough to come back for more?"

"Damn straight I am," Dillon told him. Wenzel nodded in perfect understanding. They were both Marines.

XII

XIII

Jane Armitage was beginning to think Oahu would make it. There had been times when she wondered if everybody on the island would starve to death. She'd lost at least twenty pounds herself, and she hadn't carried any extra weight to begin with. Everybody she knew had lost at least that much—except Major Hirabayashi and the rest of the Jap soldiers in and around Wahiawa. They hadn't changed a bit. That didn't surprise her, but it did infuriate her.

She knew better than to let the occupiers see what she thought. Almost everybody in Wahiawa knew better than that. Not being noticed was the best thing you could hope for these days.

A lot of what had been pineapple fields before the invasion were rice paddies now. The Japs seemed convinced the islands could grow enough rice to feed themselves. They talked about two crops a year. Yosh Nakayama didn't sound too dubious. Jane put more faith in that. What the Big Five had to say . . . What the Big Five had to say, for the first time since before Hawaii belonged to the United States, didn't matter one damn bit. And if the families who'd run the islands for so long had any brains, they didn't want the Japs noticing them, either.

As for Jane, she had a new crop of turnips and a new crop of potatoes coming in. Eating what she'd raised with her own hands, with her own sweat, gave her pride of a sort she'd never known before. If only there'd been more.

She'd also discovered that zebra doves were as tasty as they looked. Mynahs, on the other hand, were nothing to write home about. She wouldn't have eaten them by choice. Roast mynah beat the hell out of going hungry, though. Nobody was fussy any more.

One of the kids who'd been in her class before the war started came by on a scooter. The school had stayed closed since the Japanese occupied Wahiawa, and especially since Mr. Murphy's untimely demise. Mitsuru Kojima was skinnier than he had been, too, but it didn't seem to matter so much on a little kid—and he hadn't been fat to begin with.

"Hello, Mitch," Jane said. That was what she'd always called him. Most of the Japanese kids in her class had had American names that they used alongside the ones their folks had given them.

He stared at her out of black button eyes. When he said, "My name's *Mitsuru*," he sounded more arrogant than an eight-year-old kid had any business doing. He added something in Japanese. Jane didn't know exactly what it meant, but she'd heard soldiers say it. One thing she had no doubt of: it wasn't a compliment.

Away Mitch—*Mitsuru*—Kojima went. He was just a little kid, but he'd put her in her place. He'd put everything that had been going on in Hawaii before December 7 in its place. He didn't even know it. All he knew was that he wanted to use his Japanese name, not his American one, and that he was entitled to say rude things to a white woman, even if she had been his teacher.

That was plenty, wasn't it?

Jane used the hoe to get rid of a few weeds. No matter how many she murdered, new ones kept popping up. She wasn't much of a farmer, and never would be, but she'd already discovered how hard it was to keep crops alive and stay ahead of pests.

She looked down at her blue jeans. The fabric over the knees was getting very, very thin. It would split pretty soon. None of her other pairs was in any better shape. Some already had patches on the knees or at the seat. Had these been normal times, she would have needed to buy more. She *did* need to buy more, but there were none to buy. Make do or do without was the rule these days.

She suspected she would end up using one pair for fabric to keep the others going as long as she could. Then another pair would have to be cannibalized, then another, until finally she'd have one pair left, made of bits and pieces from all the rest.

And what would happen when *that* pair bit the dust? Jane used a savage slash to decapitate another weed. She might almost have been Major Hirabayashi, cutting off Mr. Murphy's . . . *Stop that*, she told herself fiercely. *Just stop it, right this minute.* But the thought wouldn't go away. Neither would the memory of the meaty thunk the sword had made biting into—biting through—the principal's neck.

Somehow, that memory joined with the way Mitch Kojima didn't want to be Mitch any more to drive home to her that the Japanese were liable to hold Hawaii for a long time. What *would* people do as things from the States wore out and broke down? Could Japan supply replacements? On the evidence so far, Japan didn't give a damn about supplying anything beyond a minimum amount of food— and the Japs grudged even that.

Sudden tears stung Jane's eyes. She stood there in the middle of her plot, clutching the hoe handle till her knuckles whitened. She didn't usually let things get to her. She went on from day to day, doing what she had to do to get by in this horribly changed world. Doing that kept her too busy and too tired to worry about anything more.

But she didn't want to be out here tending turnips and digging weeds and killing bugs when she was thirty-five, or forty-five, or sixty-five, and she was damned if she could see what to do about it. Damned was the word, all right. If this wasn't hell, it would do till she made the acquaintance of the genuine article.

Two Japanese soldiers strode by. Jane bowed and lowered her eyes to the ground. She didn't want them noticing she was upset. She didn't want them noticing her at all.

Every once in a while, they would drag somebody into the bushes and do whatever they wanted with her—to her. Several women in Wahiawa went around with dead eyes and started to shiver whenever they saw a Jap.

If they came for her . . . If they came for her, she had to run. She would have liked nothing better than splitting their skulls with the hoe. But bayonets sparkled on their rifles. If she hurt them, they wouldn't just rape her and they wouldn't just shoot her dead. They'd kill her slowly, and they'd laugh while they did it. They might kill some other people, too, so nobody got any ideas above her station.

They kept walking. She breathed again. She always felt as if she couldn't get enough air into her lungs when the Japs were close by. A man worked in the next plot. He also bowed to the soldiers, but he didn't seem on the edge of panic. As long as he followed the rules they set, he was—probably—safe. No female between ten and sixty could say even that much.

The woman beyond him tensed, the same as Jane had. Having felt the tension in her own bones, Jane recognized it when she saw it. Again, the soldiers went right on past the woman as if she didn't exist. As soon as she saw their backs, life returned to the way she stood.

Jane looked to the northeast. She wished a hundred, a thousand, American bombers were roaring towards her. At supper a few days before, somebody had whispered that the British had attacked a German town with a thousand bombers. Maybe somebody had access to a secret radio. Maybe the rumor was just wishful thinking.

Either way, the sky over Wahiawa stayed clear: bare of clouds, bare of bombers, bare of hope. Jane muttered something she'd learned from Fletch, something she never would have said even when she was all alone while she was married to him. Well, circumstances altered cases, by God. These days, she despised him much more for being part of the Army that hadn't defended Oahu than she ever had for not being much of a husband.

A fly lit on her arm. She smashed it, wiped her hand on her dungarees, and went back to weeding.

* * *

LIEUTENANT SABURO SHINDO was not a happy man. Yes, bulldozers had repaired the airstrip at Haleiwa with commendable speed. Yes, more antiaircraft guns poked their camouflaged snouts into the sky around it now. As far as Shindo was concerned, the B-25s never should have got to Oahu in the first place.

He drove down to Honolulu to make his feelings known. Parts of the Kamehameha Highway were in excellent shape, set to rights not by bulldozers but by gangs of POWs. Shindo thoroughly approved of that. Since they'd surrendered, how were they better than any other draft animals? Why shouldn't Japan use them—or use them up—as necessary?

Commander Genda and Commander Fuchida waited for him in Genda's office. He saluted both of them, then came straight to the point, as was his way: "We should have done a much better job against the Americans. The warning we got was inaccurate, and lulled us into a false sense of security. We would have been better off with no warning at all."

Had his superiors tried to deny that, he would have been very angry. He would have tried not to show it; a man without self-control would never progress in the Japanese Navy—or anywhere in Japan, come to that. But the feeling would have been there. He probably would have taken it out on his subordinates, as mothers-in-law got their own back for what they'd had to put up with when they were daughters-in-law.

But Mitsuo Fuchida only gave him a wry smile and said, "*Hai. Honto.*"

"I think we can expect more trouble from the Americans, too, now that we've poked them in the snout as they poked us," Minoru Genda added.

"I believe that. Bombing the mainland was well done." Shindo didn't have to disguise his envy as he eyed Fuchida. The commander had all the luck! Not only first over Pearl Harbor but first over San Francisco! Either one of those could make a man's career. Both? To have both seemed downright unfair.

Fuchida was modest, too. "It was Genda's idea," he said.

That didn't matter so much to Shindo. A lot of the Pearl Harbor plan had also been Genda's. So what? Fuchida was the one who'd made it real.

With an effort, Shindo brought his thoughts back to the purpose for which he'd come down to Honolulu. "We need more air cover here," he said. "I don't just mean land-based. I mean carriers. *Akagi* by herself isn't enough. That's all the more true if you really do expect the Americans to pay us another call. I don't want them to surprise us again. I want to be the one who goes hunting and finds them first."

"That may not be as easy as you hope, Lieutenant," Genda said. "They have something they call *radar*. We have the name from prisoners we have taken." He went on to explain what the word meant.

The more Shindo listened, the less happy he got. "That's terrible!" he exclaimed. "They can see us coming and guide their planes straight to us?"

"It seems so, when everything goes right," Genda answered.

"They detected us coming in when we attacked Pearl Harbor," Fuchida added.

"*Zakennayo!*" Shindo said. "They *are* idiots, then. Why didn't they scramble their planes? They could have hurt us badly."

"For one thing, they were expecting a flight of B-17s along almost the same course. The bombers came in just a little later, and we shot them up on the ground," Genda answered. He was the man with the facts at his fingertips. He went on, "And, for another, they didn't *really* believe we would attack them."

"In future operations, neither of these factors will hold true." Commander Fuchida's voice was dry.

"I should say not." No matter how phlegmatic Shindo was, he had to fight to keep dismay from his voice. He gathered himself and did his best to think about tactical implications. After a moment, he nodded. "This only makes it more urgent that we reinforce the *Akagi*. If they have a technical edge, we'll need the advantage in numbers all the more."

"Our engineers in Japan were already working on radar," Genda said. "We've flown some of the prisoners to Tokyo so they can give our people more information as that becomes necessary. The principles seem clear. We should be able to deploy sets of our own before long—in fact, we have some trial installations in place now."

"Will we have working models before the Americans try hitting us again?" Shindo asked. Genda and Fuchida looked at each other. Their elaborately casual shrugs said it was unlikely. Shindo hadn't expected anything else. He went on, "I'm just a flying officer. Nobody pays any particular attention to me, here or back in Tokyo. But the two of you, you have the ears of important people." Nobody was more important than Admiral Yamamoto, for instance. "You can persuade them we really *need* more carriers here."

The two commanders looked at each other again. They gave Shindo another matched set of slightly overacted shrugs. Once more, he had to fight not to show the anger he felt. Minoru Genda said, "Please believe me, Shindo-*san*—you aren't the only one who has seen this problem coming. The carriers had other things to do. But now that Admiral Nagumo's force has returned to home waters from its sortie into the Indian Ocean . . ."

"*Ah, so desu!*" Shindo breathed. The Japanese strike force had sunk a British carrier and smashed up ports and shipping along the east coast of India and in Ceylon. That would help Japan tighten its grip on Burma and perhaps clear the way for an invasion of India. Shindo gave back a shrug of his own. The western fringe of the Japanese Empire wasn't his special worry. The eastern edge was. "How many carriers will we get?" he asked eagerly.

"Two," Genda answered.

Shindo had hoped for three, but feared the answer would be only one. "Not bad," he said.

"Tell him the rest," Fuchida put in.

Genda did: "They're *Shokaku* and *Zuikaku*."

Those were the biggest, best, and newest carriers the

Imperial Navy boasted. Shindo wanted to jump up and down and whoop, but showing delight would have been as uncalled-for, as *American*, as showing anger. "Well," he said, "That *is* good news."

"*Hai*," Fuchida said. "If the Yankees want to make a big fight of it, let them. We'll deal with whatever carriers they send the same way as we dealt with the ones we caught off Hawaii when the Pacific War started."

"Oh, yes. Oh, my, yes. I can't wait to start flying off a carrier deck again," Shindo said. "After you've got used to doing them at sea, takeoffs and landings from an ordinary airstrip just aren't the same." He made as if to yawn. Fuchida, also a carrier pilot of great experience, laughed out loud at that. Shindo went on, "And, as we said, the Americans won't take us by surprise again."

"We will make very sure of that," Commander Genda said. "Along with the picket boats, now we'll have the new H8Ks flying long-range patrols to the north and east."

"They're really remarkable machines." Having flown in one, Fuchida could hardly contain his enthusiasm. "Wonderful endurance, good protection, lots of guns, and they aren't even all that slow. Lieutenant Muto said he wasn't afraid of taking on American fighters, not even a little bit."

"No, eh?" Shindo let it go at that. Pilots were supposed to be happy about the planes they flew. All the same, he thought this Muto, whom he didn't know, not just an optimist but a fool. No matter how fast a flying boat was, it couldn't outrun or outmaneuver a fighter. The fighter could pick an attack angle where most of the victim's guns didn't bear, and then. . . . Shindo's thumb twitched, as if on the firing button. American warplanes didn't measure up to Zeros, but they were plenty to deal with the likes of an H8K. He hoped Muto didn't discover the truth of that the hard way.

Still . . . *Shokaku* and *Zuikaku* coming to join the *Akagi*! He went back to Haleiwa a happy man.

OSCAR VAN DER KIRK met Charlie Kaapu on the beach at Waikiki. They both had their sailboards and everything else they needed for a fishing run. Oscar was proud of himself for his invention. Not for the first time, he thought he might have made a mint off it in ordinary days. The trouble with that was, in ordinary days he wouldn't have thought of it. Amazing how hunger concentrated the mind.

And he'd found a real niche no one else was exploiting. The fishing was pretty good out in that area beyond the beach but closer than sampans usually came. He hoped it would stay that way now that more and more people were putting sails on their surfboards.

He didn't begrudge Charlie his sailboard. The two of them had been through too much together for that. The *hapa*-Hawaiian grinned at him, saying, "Here comes the smart *haole*."

"Where?" Oscar looked back over his own shoulder. Charlie thought that was funnier than Oscar did himself. He made a hell of a good audience. The two of them walked down to the Pacific. As usual now, the men fishing at the edge of the surf made way for them.

As they paddled out past the breakers, Charlie said, "You really that smart?"

"What do you mean?" Oscar asked, though he had a good idea.

Sure enough, his buddy said, "You so smart, why you take up with that blond wahine from the mainland again?"

That had several possible answers, from the crudely anatomical to *None of your business*. Oscar chose a mild middle ground: "Susie's not so bad. A lot of people would've flipped, getting stuck in all this. Heck, a lot of people *did* flip. Susie's come through pretty well."

"Yeah, but you fought like cats and dogs last time she was at your place," Charlie said, which was true. "Why bang heads with a broad when it's so easy to find one that doesn't want to yell and throw stuff? Waste time."

"We're getting along pretty good now." Oscar wasn't about to claim any more than that. More would have let Charlie give him the horse laugh if things blew up in his face day after tomorrow.

They put up their sails and let the offshore breeze waft

them out into the Pacific. *Lousy name for this ocean,* Oscar thought, remembering that the word meant *peaceful.* The brief taste of oceanic war he'd got up by Waimea was plenty to sour him on it forever.

After a while, the two of them separated. Charlie swung east, towards Diamond Head, while Oscar went west, towards Pearl Harbor. He thought the fishing outside the Navy base was better than it was farther east. That stretch of ocean had been restricted before the war; sampans hadn't gone through it as they had everywhere else near Honolulu.

The Japs weren't enforcing the restricted zone. Maybe nobody'd told them about it. If they did decide to crack down, Oscar had every intention of staying away from then on out. Falling foul of U.S. authorities would have meant a fine and maybe a little time in the cooler. If a Jap patrol caught somebody where he wasn't supposed to be . . . They'd shoot first and wouldn't bother asking questions.

But as long as there was no rule against being here, Oscar intended to make the most of it. He was well out to sea as he scattered grains of rice and dropped his line in the water. He wanted a good catch, enough to keep him and Susie eating for a while, enough to let him trade some so they wouldn't have to eat nothing but fish till they wondered if they'd grow fins. Whether what he wanted was anything like what he'd get was another question. He'd find out pretty soon.

It *was* going to be a good day. He had *ahi* and *aku* and even a small *mahimahi* on the line as he drew it back onto the sailboard. He gutted the fish as fast as he could. Some of the offal would make more bait. The rest he kicked back into the Pacific. He'd put some distance between this spot and his next one. He hadn't had any trouble from big sharks yet, and he didn't want to start now.

Something splashed behind him. He turned, careful not to upset the sailboard. His jaw dropped. His eyes bugged out of his head. That was no shark, no pod of dolphins, no breaching whale. That was a goddamn submarine, its deck almost awash, its conning tower painted an oceanic blue.

I've had it, was the first thought that went through his

head. He almost jumped into the water and tried to swim for it. Only the sure knowledge that that was hopeless kept him where he was. If they were Japs, maybe they were just intrigued with his contraption. Maybe they wouldn't do him in for the fun of it.

A grubby sailor stuck his head and shoulders out of the top of the conning tower. In purest Brooklynese, he asked, "Hey, Mac, you speak English?"

Better than you do, buddy. Somehow, Oscar didn't burst into hysterical laughter. That proved he owned more strength of character than he'd suspected. He made himself nod. "Yes," he said, adding, "I grew up in California."

"Oh, yeah? Says you." The sailor sounded deeply skeptical. Oscar knew why: he was almost naked and very, very brown. Plenty of tourists figured him for at least *hapa*-Hawaiian, too; they were too dumb to know a blond Hawaiian was a lot less likely than a swarthy Swede. This guy was evidently somewhere on the same level of dumbness. "Don't go away," he said, and disappeared.

A minute later, another man took his place. This fellow looked just as unkempt, but wore an officer's cap with a large grease spot on it. "I'm Woodrow Kelley," he said. "They call me Woody. This is the *Amberjack*, and they were rash enough to put me in charge of her. Who are you, pal? Vinnie says you say you're from California." He didn't sound as if he believed it, either.

"My name is Oscar van der Kirk, and yeah, I'm from California. I graduated from Stanford, matter of fact."

"What are you doing *here*, then?" Kelley asked.

"I like it here," Oscar answered simply. "I liked it a hell of a lot better before the Japs came, but I still like it." He pointed at the sub—the *Amberjack*, Kelley had called it. "What are *you* doing here?"

"Who, me? I'm not here at all. You're talking to a wad-dayacallit—a figment of your imagination." The subma-rine's skipper had a wryly engaging grin. "If I were here, I'd just be looking around, seeing what I can find out. What the hell's that thing you're riding on, for instance?"

"I call it a sailboard," Oscar said. "It lets me fish farther from shore than a regular surfboard would."

"Your idea?" Woodrow Kelley asked. Oscar nodded. Kelley eyed the hybrid craft. "Pretty neat, I'd say. How far could you go on it?"

"Beats me," Oscar answered. "I never tried anything really fancy. All I wanted to do was get out where the fishing was better than it is by the beach."

"Could you sail to another island?" Kelley persisted.

"I suppose so, if the wind didn't let me down," Oscar said. Molokai was only about forty miles away, Lanai not much farther, and Maui a short hop from either one. Even so, he went on, "I'd sure rather do it in a real boat, though. Not much margin for error in this thing. How come?"

"Just thinking out loud," the sub's skipper said. Oscar knew bullshit when he heard it, but he was in no position to call the other man. Kelley went on, "How are things in Honolulu?"

"You don't have spies to tell you stuff like that?" Oscar asked.

"How do things look to you?" Kelley said, another answer that wasn't an answer. That was probably fair enough. A Navy officer wouldn't talk about spies with a guy on a sailboard.

Oscar thought. "People are hungry, but they aren't quite starving. You try and keep your head down so the Japs don't notice you."

"Okay." Kelly nodded. "How about the local Japs?—the ones who were living here before the invasion, I mean."

"Some of 'em—usually older ones, I'd say—like it with Japan in charge. The ones my age and younger are mostly as American as anybody else. But an awful lot of them just want to go on about their business, same as most folks. As long as they get left alone, they're happy."

"Uh-*huh*." Woody Kelley nodded again, this time as if telling himself not to forget that. "How much of the rest of the island have you seen?"

"Not much, not since the war started. There's no gas for ordinary people's cars." Oscar pointed up towards the conning tower. "Hey! Can you do something for me?"

"I dunno. Try me."

"Let my folks know I'm okay, please. Bill and Enid van der Kirk, in Visalia, California. And my brother Roger." Oscar paused. In for a penny, in for a pound, he decided. "And a gal named Susie Higgins has family in Pittsburgh. They ought to know she's all right."

"Visalia. Pittsburgh." Kelley looked down. Oscar hoped that meant he was taking notes. When he looked up again, he said, "They'll get the word. It may take a while. We'll have to clean it up so they can't tell how it came from Hawaii to the mainland."

"Gotcha," Oscar said. "Thanks, pal."

"Any time," Kelley said. "You want some real chow— canned stuff—to go along with your fish there?"

Spit flooded into Oscar's mouth. Canned stuff was precious, not least because so much of it had already been eaten. But, regretfully, he shook his head. "I better not. Anybody sees me coming off the beach with it, he's gonna know damn well I didn't catch it on a hook."

Woody Kelley chuckled. "Okay, van der Kirk. Makes sense. You're nobody's dummy, are you?"

Except for Charlie Kaapu, he was the first person who'd said anything like that in years. Most folks figured Oscar was a jerk for preferring surf-riding to making something of himself. In his occasional gloomy moments, he'd had the same thought himself. So when he said, "Thanks," he really sounded as if he meant it.

"Sure thing," Kelley said. "Listen. One more time . . . You've never seen me. You've never heard of the *Amberjack*, right?"

"Who? What?" Oscar said, and the officer—who couldn't have been any older than he was—laughed again. He touched his index finger to the brim of his grimy cap in something halfway between a wave and a salute. Then he vanished into the conning tower. A hatch clanged shut behind him.

The submarine slipped below the surface. Oscar guffawed. He'd watched subs go underwater in the movies. One thing the movies didn't tell you, though, was that the bubbling submergence sounded like the world's biggest fart in a bathtub.

He gave his attention back to the fishing line. Whether American subs were prowling around Oahu or not, he still had to eat. Keeping a full belly was everybody's number-one worry these days. When he got back to shore, he wondered if he'd hear that the *Amberjack* had surfaced and plastered a Japanese barracks or gun position. Nobody said a word about anything like that, though. He supposed the sub was just on a snooping run. *Too bad*, he thought.

"How did it go?" Susie asked when he got back to the apartment.

"Pretty well," he answered, and displayed a *mahimahi* he hadn't traded. It would be tasty tonight. He wanted to tell her he'd passed the word that she was safe. He wanted to, but he didn't. If he couldn't keep from running his own mouth, how could he expect her to manage it? Even if he couldn't talk, he'd done a good deed. Some people said the best good deeds were the ones you didn't talk about. Oscar wasn't convinced. As far as he could see, this one was just the most frustrating.

JIRO TAKAHASHI LET HIS SONS SAIL the *Oshima Maru* back towards Kewalo Basin. By now, Hiroshi and Kenzo handled the sampan's rig nearly as well as he did. When they were working, they didn't have time to grumble that he'd be taking fish to the Japanese consulate once they came ashore.

Actually, they'd almost given up nagging him about going to the consulate. He was, after all, a Japanese citizen. And he was at least as stubborn as his two blockheaded sons. They weren't about to make him change his mind. The more they tried, the harder he dug in his heels.

By now, even they seemed to have figured that out. As Kenzo swung the sail about to change tacks on the way back to Honolulu, Hiroshi changed tacks on the argument. "Father-*san*, you really shouldn't let the occupiers use you for propaganda," he said.

"Propaganda?" To Jiro, it was nothing but a fancy word. "A reporter asked me questions. I answered them. So what?"

"If the United States comes back to Hawaii, people will remember things like that. They won't like them," Hiroshi said.

"If *that's* all you're worrying about . . ." Jiro snorted. "The United States isn't coming back. These islands are Japanese now. They're going to stay that way."

"Are you sure?" Hiroshi asked. "What about the American bombers? What about that submarine?"

"What about them?" Jiro said. "We bombed San Francisco. Our submarines have shelled the mainland. It evens out. We won't put soldiers over there, and I don't think they can put soldiers over here."

"We?" But Hiroshi let it go. They'd quarreled over that ever since the day the war started. Jiro's *we* focused on his homeland and the Emperor, Hiroshi and Kenzo's on the country where they were born.

Kewalo Basin was getting close. Kenzo made a short tack, then a longer one, and slid into the basin as smoothly as Jiro could have done it. The sampan glided up to a quay. Hiroshi hopped up onto the planking and made the boat fast.

The Takahashis weighed the bulk of the catch on the scales now supervised by Japanese soldiers. The soldiers paid them by weight, as usual. With all food so scarce on Oahu, the finest *ahi* was worth no more—officially—than trash fish Jiro would have thrown back into the sea before the war.

Officially. But Jiro and Hiroshi and Kenzo didn't carry trash fish away from Kewalo Basin. Oh, no. What they carried away for "personal use" was the best of what they'd taken that day: *ahi* and *mahimahi*. They'd eat some, sell or trade some, and Jiro would take some to the Japanese consulate, as he'd got into the habit of doing.

"Waste of fish," Kenzo said as Jiro headed up Nuuanu Avenue. "Waste of money, too."

Jiro stopped and scowled at his younger son. "You mind your business," he said angrily. "You mind it, you hear me? You go sniffing round after that *haole* girl, and then you go telling *me* what to do? *Ichi-ban baka!*" He spat on the sidewalk in scorn.

He wondered whether Kenzo would come back at him as hotly as he sometimes did. If that happened, Hiroshi would pitch in on his brother's side, and Jiro would have to start screaming at both of them. Back in Japan, he told himself, such a thing would never happen. Back in Japan, youngsters respected their elders. He conveniently forgot that one of the reasons he'd been eager to come to Hawaii was so he wouldn't have to bang heads with his father any more.

But this argument collapsed instead of going on to the screaming stage. Kenzo wasn't fair-skinned to begin with. All his time on the *Oshima Maru* had browned him further. Even so, he turned red. He muttered something unintelligible under his breath and turned away from Jiro.

Ha! Jiro thought. *My shot went home like a torpedo hitting an American battleship.* He went his way, while his sons went theirs. He wanted to do some more yelling at Kenzo for sniffing after a *haole* girl *now*, of all the idiotic times. Just as he wouldn't listen to Kenzo, though, his son was unlikely to heed him.

Reiko and I should have arranged marriages for both of them. It would have happened like that in Japan. Here? Well, it might have. But the American nonsense about falling in love and living happily ever after had a grip on a lot of young Japanese in Hawaii. Who could guess whether Hiroshi and Kenzo would have gone along? No one would ever know now. That seemed plain enough.

Up the street Jiro went. The Rising Sun fluttered above and in front of the consulate. As usual, the soldiers standing guard outside both teased Jiro about the fish he'd brought and admired them. Before they went into the Army, they'd mostly been farmers or fishermen themselves—men of his own class. He laughed at their gibes, and sassed them back the same way. They understood one another.

After they got done with those friendly rituals, the soldiers passed him on to the men inside. That was a different business. Those people wore Western-style suits and had fancy educations—you could tell by the way they talked. Jiro spoke to them with careful politeness. He didn't want to seem like some backwoods buffoon.

Consul Kita was in a meeting. A secretary took Jiro to meet Chancellor Morimura. With his long face, his large eyes, and especially with his missing finger joint, Morimura always put Jiro in mind of a samurai of old. His sharp suit somehow strengthened the impression instead of detracting from it.

As always, the young chancellor admired Jiro's catch. *His* good manners seemed natural, effortlesss, not the product of care and a constant struggle against saying the wrong thing. He asked where Jiro had taken the *Oshima Maru* today and how the fishing had gone. And then he asked, "And did you notice anything out of the ordinary while you were at sea, Takahashi-*san?*"

"Out of the ordinary?" Jiro frowned. "I don't think so, sir. Can you tell me what you've got in mind?"

"Well . . ." Morimura steepled his fingers. With that missing joint, one pair didn't meet, so the steeple would have a leak when it rained. "There are reports that another American submarine has been sniffing around—rumors, really, more than reports. Did you see one today?"

"No, sir. I didn't," Jiro answered without hesitation. "I would have said so right away if I had."

"All right. I thought you would." Morimura pulled a map from one of the desk drawers. "And you were . . . here, more or less?" He used a pencil for a pointer to show just where the sampan had gone. Jiro was so impressed, he had to remind himself to nod. The consular official went on, "What time would that have been? Do you remember?"

"We got there late in the morning, and we fished till early afternoon. Then we sailed back to Kewalo Basin," Jiro said. "We made a short trip to keep the fish fresh—not so easy now that ice is hard to get—and we didn't want to spend a night on the sea. Why, sir, if you don't mind my asking?"

"Negative information isn't as good as positive, but it's better than nothing," Morimura replied. "Now at least I know one place where this submarine, if there was a submarine, wasn't."

"It didn't shoot at the island here—I would have heard about that," Jiro said. "From what you tell me, it didn't torpedo any ships. Why would a submarine come at all, if it didn't do any of those things?"

"To spy," the young man from Japan told him. "Submarines and flying boats—those are what the Americans can use. And they do. They keep sneaking around. I don't know if there really was a submarine this time, but there could have been."

"I see." Jiro wasn't altogether comfortable with what he saw. Why would the United States spy on Hawaii if it wasn't thinking about taking back the islands? And if it was, that meant his sons were right. Few fathers faced a more depressing prospect than that.

Some of what he thought must have shown on his face. Tadashi Morimura smiled at him. "Don't worry, Takahashi-*san*. If the Americans try to stick their long snouts back here again, we'll bloody those snouts for them and send them home."

"Good!" The word was an exhalation of relief. Jiro hadn't done badly under the Americans—he'd done better here than he would have in Japan. But not only did he remain loyal to the country that had given him birth, an American triumph and a Japanese defeat would be his sons' triumph and his defeat. He didn't care to think about that.

Morimura smiled again. "You are a true Japanese," he said. "One of those times when you visit us, you must record your feelings about your mother country."

"Whatever you say, sir," replied Jiro, who wasn't quite sure what he meant by that. Tadashi Morimura smiled once more.

WHENEVER THE JAP COMMANDANT STRUTTED into the POW camp that had swallowed Kapiolani Park, trouble followed. Fletch Armitage had seen that was an unbreakable rule. The local Jap who scurried along in the commandant's wake and did his translating for him reminded Fletch of nothing so much as a lapdog at the heel of some plump matron.

The prisoners assembled in neat rows. Fletch thought about how easy mobbing that arrogant Jap and tearing him to pieces would be. The POWs could do it. But the price! It wouldn't be just the soldiers with submachine guns who extracted it, or even the guards with machine guns in the towers out beyond the barbed wire. That slaughter would be bad enough. Afterwards, though . . . If the Japs didn't massacre everybody in the camp afterwards to avenge the miserable son of a bitch who ran it, Fletch would have been amazed.

The rest of the POWs must have thought the way he did. No one charged the commandant as he got up onto a table so he could look down on the sea of tall American prisoners. He barked something in Japanese. Of necessity, Fletch had started picking up a few words of the conquerors' language. He couldn't follow the commandant's harangue, though.

"You prisoners have benefited too long from the mercy and leniency of the Empire of Japan," the interpreter said. Even among the cowed throng of POWs, that produced a stir and a murmur. If this was mercy, Fletch didn't want the Japs getting mad at him. He was filthy. He stank to high heaven. He didn't know how much weight he'd lost, but guessed it was somewhere between thirty and forty pounds. His shirt hung on him like a tent. He could tie a fancy bow in the rope that held up his pants. The only reason he wished he had his belt back was so he might try to eat the leather.

"This mercy and leniency will end," the interpreter went on. "Many of you—too many of you—do not do a lick of work. And yet you still expect to be fed. You want to live off the fat of the land, and—"

After that, the interpreter had to stop. The murmurs grew to raucous jeers. Fletch gleefully joined in. With so many men mouthing off, the Japs couldn't shoot all of them. He hoped they couldn't, anyway.

Those jeers were enough to make even the commandant pause. He spoke in a low voice to the local Jap, no doubt demanding to know what the obstreperous Americans were saying. He didn't like what the translator told him. He shouted angrily and put a hand on the hilt of his samurai sword. Then he spoke again, this time with harsh purpose in his voice.

"You prisoners will be silent. You will be punished for this outrageous outburst. How dare you behave so, you who have forfeited all honor? This whole camp will go without food for three days because of your intolerable action," the interpreter said. "At the end of that time, the commandant will return to see whether you have come to your senses."

Out strode the commandant, the local Jap again in his wake. He was as good—or as bad—as his word. Three days with nothing to eat would have been no fun for men in good condition. For those already on the edge of starvation . . . They were the worst three days of Fletch's life. He didn't go quite without food: on the last day he caught a gecko about as long as his thumb, skewered it on a stick, roasted it over a tiny fire in his tent, and ate it scales, claws, guts, and all. It should have been disgusting. He remembered it as one of the most delicious things he'd ever tasted.

Several men quietly died during the enforced fast. Odds were they would have died soon anyhow. So Fletch told himself, watching two prisoners drag an emaciated corpse towards the burying ground. He half envied the dead man, who at least wasn't suffering any more. And the poor, sorry son of a bitch didn't look a whole hell of a lot skinnier than he was.

The commandant spoke again to the assembled POWs before the kitchens reopened. The warning was clear as a kick in the teeth: if the men gave him a hard time, maybe the kitchens *wouldn't* reopen. By then, Fletch was almost beyond lessons. Standing at attention took not only all his strength but also all his concentration. He didn't have much concentration left; he felt dizzy and light-headed.

Yammer, yammer, yammer. After the commandant spoke, the interpreter said, "Have you learned your lesson?"

Fuck you, you sadistic bastard! Fletch thought it, but he didn't shout it. By that standard, he supposed he had learned his lesson. Instead, he chorused, "*Hai!*" with the rest of the soldiers and managed to bow without falling on his face. It wasn't easy.

More yammering in Japanese. "Perhaps now you will understand that, as men who have surrendered, you have no rights, only the privileges the Imperial Japanese Army graciously pleases to grant you." The translator paused after saying that. If some hotheaded fool told him and the commandant where to head in, the whole camp would pay for it.

Nobody said a word. Only the wind's soft sighing broke the silence that stretched and stretched. Fletch wasn't the only one who'd learned the commandant's lesson.

"As you were told before, when your rudeness began, you eat only by the grace of the Imperial Japanese Army," the interpreter said. "Supplies are short all over these islands. The Army can no longer support idle mouths. If you do not work, you will not eat. It is as simple as that. Do you understand?"

"*Hai!*" the prisoners chorused again. Yes, they'd learned the lessons the Japs wanted to teach them, all right.

"You will be assigned your duties," the interpreter told them. "There is much damage to repair on Oahu, damage caused by your useless, vain, and senseless resistance. You will now have the chance to set it right. Work diligently at all times."

So the commandant blamed the United States for the damage to Oahu, did he? Japan had nothing to do with it, eh? *That's a hot one*, Fletch thought. No matter what he thought, his face showed none of it. The commandant's idiotic opinions weren't immediately relevant to him, the way anything that had to do with food was. The dumb Jap could think whatever he pleased.

Three or four more men keeled over waiting in the chow line once the commandant finally got done blathering. All but one came around when the men in line chafed their wrists and slapped their faces. That one, though, wouldn't get up again till the Last Trump blew. He looked absurdly peaceful, lying there on the ground. Nothing bothered him any more. Fletch wished he could say the same.

When he did get fed, it was the same inadequate ration of rice and greens the cooks had been dishing out all along. It seemed like a six-course dinner at the Royal Hawaiian. Having anything in his stomach felt almost unnatural. And then, after he'd all but inhaled it, he realized he was just about as hungry as he had been before he got it.

It was better and more filling than a seared gecko. That he was reduced to such comparisons told him more plainly than anything else how degraded he'd become since the surrender. And what did he have to look forward to? Slave labor on starvation rations. He wondered how Clancy and Dave had done since they'd bailed out instead of giving up. One thing seemed obvious: it couldn't have been a whole hell of a lot worse.

Of course, the Japs might have caught them and killed them, too. From where Fletch sat now, that didn't look a whole hell of a lot worse, either.

KENZO TAKAHASHI SPLASHED VITALIS on his hands and then ran them through his freshly washed hair. The spicy smell of the hair tonic took him back to the days before the war. The bottle had cost him two nice *aku*. Once he'd rubbed in the lotion, he combed vigorously.

His brother clucked, watching him spruce up. "You sure this is a good idea, Ken?" Hiroshi asked dubiously.

"Not you, too, Hank!" Kenzo exclaimed. He looked down at himself. He wished he had something fancier than dungarees and a work shirt to wear. At least they were clean. Thanks to a Chinaman whose laundry had survived the fighting, he wouldn't have the stink of stale fish fighting the Vitalis.

Hiroshi seemed embarrassed, but he was also stubborn. "Yeah, me, too. Taking out a *haole* girl right now isn't the smartest thing you ever did."

"Oh, Jesus Christ!" Kenzo stuck the comb in his hip pocket and threw his hands in the air. "I'm not going to marry her. I'm not going to molest her, either." He had the small satisfaction of watching his brother turn red as he went on, "All I'm going to do is take her to a movie, so what are you jumping up and down for?"

"You can say that to me. I don't have any trouble with it," Hiroshi persisted. "What if you have to say it in Japanese to a bunch of soldiers? You're asking for trouble, is what you're doing."

"Oh, yeah?" Kenzo said. "I'll tell 'em my dad's in tight with the Japanese consul. They'll leave me alone so fast, it'll make your head swim."

The scary thing was, he was probably right. Connections never hurt anybody. That had always been true, and it seemed all the more so now. Kenzo wished his father had nothing to do with Consul Kita and the rest of the Japanese at the consulate. The more often Dad went over there and talked with those people, the more self-important he seemed to get. He just wouldn't see they were using him as a collaborator. The idea of using his trips over there against the occupiers struck Kenzo as delicious. *Turnabout is fair play.* Who'd said that? He couldn't remember. His English teachers would have frowned. At least he remembered the phrase. That was what really mattered, wasn't it?

Hiroshi said, "The *haoles* won't like it, either."

"Hey, butt out, okay?" Kenzo's temper started fraying. "Let me worry about it. It's my business, not yours."

"You're as pigheaded as Dad is."

That probably—no, certainly—held more truth than Kenzo wished it did. He could either fight with Hiroshi or go get Elsie Sundberg. He chose the latter without hesitation, and without a backwards glance. Just getting out of the tent, getting out of the refugee camp, seemed wonderful. Sunday afternoon felt almost as good as it would have before the war.

Try as he would, though, he couldn't pretend December 7 and its aftermath hadn't happened. Too much reminded him of the changes Honolulu and all of Hawaii had seen. The ruins left from the fighting, oddly, often seemed the least of those changes. The gangs of scrawny POWs clearing rubble with picks and shovels under the guns of Japanese soldiers were much more alien to what Kenzo was used to than the rubble itself. Seeing all those hungry *haoles* made him feel guilty for being well fed.

Before Honolulu changed hands, it had had as much traffic as any other American city of about 200,000 people. Now moving cars and buses had disappeared from the streets, though many were parked at the curb, more often than not sitting on one or more flat tires. Gasoline and diesel fuel for civilian use had simply dried up. If the Japanese couldn't spare fuel for fishing sampans—and they couldn't—they couldn't spare it for anything.

Shank's mare, bicycles, a few horse-drawn carriages exhumed from God only knew where, rickshaws, and pedicabs did their best to take up the slack. Kenzo hated the idea of one man hauling another—by which he proved how American he was. Some of the haulers were *haoles*, which also would have been unimaginable before December 7. The smug look on a Japanese officer's face as a big blond man pulled him along Vineyard Boulevard stuck in Kenzo's memory forever.

The Stars and Stripes was gone. Hawaii's flag still flew here and there, and looked much like that of the USA at a distance, but Old Glory was as extinct as moving motorcars. The Rising Sun had replaced it. Japan's flag flew over post offices and other public buildings, and also over or in front of houses and businesses owned by people who wanted to get in good with the new occupiers. Not everyone who flew the Rising Sun was Japanese—not even close. Plenty of people of all bloods judged the Japanese Empire was here to stay.

Also gone, or nearly so, were the pigeons and the once even more numerous zebra doves. Kenzo knew what had happened to them. Lots of people were hungry these days, and zebra doves weren't hard to catch. The foolish little birds did everything but carry EAT ME! signs. Mynahs, by contrast, persisted. They were less appetizing than pigeons and doves, and also had the brains to fly away when people started sneaking up on them.

Kenzo saw plenty of soldiers and sailors heading down towards the red-light district centered on Hotel Street. The uniforms and the faces had changed. The look of greedy expectation on those faces hadn't.

When Kenzo got farther east, into the *haole* part of town, the absence of moving motorcars was the main thing that told him how times had changed. Lawns remained neatly mowed; trees were still neatly trimmed. A majority of the houses wrecked by bombs and shellfire had been pulled down by now, so their lots looked as if they were just vacant.

Elsie had always liked him fine. Before the war, her folks wouldn't have been so happy if he'd shown up to take her out. They weren't so stuffy about that kind of thing as some *haoles*, but they wouldn't have been dancing in the streets, either. Now . . . When he knocked on the door now, Elsie's mother opened the door and smiled and said, "Hello, Ken. Come in. Elsie will be ready in just a minute." The smile seemed genuine. If it wasn't, she could have gone on stage with it. She used his first name now, too, he noticed, which she hadn't the first time he'd come over.

"Thank you, Mrs. Sundberg," Kenzo answered, and did. So much room inside! He'd had that thought before. The apartment where he'd grown up couldn't have had a quarter as much space. He refused to think about the tent where he was living now.

"Would you like some lemonade?" Mrs. Sundberg asked.

"Sure, if it's not too much trouble," he said. He didn't suppose it would be. Factories had gone right on making sugar even after anybody with a brain in his head could see they weren't going to be able to ship it to the mainland. And, while you could cook with lemons and use their juice, eating them as fruit took real determination.

The lemonade was perfect: sweet and tart and cold. Kenzo had taken only a couple of sips before Elsie walked into the front room. "Hi!" he said.

"Hi, Ken." She smiled.

"You look nice," Kenzo said. She was wearing a sundress, but not one that was too revealing. Part of him was sorry. The rest, the sensible part, wasn't: why borrow trouble with leering soldiers or, worse, with soldiers who wanted to do more than leer? He sniffed. "You smell nice, too." She'd put on some kind of cologne. He could smell it in spite of the Vitalis he'd used on his own hair.

Elsie wrinkled her nose at him. "As long as I don't smell like old fish, I'd smell nice to you."

Since she was right, he grinned back at her. "Shall we go?" he said. Elsie nodded. He drained the glass of lemonade and set it down on a doily to make sure it didn't leave a ring on the furniture. "Thanks very much," he told Mrs. Sundberg.

"You're welcome, Ken," she answered. "I hope you have a nice time." If her voice held the thinnest edge of worry, he could pretend he didn't notice.

Little spatters of rain were coming down when he and Elsie stepped outside. They both ignored it, confident it would let up in a few minutes—and it did. Some adman had no doubt got a bonus for coining the phrase "liquid sunshine." Advertising for tourists or not, though, it held a lot of truth. The sun hadn't stopped shining while the rain fell, and it was warm and more refreshing than annoying.

Elsie looked up at the sky as the clouds drifted away. "If I'd just had a permanent, I'd be mad," she said, and laughed. "I don't think you can get a permanent here any more, so I don't have to worry about *that*."

"I hadn't even thought about it," Kenzo confessed.

"Men." Elsie condemned half the human race. She laughed again while she did it.

"Hey!" Kenzo played at being more wounded than he really was. "Most of what I've been worrying about lately is fish. They don't care about permanents. The rest is trying to keep Dad from . . . you know." He didn't want to say *turning into a quisling*, even if that was what it amounted to.

"Nothing you can do about that. You can't live his life for him," Elsie said. "I'm just glad you don't think that way yourself."

"Nope. I'm an American." But Kenzo looked around to make sure nobody overheard him before he said it. He trusted Elsie—and he was sure she was on the same side as he was. Some stranger? A stranger, Japanese or advantage-seeking *haole*, was liable to report him to the occupiers. He didn't like having to be careful that way, but he didn't see that he had any choice, either.

"I should hope so." Elsie spoke in a low voice, and she looked around, too. She made an unhappy face. "It's like living in France or Russia or something and worrying about the Nazis listening all the time."

"It's *just* like that," Kenzo said. His father's homeland was on the same side as Adolf Hitler. If that wasn't enough to give Dad a hint . . . But Hitler had got a much better press in the Japanese papers his father read than he did in the English-language press. *What can you do?* he thought.

The closest theater was showing a Gary Cooper Western. *What can you do?* Kenzo thought again. He gave the ticket-seller two quarters. The theater had long since run out of tickets. Kenzo and Elsie extended their hands. The fellow stamped PAID on the backs of them. They showed the stamps to the man who would have taken tickets if they'd had any. He stood aside and let them through.

Gone from the snack bar were the familiar odors of hot dogs and popcorn. All it sold were lemonade and salted macadamia nuts—another local specialty. Kenzo got some for Elsie and him. They cost more than admission had.

Japanese sailors had taken a lot of the best seats. Kenzo and Elsie sat down near the back of the theater. They wanted to draw as little notice as they could. When they started to eat their snacks, they discovered that macadamia nuts were a lot noisier to chew than popcorn. Crunching, they grinned at each other.

No coming attractions filled the screen when the house lights went down. Theaters on Oahu swapped films back

and forth among themselves, but even they didn't think
their audiences would get too excited about it. Instead, the
projectionist went straight into the newsreel.

That was a Japanese production. It seemed to have
American models, but watching it was like looking in a
mirror: everything was backwards. The Allies were the
bad guys, the armed forces of the Axis the heroes. To blar-
ing, triumphal music, Japanese soldiers advanced in China
and Burma. Japanese bombers knocked the stuffing out
of towns in Australia and Ceylon. They also pounded a
British aircraft carrier in the Indian Ocean. "*Banzai!*" the
sailors shouted as flames and smoke swallowed the carrier.

Somehow—by submarine?—the Jap newsreel makers
had also got hold of some German footage. Men in coal-
scuttle helmets dashed forward with artillery support on
the Russian front. More German soldiers led bedraggled
Englishmen into captivity in North Africa. And U-boats
sent ship after ship to the bottom off the East Coast of the
USA. Those sinking freighters drew more "*Banzai!*"s from
the Japanese sailors, who no doubt had a professional ap-
preciation of their allies' murderous competence.

By the time the newsreel got done, only a Pollyanna
would have given a nickel for the Allies' chances. "It's all
propaganda," Kenzo whispered to Elsie. She nodded, but
she was blinking rapidly, trying to hold back tears.

Then the Western came on. That was a merciful relief.
You knew Gary Cooper would drive off the Indians, save
the pretty girl, and live happily ever after. The movie had
no subtitles, but the Japanese sailors didn't need any help
figuring out what was going on.

They made a noisy audience. Before the war, ushers would
have thrown anybody that raucous right out of the theater.
Obviously, nobody was going to try throwing the sailors out.
Kenzo expected them to root for the Apaches or Comanches
or whatever the Indians were supposed to be. But they
didn't—they were all for tall, fair, white-skinned Gary
Cooper. "Shoot the savages!" they called. "Kill them all!"
Cooper earned as many "*Banzai!*"s as the German U-boat
captains had.

Elsie couldn't understand the sailors. She did frown when they made an especially loud racket, but that was all. After a while, Kenzo reached out and took her hand. She squeezed his, and squeezed it again whenever the Japanese sailors got uproarious.

"Let's leave before the lights come up," he said as the six-shooter epic drew to a close.

When they went out into the lobby, Kenzo wasn't so sure it was a good idea. Half a dozen soldiers with the Japanese Army's star on their caps were buying lemonade and macadamia nuts there. But he managed to get Elsie outside before their eyes lit on her.

Both of them blinked against the bright sunshine. "Thank you, Ken," Elsie said. "It was nice to get out of the house for something besides trying to find enough to eat."

"Can we do it again?" Kenzo asked, and he felt like jumping in the air when she nodded. He steered her away from the theater, away from trouble. As they started back towards her house, he asked, "Is it really so bad?"

She looked at him. "You're a fisherman. You don't know how lucky you are. Believe me, you don't. Nobody we know who keeps chickens lets them go outside any more. They disappear."

Kenzo suspected she didn't know anybody who'd kept chickens before December 7. He admitted to himself that he might have been wrong, though. Some *haole* families couldn't seem to forget they'd come off the farm in Iowa. He said, "It's not an easy time for anybody."

Elsie drew in a breath. She was going to scorch him. He could tell—something like, *What do you know about it, with your dad licking Kita's boots?* But her anger died before it was born. All she said, quietly, was, "I forgot about your mother for a second. I'm sorry."

Back at the theater, she'd been the one who kept squeezing his hand. Now he squeezed hers. "Thanks for remembering," he said.

When they got back to her house, they stood on the front porch. She spoke the ritual words: "Thank you for a very nice time."

He gave her a kiss. With the sun still in the sky, it was a decorous kiss. If her folks were watching—and they probably were—he didn't want them saying she couldn't go out with him any more. But a kiss it definitely was, and he wore a big, silly grin on his face all the way back to the tent in the botanical garden.

COMMANDER MINORU GENDA and Commander Mitsuo Fuchida met in front of Iolani Palace. They bowed politely to each other. Genda grinned wryly. "Here we are again," he said.

"*Hai.*" Fuchida spoke with amused resignation: "Maybe we'll have better luck this time."

"Well, it couldn't be much worse," Genda said.

The Hawaiian and Japanese flags fluttered over the palace as the two Navy officers climbed the stairs. Japanese guards at the top of the stairs saluted and stepped aside to let Genda and Fuchida in. They climbed the koa-wood interior stairway and went into the library. Their Army counterparts, Lieutenant Colonels Minami and Murakami, were waiting for them behind that Victorian battleship of a desk. The Army men looked no more hopeful about the coming interview than Genda felt.

"We'll try it again, that's all," Murakami said.

Izumi Shirakawa scurried into the library next. As usual, the local man looked nervous and unhappy about translating for the occupiers. Odds were he sympathized with the other side. If he did his job and otherwise kept his mouth shut, no one would have to ask him any questions about that. He *was* a good interpreter. Genda knew enough English to be sure of that.

A soldier stuck his head into the room. Saluting, he said, "The prince is here."

"Send him up," Genda replied. With another salute, the soldier disappeared.

As soon as Minoru Genda saw the man who called himself Prince Stanley Owana Laanui, his hopes began to rise. The swag belly, the double chin, the shrewd eyes with dark patches beneath them—all spoke of a man who thought of himself first and everyone and everything else later if at all. That was exactly the sort of man Japan needed right now.

Genda spoke to the interpreter: "Tell His Highness we are glad to see him and pleased to make his acquaintance."

After Shirakawa turned his words into English, the Hawaiian princeling muttered, "Took you long enough to get around to me." Shirakawa politely shaded his translation of that. Genda followed it even so.

And Stanley Owana Laanui wasn't wrong, even if he also wasn't particularly polite. It *had* taken the Japanese a while to get around to him. The reason was simple: he had a much more tenuous connection to the old Hawaiian royal family than did Abigail Kawananakoa and several other men and women. But they'd all declined to be involved in reviving the monarchy. He was the best candidate left.

"We are sure you are a man who thinks first of your country and only afterwards of yourself," Lieutenant Colonel Murakami said. Genda was sure of exactly the opposite, but hypocrisy was an essential part of this game.

"Yes, of course," the Hawaiian nobleman said, preening a little. In fact, he had more Anglo-Saxon blood than native Hawaiian. That was not necessarily an impediment; it was true of quite a few in the Hawaiian community. Some so-called Americans, prominent ones included, were also part Hawaiian. Intermarriage had run rampant here.

A bigger problem was Laanui's personality. If he were rendered for oil, he could go a long way towards replacing what the Japanese had destroyed in the third wave of attacks on December 8. (People here spoke of it as December 7, but Genda and the strike force had stayed on Tokyo time throughout.) Genda glanced at the photographic portraits of distinguished nineteenth-century Hawaiians on the walls of the library. Judging by Stanley Laanui, interbreeding hadn't been altogether for the best.

But, inadequate as he was, he was what the Empire of Japan had to work with at the moment. Genda said, "You must be sorry, Your Highness, that the United States has occupied these islands for so long and robbed them of their independence."

"Yes, that is very unfortunate," agreed Laanui, who'd probably still been making messes in his drawers when the Americans put an end to the Hawaiian monarchy, and who no doubt hadn't lost a minute of sleep over what had happened from that day to this.

"You can help us set a historic injustice to rights," Lieutenant Colonel Murakami said. He was smoother and more polished than his Army colleague.

Lieutenant Colonel Minami proved as much by adding, "You can give the Americans a good boot in the ass."

Izumi Shirakawa looked pained. "How am I supposed to translate that?" he asked plaintively.

"Just the way I said it," Minami snapped. Sighing, the interpreter obeyed.

And a broad smile spread over Stanley Owana Laanui's greasy face. "By God, that's just what I want to do!" he said. Genda and Fuchida exchanged faintly disgusted glances. Until the Japanese came, the useless noble's main goal in life had surely been to suck up to the Big Five in every way he could.

"You could give the islands a powerful symbol of their restored freedom," Genda said. What he was thinking was, *I hope I can get through this without being sick. It's worse than the North Atlantic in January.*

"That would be good. The Greater East Asia Co-Prosperity Sphere sounds like a real smart idea to me," Laanui said.

Now Genda eyed him in some surprise. That the nobleman knew the Greater East Asia Co-Prosperity Sphere existed proved he wasn't as dumb as he looked. But if he spoke well of it . . . "Hawaii will have its proper role to play, I assure you," Lieutenant Murakami said: a promise that promised nothing. Hawaii's proper place would be whatever Japan said it was. Would Stanley Laanui see that?

If he did, he didn't show it. He said, "The Americans have had their boot heels on us for too long. It's time for a change." If that meant, *It's high time to put a crown on my head*—well, what was the point of this exercise if not putting a crown on his head?

Commander Fuchida said, "You do understand, Your Highness, that the restored Kingdom of Hawaii would still find it advisable to cooperate closely with the Empire of Japan?" That meant, *You do understand you'll be a puppet?* Genda wanted to applaud. He couldn't have put it so delicately himself.

Stanley Owana Laanui nodded. "Oh, yes," he said. He might have been talking about the weather. "After all, you came all this way just to liberate us."

Was he an idiot after all, or only an extravagant hypocrite? Genda would have bet on the latter, but how much did it really matter? Either way, he was a tool, and Japan needed a tool right now. Genda said, "Well, Your Highness, before long your subjects will start calling you 'Your Majesty.'"

"*Yes.*" It was a whisper, Laanui talking to himself, but Genda heard the harsh hunger in it. Idiot or hypocrite, this man would definitely do.

Lieutenant Colonel Murakami must have thought the same thing, for he said, "We will arrange your coronation at a time convenient to you and to the Japanese Empire. I hope this is agreeable?"

"Oh, yes," Laanui repeated, and nodded once more. Then he seemed to take courage, adding, "It could have happened a while ago if only you'd decided to talk to me before you had anything to do with those other people."

Those people with better claims, he meant, though he probably didn't think of it in those terms. No, he was bound to be the hero in his own story—as who was not? Minoru Genda was sad for him. Even with a crown on his head, he was most unlikely to be a hero in anyone else's.

That didn't matter, though, not to anyone but Laanui. Japan would do what it needed to do with him—and would do what it needed to do to him. He might have done better to decline the honor, as other Hawaiian nobles had before him. He might have . . . except he could no more help rising to it than a trout could help rising to a fly. What did a trout know of hooks? Nothing. Nothing at all.

"I think we have an agreement here—Your Majesty,"

Genda said. He gave Stanley Owana Laanui a seated bow. Fuchida, Murakami, and Minami followed suit. Maybe the Hawaiian thought that was the ceremony they would have shown the Emperor. If so, he only proved himself an ignorant trout indeed. The Emperor was hedged round with degrees of ceremony no other mortal even approached.

Let Laanui think what he wanted, though. As long as he sat on the throne and did as he was told, he served his purpose admirably.

XIV

WITH HAWAII IN THEIR HANDS, WITH H8K SEAPLANES AND with submarines to refuel them, the Japanese could keep an eye on the West Coast of the United States. The big flying boats didn't have to carry bombs every time. Getting a look at what the Yankees were up to counted for just as much, maybe more.

Commander Mitsuo Fuchida wished he could go on more H8K missions. But he had a swarm of other duties, and that one flight had to suffice for him. He did attend every briefing by pilots coming back to the Pan Am Clipper berth in Pearl City.

"The Americans are more alert than they were the first time we visited them," Lieutenant Kinsuke Muto reported. He paused to yawn, then said, "So sorry. Please excuse me."

None of the officers who'd gathered to hear him could possibly have been offended. Even for an H8K, the round trip to the mainland took a long time. A pilot who did most of the flying had earned the right to be tired. "Go on, Muto-*san*," Fuchida urged. "You can sleep soon."

"*Hai*," Muto said. "Yes, they are more alert. The blackout is better than it was—not as good as it ought to be, but better than it was. They had fighters out looking for us. Night interceptions aren't easy, but they found one of the planes in the flight."

The officers listening to the briefing exchanged glances, but no one said anything. Like Fuchida, some of the others had to know about the USA's electronic detection gear. Until someone figured out countermeasures, Muto didn't need to.

"There was an exchange of fire," Muto continued. "The H8K has a couple of bullet holes in the tail, but nothing serious. The pilot broke off contact and escaped. After that, all the antiaircraft guns around Los Angeles harbor started going off. The tracers helped us more than they hurt; they showed exactly where the harbor was and lit it for us."

"What did you see?" Three officers asked the same question at the same time.

"More freighters and more Navy ships than we did two weeks ago," Lieutenant Muto answered. "They are building strength. What else can they be building it for but a strike against Hawaii?"

"Did you see any carriers?" Fuchida asked, ahead of anyone else.

"No, sir." Muto paused to yawn again. "I'm sure I didn't. Carriers stand out because of their size and their flight deck. Warships, yes. Freighters—maybe troopships—yes. But no carriers."

"If they aren't in Los Angeles, they will be in San Diego or San Francisco or Seattle." Fuchida spoke with complete assurance. "The question is, how many will the Americans bring against us? That will tell a large part of the story of how the fight goes."

"*Hai. Honto.* Our alliance with the Germans serves us well here." Minoru Genda sounded as precise as usual. Fuchida admired the way his friend saw not only the big picture but also how pieces of it applied to a particular situation. Genda went on, "If Germany and the USA were not at war, the Americans could move more carriers from the Atlantic and attack us with overwhelming strength."

"We're better than they are," Fuchida said.

"We've had the advantage when we met them," Genda responded. "We were lucky to get away from the fighting at the invasion with as little damage as we did. If that one torpedo hadn't been a dud, they would have sunk *Akagi* or hurt her badly. I heard the thud, and then—nothing. I was very glad."

"Gaining the advantage before going into the fight is part of being better," Fuchida said stubbornly. "Our pilots are better than theirs. Zeros are better than their Wildcats. We saw that."

"Wildcats are good enough to be dangerous with a good pilot," Genda said.

Fuchida snorted. "If the pilot is good enough, what he flies hardly matters. But our fliers are better, all in all. As for Wildcats, they can take damage and they're very fast in a dive. Otherwise, the Zero outdoes them in every way."

Major Kuro Horikawa was an Army pilot. He said, "You will have Army fighters and bombers to help you against the Americans."

Neither Fuchida nor Genda spoke right away. Major Horikawa meant well. Telling him straight out that his planes weren't as important as he thought would make him lose face. Commander Genda chose his words with obvious care: "So far, neither side has had much luck striking ships with land-based aircraft."

"Your planes will be very useful if the enemy lands on Oahu," Fuchida added. "We will certainly be fighting out of the range of land-based fighters, though, and probably out of the range of most land-based bombers as well. Our goal is to defend Hawaii as far forward as possible."

"Your G4M bombers are likely to be in the fight." Horikawa couldn't quite hide his resentment. "They're land-based, even if they're Navy aircraft."

"They were specially designed for long range," Fuchida said. "Even so, it is not yet decided whether they will go into the fight." The G4Ms got their extremely long range by carrying lots of fuel. They sacrificed crew armor, self-sealing gas tanks, and structural strength for that range . . . and raids on Australia, Burma, and India had shown them to be extremely inflammable. Fuchida didn't want to talk about that. The Navy didn't air its dirty little secrets in front of the Army, any more than the Army told the Navy about its.

"We need to find out about the American carriers," Genda told Lieutenant Muto. That was the most important order of business for him, too. Any Navy man with a gram of sense knew carriers were what really mattered. *Yamato* and *Musashi* were the biggest, most powerful battleships ever built. But if American bombers or torpedo planes flying off carriers sank them before they came within gun range of enemy battlewagons, what good were they?

As far as Fuchida was concerned, the Navy would have done better to build carriers with the steel and labor that went into the superdreadnoughts. Other opinions had prevailed, though. He couldn't do anything about that but regret it.

"We'll try our best to locate them, sir," Lieutenant Muto promised.

"Good," Fuchida said. "We caught the Americans by surprise here. They had better not do the same to us."

"They won't. We won't let them," Genda said. "If they want to take these islands back, they'll have to go through everything we can throw at them—and we can throw a lot."

THE BUZZ OF THE STEARMAN'S ENGINE grew thinner as Joe Crosetti eased back on the throttle. The runway swelled beneath and ahead of him. He checked his airspeed and angle of descent. Still a trifle steep . . . He pulled back on the stick, just a little, and the Yellow Peril's nose rose a bit. Airspeed was okay, but he checked again to make sure his flaps were down. They were. They had been the last three times he checked, too.

Here came the runway. No time for second thoughts now. He just wanted to do things right. *Ninety percent of the trouble in the last twenty feet* . . . That wasn't a second thought; his flight instructor had drilled it into him till it never left his mind.

Down! The Stearman bounced. Joe's teeth clicked together. It wasn't so smooth as he would have liked, but he *was* down. If he bounced once, he didn't bounce twice. The little biplane taxied to a stop. Joe let out a long sigh and killed the engine. He unfastened his chute and his safety belt.

Lieutenant Ralph Goodwin strode across the tarmac to him. "Not bad, Mr. Crosetti," he said. "Pretty smooth, in fact, up until the very last moment there."

"Thank you, sir," Joe said. "I'm sorry about that."

"I've seen people walk away from plenty worse after their first solo," Goodwin answered. "How does it feel?"

Realization of what he'd done washed through Crosetti. "Swell, sir!" He wasn't the first in his training squadron to solo, but he was ahead of more cadets than he was behind.

"All right, then," Goodwin said. "Let's see you walk away from it."

Joe got out of the Yellow Peril. He gave the wing an affectionate pat. "When can I go up again?"

"Oh, it won't be long," the flight instructor said. "But you'll be moving into a new squadron soon. They may transfer you to another base—they'll have to check the openings here."

As Chapel Hill had before it, Pensacola was starting to feel like home. "I hope they don't," Joe said.

"Wouldn't hurt you if they did," Goodwin told him. "You've got to be able to fly anywhere, not just at a place you know well. But you'll take a step up, any which way. You've done what you can do on this baby. Time to see how you handle a Texan."

"Yeah." Joe knew he sounded less excited than he should have. He didn't want to climb into another trainer, even a more advanced one. He wanted to get into a Wildcat and start shooting down Japs.

Longing must have been naked on his face. Goodwin laughed and clapped him on the back. "Don't look down your nose at a Texan. The Aussies use the ones they make for ground-attack planes and light bombers—Wirraways, they call 'em. And there's even talk that they'll build a version with a cleaner airframe and a bigger engine and use it for a fighter."

That struck Joe as a desperation measure. Of course, Australia was in pretty desperate shape these days. With

Hawaii lost, the USA had a devil of a time getting supplies over there. And the Japs ruled the skies above the northern part of the country. Everybody wondered when they were going to invade, though it hadn't happened yet.

"Come on," Goodwin said. "Let me buy you a beer. You've earned one, by God. Just remember, you've got to walk before you can run. Now that you've soloed, you're not taking baby steps any more."

"Yes, sir." Every word of that was true, and Joe knew it. Even so, he ached to be where the action was. He ached for there to *be* action. "Sir, when are we going to try and take Hawaii back from the Japs?"

"Your guess is as good as mine," Goodwin replied. "I've got no idea—and if I did, I probably couldn't tell you anyway. You want to be along for that, don't you?"

"You bet I do—more than anything," Joe said. "That's why I signed up for this. And after what those bastards did to my uncle and his family—"

"You still have a chance, I'd say," Lieutenant Goodwin told him. "Come on—let's see about that beer."

"Okay." Unlike some of his buddies, Joe didn't do a whole lot of drinking. For one thing, he was still underage. For another, he didn't like the taste of the stuff all that much. But this was a ceremonial occasion.

Goodwin sat him down at the bar in the officers' club and bought him a Budweiser. A couple of stools over, two lieutenant commanders were still going on about the alligator hunt of a few days past. A pair of officers had poured down more than might have been good for them and gone out into the swamp not far from the base vowing to come back with an alligator. Some time later, they'd proudly returned with a deceased snapping turtle tied to a broomstick. They'd taken it to market in Pensacola and got eleven cents a pound for it—plus ribbing that wouldn't quit.

"Here's to you, Joe," Goodwin said, hoisting his own bottle of Bud. "And here's to giving the Japs what-for."

"Thanks." Joe sipped cautiously. Once, when he was a little kid, his old man had let him take a swig from a bottle of beer. It had tasted nasty then. *Am I poisoned?* he'd squeaked. His father had laughed like hell. He still wasn't crazy about the stuff, but it didn't make him want to get his stomach pumped any more.

The colored man behind the bar asked, "This here the gentleman's first solo?"

"That's right," Goodwin told him.

He slid a dime back across the bar. "On the house."

"Thanks." The flying instructor stuck the little silver coin in his pocket. "See, Mr. Crosetti? You don't just save the country when you learn to fly. You save me money, too, so you're really a hero."

"Right." Joe felt silly. Part of him recognized that this was a piece of the celebration, too. The rest was embarrassed all the same. He worked conscientiously at the beer. He supposed one was okay. If he had more than one, he didn't think he'd be able to see straight for his afternoon classes. He had enough trouble keeping up in navigation the way things were.

When he went to the mess hall for lunch, Orson Sharp all but waylaid him. "How did it go?" his roomie demanded.

"I got up," Joe answered. "I got down. I'm still here. I bounced the landing a little, but I'm still here."

"All right!" Sharp grabbed his hand and squeezed it and pumped it up and down. Like everything else about the Mormon, his enthusiasm was perfectly genuine. He'd soloed the week before; his competence was perfectly genuine, too. He seemed delighted to have company, even though Joe was competition for a precious slot on a carrier. "We may be the first room where both guys have soloed."

"Yeah?" Joe hadn't thought about that. "I guess maybe we are. Pretty neat. Maybe we'll stay together when we switch squadrons, too."

"I think we're stuck with each other," Sharp said. "We'll probably make ace the same day."

"Yeah!" This time, the word burst from Joe's throat with savage enthusiasm. And then something else occurred to him. "When you soloed, did your instructor try to buy you a beer?"

"Sure." Orson Sharp was anything but self-conscious.

"What did you do?" Joe asked.

"I had a glass of apple juice instead," Sharp answered calmly. "He said it looked like beer from a little ways away, but that isn't why I did it."

"Why did you, then?" Joe inquired, fascinated by the way his roommate did what he thought he ought to do without worrying in the least about anybody else's opinion. He wondered if he could have matched such self-assurance. He doubted it.

Sharp looked at him. "I *like* apple juice."

Joe laughed out loud. "You break me up, buddy, I swear to God."

"That's nice." No, nothing bothered Sharp. "Before too long, we'll both be breaking up the Japs."

"Yeah!" Joe said again.

THE LANDING CRAFT BOBBED IN THE WAVES as it waddled through the Pacific towards the beach. Shells flew overhead. Lester Dillon remembered those freight-train noises only too well from the First World War. Along with the rest of the men in the clumsy landing craft, he bent down a little, as if that would help if one of those shells came down here instead of on the beach. Booms up ahead said the cruisers and destroyers doing the firing were rearranging the landscape pretty drastically.

Suddenly, the landing craft's bottom grated on sand. The swabbies who were in charge of the ship as long as it was on the water unhooked the landing ramp at the bow. It thudded down, kicking up quite a splash as it did.

Captain Bradford was hitting the beach in this landing craft, too. "Come on, y'all!" he yelled, swarming forward. "Let's go!"

"Move! Move! Move!" Dillon added, even louder. "The longer you hang around with your thumbs up your asses, the better the chance the Japs have of dropping one on a whole bunch of you."

Marines raced out of the boat. Their boots thudded on the steel ramp. Clutching his rifle, Dillon ran for the beach, too. As soon as he got off the ramp, he went into the water more than halfway up to his knees. It was cold water, too. He swore as he splashed shoreward.

As soon as he got up onto the beach, he threw himself flat and aimed his Springfield, looking for targets. "Keep moving, men!" Braxton Bradford shouted. "Can't let 'em pin us down here!"

Landing craft by the dozen were vomiting Marines onto the beach. All the officers and noncoms were screaming the same kinds of things. As Platoon Sergeant Dillon ran inland, he looked back over his shoulder. The destroyers and cruisers had ceased fire, but they were still out there, ready to drop shells on anybody who gave the leathernecks trouble.

Dillon caught up with the company commander. "How are we doing, sir?"

Bradford sprawled behind a bush going brown from lack of rain. "Well," he drawled, "it's a hell of a lot easier when they don't shoot back."

"Ain't that the truth?" Dillon agreed. "This doesn't look a hell of a lot like a Hawaii beach, either. Ocean's sorta green, sorta gray, not blue like it's supposed to be."

"Damn near froze my feet when I went in, too," Bradford said. "I remember the first time I went into the Pacific in California. Hell, it was a hot day, and there I was at the goddamn beach, so I charged right on into the water. A minute later, I charged right on out again, too. Damn near—*damn* near—froze my nuts off."

"I believe it," Dillon said. "Like you say, the weather can get hot, but the ocean never warms up."

Bradford looked up to the sky. "Other thing is, we don't have any of those goddamn Zeros strafing our asses here. If we can't get air superiority—"

"Sir, if we can't get air superiority, we'll never make it to the beach, let alone off it," Dillon said.

"Uh-huh." The company commander nodded. Dillon had seen more optimistic nods. Hell, he'd felt more optimism himself. Zeros had proved much more effective than anything anybody had dreamt the Japs owned. From Pearl

Harbor to Australia to Ceylon, they'd chewed up Wildcats and Buffaloes and Warhawks and Spitfires. Allied planes hadn't done a whole hell of a lot of chewing back, either.

"Up to the flyboys," Dillon said.

"Yeah." Captain Bradford nodded again. "They reckon they can do it—and we get to go along for the ride and find out if they're right."

"That's the sixty-four-dollar question, all right," Dillon agreed. If the Japs kept control of the air over Hawaii . . . Well, Pearl Harbor had shown what air superiority was worth. And if it hadn't, the sinking of the *Prince of Wales* and the *Repulse* and the disaster in the Philippines would have. It wasn't a battleship world, not any more—carriers had more clout.

The Marines continued their advance inland. Dillon kept shouting to his men to be careful. He kept warning them that it wouldn't be so easy when the real thing started. He kept reminding them that the Japs would shoot back, and nobody was doing any of that here. And he kept seeing that all his warnings were going in one ear and out the other. More than half the Marines he led hadn't been born when that machine-gun bullet took a bite out of his leg in 1918. They didn't know what being under fire was like. Live-fire exercises made them think they did, but those weren't the real thing. Nobody shot to kill in live-fire exercises. The Japs, on the other hand, would be playing for keeps.

Dillon wasn't worried that his Marines would turn tail when they came under fire. He wasn't even worried that they would freeze up and not shoot back. He had absolute confidence in their courage. He did fear that too many of them would stop bullets because they leaped before they looked, or because they didn't know what to look for before they leaped. A few hours—sometimes a few minutes—of real combat would teach a lot of those lessons. Sadly, he didn't know anything else that would. Some of *his* Marines would get killed before they could learn, and that pained him.

Unlike a real amphibious assault, this one ended with a

bus ride back down to Camp Elliott. Some of the men pointed to Camp Pendleton, where bulldozers and steam shovels and carpenters and masons swarmed. The big new base was going up lickety-split. Les Dillon remained glad he had nothing to do with it. The men on this bus with him—*they* were the ones who'd go into action first, and that was what he wanted to do himself.

Some of them were looking out across the Pacific instead of at the construction on land. His own eyes kept sliding west and south, too. A little more than two thousand miles away: that was where he wanted to be.

In a low voice, he asked Captain Bradford, "We really gonna ship out soon, sir? Is that the McCoy, or is it just the usual bullshit?"

"Well, you never can tell for sure," Bradford answered, just as quietly, "but I'd sure as hell be ready to sling a duffel over my shoulder and haul ass in a hurry if I was you."

"Right." Excitement flared through Dillon. He sometimes wondered why. He *did* know what combat was like—and he wanted to go back to it? But, crazy or not, he did. "I'll have the men ready, too," he promised.

"Reckoned you would," the company commander said, and not another word after those three. Dillon was proud.

He let his Marines know what was what without making a big fuss about it. He didn't want them too excited, in case the rumor turned out to be just a rumor after all. The next day, Dutch Wenzel tipped him a wink. The other platoon sergeant thought it would happen, too, then.

And it did happen. Four days later, they were ordered onto buses again, this time to the port of San Diego. They climbed aboard the *B. F. Irvine*, a converted freighter. By everything Dillon could see, the conversion was hasty and incomplete. The accommodations he and his men got were better than the railroad cars he'd used in France. Of course, those had been marked 36 MEN OR 8 HORSES. These weren't a hell of a lot better, either.

Seeing the narrow, gloomy, airless space in which he'd make the journey to Hawaii, a Marine said, "I ought to complain to the Red Cross."

"Fuck that," his buddy answered. "They're treating us like dogs, so complain to the goddamn SPCA."

They had their first abandon-ship drill a little more than an hour after leaving port. Part of Les approved; they were doing what they needed to do in case of disaster. The rest of him worried. Did they have so little confidence that they could evade Japanese subs? If they did, how much trouble was the invasion fleet liable to be in?

He shrugged, down there in the bowels of the troopship. He couldn't do anything about it, one way or the other.

CORPORAL TAKEO SHIMIZU FELT EVERY GRAM in the pack on his back. He and his men had spent too long in Honolulu, and hadn't done enough while they were there. Now they were marching again, and he could feel that they hadn't done it for too long. He could also feel that it was summertime. Oahu didn't get cold in the winter or hot in the summer, but it was warmer now than it had been when he fought his way south across the island. As the sweat streamed down his face, he felt every degree, too.

"Come on, keep it up!" he called to his men. "You've got soft! You've got fat! You've got lazy!" He'd got soft and fat and lazy himself, but he wasn't about to admit it to the soldiers in his squad. He would march till he fell over dead before he showed weakness. Noncoms had to act that way. If they didn't, if they let their men get the edge on them, they couldn't hope to do their job.

The very landscape had changed since he last came this way. It wasn't that he was heading north instead of south, either. What had been fields full of sugarcane and pineapple were now rice paddies. That gave the countryside a much more familiar feel. The men who had grown the other crops were now hard at work to feed the island. Some of them looked up from the fields as the regiment marched by. Others just kept on with what they were doing.

"I wonder if they'd rather be doing this or the work they had before," Senior Private Furusawa said. He'd always had an inquiring turn of mind.

"They'd rather eat," Shimizu said. "You can't live on that other stuff, even if it's nice once in a while. Rice, now . . ." He didn't go on, or need to. To him, to all of them, rice *was* food. Everything else added variety.

All the blown bridges on the north-south highway had been repaired. All the damage from mines and shells had been fixed, too. Cars and trucks and tanks could travel without any trouble. So could soldiers.

Shiro Wakuzawa asked, "Are the Americans really going to attack us? Didn't we teach them enough of a lesson when we took Hawaii away from them?"

"Who knows for sure?" Shimizu answered. "That's not for us to worry about. If they try to land on Oahu, what we've got to worry about is throwing them back. We can do it—if we're in the right place when they try to land. If we're there and they don't have the nerve to try anything, that's all right. But if we aren't and they do, then we've got a problem."

Mynah birds scolded the Japanese soldiers as the men marched north. Corporal Shimizu did his best to ignore them. They were noisy and pushy and had no manners. *They might as well be Americans*, he thought.

When he said that out loud, the men in his squad laughed. Of course, any joke a noncom made was automatically funny to the men he commanded. Corporals and sergeants had too many ways to avenge themselves on soldiers who didn't think so—or, more to the point, who acted as if they didn't think so.

Shimizu remembered the other birds he'd seen when he first came to Oahu: the pigeons and the little blue-faced doves. They'd got thin on the ground in Honolulu, and there weren't many of them left in the countryside, either. He had no trouble figuring out why: they were good to eat, and food had got scarce. When supplies came regularly from the U.S. mainland, nobody'd bothered the birds. Nowadays, though, they were nothing but meat.

More slowly than they should have, the Japanese soldiers reached the crossroad that led west to Schofield Barracks. A gang of American prisoners was repairing it, as the

POWs had already done on the north-south road. The prisoners were a sorry-looking lot: skinny and dirty and dressed in the tattered remnants of the uniforms they'd worn before giving up.

"See what happens when you surrender?" Shimizu said, pointing their way. "That's what you get. That's what you deserve. Better to die fighting. Better to hug a grenade to your chest and get everything over with at once. Then, at least, you don't disgrace your family. *Honto?*"

"*Honto!*" his squad chorused. No hesitation, no disagreement. Surrender was the ultimate disgrace. How could you hope to go back to your home village after falling into the enemy's hands? You couldn't. You'd bring dishonor with you, and all your kin would lose face. Yes, better by far to tap a grenade against your helmet and then hold it tight. Everything would be over in a hurry, and your spirit would go to the Yasukuni Shrine.

After the turnoff for Schofield Barracks came the town of Wahiawa, more of it to the east of the road than to the west. Locals on the street bowed, but didn't pay much attention to the regiment passing through. By now, they were bound to be used to Japanese soldiers coming and going. They were thin, too, though not so scrawny as the American prisoners. Shimizu thought most of them were skinnier than the civilians in Honolulu. He wondered how much of the fish the sampans caught came this far inland. Not much, unless he missed his guess.

No matter how skinny they were, some of the white women wore scandalously little: nothing but shorts that came more than halfway up their thighs and tops that covered their breasts but not much else. A yellow-haired woman perhaps a few years older than Shimizu walked along the sidewalk with her back very straight, doing her best to pretend the Japanese soldiers in the street didn't exist.

"They look like whores," somebody behind Shimizu said.

Soldiers nodded, though he wondered why. No whore in Japan would show herself in public wearing so little; it would shame her. From what he'd seen in the brothels in

Honolulu, the same held true here. None of the women in Wahiawa seemed the least bit ashamed.

The women did seem cool and comfortable in the warm weather. Shimizu's feet were sore. Sweat dampened his uniform. He could smell the men he marched with. They didn't have the sour, beefy reek a like number of Americans would have, but he knew they were there. He sighed, wishing he were marching with almost-naked women instead of his squadmates. That would sure liven up the day.

Not far beyond Wahiawa, the regiment took a ten-minute break. "Leave your boots on," Shimizu warned his men. "If you take them off, your feet will swell up and you won't be able to get them back on again. You wouldn't like that." Anyone who couldn't get his boots back on would have to finish the march barefoot. No, the men wouldn't like that a bit.

When the sun went down, the regiment was short of Haleiwa and had to camp by the side of the road. The officers muttered and fumed at that, which meant Shimizu and the other noncoms were obliged to mutter and fume, too. He didn't know about anybody else, but he growled at his squad more for form's sake than from conviction. If he'd had to march another hundred meters, he was sure he would have fallen over dead.

Cooks who'd brought their field kitchens on horse-drawn carts fixed rice for the men. Some of the soldiers had fallen asleep and couldn't be shaken awake even to eat. "More for the rest of us," Senior Private Furusawa said.

"Yes, why not?" Shimizu agreed. "For them, sleep is more important. As for me, I wouldn't be sorry if the cooks slaughtered the horses and fed them to us, too." *Hashi* flashing in the firelight, he emptied his bowl amazingly fast—but he wasn't the first man done. The soldiers who were hungrier than they were sleepy were *hungry*.

Shimizu told off soldiers to stand watches through the night. One of the benefits of his none-too-exalted rank was that he got to assign such duties instead of enduring them. He cocooned himself in his blanket and fell asleep. Though he'd been able to eat, exhaustion made the ground seem softer than the mattress on his cot back in the Honolulu barracks.

He wasn't so happy when he woke up a little before dawn the next morning. He felt stiff and sore. Grunting, he stretched and twisted, trying to work out the kinks. Then he undid his fly and pissed into a rice paddy. Men lined up along the paddy's muddy edge to do the same.

After more rice for breakfast, the regiment set out again. For the first little while, Shimizu felt like his own grandfather—except that his grandfather had fought in the Sino-Japanese War and always went on about how soft the modern generation was. Then his muscles loosened up and he just felt tired. Tired wasn't so bad; after yesterday's march, he'd earned the right to be tired.

"The sea! The sea!" Someone pointed north, towards the Pacific.

"It's the same sea that washes up against Japan," Yasuo Furusawa said. He was right, of course. Corporal Shimizu knew that. Like everyone else in the regiment, he'd sailed across every centimeter of it in the *Nagata Maru*. There hadn't been any place where he'd had to get out and walk. But it didn't always feel like the same sea. It was so much warmer, so much bluer, and—except on north-facing beaches in wintertime—so much calmer.

"Remember the waves we rode going up onto the beach?" Shimizu said. "Didn't that make your bottom pucker up? And it could have been worse. It could have been too nasty to let us land at all. I don't know what we would have done then." He had a pretty good idea, though. Ready or not, they would have tried to land. They hadn't come all that way to sit in the troopships.

"If the Yankees try to land now, the waves won't throw them around," Corporal Aiso said. "It's calm and peaceful during the summer. So it'll be up to us to shoot them on the beaches if they get that far."

"If the Navy's doing its job, they won't," Shimizu said.

"If the Navy was doing its job, the Americans wouldn't

have bombed us here," Aiso said. "If the Navy was doing its job, American subs wouldn't be shelling us and sinking our ships and spying on us."

"Well, that's the Navy," Shimizu said, and everyone who caught his tone of voice nodded. *What can you do about such people?* he might have asked. Of course, a sailor would have said, *Well, that's the Army*, and sounded exactly the same—half exasperated, half amused. Neither service thought the other had the faintest idea what it was doing.

When the regiment got up to Haleiwa, near the north coast of Oahu, Shimizu expected to turn right and march east. He'd come ashore near Waimea, and the march up from Honolulu had felt a little like running the film of the invasion in reverse. He was taken aback when the column turned left instead. But the beaches past which the soldiers marched were broad and friendly, the country behind them flat and inviting for an invader—flatter and more inviting than where he'd landed. Mountains rose to the south and west, yes, but behind a good stretch of plain now converted to rice paddies.

Fighters with the Rising Sun on flanks and wings rose from an airstrip not far inland. Shimizu smiled to see them as they roared overhead. The handful of planes the Americans managed to put in the air had done damage out of proportion to their numbers till Zeros dealt with them. Unlike the Americans, Japan wouldn't be caught sleeping. The planes zooming out helped guarantee that.

Grass and ferns had grown over the works the Yankees had dug near the beaches to try to hold back the Japanese Army. The plants and the rain had softened their outlines, as well as those of the bomb craters and shell holes from the Japanese bombardment that had forced the enemy soldiers away from their hastily dug holes.

Lieutenant Horino led his platoon to some of the battered, abandoned American works. "We are going to restore these, men," he said, by which he meant, *You are going to restore these*—he wasn't about to pick up a shovel himself. "We are going to restore these, and meet the enemy on the beach if the Navy screws up and lets him land. If he does, his bones will bleach on the sand. *Honto?*"

"*Hai!*" the soldiers shouted, Takeo Shimizu loud among them.

"Not one American will set foot on the grass. *Honto?*"

"*Hai!*"

"Then get to work."

A corporal wasn't above digging in with an entrenching tool, even if a lieutenant was. As Shimizu cleared trenches and built breastworks, he looked out to sea. The Americans had sited this position well. If not for destruction rained on them by airplanes and warships, they might have held it. *We* will *hold it*, Shimizu thought, and added more dirt to the breastwork.

COMMANDER MINORU GENDA STOOD BY the edge of the Wheeler Field runway. Right on schedule, two Mitsubishi G4M bombers flew in from the northwest and landed on the runway. The G4M had proved very useful. It was almost as fast as a fighter, and it had extraordinary range, which meant the Japanese Navy sometimes, as now, ferried important passengers across long stretches of ocean in G4Ms.

But the bomber wasn't perfect. Everything came with a price. The Mitsubishi plane burned like a torch if it got hit.

No danger here, though; there were no hostile aircraft within fifteen hundred kilometers of Hawaii. The G4Ms taxied to a stop, one behind the other. Vice Admiral Matome Ugaki got out of the first plane: a short man with a face so round, it was almost wider than it was long. From the second G4M descended the officer for whom Ugaki served as chief of staff: Admiral Isoroku Yamamoto. Yamamoto had a firm rule that he and his chief aide should not travel in the same aircraft, lest one disaster overwhelm them both.

Yamamoto looked around as Genda hurried across the tarmac towards him and Ugaki. "So this is Oahu," said the commander of the Combined Fleet.

"Yes, sir," Genda said, saluting. "Have you never been here before?"

"I've seen Honolulu on my way to and from the United States," Yamamoto answered. "I never got back into the countryside, though. How about you, Ugaki-*san*?"

"This is my first time here, sir," Ugaki said. "Pretty. The weather's nice, *neh*?"

"*Hai*," Genda said. "If the weather were all we had to worry about, we wouldn't have anything to worry about, if you know what I mean."

Yamamoto smiled. As always, Genda was struck by the sheer physical presence of the man. Yamamoto was short—though not quite so short as either Genda or Ugaki—but energy blazed from him. He said, "Well, we didn't come here to take on the weather."

"No, sir," Genda agreed. "We are honored that you have come to take personal charge of the defenses of Hawaii." He bowed, thinking, *And you and Ugaki both outrank General Yamashita. About time the Navy was in charge of things again.*

Shrugging broad shoulders, Yamamoto answered, "The highest-ranking officer should be in charge at the most important point, *neh*? Nothing is more important for the Empire than holding Hawaii. You were the one who first pointed that out: here we have the great shield behind which the rest of our conquests have proceeded. The Americans are not blind to this. In their hands, Hawaii is a shield no more, but a dagger aimed at our heart."

Commander Genda bowed. "You are too generous, sir."

"I don't think so," Yamamoto said. "I'll want to get out to sea as fast as I can. The Yankees are on their way, eh?"

"So it seems, sir," Genda replied. "They appear to have slipped by our submarines at night, but flying boats report that large numbers of Navy ships and transports are no longer in West Coast harbors."

"Why haven't the famous flying boats found the enemy fleet at sea, then?" Vice Admiral Ugaki asked irritably.

"My guess is, the Americans are trying something sneaky," Yamamoto said before Genda could reply. "They'll come down on us out of the north, or maybe even from the northwest, instead of making a straight run from their Pacific coast. And the straight route is the one the flying boats and the subs will be patrolling most. What do you think, Genda-*san?*"

"That's how it looks to me, too, sir," Genda said. "They'll assemble somewhere up in the north, hope they can defeat our carrier force, and try to land if they do."

"Good enough," Yamamoto said. "Well, the sooner we get out to *Akagi* and go after them, the better off we'll be. We have better planes and better pilots, and I aim to take advantage of it."

"Yes, sir," Genda said, and then, "You'll want to spend the night here on Oahu, won't you, and fly out in the morning? You've been traveling for a long time."

By the look on Vice Admiral Ugaki's face, he would have liked nothing better. But Yamamoto shook his head. "I'll rest when I get there," he said. "I want to make sure I'm in place when the fighting starts. If I wait, it may start without me. You do have aircraft here that can land on a carrier?" His bulldog expression said somebody—probably Genda—would catch it if he had to wait while planes came back to Oahu from the *Akagi.*

But Genda pointed to a pair of Aichi dive bombers. "They are at your service, sir."

"Good." There was never anything halfway about Yamamoto. If he was unhappy, he was very unhappy. If he wasn't, everything was rosy. He walked over to the edge of the runway, undid his fly, and eased himself on the grass. When he came back, he was smiling. "That's a lot better than trying to piss in a tin can while an airplane's bouncing all over the sky. Go on, Ugaki-*san*, while you've got the chance. You won't make a mess here."

"*I* didn't make a mess," Ugaki said with dignity, but he walked off the runway and turned his back, too.

Admiral Yamamoto threw back his head and laughed. Now that he saw he'd got what he wanted, he was in a good mood. He cocked his head to one side and studied Genda. "Are you feeling well, Commander? You look a little peaked."

Genda bit down on his lower lip in embarrassment. He

hadn't realized it showed. "I'm . . . all right, sir." He gave himself the lie, for he started coughing and wheezing and had trouble stopping. "I've had a little trouble with my lungs lately; nothing too bad, though."

"You ought to see a physician," Yamamoto said.

"I intend to, sir—after we beat the Americans."

"All right, as long as you're well enough to help us fight them. You won't do the Empire any good if you're flat on your back."

"Yes, sir. I understand that. I'll get through the fight." Genda knew he was trying to convince himself as well as Admiral Yamamoto. There'd been a couple of times when he almost did go to the doctor in spite of the action looming ahead. But whatever was troubling his chest had eased back, and here he was.

Here came the officer in charge of Wheeler Field: a lieutenant colonel. He bowed to Yamamoto and Ugaki in turn. "Honored to have you here, sir," he told the commander of the Combined Fleet. "I trust you'll do me the honor of dining with me tonight?"

"I'm afraid not," Yamamoto said, and the Army officer's face fell. Yamamoto did take the time to make sure the man understood it was nothing personal: "My chief of staff and I are going straight out to our flagship, as soon as you can put pilots into those Aichis. The Americans won't wait."

In the face of such formidable devotion to duty, the lieutenant colonel said the only thing he could: "Yes, sir."

Genda knew a certain amount of relief. At least Yamamoto didn't propose flying out to the *Akagi* himself. He had his wings, yes, but Genda didn't think he'd ever made a landing on the deck of a flattop. Yamamoto caught his eye and raised one eyebrow slightly. Genda gave back an almost imperceptible nod. Yamamoto said, "And make sure you have a plane for Commander Genda as well. His assistance is bound to prove invaluable."

"I'll take care of it, sir," the Army man promised. His eyes raked Genda. *Who the devil are you?* he might have asked. Genda didn't enlighten him.

Inside half an hour, Admiral Yamamoto and Vice Admiral Ugaki were winging their way north. A little later, the lieutenant colonel scraped up another Aichi D3A1 and a pilot to ferry Genda out to the *Akagi*. He still didn't know who Genda was or what he'd done to deserve singling out by name by the most famous officer in all the Japanese armed forces. That suited Genda—who cared for results much more than for renown—just fine.

The flight didn't suit him so well. The longer it went on, the less happy his chest got. He tried willing the congestion away, as he had before, but didn't have much luck. He huddled in the dive bomber's rear seat, doing his best not to move. When the plane came down in the controlled crash that was a carrier landing, he had to bite back a groan.

Getting out of the Aichi after the pilot opened the canopy took all his strength. He dragged himself down to the flight deck and stood there swaying. Captain Kaku, who'd come out of the island onto the deck to greet him, took one look at him and snapped, "Go to the dispensary."

"I'm all right, sir," Genda protested feebly.

"Go to the dispensary. That's an order, Commander." Kaku's voice had not a gram of give in it. Genda gave back a miserable salute and obeyed.

A doctor with round-lensed spectacles like Prime Minister Tojo's listened to his heart and lungs with a stethoscope. "I'm very sorry, Commander, but you have pneumonia," he announced. "It's a good thing you came to see me. You need a spell of bed rest."

"But I can't!" Genda said.

"You have to," the doctor said firmly. "Dying gloriously for the Emperor is one thing. Dying because you don't pay attention to what germs are doing to you is something else again. You'll be fine if you take it easy now. If you don't, you won't—and you won't do your country any good, either."

"But—" Commander Genda felt too rotten to work up a good argument. He supposed that went a long way towards proving the doctor's point. They put him in sick bay. He lay on an iron-framed cot staring up at the gray-painted steel ceiling not far enough overhead. For *this* he had come out to *Akagi*?

*   *   *

JIM PETERSON LOOKED DOWN AT HIS HANDS. By now, the blisters he'd got when he started road work had healed into hard yellow calluses. No, his hands didn't bother him any more. A steady diet of pick-and-shovel work had cured that.

Trouble was was, the work was the only steady diet he had. No matter what the Japs promised, they didn't feed road gangs much better than they had the prisoners back at the camp near Opana. If the American POWs starved— so what? That was their attitude.

And getting enough to eat wasn't even Peterson's chief worry. If *that* wasn't a son of a bitch, he didn't know what would be. Making sure nobody in his shooting squad—and most especially not Walter London—headed for the tall timber took pride of place, if that was the right name for it. The man didn't give a damn about anything or anybody but himself. Everybody knew it.

"He's gonna get us all killed, you know that?" Gordy Braddon said as they dumped dirt and gravel into a hole in the road near Schofield Barracks. "He's gonna get us all killed, and that ain't the worst of it. You know what the worst of it is?"

"Depends," Peterson said judiciously. "Maybe you mean he'll do something stupid and get himself caught and shot, too. Or maybe you mean he won't just get us killed— he'll laugh about it, too."

The PFC stared at him. "Shit, Corporal—you readin' my mind or what?"

"Hell, anybody with eyes can see what that London item is like," Peterson said. "He'd take money out of a blind man's cup—and then, if he thought somebody was watching, he'd toss back a nickel so he'd look good." Quietly, out of the side of his mouth, he added, "Careful. He's liable to be listening."

Gordy Braddon looked around. "Sorry. Don't reckon he heard me, though."

"Okay." Peterson checked, too, a lot more subtly. "Yeah, I guess you're right. Can't blame me for being jumpy, though."

"Only thing you can blame anybody for these days is letting his pals down. You don't do that, by Jesus," Braddon said. Two dive bombers blazoned with Rising Suns flew north over their heads, not too high. Braddon watched them till they were out of sight. "I think the Japs are jumpy, too. They've been doing a lot more flying lately than they had for quite a while. Wonder what the hell it means?"

"Just one thing I can think of." Peterson had watched the dive bombers, too, watched them with hatred in his eyes. Planes like that had done horrible things at Pearl Harbor—and, he gathered, against the *Enterprise*, too. Scowling still, he went on, "They must figure we're going to try to take the islands back."

"Christ!" Braddon said reverently. "Hope to God you're right. You think we can do it?"

Before Peterson could answer, the Japanese sergeant who did duty as straw boss for the work gang pointed at the two of them and said, "*Isogi!*" That meant something like, *Make it snappy!* As slave drivers went, he was a fair man. He warned you before he turned the goons loose on you. If you didn't get the message, it was your own damn fault. Peterson found it a good idea to busy himself with his shovel for a while. Braddon worked beside him.

After a while, the Jap found someone else to yell at. It never took real long. For one thing, the American POWs were doing work they hated, work any idiot could see would help Japan against their own countrymen. No wonder they didn't give it their finest effort. And even if they'd shown the best will in the world, they were still too weak and too hungry to work as hard as the Japs wanted them to.

"I'm with you. I *hope* we can do it," Peterson said when he judged the coast was clear. The Japanese sergeant didn't come down on him. Neither did any of the other guards. He kept busy filling in shell holes and potholes just the same. "I'm afraid of what happens if we don't send enough out to do what needs doing. Yeah, that's what scares me. Back on the mainland, have they figured out how tough the goddamn Japs really are?"

"If they haven't, they sure ain't been paying attention," Gordy Braddon said. Like Peterson, he went on talking while he worked now. "They beat the shit out of us here. They did the same thing in the Philippines. They bombed San Francisco, for cryin' out loud. What more does the mainland need?"

"Maybe they've got the message over there. I hope so. But I don't know. I remember how things were before the shooting started," Peterson said. "Hardly anybody thought they'd have the nerve to pick a fight with us, and everybody thought they'd get their heads handed to them if they tried. After all, they were just using a bunch of junk made out of our old tin cans, right?"

His laugh had a bitter edge. The Japs had used a lot of U.S. scrap metal till FDR stopped selling it to them. But they hadn't built junk out of it. He'd never got a nastier surprise in his life than when he tried dogfighting a Zero with his Wildcat. The Jap in that fighter had taken him to school, chewed him up, and spit out the pieces.

From what he'd heard since, he'd been damn lucky not to get shot while he was parachuting down to the ground, too. Plenty of pilots had been. The Japanese didn't respect the chivalry of the air. As far as he could see, they didn't respect anything but strength. If they had it and you didn't, they walked all over you. If you had it and they didn't . . . maybe they'd kowtow. Maybe. How could anybody know for sure? Nobody'd managed to make 'em say uncle yet.

Walter London laid down his pick in the middle of the road. "I've got to take a whizz," he announced, as if the bulletin were as important as one from the Russian front.

To Peterson and the other men in the shooting squad, it was a lot more important than that. He looked at his comrades in mistrust. Was it his turn? He thought it was. He let his shovel fall. "Me, too," he said.

London scowled at him. "I can't even piss without somebody looking over my shoulder."

"It's not while you piss that really scares me," Peterson answered. "But if you take off afterwards, I get shot."

"I won't do that," London whined.

"Not while I'm watching you, you won't," Peterson said.

London went off behind a bush. Peterson stood behind another one no more than ten feet away. *He* didn't need to piss. He was sweating so hard, most of his water leaked out that way. London did a fine job of watering the grass. "See?" he said to Peterson as he set his clothes to rights.

"Hot damn," Peterson said. He almost added, *Only goes to show what a pissant you are.* Almost, but not quite. If he came down on London too hard, he'd give the SOB reason to run and hope everybody else in the shooting squad, or at least one Jim Peterson, got an Arisaka round right between the eyes.

Peterson sighed as they both headed back to the roadway. Maybe having to make calculations like that was the worst part of being a POW. He went back to work while another northbound dive bomber roared by overhead. As soon as he got another hole halfway filled, he was forcibly reminded that exhaustion and starvation came in a long way ahead of calculation after all.

WHEN MITSUO FUCHIDA WENT DOWN to the *Akagi*'s sick bay to see how his friend Genda was doing, a pharmacist's mate wearing a gauze mask over mouth and nose—a *masuku*, they called it in Japanese—chased him away. "*Gomen nasai*, Commander-*san*," the petty officer said, not sounding sorry at all, "but Commander Genda is contagious. We don't want anyone else coming down with his sickness."

"I just wanted to say hello and ask how he's doing," Fuchida protested.

"I will pass on your greetings, sir." The pharmacist's mate stood in the doorway like a dragon. "Commander Genda is doing as well as can be expected."

That could mean anything or nothing. "About how long do you think he'll be laid up?" Fuchida asked.

"Until he is well enough and strong enough to resume his duties," the pharmacist's mate said. Fuchida wanted to hit him. Petty officers slapped seamen around all the time, the same way Army noncoms did with common soldiers.

Officers needed good reasons for belting noncoms, though, and a refusal—or maybe just an inability—to communicate wasn't enough, not when the pharmacist's mate was odds-on to be obeying the doctor's orders by keeping Genda isolated.

Thwarted, Fuchida turned away and went up to the officers' wardroom. The food there was better than what he'd been eating in Honolulu. Captain Kaku was also there, eating a bowl of pickled plums and sipping tea. "Any sign of the Americans, sir?" Fuchida asked.

The skipper shook his head. "Not yet, Commander. Believe me, you'll be the first to know." His voice was dry. Fuchida looked down at his own snack so Kaku wouldn't see him flush. When the Yankees *were* spotted, he would lead the strike against them, as he'd led the first strike against Pearl Harbor and then the attack on the *Lexington*. Of course he would know as soon as anyone else did.

He found another question: "How are our engineers doing on electronic ranging gear like the Americans have?"

"I'd hoped *Zuikaku* and *Shokaku* would have it," Captain Kaku answered. "No such luck, though. I think we understand the principles. Now the problem is getting it into production, installing it aboard ship, and training men to use it." He shrugged. "We have our picket sampans out there, and we have H8Ks patrolling beyond them, and we have the cruisers' floatplanes for close-in reconnaissance. Wherever the enemy comes from, he won't take us by surprise."

"That's what counts, sir," Fuchida agreed. "As long as we meet the Americans on anything like equal terms, we'll beat them."

"I see it the same way," Kaku said. "Admiral Yamamoto is less hopeful. He fears the United States will outproduce us no matter what we do."

"Let the Americans try," Fuchida said. "If we keep sinking their ships, it doesn't matter how many they build. And we'll be building, too."

"*Hai*." The captain of the *Akagi* nodded. "This is also how it seems to me, Fuchida-*san*. You're a sound man, very sound." What Kaku no doubt meant was that he and Fuchida held the same opinion. He went on, "The admiral has a different view. He says we have no idea of how much matériel the United States can produce once all its factories start going full tilt."

"And the Americans, who have so much, begrudge us the chance of getting our fair share," Fuchida said angrily. "They think they should be the only big power in the Pacific. We've taught them a thing or two, and if they want another lesson here, I'd say we're ready to give them one."

As if his words were the cue in a play, a yeoman from the radio shack stuck his head into the wardroom. "Ah, here you are, Captain-*san*!" Excitement crackled in his voice. He waved a sheet of flimsy paper. "We have a report from one of the flying boats. They've spotted the American ships, sir! The pilot reports three enemy carriers, sir, with the usual supporting ships. Range about eight hundred kilometers, bearing 017."

Three against three, Fuchida thought. *Equal terms—just what I asked for. Now to make the most of it.*

"*Domo arigato*," Kaku breathed. After thanking the yeoman, he went on, "Any sign of transports—of an invasion fleet?"

"Sir, I have no report of them," the radioman answered.

"If they are there, sir, they may be hanging back, waiting for their carriers to dispose of ours," Fuchida said. "I wouldn't want to expose troopships to air strikes."

"*Hai. Honto.* Neither would I." Captain Kaku turned back to the yeoman. "You've informed Admiral Yamamoto?"

"Oh, yes, sir," the man said. "He nodded to me and he said, 'Now it begins.' He *spoke* to me, sir!" He seemed immensely proud of himself. A Christian to whom Jesus had spoken might have sounded the same way.

Kaku got to his feet. "I'm going to sound general quarters," he said to Fuchida. "They're still out of range, but now we know where they are." To the yeoman again: "Do the Americans know that flying boat has spotted them?"

"Sir, if they do, the message didn't say," the yeoman told him. Fuchida nodded to himself, liking the response. The man wasn't trying to read anything into what he'd got from the H8K. Many radiomen might have.

"Let's tend to business, Commander," Kaku said. "You'll want to get your men ready for what's ahead of them, I'm sure. And we're all going to be busy before very long."

"Yes, sir," Fuchida said. He and Kaku both hurried out of the wardroom. The skipper of the *Akagi* headed for the bridge. Fuchida made for the pilots' briefing room on the hangar deck, right under the flight deck. Hardly knowing he was doing it, he rubbed at his belly as he hurried along. If he had a bellyache, he would just have to ignore it. More important things were going on. General quarters sounded before he was even halfway to the briefing room. He nodded to himself. This was why he'd gone to the Naval Academy at Eta Jima, to the naval aircraft training center at Kasumigaura, to war against the United States in the first place. One more strong blow . . .

Sailors and officers ran every which way, hurrying to their battle stations. Fuchida ducked into the briefing room as the mechanics and other members of the maintenance crew began making sure the level bombers, torpedo planes, dive bombers, and fighters were as ready for action as they could be.

One of the dive-bomber pilots made it to the briefing room less than fifteen seconds behind Fuchida. The man grinned and said, "I might have known you'd be here first, Commander-*san*."

"I'm not that fast," Fuchida said. "I happened to be in the wardroom with the captain when the news came in. I was on my way over here before the alert sounded."

"News? What sort of news?" the pilot asked eagerly. "The sort we've been waiting for?"

"Patience. Patience," Fuchida answered with a smile of his own. "That way I'll only have to tell the story once."

"Yes, sir." The dive-bomber pilot didn't sound patient. He sounded like a small boy reluctantly awaiting permission to open a present sitting there on a mat in front of him.

More pilots swarmed into the briefing room, along with

radiomen and bombardiers for the Nakajimas and Aichis. They were all chattering excitedly; they knew what the call to general quarters was likely to mean. They kept flinging questions at Fuchida, too, as he stood there in front of the map.

When the room was full, he held up his hand. The fliers were in such a state, they needed a little while to realize he was calling for quiet. Slowly, a centimeter at a time, they gave it to him. "Thank you, gentlemen," he said when he could make himself heard through the din. "Thank you. The news I have is the news we've all been waiting for. We have found the Americans."

That started everyone talking at once again. He'd known it would. "Where are they?" "When do we take off?" The questions rained down on him.

"We don't take off yet—they aren't in range," Fuchida answered. "They're about—here." He pointed on the map. "One of our H8Ks picked them up way out there."

"*Banzai!* for the flying boats!" somebody shouted, and a cheer filled the briefing room. *How can we lose with men like these?* Fuchida thought proudly. Another pilot called, "What are we going to do about them, sir?"

"I don't know yet, not officially," Fuchida replied. "Admiral Yamamoto and Captain Kaku haven't given the orders. But I'll tell you this—we didn't come out here to invite the Yankees to a *cha-no-yu.*"

The officers and ratings laughed. As if the round-eyed barbarians could appreciate a tea ceremony anyway! "We'll make them drink salty tea!" a pilot yelled.

"That's the spirit," Fuchida said. "Be ready. I expect we'll close with the enemy and attack. *Banzai!* for the Emperor!"

"*Banzai! Banzai!*" The shout filled the briefing room.

OUT ON THE PACIFIC, Platoon Sergeant Les Dillon was playing poker with four other noncoms when the *B. F. Irvine*'s engine fell silent, leaving the troopship bobbing in the water. "What the fuck?" He and two other sergeants said the same thing at the same time.

"It's your bet, Les," Dutch Wenzel said.

Dillon shoved money into the pot. "I'll bump it up a couple of bucks," he said. He had two pair, and nobody'd shown much strength. But the change in the background noise worried him. "What the hell are they doing? They break down? We're sitting ducks for a goddamn Jap sub if we just park here."

"Thank you, Admiral Nimitz," said Vince Monahan, who sat to Les' left. He tossed in folding money of his own. "Call."

"I'm out." Wenzel threw in his hand. So did the last two sergeants.

"Here's mine." Dillon laid down his queens and nines. Monahan said something unpleasant. He'd had jacks and fives. Dillon raked in the pot. "Whose deal is it?" he asked.

"Maybe we ought to find out what's going on," Monahan said. "We were steaming around in the North Pacific marking time, and then we started heading south like we were really going somewhere—"

"Yeah. Somewhere," Dillon said drily. The other men in the poker game grunted. A couple of them chuckled. They'd been heading for Oahu and whatever happened when they hit the beach. Now . . . Now they weren't going anywhere.

A few minutes later, the engines started up again. So did the poker game, which had stalled. The troopship swung through a turn. Dillon's inner ear told him they were heading east now, more or less, not south. The game went on. The *B. F. Irvine* went through what felt like a one-eighty half an hour later, and then another one half an hour after that.

"Jesus Christ!" Wenzel said. "Why the fuck don't they make up their minds? They send us all the way out here to march in place, for crying out loud?"

"I know what it could be," Dillon said.

"Yeah?" Wenzel and Monahan and the other two men in the game all spoke together.

"Yeah," he replied. "The Navy's got to be up ahead of us somewhere. If they don't clear the Japs out of this part of the Pacific, we aren't gonna make it to Oahu to land. If they've bumped into 'em . . ."

After some thought, Dutch Wenzel nodded. "Makes

sense," he allowed. "They wouldn't want us bumping into carrier air." He made a horrible face. "That could ruin your whole day, matter of fact." One more brief pause. "Whose deal is it?"

LIEUTENANT SABURO SHINDO PRIDED HIMSELF on never getting too excited about anything. Tomorrow morning, battle would come: Japan's most important fight since the opening blows of the war against the USA. Some people were jumping up and down about that—and making a devil of a racket doing it. Shindo ignored them. He sprawled dozing in a chair in the briefing room. He wore his flying togs. He could be inside his Zero and airborne in a matter of minutes.

Every so often, the noise around him got too loud to stand, and he'd wake up for a little while. When he did, he thought about what he would have to do. This would be no surprise attack. The Americans knew they'd been spotted. They'd sent up fighters to chase off or shoot down the first H8K that found their fleet. They'd done it, too, though the flying boat had taken out a Wildcat before going into the Pacific. By the time it went down, others were in the neighborhood.

The Yankees might try to get away under cover of darkness—try to scurry back to the West Coast of the United States. Some of the Japanese pilots thought they would. Saburo Shindo didn't believe it. Running now would be cowardly. The Americans hadn't fought very well on Oahu, but they'd fought bravely. They wouldn't run away.

If they weren't running, what would they be doing? Shindo fell asleep again after he asked himself the question and before he answered it. He realized as much only when his eyes came open some time later and he noticed half the people who had been around him were gone, replaced by others. He started chewing on things once more, just as if he hadn't stopped. What *would* the Americans do?

Stay where they were and wait to be attacked? *He* wouldn't do anything that foolish. He would storm forward, launch his own search planes as soon as it got light,

and strike with everything he had the instant he found the
Japanese fleet. If he could see that, wouldn't the Yankees
be able to see it, too? He expected they would.

They had three carriers. The Japanese also had three, including two of the newest, largest, and fastest in the Navy.
The Americans had who knows what for pilots. The Japanese had men who'd smashed everything they came up
against from Hawaii to Ceylon. The Americans used Wildcats for fighters. The Japanese used Zeros. Shindo yawned
and smiled at the same time. A Wildcat could take more
punishment than a Zero. It could, yes—and it needed to.
He dozed off one more time, laughing a little as he did.

When he woke again, it was with someone's hand on his
shoulder. Full alertness returned instantly. "Is it time?" he
asked.

"Not quite yet, sir." The man standing beside him was
one of the wardroom stewards. "We're serving out a combat meal before the fliers go up." He held out a bowl full of
nigirimeshi—rice balls wrapped in bamboo shoots, with
plums at their centers.

"*Arigato.*" Shindo took one and bit into it. The stewards
had served the same meal before the fliers set off for Pearl
Harbor. Another man carried a tray with cups of green tea.
Shindo washed down his breakfast with it.

Akagi's three elevators were lifting planes from the
hangar deck to the flight deck, getting them ready to go
into action. Flight crewmen wrestled the bombers and
fighters into position one after another. As soon as each elevator went up and came down, another plane went on. Up
above, more men from the flight crew would be fueling the
planes and making sure their engines and control surfaces
and instruments were in good working order. Armorers
would be loading bombs and torpedoes, machine-gun bullets and cannon shells. When the time came . . .

Before it came, though, Shindo gathered up the fighter
pilots he would be leading. "Some of you were stuck on
Oahu with me when the American bombers raided us," he
said. "They fooled us, and they hit us, and they made us
lose face. Now is our chance to get revenge. Are we going

to let it slip through our fingers?"

"*Iye!*" the fliers answered loudly. Not all of them had been stuck on the island, but every one had been embarrassed. Of course they would say no.

"Good," Shindo told them. "Very good. They want a lesson. It's up to us to give them one. By the time we're through with them, they won't want to come anywhere near Hawaii for the next hundred years. Let's give the Emperor a *Banzai!* and then go out there and serve him."

"*Banzai!*" the fighter pilots shouted. They hurried up to the flight deck.

Shindo climbed into his Zero. Morning twilight stained the eastern sky with gray. Somewhere out there, the enemy waited. As Shindo went through his checks, he was pretty sure he knew where. Any which way, he would get a signal from the bombers, whose radios were more fully hooked into the reconnaissance network.

Planes began roaring off the flight deck. He fired up his engine. It roared to smooth, powerful life. His turn came soon. The air officer swung his green lantern in a circle. Shindo's Zero sped along, dipped as it went off the end of the deck, and soared into the sky.

XV

IN HIS NAKAJIMA B5N1, COMMANDER MITSUO FUCHIDA listened to the reports coming in from the flying boats and from the floatplanes the fleet had launched to search for the American carriers and their surrounding vessels. He didn't think he would have long to wait; the Japanese knew about where the enemy would be.

And he proved right. He hadn't been airborne long before a floatplane pilot found the foe. "Range approximately 150 kilometers," the pilot shouted. "Bearing is 045." He paused, then shouted again: "They are launching planes! Repeat—they are launching planes!"

We're up first, Fuchida thought. *Good*. Ignoring the growing ache in his belly, he spoke to his radioman: "Relay the position to our aircraft."

"*Hai*, Commander-*san*," First Flying Petty Officer Tokunobu Mizuki said. He took care of that with his usual unflustered competence.

Fuchida worried that the Americans would intercept the floatplane's signal and learn where the fleet was. He shrugged. With their electronics, they would see from which direction the Japanese strike was coming and trace it back anyhow. *Maybe we should have thrown them a curve*, thought Fuchida, a baseball fan. Probably too late to worry about it now.

"Shindo here, Commander." The fighter pilot's voice, calm as usual, sounded in Fuchida's earphones.

"Go ahead," Fuchida said.

"Question, sir," Saburo Shindo said. "If we spot the American airplanes on their way to our fleet, do we peel off and attack them, or do we continue with you?"

"Come with us," Fuchida answered without hesitation. "We'll need your help to keep the Wildcats off us, and the Zeros up over our ships will tend to the Americans."

"All right, sir. That's the way we'll do it, then. Out." Lieutenant Shindo broke the connection. Fuchida smiled to himself. Shindo, no doubt, would be telling the fighter pilots of the decision. Just as surely, he wouldn't raise his voice while he did it. With his machinelike competence, Shindo might have come out of the Mitsubishi aircraft plant himself.

Somewhere not too far away—and drawing closer by several kilometers every minute—an American officer was likely listening to the same question from one of his subordinates. How would he answer it? How would his answer change the building battle? *We'll see*, Fuchida thought.

As when planes from the Japanese carriers attacked the *Enterprise* and then the *Lexington*—and as when aircraft from the *Lexington* delivered their alarming counterstroke— the two fleets here would not draw close enough to see each other and turn their guns on each other. This war was overturning centuries of naval tradition.

Sudden excited gabble filled Fuchida's earphones. Dryly, Petty Officer Mizuki said, "Some of our men have spotted the Americans' airplanes, sir."

"Really?" Fuchida matched dry for dry. "I never would have guessed." Mizuki chuckled.

A moment later, Fuchida saw the Americans himself. They were flying a little lower than the Japanese, and noticeably slower: their torpedo planes were lumbering pigs, obsolete when compared to the sleek Nakajima B5N2s in Fuchida's strike force. American torpedoes weren't all they might have been, either. Several duds had proved a hit from them wasn't necessarily fatal, or even damaging.

Would the Wildcats climb up and try to strike the Japanese? Fuchida hoped so. They were slower than Zeros in everything but an emergency dive, and gaining altitude would cost them still more speed. Shindo and the rest of the Japanese fighter pilots had to be licking their chops.

But the Wildcats pressed on to the south, not leaving the attack aircraft they were assigned to shepherd. Fuchida nodded to himself. He would have made the same choice. He *had* made the same choice for his side. He ordered Mizuki to radio word of the sighting back to the fleet.

"Aye aye, sir," the radioman answered. "I would have done it without orders in a minute if you hadn't spoken up." From a lot of ratings, that would have been a shocking breach of discipline. Mizuki and Fuchida had been together for a long time. The petty officer knew what needed doing in his small sphere as well as Fuchida did in the larger one.

Each strike force slightly adjusted its course based on the direction in which the other had been flying. If the Americans had thrown a curve . . . Fuchida refused to worry about it. He already had the approximate bearing from the Japanese reconnaissance aircraft.

He had the bearing. He knew how far he'd come. Where were the Americans, then? All he saw was the vast blue expanse of the Pacific. He didn't want the men he led spotting the fleet ahead of him. He was their leader. Didn't that mean he ought to be first at everything?

No matter what he wanted, he wasn't quite first. But he spied the enemy warships just after the first radio calls rang out. Like the Japanese, the Americans used cruisers and destroyers to surround the all-important carriers. The smaller vessels started throwing up antiaircraft fire. Puffs of black smoke marred the smooth blue of the sky.

A couple of shells burst not far from Fuchida's bomber. Blast made the Nakajima shake and jerk in the air. A chunk of shrapnel clattered off a wingtip. It seemed to do no harm. The B5N1 kept flying.

"Torpedo planes, dive bombers—work together," Fuchida called. "Don't let the enemy fighters concentrate on one group. Fighters, protect the attack planes. *Banzai!* for the Emperor."

Answering *"Banzai!"*'s filled all strike-force frequencies. Here came the Wildcats that had been orbiting above the American fleet. Muzzle flashes showed they'd started shooting. The four heavy machine guns they carried were not to be despised. If they hit, they hit hard.

As if to prove as much, a burning Zero spun towards the Pacific far below. A Wildcat followed. It was out of control, the pilot surely dead, but it didn't show nearly so many flames as the Zero. Wildcats could take more damage than their Japanese counterparts. They could—and they needed to, for the Japanese had an easier time hitting than they did.

"Level bombers, line up behind your guide aircraft," Fuchida called out over the radio. The tactic had worked extremely well above Pearl Harbor. The level bombers scored a surprising number of hits there. Back in December, though, their targets lay at anchor in a crowded harbor. Now they were twisting and dodging all over the sea. Hits wouldn't come easy. *We can only do our best*, Fuchida thought.

Down below, antiaircraft fire caught an Aichi dive bomber as it was about to heel over and swoop on a carrier. Instead of diving, the Aichi fell out of the sky, rolling over and over and breaking up before it hit the water. Two more brave men gone. Two more spirits in Yasukuni Shrine.

Fuchida switched places with the second plane in his group of five. First Flying Petty Officer Akira Watanabe was the best pilot in the Japanese Navy, and his bombardier, First Flying Petty Officer Yanosuke Aso, was also the best. They needed to pass right over the center of the enemy fleet. As always, hitting carriers came first.

"Be ready!" Watanabe called to the pilots behind him. His plane bounced upward as the bombardier released the load. Fuchida's B5N1 also lurched in the air as its bombs fell free. More bombs tumbled down from the planes that followed him. Suddenly, the aircraft was lighter, more maneuverable. And it needed to be. Mizuki, who handled the rear-facing machine gun as well as the radio, opened up on something—presumably a Wildcat—behind the bomber.

Now that Fuchida didn't have to fly slow and straight for the bombardier's sake, he threw his Nakajima into aerobatics as violent as its engine and frame could stand. The rest of the planes in his group were doing the same thing—all but one. That one, flames shooting from the wing root and the engine cowling, plummeted down towards the sea.

Petty Officer Mizuki let out a wordless shout. Fuchida corkscrewed away to the left. Planes usually broke to the right, to take advantage of the torque from their props. He hoped his maneuver would catch the Yankee on his tail by surprise. And it did—the Wildcat shot past him, close enough for him to see the American's startled face. If only he had a forward-facing machine gun . . . But he didn't, and the Wildcat got away.

Now—what had the bombs done?

LIEUTENANT SABURO SHINDO was not a happy man. His Zero was still a better plane than the Wildcats he faced, but the Yankees had come up with something new, something that made them harder to shoot down. They flew in groups of four, two pairs of two separated by the radius of a tight turn. Whenever he drew a bead on one plane, the enemy pilots in the more distant pair would turn sharply towards him. That move warned the man he'd targeted to turn away sharply, spoiling his aim. And if he pursued too far trying to get it back, he came right into the line of fire of the more distant pair.

The first time the Americans tried that weave on him, he almost shot himself down walking right into it. He thought they'd got lucky then. When they did it twice more in quick succession, he realized it wasn't luck. They'd worked out a tactic to take advantage of the Wildcat's powerful guns and give it a chance to survive against the otherwise superior Zero.

"Be careful!" he shouted to the pilots he led, and

warned them what to look for. He hoped they would listen. In the heat of battle, who could tell?

Not all the Japanese had the chance to listen. Several Zeros had already gone down. The Americans' weave, no doubt, had done to them what it almost did to Shindo.

But Wildcats were also falling out of the sky. And the ones that mixed it up with Shindo's Zeros weren't attacking the Aichis and Nakajimas that accompanied them. Those were the ship-killers, the planes that had to get through at any cost.

Bombs burst around the American carriers. Shindo saw no hits, but even near misses would cause damage from casing fragments and from the effects of blast on enemy hulls. A Nakajima B5N2 raced towards a carrier. Its torpedo splashed into the sea. A heartbeat later, the torpedo bomber turned into a fireball. The torpedo *was* away, though.

The carrier started to slew to starboard. Too late, too slow. The torpedo struck home just aft of amidships. Nothing wrong with Japanese ordnance—Shindo watched the explosion. The enemy ship staggered like a prizefighter who'd just taken a right to the chin.

"*Banzai!*" Shindo yelled, there in the cockpit. "*Banzai!*"

He lost sight of the carrier for a little while after that. He was dealing with a Wildcat that had somehow got separated from its comrades. The pilot tried to dogfight him instead of diving away from trouble. The Yankee discovered what a lot of his countrymen had before him: that didn't work. A Zero could turn inside a Wildcat. A Zero could, and Shindo did. He shot up the American plane till at last it nosed down and crashed into the ocean.

By then, the Americans on the carrier had got her moving again, even if not at top speed. Saburo Shindo gave American engineers and damage-control parties reluctant respect. They knew their business. Here, knowing it didn't help. An Aichi dive bomber swooped down out of the sky, releasing its bomb at what seemed just above the height of the bridge. As the Aichi screamed away, its prop and fixed landing gear almost skimming the waves, the bomb hit dead center.

Where the ship had staggered before, she shuddered

now. She lost power and lay there dead in the water as flames leaped up from her. That, of course, was an invitation to the Japanese pilots. Another torpedo and what Shindo thought was a bomb from a level bomber slammed home. The carrier began to list heavily to port.

One down, Shindo thought. *Two to go.*

WHEN MINORU GENDA HEARD AMERICAN PLANES were on the way, he climbed out of the sick-bay cot where he'd been lying. Weak as he was, it felt like a long climb, too. He found a box of gauze masks like the ones the pharmacist's mates wore, and fastened the ties around his ears. *Masuku* was the Japanese name, borrowed from the English.

"Here, what are you doing? You shouldn't be up and about! *Kinjiru!*" One of those pharmacist's mates caught him in the act of leaving. "Get back where you belong, right this minute!" He was just a rating, but thought his station gave him the right to boss officers around.

He was usually right, too. Not here. Not now. Slowly but firmly, Genda shook his head. "No. We're going into battle. They need me up there." He had to stop and cough halfway through that, but he spoke with great determination.

"In your pajamas?" the pharmacist's mate said.

Genda looked down at himself. Then he spied his uniform jacket hanging on a hook welded to the sick-bay door. He threw it on over the thin cotton pajamas. "This will do. Now get out of my way."

If the pharmacist's mate tried to stop him by force, the man could. Genda didn't have the physical strength to oppose him. But he had a blazing strength of will, and the bigger, healthier man gave way before him. *I might as well be Japan against the United States*, he thought, and headed for his battle station.

When he reached the bridge, Captain Tomeo Kaku took one look at him and snapped, "Go below."

An order was an order. Dejectedly, Genda turned to go. "Wait," Admiral Yamamoto told him. To Kaku, Yamamoto went on, "Genda-*san* is not as well as I wish he were. But the illness affects only his body. His mind remains what it always was, and it is keen enough that I think he will be valuable here."

"As you wish, sir," Kaku answered. Most Japanese officers would have left it there, especially when a godlike man like Yamamoto had spoken. But *Akagi*'s new skipper showed he had nerve, for he continued. "I was concerned for the commander's well-being, sir. He would be safer down in sick bay."

Yamamoto laughed raucously. "If we are hit, Captain, nothing and no one on this ship is safe. Or will you tell me I'm wrong?" He waited. With a small, sheepish smile, Kaku shook his head. "All right, then," Yamamoto said. "Let's get down to business, shall we?" He moved aside half a pace to make room for Genda beside him. Genda bowed and took his place. Yamamoto barked a question at a signals officer: "*Zuikaku* and *Shokaku* are properly dispersed from us and from each other?"

"Oh, yes, sir," the young lieutenant replied. "They are following your orders, just as you gave them."

"Good." Yamamoto turned the word into a satisfied grunt. "We won't leave all our eggs in one basket for the Yankees." For Genda's benefit, he added, "They've grouped their carriers very close together. We have them all under attack, and we've struck a hard blow against at least one."

"I'm glad to hear it, sir," Genda said, wishing he could have had more to do with the operation under way. Before he could say anything else, the thunder of antiaircraft guns from the screening ships and, a moment later, from *Akagi* herself penetrated the steel and bulletproof glass armoring the carrier's bridge.

"All ahead full," Captain Kaku called down the speaking tube to the engine rooms. He stepped to the wheel. "*I* have the conn."

Genda didn't like Kaku as much as he'd liked Captain Hasegawa, whose outspokenness had got him sent back to Japan. No denying Kaku could handle a ship, though. *Akagi* was a converted battle-cruiser, but he handled her as if she were a destroyer, sending her twisting this way and that across the broad expanse of the Pacific.

None of which might matter even a sen's worth. No matter how swift she was, no matter what kind of evasive action she took, *Akagi* was a tortoise when measured against the airplanes attacking her. Antiaircraft guns and, most of all, the Zeros overhead would have the biggest say in whether she lived or died.

Admiral Yamamoto folded his arms across his broad chest. "We've done our part," he said. "We have put this force in a position where it can achieve victory. Now we rely on the brave young men we have trained to give it to us."

"Yes, sir," Genda said. *Maybe I should have stayed below*, he thought. *What can I do up here? The fight will go as it goes, with me or without me.*

A plane smashed into the Pacific, two or three hundred meters ahead of the *Akagi*. Genda couldn't be sure whether it was American or Japanese. American, he thought, for after the column of seawater it kicked up subsided there was no flame floating on the ocean. As if to show the contrast, a Zero went into the sea a moment later. The stricken Japanese fighter lit its own brief funeral pyre.

"A second Yankee carrier under attack, sir," the signals officer reported. "Heavy American resistance."

"They need to make a coordinated attack," Genda said: "torpedo planes and dive bombers together. That way, the enemy won't be able to concentrate on any one group."

"Send the message," Yamamoto told the signals officer. "Send it in Genda's name."

"Sir?" the lieutenant said in surprise.

"I'm sure it's not necessary, Admiral," Genda said quickly. "Commander Fuchida will have given the same order—he knows all there is to know about these attacks."

"Send it," Yamamoto repeated. "The Americans already know where *Akagi* is—they've proved that. And Fuchida and everyone to whom he relays the message will be glad to hear Genda-*san* is on his feet."

"*Domo arigato*," Genda whispered, and punctuated the words with a couple of coughs.

"*Torpedo in the water on the port side!*" Captain Kaku was swinging the helm hard to port even before that alarmed cry rang out. Genda didn't know whether he would have swung the carrier into the torpedo's track or away from it. His specialties were air power and attack planning. He'd never been anything more than an ordinary ship-handler.

Tomeo Kaku was definitely out of the ordinary. He hesitated not even for an instant, wrenching *Akagi* around so she offered the torpedo the smallest possible target. Now Genda could see the wake, drawing closer with hideous inevitability. The track looked very straight—but the torpedo slid past, missing by no more than five or ten meters.

"Not bad, Captain." For all the excitement in Yamamoto's voice, he might have been talking about the soup course at a fancy dinner.

Two American torpedo planes went into the drink in quick succession, both before they could launch. The Yankees were still flying the hopelessly slow Douglas Devastators they'd used when the war broke out. The pilots in them were brave men. They had to be, because they attacked in flying death traps. The Devastator was far slower and less agile than the Nakajima B5N2. Like most American planes, it could take a lot of battle damage—but not as much as the Zeros and the ships' antiaircraft guns were dishing out. Another torpedo plane crashed, and then another.

"I hope they haven't drawn all the fighters down to the deck with them," Genda said. "We'll need some up high for top cover against dive bombers."

"Send that, too," Yamamoto told the signals officer. He gave Genda a smile. "You see? You are earning your keep. Thank you for coming up."

"Thank *you*, sir," Genda said. "I'm sure someone else would have thought of it if I hadn't."

Admiral Yamamoto shook his head. "I'm not. Too much going on in the heat of battle. People get excited pursuing the enemy and make mistakes. They get so caught up in the *now*, they forget what may happen five minutes further down the line."

"*Torpedo!*" The cry rang out again. In spite of everything the Japanese could do, another Devastator had got a fish in the water.

"I'll tend to it," Captain Kaku said. Then he laughed. It was gallows humor, as he proved a moment later: "And if I don't, you can tie me to the wheel, and I'll go down with the ship."

"That is not a good tradition," Yamamoto said severely. "Not at all. The Empire loses brave, able men who could still serve it well."

Kaku only shrugged. "You may be right, sir, but it's a way for officers to atone for failure. Better than living in disgrace, *neh?*" He didn't wait for an answer, but spun the wheel hard. *Akagi* answered the helm more slowly than a destroyer would have, but still turned into the path of the oncoming torpedo. As she swung that way, her new skipper let out a sigh of relief. "Track on this one's not as straight as the last one was. She'll miss us by plenty." *Plenty* was about a hundred meters, or less than half the carrier's length. Maybe Captain Kaku was trying to impress Yamamoto with his coolness, or maybe he really did have more than his fair share.

So far, so good, Genda thought. Then, in almost the same instant, he heard the shout he really dreaded: "*Helldivers!*"

MITSUO FUCHIDA'S B5B1 STILL HAD BOMBS left in the bomb bay. That kept him loitering over the battle above the American fleet in the hope of doing more harm. Actually, he wasn't sure he or any of the other level bombers had done the Yankees any harm yet. He knew they'd scored near misses. Hits? He shrugged in the cockpit. Moving targets were much tougher than ships tied up in a harbor.

Next time, it'll be all torpedo planes and dive bombers, he thought with a twinge of regret. *We'll save the level bombers for shore installations.*

"See anything behind us, Mizuki?" he called through the intercom. He checked six whenever he could, but Mizuki faced that way all the time.

"No, sir," the radioman answered. "Pretty quiet up here. Not a lot of Wildcats left."

He was right. Most of the fighters that had flown over the American fleet had gone into the Pacific. Too many Zeros and Japanese attack aircraft had gone down with them, though—too many skilled pilots, too. No one could say the Americans hadn't fought hard. No one could say they weren't brave, either. They'd done everything with their Wildcats anyone could imagine, and a little more besides.

And it hadn't been enough. One of their aircraft carriers, smashed by torpedoes and bombs, had already sunk. Another lay dead in the water, burning from stem to stern. They were abandoning ship there. And the last enemy carrier had taken at least two bomb hits. Damage-control parties on that ship must have worked like fiends, for she wasn't burning. But she wouldn't be operating aircraft for quite a while, either, not with those holes in her flight deck she wouldn't.

Two U.S. destroyers and a bigger ship—a cruiser or a battlewagon—had also taken damage. Fuchida was inclined to shrug them off. They were small change in a modern naval battle.

An Aichi dove on the surviving carrier. It got shot down before it could drop its bomb. Fuchida cursed. He spoke to his bombardier: "I'm going to make one last run at that ship myself. Give it what we have left."

"*Hai*, Commander," the bombardier answered. "I am ashamed not to have served my country and the Emperor better."

"Don't be," Fuchida said. "You've done everything as best you could. War is a hard business, and we're going to have to revise some of our doctrine. No shame, no blame. If there is blame, it goes to me for not flying the plane straighter."

"Thank you, sir. Thank you very much," the bombardier said. "You're kinder than I deserve."

Fuchida concentrated on going straight over the surviving U.S. carrier. He had no more bombers following him; formations had broken down during the past wild. . . . He looked at his wristwatch. Could this fight have lasted only forty-five minutes? So the watch insisted. He couldn't say it was wrong, but he felt as if he'd aged years.

"Ready there?" he called to the bombardier. "Coming up on the target."

"Yes, sir. . . . Bombs free!"

The Nakajima rose as the bombs fell. With the whole bomb load and a lot of its fuel gone, it was as light and lively as it would ever be. "We've done everything we can do here," Fuchida said. "Time to go home now."

"Yes, sir," the bombardier said again, and then, in sudden excitement, "Hit! That's a hit!"

Was it? Fuchida had thought they'd made hits before, only to watch U.S. warships steam on, apparently undamaged. Why should it be any different here? Another look at his fuel gauge told him he didn't really want to linger to find out.

He swung the B5N1 south. Japanese warplanes were leaving the battle by ones and twos and forming into larger groups as they flew: Aichis and Nakajimas protected by Zeros. Too many Japanese planes and pilots weren't leaving the battle at all. But they'd done what they set out to do. Without air cover, the Yankees couldn't possibly hope to invade Hawaii. And their air cover was smashed to smithereens.

Then another question occurred to him. How were *his* side's carriers faring?

THE FIRST DIVE BOMBERS CALLED HELLDIVERS had been biplanes. A movie about them was one of the things that interested the Japanese in the technique. Not least because of the film, Japanese Navy men still often called any dive bomber a Helldiver. Only in nightmares had Minoru Genda ever imagined Helldivers screaming down on a ship in which he served.

A bomb burst just off to port. The great gout of water it threw up drenched everyone on the bridge. It soaked Genda's *masuku*, too. He took the worthless cloth thing off and threw it away. An ensign was rubbing at Admiral Yamamoto's dress uniform with a towel. Yamamoto shoved the youngster away, saying, "Never mind. I don't have to be pretty to fight a war."

Engine roaring, the dive bomber streaked away just above wavetop height. Two Zeros pursued it. They quickly shot it down, but it had already done what it set out to do.

Captain Kaku swung *Akagi* hard to port. Someone on the bridge made a questioning noise. Kaku said, "They will expect me to turn away from the bomb burst, so I will turn towards it. Maybe I will throw off their aim."

No one else said a word, not even Yamamoto. Kaku was *Akagi*'s skipper; how she was handled rested on his shoulders. And when a bomb burst to starboard, even closer than the first one had to port, everybody cheered. An explosion so close was liable to damage the hull, but the carrier's crew could repair wounds like that at their leisure.

"Sir, *Zuikaku* is hit!" the signals officer reported to Yamamoto. "Two bombs through the flight deck—major damage."

Before Yamamoto could answer, another American dive bomber stooped on *Akagi*. Captain Kaku was already swinging the carrier towards the last burst.

Maybe the American pilot guessed with him this time. Maybe his luck just ran out. Either way, the bomb hit the carrier a few meters ahead of the forwardmost elevator. Deck planking, jagged chunks of the steel beneath it, and flight crewmen all flew through the air.

Genda braced for yet another bomb, but no more came. A plane crashed into the sea not far from the wounded *Akagi*. Genda thought it was a dive bomber, but he couldn't be sure. Flight crewmen dragged hoses across the deck towards the hole in the ship. Down below, damage-control parties would be doing what they could to restore and repair.

"Can we land planes?" the signals officer asked. "Our strike force is coming home."

"We can land them," Genda said. "I wouldn't want to try to launch, but we can land—if we don't get hit again, that is."

He cast a wary eye up to the heavens, but it seemed as if no more dive bombers would come roaring down on the *Akagi*. He dared hope not, anyhow. And then word came from the flight deck: the surviving American planes were flying north. Genda wondered where they would land with two of their carriers destroyed and the third crippled. Maybe they would ditch in the Pacific, as the crews from the B-25s had done. That would save some of the fliers, even if the planes were lost.

He looked out at the flight crewmen and damage-control parties working on *Akagi*. He thought of the pounding *Zuikaku* had taken. And he thought of what the Japanese strike force had done to the American carriers. Turning to Admiral Yamamoto, he said, "Sir, this fight reminds me too much of a duel of submachine guns at three paces."

Somber pride in his voice, Captain Kaku said, "Maybe so, but we had the better gunners today."

"Today, yes," Yamamoto said. But it wasn't quite agreement, for he went on, "What will the Americans throw at us the next time? What will we have to answer?"

SABURO SHINDO WASN'T SURE HOW MANY WILDCATS he'd shot down. Three, he thought, but it might have been two or four or maybe, if he was very lucky, even five. All knew was, his Zero still flew, and some Americans didn't.

Quite a few Japanese didn't, either. Nothing had come cheap today. The Americans had fought ferociously. They'd fought ferociously—and they'd lost. What Japan had paid was worth the price. The invasion fleet behind the carriers, wherever it was, would come no farther. Shindo was sure of that. Without air superiority, trying a landing on Oahu was an invitation to suicide.

"Attention! Attention!" A radio alert blared in his earphones. "Planes from *Zuikaku*, divert to *Shokaku* or *Akagi*! Attention! Attention! Planes from *Zuikaku*, divert to *Shokaku* or *Akagi*!"

"*Zakennayo!*" he muttered. So the Yankees' strike force had done damage, too. That was . . . unfortunate. The Americans might be—were—clumsy and none too skillful, but they'd given it everything they had. Not enough, though. They had no carriers left that could land planes, while Japan still had two.

If all the Japanese planes from the strike force had come home safely, *Akagi* and *Shokaku* wouldn't have been able to accommodate them. As things were, that wouldn't be a problem.

And here came the survivors from the U.S. attack, heading north towards who could say what? They were scattered all over the sky. Shindo saw enemy fighters and dive bombers—no torpedo planes. Had the defenders knocked down all of them? He wouldn't have been surprised; the Devastator couldn't get out of its own way.

Shindo dove on a dive bomber. He didn't think the Douglas Dauntless' pilot saw him till he opened fire, and maybe not even then. The American plane never tried to take evasive action. It heeled to the right and arced down into the sea.

One more small victory. Shindo flew on towards *Akagi*.

WHILE MITSUO FUCHIDA WAS IN COMBAT, he'd—mostly—forgotten about the ache in the right side of his belly. He couldn't ignore it any more. It felt as if an angry dragon had sunk its teeth in there and didn't want to let go.

I have one thing left to do, he told himself. *I have to get this plane down. My radioman and my bombardier are depending on me*. After that . . . After that, he intended to head for sick bay as fast as he could go. *Genda and me*, he thought. *We're two of a kind*. He wondered how his friend was doing.

His first glimpse of *Akagi* came as a shock. Because she was landing planes, he'd assumed she'd come through the American attack unscathed. Now he found out what such assumptions were worth. Had that bomb struck near the stern instead of at the bow, the whole strike force would have been trying to come down on *Shokaku*—and wouldn't that have been a lovely mess?

A Zero landed on *Akagi*. Fuchida circled, waiting his turn and watching the fuel gauge. He was low, but not too low. He could last long enough—he hoped. An Aichi dive bomber followed the fighter down. Men from the flight crew hustled to get each new arrival off to one side and clear the flight deck for the next. Another Zero landed. Was that Lieutenant Shindo's plane? Fuchida thought so, but he couldn't be sure. He couldn't be sure of anything except how much he hurt—and that his turn came next.

He lined up on *Akagi*'s stern with extra-fussy care. He always hated to get waved off and have to go around again. Feeling the way he did right now, he hated the idea ten times as much. The landing officer signaled that he was a little high. Obediently, he brought the B5N1's nose down. No arguments today. Whatever the landing officer wanted, the landing officer would get.

Down came the bomber, straight and true. Fuchida checked once more—yes, he'd lowered his wheels. The landing officer signaled for him to land. He dove for the deck. A carrier landing was always a controlled crash. Most of the time, *controlled* was the key word. Here, for Fuchida, *crash* counted for more. The impact made him groan. The world turned gray for a moment. The Nakajima's tailhook caught an arrester wire. The bomber jerked to a stop. As color returned to things, Fuchida remembered to kill the engine. He was proud of himself for that.

He slid back the canopy and, moving like an old man, got down from the plane. One of the flight crew who'd come to push the bomber out of the landing path looked at him and exclaimed, "Are you all right, Commander?"

"So sorry, but no," Fuchida answered as his crewmen also left the B5N1.

"Are you wounded?"

"No. Sick. Belly." Every word took effort.

"Don't worry, sir. We'll get you to sick bay," the man from the flight crew said. And the sailors did, helping him down to the compartment. Usually, it was almost empty; wounded men crowded it now. Had *Akagi* caught fire, the place would have been a death trap. Damage control must have done a good job.

A doctor in surgical whites eyed Fuchida from over a *masuku*. "What's the trouble?" he asked. Fuchida explained his symptoms in a few words. The doctor said, "*Ah, so desu. Could be your appendix. Lie down.*"

"Where?" Fuchida asked—the beds were all full.

"On the deck." The doctor sounded impatient. Fuchida obeyed. The doctor peeled him out of his flight suit and jabbed a thumb into his belly between his navel and his right hipbone. "Does that hurt?"

Fuchida didn't bounce off the steel ceiling, though why he didn't he couldn't have said. He didn't scream, either—another marvel. In lieu of that shriek, he gasped, "*Hai.*"

"Well, it's got to come out. Can't leave it in there—liable to kill you if we do." The doctor sounded perfectly cheerful. Why not? It wasn't *his* appendix. Fuchida lay on the deck till the doctors got another surgical case off one of the operating tables. They helped him onto it. The fellow who'd poked him in the belly stuck an ether cone over his face. The stuff made him think he was being asphyxiated. He feebly tried to fight back. The struggle was the last thing he remembered as blackness swept over him.

THE *B. F. IRVINE*'S ENGINE started thudding away again for all it was worth. Lester Dillon had served aboard warships. He didn't think much of freighters. He doubted this one could make better than fifteen knots unless you threw her off a cliff. By the racket and the vibration, she was sure as hell trying now.

He'd gone to the head a couple of times. Otherwise, he'd stayed in the poker game. He would have been a fool to bail out; he was up close to two hundred bucks. You could have a hell of a good time in Honolulu for a couple of hundred bucks.

When he said as much, though, Dutch Wenzel looked up from his cards and asked, "Who says we're still heading for Hawaii?"

"Well, fuck," Dillon said. That was a damn good question. He waited till the hand was done. He dropped out early; Dutch ended up taking it with three queens. Then Les stood and stretched. "I'm going up on deck, see what I can find out."

"I'll come with you," Wenzel said, which effectively broke up the poker game. Everybody pocketed his cash. The cards belonged to Dillon. He stuck them in his hip pocket and headed for the narrow steel stairway up to the *B. F. Irvine*'s deck.

Sailors in tin hats manned hastily mounted antiaircraft guns. Les didn't laugh out loud, even if he felt like it. The swabbies didn't look as if they'd ever drawn that duty before. Marines could have done it a hell of a lot better. But Dillon hadn't come up there to scoff at the sailors.

He glanced at his watch: half past three. He looked at the sun: astern and a little to starboard. He swore in disgust. "We're heading east," he said, spitting out the words as if they tasted bad—and they did. "Fucking east, goddammit. We're running away like sons of bitches."

A petty officer hurrying by paused. He might have been thinking about chewing Dillon out. But either a look at the platoon sergeant's stripes or a look at the other Marine with him changed the rating's mind. All he said was, "You ain't got the word?"

"Down there?" Dillon jerked a thumb towards the passageway from which he'd just emerged. "Shit, no, Navy. They don't even give us the time of day down there. What *is* the skinny?"

"Two carriers sunk—two of ours, I mean—and the third one smashed to hell and gone. God only knows how many pilots lost." The petty officer spoke with the somber relish contemplating a really large disaster can bring. He went on, "We hurt the Japs some—don't know just how much. It doesn't *look* like they're chasing us. Why the hell should they, when we ain't got any air support left? Sure as hell can't go on without it. So we're heading back to port, fast as we can go."

"Oughta be zigzagging, then," said Dillon, remembering

his trip Over There as a young man. "Otherwise, we're liable to make some Jap sub driver's day."

The Navy man pointed to the bridge. "You wanna go talk to the skipper? He's just dying to hear from you, I bet."

"We're all liable to be dying," Dillon said. But he took not one step in the direction the petty officer had indicated. Would a Navy officer listen to a jarhead sergeant? Fat chance. Anyhow, all the troopships should have been zigzagging, not just the *B. F. Irvine*.

He took another look down the deck. Along with the men at the antiaircraft guns, the ship did have sailors at the rail, some with binoculars, looking for periscopes. That was better than nothing. How much better? Time would tell.

Behind him, Dutch Wenzel started swearing with a sudden impassioned fury. "What's eating you?" Les asked.

"If I'd known we were gonna get our butts kicked here, I would've let 'em make me a gunny," Wenzel answered. "We won't be coming back this way for a while—better believe we won't. When we do, we'll have some of the new fish with us, too. I could've got that new rocker and still had a chance to hit Hawaii."

"Oh," Dillon said. "Yeah. Hadn't even thought of that." He too contemplated rank gone glimmering. "Too late to worry about it now, and it ain't the biggest worry we've got right now, either. Maybe we'll get another crack at it once we make it back to base." *If we make it back to base*, he added to himself.

Vince Monahan came up on deck. "Let's pick up the game again. You guys have got a chunk of my money, and I aim to get it back again."

Les said, "Just don't shoot at the Japs with aim like that." They went below, reclaimed their spot—no mere privates had presumed to occupy it—and got down to business. Dillon took out the cards. "My deal this time, I think."

JOE CROSETTI AND ORSON SHARP listened to the bad news coming out of the radio in their room. "The *Saratoga* and the *Yorktown* are definitely known to be lost," Lowell

Thomas said in mournful, even sepulchral, tones. "The *Hornet* has suffered severe damage at the hands of the Japanese, while two cruisers and a destroyer were also hit by Jap aircraft. Our own gallant fliers inflicted heavy blows on the enemy fleet. They struck at least two and maybe three Jap carriers, as well as several other enemy warships."

That was all good, but nowhere near good enough. The American carriers should have knocked out their Japanese rivals, then gone on to gain dominance over whatever land-based planes the Japs had in Hawaii. The plan must have looked good when the American fleet set out from the West Coast. Unfortunately, the Japs had had plans of their own.

Thomas continued, "Admiral Chester W. Nimitz, who commanded the American task force, has issued the following statement: 'Our movement towards the Hawaiian Islands has failed to gain a satisfactory position, and I have withdrawn our ships. My decision to attack at this time and in this way was based on the best information available. The Navy and the air did all that bravery and devotion to duty could do. If any blame or fault attaches to the attempt, it is mine alone.'"

A singing commercial extolling the virtues of shaving cream came on. Orson Sharp said, "Well, you can't stand up and take the heat any better than that."

"Yeah," Joe said glumly. "I only wish he didn't have to. What the *hell* went wrong?" He often felt funny about cussing around his roommate, because Sharp so scrupulously didn't. He couldn't help himself today. "Goddamnit, we were supposed to *whip* them."

"I think we sold them short again," Sharp said. "We didn't figure they'd have the nerve to attack Hawaii at all, and then they did. And they licked us there and in the Philippines and down in the South Seas, but they had numbers and surprise on their side. We'd lick 'em if we ever got 'em even-Steven."

"Well, sure," Joe said. But it hadn't turned out to be *well, sure*. The American carrier force and the Japanese had met on equal terms, and the Japs had come out on top. That wasn't just shocking. It was mortifying.

Patiently, Sharp said, "Looks to me like we sent a boy to do a man's job. We wanted to do something fast, pay the Japs back for what they did to us. And we tried it, and it didn't work. We'll try again—we have to try again. I just hope we do it right next time instead of fast."

Joe eyed his roomie. "When the next war comes, you want Thomas or H. V. Kaltenborn or whoever's in back of the microphone to go, 'Admiral Sharp has issued the following statement,' don't you?"

"Not if it's a statement explaining why what we tried didn't work," Sharp replied.

He didn't make a big fuss about things. He hardly ever did. But he had his eye on one of the top prizes, sure as the devil. Joe owned no ambition higher than roaring off the deck of a carrier and mowing down Zeros one after another. The way Sharp thought about the bigger picture and how things fit together made him want to do the same.

Lowell Thomas returned. He talked about big German advances in southern Russia, and about the *Afrika Korps'* push to Alamein. The next stop after that was Alexandria and the Nile. "The upcoming Fourth of July holiday," he went on, "promises to be the most anxious for this great nation since that of 1863, when Meade's army met Robert E. Lee's at a little Pennsylvania town called Gettysburg."

"Gettysburg," Joe echoed. To all but a dying handful of graybeards, it was only a name from a history book. None of his family had been on this side of the Atlantic when men in blue and men in gray tried to kill one another with muzzle-loading muskets and cannon. The weapons, by modern standards, were laughable. The fury with which the soldiers on both sides had wielded them was anything but.

"We'll do what we need to do," Sharp said. "If it takes a little longer than we figured at first—then it does, that's all. When the Federals marched down to Bull Run, they thought they'd win in a hurry, too. It didn't work like that, but they didn't lose, either, not in the end."

"You've got a good way of looking at things, you know?" Joe said.

His roomie shrugged. "Hey, I wish we'd done it the easy way, believe me. If we have to do it the hard way, then we do, that's all."

Joe eyed him. "Anybody ever tell you you're too sensible for your own good?"

"Besides you, you mean?" Sharp asked. Laughing, Joe nodded. The other cadet said, "Oh, I've heard it a few times. But my guess is, the people who say it aren't sensible enough."

He sounded dead serious. That only made Joe laugh harder. He said, "God help the Japs when we turn you loose on them."

Now Orson Sharp was the one who laughed. And Joe had been joking. But, while he'd been joking, he probably hadn't been kidding. How many pilots had the Navy lost in the failed attack on Hawaii? Too damn many—Joe was sure of that. A lot of what had been the first team wasn't there any more. If the United States tried again—no, *when* the United States tried again, for he too was sure the country would—a lot of the guys who flew off the flattops would be rookies like him.

Yeah, he thought. *Just like me.*

FOR THE FIRST TIME in Kenzo Takahashi's life, the Fourth of July wasn't a holiday. It was a little slower than usual, because it was a Saturday. But no firecrackers spit and snarled. No fireworks displays were scheduled for the evening. No admirals and generals made pompous, boring speeches about the land of the free and the home of the brave.

Instead, both the *Advertiser* and the *Star-Bulletin* ran banner headlines: GREAT JAPANESE VICTORY! and JAPAN SAVES HAWAII!, respectively. Both got more paper than the occupying authorities normally doled out to them. The Japanese wanted them to make a big fuss about this. Japanese-language newspapers shouted even louder.

Kenzo wanted to believe all the shouts were a pack of lies. He wanted to, but he couldn't. It wasn't just that no

American planes appeared over Oahu and no American fighting men splashed ashore. Word always got around when the Japanese were telling tall tales. Kenzo wasn't sure how. He supposed some people still had shortwave sets and listened to news from the mainland, even if they took their lives in their hands when they did it.

He kept hoping he would hear that Japan was inventing a battle that hadn't happened or exaggerating about one that hadn't gone so well. He kept hoping, but nobody said anything like that. It looked as if those gloating headlines were nothing but the truth.

His father had no doubts. Jiro Takahashi rubbed it in. "You see?" he said as he and Kenzo and Hiroshi lined up for their rice that evening. "You see? This is what happens when the United States fights Japan. Twice now, big battles—and who won? Who won, eh? Japan won, that's who!"

"*Banzai*," Kenzo said sourly.

That only made his old man mad. He'd known it would, which was why he did it. "You should always say that with respect! With spirit!" Jiro growled. "You don't joke around with it!"

Kenzo hadn't been joking. Before he could say so, Hiroshi stuck an elbow in his ribs. He gave his brother an *Et tu, Brute?* look. But Hiroshi only shook his head, ever so slightly. And Kenzo realized his brother was right. If he sounded too American, somebody in earshot was liable to report him to the occupying authorities. His father wouldn't—they might disagree, they might quarrel, but he knew his old man would never betray him. Some stranger who might get some cash or some extra food, though . . .

"Yeah," Kenzo said in English. "Thanks."

"Don't worry about it," Hiroshi told him.

"What are you two going on about?" their father asked. Neither one of them answered. He sniffed. "You're so proud of your English. How much good does English do you now?"

They didn't answer that sally, either. The line snaked forward. Kenzo held out his bowl for rice and vegetables. Some people had to live on this and nothing else. Kenzo would have been happy out on the Pacific now, not just for the sake of food but because he and his father didn't fight so much when they had bait and hooks and *ahi* and *aku* and lines and sails to talk about. Everything came back to politics on dry land . . . and everything that had to do with politics was going his old man's way.

Once he got fed, he took the bowl off by himself to eat in peace. He even waved Hiroshi away when his brother started to follow him. Hiroshi just shrugged and found somewhere else to go. To Kenzo's relief, his father didn't come after him.

A lot of the trees that had been proud parts of the botanical garden were long since gone to firewood. Shrubs and bushes and ferns persisted. Why not? They weren't worth pulling up and burning. He sat down on the grass close by a jungly clump and started eating. With automatic ease, he scooped up rice with his *hashi* and brought it to his mouth.

He started to laugh, not that it was funny. He told anybody who'd listen that he was an American. No matter what he told people, what was he doing? Sitting on the ground and eating rice with chopsticks. Circumstances seemed to be conspiring to turn him into a Jap no matter what he wanted.

He told himself Elsie Sundberg wouldn't think so. No matter what he told himself, he had a hard time believing it. After what had happened out in the Pacific, she'd probably figure him for a Jap now, no matter what he'd told her. And if she didn't, her folks would.

At just short of twenty, gloom came easily. Getting rid of it was harder. Kenzo washed his bowl after he finished eating. The chopsticks were cheap bamboo. Even here, even now, they weren't in short supply. He threw them in a corrugated-metal trash can.

Then he looked west, towards Pearl Harbor. No, no fireworks tonight. The U.S. Navy was gone from these parts. Everything else that had to do with the United States seemed gone, too. So where was there a place for a person of Japanese blood who thought he had the right to be an American?

Anywhere at all?

MINORU GENDA COUGHED BEHIND HIS *MASUKU*. Admiral Yamamoto looked around *Akagi*'s wardroom with affectionate amusement. "Is this an after-action conference or a sick-bay gathering?" he asked.

"Sorry, sir," Genda said. If not for the conference, he would have been back in sick bay. Commander Fuchida sprawled across three chairs at the doctor's orders. He was a long way from being over his appendectomy. Captain Ichibei Yokokawa of *Zuikaku* had a bandaged left shoulder. A ricocheting bullet from a Wildcat had wounded him. He was lucky it had lost most of its momentum before striking; a .50-caliber round could kill from shock without penetrating anything vital. Of course, if he were really lucky he wouldn't have been wounded at all.

"We did what we set out to do when we sought this battle," Yamamoto said. "The Americans will not come forward. They will not invade Hawaii. The islands will remain our bastion, not theirs."

"Well done!" Captain Tomeo Kaku said. "And I say, 'Well done!' to the crews of *Shokaku* and *Zuikaku* in particular. However fine the ships are, they are new, and their crews do not have so much experience working as a team as *Akagi*'s does. But no one will say they are not veterans now."

"*Arigato*," said Captain Jojima Takatsugu of *Shokaku*. Captain Yokokawa started to nod his thanks, then grimaced and thought better of it. Eyeing that thick pad of bandages on his shoulder, Genda couldn't blame him.

"We are not finished, though," Yamamoto said sternly. "This is a victory, but not one that will end the war. The Americans paid a high price, but they will be back when they feel strong enough. We have to see what *we* paid, what we can do to make good our losses, and how best to face the Yankees when they return—for they will."

"Are you sure, sir?" Captain Kaku asked. "How many times must we crush them before they know we are their masters?"

"How many times?" Yamamoto shrugged. "I don't know. I do know that what we've done so far isn't enough. We have awakened a sleeping giant, and we have yet to see everything he can do."

"What is our best course, then, sir?" Genda asked.

"To make these islands strong. To make the fleet that protects them strong," Yamamoto replied. "American arms factories and shipyards are just now getting up to full war production. What we have seen is not a patch on what we will see. Fuchida-*san!*"

"Yes, sir!" Fuchida still sounded fuzzy—from painkillers, Genda suspected—but Yamamoto's voice could and would galvanize anybody.

"What were our aircraft losses?" asked the commander of the Combined Fleet.

"Just over a hundred planes, Admiral." Fuzzy or not, Fuchida had the numbers he needed at his fingertips. Anyone who came to a meeting with Yamamoto unprepared deserved whatever happened to him.

The admiral grunted. "Could have been worse, I suppose. But these were highly trained men, some of the best we had. How soon can we replace them, and how good will the replacements be?"

"As for numbers, sir, we can replace them as soon as the new pilots and radiomen and bombardiers arrive from Japan," Fuchida replied. "Quality . . . Quality is harder to gauge. Nothing but experience can make a man a veteran. The fliers from *Shokaku* and *Zuikaku* know this now."

"*Hai,*" Yamamoto said noncommittally. He rounded on Captain Yokokawa. "How long before *Zuikaku* is back in service?"

"Sir, she'll have to return to Japan for repairs," Yokokawa answered. "There's no help for it. We're lucky we kept her afloat after the pounding she took. The Americans pressed their attacks with all their strength."

Another grunt from Yamamoto. He hadn't been aboard *Zuikaku* or seen for himself how she was fought. All he could know was that she'd taken much more damage than either of the other Japanese carriers. He said, "A pity the Americans did such a good job of wrecking the navy yard here before they surrendered."

"They were thorough," Genda agreed.

"Have the engineers looked at what we'd need to do to get the yard operational?"

Genda's specialty was air operations. But he was also the man with the answers; Yamamoto's wasn't the only head to turn his way. He said, "Sir, I'm told it's not practical, since we would have to bring all our fuel from Japan. You might want to talk with the engineers, though, to see if things have changed since the last time I checked with them."

"I'll do that," Yamamoto said. "Having to take a ship back more than five thousand kilometers to get it repaired is inefficient, to say the least."

"The Americans had no trouble maintaining a yard here," Captain Takatsugu said. "What they can do, we should be able to do, too."

Just for a moment, Admiral Yamamoto looked angry. Genda knew what to watch for, and when to look. The eyebrows that came together, the lips that thinned . . . The expression vanished almost as fast as it appeared, but Yamamoto did not care for officers who failed to think things through before they spoke. "The Americans are only a little more than half as far from Hawaii as we are. And they have more fuel than they know what to do with. They had no trouble shipping some of it here. We, on the other hand . . ."

He didn't go on, or need to. Had the USA not cut off oil shipments to Japan, the war never would have started. If everything went well from here on out, Japan wouldn't have to depend on a rival for the oil she desperately needed. The formerly Dutch East Indies would see to that.

Yamamoto let Captain Takatsugu down easy. "We

fought well," he said. "As long as we do that, all will be well for us."

"*Hai.*" Several officers agreed with that. Some of them sounded relieved, too.

Turning to Captain Kaku, Yamamoto said, "I am pleased at how well the damage-control parties have worked here on *Akagi*. That she can launch planes again is a credit to her officers and men."

"Thank you very much, sir." Kaku modestly looked down at his hands. "We were lucky that only one bomb hit us. And the repairs, of course, are emergency makeshifts. She needs much more work."

That was an understatement. Genda had seen the gaping hole in the hangar deck. The bomb would have done even more damage had it struck while planes were stored there and not in combat.

"I understand," Yamamoto said. "But you've done what's essential. If the ship has to fight, she can. I don't expect the Americans to come back to these waters for some time, but I might be wrong. In case I am, we'll need every carrier and every plane we can get our hands on."

Genda looked north and east. He didn't expect the Americans back any time soon, either. They'd just had a lesson. Now they knew how much they didn't know about conducting carrier operations. With luck, that would be enough to keep them thoughtful for some time. In the meanwhile, Japan would grow stronger, and so would her grip on Hawaii.

Admiral Yamamoto dismissed the meeting. *Shokaku*'s skipper, and *Zuikaku*'s, went over the side and down to the boats waiting to carry them back to their carriers. Genda stood with Fuchida on the *Akagi*'s battered flight deck. Because of the stitches in his belly, Fuchida listed to starboard. The deck put Genda in mind of a man who'd had a head injury and went around forever afterwards with a steel plate in his skull. The repairs here were ugly, but they were functional.

Even through the *masuku*, Genda tasted the sweetness of the tropical air. He asked Fuchida, "How are you doing?"

"Not so well," his friend answered. "But I'm getting better. How about you?"

"The same, more or less," Genda said. "We made it through the fight. That's the most important thing. Now we take our time recovering."

Fuchida nodded. "That's right." He looked back towards some of the planes parked on the flight deck near *Akagi*'s stern. "From now on, I think we'd better equip all the Nakajimas with torpedoes. In a sea fight, they have a much better chance of scoring a hit than level bombers do."

"Put it in your action report, Fuchida-*san*," Genda said. "It makes good sense to me. As long as we don't dither between one and the other, we'll be all right."

"That would be bad, wouldn't it?" Fuchida said. "Suppose the enemy caught us while we were switching from bombs to torpedoes in combat. Can you imagine what a Helldiver hit would do then?" He shuddered at the idea.

So did Genda. A carrier caught betwixt and between like that would go up like an ammunition dump—which, in effect, she would be. No damage-control party in the world could hope to save her. With a deliberate effort of will, he made himself dismiss the frightening possibility. "It didn't happen," he said firmly. "It won't happen, either."

BEING ABLE TO WALK STRAIGHT felt wonderful to Mitsuo Fuchida. The three weeks since his appendectomy felt like forever, but the doctors had finally taken the stitches out of his abdomen. The one who did the work said, "If people look at you when you go to the public baths, you can tell them you started to commit *seppuku* but changed your mind."

He'd chortled loudly. Fuchida didn't think it was so funny. For one thing, the scar wasn't quite in the right place for that. For another, the feel of the sutures sliding through his flesh as the doctor snipped them and pulled them out one by one was—not painful, but distinctly unpleasant.

Now he strode across the lawn to one side of Iolani Palace towards the folding chairs set up there. Genda and the two lieutenant colonels, Minami and Murakami, rose to greet him. They bowed. So did he. It made his belly twinge, but only a little.

The Coronation Pavilion hadn't been used for its original function for most of a lifetime. It hadn't gone altogether unused since then, though. King David Kalakaua had built it directly in front of the palace, connecting it to the veranda there with a bridge. After he held his coronation ceremony in 1883, the pavilion was moved to the side and became the home of the Royal Hawaiian Band. Now it would again see the crowning of a monarch . . . of sorts.

Fuchida wasn't sorry to sink into a chair by Genda—who still wore his *masuku*—and the two Army officers. Other Japanese military men, including Admiral Yamamoto (who'd stayed in Honolulu for the ceremony) and General Yamashita, filled most of the seats on the left side of the aisle. Others were taken by representatives from the Foreign Ministry and by allied diplomats: men from Germany and Italy, from Romania and Hungary and Bulgaria, from Croatia and Vichy France, from Manchukuo and Siam, from the Japanese puppet government of China in Nanking, and from the even less powerful authorities Japan had set up with the aid of nationalists in Burma, Malaya, and the Philippines.

On the right side of the aisle sat local dignitaries: some Hawaiian noblemen and -women, some members of the former Territorial Legislature (most but not all of them of Japanese blood), a couple of justices from the former Territorial Supreme Court, judges from lesser courts (some of them were Japanese, too, and one an immense Hawaiian), and various other prominent people. Fuchida was a little surprised at how many *haoles* had chosen to attend, the men in formalwear, often even including top hats, the woman in fancy gowns, most of them of glowing silk.

Some people were conspicuous by their absence. Fuchida leaned towards Genda and murmured, "I see Abigail Kawananakoa decided not to come."

Genda nodded. "None of the other candidates we interviewed is here, either. Did you expect anything different?"

"No, not really," Fuchida admitted. "I'm glad this many of the Hawaiian *alii* did show up." He chuckled. "Now the ones who did and the ones who didn't can start cutting each other dead at parties."

His friend laughed at that till he started to cough. He sent Fuchida a reproachful stare once the spasm passed. "See what you made me do."

"So sorry," Fuchida said. They grinned at each other.

Under the ribbed copper dome of the Coronation Pavilion—decorated with Hawaiian coats of arms and supported by eight concrete columns—stood the Anglican Bishop of Honolulu in full ecclesiastical regalia. Fuchida wondered how the *haole* had been persuaded to officiate. Maybe Stanley Owana Laanui had taken care of that. Fuchida suspected the bishop would have been more likely to listen to him than to the Japanese occupying authorities. Or maybe the occupiers had just held a gun to his head and told him that doing what he needed to do would improve his chances of living to get a little grayer. He was here. That was what counted.

The Royal Hawaiian Band was here, too, though displaced from its usual venue. The bandmaster raised his baton. The band struck up a tune. Fuchida would not have recognized it, but he knew what it was: "Hawaii Ponoi." The Hawaiian national anthem was particularly appropriate to the occasion, with words by King David Kalakaua and music by Henry Berger, the fork-bearded Prussian who'd created the Royal Hawaiian Band.

On the right side of the aisle, people sang in both Hawaiian and English. Fuchida caught some of the latter:

> "Hawaii's own true sons
> Be loyal to your chief
> The country's liege and lord
> The chief."

He nodded to himself. Yes, that fit the spirit of the day very well.

And here came the coronation procession. First were

the bearers of the royal insignia, both imported and native. One man carried the dove-topped royal scepter; another, on a velvet cushion, the golden ring of state; two more bore *puloulous*—tabu staffs ornamented by crowns of black-and-white cloth that showed the world the king's sacrosanctity.

Behind them walked a Hawaiian noblewoman carrying the royal cloak made entirely of yellow *mamo* feathers. The *mamo* had been hunted into extinction for those feathers, of which each bird had only tiny patches under the wings. The feather cloak was almost extinct, too; it had been taken out of the Bishop Museum—over the curator's loud objections—for the occasion.

More Hawaiian nobles followed. They had attendants bearing *kahili*, which reminded Fuchida of nothing so much as the sponges on sticks used to swab out cannon. Here, though, the sponge part was replaced by red and yellow feathers, which produced a much more pleasing effect. Two of the nobles carried the royal crowns, which were made on the European pattern (though decorated with golden taro leaves) and studded with diamonds, opals, emeralds, rubies, pearls—and *kukui* nuts.

And behind them marched Stanley Owana Laanui himself, in white tie and tails. With him came the prospective Queen of the restored Kingdom of Hawaii. Cynthia Laanui was a smiling, busty redhead only a little more than half her husband's age. Fuchida had no trouble figuring out what he saw in her. What she saw in him might be a different question altogether.

The new royal couple went up the half-dozen steps that led into the Coronation Pavilion. The noblewoman who bore the royal cloak carefully draped it over Stanley Owana Laanui's shoulders. The cloak fell to his ankles. It was, without a doubt, an impressive garment, and one no sovereign anywhere in the world could match. Stanley Laanui took the ring of state and set it on his right index finger. He grasped the scepter in his right hand.

"Let us pray," the Bishop of Honolulu said. Raising his hands in benediction, he went on, "May the Lord bless us and keep us. May He make His face shine upon us and give us peace. And may He find good what we do here today. This we ask in the holy name of our Savior, His Son, Jesus Christ. Amen."

"Amen." The response came from the right side of the audience, from some of the diplomats on the left side, and from the new royal couple. Fuchida nodded once more. The prayer said enough to satisfy the occupying authorities, yet not so much as to make a mockery of the bishop's conscience if, as was likely, he didn't favor the Japanese cause.

Wearing no expression whatever, the bishop set one crown on Stanley Owana Laanui's head, the other on Cynthia Laanui's flaming locks. "God bless the King and Queen of Hawaii," he said in a voice also empty of everything.

Flashbulbs popped. Newsreel cameras had been grinding away all along. The audience applauded, perhaps more politely than enthusiastically. Fuchida and Genda, Minami and Murakami looked at one another and smiled as they clapped. They'd got the job done.

"I thank you," King Stanley said, looking out over his subjects—and his masters. "The American annexation and occupation of Hawaii were not only illegal and immoral but also disastrous for the Hawaiian people. There are less than half as many Hawaiians alive today as there were fifty years ago."

Is that why you have a redheaded Queen? Fuchida wondered. Stanley Owana Laanui went on, "Now that these islands are free again, I intend to make them into a kingdom that can feed itself and support itself instead of being caught like a fly in a spiderweb of ties to the mainland. Cooperation with the Greater East Asia Co-Prosperity Sphere will help Hawaii to achieve this goal." That was nicely done: he admitted being a puppet without ever naming Japan.

"Now we do not have to pretend to be Americans any more," he said—in English. Did he notice the irony, or did it slide past him? Fuchida couldn't be sure. The new King was shrewd, but whether he was really clever was much less obvious. He finished, "We may choose our own friends once more. With the help of those friends, we will continue to live untroubled lives here in the heart of the Pacific. Thank you."

The Kingdom of Hawaii's . . . friends had sunk two U.S. carriers and smashed up a third. As long as they could keep that up, Hawaii would remain untroubled—by the Americans, anyhow. As Fuchida applauded once more, he caught Genda's eye. Now they had to make sure the newly revived kingdom stayed as independent as Japan wanted it to be—and not a bit more.

DON'T MISS THE SEQUEL TO *DAYS OF INFAMY*,
NOW AVAILABLE IN HARDCOVER

NEW YORK TIMES BESTSELLING AUTHOR OF *DAYS OF INFAMY*

HARRY TURTLEDOVE

END OF THE BEGINNING

⊹ A NOVEL OF ALTERNATE HISTORY ⊹

NAL • 0-451-21668-7